D0433887

EVERYMAN'S LIBRARY

EVERYMAN,
I WILL GO WITH THEE,
AND BE THY GUIDE,
IN THY MOST NEED
TO GO BY THY SIDE

STENDHAL

Scarlet and
Black

Translated from the French by
C. K. Scott Moncrieff
with an Introduction by Jonathan Keates

EVERYMAN'S LIBRARY

38

This book is one of 250 volumes in Everyman's Library
which have been distributed to 4500 state schools
throughout the United Kingdom.
The project has been supported by a grant of £4 million
from the Millennium Commission.

First included in Everyman's Library, 1938
Introduction, Bibliography and Chronology © David Campbell
Publishers Ltd., 1991
Typography by Peter B. Willberg

ISBN 1-85715-038-4

A CIP catalogue record for this book is available from the
British Library

Published by David Campbell Publishers Ltd.,
Gloucester Mansions, 140A Shaftesbury Avenue,
London WC2H 8HD

Distributed by Random House (UK) Ltd.,
20 Vauxhall Bridge Road, London SW1V 2SA

SCARLET AND BLACK

INTRODUCTION

The traditional role of the artist in nineteenth-century France was that of a disdainful rebel, swimming resolutely against the tide of received wisdom, political orthodoxy and bourgeois prejudice, determinedly unconventional in morals and life-style, and always carefully distanced from the banal rhythms and lowly expectations of other people's daily existence. Through no special irony, this dogged refusal to keep in step evolved its own norms – an orthodoxy of unorthodoxy – so that by the end of the century Paris had become, *par excellence*, the city in which you could satisfy your craving to lead an artist's life, even if none of your concepts ever reached the stage of a finished creation.

It is hard to think of a single French writer, painter or musician of that entire cultural epoch who did not adopt this pose of self-conscious alienation. For every Matthew Arnold the school inspector, Anthony Trollope the post office superintendent or Nathaniel Hawthorne the consul, there is a Victor Hugo in his Channel Island exile, a Gauguin syphilitic in the South Seas, a Flaubert energized by a perpetual rage against the bourgeoisie, a George Sand smoking and wearing trousers or a Berlioz furiously dramatizing in music the light of the heroic artist *contra mundum*.

Plenty of good reasons exist for seeing Stendhal as a pioneer, perhaps even as an originator, of this essentially combative persona, which has remained, in one form or another, stereotypical ever since. He needed the stimulus of his own wary detachment from the world so ruthlessly scrutinized by his novels, finished or unfinished, and the circumstances of his life and professional career were, in this as in other respects, thoroughly obliging to him.

The pseudonym 'Stendhal' by which he is known to the world was simply another symptom of the condition. Since hitherto unexamined correspondence and scribbled marginalia are even now coming to light, nobody has yet been able to make the final count of his myriad aliases, but a conservative estimate puts them at well over a hundred. Louis Alexandre Bombet, Lisio Visconti, Cornichon, Dominique, Timoleon du Bois, William Crocodile were a mere handful among the names used largely in the belief that anything he wrote would automatically be unacceptable to the government censorship of the day and that a perpetually suspicious police surveillance would be forever prying into his letters and personal papers. It was these apprehensions, as much as any more personal idiosyncracy, which caused him to switch, in his notebooks and in the innumerable jottings scribbled across the books he read, into sudden snatches of English, a language over which he never exercised an adequate oral command, but which provided continual escape values for an irrepressibly effervescent intellect.

Behind all these literary false beards and artistic coded messages, however, lay something more than a fear of reaction and repression in the obscurantist Europe of resuscitated despots which followed the fall of Napoleon in 1815. Bonaparte indeed furnishes a clue to much that animated and absorbed the mature Stendhal, as a man or as a literary artist, and the cult of the exiled Emperor is central to an understanding of his two most perfect novels. The question often asked is whether this erstwhile commissariat officer with the Grande Armée, who had followed his master with considerable distinction through the disastrous Russian campaign of 1812, this former Auditor of the Council of State, with his splendid official uniform and two carriages, would have been quite as good a writer or have written at all, if the Empire itself had not fallen. Just as defeat at Waterloo ironically crowned the Emperor's achievement with the imperishable allure of the romantic loser, so Stendhal, proclaiming with characteristic disingenuousness that he had fallen with Napoleon, was free at last to assume the glamour of the subversive, the maverick, the renegado, which defined his unique gifts. He needed, in short, to feel that he was unacceptable, even while so much of his life was devoted to seeking official acceptance.

The crucial difference between Stendhal and his great contemporaries, Balzac, Hugo or – yes, why not? – Dumas, was that he was old enough to recall the French Revolution.

INTRODUCTION

Born Marie-Henri Beyle at Grenoble in 1783, he stood grounded irremovably in that seventeenth- and eighteenth-century culture of light and clarity whose crucial impact on France is apparently eternal. His friend Prosper Mérimée recalled him loudly extolling the supremacy of what he called 'la lo-gique', and his literary tastes, whether in French, English or Italian, centred upon the authors of the Grand Siècle and the Enlightenment rather than upon his Romantic contemporaries.

Yet his childhood was archetypally Romantic in its atmosphere of alienated unhappiness, scorn and misunderstanding. He hated his father, Chérubin Beyle, a royalist lawyer who frittered money away in useless agricultural speculations and failed to make adequate emotional contact with his children. Conversely, he adored his mother, Henriette Gagnon, with whom, though she died when young Henri was only seven, he claimed that he was 'amoureux'. It was his grandfather, Doctor Gagnon, with his extensive library and passion for Voltaire, and his great-aunt Elisabeth, with her ferocious sense of honour and disdain of cant and false sentiment, who gave the boy's character its essential toughness and resilience.

After a dismal spell under the tutelage of a local abbé, on whom he scarifyingly pronounced 'I do not pretend that he was actually a criminal, but it is difficult to imagine a soul more dead, more a foe to everything honest, more perfectly devoid of any humane feeling', Stendhal entered the Ecole Centrale at Grenoble, one of a series of such schools established under national laws in 1795. Even though disillusioned by his schoolfellows, 'a bunch of selfish rascals', he was sufficiently well drilled in the heavily mathematical curriculum to gain a place at the Ecole Polytechnique in Paris, thereby making one of those classic rejections of provincial stuffiness and parochialism in favour of metropolitan sophistication which form a *sine qua non* in many a French literary career.

What Stendhal's youthful frustrations, whether real or imagined, had taught him was the supreme value of personal happiness. His entire existence thereafter was devoted to pursuing *la bonheur*, even if, in its supreme form, that of a woman's unfettered love, it was often hard to come by. More accessible altogether were the excitement and adventure guaranteed to young Frenchmen by the dazzling military successes of Napoleon Bonaparte, to whose Army of Italy Henri Beyle soon found himself attached under the patronage of his influential cousin Pierre Daru. Crossing the Alps in the early summer of 1800 as a cavalry subaltern, the seventeen-year-old boy made what was to prove the crucial encounter of his life with the culture, language and society of a people exclusively devoted, as it seemed, to the successful pursuit of happiness.

Besides falling in love with Italy, he formed a series of deep sentimental attachments, subsequently transmuted into subjects for fiction but never losing their power to stir him, even long after they were over. Few if any of these were love affairs in the ordinary sense of the term. The women concerned were seldom as wholeheartedly involved in the business, either because this ugly fellow, with his plump cheeks, bad teeth and thinning hair (he finally resorted to wearing a toupee), in no way attracted them, or because, unlike Stendhal himself, they were not perpetually dazzled by the very notion of being in love. Their presence in his life is nevertheless of enormous significance, and about several of them, Mathilde Viscontini Dembowski, Alberthe de Rubempre, Giulia Rinieri, we now know enough to appreciate the special impact made by each on his creative imagination.

With the final collapse of the Empire in 1815, Stendhal, left without any sort of permanent employment, spent the next six years as a wanderer between France and Italy. In his beloved Milan (for his tomb he requested the inscription 'Arrigo Beyle, Milanese') he pursued love and literature with equal pleasure, meeting Byron and Rossini, haunting café society and the fashionable audiences of La Scala. Renouncing his earlier ambition to become a dramatist, he published a history of Italian painting, embarked on a life of Napoleon and completed *Rome, Naples et Florence en 1817*, the first of his works in which we can catch the unmistakable resonance of the Stendhalian voice, fearlessly opinionated, pugnacious, allusive, witty, elegant and unsparing.

'I think about everything before I write it down: of how

many other writers in Paris may the same be said?' Always
ambivalent in his attitudes towards the city and its artistic life,
Stendhal returned to Paris in 1821 to earn a living as a journalist
and reviewer for various French and English newspapers and
magazines and to gain himself a reputation as 'un homme
d'esprit' in the great salons of the capital. Not all their hostesses
and habitués appreciated his caustic tongue or his passion
for argument and paradox. Mary Clarke, friend of everyone
from Manzoni to Turgenev, loathed him almost from the
outset. 'He is like the harpies,' she wrote, 'he has the gift
of spoiling all he touches.' Nevertheless, his real genius for
making and maintaining firm friendships flourished during
these nine Parisian years, leavened as they were by a journey
to England which took him everywhere, from the Lake District
to Black Country factories to a highly genteel brothel in
Westminster.

It was a uniquely Stendhalian combination of political
change and the quirks of his own personality which ushered in
the final, momentous phase of his career. With the fall of
Charles X in 1830 and his replacement on the French throne
by the 'citizen king', Louis-Philippe, Stendhal, strapped for
cash, felt conscientiously able once again to seek an official
government position. If a provincial prefecture was too much
to expect, an Italian consulate was not, but his Napoleonic past
and combative literary personality were not unknown to the
agents of Austria, then the dominant superpower throughout
Italy, and his spell as consul at Trieste was destined to last a
mere three months before acceptance of his official position
was refused and he was transferred to the port of Civitavecchia
in the Papal States.

Nobody has ever claimed anything for Civitavecchia in the
way of artistic beauty or special excitement, and for Stendhal
it represented the seat of a dreary exile. Though reprimanded
by his superiors for his long absences in Rome, he was
nevertheless an exceptionally efficient bureaucrat, in charge of
a district extending right across Italy to Ancona on the Adriatic
coast, a notable martinet in his strict supervision of consular
expenses and assiduous in gleaning political information.
The Papal government, however, taking its cue from the

Austrians, was still wary of the former Bonapartist and suspected free thinker, while the French authorities were unlikely to view with much favour Stendhal's periodic expressions of cynical disillusionment with the atmosphere created in France by the bourgeois industrialism of the July Monarchy.

There were consolations. The breadth of his enthusiasms led him to try his hand as an amateur archaeologist among Etruscan tombs, and to develop an interest in Italy's more recent history buried among the archives and libraries of Rome. Most important of all was the impetus given to Stendhal's literary ambitions by his sense of distance, both figurative and actual, from that metropolitan French culture to which he had never uncritically belonged. Is there an element of meaningful coincidence in the fact that the first edition of *Le Rouge et le Noir* (*Scarlet and Black*), published in two volumes by the Parisian firm of Levavasseur in November 1830, appeared a week after he had set off for Trieste?

Le Rouge et le Noir was not Stendhal's first complete novel – *Armance*, an absorbing but necessarily flawed investigation of sexual impotence, had appeared in 1827 – nor was it the work of a writer altogether inexperienced in trying to make fiction serve his singular artistic purposes. There exists an entire volume of the author's botched jobs, false starts, rough sketches and unrealized projects, and fascinating reading this makes, the more so since it helps us to understand why his worldwide reputation rests on only two works, the present novel and *La Chartreuse de Parme*, published in 1839. True Stendhal enthusiasts would naturally add to this *Rome, Naples et Florence*, the autobiographical *Vie de Henry Brulard* and the unfinished masterpiece *Lucien Leuwen*, begun in 1834, but none of these has gained such universal popularity.

The fact is that Stendhal was not a novelist by disposition, in the manner of George Sand, with whom he travelled down the Rhône in 1833, or of Balzac, who penned an admiring notice of *La Chartreuse de Parme*. Lacking the boundless facility and inventiveness of either writer, he was impatient of contemporary fictional conventions. He shared Jane Austen's reluctance to describe places and people except where such description might be directly relevant to the ideas he was trying to convey with regard to a particular state of mind or social atmosphere. For this reason, where a descriptive passage does appear, it lacks that extraordinary conversational ease of manner, that fluency and directness of engagement, which are the hallmarks of his style at its best.

What he needed was the kind of kick-start inspiration which would carry him through the dangerous initial creative phase to a point safely beyond the reach of his own ruthless and unflinching self-awareness. Years before starting work on the novel which began in 1829 as 'Julien' and ended with the altogether more enigmatic title of *Le Rouge et le Noir*, he had written to a friend of 'this species of froth known as fine art, the necessary product of a certain sort of fermentation'.

The fermentation in the present case was set going by Stendhal's interest in two recent court cases which had been given widespread publicity in France. The first of these, the 'affaire Lafargue', he had already recounted in his travel book *Promenades dans Rome* (1829) a typically Stendhalian *mélange* of observations and opinions, in which the story scarcely seems out of place among tales of scandalous convent assignations, café gossip and Roman murders. Lafargue, a young cabinet-maker, having suspected and proved his mistress's infidelity, shot at her twice and then cut her throat. Found guilty, he was given a comparatively brief prison sentence, a fact which seems not to have impressed Stendhal so much as the sheer zeal and fearlessness with which Lafargue carried out his murderous revenge. It was this, he noted, which contrasted the lower-middle-class Lafargue with the strikingly passionless aristocracy of modern France. Poor and without social advantages the cabinet-maker might have been, but at least he was energetic, imaginative and well educated.

The second case, whose outlines more clearly influenced the plot of *Le Rouge et le Noir*, took place in 1827 in the novelist's native city of Grenoble. The good-looking and ambitious Antoine Berthet, son of a blacksmith, entered the household of the prosperous bourgeois Michoud family as tutor to their children, but was dismissed after a few months. His attempts to train for the priesthood were similarly unsuccessful, and he was dismissed from two local seminaries. Angry and desperate, he sent a series of threatening letters to Madame Michoud, a successful piece of blackmailing which prompted her husband to find him a post in the family of a Monsieur Cordon. With the Cordons, Berthet was equally unlucky. Madame Michoud took care to denounce him to his new employers, who were in any case suspicious of his growing interest in their daughter.

Dismissed once more, the young man, feeling himself well and truly spurned by the society from which he craved advancement, lost no time in declaring his intention to murder Madame Michoud. One Sunday morning he entered the church where she was at mass and wounded her mortally with a double-shotted pistol. Turning the gun on himself, he fired but only contrived to break his jaw. The courtroom at his trial was thronged with smartly dressed *grenobloises*, attracted by the murderer's 'interesting pallor'. Any hopes they might have entertained of judicial leniency, however, were dashed by the death sentence for premeditated homicide, and Berthet was executed, notwithstanding several efforts at obtaining a royal pardon.

If the Lafargue and Berthet cases offered the most direct inspiration for the story of Julien Sorel, the doomed hero of *Le Rouge et le Noir*, its essential immediacy for Stendhal's contemporaries was emphasized by the subtitle, 'A Chronicle of 1830'. In fact the novelist had been overtaken by events, for 1830 is notable in French history as the year in which a bourgeois revolution sent Charles X into exile and brought his distant cousin Louis-Philippe of Bourbon Orléans to the throne as a fully constitutional monarch. As a result, Stendhal changed his subtitle to 'A Chronicle of the Nineteenth Century', but the July Revolution, while not actually brought into the story, undoubtedly colours the narrative in the sense that the political and social background to the principal characters and episodes is littered with portents whose implications Stendhal's readers might easily pick up. The famous 'Secret Note' chapters of Volume 2, for example, in which Julien's phenomenal memorizing skills are exploited by the Marquis de la Mole as part of a reactionary conspiracy designed to purge the kingdom of pernicious liberalism, are an uncannily accurate reflection of the prevailing mood among the 'ultras', the extreme conservative element whose encouragement of Charles X in his more drastic legislative measures, especially those connected with strengthening the power of the Church, ultimately brought about his downfall.

Like many other novels of its period, *Le Rouge et le Noir* is thus self-consciously historical. Whatever his strictures on the romances of Sir Walter Scott, Stendhal, in common with every other contemporary writer of fiction, acknowledged their pervasive influence, especially in his enduring preoccupation with the links between the hero and the tide of political circumstance which laps around him. Yet the historicity of *Le Rouge et le Noir* is emphatically not that of *Waverley*, *Ivanhoe* or *The Bride of Lammermoor*. The atmosphere recaptured is that of recent experience, the common heritage of provincial France at the beginning of the nineteenth century. With little real sensitivity towards the past as something purely decorative and antiquarian, Stendhal was conscious, like many of his generation, of having lived through an astonishing and, as it increasingly seemed, unrepeatable era, in which history was made, unmade and made once more only to be finally destroyed, the age of Napoleon Bonaparte.

The spirit of Bonapartism, or to be more precise, of the Emperor defeated, exiled and dead, as a symbol of France's dissipated energies, dominates the novel. For the brooding Julien, whose favourite reading is the hagiographical *Memorial de Sainte Hélène*, Napoleon becomes a symbol of fateful possibilities, of the chance to turn reverie into reality. 'For many years, perhaps not an hour of his life had gone by without him telling himself that Bonaparte, a penniless and unknown lieutenant, had made himself ruler of the world with his sword.'

As well as providing a role model and an evil genius for Julien, Bonaparte, in his capacity of Grand Subversive, becomes part of that family drama which is played out in all Stendhal's fiction and which relates clearly to the writer's own view of himself and his attitude towards his parents. An enthusiasm for Napoleon is inculcated in Julien by the old army surgeon who teaches him 'all the history he knew – that is to say, the history of the Italian campaign of 1797' and who is one of various surrogate parents of either sex whom Julien acquires in the book. True fatherhood becomes identified, as in Stendhal's own case, with detested orthodoxy and legitimate authority. Julien himself, throughout the book, searches for, indeed insists upon, the kind of absolute freedom which rejects traditional family ties. At one point he even gleefully accepts the high-born origins which the Marquis de la Mole, partly for social convenience and partly because he cannot believe that so naturally noble a youth is merely the son of the proprietor of a saw-mill, thrusts upon him. 'Can it truly be,' asks Julien, 'that I am the son of an aristocrat exiled among our mountains by the dreaded Napoleon?'

This theme of doubtful paternity and its personal link with Stendhal's complex preoccupation with the whole issue of parents and children begs the question of how Julien may be identified with his creator. Everything by the writer of *Souvenirs d'égotisme* celebrates the Stendhalian self, the *moi-même* by whose singularity he was absorbed, with the absorption of a naturalist logging the behaviour of a creature in its natural habitat. His heroes, Lucien Leuwen, Fabrizio del Dongo in *La Chartreuse de Parme*, Octave in *Armance*, and his heroines besides, reflect different facets of their author, and Julien is no exception. The self-control applied as a test of will, the notion of duty as part of a stern code of private honour, the rigorously maintained independence so marked in the young man, were all features of Stendhal's own character which his friends and associates found attractive or problematical according to circumstance. So too was an obsession with reading which made him one of the best-read writers of his own age or any other, armed with a voracious curiosity and a photographic memory, both quali-ties he accords to his hero.

Yet it would be a mistake to see *Le Rouge et le Noir*, for all that 'Verrières' is a thinly disguised Grenoble, simply as slice of the ongoing Stendhalian autobiography which, in the form of notebooks, journals and numberless marginalia, forms such a significant element in his literary output. Other characters in the novel, it is true, have been readily matched against real-life counterparts. Madame de Rênal and Mathilde de la Mole are

linked with women in Stendhal's own life, including Mathilde
Viscontini Dembowski, the spirited Milanese wife of a Polish
general, and Giulia Rinieri de' Rocchi, ward of the Tuscan
minister to Paris, with whom he was to maintain amorous
relations until his death. The episode in Chapter 18, 'A King
at Verrières', imitated by Thomas Hardy in *The Mayor of
Casterbridge*, in which Charles X visits the splendidly restored
medieval abbey of Bray-le-Haut, is founded on a real incident
reported in a contemporary newspaper from which Stendhal
even lifted most of a sentence describing the light streaming
through the church windows.

Le Rouge et le Noir is not, however, a realist novel in the
tradition of absolute fidelity to sensation established later in
the century by Zola, Daudet and the Goncourts, though all of
them acknowledged what they owed to Stendhal. Its realism is
that of tone rather than atmosphere. Stendhal is less interested
in how things feel, sound and smell than in finding and sustain-
ing the appropriate idiom in which to express what he knows
about his characters and their world. This is why the novel's
famous 'dry' style made, and continues to make, such an enduring impression on its readers. It is the fact that we expect far
more from Stendhal than he is prepared to give us in the way
of melodrama and heightened emotion which makes him so
unmistakable and idiosyncratic a writer.

A lesser novelist would, for example, have exploited to the
full the operatic potential implicit in Madame de Rênal's
interview with Julien in the condemned cell in Chapter 73. In
Stendhal's hands their exchange becomes an entirely believable
mixture of fervent protestations with flat matters of fact,
touched with details whose realism subtly mingles the comic
and the pathetic. When Julien embraces Madame de Rênal,
he hugs her so hard that she cries out.

> 'It is nothing,' she told him, 'you hurt me.'
> 'In your shoulder,' cried Julien, bursting into tears.

What other writer could so skilfully underplay the moment's
essential theatricality?

A similar blend of ludicrous and touching elements inspires
the marvellous moment in which Julien catches the youthful

Bishop of Agde practising his episcopal role in front of a long mirror, making a series of appropriate priestly gestures. He asks Julien whether his mitre is on straight, and then, making the disarming excuse that he might not seem old or venerable enough to the King, goes on 'describing benedictions'.

The hint of indulgence towards human foibles here is typical of Stendhal. One of the saving graces of his personality was that he seldom managed to appear quite as merciless as he might have wished in his outlook on the world. His moments of tenderness towards his characters, by being so unforced, appear to greater advantage in the context of the 'truth – truth in all her rugged harshness' which stands as an epigraph to the novel.

'I make every effort possible to appear dry,' he wrote in *De l'Amour*, 'I want to impose silence on my heart which imagines it has so much to say. I always tremble in case I may only have written a sigh when I wished to note down a truth.' The impact of Stendhal's unique fictional voice, heard for the first time at its full resonance in *Le Rouge et le Noir*, was not as powerful as he had hoped, either upon Parisian critics, divided as to the merits of the book, or on contemporary readers. He was correct in believing that a real audience for his work would gather only after his death, as the nineteenth-century novel achieved its maturity, when artists of the calibre of Tolstoy, George Eliot and Henry James acknowledged his influence, when Nietzsche hailed him as 'the last great French psychologist' and Conrad saw in him an apostle of unfettered liberty.

Only in the present century, obsessed as it is with criteria of authenticity in art, has the totality of Stendhal's achievement in *Le Rouge et le Noir* been adequately grasped. His famous description in Volume 2 of the novel genre as 'a mirror walking along a high road', sometimes reflecting the blue sky and at others the mud, encapsulates his idea of this book as something which should strike out far beyond the reach of his fiction-writing contemporaries, both in its uncompromising clarity of style and its awareness that our humanity is moulded, refined, battered or distorted by environment, education, society and the incalculable fluctuations of politics, war or revolution. If

such truths seem self-evident nowadays, Stendhal's own era
had scarcely begun to acknowledge them. Our modern age
pays *Le Rouge et le Noir* its due of admiration for an artistic
integrity which seems at first glance to have been shaped out
of nothing at all in the way of practice, experience or the
painstaking acquisition of professional expertise. The greatest
tribute we can pay this book is to say that it has no fathers or
mothers but an infinity of heirs.

Jonathan Keates

SELECT BIBLIOGRAPHY

STENDHAL'S LITERARY WORKS

Vies de Haydn, Mozart et Métastase, 1814.
L'Histoire de la peinture en Italie, 1817.
Rome, Naples et Florence, 1817.
De l'Amour, 1822.
Racine et Shakespeare, 1823.
La Vie de Rossini, 1823.
Armance, 1827.
Le Rouge et le Noir, 1830.
Souvenirs d'égotisme, 1832.
Lucien Leuwen, 1834.
La Vie de Henry Brulard, 1835.
Chroniques italiennes, 1837–8.
Mémoires d'un touriste, 1837.
La Chartreuse de Parme, 1839.

GENERAL STUDIES OF STENDHAL

Biographical
Reliable accounts are those of VICTOR DEL LITTO, 1965; JOANNA
RICHARDSON, 1974; ROBERT ALTER, 1979; and MICHAEL CROUZET,
1990.

Critical
ADAMS, ROBERT M., *Stendhal, Notes on a Novelist*, 1959.
BEAUVOIR, SIMONE DE, 'Women in Stendhal' in *The Second Sex* (1949),
English trans. 1951.
BERTHIER, PHILIPPE, *Stendhal et la sainte famille*, 1983.
BROMBERT, VICTOR, *Stendhal, Fiction and the Themes of Freedom*, 1968.
DIDIER, BEATRICE, *Stendhal, autobiographe*, 1983.
HEMMINGS, F. W. J., *Stendhal, A Study of His Novels*, 1964.
JEFFERSON, ANN, *Reading Realism in Stendhal*, 1989.
MARTINEAU, HENRI, *L'Oeuvre de Stendhal*, 1945.
PRÉVOST, JEAN, *La Création chez Stendhal*, 1951.
REID, MARTINE, *Correspondances: Stendhal en toutes lettres*, Yale French
Studies no. 71, 1986.
TILLETT, MARGARET, *Stendhal, The Background to the Novels*, 1971.

ON *LE ROUGE ET LE NOIR*

CASTEX, P-G, *Le Rouge et Noir de Stendhal*, 1970.
FELMAN, SHOSHANA, *La 'Folie' dans l'oeuvre romanesque de Stendhal*, 1971.
HAIG, STIRLING, *Stendhal, The Red and The Black*, 1989.
MITCHELL, JOHN, *Stendhal, Le Rouge et le Noir*, 1973.
ROBERT, MARTHE, *Roman des origines et origines du roman*, 1972.

CHRONOLOGY

DATE	AUTHOR'S LIFE	LITERARY CONTEXT
1782		Laclos: *Les Liaisons dangereuses*. Rousseau: *Confessions*.
1783	Birth of Marie-Henri Beyle in Grenoble, 23 January, the eldest of three children of Chérubin Beyle, a lawyer, and Henriette Gagnon. Two sisters are born in 1786 and 1788.	
1784		Beaumarchais: *Le Mariage de Figaro*. Death of Diderot.
1788		Restif de la Bretonne: *Les Nuits de Paris* (to 1794). Bernardin de Saint Pierre: *Paul et Virginie*.
1789		Mme de Staël: *Lettres sur Rousseau*.
1790	Death of his mother in childbirth.	Birth of Lamartine.
1791		Sade: *Justine*.
1792		Florian: *Fables*.
1793	During the Terror, his father, a royalist, is arrested and imprisoned three times (to 1794).	Mme Roland: *Mémoires* (pub. 1820).
1794	The young Henri, his imagination fired by the Revolution, tries to join the Battalion of Hope, a Jacobin organization for children in Grenoble.	Ann Radcliffe: *The Mysteries of Udolpho*.
1795		Goethe: *Wilhelm Meister's Apprenticeship* (to 1796); *Roman Elegies*.
1796	Attends Ecole Centrale in Grenoble.	Diderot: *Jacques le fataliste*. Maistre: *Considérations sur la révolution française*.
1797		Chateaubriand: *Essais sur les révolutions*. Ann Radcliffe: *The Italian*. Birth of Alfred de Vigny.

Treaty of Versailles ends American war, in which the French had been involved on the side of the colonists since 1778. Britain recognizes US independence.

Meeting of States General. French Revolution. Storming of Bastille. Secularization of Church lands.

Death of Mirabeau. Louis XVI attempts to flee and is arrested at Varennes. Constitution of 1791 voted. New Legislative Assembly set up.
France at war with Austria and Prussia. Prison massacres in Paris. National Convention established. French Republic proclaimed.
Execution of Louis XVI. France and Britain at war. Reign of Terror (to 1794). War in Vendée (to 1796). Marat assassinated. Execution of Marie Antoinette.
Fall of Robespierre (July): end of Terror.

Defeat of émigrés at Quiberon. Revolt of 13 vendémiaire: Dissolution of the Convention (October), and its replacement by the Directory (November).

Napoleon leads French army to victory against the Austrians in northern Italy: Peace of Campo Formio. Constitutional monarchists gain majority in Directory (April). Republican *coup d'état* of 18 fructidor (October).

DATE	AUTHOR'S LIFE	LITERARY CONTEXT
1799	Studying mathematics with a view to entering the Ecole Polytechnique in Paris. Goes to Paris (November), fails to enrol but stays in the capital. Is taken up by the Daru family, aristocratic cousins of his grandfather.	Schiller: *Wallenstein*. Birth of Balzac.
1800	Pierre Daru, a high-ranking bureaucrat in the Ministry of War, secures him a clerical post in his department. Accompanies Daru to the Italian front. His cousin's influence obtains for him a commission in the Dragoons. Returns to Paris, and after a period of training in Switzerland arrives back in Italy (May) as part of the occuping army. Based in Milan, he is captivated by Italian opera, architecture, and women. Meets Angela Pietragrua.	Mme de Staël: *De la Littérature*.
1801	After a brief spell as aide-de-camp to his divisional commander, returns to his regiment in Turin.	Chateaubriand: *Atala*. Destutt de Tracy: *Eléments d'idéologie*.
1802	An allowance from his father enables him to return to Paris and start writing. His ambition is to write for the theatre.	Chateaubriand: *Le Génie de christianisme*. Mme de Staël: *Delphine*. Cabanis: *Rapports du physique et du moral de l'homme*. Foscolo: *Last Letters of Jacopo Ortis*. Birth of Hugo.
1803		Death of Laclos. Birth of Mérimée.
1804	Meets the actress Mélanie Guilbert.	Senancour: *Obermann*. Schiller: *William Tell*.
1805	Follows her to Marseilles, where he works as a clerk in a trading house.	Chateaubriand: *René*.
1806	Through Daru's influence, obtains an administrative post in Napoleon's army, based at Brunswick (November). Spends the next four years behind the lines in Germany and Austria.	

CHRONOLOGY

War of the Second Coalition. Russians and Austrians achieve initial successes against the French in Italy, but are driven back and defeated in Switzerland. Napoleon's *coup d'état* of 18 brumaire (9-10 November): overthrow of the Directory. Constitution of the year VIII. Bonaparte First Consul.

Bank of France founded (February). Prefectoral system established. Pacification of the west. French defeat Austrians at the battles of Marengo and Hohenlinden. Royalist bomb plot.

Treaty of Lunéville between France and Austria (February). French defeated in Egypt (August).

Peace of Amiens between France and Britain (March). Concordat between France and the papacy promulgated (April). Bonaparte is made a Consul for life (May). The Legion of Honour created. Incorporation of Piedmont with France (September).

War breaks out once more between France and Britain. France sells Louisiana to the United States.
Code Napoléon. Napoleon becomes Emperor.

Napoleon becomes King of Italy. *Code Napoléon* extended to Italy. Third Coalition against France. Nelson victorious at battle of Trafalgar. French occupation of Vienna, and victory at Austerlitz. France annexes Genoa. Joseph Bonaparte becomes King of Naples and Sicily. Louis Bonaparte becomes King of Holland. Confederation of the Rhine constituted. End of Holy Roman Empire. Prussian army broken at Jena. Napoleon annexes Prussia. Napoleon's Berlin Decrees. Blockade of Britain begins. Venice added to Napoleon's Italian kingdom.

DATE	AUTHOR'S LIFE	LITERARY CONTEXT
1807		Foscolo: *Of Sepulchres*.
1808		Goethe: Faust, part I.
1809	His post takes him to occupied Vienna (May–December).	Goethe: *Elective Affinities*.
1810	Returns to Paris. Enjoys active social life. Affair with opera singer Angéline Béreyter.	Mme de Staël: *De l'Allemagne*. Scott: *The Lady of the Lake*.
1811	On leave in Milan, he resumes affair with Angela Pietragrua. Brief tour of Italy. Starts working on a history of Italian painting.	Jane Austen: *Sense and Sensibility*.
1812	Obtains appointment as a courier during Napoleon's Russian campaign. Takes part in retreat from Moscow.	Byron: *Childe Harold* (to 1818).
1813	Paris. Briefly posted to Prussian front; witnesses battle of Bautzen. Posted to Silesia (June) but returns to Paris, ill, in July. On sick leave, visits Milan (September); in Paris again (November). During state of emergency, sent to Grenoble to organize defence of Dauphiné (December).	Jane Austen: *Pride and Prejudice*. Byron: *Le Corsair*; *Le Giaour*.
1814	Returns, ill again, to Paris (March), in time to witness battle of Montmartre, won by the Russians, and the allies' triumphant march down the Champs Elysées. Frustrated in his attempts to gain employment under the new regime, leaves for Italy (July), heavily in debt.	Scott: *Waverley*. Jane Austen: *Mansfield Park*. Hoffmann: *Tales* (to 1815).
1815	Lives in Milan, also exploring all the major Italian cities (to 1821). First book published: *Vies de Haydn, Mozart et Métastase*, little of it original work. Breaks with Angela Pietragrua.	Béranger: *Chansons morales et autres* (first of five collections of Chansons, 1815–33). Destutt de Tracy: *Traité de la volonté et de ses effets*. Scott: *The Lord of the Isles*; *Guy Mannering*. Wordsworth: *Poems*.

CHRONOLOGY

After Russian defeats at Eylau and Friedland, Alexander I makes peace with Napoleon (Treaty of Tilsit). Prussian Edict of Emancipation. Scharnhorst's military reforms.

Tuscany added to France. Joseph Bonaparte King of Spain. Peninsular campaign begins.

Revolt in Tyrol. Outbreak of war between France and Austria. Annexation of Papal States. Napoleon enters Vienna. Austrians defeated at Wagram: Peace of Schönbrunn. Battle of Talavera: Wellesley expels French from Portugal. Napoleon divorces Josephine and marries Archduchess Marie-Louise.

Napoleon invades Russia. Battle of Borodino. Retreat from Moscow. Wellington takes Madrid.

War of Liberation opens (February): battle of Bautzen (May); armistice in Germany (May–August); battles of Dresden (August) and Kulm (September). Napoleon's defeat by allied forces at Leipzig (October). Wellington crosses Pyrenees into France (October–November). Carbonari (secret societies of Italian nationalists) rise against French invaders in Naples; movement suppressed and its leader, Vincenzo Federici, put to death.

Allies enter Paris and establish a provisional government (March). Abdication of Napoleon and exile to Elba; Louis XVIII returns to Paris; French Constitutional Charter (April). First Peace of Paris (May). Congress of Vienna opens (September).

Napoleon's 'Hundred Days' and defeat at Waterloo (June). Adoption of Final Act by Congress of Vienna (June): Austria regains control of most of Italy; Papal States restored; Ferdinand IV recognized as King of the Two Sicilies. Second Restoration and return of Louis XVIII (July). 'White Terror' (July–September). Election of ultra-Royalist *Chambre introuvable* (August). Resignation of Talleyrand and Fouché (September). First Richelieu ministry. Napoleon lands on St Helena (October). Second Peace of Paris (November).

DATE	AUTHOR'S LIFE	LITERARY CONTEXT
1816	Meets Byron at La Scala.	Constant: *Adolphe*. Coleridge: *Christabel and other Poems*.
1817	*Histoire de la peinture en Italie* (2 vols). *Rome, Naples et Florence en 1817* (for which he first uses the name Stendhal). First trip to London.	Byron: *Manfred*. Keats: *Poems*.
1818	Works on a life of Napoleon. Falls in love – which is unreciprocated – with Mathilde Dembowski in Milan.	Jane Austen: *Northanger Abbey*; *Persuasion*. Mary Shelley: *Frankenstein*.
1819	Death of his father. Disappointed in his hopes of a substantial inheritance: the estate is encumbered with debt. Writing *De l'Amour*, inspired by his unhappy passion for 'Métilde'.	Maistre: *Du Pape*. Byron: *Don Juan* (to 1824). Shelley: *The Cenci* (to 1821). Scott: *Ivanhoe*. Hoffmann: *The Serapion Brethren* (to 1821).
1820		Lamartine: *Premières méditations poétiques*. Keats: *Lamia ... and other Poems*. Shelley: 'To Liberty'; 'To Naples'. Manzoni: *The Count of Carmagnola*.
1821	His position in Austrian-dominated Milan becoming untenable. Suspected of Carbonarism, he is obliged to leave Italy for Paris. Second trip to London (autumn).	Maistre: *De l'église gallicane*; *Soirées de St Petersbourg*. Scott: *Kenilworth*. Goethe: *Wilhelm Meister's Travels* (to 1829).
1822	Becomes involved in the artistic and intellectual life of Paris. During the 1820s meets many of the great figures in literature, science and politics – Hugo, Sainte-Beuve, Béranger, Mérimée, Tracy, Cuvier, Thiers, Lafayette, etc. *De l'Amour* published. Writes for English journals.	Hugo: *Odes et Poésies diverses*. Vigny: *Poèmes*. Les Cases: *Mémorial de Sainte-Hélène*. de Quincey: *Confessions of an English Opium Eater*.

HISTORICAL EVENTS

Dissolution of *Chambre introuvable.*

Congress of Aix-la-Chapelle: end of allied occupation of France. France readmitted to 'Concert of Powers'. Richelieu replaced by Decazes.

Assassination of conservative playwright Kotzebue by student Karl Sand in Mannheim. Metternich responds by repressive Carlsbad Decrees, designed to stamp out liberal opposition in German Confederation. Massacre of Peterloo in Britain, followed by repressive Six Acts. Géricault: *The Raft of the Medusa.*

Accession of George IV in Britain (January). Revolution in Spain (January–March). Assassination of the duc de Berry, heir presumptive to French throne (February). Recall of Richelieu. In Naples, a military rising against King Ferdinand is joined by members of the Carbonari led by General Pepe (July); they are granted a constitution but success is only temporary. In response, Metternich convokes Conference of Troppau (October). Local uprisings by the Charbonnerie in France (1820–21) are quickly suppressed.

Conference of Laibach (January): Austria authorized to suppress Neapolitan revolution (March). Insurrection in Piedmont; abdication of Victor Emmanuel. Outbreak of Greek War of Independence. Resignation of Richelieu ministry; Ultras (Villèle and Corbière) take office (December). Education gradually put under clerical control (to 1824). Death of Napoleon.

Massacre of Scio. Congress of Verona. Attempt of the four sergeants at La Rochelle.

DATE	AUTHOR'S LIFE	LITERARY CONTEXT
1823	Defends Romanticism in his pamphlet *Racine et Shakespeare*. Publishes *La Vie de Rossini*. Three-month tour of Italy.	Lamartine: *Nouvelles méditations poétiques*. Hugo: *Han d'Islande*. Guizot: *Essais sur l'histoire de France*. Thiers: *Histoire de la révolution française* (to 1827).
1824	Writes for the *Journal de Paris* and other French periodicals. Affair with Comtesse Clémentine Curial.	Scott: *Redgauntlet*. Death of Byron at Missolonghi.
1825	*Racine et Shakespeare* II. Death of 'Métilde' in Milan.	Mérimée: *Le Théâtre de Clara Gazul*. Saint-Simon: *Nouveau Christianisme*. Thierry: *Histoire de la conquête de l'Angleterre par les Normands*.
1826	Writes his first novel, *Armance*. Breaks with Clémentine Curial. Travels in England (June–September).	Scott: *Woodstock*. Vigny: *Cinque-mars*; *Poèmes antiques et modernes*. Hugo: *Odes et Ballades*; *Bug-Jargal*.
1827	*Armance* published. Leaves for six-month tour of Italy (August), during which he spends some time with Lamartine in Florence. Returns to Milan for the first time since 1821 but is immediately expelled by Austrian authorities.	Mérimée: *La Guzla*. Hugo: *Cromwell*. Guizot: *La Révolution d'Angleterre*. Nerval: translation of Goethe's *Faust*. Manzoni: *The Betrothed*.
1828	Returns to Paris (January).	Mickiewicz: *Konrad Wallenrod*. Casanova: *Mémoires*. Mérimée: *Jacquerie*.
1829	Publishes *Promenades dans Rome*. Affair with Alberthe de Rubempré. Spends three months in the south of France (autumn); in Marseilles, starts working on *Le Rouge et le Noir*. Produces three stories for periodical publication: 'Vanina Vanini', 'Le Philstre' and 'Le Coffre et le revenant' (to 1830).	Balzac: *Les Chouans*; *Physiologie du mariage*. Hugo: *Les Orientales*; *Le Dernier Jour d'un condamné*. Dumas: *Henri III et sa cour*. Mérimée: *Chronique du règne de Charles IX*, 'Matteo Falcone'. Lamennais: *Des progrès de la révolution et de la guerre contre l'église*.

CHRONOLOGY

DATE	AUTHOR'S LIFE	LITERARY CONTEXT
1830	Breaks with Alberthe. Affair with Giulia Rinieri, a patrician Sienese living in Paris. Witnesses July Revolution; is refused an appointment as a Prefect but offered a post as Consul in Trieste. Seeks marriage with Giulia Rinieri, but is turned down by her guardian. Writes fragment *Mina de Vanghel*. *Le Rouge et le Noir* published (November), a week after his departure for Italy.	Hugo: *Hernani*. Lamartine: *Harmonies poétiques et religieuses*. Musset: *Contes d'Espagne et d'Italie*. Gautier: *Premières poésies*. Comte: *Cours de philosophie positive* (6 vols to 1842).
1831	Transferred to Civitavecchia in the Papal States after Metternich himself refuses to accept his appointment to Trieste. Immediately befriends Republicans in the town.	Balzac: *Le Peau de chagrin*. Dumas: *Antony*.
1832	Bored by life in Civitavecchia, contrives to spend much of the year travelling in Italy or at his Roman *pied-à-terre*. Writes the autobiographical *Souvenirs d'égotisme* (published posthumously). Dispatched as military intendant to Ancona in March, at the time of the French expeditionary force.	George Sand: *Indiana*. Hugo: *Le Roi s'amuse*. Balzac: *Le Curé de Tours*. Sainte-Beuve: *Critiques et portraits littéraires* (to 1839). Goethe: *Faust*, part II. Clausewitz: *On War*. Death of Goethe and Scott.
1833	Leave in France (September–December). Travels down the Rhône with George Sand and Alfred de Musset (December).	Balzac: *Eugénie Grandet*; *Le Médecin de campagne*. Hugo: *Lucrèce Borgia*; *Marie Tudor*. George Sand: *Lélia*. Heine: *De la France*. Béranger: *Chansons nouvelles et dernières*. Michelet: *L'Histoire de France* (17 vols to 1867). Carlyle: *Sartor Resartus*.
1834	Starts working on *Lucien Leuwen* (which is never completed).	Mickiewicz: *Pan Tadeusz*. Musset: *Fantasio*; *On ne badine pas avec l'amour*; *Lorenzaccio*. George Sand: *Jacques*.

CHRONOLOGY

HISTORICAL EVENTS

Conquest of Algiers. The Four Ordinances: king dissolves newly elected Chamber, restricts the franchise and suppresses freedom of the press. July Revolution. Abdication of Charles X; duc d'Orléans accepts lieutenant-generalcy of France, afterwards becoming 'King of the French' as Louis-Philippe. New constitutional Charter. Revolt of Belgians against King of Holland. Accession of William IV in Britain. Revolutions in Germany and risings in central Italy. Berlioz: *Symphonie fantastique*. Delacroix: *Liberty leading the People*.

Anti-clerical riots in Paris. Casimir-Périer ministry. French expel Dutch from Belgium. Insurrection of Lyons silk-workers. Risings in Modena, Bologna, Parma and Romagna: the rebels count on support from France, but Louis-Philippe, pressurized by Metternich, declines to intervene, and Austrian troops suppress rebellion (March–April). Mazzini founds 'Young Italy'. Russia crushes revolution in Poland.
Austrian troops recalled to the Papal States by Legate-Cardinal Albani (January); Casimir-Périer dispatches French fleet to Ancona to resist Austrian encroachment. Duchesse de Berry attempts to rouse Vendée. Death of Casimir-Périer. New ministry includes Broglie, Thiers and Guizot, with Marshal Soult as nominal head. European recognition of new Greek state. Parliamentary Reform Act in Britain.

Guizot's education law. Quadruple Alliance between France, Britain, Spain and Portugal.

Revolt in Lyons. Unrest in Paris suppressed (rue Transnonain massacre). Berlioz: *Harold en Italie*.

DATE	AUTHOR'S LIFE	LITERARY CONTEXT
1835	Starts work on the autobiographical *Vie de Henry Brulard*. Awarded the Croix de la Légion d'Honneur for his contribution to French literature.	Balzac: *Le Père Goriot*. Musset: *Les Nuits* (to 1837). Vigny: *Servitude et grandeur militaires*; *Chatterton*. Hugo: *Les Chants du crépuscule*. Gautier: *Mademoiselle de Maupin*. Tocqueville: *De la Démocratie en Amérique* (and 1840).
1836	For the second time, attempts to write the *Vie de Napoléon* (which remains unfinished). On leave in France (to 1839).	Lamartine: *Jocelyn*. Dumas: *Kean*. Musset: *Confessions d'un enfant du siècle*.
1837	Travels within France and writes *Mémoires d'un touriste*. Writes and publishes *Vittoria Accoramboni* and *Les Cencis* in *Le Revue des Deux Mondes* – the first two stories of what are now known as the *Chroniques italiennes* (based on Italian manuscripts). Writes fragment *Le Rose et le Vert*.	Balzac: *Illusions perdues* (to 1843). Hugo: *Les Voix intérieures*. George Sand: *Mauprat*. Dickens: *The Pickwick Papers*. Carlyle: *History of the French Revolution*.
1838	Travels in Switzerland, Low Countries and Germany. *Mémoires d'un touriste* published (June). Starts gathering material for *Voyage dans le midi de la France* (published posthumously). Two further Italian stories, *La Duchesse de Palliano* and *L'Abbesse de Castro* (Part One) published. Writes *La Chartreuse de Parme* in six weeks (November–December).	Hugo: *Ruy Blas*. Gautier: *La Comédie de la mort*. Dickens: *Oliver Twist*.
1839	*La Chartreuse de Parme* and second part of *L'Abbesse de Castro* published (spring). In June, obliged to return to Civitavecchia. Starts work on a novel, *Lamiel* (unfinished). Spends a month with Mérimée in Rome and Naples.	Lamartine: *Recueillements poétiques*. Blanc: *Organisation du travail*. Louis Napoleon: *Les Idées napoléoniennes*. Dickens: *Nicholas Nickleby*.
1840	Civitavecchia and Rome. Reads Balzac's enthusiastic review of *La Chartreuse de Parme* and considers revising it in the light of his criticisms.	Hugo: *Les Rayons et les Ombres*. Sainte-Beuve: *Port-Royal* (6 books, to 1859). Mérimée: 'Colomba'. Proudhon: *Qu'est-ce que la propriété?*

CHRONOLOGY

Fieschi's assassination attempt on Louis-Philippe. Abortive invasion of Savoy by followers of Mazzini.

Attempted uprising by Louis Napoleon at Strasbourg. Molé forms government. Death of Charles X in exile. Meyerbeer: *The Huguenots*.

Paris–Saint-Germain railway opened. Capture of Constantine (Algeria). Accession of Queen Victoria.

Death of Talleyrand. Berlioz: *Benvenuto Cellini*.

Revolt of Abd-el-Kader. Fall of Molé. Berlioz: *Roméo et Juliette*.

Inauguration of Bastille Column. Napoleon's ashes returned to Paris. Attempt of Louis Napoleon at Boulogne. Government of Thiers (March–October). Mehemet Ali crisis. Guizot forms ministry (to 1848).

DATE	AUTHOR'S LIFE	LITERARY CONTEXT
1841	Suffers a stroke. Returns to Paris.	Musset: *Le Souvenir*. Lamennais: *Le Livre du peuple*. Dickens: *The Old Curiosity Shop*.
1842	Suffers a second stroke in the street, from which he dies the following day (23 March).	Sue: *Les Mystères de Paris*. George Sand: *Consuelo*.

HISTORICAL EVENTS

Franco-British entente cordiale.

Duc d'Orléans killed in accident. Guizot's railway law. Railway mania in France (to 1846).

To O. H. H.
who had every word of both volumes
read to her when she was powerless to resist.

C. K. S. M.
Leghorn and Pisa
July–December 1925

TRANSLATOR'S NOTE

This translation has been made from the text of *Le Rouge et le Noir, Chronique du XIXe Siècle*, texte établi et annoté avec une préface et une bibliographie par Henri Martineau … Éditions Bossard, Boulevard Saint-Germain, 140, Paris, 1925. This is a reprint of the first edition; the footnotes, giving the corrections and alterations afterwards made in manuscript by Beyle himself, have been incorporated in the text of the translation, the proofs of which have also been collated with the text edited by M. Jules Marsan and published by M. Édouard Champion (1923).

C.K.S.M.

PUBLISHER'S NOTE

This work was on the point of publication
when the great events of July took place and
turned every mind in a direction which does
not encourage the play of the imagination.
We have reason to believe that the following
pages were written in 1827.

(Stendhal's note in first French edition)

SCARLET AND BLACK

A CHRONICLE OF
THE NINETEENTH CENTURY

TO THE HAPPY FEW

The drawback of the reign of opinion, which however procures *liberty*, is that it interferes in matters with which it has no concern; such as private life. Hence the gloom of America and England. To avoid touching upon private life, the author has invented a small town, *Verrières*, and when he required a Bishop, a jury, an Assize Court, has placed them all in Besançon, where he has never been.

CONTENTS

CONTENTS

SCARLET AND BLACK

VOLUME ONE

Truth—Truth in all her rugged harshness.
DANTON

SCARLET AND BLACK

CHAPTER ONE

A SMALL TOWN

Put thousands together
Less bad,
But the cage less gay.
HOBBES.

T HE small town of Verrières may be regarded as one
of the most attractive in the Franche-Comté. Its white
houses with their high pitched roofs of red tiles are
spread over the slope of a hill, the slightest contours of which
are indicated by clumps of sturdy chestnuts. The Doubs runs
some hundreds of feet below its fortifications, built in times
past by the Spaniards, and now in ruins.

Verrières is sheltered on the north by a high mountain, a
spur of the Jura. The jagged peaks of the Verra put on a
mantle of snow in the first cold days of October. A torrent
which comes tearing down from the mountain passes through
Verrières before emptying its waters into the Doubs, and sup-
plies power to a great number of sawmills; this is an
extremely simple industry, and procures a certain degree of
comfort for the majority of the inhabitants, who are of the
peasant rather than of the burgess class. It is not, however,
the sawmills that have made this little town rich. It is to the
manufacture of printed calicoes, known as Mulhouse stuffs,
that it owes the general prosperity which, since the fall of
Napoleon, has led to the refacing of almost all the houses in
Verrières.

No sooner has one entered the town than one is startled

by the din of a noisy machine of terrifying aspect. A score of weighty hammers, falling with a clang which makes the pavement tremble, are raised aloft by a wheel which the water of the torrent sets in motion. Each of these hammers turns out, daily, I cannot say how many thousands of nails. A bevy of fresh, pretty girls subject to the blows of these enormous hammers, the little scraps of iron which are rapidly transformed into nails. This work, so rough to the outward eye, is one of the industries that most astonish the traveller who ventures for the first time among the mountains that divide France from Switzerland. If, on entering Verrières, the traveller inquires to whom belongs that fine nail factory which deafens everybody who passes up the main street, he will be told in a drawling accent: 'Eh! It belongs to the Mayor.'

Provided the traveller halts for a few moments in this main street of Verrières, which runs from the bank of the Doubs nearly to the summit of the hill, it is a hundred to one that he will see a tall man appear, with a busy, important air.

At the sight of him every hat is quickly raised. His hair is turning grey, and he is dressed in grey. He is a Companion of several Orders, has a high forehead, an aquiline nose, and on the whole his face is not wanting in a certain regularity: indeed, the first impression formed of it may be that it combines with the dignity of a village mayor that sort of charm which may still be found in a man of forty-eight or fifty. But soon the visitor from Paris is annoyed by a certain air of self-satisfaction and self-sufficiency mingled with a suggestion of limitations and want of originality. One feels, finally, that this man's talent is confined to securing the exact payment of whatever is owed to him and to postponing payment till the last possible moment when he is the debtor.

Such is the Mayor of Verrières, M. de Rênal. Crossing the street with a solemn step, he enters the town hall and passes from the visitor's sight. But, a hundred yards higher up, if the visitor continues his stroll, he will notice a house of quite imposing appearance, and, through the gaps in an iron railing belonging to the house, some splendid gardens. Beyond, there is a line of horizon formed by the hills of Burgundy, which seem to have been created on purpose to delight the eye. This view makes the visitor forget the pestilential atmosphere of small financial interests which was beginning to stifle him.

He is told that this house belongs to M. de Rênal. It is to the profits that he has made from his great nail factory that the Mayor of Verrières is indebted for this fine free-stone house which he has just finished building. His family, they say, is Spanish, old, and was or claims to have been established in the country long before Louis XIV conquered it.

Since 1815 he has blushed at his connexion with industry: 1815 made him Mayor of Verrières. The retaining walls that support the various sections of this splendid garden, which, in a succession of terraces, runs down to the Doubs, are also a reward of M. de Rênal's ability as a dealer in iron.

You must not for a moment expect to find in France those picturesque gardens which enclose the manufacturing towns of Germany; Leipsic, Frankfort, Nuremberg, and the rest. In the Franche-Comté, the more walls a man builds, the more he makes his property bristle with stones piled one above another, the greater title he acquires to the respect of his neighbours. M. de Rênal's gardens, honeycombed with walls, are still further admired because he bought, for their weight in gold, certain minute scraps of ground which they cover. For instance that sawmill, whose curious position on the bank of the Doubs struck you as you entered Verrières, and on which you noticed the name *Sorel*, inscribed in huge letters on a board which overtops the roof, occupied, six years ago, the ground on which at this moment they are building the wall of the fourth terrace of M. de Rênal's gardens.

For all his pride, the Mayor was obliged to make many overtures to old Sorel, a dour and obstinate peasant; he was obliged to pay him in fine golden louis before he would consent to remove his mill elsewhere. As for the *public* lade which supplied power to the saw, M. de Rênal, thanks to the influence he wielded in Paris, obtained leave to divert it. This favour was conferred upon him after the 182— elections.

11

He gave Sorel four acres in exchange for one, five hundred yards lower down by the bank of the Doubs. And, albeit this site was a great deal more advantageous for his trade in planks of firwood, Père Sorel, as they have begun to call him now that he is rich, contrived to screw out of the impatience and *land-owning mania* which animated his neighbour a sum of 6,000 francs.

It is true that this arrangement was adversely criticised by the local wiseacres. On one occasion, it was a Sunday, four years later, M. de Rênal, as he walked home from church in his mayoral attire, saw at a distance old Sorel, supported by his three sons, watching him with a smile. That smile cast a destroying ray of light into the Mayor's soul; ever since then he has been thinking that he might have brought about the exchange at less cost to himself.

To win popular esteem at Verrières, the essential thing is not to adopt (while still building plenty of walls) any plan of construction brought from Italy by those masons who in spring pass through the gorges of the Jura on their way to Paris. Such an innovation would earn the rash builder an undying reputation for *wrong-headedness*, and he would be lost forever among the sober and moderate folk who create reputations in the Franche-Comté.

As a matter of fact, these sober folk wield there the most irritating form of *despotism*; it is owing to that vile word that residence in small towns is intolerable to anyone who has lived in that great republic which we call Paris. The tyranny of public opinion (and what an opinion!) is as fatuous in the small towns of France as it is in the United States of America.

CHAPTER TWO

A MAYOR

L'importance! Monsieur, n'est-ce rien? Le respect des sots,
l'ébahissement des enfants, l'envie des riches, le mépris du
sage.

BARNAVE.

FORTUNATELY for M. de Rênal's reputation as an administrator, a huge retaining wall was required for the public avenue which skirts the hillside a hundred feet above the bed of the Doubs. To this admirable position it is indebted for one of the most picturesque views in France. But, every spring, torrents of rainwater made channels across the avenue, carved deep gullies in it and left it impassable. This nuisance, which affected everybody alike, placed M. de Rênal under the fortunate obligation to immortalize his administration by a wall twenty feet in height and seventy or eighty yards long.

The parapet of this wall, to secure which M. de Rênal was obliged to make three journeys to Paris, for the Minister of the Interior before last had sworn a deadly enmity to the Verrières avenue; the parapet of this wall now rises four feet above the ground. And, as though to defy all Ministers past and present, it is being finished off at this moment with slabs of dressed stone.

How often, my thoughts straying back to the ball-rooms of Paris, which I had forsaken overnight, my elbows leaning upon those great blocks of stone of a fine grey with a shade of blue in it, have I swept with my gaze the vale of the

13

Doubs! Over there, on the left bank, are five or six winding valleys, along the folds of which the eye can make out quite plainly a number of little streams. After leaping from rock to rock, they may be seen falling into the Doubs. The sun is extremely hot in these mountains; when it is directly overhead, the traveller's rest is sheltered on this terrace by a row of magnificent planes. Their rapid growth, and handsome foliage of a bluish tint are due to the artificial soil with which the Mayor has filled in the space behind his immense retaining wall, for, despite the opposition of the town council, he has widened the avenue by more than six feet (although he is a True-Blue and I myself a Liberal, I give him credit for it), that is why, in his opinion and in that of M. Valenod, the fortunate governor of the Verrières poorhouse, this terrace is worthy to be compared with that of Saint-Germain-en-Laye.

For my part, I have only one fault to find with the *Cours de la Fidélité*; one reads this, its official title, in fifteen or twenty places, on marble slabs which have won M. de Rênal yet another Cross; what I should be inclined to condemn in the Cours de la Fidélité is the barbarous manner in which the authorities keep these sturdy plane trees trimmed and pollarded. Instead of suggesting, with their low, rounded, flattened heads, the commonest of kitchen garden vegetables, they would like nothing better than to assume those magnificent forms which one sees them wear in England. But the Mayor's will is despotic, and twice a year every tree belonging to the commune is pitilessly lopped. The Liberals of the place maintain, but they exaggerate, that the hand of the official gardener has grown much more severe since the Reverend Vicar Maslon formed the habit of appropriating the clippings.

This young cleric was sent from Besançon, some years ago, to keep an eye upon the Abbé Chélan and certain parish priests of the district. An old Surgeon-Major of the Army of Italy, in retirement at Verrières, who in his time had been simultaneously, according to the Mayor, a Jacobin and a Bonapartist, actually ventured one day to complain to him of the periodical mutilation of these fine trees.

'I like shade,' replied M. de Rênal with the touch of arrogance appropriate when one is addressing a surgeon, a Member of the Legion of Honour; 'I like shade, I have *my* trees cut so as to give shade, and I do not consider that a tree is made for any other purpose, unless, like the useful walnut, it *yields a return*.'

There you have the great phrase that decides everything at Verrières: YIELD A RETURN; it by itself represents the habitual thought of more than three fourths of the inhabitants.

Yielding a return is the consideration that settles everything in this little town which seemed to you, just now, so attractive. The stranger arriving there, beguiled by the beauty of the cool, deep valleys on every side, imagines at first that the inhabitants are influenced by the idea of *beauty*; they are always talking about the beauty of their scenery: no one can deny that they make a great to-do about it; but this is because it attracts a certain number of visitors whose money goes to enrich the innkeepers, and thus, through the channel of the rate-collector, *yields a return to the town*.

It was a fine day in autumn and M. de Rênal was strolling along the Cours de la Fidélité, his lady on his arm. While she listened to her husband, who was speaking with an air of gravity, Madame de Rênal's eye was anxiously following the movements of three little boys. The eldest, who might be about eleven, was continually running to the parapet as though about to climb on top. A gentle voice then uttered the name Adolphe, and the child abandoned his ambitious project. Madame de Rênal looked like a woman of thirty, but was still extremely pretty.

'He may live to rue the day, that fine gentleman from Paris,' M. de Rênal was saying in a tone of annoyance, his cheek paler even than was its wont. 'I myself am not entirely without friends at Court....'

But albeit I mean to speak to you of provincial life for two hundred pages, I shall not be so barbarous as to inflict upon you the tedium and all the *clever turns* of a provincial dialogue.

This fine gentleman from Paris, so odious to the Mayor of

Verrières, was none other than M. Appert,[1] who, a couple of days earlier, had contrived to make his way not only into the prison and the poorhouse of Verrières, but also into the hospital, administered gratuitously by the Mayor and the principal landowners of the neighbourhood.

'But,' Madame de Rênal put in timidly, 'what harm can this gentleman from Paris do you, since you provide for the welfare of the poor with the most scrupulous honesty?'

'He has only come to cast blame, and then he'll go back and have articles put in the Liberal papers.'

'You never read them, my dear.'

'But people tell us about those Jacobin articles; all that distracts us, and *hinders us from doing good.*[2] As for me, I shall never forgive the curé.'

1 A contemporary philanthropist and prison visitor.
2 Authentic.

16

CHAPTER THREE

THE BREAD OF THE POOR

Un curé vertueux et sans intrigue est une Providence pour
le village.

FLEURY.

I T should be explained that the curé of Verrières, an old
man of eighty, but blessed by the keen air of his mountains with an iron character and strength, had the right
to visit at any hour of the day the prison, the hospital, and
even the poorhouse. It was at six o'clock in the morning
precisely that M. Appert, who was armed with an introduction to the curé from Paris, had had the good sense to arrive
in an inquisitive little town. He had gone at once to the
presbytery.

As he read the letter addressed to him by M. le Marquis
de La Mole, a Peer of France, and the wealthiest landowner
in the province, the curé Chélan sat lost in thought.

'I am old and liked here,' he murmured to himself at
length, 'they would never dare!' Turning at once to the gentleman from Paris, with eyes in which, despite his great age,
there burned that sacred fire which betokens the pleasure of
performing a fine action which is slightly dangerous:

'Come with me, Sir, and, in the presence of the gaoler and
especially of the superintendents of the poorhouse, be so
good as not to express any opinion of the things we shall
see.' M. Appert realized that he had to deal with a man of
feeling; he accompanied the venerable curé, visited the
prison, the hospital, the poorhouse, asked many questions

and, notwithstanding strange answers, did not allow himself to utter the least word of reproach.

This visit lasted for some hours. The curé invited M. Appert to dine with him, but was told that his guest had some letters to write: he did not wish to compromise his kind friend any further. About three o'clock, the gentlemen went back to complete their inspection of the poorhouse, after which they returned to the prison. There they found the gaoler standing in the doorway; a giant six feet tall, with bandy legs; terror had made his mean face hideous.

'Ah, Sir,' he said to the curé, on catching sight of him, 'is not this gentleman, that I see with you, M. Appert?'

'What if he is?' said the curé.

'Because yesterday I received the most definite instructions, which the Prefect sent down by a gendarme who had to gallop all night long, not to allow M. Appert into the prison.'

'I declare to you, M. Noiroud,' said the curé, 'that this visitor, who is in my company, is M. Appert. Do you admit that I have the right to enter the prison at any hour of the day or night, bringing with me whom I please?'

'Yes, M. le curé,' the gaoler murmured in a subdued tone, lowering his head like a bulldog brought reluctantly to obedience by fear of the stick. 'Only, M. le curé, I have a wife and children, if I am reported I shall be dismissed; I have only my place here to live on.'

'I too should be very sorry to lose mine,' replied the worthy curé, in a voice swayed by ever increasing emotion.

'What a difference!' the gaoler answered promptly; 'why you, M. le curé, we know that you have an income of 800 livres, a fine place in the sun. . . .'

Such are the events which, commented upon, exaggerated in twenty different ways, had been arousing for the last two days all the evil passions of the little town of Verrières. At that moment they were serving as text for the little discussion which M. de Rênal was having with his wife. That morning, accompanied by M. Valenod, the governor of the poorhouse, he had gone to the curé's house, to inform him of their

18

extreme displeasure. M. Chélan was under no one's protection; he felt the full force of their words.

'Well, gentlemen, I shall be the third parish priest, eighty years of age, whom the faithful will have seen deprived of his living in this district. I have been here for six and fifty years; I have christened almost all the inhabitants of the town, which was no more than a village when I came. Every day I marry young couples whose grandparents I married long ago. Verrières is my family, but the fear of leaving it will never make me traffic with my conscience, or admit any other influence over my actions; I said to myself, when I saw the stranger: "This man, who has come from Paris, may indeed be a Liberal, there are far too many of them; but what harm can he do to our poor people and our prisoners?"'

The reproaches of M. de Rênal, and above all those of M. Valenod, the governor of the poorhouse, becoming more and more bitter:

'Very well, gentlemen, have me deprived,' the old curé had cried, in a quavering voice. 'I shall live in the town all the same. You all know that forty-eight years ago I inherited a piece of land which brings me 800 livres; I shall live on that income. I save nothing out of my stipend, gentlemen, and that may be why I am less alarmed when people speak of taking it from me.'

M. de Rênal lived on excellent terms with his wife; but not knowing what answer to make to the question, which she timidly repeated: 'What harm can this gentleman from Paris do to the prisoners?' he was just about to lose his temper altogether when she uttered a cry. Her second son had climbed upon the parapet of the wall of the terrace, and was running along it, though this wall rose more than twenty feet from the vineyard beneath. The fear of alarming her son and so making him fall restrained Madame de Rênal from calling him. Finally the child, who was laughing at his own prowess, turned to look at his mother, noticed how pale she was, sprang down upon the avenue and ran to join her. He was well scolded.

This little incident changed the course of the conversation.

'I am quite determined to engage young Sorel, the saw-
yer's son,' said M. de Rênal; 'he will look after the children,
who are beginning to be too much of a handful for us. He
is a young priest or thereabouts, a good Latin scholar, and
will bring the children on; for he has a strong character, the
curé says. I shall give him 300 francs and his board. I had
some doubts as to his morals; for he was the Benjamin of
that old surgeon, the Member of the Legion of Honour, who
on pretence of being their cousin came to live with the
Sorels. He might quite well have been nothing better than a
secret agent of the Liberals; he said that our mountain air
was good for his asthma; but that has never been proved. He
had served in all *Buonaparté's* campaigns in Italy, and they
even say that he voted against the Empire in his day. This
Liberal taught young Sorel Latin, and left him all the pile of
books he brought here with him. Not that I should ever have
dreamed of having the carpenter's son with my children; but
the curé, only the day before the scene which has made a
permanent breach between us, told me that this Sorel has
been studying theology for the last three years, with the idea
of entering the Seminary; so he is not a Liberal, and he is a
Latin scholar.

'This arrangement suits me in more ways than one,' M. de
Rênal went on, looking at his wife with an air of diplomacy;
'Valenod is tremendously proud of the two fine Norman
horses he has just bought for his calash. But he has not got
a tutor for his children.'

'He is quite capable of taking this one from us.'

'Then you approve of my plan?' said M. de Rênal, thanking his wife, with a smile, for the excellent idea that had just
occurred to her. 'There, that's settled.'

'Oh, good gracious, my dear, how quickly you make up
your mind!'

'That is because I have a strong character, as the curé has
had occasion to see. Let us make no pretence about it, we
are surrounded by Liberals here. All these cloth merchants
are jealous of me, I am certain of it; two or three of them
are growing rich; very well, I wish them to see M. de Rênal's

children go by, out walking in the care of *their tutor*. It will make an impression. My grandfather used often to tell us that in his young days he had had a tutor. It's a hundred crowns he's going to cost me, but that will have to be reckoned as a necessary expense to keep up our position.'

This sudden decision plunged Madame de Rênal deep in thought. She was a tall, well made woman, who had been the beauty of the place, as the saying is in this mountain district. She had a certain air of simplicity and bore herself like a girl; in the eyes of a Parisian, that artless grace, full of innocence and vivacity, might even have suggested ideas of a mildly passionate nature. Had she had wind of this kind of success, Madame de Rênal would have been thoroughly ashamed of it. No trace either of coquetry or of affectation had ever appeared in her nature. M. Valenod, the wealthy governor of the poorhouse, was supposed to have paid his court to her, but without success, a failure which had given a marked distinction to her virtue; for this M. Valenod, a tall young man, strongly built, with a vivid complexion and bushy black whiskers, was one of those coarse, brazen, noisy creatures who in the provinces are called fine men.

Madame de Rênal, being extremely shy and liable to be swayed by her moods, was offended chiefly by the restless movements and loud voice of M. Valenod. The distaste that she felt for what at Verrières goes by the name of gaiety had won her the reputation of being extremely proud of her birth. She never gave it a thought, but had been greatly pleased to see the inhabitants of Verrières come less frequently to her house. We shall not attempt to conceal the fact that she was reckoned a fool in the eyes of *their* ladies, because, without any regard for her husband's interests, she let slip the most promising opportunities of procuring fine hats from Paris or Besançon. Provided that she was left alone to stroll in her fine garden, she never made any complaint.

She was a simple soul, who had never risen even to the point of criticising her husband, and admitting that he bored her. She supposed, without telling herself so, that between husband and wife there could be no more tender relations.

21

She was especially fond of M. de Rênal when he spoke to her of his plans for their children, one of whom he intended to place in the army, the second on the bench, and the third in the church. In short, she found M. de Rênal a great deal less boring than any of the other men of her acquaintance.

This wifely opinion was justified. The Mayor of Verrières owed his reputation for wit, and better still for good tone to half a dozen pleasantries which he had inherited from an uncle. This old Captain de Rênal had served before the Revolution in the Duke of Orleans's regiment of infantry, and, when he went to Paris, had had the right of entry into that Prince's drawing-rooms. He had there seen Madame de Montesson, the famous Madame de Genlis, M. Ducrest, the 'inventor' of the Palais-Royal. These personages figured all too frequently in M. de Rênal's stories. But by degrees these memories of things that it required so much delicacy to relate had become a burden to him, and for some time now it was only on solemn occasions that he would repeat his anecdotes of the House of Orleans. As he was in other respects most refined, except when the talk ran on money, he was regarded, and rightly, as the most aristocratic personage in Verrières.

CHAPTER FOUR

FATHER AND SON

E sarà mia colpa,
Se così è?
MACHIAVELLI.

'MY wife certainly has a head on her shoulders!' the Mayor of Verrières remarked to himself the following morning at six o'clock, as he made his way down to Père Sorel's sawmill. 'Although I said so to her, to maintain my own superiority, it had never occurred to me that if I do not take this little priest Sorel, who, they tell me, knows his Latin like an angel, the governor of the poorhouse, that restless spirit, might very well have the same idea, and snatch him from me. I can hear the tone of conceit with which he would speak of his children's tutor!... This tutor, once I've secured him, will he wear a cassock?'

M. de Rênal was absorbed in this question when he saw in the distance a peasant, a man of nearly six feet in height, who, by the first dawning light, seemed to be busily occupied in measuring pieces of timber lying by the side of the Doubs, upon the towpath. The peasant did not appear any too well pleased to see the Mayor coming towards him; for his pieces of wood were blocking the path, and had been laid there in contravention of the law.

Père Sorel, for it was he, was greatly surprised and even more pleased by the singular offer which M. de Rênal made him with regard to his son Julien. He listened to it neverthe-less with that air of grudging melancholy and lack of interest which the shrewd inhabitants of those mountains know so well how to assume. Slaves in the days of Spanish rule, they still retain this facial characteristic of the Egyptian fellahin.

Sorel's reply was at first nothing more than a long-winded recital of all the formal terms of respect which he knew by heart. While he was repeating these vain words, with an awkward smile which enhanced the air of falsehood and almost of rascality natural to his countenance, the old peasant's active mind was seeking to discover what reason could be inducing so important a personage to take his scapegrace of a son into his establishment. He was thoroughly dissatisfied with Julien, and it was for Julien that M. de Rênal was offering him the astounding wage of 300 francs annually, in addition to his food and even his clothing. This last condition, which Père Sorel had had the intelligence to advance on the spur of the moment, had been granted with equal readiness by M. de Rênal.

This demand impressed the Mayor. 'Since Sorel is not delighted and overwhelmed by my proposal, as he ought naturally to be, it is clear,' he said to himself, 'that overtures have been made to him from another quarter; and from whom can they have come, except from Valenod?' It was in vain that M. de Rênal urged Sorel to conclude the bargain there and then: the astute old peasant met him with an obstinate refusal; he wished, he said, to consult his son, as though, in the country, a rich father ever consulted a penniless son, except for form's sake.

A sawmill consists of a shed by the side of a stream. The roof is held up by rafters supported on four stout wooden pillars. Nine or ten feet from the ground, in the middle of the shed, one sees a saw which moves up and down, while an extremely simple mechanism thrusts forward against this saw a piece of wood. This is a wheel set in motion by the mill lade which drives both parts of the machine; that of the saw which moves up and down, and the other which pushes the piece of wood gently towards the saw, which slices it into planks.

As he approached his mill, Père Sorel called Julien in his

stentorian voice; there was no answer. He saw only his two elder sons, young giants who, armed with heavy axes, were squaring the trunks of fir which they would afterwards carry to the saw. They were completely engrossed in keeping exactly to the black line traced on the piece of wood, from which each blow of the axe sent huge chips flying. They did not hear their father's voice. He made his way to the shed; as he entered it, he looked in vain for Julien in the place where he ought to have been standing, beside the saw. He caught sight of him five or six feet higher up, sitting astride upon one of the beams of the roof. Instead of paying careful attention to the action of the machinery, Julien was reading a book. Nothing could have been less to old Sorel's liking; he might perhaps have forgiven Julien his slender build, little adapted to hard work, and so different from that of his elder brothers; but this passion for reading he detested: he himself was unable to read.

It was in vain that he called Julien two or three times. The attention the young man was paying to his book, far more than the noise of the saw, prevented him from hearing his father's terrifying voice. Finally, despite his years, the father sprang nimbly upon the trunk that was being cut by the saw, and from there on to the cross beam that held up the roof. A violent blow sent flying into the mill lade the book that Julien was holding; a second blow no less violent, aimed at his head, in the form of a box on the ear, made him lose his balance. He was about to fall from a height of twelve or fifteen feet, among the moving machinery, which would have crushed him, but his father caught him with his left hand as he fell.

'Well, idler! So you keep on reading your cursed books, when you ought to be watching the saw? Read them in the evening, when you go and waste your time with the curé.'

Julien, although stunned by the force of the blow, and bleeding profusely, went to take up his proper station beside the saw. There were tears in his eyes, due not so much to his bodily pain as to the loss of his book, which he adored.

'Come down, animal, till I speak to you.' The noise of the

25

machine again prevented Julien from hearing this order. His father who had stepped down not wishing to take the trouble to climb up again on to the machine, went to find a long pole used for knocking down walnuts, and struck him on the shoulder with it. No sooner had Julien reached the ground than old Sorel, thrusting him on brutally from behind, drove him towards the house. 'Heaven knows what he's going to do to me!' thought the young man. As he passed it, he looked sadly at the mill lade into which his book had fallen; it was the one that he valued most of all, the *Mémorial de Sainte-Hélène*.

His cheeks were flushed, his eyes downcast. He was a slim youth of eighteen or nineteen, weak in appearance, with irregular but delicate features and an aquiline nose. His large dark eyes, which, in moments of calm, suggested a reflective, fiery spirit, were animated at this instant with an expression of the most ferocious hatred. Hair of a dark chestnut, growing very low, gave him a narrow brow, and in moments of anger a wicked air. Among the innumerable varieties of the human countenance, there is perhaps none that is more strikingly characteristic. A slim and shapely figure betokened suppleness rather than strength. In his childhood, his extremely pensive air and marked pallor had given his father the idea that he would not live, or would live only to be a burden upon his family. An object of contempt to the rest of the household, he hated his brothers and father; in the games on Sundays, on the public square, he was invariably beaten.

It was only during the last year that his good looks had begun to win him a few supporters among the girls. Universally despised, as a feeble creature, Julien had adored that old Surgeon-Major who one day ventured to speak to the Mayor on the subject of the plane trees.

This surgeon used now and then to pay old Sorel a day's wage for his son, and taught him Latin and history, that is to say all the history that he knew, that of the 1796 campaign in Italy. On his death, he had bequeathed to him his Cross of the Legion of Honour, the arrears of his pension, and thirty or forty volumes, the most precious of which had just taken a plunge into the *public lade*, diverted by the Mayor's influence.

As soon as he was inside the house, Julien felt his shoulder gripped by his father's strong hand; he trembled, expecting to receive a shower of blows.

'Answer me without lying,' the old peasant's harsh voice shouted in his ear, while the hand spun him round as a child's hand spins a lead soldier. Julien's great dark eyes, filled with tears, found themselves staring into the little grey eyes of the old peasant, who looked as though he sought to penetrate to the depths of his son's heart.

CHAPTER FIVE

DRIVING A BARGAIN

Cunctando restituit rem.
ENNIUS.

'ANSWER me, without lying, if you can, you miserable bookworm; how do you come to know Madame de Rênal? When have you spoken to her?'

'I have never spoken to her,' replied Julien, 'I have never seen the lady except in church.'

'But you must have looked at her, you shameless scoundrel?'

'Never! You know that in church I see none but God,' Julien added with a hypocritical air, calculated, to his mind, to ward off further blows.

'There is something behind this, all the same,' replied the suspicious peasant, and was silent for a moment; 'but I shall get nothing out of you, you damned twister. The fact is, I'm going to be rid of you, and my saw will run all the better without you. You have made a friend of the parson or some one, and he's got you a fine post. Go and pack your traps, and I'll take you to M. de Rênal's where you're to be tutor to the children.'

'What am I to get for that?'

'Board, clothing and three hundred francs in wages.'

'I do not wish to be a servant.'

'Animal, who ever spoke of your being a servant? Would I allow my son to be a servant?'

'But, with whom shall I have my meals?'

This question left old Sorel at a loss; he felt that if he

spoke he might be guilty of some imprudence; he flew into a rage with Julien, upon whom he showered abuse, accusing him of greed, and left him to go and consult his other sons.

Presently Julien saw them, each leaning upon his axe and deliberating together. After watching them for some time, Julien, seeing that he could make out nothing of their discussion, went and took his place on the far side of the saw, so as not to be taken by surprise. He wanted time to consider this sudden announcement which was altering his destiny, but felt himself to be incapable of prudence; his imagination was wholly taken up with forming pictures of what he would see in M. de Rênal's fine house.

'I must give up all that,' he said to himself, 'rather than let myself be brought down to feeding with the servants. My father will try to force me; I would sooner die. I have saved fifteen francs and eight sous, I shall run away to-night; in two days, by keeping to side-roads where I need not fear the police, I can be at Besançon; there I enlist as a soldier, and, if necessary, cross the border into Switzerland. But then, good-bye to everything, good-bye to that fine clerical profession which is a stepping-stone to everything.'

This horror of feeding with the servants was not natural to Julien; he would, in seeking his fortune, have done other things far more disagreeable. He derived this repugnance from Rousseau's *Confessions*. It was the one book that helped his imagination to form any idea of the world. The collection of reports of the Grand Army and the *Mémorial de Sainte-Hélène* completed his Koran. He would have gone to the stake for those three books. Never did he believe in any other. Remembering a saying of the old Surgeon-Major, he regarded all the other books in the world as liars, written by rogues in order to obtain advancement.

With his fiery nature Julien had one of those astonishing memories so often found in foolish people. To win over the old priest Chélan, upon whom he saw quite clearly that his own future depended, he had learned by heart the entire New Testament in Latin; he knew also M. de Maistre's book *Du Pape*, and had as little belief in one as in the other.

29

As though by a mutual agreement, Sorel and his son avoided speaking to one another for the rest of the day. At dusk, Julien went to the curé for his divinity lesson, but did not think it prudent to say anything to him of the strange proposal that had been made to his father. 'It may be a trap,' he told himself; 'I must pretend to have forgotten about it.'

Early on the following day, M. de Rênal sent for old Sorel, who, after keeping him waiting for an hour or two, finally appeared, beginning as he entered the door a hundred excuses interspersed with as many reverences. By dint of giving voice to every sort of objection, Sorel succeeded in gathering that his son was to take his meals with the master and mistress of the house, and on days when they had company in a room by himself with the children. Finding an increasing desire to raise difficulties the more he discerned a genuine anxiety on the Mayor's part, and being moreover filled with distrust and bewilderment, Sorel asked to see the room in which his son was to sleep. It was a large chamber very decently furnished, but the servants were already engaged in carrying into it the beds of the three children.

At this the old peasant began to see daylight; he at once asked with assurance to see the coat which would be given to his son. M. de Rênal opened his desk and took out a hundred francs.

'With this money, your son can go to M. Durand, the clothier, and get himself a suit of black.'

'And supposing I take him away from you,' said the peasant, who had completely forgotten the reverential forms of address. 'Will he take this black coat with him?'

'Certainly.'

'Oh, very well!' said Sorel in a drawling tone, 'then there's only one thing for us still to settle: the money you're to give him.'

'What!' M. de Rênal indignantly exclaimed, 'we agreed upon that yesterday: I give three hundred francs; I consider that plenty, if not too much.'

'That was your offer, I do not deny it,' said old Sorel, speaking even more slowly; then, by a stroke of genius which

will astonish only those who do not know the Franc-Comtois
peasant, he added, looking M. de Rênal steadily in the face:
'*We can do better elsewhere.*'

At these words the Mayor was thrown into confusion. He
recovered himself, however, and, after an adroit conversation
lasting fully two hours, in which not a word was said without
a purpose, the peasant's shrewdness prevailed over that of
the rich man, who was not dependent on his for his living.
All the innumerable conditions which were to determine
Julien's new existence were finally settled; not only was his
salary fixed at four hundred francs, but it was to be paid in
advance, on the first day of each month.

'Very well! I shall let him have thirty-five francs,' said M.
de Rênal.

'To make a round sum, a rich and generous gentleman
like our Mayor,' the peasant insinuated in a coaxing voice,
'will surely go as far as thirty-six.'

'All right,' said M. de Rênal, 'but let us have no more
of this.'

For once, anger gave him a tone of resolution. The peasant
saw that he could advance no farther. Thereupon M. de
Rênal began in turn to make headway. He utterly refused to
hand over the thirty-six francs for the first month to old
Sorel, who was most eager to receive the money on his son's
behalf. It occurred to M. de Rênal that he would be obliged
to describe to his wife the part he had played throughout
this transaction.

'Let me have back the hundred francs I gave you,' he said
angrily. 'M. Durand owes me money. I shall go with your
son to choose the black cloth.'

After this bold stroke, Sorel prudently retired upon his
expressions of respect; they occupied a good quarter of an
hour. In the end, seeing that there was certainly nothing
more to be gained, he withdrew. His final reverence ended
with the words:

'I shall send my son up to the *château*.'

It was thus that the Mayor's subordinates spoke of his
house when they wished to please him.

Returning to his mill, Sorel looked in vain for his son. Doubtful as to what might be in store for him, Julien had left home in the dead of night. He had been anxious to find a safe hiding-place for his books and his Cross of the Legion of Honour. He had removed the whole of his treasures to the house of a young timber-merchant, a friend of his, by the name of Fouqué, who lived on the side of the high mountain overlooking Verrières.

When he reappeared: 'Heaven knows, you damned idler,' his father said to him, 'whether you will ever have enough honour to pay me for the cost of your keep, which I have been advancing to you all these years! Pack up your rubbish, and off with you to the Mayor's.'

Julien, astonished not to receive a thrashing, made haste to set off. But no sooner was he out of sight of his terrible father than he slackened his pace. He decided that it would serve the ends of his hypocrisy to pay a visit to the church.

The idea surprises you? Before arriving at this horrible idea, the soul of the young peasant had had a long way to go.

When he was still a child, the sight of certain dragoons of the 6th, in their long, white cloaks, and helmets adorned with long crests of black horsehair, who were returning from Italy, and whom Julien saw tying their horses to the barred window of his father's house, drove him mad with longing for a military career. Later on he listened with ecstasy to the accounts of the battles of the Bridge of Lodi, Arcole and Rivoli given him by the old Surgeon-Major. He noticed the burning gaze which the old man directed at his Cross.

But when Julien was fourteen, they began to build a church at Verrières, one that might be called magnificent for so small a town. There were, in particular, four marble pillars the sight of which impressed Julien; they became famous throughout the countryside, owing to the deadly enmity which they aroused between the Justice of the Peace and the young Vicar, sent down from Besançon, who was understood to be the spy of the *Congregation*. The Justice of the Peace came within an ace of losing his post, such at least was the common report. Had he not dared to have a difference of opinion with a priest who, almost every fortnight, went to Besançon, where he saw, people said, the Right Reverend Lord Bishop?

In the midst of all this, the Justice of the Peace, the father of a large family, passed a number of sentences which appeared unjust; all of these were directed against such of the inhabitants as read the *Constitutionnel*. The right party was triumphant. The sums involved amounted, it was true, to no more than four or five francs; but one of these small fines was levied upon a nailsmith, Julien's godfather. In his anger, this man exclaimed: 'What a change! And to think that, for twenty years and more, the Justice was reckoned such an honest man!' The Surgeon-Major, Julien's friend, was dead.

All at once Julien ceased to speak of Napoleon; he announced his intention of becoming a priest, and was constantly to be seen, in his father's sawmill, engaged in learning by heart a Latin Bible which the curé had lent him. The good old man, amazed at his progress, devoted whole evenings to instructing him in divinity. Julien gave utterance in his company to none but pious sentiments. Who could have supposed that that girlish face, so pale and gentle, hid the unshakable determination to expose himself to the risk of a thousand deaths rather than fail to make his fortune?

To Julien, making a fortune meant in the first place leaving Verrières; he loathed his native place. Everything that he saw there froze his imagination.

From his earliest boyhood, he had had moments of exaltation. At such times he dreamed with rapture that one day he would be introduced to the beautiful ladies of Paris; he would manage to attract their attention by some brilliant action. Why should he not be loved by one of them, as Bonaparte, when still penniless, had been loved by the brilliant Madame de Beauharnais? For many years now, perhaps not an hour of Julien's life had passed without his reminding himself that Bonaparte, an obscure subaltern with no fortune, had made himself master of the world with his sword. This thought consoled him for his misfortunes which he deemed to be great, and enhanced his joy when joy came his way.

The building of the church and the sentences passed by the Justice brought him sudden enlightenment; an idea which occurred to him drove him almost out of his senses for some weeks, and finally took possession of him with the absolute power of the first idea which a passionate nature believes itself to have discovered.

'When Bonaparte made a name for himself, France was in fear of being invaded; military distinction was necessary and fashionable. To-day we see priests at forty drawing stipends of a hundred thousand francs, that is to say three times as much as the famous divisional commanders under Napoleon. They must have people to support them. Look at the Justice here, so wise a man, always so honest until now, sacrificing his honour, at his age, from fear of offending a young vicar of thirty. I must become a priest.'

On one occasion, in the midst of his new-found piety, after Julien had been studying divinity for two years, he was betrayed by a sudden blaze of the fire that devoured his spirit. This was at M. Chélan's; at a dinner party of priests, to whom the good curé had introduced him as an educational prodigy, he found himself uttering frenzied praise of Napoleon. He bound his right arm across his chest, pretending that he had put the arm out of joint when shifting a fir trunk, and kept it for two months in this awkward position. After this drastic penance, he forgave himself. Such is the young man of eighteen, but weak in appearance, whom you would have said to be, at the most, seventeen, who, carrying a small parcel under his arm, was entering the magnificent church of Verrières.

He found it dark and deserted. In view of some festival, all the windows in the building had been covered with crimson cloth; the effect of this, when the sun shone, was a dazzling blaze of light, of the most imposing and most religious character. Julien shuddered. Being alone in the church, he took his seat on the bench that had the most handsome appearance. It bore the arms of M. de Rênal.

On the desk in front, Julien observed a scrap of printed paper, spread out there as though to be read. He looked at it closely and saw:

'Details of the execution and of the last moments of Louis Jenrel, executed at Besançon, on the ...'

The paper was torn. On the other side he read the opening words of a line, which were: 'The first step.'

'Who can have put this paper here?' said Julien. 'Poor wretch!' he added with a sigh, 'his name has the same ending as mine.' And he crumpled up the paper.

On his way out, Julien thought he saw blood by the holy water stoup; it was some of the water that had been spilt: the light from the red curtains which draped the windows made it appear like blood.

Finally, Julien felt ashamed of his secret terror.

'Should I prove coward?' he said to himself. '*To arms!*'

This phrase, so often repeated in the old Surgeon's accounts of battles, had a heroic sound in Julien's ears. He rose and walked rapidly to M. de Rênal's house.

Despite these brave resolutions, as soon as he caught sight of the house twenty yards away he was overcome by an unconquerable shyness. The iron gate stood open; it seemed to him magnificent. He would have now to go in through it.

Julien was not the only person whose heart was troubled by his arrival in this household. Madame de Rênal's extreme timidity was disconcerted by the idea of this stranger who, in the performance of his duty, would be constantly coming between her and her children. She was accustomed to having her sons sleep in her own room. That morning, many tears had flowed when she saw their little beds being carried into the apartment intended for the tutor. In vain did she beg her husband to let the bed of Stanislas Xavier, the youngest boy, be taken back to her room.

Womanly delicacy was carried to excess in Madame de Rênal. She formed a mental picture of a coarse, unkempt creature, employed to scold her children, simply because he knew Latin, a barbarous tongue for the sake of which her sons would be whipped.

CHAPTER SIX

DULNESS

Non so più cosa son,
Cosa facio.
MOZART (*Figaro*).

WITH the vivacity and grace which came naturally to her when she was beyond the reach of male vision, Madame de Rênal was coming out through the glass door which opened from the drawing-room into the garden, when she saw, standing by the front door, a young peasant, almost a boy still, extremely pale and shewing traces of recent tears. He was wearing a clean white shirt and carried under his arm a neat jacket of violet ratteen.

This young peasant's skin was so white, his eyes were so appealing, that the somewhat romantic mind of Madame de Rênal conceived the idea at first that he might be a girl in disguise, come to ask some favour of the Mayor. She felt sorry for the poor creature, who had come to a standstill by the front door, and evidently could not summon up courage to ring the bell. Madame de Rênal advanced, oblivious for the moment of the bitter grief that she felt at the tutor's coming. Julien, who was facing the door, did not see her approach. He trembled when a pleasant voice sounded close to his ear:

'What have you come for, my boy?'

Julien turned sharply round, and, struck by the charm of Madame de Rênal's expression, forgot part of his shyness. A moment later, astounded by her beauty, he forgot everything, even his purpose in coming. Madame de Rênal had repeated her question.

'I have come to be tutor, Madame,' he at length informed her, put to shame by his tears which he dried as best he might.

Madame de Rênal remained speechless; they were standing close together, looking at one another. Julien had never seen a person so well dressed as this, let alone a woman with so exquisite a complexion, to speak to him in a gentle tone. Madame de Rênal looked at the large tears which lingered on the cheeks (so pallid at first and now so rosy) of this young peasant. Presently she burst out laughing, with all the wild hilarity of a girl; she was laughing at herself, and trying in vain to realise the full extent of her happiness. So this was the tutor whom she had imagined an unwashed and ill-dressed priest, who was coming to scold and whip her children.

'Why, Sir!' she said to him at length, 'do you know Latin?'

The word 'Sir' came as such a surprise to Julien that he thought for a moment before answering.

'Yes, ma'am,' he said shyly.

Madame de Rênal felt so happy that she ventured to say to Julien:

'You won't scold those poor children too severely?'

'Scold them? I?' asked Julien in amazement. 'Why should I?'

'You will, Sir,' she went on after a brief silence and in a voice that grew more emotional every moment, 'you will be kind to them, you promise me?'

To hear himself addressed again as 'Sir,' in all seriousness, and by a lady so fashionably attired, was more than Julien had ever dreamed of; in all the cloud castles of his boyhood, he had told himself that no fashionable lady would deign to speak to him until he had a smart uniform. Madame de Rênal, for her part, was completely taken in by the beauty of Julien's complexion, his great dark eyes and his becoming hair which was curling more than usual because, to cool himself, he had just dipped his head in the basin of the public fountain. To her great delight, she discovered an air of girlish shyness in this fatal tutor, whose severity and savage tone she had so greatly dreaded for her children's sake. To Madame de Rênal's peace-loving nature the contrast between her fears and what she now saw before her was a great event. Finally she recovered from her surprise. She was astonished to find herself standing like this at the door of her house with this young man almost in his shirtsleeves and so close to her.

'Let us go indoors, Sir,' she said to him with an air of distinct embarrassment.

Never in her life had a purely agreeable sensation so profoundly stirred Madame de Rênal; never had so charming an apparition come in the wake of more disturbing fears. And so those sweet children, whom she had tended with such care, were not to fall into the hands of a dirty, growling priest. As soon as they were in the hall, she turned to Julien who was following her shyly. His air of surprise at the sight of so fine a house was an additional charm in the eyes of Madame de Rênal. She could not believe her eyes; what she felt most of all was that the tutor ought to be wearing a black coat.

'But is it true, Sir,' she said to him, again coming to a halt, and mortally afraid lest she might be mistaken, so happy was the belief making her, 'do you really know Latin?'

These words hurt Julien's pride and destroyed the enchantment in which he had been living for the last quarter of an hour.

'Yes, Ma'am,' he informed her, trying to adopt a chilly air; 'I know Latin as well as M. le curé; indeed, he is sometimes so kind as to say that I know it better.'

Madame de Rênal felt that Julien had a very wicked air; he had stopped within arm's length of her. She went nearer to him, and murmured:

'For the first few days, you won't take the whip to my children, even if they don't know their lessons?'

This gentle, almost beseeching tone coming from so fine a lady at once made Julien forget what he owed to his reputation as a Latin scholar. Madame de Rênal's face was close to his own, he could smell the perfume of a woman's summer attire, so astounding a thing to a poor peasant. Julien blushed deeply, and said with a sigh and in a faint voice:

'Fear nothing, Ma'am, I shall obey you in every respect.'

It was at this moment only, when her anxiety for her children was completely banished, that Madame de Rênal was struck by Julien's extreme good looks. The almost feminine cast of his features and his air of embarrassment did not seem in the least absurd to a woman who was extremely timid herself. The manly air which is generally considered essential to masculine beauty would have frightened her.

'How old are you, Sir?' she asked Julien.

'I shall soon be nineteen.'

'My eldest son is eleven,' went on Madame de Rênal, completely reassured; 'he will be almost a companion for you, you can talk to him seriously. His father tried to beat him once, the child was ill for a whole week, and yet it was quite a gentle blow.'

'How different from me,' thought Julien. 'Only yesterday my father was thrashing me. How fortunate these rich people are!'

Madame de Rênal had by this time arrived at the stage of remarking the most trivial changes in the state of the tutor's mind; she mistook this envious impulse for shyness, and tried to give him fresh courage.

'What is your name, Sir?' she asked him with an accent and a grace the charm of which Julien could feel without knowing from whence it sprang.

'They call me Julien Sorel, Ma'am; I am trembling as I enter a strange house for the first time in my life; I have need of your protection, and shall require you to forgive me many things at first. I have never been to College, I was too poor; I have never talked to any other men, except my cousin the Surgeon-Major, a Member of the Legion of Honour, and the Reverend Father Chélan. He will give you a good account of me. My brothers have always beaten me, do not listen to them if they speak evil of me to you; pardon my faults, Ma'am, I shall never have any evil intention.'

Julien plucked up his courage again during this long speech; he was studying Madame de Rênal. Such is the effect of perfect grace when it is natural to the character, particularly when she whom it adorns has no thought of being graceful. Julien, who knew all that was to be known about feminine beauty, would have sworn at that moment that she was no more than twenty. The bold idea at once occurred to him of kissing her hand. Next, this idea frightened him; a moment later, he said to himself: 'It would be cowardly on my part not to carry out an action which may be of use to me, and diminish the scorn which this fine lady probably feels for a poor workman, only just taken from the saw-bench.' Perhaps Julien was somewhat encouraged by the words 'good looking boy' which for the last six months he had been used to hearing on Sundays on the lips of various girls. While he debated thus with himself, Madame de Rênal offered him a few suggestions as to how he should begin to handle her children. The violence of Julien's effort to control himself made him turn quite pale again; he said, with an air of constraint:

'Never, Ma'am, will I beat your children; I swear it before God.'

And so saying he ventured to take Madame de Rênal's hand and carry it to his lips. She was astonished at this action, and, on thinking it over, shocked. As the weather was very warm, her arm was completely bare under her shawl, and Julien's action in raising her hand to his lips had uncovered it to the shoulder. A minute later she scolded herself; she felt that she had not been quickly enough offended.

M. de Rênal, who had heard the sound of voices, came out of his study; with the same majestic and fatherly air that he assumed when he was conducting marriages in the Town Hall, he said to Julien:

'It is essential that I speak to you before the children see you.'

He ushered Julien into one of the rooms and detained his wife, who was going to leave them together. Having shut the door, M. de Rênal seated himself with gravity.

'The curé has told me that you were an honest fellow, everyone in this house will treat you with respect, and if I am satisfied I shall help you to set up for yourself later on. I wish you to cease to see anything of either your family or your friends, their tone would not be suited to my children. Here are thirty-six francs for the first month; but I must have your word that you will not give a penny of this money to your father.'

M. de Rênal was annoyed with the old man, who, in this business, had proved more subtle than he himself.

'And now, *Sir*, for by my orders everyone in this house is to address you as Sir, and you will be conscious of the advantage of entering a well ordered household; now, Sir, it is not proper that the children should see you in a jacket. Have the servants seen him?' M. de Rênal asked his wife.

'No, dear,' she replied with an air of deep thought.

'Good. Put on this,' he said to the astonished young man, handing him one of his own frock coats. 'And now let us go to M. Durand, the clothier.'

More than an hour later, when M. de Rênal returned with the new tutor dressed all in black, he found his wife still seated in the same place. She felt soothed by Julien's presence; as she studied his appearance she forgot to feel afraid. Julien was not giving her a thought; for all his mistrust of destiny and of mankind, his heart at that moment was just like a child's; he seemed to have lived whole years since the moment when, three hours earlier, he stood trembling in the church. He noticed Madame de Rênal's frigid manner, and gathered that she was angry because he had ventured to kiss her hand. But the sense of pride that he derived from the contact of garments so different from those which he was accustomed to wear caused him so much excitement, and he was so anxious to conceal his joy that all his gestures were more or less abrupt and foolish. Madame de Rênal gazed at him with eyes of astonishment.

'A little gravity, Sir,' M. de Rênal told him, 'if you wish to be respected by my children and my servants.'

'Sir,' replied Julien, 'I am uncomfortable in these new

41

clothes; I, a humble peasant, have never worn any but short jackets; with your permission, I shall retire to my bedroom.'

'What think you of this new acquisition?' M. de Rênal asked his wife.

With an almost instinctive impulse, of which she herself certainly was not aware, Madame de Rênal concealed the truth from her husband.

'I am by no means as enchanted as you are with this little peasant; your kindness will turn him into an impertinent rascal whom you will be obliged to send packing within a month.'

'Very well! We shall send him packing; he will have cost me a hundred francs or so, and Verrières will have grown used to seeing a tutor with M. de Rênal's children. That point I should not have gained if I had let Julien remain in the clothes of a working man. When I dismiss him, I shall of course keep the black suit which I have just ordered from the clothier. He shall have nothing but the coat I found ready made at the tailor's, which he is now wearing.'

The hour which Julien spent in his room seemed like a second to Madame de Rênal. The children, who had been told of their new tutor's arrival, overwhelmed their mother with questions. Finally Julien appeared. He was another man. It would have been straining the word to say that he was grave; he was gravity incarnate. He was introduced to the children, and spoke to them with an air that surprised M. de Rênal himself.

'I am here, young gentlemen,' he told them at the end of his address, 'to teach you Latin. You know what is meant by repeating a lesson. Here is the Holy Bible,' he said, and shewed them a tiny volume in 32mo, bound in black. 'It is in particular the story of Our Lord Jesus Christ, that is the part which is called the New Testament. I shall often make you repeat lessons; now you must make me repeat mine.'

Adolphe, the eldest boy, had taken the book.

'Open it where you please,' Julien went on, 'and tell me the first three words of a paragraph. I shall repeat by heart the sacred text, the rule of conduct for us all, until you stop me.'

Adolphe opened the book, read a couple of words, and Julien repeated the whole page as easily as though he were speaking French. M. de Rênal looked at his wife with an air of triumph. The children, seeing their parents' amazement, opened their eyes wide. A servant came to the door of the drawing-room, Julien went on speaking in Latin. The servant at first stood motionless and then vanished. Presently the lady's maid and the cook appeared in the doorway; by this time Adolphe had opened the book at eight different places, and Julien continued to repeat the words with the same ease.

'Eh, what a bonny little priest,' the cook, a good and truly devout girl, said aloud.

M. de Rênal's self-esteem was troubled; so far from having any thought of examining the tutor, he was engaged in ransacking his memory for a few words of Latin; at last, he managed to quote a line of Horace. Julien knew no Latin apart from the Bible. He replied with a frown:

'The sacred ministry to which I intend to devote myself has forbidden me to read so profane a poet.'

M. de Rênal repeated a fair number of alleged lines of Horace. He explained to his children what Horace was; but the children, overcome with admiration, paid little attention to what he was saying. They were watching Julien.

The servants being still at the door, Julien felt it incumbent upon him to prolong the test.

'And now,' he said to the youngest boy, 'Master Stanislas Xavier too must set me a passage from the Holy Book.'

Little Stanislas, swelling with pride, read out to the best of his ability the opening words of a paragraph, and Julien repeated the whole page. That nothing might be wanting to complete M. de Rênal's triumph, while Julien was reciting, there entered M. Valenod, the possessor of fine Norman horses, and M. Charcot de Maugiron, Sub-Prefect of the district. This scene earned for Julien the title 'Sir'; the servants themselves dared not withhold it from him.

That evening, the whole of Verrieres flocked to M. de Rênal's to behold the marvel. Julien answered them all with an air of gloom which kept them at a distance. His fame spread so rapidly through the town that, shortly afterwards, M. de Rênal, afraid of losing him, suggested his signing a contract for two years.

'No, Sir,' Julien replied coldly, 'if you chose to dismiss me I should be obliged to go. A contract which binds me without putting you under any obligation is unfair, I must decline.'

Julien managed so skilfully that, less than a month after his coming to the house, M. de Rênal himself respected him. The curé having quarrelled with MM. de Rênal and Valenod, there was no one who could betray Julien's former passion for Napoleon, of whom he was careful to speak with horror.

CHAPTER SEVEN

ELECTIVE AFFINITIES

Ils ne savent toucher le cœur qu'en le froissant.
                                        A MODERN.

T HE children adored him, he did not care for them; his
thoughts were elsewhere. Nothing that these urchins
could do ever tried his patience. Cold, just, impassive,
and at the same time loved, because his coming had in a
measure banished dulness from the house, he was a good
tutor. For his part, he felt only hatred and horror for the
high society in which he was allowed to occupy the very foot
of the table, a position which may perhaps explain his hatred
and horror. There were certain formal dinners at which he
could barely contain his loathing of everything round about
him. On Saint Louis's day in particular, M. Valenod was
laying down the law at M. de Rênal's; Julien almost gave
himself away; he escaped into the garden, saying that he
must look after the children. 'What panegyrics of honesty!'
he exclaimed; 'anyone would say that was the one and only
virtue; and yet what consideration, what a cringing respect
for a man who obviously has doubled and tripled his fortune
since he has been in charge of the relief of the poor! I would
wager that he makes something even out of the fund set apart
for the foundlings, those wretches whose need is even more
sacred than that of the other paupers. Ah, monsters! Monsters! And I too, I am a sort of foundling, hated by my father,
my brothers, my whole family.'

Some days earlier, Julien walking by himself and saying

45

his office in a little wood, known as the Belvedere, which overlooks the Cours de la Fidélité, had tried in vain to avoid his two brothers, whom he saw approaching him by a solitary path. The jealousy of these rough labourers had been so quickened by the sight of their brother's handsome black coat, and air of extreme gentility, as well as by the sincere contempt which he felt for them, that they had proceeded to thrash him, leaving him there unconscious and bleeding freely. Madame de Rênal, who was out walking with M. Valenod and the Sub-Prefect, happened to turn into the little wood; she saw Julien lying on the ground and thought him dead. She was so overcome as to make M. Valenod jealous.

His alarm was premature. Julien admired Madame de Rênal's looks, but hated her for her beauty; it was the first reef on which his fortune had nearly foundered. He spoke to her as seldom as possible, in the hope of making her forget the impulse which, at their first encounter, had led him to kiss her hand.

Elisa, Madame de Rênal's maid, had not failed to fall in love with the young tutor; she often spoke of him to her mistress. Miss Elisa's love had brought upon Julien the hatred of one of the footmen. One day he heard this man say to Elisa: 'You won't speak to me any more, since that greasy tutor has been in the house.' Julien did not deserve the epithet; but, with the instinct of a good looking youth, became doubly attentive to his person. M. Valenod's hatred was multiplied accordingly. He said in public that such effeminate ways were not becoming in a young cleric. Barring the cassock, Julien now wore clerical attire.

Madame de Rênal observed that he was speaking more often than before to Miss Elisa; she learned that these conversations were due to the limitations of Julien's extremely small wardrobe. He had so scanty a supply of linen that he was obliged to send it out constantly to be washed, and it was in performing these little services that Elisa made herself useful to him.

This extreme poverty, of which she had had no suspicion, touched Madame de Rênal; she longed to make him presents, but did not dare; this inward resistance was the first feeling of regret that Julien caused her. Until then the name of Julien and the sense of a pure and wholly intellectual joy had been synonymous to her. Tormented by the idea of Julien's poverty, Madame de Rênal spoke to her husband about making him a present of linen:

'What idiocy!' he replied. 'What! Make presents to a man with whom we are perfectly satisfied, and who is serving us well? It is when he neglects his duty that we should stimulate his zeal.'

Madame de Rênal felt ashamed of this way of looking at things; before Julien came she would not have noticed it. She never saw the young cleric's spotless, though very simple, toilet without asking herself: 'Poor boy, how ever does he manage?'

As time went on she began to feel sorry for Julien's deficiencies, instead of being shocked by them.

Madame de Rênal was one of those women to be found in the provinces whom one may easily take to be fools until one has known them for a fortnight. She had no experience of life, and made no effort at conversation. Endowed with a delicate and haughty nature, that instinct for happiness natural to all human beings made her, generally speaking, pay no attention to the actions of the coarse creatures into whose midst chance had flung her.

She would have been remarkable for her naturalness and quickness of mind, had she received the most scanty education; but in her capacity as an heiress she had been brought up by nuns who practised a passionate devotion to the Sacred Heart of Jesus, and were animated by a violent hatred of the French as being enemies of the Jesuits. Madame de Rênal had sufficient sense to forget at once, as absurdities, everything she had learned in the convent; but she put nothing else in its place, and ended by knowing nothing. The flatteries of which she had been the precocious object, as the heiress to a large fortune, and a marked tendency towards passionate devotion, had bred in her an attitude towards life that was wholly inward. With an outward shew of the most perfect submission, and a self-suppression which the husbands of Verrières used to quote as an example to their wives, and which was a source of pride to M. de Rênal, her inner life was, as a matter of fact, dictated by the most lofty disdain. Any princess who is quoted as an illustration of pride pays infinitely more attention to what her gentlemen are doing round about her than this meekest of women, so modest in appearance, gave to anything that her husband said or did. Until Julien arrived, she had really paid no attention to anyone but her children. Their little illnesses, their sorrows, their little pleasures absorbed the whole sensibility of this human soul, which had never, in the whole of her life, adored anyone save God, while she was at the Sacred Heart in Besançon.

Although she did not condescend to say so to anyone, a feverish attack coming to one of her sons threw her almost into the same state as if the child had died. A burst of coarse laughter, a shrug of the shoulders, accompanied by some trivial maxim as to the foolishness of women, had regularly greeted the confessions of grief of this sort which the need of an outlet had led her to make to her husband during the first years of their married life. Witticisms of this sort, especially when they bore upon the illnesses of the children, turned the dagger in Madame de Rênal's heart. This was all the substitute she found for the obsequious, honeyed flatteries of the Jesuitical convent in which she had passed her girlhood. She was educated in the school of suffering. Too proud to speak of griefs of this sort, even to her friend Madame Derville, she imagined that all men resembled her husband, M. Valenod, and the Sub-Prefect Charcot de Maugiron. Coarse wit and the most brutal insensibility to everything that did not promise money, promotion or a Cross; a blind hatred of every argument that went against them seemed to her to be things natural to the male sex, like the wearing of boots and felt hats.

After many long years, Madame de Rênal had not yet grown accustomed to these money-grubbing creatures among whom she had to live.

Hence the success of the little peasant Julien. She found

much pleasant enjoyment, radiant with the charm of novelty, in the sympathy of this proud and noble spirit. Madame de Rênal had soon forgiven him his extreme ignorance, which was an additional charm, and the roughness of his manners, which she succeeded in improving. She found that it was worth her while to listen to him, even when they spoke of the most ordinary things, even when it was a question of a poor dog that had been run over, as it was crossing the street, by a peasant's cart going by at a trot. The sight of such a tragedy made her husband utter his coarse laugh, whereas she saw Julien's fine, beautifully arched black eyebrows wince. Generosity, nobility of soul, humanity, seemed to her, after a time, to exist only in this young cleric. She felt for him alone all the sympathy and even admiration which those virtues arouse in well-bred natures.

In Paris, Julien's position with regard to Madame de Rênal would very soon have been simplified; but in Paris love is the child of the novels. The young tutor and his timid mistress would have found in three or four novels, and even in the lyrics of the Gymnase a clear statement of their situation. The novels would have outlined for them the part to be played, shewn them the model to copy; and this model, sooner or later, albeit without the slightest pleasure, and perhaps with reluctance, vanity would have compelled Julien to follow.

In a small town of the Aveyron or the Pyrenees, the slightest incident would have been made decisive by the ardour of the climate. Beneath our more sombre skies, a penniless young man, who is ambitious only because the refinement of his nature puts him in need of some of those pleasures which money provides, is in daily contact with a woman of thirty who is sincerely virtuous, occupied with her children, and never looks to novels for examples of conduct. Everything goes slowly, everything happens by degrees in the provinces: life is more natural.

Often, when she thought of the young tutor's poverty, Madame de Rênal was moved to tears. Julien came upon her, one day, actually crying.

'Ah, Ma'am, you have had some bad news!'

'No, my friend,' was her answer: 'Call the children, let us go for a walk.'

She took his arm and leaned on it in a manner which Julien thought strange. It was the first time that she had called him 'my friend.'

Towards the end of their walk, Julien observed that she was blushing deeply. She slackened her pace.

'You will have heard,' she said without looking at him, 'that I am the sole heiress of a very rich aunt who lives at Besançon. She loads me with presents. My sons are making ... such astonishing progress ... that I should like to ask you to accept a little present, as a token of my gratitude. It is only a matter of a few louis to supply you with linen. But——' she added, blushing even more deeply, and was silent.

'What, Ma'am?' said Julien.

'It would be unnecessary,' she went on, lowering her head, 'to speak of this to my husband.'

'I may be humble, Ma'am, but I am not base,' replied Julien coming to a standstill, his eyes ablaze with anger, and drawing himself up to his full height. 'That is a point which you have not sufficiently considered. I should be less than a footman if I put myself in the position of hiding from M. de Rênal anything that had to do with *my money*.'

Madame de Rênal was overwhelmed.

'The Mayor,' Julien went on, 'has given me thirty-six francs five times since I came to live in his house; I am prepared to shew my account-book to M. de Rênal or to anyone else, including M. Valenod who hates me.'

This outburst left Madame de Rênal pale and trembling, and the walk came to an end before either of them could find an excuse for renewing the conversation. Love for Madame de Rênal became more and more impossible in the proud heart of Julien: as for her, she respected, she admired him; she had been scolded by him. On the pretext of making amends for the humiliation which she had unintentionally caused him, she allowed herself to pay him the most delicate attentions. The novelty of this procedure kept her happy for a week. Its effect was to some extent to appease Julien's anger; he was far from seeing anything in it that could be mistaken for personal affection.

'That,' he said to himself, 'is what rich people are like: they humiliate one, and then think they can put things right by a few monkey-tricks.'

Madame de Rênal's heart was too full, and as yet too innocent for her, notwithstanding the resolutions she had made, not to tell her husband of the offer she had made to Julien and the manner in which she had been repulsed.

'What,' M. de Rênal retorted, with keen annoyance, 'could you tolerate a refusal from a *servant*?'

And as Madame de Rênal protested at this word:

'I speak, Ma'am, as the late Prince de Condé spoke, when presenting his Chamberlains to his bride: "All these people," he told her, "are our servants." I read you the passage from Besenval's *Memoirs*, it is essential in questions of precedence. Everyone who is not a gentleman, who lives in your house and receives a salary, is your servant. I shall say a few words to this Master Julien, and give him a hundred francs.'

'Ah, my dear,' said Madame de Rênal trembling, 'please do not say anything in front of the servants.'

'Yes, they might be jealous, and rightly,' said her husband as he left the room, thinking of the magnitude of the sum.

Madame de Rênal sank down on a chair, almost fainting with grief. 'He is going to humiliate Julien, and it is my fault!' She felt a horror of her husband, and hid her face in her hands. She promised herself that she would never confide anything in him again.

When she next saw Julien, she was trembling all over, her bosom was so contracted that she could not manage to utter a single word. In her embarrassment she took his hands and wrung them.

'Well, my friend,' she said to him after a little, 'are you pleased with my husband?'

'How should I not be?' Julien answered with a bitter smile; 'he has given me a hundred francs.'

Madame de Rênal looked at him as though uncertain what to do.

'Give me your arm, she said at length with an accent of courage which Julien had never yet observed in her.

She ventured to enter the shop of the Verrières bookseller, in spite of his terrible reputation as a Liberal. There she chose books to the value of ten louis which she gave to her sons. But these books were the ones which she knew that Julien wanted. She insisted that there, in the bookseller's shop, each of the children should write his own name in the books that fell to his share. While Madame de Rênal was rejoicing at the partial reparation which she had had the courage to make to Julien, he was lost in amazement at the quantity of books which he saw on the bookseller's shelves. Never had he dared to set foot in so profane a place; his heart beat violently. So far from his having any thought of trying to guess what was occurring in the heart of Madame de Rênal, he was plunged in meditation as to how it would be possible for a young student of divinity to procure some of these books. At length the idea came to him that it might be possible, by a skilful approach, to persuade M. de Rênal that he ought to set his sons, as the subject for an essay, the lives of the celebrated gentlemen who were natives of the province. After a month of careful preliminaries, he saw his idea prove successful, so much so that, shortly afterwards, he ventured, in speaking to M. de Rênal, to mention an action considerably more offensive to the noble Mayor; it was a matter of contributing to the prosperity of a Liberal, by taking out a subscription at the library. M. de Rênal entirely agreed that it was wise to let his eldest son have a visual *impression* of various works which he would hear mentioned in conversation when he went to the Military School; but Julien found the Mayor obdurate in refusing to go any farther. He suspected a secret reason, which he was unable to guess.

'I was thinking, Sir,' he said to him one day, 'that it would be highly improper for the name of a respectable gentleman like a Rênal to appear on the dirty ledger of the librarian.'

M. de Rênal's face brightened.

'It would also be a very bad mark,' Julien went on, in a

humbler tone, 'against a poor divinity student, if it should one day be discovered that his name had been on the ledger of a bookseller who keeps a library. The Liberals might accuse me of having asked for the most scandalous books; for all one knows they might even go so far as to write in after my name the titles of those perverse works.'

But Julien was going off the track. He saw the Mayor's features resume their expression of embarrassment and ill humour. Julien was silent. 'I have my man hooked,' he said to himself.

A few days later, on the eldest boy's questioning Julien as to a book advertised in the *Quotidienne*, in M. de Rênal's presence:

'To remove all occasion for triumph from the Jacobin Party,' said the young tutor, 'and at the same time to enable me to answer Master Adolphe, one might open a subscription at the library in the name of the lowest of your servants.'

'That is not at all a bad idea,' said M. de Rênal, obviously delighted.

'Only it would have to be specified,' said Julien with that grave and almost sorrowful air which becomes certain people so well, when they see the success of the projects which have been longest in their minds, 'it would have to be specified that the servant shall not take out any novels. Once they were in the house, those dangerous works might corrupt Madame's maids, not to speak of the servant himself.'

'You forget the political pamphlets,' added M. de Rênal, in a haughty tone. He wished to conceal the admiration that he felt for the clever middle course discovered by his children's tutor.

Julien's life was thus composed of a series of petty negotiations; and their success was of far more importance to him than the evidence of a marked preference for himself which was only waiting for him to read it in the heart of Madame de Rênal.

The moral environment in which he had been placed all his life was repeated in the household of the worshipful Mayor of Verrières. There, as in his father's sawmill, he profoundly despised the people with whom he lived, and was hated by them. He saw every day, from the remarks made by the Sub-Prefect, by M. Valenod and by the other friends of the family, with reference to the things that had just happened under their eyes, how remote their ideas were from any semblance of reality. Did an action strike him as admirable, it was precisely what called forth blame from the people round about him. His unspoken retort was always: 'What monsters!' or 'What fools!' The amusing thing was that, with all his pride, frequently he understood nothing at all of what was being discussed.

In his whole life, he had never spoken with sincerity except to the old Surgeon-Major; the few ideas that he had bore reference to Napoleon's campaigns in Italy, or to surgery. His youthful courage took delight in detailed accounts of the most painful operations; he said to himself: 'I should not have flinched.'

The first time that Madame de Rênal attempted a conversation with him on a subject other than that of the children's education, he began to talk of surgical operations; she turned pale, and begged him to stop.

Julien knew nothing apart from these matters. And so, as he spent his time with Madame de Rênal, the strangest silence grew up between them as soon as they were alone together. In her own drawing-room, humble as his bearing was, she found in his eyes an air of intellectual superiority over everyone that came to the house. Were she left alone for a moment with him, she saw him grow visibly embarrassed. This troubled her, for her womanly instinct made her realize that his embarrassment was not in the least degree amorous.

In consequence of some idea derived from a description of good society, as the old Surgeon-Major had beheld it, as soon as conversation ceased in a place where he found himself in the company of a woman, Julien felt abashed, as though he himself were specially to blame for this silence. This sensation was a hundred times more painful when they were alone. His imagination, full of the most extravagant, the most Spanish notions as to what a man ought to say, when he is alone with a woman, offered him in his agitation none but inadmissible ideas. His soul was in the clouds, and yet he was incapable of breaking the most humiliating silence. Thus his air of severity, during his long walks with Madame de Rênal and the children, was intensified by the most cruel sufferings. He despised himself hideously. If by mischance he forced himself to speak, he found himself saying the most ridiculous things. To increase his misery, he saw and exaggerated his own absurdity; but what he did not see was the expression in his eyes, they were so fine and revealed so burning a soul that, like good actors, they imparted at times a charming meaning to what was meaningless. Madame de Rênal remarked that, when alone with her, he never expressed himself well except when he was distracted by some unforeseen occurrence, he never thought of turning a compliment. As the friends of the family did not spoil her by offering her new and brilliant ideas, she took a delight in the flashes of Julien's intellect.

Since the fall of Napoleon, all semblance of gallantry in speech has been sternly banished from the code of provincial behaviour. People are afraid of losing their posts. The unscrupulous seek support from the *Congregation*; and hypocrisy has made the most brilliant advances even among the Liberal classes. Dulness increases. No pleasure is left, save in reading and agriculture.

Madame de Rênal, the wealthy heiress of a religious aunt, married at sixteen to a worthy gentleman, had never in her life felt or seen anything that bore the faintest resemblance to love. Her confessor, the good curé Chélan, was the only person almost who had ever spoken to her of love, with reference to the advances of M. Valenod, and he had drawn so revolting a picture of it that the word conveyed nothing to her but the idea of the most abject immorality. She regarded as an exception, or rather as something quite apart from nature, love such as she had found it in the very small number of novels that chance had brought to her notice. Thanks to this ignorance, Madame de Rênal, entirely happy, occupied incessantly with the thought of Julien, was far from reproaching herself in the slightest degree.

CHAPTER EIGHT

MINOR EVENTS

Then there were sighs, the deeper for suppression,
    And stolen glances, sweeter for the theft,
And burning blushes, though for no transgression.
                                        Don Juan, I. 74.

T HE angelic sweetness which Madame de Rênal
        derived from her own character as well as from her
        present happiness was interrupted only when she
happened to think of her maid Elisa. This young woman
received a legacy, went to make her confession to the curé
Chélan, and revealed to him her intention to marry Julien.
The curé was genuinely delighted at his friend's good fortune; but his surprise was great when Julien informed him
with a resolute air that Miss Elisa's offer could not be
accepted.

'Pay good heed, my son, to what is taking place in your
heart,' said the curé, frowning; 'I congratulate you on your
vocation, if it is to it alone that must be ascribed your scorn
of a more than adequate provision. For fifty-six years and
more have I been curé at Verrières, and yet, so far as one
can see, I am going to be deprived. This distresses me, albeit
I have an income of eight hundred livres. I tell you of this
detail in order that you may not be under any illusion as to
what is in store for you in the priestly calling. If you think
of paying court to the men in power, your eternal ruin is
assured. You may make your fortune, but you will have to
injure the poor and needy, flatter the Sub-Prefect, the Mayor,

56

the important person, and minister to his passions: such conduct, which in the world is called the art of life, may, in a layman, be not wholly incompatible with salvation; but in our calling, we have to choose; we must make our fortune either in this world or in the next, there is no middle way. Go, my dear friend, reflect, and come back in three days' time with a definite answer. I am sorry to see underlying your character, a smouldering ardour which does not suggest to my mind the moderation and complete renunciation of earthly advantages necessary in a priest; I augur well from your intelligence; but, allow me to tell you,' the good curé went on, with tears in his eyes, 'in the calling of a priest, I shall tremble for your salvation.'

Julien was ashamed of his emotion; for the first time in his life, he saw himself loved; he wept for joy, and went to hide his tears in the great woods above Verrières.

'Why am I in this state?' he asked himself at length; 'I feel that I would give my life a hundred times over for that good Father Chélan, and yet he has just proved to me that I am no better than a fool. It is he above all that I have to deceive, and he sees through me. That secret ardour of which he speaks is my plan for making my fortune. He thinks me unfit to be a priest, at the very moment when I imagined that the sacrifice of an income of fifty louis was going to give him the most exalted idea of my piety and my vocation.

'For the future,' Julien continued, 'I shall rely only upon those elements of my character which I have tested. Who would ever have said that I should find pleasure in shedding tears? That I should love the man who proves to me that I am nothing more than a fool?'

Three days later, Julien had found the pretext with which he should have armed himself from the first; this pretext was a calumny, but what of that? He admitted to the curé, after much hesitation, that a reason which he could not explain to him, because to reveal it would injure a third party, had dissuaded him from the first from the projected marriage. This was tantamount to an indictment of Elisa's conduct. M. Chélan detected in his manner a fire that was wholly mundane, and very different from that which should have inspired a young Levite.

'My friend,' he appealed to him again, 'be an honest yeoman, educated and respected, rather than a priest without a vocation.'

Julien replied to these fresh remonstrances extremely well, so far as words went; he hit upon the expressions which a fervent young seminarist would have employed; but the tone in which he uttered them, the ill-concealed fire that smouldered in his eyes alarmed M. Chélan.

We need not augur ill for Julien's future; he hit upon the correct form of words of a cunning and prudent hypocrisy. That is not bad at his age. As for his tone and gestures, he lived among country folk; he had been debarred from seeing the great models. In the sequel, no sooner had he been permitted to mix with these gentlemen than he became admirable as well in gesture as in speech.

Madame de Rênal was surprised that her maid's newly acquired fortune had not made the girl more happy; she saw her going incessantly to the curé's, and returning with tears in her eyes; finally Elisa spoke to her mistress of her marriage.

Madame de Rênal believed herself to have fallen ill; a sort of fever prevented her enjoying any sleep; she was alive only when she had her maid or Julien before her eyes. She could think of nothing but them and the happiness they would find in their married life. The poverty of the small house in which people would be obliged to live, with an income of fifty louis, portrayed itself to her in enchanting colours. Julien might very well become a lawyer at Bray, the Sub-Prefecture two leagues from Verrières; in that event she would see something of him.

Madame de Rênal sincerely believed that she was going mad; she said so to her husband, and finally did fall ill. That evening, as her maid was waiting upon her, she noticed that the girl was crying. She loathed Elisa at that moment, and had spoken sharply to her; she begged the girl's pardon. Elisa's tears increased; she said that if her mistress would allow it, she would tell her the whole tale of her distress.

'Speak,' replied Madame de Rênal.

'Well, the fact is, Ma'am, he won't have me; wicked people must have spoken evil of me to him, and he believes them.'

'Who won't have you?' said Madame de Rênal, scarcely able to breathe.

'And who could it be, Ma'am, but M. Julien?' the maid replied through her sobs. 'His Reverence has failed to overcome his resistance; for His Reverence considers that he ought not to refuse a decent girl, just because she has been a lady's maid. After all, M. Julien's own father is no better than a carpenter; and he himself, how was he earning his living before he came to Madame's?'

Madame de Rênal had ceased to listen; surfeit of happiness had almost deprived her of the use of her reason. She made the girl repeat to her several times the assurance that Julien had refused in a positive manner, which would not permit of his coming to a more reasonable decision later on.

'I wish to make a final effort,' she said to her maid. 'I shall speak to M. Julien.'

Next day after luncheon, Madame de Rênal gave herself the exquisite sensation of pleading her rival's cause, and of seeing Elisa's hand and fortune persistently refused for an hour on end.

Little by little Julien abandoned his attitude of studied reserve, and ended by making spirited answers to the sound arguments advanced by Madame de Rênal. She could not hold out against the torrent of happiness which now poured into her heart after all those days of despair. She found herself really ill. When she had come to herself, and was comfortably settled in her own room, she asked to be left alone. She was in a state of profound astonishment.

'Can I be in love with Julien?' she asked herself at length.

This discovery, which at any other time would have filled her with remorse and with a profound agitation, was no more to her than a singular spectacle, but one that left her indifferent. Her heart, exhausted by all that she had just undergone, had no sensibility left to place at the service of her passions.

Madame de Rênal tried to work, and fell into a deep sleep; when she awoke, she was less alarmed than she should have been. She was too happy to be able to take anything amiss. Artless and innocent as she was, this honest provincial had never tormented her soul in an attempt to wring from it some little sensibility to some novel shade of sentiment or distress. Entirely absorbed, before Julien came, in that mass of work which, outside Paris, is the lot of a good wife and mother, Madame de Rênal thought about the passions, as we think about the lottery: a certain disappointment and a happiness sought by fools alone.

The dinner bell rang; Madame de Rênal blushed deeply when she heard Julien's voice as he brought in the children. Having acquired some adroitness since she had fallen in love, she accounted for her colour by complaining of a splitting headache.

'There you have women,' put in M. de Rênal, with a coarse laugh. 'There's always something out of order in their machinery.'

Accustomed as she was to this form of wit, the tone of his voice hurt Madame de Rênal. She sought relief in studying Julien's features; had he been the ugliest man in the world, he would have charmed her at that moment.

Always zealous in imitating the habits of the Court, with the first fine days of spring M. de Rênal removed his household to Vergy; it is the village rendered famous by the tragic adventure of Gabrielle.[1] A few hundred yards from the picturesque ruins of the old gothic church, M. de Rênal owned an old castle with its four towers, and a garden laid out like that of the Tuileries, with a number of box borders, and chestnut alleys trimmed twice in the year. An adjoining field, planted with apple trees, allowed the family to take the air. Nine or ten splendid walnuts grew at the end of the orchard; their massive foliage rose to a height of some eighty feet.

'Each of those damned walnuts,' M. de Rênal would say

1 Gabrielle de Vergy, the heroine of a mediæval romance. C. K. S. M.

when his wife admired them, 'costs me half an acre of crop; the corn will not grow in their shade.'

The rustic scene appeared to come as a novelty to Madame de Rênal; her admiration knew no bounds. The feeling that animated her gave her a new spirit and determination. On the second day after their removal to Vergy, M. de Rênal having returned to town upon some official business, his wife engaged labourers at her own expense. Julien had given her the idea of a little gravelled path, which should run round the orchard and beneath the big walnuts, and would allow the children to walk there in the early morning without wetting their shoes in the dew. This plan was put into execution within twenty-four hours of its conception. Madame de Rênal spent a long and happy day with Julien supervising the labourers.

When the Mayor of Verrières returned from the town, he was greatly surprised to find the path finished. His coming surprised Madame de Rênal also; she had forgotten that he existed. For the next two months, he continued to speak with annoyance of their presumption in having carried out, without consulting him, so important a repair, but Madame de Rênal had done it at her own expense, and this to some extent consoled him.

She spent her days running about the orchard with her children, and chasing butterflies. They had made a number of large nets of light-coloured gauze, with which they caught the unfortunate *lepidoptera*. This was the outlandish name which Julien taught Madame de Rênal. For she had sent to Besançon for the handsome work on the subject by M. Godart; and Julien read to her the strange habits of these insects.

They fastened them, without compunction, with pins upon a large sheet of pasteboard, also prepared by Julien.

At last Madame de Rênal and Julien had a subject for conversation; he was no longer exposed to the frightful torture inflicted on him by intervals of silence.

They conversed incessantly, and with extreme interest, although always of the most innocent things. This life, active, occupied and cheerful, suited everyone, except Miss Elisa, who found herself worked to death. 'Even at carnival-time,' she said, 'when there is a ball at Verrières, Madame has never taken so much trouble over her dress; she changes her clothes two or three times a day.'

As it is our intention to flatter no one, we shall not conceal the fact that Madame de Rênal, who had a superb skin, had dresses made for her which exposed her arms and bosom freely. She was very well made, and this way of dressing suited her to perfection.

'You have never *been so young*, Ma'am,' her friends from Verrières used to tell her when they came to dine at Vergy. (It is a local form of speech.)

A curious point, which our readers will scarcely believe, was that Madame de Rênal had no deliberate intention in taking such pains with her appearance. She enjoyed doing so; and, without giving the matter any particular thought, whenever she was not chasing butterflies with the children and Julien, she was engaged with Elisa making dresses. Her one expedition to Verrières was due to a desire to purchase new summer clothes which had just arrived there from Mulhouse.

She brought back with her to Vergy a young woman, one of her cousins. Since her marriage, Madame de Rênal had gradually formed an intimate friendship with Madame Derville, who in their younger days had been her school-fellow at the Sacré-Cœur.

Madame Derville laughed heartily at what she called her cousin's absurd ideas. 'If I were alone, they would never occur to me,' she used to say. These sudden ideas, which in Paris would have been called sallies, made Madame de Rênal feel ashamed, as of something foolish, when she was with her husband; but Madame Derville's presence gave her courage. She began by telling her what she was thinking in a timid voice; when the ladies were by themselves for any length of time, Madame de Rênal would become animated, and a long, undisturbed morning passed in a flash and left the friends quite merry. On this visit, the sensible Madame

Derville found her cousin much less merry and much happier.

Julien, meanwhile, had been living the life of a child since he had come to the country, as happy to be running after butterflies as were his pupils. After so much constraint and skilful diplomacy, alone, unobserved by his fellow-men, and, instinctively, feeling not in the least afraid of Madame de Rênal, he gave himself up to the pleasure of being alive, so keen at his age, and in the midst of the fairest mountains in the world.

As soon as Madame Derville arrived, Julien felt that she was his friend; he hastened to shew her the view that was to be seen from the end of the new path; as a matter of fact it was equal, if not superior to the most admirable scenery which Switzerland and the Italian lakes have to offer. By climbing the steep slope which began a few yards farther on, one came presently to high precipices fringed with oakwoods, which projected almost over the bed of the river. It was to the summits of these sheer rocks that Julien, happy, free, and indeed something more, lord of the house, led the two friends, and relished their admiration of those sublime prospects.

'To me it is like Mozart's music,' said Madame Derville.

His brothers' jealousy, the presence of a despotic and ill tempered father had spoiled the country round Verrières in Julien's eyes. At Vergy, he found no trace of these unpleasant memories; for the first time in his life, he could see no one that was his enemy. When M. de Rênal was in town, as frequently happened, he ventured to read; soon, instead of reading at night, and then taking care, moreover, to shade his lamp with an inverted flowerpot, he could take his full measure of sleep; during the day, in the interval between the children's lessons, he climbed up among these rocks with the book that was his sole rule of conduct, and the sole object of his transports. He found in it at once happiness, ecstasy and consolation in moments of depression.

Certain things which Napoleon says of women, various discussions of the merits of the novels in vogue during his reign, furnished him now, for the first time, with several ideas which would long since have been familiar to any other young man of his age.

The hot weather came. They formed the habit of spending the evening under a huge lime a few yards from the house. There the darkness was intense. One evening, Julien was talking with emphasis, he was revelling in the pleasure of talking well and to young married women; as he gesticulated, he touched the hand of Madame de Rênal, who was leaning on the back of one of those chairs of painted wood that are placed in gardens.

The hand was hurriedly withdrawn; but Julien decided that it was his *duty* to secure that the hand should not be withdrawn when he touched it. The idea of a duty to be performed, and of making himself ridiculous, or rather being left with a sense of inferiority if he did not succeed in performing it, at once took all the pleasure from his heart.

CHAPTER NINE

AN EVENING IN THE COUNTRY

La Didon de M. Guérin, esquisse charmant!
STROMBECK.

WHEN he saw Madame de Rênal again, the next morning, there was a strange look in his eyes; he watched her like an enemy with whom he would presently be engaged. This expression, so different from his expression overnight, made Madame de Rênal lose her head; she had been kind to him, and he appeared vexed. She could not take her eyes from his.

Madame Derville's presence excused Julien from his share of the conversation, and enabled him to concentrate his attention upon what he had in mind. His sole occupation, throughout the day, was that of fortifying himself by reading the inspired text which refreshed his soul.

He greatly curtailed the children's lessons, and when, later on, the presence of Madame de Rênal recalled him to the service of his own vanity, decided that it was absolutely essential that this evening she should allow her hand to remain in his.

The sun as it set and so brought nearer the decisive moment made Julien's heart beat with a strange excitement. Night fell. He observed, with a joy that lifted a huge weight from his breast, that it was very dark. A sky packed with big clouds, kept in motion by a hot breeze, seemed to forebode a tempest. The two women continued strolling until a late hour. Everything that they did this evening seemed strange to Julien. They were enjoying this weather, which, in certain delicate natures, seems to enhance the pleasure of love.

At last they sat down, Madame de Rênal next to Julien, and Madame Derville on the other side of her friend. Preoccupied with the attempt he must shortly make, Julien could think of nothing to say. The conversation languished.

'Shall I tremble like this and feel as uncomfortable the first time I have to fight a duel?' Julien wondered; for he had too little confidence either in himself or in others not to observe the state he was in.

In this agonising uncertainty, any danger would have seemed to him preferable. How often did he long to see Madame de Rênal called by some duty which would oblige her to return to the house and so leave the garden! The violence of the effort which Julien had to make to control himself was such that his voice was entirely altered; presently Madame de Rênal's voice became tremulous also, but Julien never noticed this. The ruthless warfare which his sense of duty was waging with his natural timidity was too exhausting for him to be in a condition to observe anything outside himself. The quarter before ten had sounded from the tower clock, without his having yet ventured on anything. Julien, ashamed of his cowardice, told himself: 'At the precise moment when ten o'clock strikes, I shall carry out the intention which, all day long, I have been promising myself that I would fulfil this evening, or I shall go up to my room and blow my brains out.'

After a final interval of tension and anxiety, during which the excess of his emotion carried Julien almost out of his senses, the strokes of ten sounded from the clock overhead. Each stroke of that fatal bell stirred an echo in his bosom, causing him almost a physical revulsion.

Finally, while the air was still throbbing with the last stroke of ten, he put out his hand and took that of Madame de Rênal, who at once withdrew it. Julien, without exactly knowing what he was doing, grasped her hand again. Although greatly moved himself, he was struck by the icy coldness of the hand he was clasping; he pressed it with convulsive force; a last attempt was made to remove it from him, but finally the hand was left in his grasp.

His heart was flooded with joy, not because he loved Madame de Rênal, but because a fearful torment was now at an end. So that Madame Derville should not notice anything, he felt himself obliged to speak; his voice, now, was loud and ringing. Madame de Rênal's, on the other hand, betrayed such emotion that her friend thought she must be ill and suggested to her that they should go indoors. Julien saw the danger: 'If Madame de Rênal returns to the drawing-room, I am going to fall back into the horrible position I have been in all day. I have not held this hand long enough to be able to reckon it as a definite conquest.'

When Madame Derville repeated her suggestion that they should go into the drawing-room, Julien pressed the hand that lay in his.

Madame de Rênal, who was preparing to rise, resumed her seat, saying in a faint tone:

'I do, as a matter of fact, feel a little unwell, but the fresh air is doing me good.'

These words confirmed Julien's happiness, which, at this moment, was extreme: he talked, forgot to dissimulate, appeared the most charming of men to his two hearers. And yet there was still a slight want of courage in this eloquence which had suddenly come to him. He was in a deadly fear lest Madame Derville, exhausted by the wind which was beginning to rise, and heralded the storm, might decide to go in by herself to the drawing-room. Then he would be left alone with Madame de Rênal. He had found almost by accident the blind courage which was sufficient for action; but he felt that it lay beyond his power to utter the simplest of words to Madame de Rênal. However mild her reproaches might be, he was going to be defeated, and the advantage which he had just gained wiped out.

Fortunately for him, this evening, his touching and emphatic speeches found favour with Madame Derville, who as a rule found him as awkward as a schoolboy, and by no means amusing. As for Madame de Rênal, her hand lying clasped in Julien's, she had no thought of anything; she was allowing herself to live. The hours they spent beneath this huge lime, which, local tradition maintained, had been planted by Charles the Bold, were for her a time of happiness. She listened with rapture to the moaning of the wind in the thick foliage of the lime, and the sound of the first few drops that were beginning to fall upon its lowest leaves. Julien did not notice a detail which would have greatly reassured him; Madame de Rênal, who had been obliged to remove her hand from his, on rising to help her cousin to pick up a pot of flowers which the wind had overturned at their feet, had no sooner sat down again than she gave him back her hand almost without difficulty, and as though it had been an understood thing between them.

Midnight had long since struck; at length it was time to leave the garden: the party broke up. Madame de Rênal, transported by the joy of being in love, was so ignorant that she hardly reproached herself at all. Happiness robbed her of sleep. A sleep like lead carried off Julien, utterly worn out by the battle that had been raging all day in his heart between timidity and pride.

Next morning he was called at five o'clock; and (what would have been a cruel blow to Madame de Rênal had she known of it) he barely gave her a thought. He had done *his duty, and a heroic duty.* Filled with joy by this sentiment, he turned the key in the door of his bedroom and gave himself up with an entirely new pleasure to reading about the exploits of his hero.

When the luncheon bell sounded, he had forgotten, in reading the reports of the Grand Army, all the advantages he had won overnight. He said to himself, in a careless tone, as he went down to the drawing-room: 'I must tell this woman that I love her.'

Instead of that gaze charged with passion which he expected to meet, he found the stern face of M. de Rênal, who, having arrived a couple of hours earlier from Verrières, did not conceal his displeasure on finding that Julien was wasting the whole morning without attending to the children.

No sight could have been so unprepossessing as that of this self-important man, conscious of a grievance and confident of his right to let it be seen.

Each of her husband's harsh words pierced Madame de Rênal to the heart. As for Julien, he was so plunged in ecstasy, still so absorbed in the great events which for the last few hours had been happening before his eyes, that at first he could barely lower the pitch of his attention to listen to the stern voice of M. de Rênal. At length he answered him, sharply enough:

'I was unwell.'

The tone of this reply would have stung a man far less susceptible than the Mayor of Verrières; it occurred to him to reply to Julien with an immediate dismissal. He was restrained only by the maxim which he had laid down for himself, never to be too hasty in business matters.

'This young fool,' he soon reminded himself, 'has made himself a sort of reputation in my house; Valenod may take him on, or else he will marry Elisa, and, in either case, he can afford to laugh at me in his heart.'

Despite the wisdom of these reflexions, M. de Rênal's displeasure found an outlet nevertheless in a succession of coarse utterances which succeeded in irritating Julien. Madame de Rênal was on the point of subsiding in tears. As soon as the meal was ended, she asked Julien to give her his arm for their walk; she leaned upon it in a friendly way. To all that Madame de Rênal said to him, Julien could only murmur in reply:

'This is what rich people are like!'

M. de Rênal kept close beside them; his presence increased Julien's anger. He noticed suddenly that Madame de Rênal was leaning upon his arm in a marked manner; this action horrified him, he repulsed her violently, freeing his arm from hers.

Fortunately M. de Rênal saw nothing of this fresh impertinence; it was noticed only by Madame Derville; her friend burst into tears. At this moment M. de Rênal began flinging stones at a little peasant girl who was trespassing by taking a short cut across a corner of the orchard.

'Monsieur Julien, kindly control yourself, remember that we are all of us liable to moments of ill temper,' Madame Derville said hastily.

Julien looked at her coldly with eyes in which the loftiest contempt was portrayed.

This look astonished Madame Derville, and would have surprised her far more could she have guessed its full meaning; she would have read in it a vague hope of the most terrible revenge. It is doubtless to such moments of humiliation that we owe men like Robespierre.

'Your Julien is very violent, he frightens me,' Madame Derville murmured to her friend.

'He has every reason to be angry,' the other replied. 'After the astonishing progress the children have made with him, what does it matter if he spends a morning without speaking to them? You must admit that gentlemen are very hard.'

For the first time in her life, Madame de Rênal felt a sort of desire to be avenged on her husband. The intense hatred that animated Julien against rich people was about to break forth. Fortunately M. de Rênal called for his gardener, with whom for the rest of the time he busied himself in stopping up with faggots of thorn the short cut that had been made across the orchard. Julien did not utter a single word in reply to the attentions that were shewn him throughout the remainder of the walk. As soon as M. de Rênal had left them, the two ladies, on the plea that they were tired, had asked him each for an arm.

As he walked between these women whose cheeks were flushed with the embarrassment of an intense discomfort, Julien's sombre and decided air formed a striking contrast. He despised these women, and all tender feelings.

'What!' he said to himself, 'not even an allowance of five hundred francs to complete my studies! Ah! How I should send her packing!'

Absorbed in these drastic thoughts, the little that he deigned to take in of the polite speeches of the two ladies displeased him as being devoid of meaning, silly, feeble, in a word *feminine*.

By dint of talking for talking's sake, and of trying to keep the conversation alive, Madame de Rênal found herself saying that her husband had come from Verrières because he had made a bargain, for the purchase of maize straw, with one of his farmers. (In this district maize straw is used to stuff the palliasses of the beds.)

'My husband will not be joining us again,' Madame de Rênal went on: 'he will be busy with the gardener and his valet changing the straw in all the palliasses in the house. This morning he put fresh straw on all the beds on the first floor, now he is at work on the second.'

Julien changed colour; he looked at Madame de Rênal in an odd manner, and presently drew her apart, so to speak, by increasing his pace. Madame Derville allowed them to move away from her.

'Save my life,' said Julien to Madame de Rênal, 'you alone can do it; for you know that the valet hates me like poison. I must confess to you, Ma'am, that I have a portrait; I have hidden it in the palliasse on my bed.'

At these words, Madame de Rênal in turn grew pale.

'You alone, Ma'am, can go into my room at this moment; feel, without letting yourself be observed, in the corner of the palliasse nearest to the window; you will find there a small box of shiny black pasteboard.'

'It contains a portrait?' said Madame de Rênal, barely able to stand.

Her air of disappointment was noticed by Julien, who at once took advantage of it.

'I have a second favour to ask of you, Ma'am; I beg you not to look at the portrait, it is my secret.'

'It is a secret!' repeated Madame de Rênal, in faint accents.

But, albeit she had been reared among people proud of their wealth, and sensible of pecuniary interests alone, love had already instilled some generosity into her heart. Though cruelly wounded, it was with an air of the simplest devotion that Madame de Rênal put to Julien the questions necessary to enable her to execute his commission properly.

'And so,' she said, as she left him, 'it is a little round box, of black pasteboard, and very shiny.'

'Yes, Ma'am,' replied Julien in that hard tone which danger gives a man.

She mounted to the second floor of the house, as pale as though she were going to her death. To complete her misery she felt that she was on the point of fainting, but the necessity of doing Julien a service restored her strength.

'I must have that box,' she said to herself as she quickened her pace.

She could hear her husband talking to the valet, actually in Julien's room. Fortunately they moved into the room in which the children slept. She lifted the mattress and plunged her hand into the straw with such force as to scratch her fingers. But, although extremely sensitive to slight injuries of this sort, she was now quite unconscious of the pain, for almost immediately she felt the polished surface of the pasteboard box. She seized it and fled.

No sooner was she rid of the fear of being surprised by her husband, than the horror inspired in her by this box made her feel that in another minute she must unquestionably faint.

'So Julien is in love, and I have here the portrait of the woman he loves.'

Seated on a chair in the sitting-room of this apartment, Madame de Rênal fell a prey to all the horrors of jealousy. Her extreme ignorance was of service to her again at this moment; astonishment tempered her grief. Julien appeared, snatched the box, without thanking her, without saying a word, and ran into his bedroom, where he struck a light and immediately destroyed it. He was pale, speechless; he exaggerated to himself the risk he had been running.

'The portrait of Napoleon,' he said to himself with a toss of the head, 'found hidden in the room of a man who professes such hatred for the usurper! Found by M. de Rênal, so *ultra* and so angry! and, to complete the imprudence, on the white card at the back of the portrait, lines in my writing! And lines that can leave no doubt as to the warmth of my admiration! And each of those transports of love is dated! There was one only two days ago!

'All my reputation brought down, destroyed in a moment!' Julien said to himself as he watched the box burn, 'and my reputation is all I have, I live by it alone ... and what a life at that, great God!'

An hour later, his exhaustion and the pity he felt for himself disposed him to feel affection. He met Madame de Rênal and took her hand which he kissed with more sincerity than he had ever yet shewn. She coloured with delight, and almost simultaneously repulsed Julien with the anger of a jealous woman. Julien's pride, so recently wounded, made a fool of him at that moment. He saw in Madame de Rênal only a rich woman. He let fall her hand with contempt, and strode away. He went out and walked pensively in the garden; presently a bitter smile appeared on his lips.

'Here I am walking about as calm as a man who is his own master! I am not looking after the children! I am exposing myself to the humiliating remarks of M. de Rênal, and he will be justified.' He hastened to the children's room.

The caresses of the youngest boy, to whom he was greatly attached, did something to soothe his agonizing pain.

'This one does not despise me yet,' thought Julien. But presently he blamed himself for this relief from pain, as for a fresh weakness. 'These children fondle me as they might fondle the puppy that was bought yesterday.'

CHAPTER TEN

A LARGE HEART AND A SMALL FORTUNE

But passion most dissembles, yet betrays,
    Even by its darkness; as the blackest sky
Foretells the heaviest tempest.
                            Don Juan, I. 73.

M. DE RÊNAL, who was visiting every room in the house, reappeared in the children's room with the servants who brought back the palliasses refilled. The sudden entry of this man was the last straw to Julien.

Paler, more sombre than usual, he advanced towards him. M. de Rênal stood still and looked at his servants.

'Sir,' Julien began, 'do you suppose that with any other tutor your children would have made the same progress that they have made with me? If your answer is no,' he went on without giving M. de Rênal time to speak, 'how dare you presume to reproach me with neglecting them?'

M. de Rênal, who had barely recovered from his alarm, concluded from the strange tone which he saw this young peasant adopt that he had in his pocket some more attractive offer and was going to leave him. Julien's anger increasing as he spoke:

'I can live without you, Sir,' he concluded.

'I am extremely sorry to see you so agitated,' replied M. de Rênal, stammering a little. The servants were a few feet away, and were occupied in making the beds.

'That is not enough for me, Sir,' Julien went on, beside

himself with rage; 'think of the abominable things you said to me, and in the presence of ladies, too!'

M. de Rênal was only too well aware of what Julien was asking, and conflicting passions did battle in his heart. It so happened that Julien, now really mad with rage, exclaimed:

'I know where to go, Sir, when I leave your house.'

On hearing these words, M. de Rênal had a vision of Julien established in M. Valenod's household.

'Very well, Sir,' he said at length with a sigh, and the air of a man calling in a surgeon to perform the most painful operation, 'I agree to your request. From the day after to-morrow, which is the first of the month, I shall give you fifty francs monthly.'

Julien wanted to laugh and remained speechless: his anger had completely vanished.

'I did not despise the animal enough,' he said to himself. 'This, no doubt, is the most ample apology so base a nature is capable of making.'

The children, who had listened to this scene open-mouthed, ran to the garden to tell their mother that M. Julien was in a great rage, but that he was to have fifty francs a month.

Julien went after them from force of habit, without so much as a glance at M. de Rênal, whom he left in a state of intense annoyance.

'That's a hundred and sixty-eight francs,' the Mayor said to himself, 'that M. Valenod has cost me. I must really say a few firm words to him about his contract to supply the foundlings.'

A moment later, Julien again stood before him.

'I have a matter of conscience to discuss with M. Chélan. I have the honour to inform you that I shall be absent for some hours.'

'Ah, my dear Julien,' said M. de Rênal, laughing in the most insincere manner, 'the whole day, if you wish, the whole of to-morrow, my worthy friend. Take the gardener's horse to go to Verrières.

'There,' M. de Rênal said to himself, 'he's going with an

answer to Valenod; he's given me no promise, but we must let the young hothead cool down.'

Julien made a speedy escape and climbed up among the big woods through which one can go from Vergy to Verrières. He was in no hurry to reach M. Chélan's. So far from desiring to involve himself in a fresh display of hypocrisy, he needed time to see clearly into his own heart, and to give audience to the swarm of conflicting feelings that disturbed it.

'I have won a battle,' he said to himself as soon as he found himself in the shelter of the woods and out of sight of anyone, 'I have really won a battle!'

The last word painted his whole position for him in glowing colours, and restored some degree of tranquillity to his heart.

'Here I am with a salary of fifty francs a month; M. de Rênal must be in a fine fright. But of what?'

His meditation as to what could have frightened the prosperous and powerful man against whom, an hour earlier, he had been seething with rage completely restored Julien's serenity. He was almost conscious, for a moment, of the exquisite beauty of the woods through which he was walking. Enormous fragments of bare rock had in times past fallen into the heart of the forest from the side of the mountain. Tall beeches rose almost as high as these rocks whose shadow provided a delicious coolness within a few yards of places where the heat of the sun's rays would have made it impossible to stop.

Julien paused for a breathing-space in the shadow of these great rocks, then went on climbing. Presently, by following a narrow path, barely visible and used only by goatherds, he found himself standing upon an immense rock, where he could be certain of his complete isolation from his fellow-men. This natural position made him smile, it suggested to him the position to which he was burning to attain in the moral sphere. The pure air of these lofty mountains breathed serenity and even joy into his soul. The Mayor of Verrières might still, in his eyes, be typical of all the rich and insolent denizens of the earth, but Julien felt that the hatred which had convulsed him that afternoon contained, notwithstanding its violence, no element of personal ill-feeling. Should he cease to see M. de Rênal, within a week he would have forgotten him, the man himself, his house, his dogs, his children and all that was his. 'I have forced him, I do not know how, to make the greatest of sacrifices. What, more than fifty crowns a year? A moment earlier I had just escaped from the greatest danger. That makes two victories in one day; the second contains no merit, I must try to discover the reason. But we can leave such arduous research for to-morrow.'

Julien, erect upon his mighty rock, gazed at the sky, kindled to flame by an August sun. The grasshoppers were chirping in the patch of meadow beneath the rock; when they ceased everything around him was silence. Twenty leagues of country lay at his feet. From time to time a hawk, risen from the bare cliffs above his head, caught his eye as it wheeled silently in its vast circles. Julien's eye followed mechanically the bird of prey. Its calm, powerful motion impressed him, he envied such strength, he envied such isolation.

It was the destiny of Napoleon, was it one day to be his own?

CHAPTER ELEVEN

NIGHT THOUGHTS

> Yet Julia's very coldness still was kind,
>   And tremulously gentle her small hand
> Withdrew itself from his, but left behind
>   A little pressure, thrilling, and so bland
> And slight, so very slight, that to the mind
>   'Twas but a doubt.
>   *Don Juan*, I. 71.

H E must, however, let himself be seen at Verrières. As he left the Presbytery the first person he met was, by a happy chance, M. Valenod, whom he hastened to inform of the increase in his salary.

On his return to Vergy, Julien did not go down to the garden until night had set in. His heart was worn out by the multitude of powerful emotions that had assailed it in the course of the day. 'What shall I say to them?' he asked himself anxiously, thinking of the ladies. It never occurred to him that his spirits were precisely at the level of the trivial happenings that as a rule occupy the whole interest of women. Often Julien was unintelligible to Madame Derville, and even to her friend, while he in turn only half understood all that they were saying to him. Such was the effect of the force, and, if I may use the word, of the magnitude of the waves of passion on which the heart of this ambitious youth was being tossed. In this strange creature almost every day was one of storm.

When he went into the garden that evening, Julien was ready to listen with interest to the thoughts of the fair cousins. They awaited his coming with impatience. He took his accustomed seat, by Madame de Rênal's side. The darkness soon became intense. He attempted to clasp a white hand which for some time he had seen close beside him, resting on the back of a chair. There was some hesitation shewn, but finally the hand was withdrawn from him in a manner which betokened displeasure. Julien was prepared to regard this as final, and to continue the conversation in a light tone, when he heard M. de Rênal approach.

The rude words of the morning still rang in Julien's ears. 'Would it not,' he said to himself, 'be a good way of scoring off this creature, so lavishly endowed with every material advantage, to take possession of his wife's hand under his very eyes? Yes, I will do it, I, for whom he has shewn such contempt.'

From that moment peace of mind, so ill assorted to Julien's character, speedily vanished; he desired most anxiously, and without being able to fix his mind on anything else, that Madame de Rênal might consent to let him hold her hand.

M. de Rênal talked politics in an angry tone: two or three manufacturers at Verrières were becoming decidedly richer than himself, and wished to oppose him at the elections. Madame Derville listened to him. Julien, irritated by this talk, moved his chair nearer to Madame de Rênal's. The darkness hid every movement. He ventured to place his hand close to the pretty arm which her gown left bare. Troubled, no longer conscious of what he was doing, he moved his cheek in the direction of this pretty arm, and made bold to press his lips to it.

Madame de Rênal shuddered. Her husband was a few feet away, she hastened to give Julien her hand, at the same time thrusting him slightly from her. While M. de Rênal continued his abuse of the good-for-nothings and Jacobins who were making fortunes, Julien covered the hand which had been left in his with passionate kisses, or so at least they seemed to Madame de Rênal. And yet the poor woman had been furnished with proof, on this fatal day, that the heart of the man whom she adored without confessing it was pledged elsewhere! Throughout the hours of Julien's absence, she had been a prey to the most abject misery, which had made her think.

'What,' she said to herself, 'am I to love, to have love offered to me? Am I, a married woman, to fall in love? But,' she reminded herself, 'I have never felt that dark passion for my husband, and so I cannot tear my mind from Julien. At heart he is only a boy filled with respect for me! This folly will pass. How can it concern my husband what feelings I may entertain for this young man? M. de Rênal would be bored by the talks I have with Julien, about things of the imagination. He himself thinks only about his business. I am taking nothing from him to give to Julien.'

No trace of hypocrisy came to sully the purity of this simple soul, carried away by a passion such as she had never felt. She was deceived, but quite unawares, and at same time a virtuous instinct had taken alarm. Such were the conflicts that were agitating her when Julien appeared in the garden. She heard his voice, almost at the same moment she saw him sit down by her side. Her heart was so to speak carried away by this charming happiness which for the last fortnight had astonished even more than it had bewitched her. Everything was unexpected to her. And yet after a few moments: 'So Julien's presence is enough,' she said to herself, 'to wipe out all memory of his misconduct?' She took fright; then it was that she withdrew her hand from his.

His kisses, filled with passion and such as she had never yet received, made her at once forget the possibility of his loving another woman. Soon he was no longer guilty in her eyes. The cessation of her poignant grief, born of suspicion, the presence of a happiness of which she had never even dreamed, plunged her in transports of affection and wild gaiety. That evening was delightful for them all, except for the Mayor of Verrières, who could not forget the growing wealth of his competitors. Julien no longer thought of his dark ambition, nor of his plans that would be so difficult of execution. For the first time in his life, he was carried away by the power of beauty. Lost in a vague and pleasant dream, so foreign to his nature, gently pressing that hand which pleased him as an example of perfect beauty, he gave a divided attention to the rustle of the leaves of the lime, stirred by the gentle night breeze, and to the dogs at the mill by the Doubs, barking in the distance.

But this emotion was a pleasure and not a passion. On returning to his room he thought of one happiness only, that of going on with his favourite book; at twenty, the thought of the world and of the impression one is going to make on it, prevails over everything else.

Presently, however, he put down the book. By dint of dreaming of Napoleon's victories, he had discerned a new element in his own. 'Yes, I have won a battle,' he told himself, 'but I must follow it up, I must crush the arrogance of this proud gentleman while he is still retreating. That is Napoleon out and out. He reproaches me with neglecting his children. I must ask him for three days' holiday, to go and see my friend Fouqué. If he refuses, I again offer to break the agreement; but he will give way.'

Madame de Rênal could not close an eye. She felt that she had never lived until that moment. She could not tear her mind from the happiness of feeling Julien cover her hand with burning kisses.

Suddenly the horrid word *adultery* occurred to her. All the most disgusting implications that the vilest debauchery can impart to the idea of sensual love came crowding into her imagination. These ideas sought to tarnish the tender and godlike image that she had made for herself of Julien and of the pleasure of loving him. The future portrayed itself in terrible colours. She saw herself an object of scorn.

It was a frightful moment; her soul journeyed into strange lands. That evening she had tasted an unknown happiness; now she suddenly found herself plunged in appalling misery. She had no conception of such sufferings; they began to affect her reason. The thought occurred to her for a moment of confessing to her husband that she was afraid of falling in love with Julien. It would have allowed her to speak of him. Fortunately she recalled a piece of advice given her long ago by her aunt, on the eve of her marriage. It warned her of the danger of confiding in a husband, who is after all a master. In the intensity of her grief she wrung her hands.

She was carried away indiscriminately by conflicting and painful imaginings. At one moment she was afraid of not being loved in return, at another the fearful thought of the crime tortured her as though on the morrow she would have to be exposed in the pillory, on the public square of Verrières, with a placard proclaiming her adultery to the populace.

Madame de Rênal was without any experience of life; even when wide awake and in the full exercise of her reason, she would have seen no distinction between being guilty in the sight of God and finding herself publicly greeted with all the most flagrant marks of general opprobrium.

When the frightful idea of adultery and of all the ignominy which (she supposed) that crime brings in its train gave her at length a respite, and she began to dream of the delight of living with Julien innocently, as in the past, she found herself swept away by the horrible thought that Julien was in love with another woman. She saw once again his pallor when he was afraid of losing her portrait, or of compromising her by letting it be seen. For the first time, she had surprised signs of fear on that calm and noble countenance. Never had he shewn himself in such a state for her or for her children. This additional grief carried her to the utmost intensity of anguish which the human soul is able to endure. Unconsciously, Madame de Rênal uttered cries which roused her maid. Suddenly she saw appear by her bedside the light of a lamp, and recognised Elisa.

'Is it you that he loves?' she cried in her frenzy.

The maid, amazed at the fearful distress in which she found her mistress, paid no attention fortunately to this singular utterance. Madame de Rênal realized her own imprudence: 'I am feverish,' she told her, 'and I think, a little light-headed; stay beside me.'

Thoroughly awakened by the necessity of controlling herself, she felt less wretched; reason resumed the sway of which her state of drowsiness had deprived it. To escape from the fixed stare of her maid, she ordered her to read the newspaper aloud, and it was to the monotonous sound of the girl's voice, reading a long article from the *Quotidienne*, that Madame de Rênal formed the virtuous resolution to treat Julien with absolute coldness when next she saw him.

CHAPTER TWELVE

A JOURNEY

On trouve à Paris des gens élégants, il peut y avoir
en province des gens à caractère.

SIEYÉS.

NEXT morning, at five o'clock, before Madame de
Rênal was visible, Julien had obtained from her husband three days' leave of absence. Contrary to his
expectation, Julien found himself longing to see her again,
and could think of nothing but that shapely hand. He went
down to the garden, Madame de Rênal was long in coming.
But if Julien had been in love with her he would have seen
her, behind her half-closed shutters on the first floor, her face
pressed to the glass. She was watching him. At length, in
spite of her resolutions, she decided to shew herself in the
garden. Her customary pallor had given place to the most
glowing colour. This simple-minded woman was evidently
agitated: a feeling of constraint and even of resentment
marred that expression of profound serenity, as though raised
above all the common interests of life, which gave such
charm to that heavenly face.

Julien lost no time in joining her; he admired those fine
arms which a shawl flung in haste across her shoulders left
visible. The coolness of the morning air seemed to increase
the brilliance of a complexion which the agitation of the past
night made all the more sensible to every impression. This
beauty, modest and touching, and yet full of thoughts which
are nowhere to be found among the lower orders, seemed to

reveal to Julien an aspect of her nature of which he had never yet been aware. Wholly absorbed in admiration of the charms which his greedy eye surprised, Julien was not thinking of the friendly greeting which he might expect to receive. He was all the more astonished by the icy coldness that was shewn him, beneath which he even thought he could make out a deliberate intention to put him in his place.

The smile of pleasure faded from his lips; he remembered the rank that he occupied in society, especially in the eyes of a noble and wealthy heiress. In a moment, his features shewed nothing but pride and anger with himself. He felt a violent disgust at having been so foolish as to postpone his departure by more than an hour, only to receive so humiliating a greeting.

'Only a fool,' he told himself, 'loses his temper with other people: a stone falls because it is heavy. Am I always to remain a boy? When am I going to form the good habit of giving these people their exact money's worth and no more of my heart and soul? If I wish to be esteemed by them and by myself, I must shew them that it is my poverty that deals with their wealth, but that my heart is a thousand leagues away from their insolence, and is placed in too exalted a sphere to be reached by their petty marks of contempt or favour.'

While these sentiments came crowding into the young tutor's mind, his features assumed an expression of injured pride and ferocity. Madame de Rênal was greatly distressed by this. The virtuous coldness which she had meant to impart to her greeting gave way to an expression of interest, and of an interest animated by the surprise of the sudden change which she had just beheld in him. The flow of idle words that people exchange in the morning with regard to one another's health, to the beauty of the day, and so forth, dried up at once in them both. Julien, whose judgment was not disturbed by any passion, soon found a way of letting Madame de Rênal see how little he regarded himself as being on terms of friendship with her; he said nothing to her of the little expedition on which he was starting, bowed to her, and set off.

As she watched him go, overwhelmed by the sombre pride which she read in that glance, so friendly the evening before, her eldest son, who came running up from the other end of the garden, said to her as he embraced her:

'We have a holiday, M. Julien is going on a journey.'

At these words Madame de Rênal felt herself frozen by a deadly chill; she was unhappy in her virtue, and more unhappy still in her weakness.

This latest development now occupied the whole of her imagination; she was carried far beyond the wise resolutions which were the fruit of the terrible night she had passed. It was a question no longer of resisting this charming lover, but of losing him for ever.

She was obliged to take her place at table. To add to her misery, M. de Rênal and Madame Derville spoke of nothing but Julien's departure. The Mayor of Verrières had remarked something unusual in the firm tone with which he had demanded a holiday.

'The young peasant has doubtless an offer from some one in his pocket. But that some one, even if it should be M. Valenod, must be a little discouraged by the sum of 600 francs, which he must now be prepared to spend annually. Yesterday, at Verrières, he will have asked for three days in which to think things over; and this morning, so as not to be obliged to give me an answer, the young gentleman goes off to the mountains. To have to reckon with a wretched workman who puts on airs, that's what we've come to!'

'Since my husband, who does not know how deeply he has wounded Julien, thinks he is going to leave us, what am I to suppose?' Madame de Rênal asked herself. 'Ah! It is all settled!'

So as to be able at least to weep in freedom, and without having to answer Madame Derville's questions, she pleaded a splitting headache, and retired to bed.

'There you have a woman all over,' M. de Rênal repeated; 'there's always something wrong with those complicated machines.' And he went on his way jeering.

While Madame de Rênal was at the mercy of the most

cruel inflictions of the terrible passion into which accident had led her, Julien was making his way light-heartedly amid the loveliest views that mountain scenery has to offer. He was obliged to pass over the high range to the north of Vergy. The path which he followed, rising gradually amid great beechwoods, forms an endless series of zigzags on the side of the high mountain which bounds the valley of the Doubs on the north. Presently the traveller's gaze, passing over the lower ridges which confine the course of the Doubs on the south, was able to sweep the fertile plains of Burgundy and Beaujolais. Irresponsive as the heart of this ambitious youth might be to this kind of beauty, he could not refrain from stopping now and again to gaze at so vast and so imposing a prospect.

At length he came to the summit of the high mountain, beneath which he must pass in order to arrive, by this diagonal route, at the lonely valley in which his friend Fouqué, the young timber-merchant, lived. Julien was in no hurry to see him, or any other human being for that matter. Concealed like a bird of prey, amid the bare rocks which crowned the high mountain, he could see a long way off anyone that might be coming his way. He discovered a small cave in the almost perpendicular face of one of the rocks. He set his course for it, and presently was ensconced in this retreat. 'Here,' he said, his eyes sparkling with joy, 'men can do me no harm.' It occurred to him to indulge in the pleasure of writing down his thoughts, so dangerous to him in any other place. A smooth block of stone served as his table. His pen flew: he saw nothing of the scene round about him. At length he noticed that the sun was setting behind the distant mountains of Beaujolais.

'Why should I not spend the night here?' he asked himself; 'I have bread, and *I am free*!' At the sound of that great word his heart leaped, his hypocrisy meant that he was not free even with Fouqué. His head supported on both his hands, Julien stayed in this cave happier than he had ever been in his life, engrossed in his dreams and in the joy of freedom. Without heeding it he saw fade and die, one after another, the last rays of evening light. In the midst of that vast darkness, his soul wandered in contemplation of what he imagined that he would one day find in Paris. This was first and foremost a woman far more beautiful and of a far higher intelligence than any it had been his lot to see in the country. He loved with passion, he was loved in return. If he tore himself from her for a few moments, it was to cover himself with glory and earn the right to be loved more warmly still.

Even if we allow him Julien's imagination, a young man brought up among the melancholy truths of Paris would have been aroused at this stage in his romance by the cold touch of irony; the mighty deeds would have vanished with the hope of performing them, to give place to the well-known maxim: 'When a man leaves his mistress, he runs the risk of being betrayed two or three times daily.' The young peasant saw no obstacle between himself and the most heroic actions, save want of opportunity.

But black night had succeeded the day, and he had still two leagues to cover before coming down to the hamlet in which Fouqué lived. Before leaving the little cave, Julien struck a light and carefully destroyed all that he had written.

He greatly astonished his friend by knocking at his door at one o'clock in the morning. He found Fouqué engaged in making up his accounts. He was a young man of tall stature, none too well made, with large, hard features, a huge nose, and plenty of good nature concealed beneath this repellent aspect.

'You've quarrelled with your M. de Rênal, then, that you come here of a sudden like this?'

Julien related to him, with suitable omissions, the events of the previous evening.

'Stay with me,' Fouqué said to him; 'I see that you know M. de Rênal, M. Valenod, the Sub-Prefect Maugiron, the curé Chélan; you have grasped all the subtle points of their natures; you're ripe now to put yourself up for auction. You know arithmetic better than I do, you shall keep my books; I am making a big profit from my business. The impossibility of doing everything by myself and the fear of hitting upon a rogue in the man I might take as my partner prevent me every day from doing the most profitable deals. Not a month ago I put six thousand francs in the pocket of Michaud of Saint-Amand, whom I had not seen for six years, and met quite by chance at the Pontarlier sale. Why should not you have made those six thousand francs yourself, or three thousand at least? For if I had had you with me that day, I should have gone on bidding for that lot of timber, and the other would soon have left me with it. Be my partner.'

This offer annoyed Julien; it unsettled his erratic mind; throughout supper, which the friends cooked for themselves, like Homeric heroes, for Fouqué lived by himself, he shewed Julien his books, and proved to him what advantages his trade in timber offered. Fouqué had the highest opinion of Julien's intelligence and character.

When at length the latter found himself alone in his little room walled with planks of firwood, 'It is true,' he said to himself, 'I can make a few thousand francs here, then return with advantage to the calling of soldier or priest, according to the fashion prevailing in France at the time. The little hoard that I shall have amassed will remove all difficulties of detail. Alone on this mountainside, I can do something to dispel my present appalling ignorance of so many of the things that occupy the minds of all these fashionable gentlemen. But Fouqué is giving up the thought of marriage, he has told me again and again that solitude is making him melancholy. It is obvious that if he is taking a partner who has no money to put into his business, it is in the hope of providing himself with a companion who will never leave him.

'Shall I prove false to my friend?' exclaimed Julien angrily. This creature, for whom hypocrisy and the absence of all fellow feeling were the ordinary line of conduct, could not on this occasion bear the thought of the slightest want of delicacy towards a man who loved him.

But all at once Julien became happy, he had a reason for refusing. 'What, I should be idly wasting seven or eight years! I should thus arrive at eight and twenty; but, at that age,

Napoleon had already done his greatest deeds! After I have obscurely scraped together a little money by going round all these timber sales, and winning the favour of various minor rascals, who can say whether I shall still preserve the sacred fire with which one makes oneself a name?'

The following morning, Julien replied with great coolness to the worthy Fouqué, who looked upon the matter of their partnership as settled, that his vocation to the sacred ministry of the altar did not allow him to accept. Fouqué could not believe his ears.

'But do you realize,' he kept on saying, 'that I make you my partner, or, if you prefer, give you four thousand francs a year? And you want to go back to your M. de Rênal, who despises you like the mud on his shoes! When you have two hundred louis in hand, what is to prevent you from entering the Seminary? I will say more, I undertake to procure for you the best parish in the district. For,' Fouqué went on, lowering his voice, 'I supply firewood to the ——, and the ——, and M. ——. I give them the best quality of oak, for which they pay me the price of white wood, but never was money better invested.'

Nothing could prevail against Julien's vocation. In the end Fouqué decided that he must be slightly mad. On the third day, at dawn, Julien left his friend to pass the day among the rocks of the big mountain. He found his little cave again, but he no longer enjoyed peace of mind, his friend's offers had destroyed it. Like Hercules he found himself called upon to choose not between vice and virtue, but between mediocrity ending in an assured comfort and all the heroic dreams of his youth. 'So I have no real firmness of character,' he told himself; and this was the doubt that pained him most. 'I am not of the stuff of which great men are made, since I am afraid that eight years spent in providing myself with bread may rob me of that sublime energy which makes men do extraordinary things.'

CHAPTER THIRTEEN

OPEN-WORK STOCKINGS

Un roman: c'est un miroir qu'on promène le long
d'un chemin.

SAINT-RÉAL.

WHEN Julien caught sight of the picturesque ruins of
the old church of Vergy, it occurred to him that
for two whole days he had not once thought of
Madame de Rênal. 'The other day, as I was leaving, that
woman reminded me of the vast gulf that separates us, she
treated me like a workman's son. No doubt she wished to
shew me that she repented of having let me hold her hand
the night before. . . . It is a lovely hand, all the same! What
charm, what nobility dwells in that woman's glance!'

The possibility of making a fortune with Fouqué gave a
certain facility to the course of Julien's reasoning; it was less
often interrupted by irritation, and the keen sense of his own
poverty and humble position in the eyes of the world. As
though perched on a lofty promontory, he was able to judge,
and, so to speak, overlooked extreme poverty on the one
hand and that life of comfort which he still called riches on
the other. He was far from considering his position like a
philosopher, but he had sufficient perception to feel that he
was *different* after this little expedition among the mountains.

He was struck by the extreme uneasiness with which
Madame de Rênal listened to the short account of his journey, for which she had asked him.

Fouqué had had thoughts of marriage, unhappy love

affairs; the conversation between the friends had been filled with long confidences of this nature. After finding happiness too soon, Fouqué had discovered that he was not the sole possessor of his mistress's heart. These disclosures had astonished Julien; he had learned much that was new to him. His solitary life, compounded of imagination and suspicion, had kept him aloof from everything that could have enlightened him.

During his absence, life had been for Madame de Rênal nothing more than a succession of torments, each different but all alike intolerable; she was really ill.

'You must not, on any account,' Madame Derville told her when she saw Julien return, 'feeling as you do, sit in the garden this evening, the damp air would make you worse.'

Madame Derville was surprised to see that her friend, who was always being scolded by M. de Rênal for the undue simplicity of her attire, had put on open-work stockings and a pair of charming little shoes that had arrived from Paris. For the last three days Madame de Rênal's sole distraction had been to cut out and make Elisa put together in all haste a summer gown, of a charming little fabric greatly in fashion. It was just possible to finish this gown a few minutes after Julien's arrival; Madame de Rênal at once put it on. Her friend had no longer any doubt. 'She is in love, poor woman!' Madame Derville said to herself. She understood all the strange symptoms of her illness.

She saw her speak to Julien. Pallor took the place of the most vivid blushes. Anxiety stood revealed in her eyes, fastened on those of the young tutor. Madame de Rênal expected every moment that he was going to offer an explanation, and announce that he was leaving the house, or would remain. It never occurred to Julien to say anything about this subject, which had not entered his thoughts. After a terrible struggle, Madame de Rênal at last ventured to say to him, in a tremulous voice, in which the whole extent of her passion lay revealed:

'Are you going to leave your pupils to take a post elsewhere?'

Julien was struck by her quavering voice and by the look in her eyes. 'This woman loves me,' he said to himself; 'but after this passing weakness for which her pride is reproaching her, and as soon as she is no longer afraid of my going, she will return to her arrogance.' This glimpse of their respective positions came to Julien like a flash of lightning; he replied, hesitatingly:

'I should greatly regret leaving such attractive and *well born* children, but perhaps it will be inevitable. A man has duties towards himself also.'

As he uttered the words *well born* (this was one of the aristocratic expressions which Julien had recently acquired), he burned with a strong feeling of antipathy.

'To this woman,' he said to himself, 'I am not well born.'

Madame de Rênal, as she listened to him, was admiring his intelligence, his beauty, her heart was pierced by the possibility of departure which he dangled before her. All her friends from Verrières who, during Julien's absence, had come out to dine at Vergy, had almost vied in complimenting her upon the astonishing young man that her husband had had the good fortune to unearth. This was not to say that they understood anything of the progress that the children had made. The fact of his knowing the Bible by heart, and in Latin, too, had provoked in the inhabitants of Verrières an admiration that will endure for, it may be, a century.

Julien, who spoke to no one, knew nothing of all this. If Madame de Rênal had had the slightest self-control, she would have congratulated him on the reputation he had won, and Julien, his pride set at rest, would have been pleasant and affable to her, all the more as her new gown seemed to him charming. Madame de Rênal, also pleased with her pretty gown, and with what Julien said to her about it, had proposed a turn in the garden; soon she had confessed that she was not well enough to walk. She had taken the returned traveller's arm, and, far from restoring her strength, the contact of that arm deprived her of what little strength remained to her.

It was dark; no sooner were they seated than Julien, relying on the privilege he had already won, ventured to press his lips to the arm of his pretty neighbour, and to take her hand. He was thinking of the boldness which Fouqué had used with his mistresses, and not of Madame de Rênal; the phrase *well born* still weighed upon his heart. His own hand was pressed, but this afforded him no pleasure. Far from his being proud, or even grateful for the affection which Madame de Rênal betrayed this evening by unmistakable signs, beauty, elegance, freshness found him almost unconscious of their appeal. Purity of heart, freedom from any feeling of hatred, serve doubtless to prolong the duration of youth. It is the face that ages first in the majority of beautiful women.

Julien was sullen all the evening; hitherto he had been angry only with fortune and with society; now that Fouqué had offered him an ignoble way of arriving at comfort, he was angry with himself. Absorbed in his own thoughts, although now and then he addressed a few words to the ladies, Julien ended by unconsciously letting go Madame de Rênal's hand. This action completely nonplussed the poor woman; she saw in it an indication of her fate.

Had she been certain of Julien's affection, her virtue might perhaps have found strength to resist him. Trembling at the thought of losing him for ever, her passion carried her to the point of seizing Julien's hand, which, in his distraction, he had allowed to rest upon the back of a chair. This action stirred the ambitious youth; he would have liked it to be witnessed by all those proud nobles who, at table, when he was at the lower end with the children, used to look at him with so patronizing a smile. 'This woman cannot despise me any longer: in that case,' he said to himself, 'I ought to be stirred by her beauty; I owe it to myself to be her lover.' Such an idea would never have occurred to him before he received the artless confidences of his friend.

The sudden resolution he had just made formed a pleasing distraction. He said to himself: 'I must have one of these two women'; he realized that he would greatly have preferred to pay his court to Madame Derville; it was not that she was more attractive, but she had seen him always as a tutor honoured for his learning, and not as a working carpenter, with a ratteen jacket folded under his arm, as he had first appeared to Madame de Rênal.

It was precisely as a young workman, blushing to the whites of his eyes, hesitating outside the door of the house and not venturing to ring the bell, that Madame de Rênal delighted most to picture him. This woman, whom the townsfolk called so haughty, rarely thought of rank, and the slightest achievement went a long way farther, in her mind, than the promise of character held out by the rank of a man. A carter who had shown valour would have been more gallant to her mind than a terrible captain of hussars adorned with moustaches and pipe. She believed Julien's heart to be nobler than that of any of her cousins, all of whom were gentlemen of family, and many of them bearing titles.

As he followed up this survey of his position, Julien saw that he must not think of attempting the conquest of Madame Derville, who had probably noticed the weakness that Madame de Rênal shewed for him. Forced to return to the latter: 'What do I know of this woman's character?' Julien asked himself. 'Only this: before I went away, I took her hand, she withdrew it; to-day I withdraw my hand, she seizes it and presses it. A good opportunity to repay her all the contempt she has shewn for me. God knows how many lovers she has had! Perhaps she is deciding in my favour only because of the facilities for our meeting.'

Such is, alas, the drawback of an excessive civilization. At the age of twenty, the heart of a young man, if he has any education, is a thousand leagues from that devil-may-care attitude without which love is often only the most tedious duty.

'I owe it to myself all the more,' went on Julien's petty vanity, 'to succeed with this woman, so that if I ever make my fortune, and some one reproaches me with having filled the humble post of tutor, I may let it be understood that it was love that brought me into that position.'

Julien once more withdrew his hand from that of Madame de Rênal, then took her hand again and pressed it. As they returned to the drawing-room, towards midnight, Madame de Rênal murmured in his ear:

'Are you leaving us, are you going away?'

Julien answered with a sigh:

'I must indeed go away, for I love you passionately; it is a sin ... and what a sin for a young priest!'

Madame de Rênal leaned upon his arm, bending towards him until her cheek felt the warmth of his.

The night passed for these two people very differently. Madame de Rênal was exalted by transports of the most lofty moral pleasure. A coquettish girl who falls in love early grows accustomed to the distress of love; when she comes to the age of true passion, the charm of novelty is lacking. As Madame de Rênal had never read any novels, all the refinements of her happiness were new to her. No melancholy truth came to freeze her heart, not even the spectre of the future. She saw herself as happy in ten years' time as she was at that moment. Even the thought of virtue and of the fidelity she had vowed to M. de Rênal, which had distressed her some days before, presented itself in vain, she dismissed it like an importunate stranger. 'Never will I allow Julien to take any liberty,' Madame de Rênal told herself, 'we shall live in future as we have been living for the last month. He shall be a friend.'

CHAPTER FOURTEEN
THE ENGLISH SCISSORS

A girl of sixteen had a rosy complexion, and put on rouge.

POLIDORI.

As for Julien, Fouqué's offer had indeed destroyed all his happiness; he could not decide upon any course.

'Alas! Perhaps I am wanting in character, I should have made Napoleon a bad soldier. Anyhow,' he went on, 'my little intrigue with the lady of the house is going to distract me for the moment.'

Fortunately for him, even in this minor incident, his inward feelings bore no relation to his cavalier language. He was afraid of Madame de Rênal because of her pretty gown. This gown was in his eyes the advance guard of Paris. His pride was determined to leave nothing to chance and to the inspiration of the moment. Drawing upon Fouqué's confessions and the little he had read about love in the Bible, he prepared a plan of campaign in great detail. Since, though he did not admit it to himself, he was extremely anxious, he committed this plan to writing.

The following morning, in the drawing-room, Madame de Rênal was alone with him for a moment.

'Have you no other name besides Julien?' she asked him.

Our hero did not know what answer to give to so flattering a question. No provision had been made in his plan for such an event. But for the stupid mistake of making a plan, Julien's quick mind would soon have come to his rescue,

97

his surprise would only have added to the keenness of his perceptions.

He was awkward and exaggerated his own awkwardness. Madame de Rênal soon forgave him that. She saw in it the effect of a charming candour. And the one thing lacking, to her mind, in this man, who was considered so brilliant, was an air of candour.

'I don't at all trust your little tutor,' Madame Derville said to her on several occasions. 'He seems to me to be always thinking and to act only from motives of policy. He's crafty.'

Julien remained deeply humiliated by the disaster of not having known what answer to make to Madame de Rênal.

'A man of my sort owes it to himself to make up for this check'; and, seizing the moment at which she passed from one room to another, he did what he considered his duty by giving Madame de Rênal a kiss.

Nothing could have been less appropriate, less agreeable either to himself or to her, nor could anything have been more imprudent. They barely escaped being caught. Madame de Rênal thought him mad. She was frightened and even more shocked. This stupidity reminded her of M. Valenod.

'What would happen to me,' she asked herself, 'if I were left alone with him?' All her virtue returned, for her love was in eclipse.

She arranged matters so that there should always be one of her children with her.

The day passed slowly for Julien, he spent the whole of it in clumsily carrying out his plan of seduction. He never once looked at Madame de Rênal without embodying a question in his look; he was not, however, such a fool as not to see that he was failing completely to be agreeable, let alone seductive.

Madame de Rênal could not get over her astonishment at finding him so awkward and at the same time so bold. 'It is the timidity of love in a man of parts!' she said to herself at length, with an inexpressible joy. 'Can it be possible that he has never been loved by my rival!'

After luncheon, Madame de Rênal returned to the drawing-room to entertain M. Charcot de Maugiron, the Sub-Prefect of Bray. She was working at a little tapestry frame on a tall stand. Madame Derville was by her side. It was in this position, and in the full light of day, that our hero thought fit to thrust forward his boot and press the pretty foot of Madame de Rênal, whose open-work stocking and smart Parisian shoe were evidently attracting the gaze of the gallant Sub-Prefect.

Madame de Rênal was extremely alarmed; she let fall her scissors, her ball of wool, her needles, and Julien's movement could thus pass for a clumsy attempt to prevent the fall of the scissors, which he had seen slipping down. Fortunately these little scissors of English steel broke, and Madame de Rênal could not sufficiently express her regret that Julien had not been nearer at hand.

'You saw them falling before I did, you might have caught them; your zeal has only succeeded in giving me a violent kick.'

All this play-acting took in the Sub-Prefect, but not Madame Derville. 'This pretty youth has very bad manners!' she thought; the worldly-wisdom of a provincial capital can never pardon mistakes of this sort. Madame de Rênal found an opportunity of saying to Julien:

'Be careful, I order you.'

Julien realized his own clumsiness, and was annoyed. For a long time he debated within himself whether he ought to take offence at the words: 'I order you.' He was foolish enough to think: 'She might say to me "I order you" if it was something to do with the children's education but in responding to my love, she assumes equality. One cannot love without *equality*'; and he lost himself in composing commonplaces on the subject of equality. He repeated angrily to himself the verse of Corneille which Madame Derville had taught him a few days earlier:

Love creates equalities, it does not seek them.

Julien, insisting upon playing the part of a Don Juan, he who had never had a mistress in his life, was deadly dull for the rest of the day. He had only one sensible idea; bored with himself and with Madame de Rênal, he saw with alarm the evening approach when he would be seated in the garden, by her side and in the dark. He told M. de Rênal that he was going to Verrières to see the curé; he set off after dinner, and did not return until late at night.

At Verrières, Julien found M. Chélan engaged in packing up; he had at last been deprived of his benefice; the vicar Maslon was to succeed him. Julien helped the good curé, and it occurred to him to write to Fouqué that the irresistible vocation which he felt for the sacred ministry had prevented him at first from accepting his friend's obliging offer, but that he had just witnessed such an example of injustice, that perhaps it would be more advantageous to his welfare were he not to take holy orders.

Julien applauded his own deftness in making use of the deprivation of the curé of Verrières to leave a door open for himself and so return to commerce, should the sad voice of prudence prevail, in his mind, over heroism.

CHAPTER FIFTEEN

COCK-CROW

Amour en latin faict amor;
Or donc provient d'amour la mort,
Et, par avant, soulcy qui mord,
Deuil, plours, pieges, forfaitz, remord....
Blason d'amour.

IF Julien had had a little of that discernment which he so
gratuitously supposed himself to possess, he might have
congratulated himself next day on the effect produced by
his visit to Verrières. His absence had made his clumsiness
be forgotten. All that day too, he was inclined to sulk;
towards nightfall a preposterous idea occurred to him, and
he imparted it to Madame de Rênal with a rare intrepidity.

No sooner had they sat down in the garden than, without
waiting for a sufficient cloak of darkness, Julien put his lips
to Madame de Rênal's ear, and, at the risk of compromising
her horribly, said to her:

'To-night, Ma'am, at two o'clock, I am coming to your
room, I have something to say to you.'

Julien was trembling lest his request should be granted;
the part of a seducer was so horrible a burden that if he had
been free to follow his own inclination, he would have retired
to his room for some days, and not set eyes on the ladies
again. He realized that, by his clever tactics of yesterday, he
had squandered all the promise of the day before, and really
he did not know where to turn.

Madame de Rênal replied with a genuine and by no

101

means exaggerated indignation to the impertinent announcement which Julien had had the audacity to make. He thought
he could read scorn in her brief answer. It was certain that
in this answer, uttered in the lowest of tones, the word 'Fie!'
had figured. Making the excuse that he had something to say
to the children, Julien went up to their room, and on his
return placed himself by the side of Madame Derville and
at a distance from Madame de Rênal. He thus removed from
himself all possibility of taking her hand. The conversation
took a serious turn, and Julien held his own admirably, apart
from a few intervals of silence during which he cudgelled his
brains. 'Why cannot I think of some fine plan,' he asked
himself, 'to force Madame de Rênal to shew me those unmistakable marks of affection which made me imagine, three
days ago, that she was mine!'

Julien was extremely disconcerted by the almost desperate
situation into which he had been led. And yet nothing could
have embarrassed him so much as success.

When the party broke up at midnight, his pessimism led
him to believe that Madame Derville looked upon him with
contempt, and that probably he stood no higher in the favour
of Madame de Rênal.

Being in an extremely bad temper and deeply humiliated,
Julien could not sleep. He was a thousand leagues from any
thought of abandoning all pretence, all his plans, and of living from day to day with Madame de Rênal, contenting himself like a child with the happiness that each day would bring.

He wearied his brain in devising clever stratagems; a
moment later, he felt them to be absurd; he was in short
extremely wretched, when two struck from the clock tower.

This sound aroused him as the crow of the cock aroused
Saint Peter. He saw himself arrived at the moment of the
most distressing event. He had not thought once again of his
impertinent suggestion, from the moment in which he had
made it. It had met with so hostile a reception!

'I told her that I should come to her at two o'clock,' he
said to himself as he rose; 'I may be inexperienced and
coarse, as is natural in the son of a peasant, Madame Derville

has let me see that plainly enough; but at any rate I will not be weak.'

Julien had every right to praise his own courage, never had he set himself a more painful task. As he opened the door of his room, he trembled so much that his knees gave way beneath him, and he was obliged to lean against the wall.

He was in his stocking feet. He went to listen at M. de Rênal's door, through which he could hear him snoring. This dismayed him. He had no longer any excuse for not going to her. But, great God! What should he do when he got there? He had no plan, and even if he had had one, he was in such distress of mind that he would not have been in a fit state to put it into practice.

Finally, with an anguish a thousand times keener than if he had been going to the scaffold, he entered the little corridor that led to Madame de Rênal's room. He opened the door with a trembling hand, making a fearful noise as he did so.

There was a light in the room, a nightlight was burning in the fireplace; he had not expected this fresh calamity. Seeing him enter, Madame de Rênal sprang quickly out of bed. 'Wretch!' she cried. There was some confusion. Julien forgot his futile plans and returned to his own natural character. Not to please so charming a woman seemed to him the greatest disaster possible. His only answer to her reproaches was to fling himself at her feet, clasping her round the knees. As she spoke to him with extreme harshness, he burst into tears.

Some hours later, when Julien emerged from Madame de Rênal's room, one might have said, in the language of romance, that there was nothing more left for him to wish. And indeed, he was indebted to the love he had inspired and to the uncontrollable impression made on him by her seductive charms for a victory to which not all his misplaced ingenuity would ever have led him.

But, in the most delicious moments, the victim of a freakish pride, he still attempted to play the part of a man in the habit of captivating women: he made incredible efforts to

destroy his natural amiability. Instead of his paying attention
to the transports which he excited, and to the remorse that
increased their vivacity, the idea of *duty* was continually
before his eyes. He feared a terrible remorse, and undying
ridicule, should he depart from the ideal plan that he had
set himself to follow. In a word, what made Julien a superior
being was precisely what prevented him from enjoying the
happiness that sprang up at his feet. He was like a girl of
sixteen who has a charming complexion and, before going
to a ball, is foolish enough to put on rouge.

In mortal terror at the apparition of Julien, Madame de
Rênal was soon a prey to the cruellest alarms. Julien's tears
and despair distressed her greatly.

Indeed, when she had no longer anything to refuse him,
she thrust him from her, with genuine indignation, and then
flung herself into his arms. No purpose was apparent in all
this behaviour. She thought herself damned without remis-
sion, and sought to shut out the vision of hell by showering
the most passionate caresses on Julien. In a word, nothing
would have been wanting to complete our hero's happiness,
not even a burning sensibility in the woman he had just van-
quished, had he been capable of enjoying it. Julien's departure brought no cessation of the transports which were
shaking her in spite of herself, nor of her struggle with the
remorse that was tearing her.

'Heavens! Is to be happy, to be loved, no more than that?'
Such was Julien's first thought on his return to his own room.
He was in that state of astonishment and uneasy misgivings
into which a heart falls when it has just obtained what it has
long desired. It has grown used to desiring, finds nothing left
to desire, and has not yet acquired any memories. Like a
soldier returning from a parade, Julien was busily engaged
in reviewing all the details of his conduct. 'Have I failed in
one of the duties I owe to myself? Have I really played my
part?'

And what a part! The part of a man accustomed to shine
before women.

CHAPTER SIXTEEN

THE DAY AFTER

He turn'd his lips to hers, and with his hand
Call'd back the tangles of her wandering hair.
Don Juan I. 170.

FORTUNATELY for Julien's pride, Madame de Rênal had been too greatly agitated and surprised to notice the fatuity of the man who in a moment had become everything in the world to her.

As she was imploring him to withdraw, seeing the day begin to break:

'Oh, Heavens!' she said, 'if my husband has heard any sound, I am lost.'

Julien, who had leisure for composing phrases, remembered one to the point:

'Should you regret your life?'

'Ah! Very much at this moment, but I should not regret having known you.'

Julien found that his dignity required him to return to his room in broad daylight and with deliberate want of precaution.

The continuous attention with which he watched his own slightest actions, in the insane idea of being taken for a man of experience, had this one advantage; when he saw Madame de Rênal again, at luncheon, his behaviour was a miracle of prudence.

As for her, she could not look at him without blushing to the whites of her eyes, and could not live for an instant without looking at him; she noticed her own confusion, and her efforts to conceal it increased. Julien raised his eyes to hers once only. At first, Madame de Rênal admired his prudence. Presently, seeing that this solitary glance was not repeated, she took alarm: 'Can it be that he does not love me any more,' she asked herself; 'alas, I am far too old for him; I am ten years his senior.'

On the way from the dining-room to the garden, she pressed Julien's hand. In the surprise that he felt at so extraordinary a token of affection, he gazed at her with passion; for she had struck him as looking very pretty at luncheon, and, without raising his eyes, he had spent his time making a detailed catalogue of her charms. This look consoled Madame de Rênal; it did not remove all her uneasiness; but her uneasiness removed, almost entirely, the remorse she felt when she thought of her husband.

At luncheon, the said husband had noticed nothing; not so with Madame Derville; she feared Madame de Rênal to be on the point of succumbing. All through the day, her bold, incisive friendship did not spare the other those hinted suggestions intended to portray in hideous colours the danger that she was running.

Madame de Rênal was burning to be left alone with Julien; she wanted to ask him whether he still loved her. Despite the unalterable gentleness of her nature, she was more than once on the point of letting her friend know what a nuisance she was making of herself.

That evening, in the garden, Madame Derville arranged things so skilfully that she found herself placed between Madame de Rênal and Julien. Madame de Rênal, who had formed a delicious image of the pleasure of pressing Julien's hand and carrying it to her lips, could not so much as address a word to him.

This catastrophe increased her agitation. Remorse for one thing was gnawing her. She had so scolded Julien for the imprudence he had shewn in coming to her room the night before, that she trembled lest he might not come that night. She left the garden early, and went up to wait in her room.

But, beside herself with impatience, she rose and went to glue her ear to Julien's door. Despite the uncertainty and passion that were devouring her, she did not dare enter. This action seemed to her the last word in lowness, for it serves as text to a country maxim.

The servants were not all in bed. Prudence obliged her finally to return to her own room. Two hours of waiting were two centuries of torment.

But Julien was too loyal to what he called his duty, to fail in the execution, detail by detail, of what he had laid down for himself.

As one o'clock struck, he slipped quietly from his room, made sure that the master of the house was sound asleep, and appeared before Madame de Rênal. On this occasion he found greater happiness with his mistress, for he was less continually thinking of the part he had to play. He had eyes to see and ears to hear. What Madame de Rênal said to him about his age contributed to give him some degree of self-assurance.

'Alas! I am ten years older than you! How can you love me?' she repeated without any object, simply because the idea oppressed her.

Julien could not conceive such a thing, but he saw that her distress was genuine, and almost entirely forgot his fear of being ridiculous.

The foolish idea of his being regarded as a servile lover, at his mistress's beck and call, on account of his humble birth, vanished likewise. In proportion as Julien's transports reassured his coy mistress, she recovered some degree of happiness and the faculty of criticising her lover. Fortunately, he shewed almost nothing, on this occasion, of that borrowed air which had made their meeting the night before a victory, but not a pleasure. Had she noticed his intentness upon playing a part, the painful discovery would have robbed her of all happiness for ever. She could have seen in it nothing else than a painful consequence of their disparity of age.

Albeit Madame de Rênal had never thought about theories of love, difference of age is, next to difference of fortune, one of the great commonplaces of provincial humour, whenever there is any talk of love.

In a few days, Julien, all the ardour of his youth restored, was madly in love.

'One must admit,' he said to himself, 'that her kindness of heart is angelic, and that no one could be prettier.'

He had almost entirely lost the idea of a part to be played. In a moment of unrestrained impulse, he even confessed to her all his anxieties. This confidence raised to its climax the passion that he inspired. 'So I have not had any fortunate rival,' Madame de Rênal said to herself with ecstasy. She ventured to question him as to the portrait in which he took such an interest; Julien swore to her that it was that of a man.

When Madame de Rênal was calm enough to reflect, she could not get over her astonishment that such happiness could exist and that she had never had the slightest idea of it.

'Ah!' she said to herself, 'if I had known Julien ten years ago, when I might still be considered pretty!'

Julien's thoughts were worlds apart from these. His love was still founded in ambition: it was the joy of possessing— he, a poor creature so unfortunate and so despised—so noble and beautiful a woman. His acts of adoration, his transports at the sight of his mistress's charms, ended by reassuring her somewhat as to the difference in age. Had she possessed a little of that worldly wisdom a woman of thirty has long enjoyed in more civilized lands, she would have shuddered for the continuance of a love which seemed to exist only upon surprise and the titillation of self-esteem.

In the moments when he forgot his ambition, Julien went into transports over everything that Madame de Rênal possessed, including her hats and gowns. He could not tire of the pleasure of inhaling their perfume. He opened her wardrobe and stood for hours on end marvelling at the beauty and neat arrangement of everything inside. His mistress, leaning upon his shoulder, gazed at him; he himself gazed at those ornaments and fripperies which on a wedding day are displayed among the presents.

'I might have married a man like this!' Madame de Rênal

sometimes thought; 'What a fiery spirit! What a rapturous life with him!'

As for Julien, never had he found himself so close to those terrible weapons of feminine artillery. 'It is impossible,' he told himself, 'that in Paris there can be anything finer!' After which he could find no objection to his happiness. Often his mistress's sincere admiration, and her transports of passion made him forget the fatuous theory that had kept him so restrained and almost ridiculous in the first moments of their intimacy. There were moments when, despite his hypocritical habits, he found an intense pleasure in confessing to this great lady who admired him his ignorance of any number of little usages. His mistress's rank seemed to raise him above himself. Madame de Rênal, for her part, found the most exquisite moral satisfaction in thus instructing in a heap of little things this young man endowed with genius whom everyone regarded as bound one day to go so far. Even the Sub-Prefect and M. Valenod could not help admiring him: she thought the better of them accordingly. As for Madame Derville, these were by no means her sentiments. In despair at what she thought she could discern, and seeing that her wise counsel was becoming hateful to a woman who had positively lost her head, she left Vergy without offering an explanation for which she was not asked. Madame de Rênal shed a few tears at her departure, and soon it seemed to her that her happiness was doubled. By the withdrawal of her guest she found herself left alone with her lover almost all day long.

Julien gave himself all the more readily to the pleasant society of his mistress inasmuch as, whenever he was left too long by himself, Fouqué's fatal offer recurred to his mind to worry him. In the first days of this new life, there were moments when he, who had never loved, who had never been loved by anyone, found so exquisite a pleasure in being sincere, that he was on the point of confessing to Madame de Rênal the ambition which until then had been the very essence of his existence. He would have liked to be able to consult her as to the strange temptation which he felt in Fouqué's offer, but a trifling occurrence put a stop to all frankness.

CHAPTER SEVENTEEN
THE PRINCIPAL DEPUTY

O! how this spring of love resembleth
The uncertain glory of an April day,
Which now shews all the beauty of the sun,
And by and by a cloud takes all away!
The Two Gentlemen of Verona.

ONE evening as the sun set, sitting by his mistress, at the end of the orchard, safe from disturbance, he was deep in thought. 'Will such delicious moments,' he was wondering, 'last for ever?' His thoughts were absorbed in the difficulty and necessity of adopting a profession, he was deploring this great and distressing problem which puts an end to boyhood and spoils the opening years of manhood when one has no money.

'Ah!' he cried, 'Napoleon was indeed the man sent by God to help the youth of France! Who is to take his place? What will the poor wretches do without him, even those who are richer than I, who have just the few crowns needed to procure them a good education, and then not enough money to purchase a man at twenty and launch themselves in a career! Whatever happens,' he added with deep sigh, 'that fatal memory will for ever prevent us from being happy!'

He saw Madame de Rênal frown suddenly; she assumed a cold, disdainful air; this line of thought seemed to her worthy of a servant. Brought up in the idea that she was extremely rich, it seemed to her a thing to be taken for granted that Julien was also. She loved him a thousand times

110

more than life itself, she would have loved him even had be been ungrateful and faithless, and money to her meant nothing.

Julien was far from guessing what was in her mind. This frown brought him back to earth. He had presence of mind enough to arrange his sentence and to make it plain to the noble lady, seated so close beside him on the bank of verdure, that the words he had just uttered were some that he had heard during his expedition to his friend the timber merchant. This was the reasoning of the impious.

'Very well! Don't mix any more with such people,' said Madame de Rênal, still preserving a trace of that glacial air which had suddenly taken the place of an expression of the tenderest and most intimate affection.

This frown, or rather his remorse for his imprudence, was the first check administered to the illusion that was bearing Julien away. He said to himself: 'She is good and kind, her feeling for me is strong, but she has been brought up in the enemy's camp. They are bound to be specially afraid of that class of men of spirit who, after a good education, have not enough money to enter upon a career. What would become of these nobles, if it were granted us to fight them with equal weapons? Myself, for instance, as Mayor of Verrières, well intentioned, honest as M. de Rênal is at heart, how I should deal with the vicar, M. Valenod and all their rascalities! How justice should triumph in Verrières. It is not their talents that would prove an obstacle. They are endlessly feeling their way.'

Julien's happiness was, that day, on the point of becoming permanent. What our hero lacked was the courage to be sincere. He needed the courage to give battle, but *on the spot*; Madame de Rênal had been surprised by his speech, because the men whom she was in the habit of meeting were always saying that the return of Robespierre was made possible especially by these young men of the lower orders, who had been too well educated. Madame de Rênal's cold manner persisted for some time, and seemed to Julien to be marked. This was because the fear of having said to him indirectly something unpleasant followed her repugnance at his unfortunate speech. This distress was clearly shewn on her pure countenance; so simple when she was happy and away from bores.

Julien no longer dared give himself up freely to his dreams. More calm and less amorous, he decided that it was imprudent in him to go to Madame de Rênal in her room. It would be better if she came to him; if a servant saw her moving about the house, there would be a score of possible reasons to account for her action.

But this arrangement also had its drawbacks. Julien had received from Fouqué certain books for which he, as a student of divinity, could never have asked a bookseller. He ventured to open them only at night. Often he would have been just as well pleased not to be interrupted by an assignation, the tension of waiting for which, even before the little scene in the orchard, would have left him incapable of reading.

He was indebted to Madame de Rênal for an entirely new understanding of the books he read. He had ventured to ply her with questions as to all sorts of little things ignorance of which seriously handicaps the intelligence of a young man born outside the ranks of society, whatever natural genius one may choose to attribute to him.

This education in love, given by an extremely ignorant woman, was a blessing. Julien was at once enabled to see society as it is to-day. His mind was not perplexed by accounts of what it was in the past, two thousand years ago, or sixty years ago merely, in the days of Voltaire and Louis XV. To his unspeakable joy a cloud passed from before his eyes; he understood at last the things that were happening at Verrières.

In the foreground appeared the highly complicated intrigues woven, for the last two years, round the Prefect at Besançon. They were supported by letters that came from Paris, and bore all the most illustrious signatures. It was a question of making M. de Moirod, the most bigoted man in the place, the Principal instead of the Second Deputy to the Mayor of Verrières.

His rival was an extremely rich manufacturer, whom it was absolutely essential to confine to the post of Second Deputy.

Julien at last understood the hints that he had overheard, when the cream of local society came to dine with M. de Rênal. This privileged class was greatly taken up with this selection of a Principal Deputy, of which the rest of the town and especially the Liberals did not even suspect the possibility. What gave it its importance was that, as everybody knew, the eastern side of the main street of Verrières must be carried back more than nine feet, for this street was now a royal highway.

Well, if M. de Moirod, who owned three houses that would have to be carried back, succeeded in becoming Principal Deputy, and so Mayor in the event of M. de Rênal's being returned to Parliament, he would shut his eyes, and it would be possible to make little, imperceptible repairs to the houses that encroached on the public thoroughfare, as a result of which they would be good for a hundred years. Despite the great piety and admitted probity of M. de Moirod, it was certain that he *could be managed*, for he had a large family. Among the houses that would have to be carried back, nine belonged to the very best people in Verrières.

In Julien's eyes, this intrigue was far more important than the history of the battle of Fontenoy, a name which he saw for the first time in one of the books that Fouqué had sent him. Many things had astonished Julien during the five years since he had begun to spend his evenings with the curé. But discretion and a humble spirit being the chief qualities required in a divinity student, it had always been impossible for him to ask any questions.

One day, Madame de Rênal had given an order to her husband's valet, Julien's enemy.

'But, Ma'am, to-day is the last Friday of the month,' the man answered her with a curious expression.

'Go,' said Madame de Rênal.

'Well,' said Julien, 'he is going to that hay store, which used to be a church, and was recently restored to the faith; but why? That is one of the mysteries which I have never been able to penetrate.'

'It is a most beneficial, but a very strange institution,' replied Madame de Rênal. 'Women are not admitted; all that I know of it is that they all address one another as *tu*. For instance, this servant will find M. Valenod there, and that conceited fool will not be in the least annoyed at hearing himself called *tu* by Saint-Jean, and will answer him in the same tone. If you really want to know what they do there, I can ask M. de Maugiron and M. Valenod for details. We pay twenty francs for each servant so that if there should be another '93 they may not cut our throats.'

The time flew. The memory of his mistress's charms distracted Julien from his black ambition. The necessity to refrain from speaking to her of serious, reasonable matters, since they were on opposite sides, added, without his suspecting it, to the happiness that he owed to her and to the power which she was acquiring over him.

At those moments when the presence of quick-eared children confined them to the language of cold reason, it was with a perfect docility that Julien, gazing at her with eyes that burned with love, listened to her explanations of the world as it really was. Often, in the middle of an account of some clever piece of roguery, in connexion with the laying out of a road, or of some astounding contract, Madame de Rênal's attention would suddenly go completely astray; Julien was obliged to scold her, she allowed herself to caress him in the same way as she caressed her children. This was because there were days on which she imagined that she loved him like a child of her own. Had she not to reply incessantly to his artless questions about a thousand simple matters of which a child of good family is not ignorant at fifteen? A moment later, she was admiring him as her master. His intelligence positively frightened her; she thought she could perceive more clearly every day the future great man in this young cleric. She saw him as Pope, she saw him as First Minister, like Richelieu.

'Shall I live long enough to see you in your glory?' she said to Julien; 'there is a place waiting for a great man; the Monarchy, the Church need one; these gentlemen say so every day. If some Richelieu does not stem the torrent of private judgment, all is lost.'

CHAPTER EIGHTEEN
A KING AT VERRIÈRES

N'êtes-vous bons qu'à jeter là comme un cadavre de
peuple, sans âme, et dont les veines n'ont plus de sang?
*(From the Bishop's address, delivered in
the Chapel of Saint Clement.)*

O N the third of September, at ten o'clock in the evening, a mounted constable aroused the whole of Verrières by galloping up the main street; he brought
the news that His Majesty the King of —— was coming
the following Sunday, and it was now Tuesday. The Prefect
authorized, that is to say ordered, the formation of a Guard
of Honour; he must be received with all the pomp possible.
A courier was sent to Vergy. M. de Rênal arrived during the
night and found the whole town in a ferment. Everybody
was claiming a right to something; those who had no other
duty were engaging balconies to see the King enter the town.

Who was to command the Guard of Honour? M. de Rênal
saw at once how important it was, in the interest of the
houses that would have to be carried back, that M. de
Moirod should fill this post. It might be held to constitute a
claim to the place of Principal Deputy. There was nothing
to be said against M. de Moirod's devotion; it went beyond
all comparison, but he had never ridden a horse in his life.
He was a man of six and thirty, timid in every way, and
equally afraid of falls and of being laughed at.

The Mayor sent for him at five o'clock in the morning.

'You see, Sir, that I am asking your advice, as though you

115

already occupied the post in which all right-minded people would gladly see you. In this unfortunate town the manufacturers prosper, the Liberal Party are becoming millionaires, they aspire to power, they will forge themselves weapons out of everything. We must consider the King's interests, those of the Monarchy, and above all those of our holy religion. To whom do you think, Sir, that we ought to entrust the command of the Guard of Honour?'

In spite of the horrible fear that a horse inspired in him, M. de Moirod ended by accepting this honour like a martyr. 'I shall manage to adopt the right manner,' he told the Mayor. There was barely time to overhaul the uniforms which had been used seven years before on the passage of a Prince of the Blood.

At seven, Madame de Rênal arrived from Vergy with Julien and the children. She found her drawing-room full of Liberal ladies who were preaching the union of parties, and had come to implore her to make her husband find room in the Guard of Honour for theirs. One of them asserted that if her husband were not chosen he would go bankrupt from grief. Madame de Rênal sent them all packing at once. She seemed greatly occupied.

Julien was surprised and even more annoyed by her making a mystery to him of what was disturbing her. 'I thought as much,' he told himself bitterly, 'her love is eclipsed by the joy of receiving a King in her house. All this excitement dazzles her. She will begin to love me again when her brain is no longer troubled by ideas of caste.'

The surprising thing was that he loved her all the more for this.

The upholsterers began to invade the whole house, he long watched in vain for an opportunity of saying a word to her. At length he found her coming out of his own room, carrying one of his coats. They were alone. He tried to speak to her. She made off, declining to listen to him. 'What a fool I am to be in love with a woman like that, ambition makes her just as stupid as her husband.'

She was even more so: one of her great wishes, which she

had never confessed to Julien, for fear of shocking him, was to see him discard, if only for a day, his gloomy black coat. With an ingenuity truly admirable in so natural a woman, she secured, first from M. de Moirod, and then from the Sub-Prefect M. de Maugiron, that Julien should be appointed to the Guard of Honour in preference to five or six young men, sons of manufacturers in easy circumstances, at least two of whom were of an exemplary piety. M. Valenod, who was reckoning on lending his carriage to the prettiest women of the town, in order to have his fine Norman horses admired, agreed to let Julien, the person he hated most, have one of them. But each of the members of the Guard of Honour possessed or had borrowed one of those sky-blue coats with a pair of colonel's epaulettes in silver, which had shone in public seven years before. Madame de Rênal wanted a new coat, and she had but four days in which to send to Besançon, and to procure from there the uniform, the weapons, the hat, and all the other requisites for a Guard of Honour. What is rather amusing is that she thought it imprudent to have Julien's coat made at Verrières. She wished to take him by surprise, him and the town.

The work of organizing the Guard of Honour and popular feeling finished, the Mayor had next to deal with a great religious ceremony; the King of —— refused to pass through Verrières without paying a visit to the famous relic of Saint Clement which is preserved at Bray-le-Haut, a short league from the town. The clergy must be present in full force, and this was the most difficult thing to arrange; M. Maslon, the new curé, was determined, at any price, to keep M. Chélan out. In vain did M. de Rênal point out to him the imprudence of this action. The Marquis de La Mole, whose ancestors for so long were Governors of the Province, had been chosen to accompany the King of ——. He had known the abbé Chélan for thirty years. He would be certain to inquire for him on arriving at Verrières, and, if he found that he was in disgrace, was quite capable of going in search of him, to the little house to which he had retired, accompanied by such of the procession as were under his orders. What a rebuff that would be!

'I am dishonoured here and at Besançon,' replied the abbé Maslon, 'if he appears among my clergy. A Jansenist, great heavens!'

'Whatever you may say, my dear abbé,' M. de Rênal assured him, 'I shall not expose the municipal government of Verrières to the risk of an insult from M. de La Mole. You don't know the man, he is sound enough at court; but here, in the country, he has a satirical, mocking spirit, and likes nothing so much as to embarrass people. He is capable, simply for his own amusement, of covering us with ridicule in the eyes of the Liberals.'

It was not until the night between Saturday and Sunday, after three days of discussion, that the abbé Maslon's pride gave way before the Mayor's fear, which had turned to courage. The next thing was to write a honeyed note to the abbé Chélan, inviting him to be present at the veneration of the relic at Bray-le-Haut, his great age and infirmities permitting. M. Chélan asked for and obtained a letter of invitation for Julien, who was to accompany him in the capacity of sub-deacon.

Early on Sunday morning, thousands of peasants, arriving from the neighbouring mountains, flooded the streets of Verrières. It was a day of brilliant sunshine. At length, about three o'clock, a tremor ran through the crowd; they had caught sight of a beacon blazing on a rock two leagues from Verrières. This signal announced that the King had just entered the territory of the Department. Immediately the sound of all the bells and the repeated discharge of an old Spanish cannon belonging to the town proclaimed its joy at this great event. Half the population climbed up on the roofs. All the women were on the balconies. The Guard of Honour began to move. The brilliant uniforms were greatly admired, each of the onlookers recognized a relative or friend. There was general laughter at the alarm of M. de Moirod, whose cautious hand lay ready at any moment to clutch hold of his saddle. But one thing made them forget all the others: the left hand man in the ninth section was a handsome lad, very slender, who at first was not identified. Presently a cry of indignation from some, the astonished silence of others announced a general sensation. The onlookers recognized in this young man, riding one of M. Valenod's Norman horses, young Sorel, the carpenter's son. There was one unanimous outcry against the Mayor, especially among the Liberals. What, because this young labourer dressed up as a priest was tutor to his brats, he had the audacity to appoint him to the Guard of Honour, to the exclusion of M. This and M. That, wealthy manufacturers! 'Those gentlemen,' said a banker's wife, 'ought really to offer an affront to the little upstart, born in the gutter.'

'He has a wicked temper and he is wearing a sabre,' replied her companion; 'he would be quite treacherous enough to slash them across the face.'

The comments made by the aristocratic element were more dangerous. The ladies asked themselves whether the Mayor alone was responsible for this grave breach of etiquette. On the whole justice was done to his contempt for humble birth.

While he was giving rise to so much comment, Julien was the happiest man alive. Bold by nature, he had a better seat on a horse than most of the young men of this mountain town. He saw in the eyes of the women that they were talking about him.

His epaulettes were more brilliant because they were new. At every moment his horse threatened to rear; he was in the seventh heaven of joy.

His happiness knew no bounds when, as they passed near the old rampart, the sound of the small cannon made his horse swerve out of the ranks. By the greatest accident, he did not fall off; from that moment he felt himself a hero. He was Napoleon's orderly officer and was charging a battery.

There was one person happier than he. First of all she had watched him pass from one of the windows of the town hall; then, getting into her carriage, and rapidly making a wide detour, she was in time to tremble when his horse carried him out of the ranks. Finally, her carriage passing out at a gallop through another of the gates of the town, she made her way back to the road along which the King was to pass, and was able to follow the Guard of Honour at a distance of twenty paces, in a noble cloud of dust. Ten thousand peasants shouted: 'Long live the King' when the Mayor had the honour of addressing His Majesty. An hour later, when, having listened to all the speeches, the King was about to enter the town, the small cannon began to fire again with frenzied haste. But an accident occurred, not to the gunners who had learned their trade at Leipsic and Montmirail, but to the future Principal Deputy, M. de Moirod. His horse dropped him gently into the one puddle to be found along the whole road, which created a scandal, because he had to be pulled out of the way to enable the King's carriage to pass.

His Majesty alighted at the fine new church, which was decked out for the occasion with all its crimson hangings. The King was to halt for dinner, immediately after which he would take the road again to go and venerate the famous relic of Saint Clement. No sooner was the King inside the church than Julien went off at a gallop to M. de Rênal's. There he discarded with a sigh his fine sky-blue coat, his sabre, his epaulettes, to resume the little threadbare black coat. He mounted his horse again, and in a few minutes was at Bray-le-Haut, which stands on the summit of an imposing hill. 'Enthusiasm is multiplying these peasants,' thought Julien. 'One cannot move at Verrières, and here there are more than ten thousand of them round this old abbey.' Half ruined by the vandalism of the Revolution, it had been magnificently restored since the Restoration, and there was already some talk of miracles. Julien joined the abbé Chélan, who scolded him severely, and gave him a cassock and surplice. He vested himself hurriedly in these and followed M. Chélan, who was going in search of the youthful Bishop of Agde. This was a nephew of M. de La Mole, recently appointed to the See, who had been selected to exhibit the relic to the King. But the Bishop was not to be found.

The clergy were growing impatient. They awaited their leader in the sombre, gothic cloister of the ancient abbey. Four and twenty parish priests had been collected to represent the original chapter of Bray-le-Haut which prior to 1789 had consisted of four and twenty canons. Having spent three quarters of an hour in deploring the youthfulness of the Bishop, the priests decided that it would be a good thing if their Dean were to go and inform His Lordship that the King was on his way, and that it was time they were in the choir. M. Chélan's great age had made him Dean; despite the anger he shewed with Julien, he made a sign to him to follow him. Julien carried his surplice admirably. By some secret process of the ecclesiastical toilet-table, he had made his fine curly hair lie quite flat; but, by an oversight which intensified the anger of M. Chélan, beneath the long folds of his cassock one could see the spurs of the Guard of Honour.

When they reached the Bishop's apartment, the tall lackeys smothered in gold lace barely condescended to inform the old curé that His Lordship could not be seen. They laughed at him when he tried to explain that in his capacity as Dean of the Noble Chapter of Bray-le-Haut, it was his privilege to be admitted at all times to the presence of the officiating Bishop.

Julien's proud spirit was offended by the insolence of the lackeys. He set off on a tour of the dormitories of the old abbey, trying every door that he came to. One quite small door yielded to his efforts and he found himself in a cell in the midst of His Lordship's body-servants, dressed in black with chains round their necks. Seeing his air of haste, these gentlemen supposed that the Bishop had sent for him and allowed him to pass. He went a little way and found himself in an immense gothic chamber, very dark and panelled throughout in black oak; with a single exception, its pointed windows had been walled up with bricks. There was nothing to conceal the coarse surface of this masonry, which formed a sorry contrast to the venerable splendour of the woodwork. Both sides of this room, famous among the antiquarians of Burgundy, which the Duke Charles the Bold built about the year 1470 in expiation of some offence, were lined with wooden stalls, richly carved. These displayed, inlaid in wood of different colours, all the mysteries of the Apocalypse.

This melancholy splendour, degraded by the intrusion of

the bare bricks and white plaster, impressed Julien. He stood there in silence. At the other end of the room, near the only window through which any light came, he saw a portable mirror framed in mahogany. A young man, robed in violet with a lace surplice, but bare-headed, was standing three paces away from the mirror. This article appeared out of place in such a room, and had doubtless been brought there from the town. Julien thought that the young man seemed irritated; with his right hand he was gravely giving benedictions in the direction of the mirror.

'What can this mean?' he wondered. 'Is it a preliminary ceremony that this young priest is performing? He is perhaps the Bishop's secretary ... he will be rude like the lackeys ... but what of that, let us try him.'

He went forward and passed slowly down the length of the room, keeping his eyes fixed on that solitary window and watching the young man who continued to give benedictions, with a slow motion but in endless profusion, and without pausing for a moment.

As he drew nearer he was better able to see the other's look of annoyance. The costliness of his lace-bordered surplice brought Julien to a standstill some distance away from the magnificent mirror.

'It is my duty to speak,' he reminded himself at length; but the beauty of the room had touched his feelings and he was chilled in anticipation by the harsh words that would be addressed to him.

The young man caught sight of him in the glass, turned round, and suddenly discarding his look of irritation said to him in the pleasantest tone:

'Well, Sir, is it ready yet?'

Julien remained speechless. As this young man turned towards him, Julien saw the pectoral cross on his breast: it was the Bishop of Agde. 'So young,' thought Julien; 'at the most, only six or eight years older than myself!'

And he felt ashamed of his spurs.

'Monseigneur,' he replied timidly. 'I am sent by the Dean of the Chapter, M. Chélan.'

'Ah! I have an excellent account of him,' said the bishop in a courteous tone which left Julien more fascinated than ever. 'But I beg your pardon, Sir, I took you for the person who is to bring me back my mitre. It was carelessly packed in Paris; the silver tissue has been dreadfully frayed at the top. It will create a shocking effect,' the young Bishop went on with a sorrowful air, 'and they are keeping me waiting too.'

'Monseigneur, I shall go and find the mitre, with Your Lordship's permission.'

Julien's fine eyes had their effect.

'Go, Sir,' the Bishop answered with exquisite courtesy; 'I must have it at once. I am sorry to keep the gentlemen of the Chapter waiting.'

When Julien was halfway down the room, he turned to look at the Bishop and saw that he was once more engaged in giving benedictions. 'What can that be?' Julien asked himself; 'no doubt, it is a religious preparation necessary to the ceremony that is to follow.' When he came to the cell in which the servants were waiting, he saw the mitre in their hands. These gentlemen, yielding in spite of themselves to Julien's imperious glance, surrendered it to him.

He felt proud to be carrying it: as he crossed the room, he walked slowly; he held it with respect. He found the Bishop seated before the glass; but, from time to time, his right hand, tired as it was, still gave the benediction. Julien helped him to put on the mitre. The Bishop shook his head.

'Ah! It will keep on,' he said to Julien with a satisfied air. 'Will you go a little way off?'

Whereupon the Bishop walked at a smart pace to the middle of the room, then returning towards the mirror with a slow step, he resumed his air of irritation and went on solemnly giving benedictions.

Julien was spellbound with astonishment; he was tempted to guess what this meant, but did not dare. The Bishop stopped, and looking at him with an air from which the solemnity rapidly vanished:

'What do you say to my mitre, Sir, does it look right?'

'Quite right, Monseigneur.'

'It is not too far back? That would look rather silly; but it does not do, either, to wear them pulled down over one's eyes like an officer's shako.'

'It seems to me to be quite right.'

'The King of —— is accustomed to venerable clergy who are doubtless very solemn. I should not like, especially in view of my age, to appear too frivolous.'

And the Bishop once more began to walk about the room scattering benedictions.

'It is quite clear,' said Julien, at last venturing to understand, 'he is practising the benediction.'

A few moments later:

'I am ready,' said the Bishop. 'Go, Sir, and inform the Dean and the gentlemen of the Chapter.'

Presently M. Chélan, followed by the two oldest of the curés, entered by an immense door, magnificently carved, which Julien had not noticed. But this time he remained in his place in the extreme rear, and could see the Bishop only over the shoulders of the ecclesiastics who crowded towards this door.

The Bishop crossed the room slowly; when he came to the threshold the curés formed in processional order. After a momentary confusion the procession began to move, intoning a psalm. The Bishop came last, between M. Chélan and another curé of great age. Julien found a place for himself quite close to His Lordship, as being attached to the abbé Chélan. They moved down the long corridors of the abbey of Bray-le-Haut; in spite of the brilliant sunshine, these were dark and damp. At length they arrived at the door of the cloister. Julien was speechless with admiration of so fine a ceremony. His heart was divided between the ambition aroused by the Bishop's youthfulness, and the sensibility and exquisite manners of this prelate. His courtesy was of a very different kind from M. de Rênal's, even on his good days. 'The more one rises towards the highest rank of society,' thought Julien, 'the more one finds these charming manners.'

They entered the church by a side door; suddenly an

124

appalling crash made its ancient vaults resound; Julien thought that the walls were collapsing. It was again the small cannon; drawn by eight horses at a gallop, it had just arrived; and immediately on its arrival, brought into action by the gunners of Leipsic, it was firing five rounds a minute, as though the Prussians had been in front of it.

But this stirring sound no longer had any effect upon Julien, he dreamed no more of Napoleon and martial glory. 'So young,' he was thinking, 'to be Bishop of Agde! But where is Agde? And how much is it worth? Two or three hundred thousand francs, perhaps.'

His Lordship's servants appeared, carrying a magnificent dais; M. Chélan took one of the poles, but actually it was Julien that bore it. The Bishop took his place beneath it. He had really succeeded in giving himself the air of an old man; our hero's admiration knew no bounds. 'What cannot one do if one is clever!' he thought.

The King made his entry. Julien was so fortunate as to see him at close range. The Bishop addressed him with unction, and did not forget to include a slight touch of confusion, extremely flattering to His Majesty. We shall not repeat the account of the ceremonies at Bray-le-Haut; for a fortnight they filled the columns of all the newspapers of the Department. Julien learned, from the Bishop's speech, that the King was descended from Charles the Bold.

Later on it was one of Julien's duties to check the accounts of what this ceremony had cost. M. de La Mole, who had secured a bishopric for his nephew, had chosen to pay him the compliment of bearing the whole of the expense himself. The ceremony at Bray-le-Haut alone cost three thousand eight hundred francs.

After the Bishop's address and the King's reply, His Majesty took his place beneath the dais; he then knelt down most devoutly upon a cushion close to the altar. The choir was enclosed with stalls, and these stalls were raised two steps above the pavement. It was on the second of these steps that Julien sat at the feet of M. Chélan, not unlike a train-bearer at the feet of his Cardinal, in the Sistine Chapel, in Rome.

There were a Te Deum, clouds of incense, endless volleys of musketry and artillery; the peasants were frantic with joy and piety. Such a day undoes the work of a hundred numbers of the Jacobin papers.

Julien was within six paces of the King, who was praying with genuine fervour. He noticed for the first time a small man of intelligent appearance, whose coat was almost bare of embroidery. But he wore a sky-blue riband over this extremely simple coat. He was nearer to the King than many other gentlemen, whose coats were so covered with gold lace that, to use Julien's expression, one could not see the cloth. He learned a minute later that this was M. de La Mole. He decided that he wore a haughty, indeed an insolent air.

'This Marquis would not be polite like my dear Bishop,' he thought. 'Ah! The career of a churchman makes one gentle and wise. But the King has come to venerate the relic, and I see no relic. Where can Saint Clement be?'

A little clerk, who was next to him, informed him that the venerable relic was in the upper part of the building, in a *chapelle ardente.*

'What is a *chapelle ardente*?' Julien asked himself.

But he would not ask for an explanation of the words. He followed the proceedings with even closer attention.

On the occasion of a visit from a sovereign prince, etiquette requires that the canons shall not accompany the Bishop. But as he started for the *chapelle ardente* His Lordship of Agde summoned the abbé Chélan; Julien ventured to follow him.

After climbing a long stair, they came to a very small door, the frame of which was sumptuously gilded. This work had a look of having just been completed.

Outside the door were gathered on their knees four and twenty girls, belonging to the most distinguished families of Verrières. Before opening the door, the Bishop sank on his knees in the midst of these girls, who were all pretty. While he was praying aloud, it seemed as though they could not sufficiently admire his fine lace, his charm, his young and pleasant face. This spectacle made our hero lose all that

126

remained of his reason. At that moment, he would have fought for the Inquisition, and in earnest. Suddenly the door flew open. The little chapel seemed to be ablaze with light. One saw upon the altar more than a thousand candles arranged in eight rows, separated from one another by clusters of flowers. The sweet odour of the purest incense rose in clouds from the gate of the sanctuary. The newly gilded chapel was quite small, but very lofty. Julien noticed that there were on the altar candles more than fifteen feet long. The girls could not restrain a cry of admiration. No one had been admitted to the tiny ante-chapel save the twenty-four girls, the two priests and Julien.

Presently the King arrived, followed only by M. de La Mole and his Great Chamberlain. The guards themselves remained outside, on their knees, presenting their arms.

His Majesty flung himself rather than knelt down on the faldstool. It was then only that Julien, pressed against the gilded door, caught sight, beneath a girl's bare arm, of the charming statue of Saint Clement. It was hidden beneath the altar, in the garb of a young Roman soldier. He had in his throat a large wound from which the blood seemed to be flowing. The artist had surpassed himself; the eyes, dying but full of grace, were half closed. A budding moustache adorned the charming mouth, which being slightly open had the effect of being still engaged in prayer. At the sight of this statue, the girl nearest to Julien wept hot tears; one of her tears fell upon Julien's hand.

After an interval of prayer in the most profound silence, disturbed only by the distant sound of the bells of all the villages within a radius of ten leagues, the Bishop of Agde asked the King's permission to speak. He concluded a brief but highly edifying discourse with these words, simple in themselves, but thereby all the better assured of their effect.

'Never forget, young Christian women, that you have seen one of the great Kings of the earth upon his knees before the servants of this all-powerful and terrible God. These servants, frail, persecuted, martyred upon earth, as you can see from the still bleeding wound of Saint Clement, are triumphant in heaven. All your lives, I think, young Christians, you will remember this day. You will detest impiety. Always you will remain faithful to this God who is so great, so terrible, but so good.'

At these words, the Bishop rose with authority.

'You promise me?' he said, extending his arm with an air of inspiration.

'We promise,' said the girls, bursting into tears.

'I receive your promise, in the name of our terrible God!' the Bishop concluded in a voice of thunder. And the ceremony was at an end.

The King himself was in tears. It was not until long afterwards that Julien was calm enough to inquire where were the bones of the Saint, sent from Rome to Philip the Bold, Duke of Burgundy. He was told that they were embodied in the charming wax figure.

His Majesty deigned to permit the girls who had accompanied him into the chapel to wear a red riband upon which were embroidered the words: 'HATRED OF IMPIETY, PERPETUAL ADORATION.'

M. de La Mole ordered ten thousand bottles of wine to be distributed among the peasants. That evening, at Verrières, the Liberals found an excuse for illuminating their houses a hundred times more brilliantly than the Royalists. Before leaving the town, the King paid a visit to M. de Moirod.

CHAPTER NINETEEN

TO THINK IS TO BE FULL OF SORROW

Le grotesque des évènements de tous les jours vous
cache le vrai malheur des passions.

BARNAVE.

WHILE he was replacing its ordinary furniture in the
room that M. de La Mole had occupied, Julien
found a piece of stout paper, folded twice across.
He read at the foot of the first page:

To H.E., M. le Marquis de La Mole, Peer of France,
Knight of the Royal Orders, etc., etc.

It was a petition in the rude handwriting of a cook.
'Monsieur le Marquis,

'All my life I have held religious principles. I was in Lyons,
exposed to the bombs, at the time of the siege, in '93, of
execrable memory. I am a communicant, I go every Sunday
to mass in my parish church. I have never failed in my Easter
duty, not even in '93, of execrable memory. My cook, for
before the revolution I kept servants, my cook observes Friday. I enjoy in Verrières a general and I venture to say merited respect. I walk beneath the dais in processions, beside
the curé and the mayor. I carry, on solemn occasions, a big
candle bought at my own cost. The certificates of all of which
are in Paris at the Ministry of Finance. I ask Monsieur le
Marquis for the Verrières lottery office, which cannot fail to
be vacant soon in one way or another, the present holder
being seriously ill, and besides voting the wrong way at the
elections; etc.   DE CHOLIN.'

On the margin of this petition was an endorsement signed *de Moirod*, which began with the words:

'I had the honour *yesterday* to mention the respectable person who makes this request,' and so forth.

'And so even that imbecile Cholin shews me the way that I must follow,' Julien said to himself.

A week after the visit of the King of —— to Verrières, the chief thing to emerge from the innumerable falsehoods, foolish interpretations, absurd discussions, etc., etc., to which the King, the Bishop of Agde, the Marquis de La Mole, the ten thousand bottles of wine, the unseated Moirod (who, in the hope of a Cross, did not set foot outside his own door for a whole month after his fall) were in turn subjected, was the utter indelicacy of having jockeyed into the Guard of Honour, Julien Sorel, the son of a carpenter. You ought to have heard, on this topic, the wealthy calico printers, who, morning, noon and night, used to talk themselves hoarse in preaching equality. That proud woman, Madame de Rênal, was the author of this abomination. Her reason? The flashing eyes and pink cheeks of that young parson Sorel were reason enough and to spare.

Shortly after their return to Vergy, Stanislas Xavier, the youngest of the children, took fever; at once Madame de Rênal was seized by the most fearful remorse. For the first time she blamed herself for falling in love in a coherent fashion. She seemed to understand, as though by a miracle, the appalling sin into which she had let herself be drawn. Although deeply religious by nature, until this moment she had never thought of the magnitude of her crime in the eyes of God.

Long ago, at the convent of the Sacred Heart, she had loved God with a passionate love; she feared Him in the same way in this predicament. The struggles that rent her heart asunder were all the more terrible in that there was nothing reasonable in her fear. Julien discovered that any recourse to argument irritated instead of calming her; she saw in it the language of hell. However, as Julien himself was greatly attached to little Stanislas, he was more welcome to speak to her of the child's illness: presently it assumed a grave character. Then her incessant remorse deprived Madame de Rênal even of the power to sleep; she never emerged from a grim silence: had she opened her mouth, it would have been to confess her crime to God and before men.

'I beg of you,' Julien said to her, as soon as they were alone, 'say nothing to anyone; let me be the sole confidant of your griefs. If you still love me, do not speak! your words cannot cure our Stanislas of his fever.'

But his attempts at consolation produced no effect; he did not know that Madame de Rênal had taken it into her head that, to appease the anger of a jealous God, she must either hate Julien or see her son die. It was because she felt that she could not hate her lover that she was so unhappy.

'Avoid my presence,' she said to Julien one day; 'in the name of God, leave this house: it is your presence here that is killing my son.

'God is punishing me,' she added in a whisper; 'He is just; I adore His equity; my crime is shocking, and I was living without remorse! It was the first sign of departure from God: I ought to be doubly punished.'

Julien was deeply touched. He was unable to see in this attitude either hypocrisy or exaggeration. 'She believes that she is killing her son by loving me, and yet the unhappy woman loves me more than her son. That, how can I doubt it, is the remorse that is killing her; there is true nobility of feeling. But how can I have inspired such love, I, so poor, so ill-bred, so ignorant, often so rude in my manners?'

One night the child's condition was critical. About two o'clock in the morning, M. de Rênal came to see him. The boy, burning with fever, was extremely flushed and did not recognize his father. Suddenly Madame de Rênal threw herself at her husband's feet: Julien saw that she was going to reveal everything and to ruin herself for ever.

Fortunately, this strange exhibition annoyed M. de Rênal.

'Good night! Good night!' he said and prepared to leave the room.

'No, listen to me,' cried his wife on her knees before him, seeking to hold him back. 'Learn the whole truth. It is I that am killing my son. I gave him his life, and I am taking it from him. Heaven is punishing me; in the eyes of God, I am guilty of murder. I must destroy and humble myself; it may be that such a sacrifice will appease the Lord.'

If M. de Rênal had been a man of imagination, he would have guessed everything.

'Romantic stuff,' he exclaimed, thrusting away his wife who sought to embrace his knees. 'Romantic stuff, all that! Julien, tell them to fetch the doctor at daybreak.'

And he went back to bed. Madame de Rênal sank on her knees, half unconscious, with a convulsive movement thrusting away Julien, who was coming to her assistance.

Julien stood watching her with amazement.

'So this is adultery!' he said to himself.... 'Can it be possible that those rascally priests are right after all? That they, who commit so many sins, have the privilege of knowing the true theory of sin? How very odd!'

For twenty minutes since M. de Rênal had left the room, Julien had seen the woman he loved, her head sunk on the child's little bed, motionless and almost unconscious. 'Here we have a woman of superior intelligence reduced to the last extremes of misery, because she has known me,' he said to himself.

The hours passed rapidly. 'What can I do for her? I must make up my mind. I have ceased to count here. What do I care for men, and their silly affectations? What can I do for her? ... Go from her? But I shall be leaving her alone, torn by the most frightful grief. That automaton of a husband does her more harm than good. He will say something offensive to her, in his natural coarseness; she may go mad, throw herself from the window.

'If I leave her, if I cease to watch over her, she will tell him everything. And then, for all one knows, in spite of the fortune he is to inherit through her, he will make a scandal. She may tell everything, great God, to that —— abbé Maslon, who makes the illness of a child of six an excuse for

132

never stirring out of this house, and not without purpose. In her grief and her fear of God, she forgets all that she knows of the man; she sees only the priest.'

'Leave me,' came suddenly from Madame de Rênal as she opened her eyes.

'I would give my life a thousand times to know how I can be of most use to you,' replied Julien; 'never have I so loved you, my dear angel, or rather, from this instant only, I begin to adore you as you deserve to be adored. What is to become of me apart from you, and with the knowledge that you are wretched by my fault! But I must not speak of my own sufferings. I shall go, yes, my love. But, if I leave you, if I cease to watch over you, to be constantly interposing myself between you and your husband, you will tell him everything, you will be ruined. Think of the ignominy with which he will drive you from the house; all Verrières, all Besançon will ring with the scandal. All the blame will be cast on you; you will never be able to lift up your head again.'

'That is all that I ask,' she cried, rising to her feet. 'I shall suffer, all the better.'

'But, by this appalling scandal, you will be harming him as well!'

'But I humble myself, I throw myself down in the mud; and in that way perhaps I save my son. This humiliation, in the sight of all, is perhaps a public penance. So far as my frailty can judge, is it not the greatest sacrifice that I can make to God? Perhaps he will deign to accept my humiliation and to spare me my son! Shew me a harder sacrifice and I will hasten to perform it.'

'Let me punish myself. I too am guilty. Would you have me retire to La Trappe? The austerity of the life there may appease your God ... Oh, heaven! Why can I not take upon myself Stanislas's illness?'

'Ah! You love him,' said Madame de Rênal, rising and flinging herself into his arms.

Immediately she thrust him from her with horror.

'I believe you! I believe you!' she went on, having fallen once more on her knees; 'O my only friend, why are not you

133

Stanislas's father? Then it would not be a horrible sin to love you more than your son.'

'Will you permit me to stay, and henceforward only to love you as a brother? It is the only reasonable expiation; it may appease the wrath of the Most High.'

'And I,' she exclaimed, rising, and taking Julien's head in her hands, and holding it at arm's length before her eyes, 'and I, shall I love you like a brother? Is it in my power to love you like a brother?'

Julien burst into tears.

'I will obey you,' he said as he fell at her feet. 'I will obey you, whatever you may bid me do; it is the one thing left for me. My brain is smitten with blindness; I can see no course to take. If I leave you, you tell your husband all; you ruin yourself, and him at the same time. After such a disgrace he will never be elected Deputy. If I stay, you regard me as the cause of your son's death, and you yourself die of grief. Would you like to test the effect of my going? If you like, I will punish myself for our sin by leaving you for a week. I shall pass the time in retreat wherever you choose. At the abbey of Bray-le-Haut, for instance; but swear to me that during my absence you will reveal nothing to your husband. Remember that I can never return if you speak.'

She promised; he departed, but was recalled after two days.

'It is impossible for me to keep my oath without you. I must speak to my husband, if you are not constantly there to order me with your eyes to be silent. Each hour of this abominable life seems to me to last a day.'

In the end, heaven took pity on this unhappy mother. Gradually Stanislas passed out of danger. But the ice was broken, her reason had learned the magnitude of her sin, she could no more recover her equilibrium. Remorse still remained, and took the form that it was bound to take in so sincere a heart. Her life was heaven and hell; hell when she did not see Julien, heaven when she was at his feet.

'I am no longer under any illusion,' she told him, even at the moments when she ventured to give absolute rein to her love: 'I am damned, irredeemably damned. You are young, you have yielded to my seduction, heaven may pardon you; but as for me, I am damned. I know it by an infallible sign. I am afraid: who would not be afraid at the sight of hell? But at heart, I am not in the least repentant. I would commit my sin again, were it to be committed. Let heaven only refrain from punishing me in this world and in my children, and I shall have more than I deserve. But you, at least, my Julien,' she cried at other moments, 'are you happy? Do you feel that I love you enough?'

Julien's distrust and suffering pride, which needed above all a love that made sacrifices, could not stand out against the sight of so great, so indubitable a sacrifice, and one that was made afresh every moment. He adored Madame de Rênal. 'She may well be noble, and I the son of a working man; she loves me ... I am not to her a footman employed in the part of lover.' Once rid of this fear, Julien fell into all the follies of love, into its mortal uncertainties.

'At least,' she cried when she saw that he doubted her love, 'let me make you happy during the few days we still have to spend together! Let us make haste; to-morrow perhaps I shall be no longer yours. If heaven strikes me through my children, in vain shall I seek to live only for love of you, not to see that it is my crime that is killing them. I shall not be able to survive that blow. Even if I would, I could not; I should go mad.

'Ah! If I could take your sin upon my conscience, as you so generously wished that you might take Stanislas's fever!'

This great moral crisis changed the nature of the sentiment that united Julien to his mistress. His love was no longer merely admiration of her beauty, pride in the possession of her.

Their joy was thenceforward of a far higher nature, the flame that devoured them was more intense. They underwent transports of utter madness. Their happiness would have seemed great in the eyes of other people. But they never recaptured the delicious serenity, the unclouded happiness, the spontaneous joy of the first days of their love, when

Madame de Rênal's one fear was that of not being loved enough by Julien. Their happiness assumed at times the aspect of crime.

In what were their happiest, and apparently their calmest moments: 'Oh! Great God! I see hell before me,' Madame de Rênal would suddenly exclaim, gripping Julien's hand with a convulsive movement. 'What fearful torments! I have well deserved them.' She clutched him, clinging to him like the ivy to the wall.

Julien tried in vain to calm this agitated soul. She took his hand, which she covered with kisses. Then, relapsing into a sombre meditation; 'Hell,' she said, 'hell would be a blessing to me; I should still have some days in this world to spend with him, but hell here on earth, the death of my children.... Yet, at that price, perhaps my crime would be forgiven me.... Oh! Great God! Grant me not my pardon at that price. These poor children have done nothing to offend thee; 'tis I, I, the guilt is mine alone! I love a man who is not my husband.'

Julien next saw Madame de Rênal reach a state that was outwardly tranquil. She sought to take the burden upon herself, she wished not to poison the existence of him whom she loved.

In the midst of these alternations of love, remorse and pleasure, the days passed for them with lightning rapidity. Julien lost the habit of reflexion.

Miss Elisa went to conduct a little lawsuit which she had at Verrières. She found M. Valenod greatly annoyed with Julien. She hated the tutor and often spoke about him to M. Valenod.

'You would ruin me, Sir, if I told you the truth!' she said to him one day. 'Employers all hang together in important things. They never forgive us poor servants for certain revelations....'

After these conventional phrases, which the impatient curiosity of M. Valenod found a way of cutting short, he learned the most mortifying things in the world for his own self-esteem.

This woman, the most distinguished in the place, whom for six years he had surrounded with every attention, and, unluckily, before the eyes of all the world; this proudest of women, whose disdain had so often made him blush, had taken as her lover a little journeyman dressed up as a tutor. And that nothing might be wanting to the discomfiture of the governor of the poorhouse, Madame de Rênal adored this lover.

'And,' the maid added with a sigh, 'M. Julien went to no pains to make this conquest, he has never departed from his habitual coldness with Madame.'

It was only in the country that Elisa had become certain of her facts, but she thought that this intrigue dated from far earlier.

'That, no doubt, is why,' she continued bitterly, 'he refused at the time to marry me. And I, like a fool, going to consult Madame de Rênal, begging her to speak to the tutor!'

That same evening M. de Rênal received from the town, with his newspaper, a long anonymous letter which informed him in the fullest detail of all that was going on under his roof. Julien saw him turn pale as he read this letter, which was written on blue paper, and cast angry glances at himself. For the rest of the evening the Mayor never recovered his peace of mind; it was in vain that Julien tried to flatter him by asking him to explain obscure points in the pedigrees of the best families of Burgundy.

CHAPTER TWENTY

THE ANONYMOUS LETTERS

> Do not give dalliance
> Too much the rein; the strongest oaths are straw
> To the fire i' the blood.
>
> *The Tempest.*

As they left the drawing-room about midnight, Julien found time to say to his mistress:

'Do not let us meet to-night, your husband has suspicions; I would swear that that long letter he was reading with such displeasure is an anonymous one.'

Fortunately, Julien locked himself into his room. Madame de Rênal conceived the mad idea that this warning was simply a pretext for not coming to see her. She lost her head absolutely, and at the usual hour came to his door. Julien, hearing a sound in the corridor, instantly blew out his lamp. Some one was attempting to open his door; was it Madame de Rênal, was it a jealous husband?

Early the next morning, the cook, who took an interest in Julien, brought him a book on the cover of which he read these words written in Italian: *Guardate alla pagina 130.*

Julien shuddered at the imprudence, turned to page one hundred and thirty and found fastened to it with a pin the following letter written in haste, bedewed with tears, and without the least attempt at spelling. Ordinarily Madame de Rênal spelt quite well; he was moved by this detail and began to forget the frightful imprudence.

'So you would not let me in to-night? There are moments

when I feel that I have never seen into the depths of your heart. Your look frightens me. I am afraid of you. Great God! Can it be, you have never loved me? In that case, my husband can discover our love, and shut me up in lifelong imprisonment, in the country, apart from my children. Perhaps God wills it so. I shall soon die; but you will be a monster.

'Do you not love me? Are you tired of my follies, of my remorse, impious one? Do you wish to ruin me? I give you an easy method. Go, shew this letter to all Verrières, or rather shew it to M. Valenod alone. Tell him that I love you; but no, utter no such blasphemy; tell him that I adore you, that life only began for me on the day when I first saw you; that in the wildest moments of my girlhood, I had never even dreamed of the happiness that I owe to you; that I have sacrificed my life to you, that I am sacrificing my soul to you. You know that I am sacrificing far more.

'But what does he know of sacrifices, that man? Tell him, tell him, to make him angry, that I defy all evil-speakers, and that there is but one misfortune in the world for me, that of beholding a change in the one man who holds me to life. What a blessing for me to lose it, to offer it in sacrifice, and to fear no longer for my children!

'Doubt not, dear friend, if there be an anonymous letter, it comes from that odious being who, for the last six years, has pursued me with his loud voice, with a list of the jumps his horse has taken, with his fatuity and with the endless enumeration of all his advantages.

'Is there an anonymous letter? Wicked one, that is what I wished to discuss with you; but no, you were right. Clasping you in my arms, for the last time perhaps, I could never have discussed the matter calmly, as I do when I am alone. From this moment our happiness will not be so easily secured. Will that be an annoyance to you? Yes, on the days when you have not received some amusing book from M. Fouqué. The sacrifice is made; to-morrow, whether there be an anonymous letter or not, I shall tell my husband that I have received an anonymous letter, that he must instantly provide

139

you with a golden ladder, find some decent pretext, and send you back without delay to your family.

'Alas, dear friend, we are going to be parted for a fortnight, perhaps a month! But there, I do you justice, you will suffer as much as I. Still, this is the only way to counteract the effect of this anonymous letter; it is not the first that my husband has received, and on my account too. Alas! How I have laughed at them!

'The whole purpose of my scheme is to make my husband think that the letter comes from M. Valenod; I have no doubt that he is its author. If you leave the house, do not fail to go and establish yourself at Verrières. I shall contrive that my husband conceives the idea of spending a fortnight there, to prove to the fools that there is no coolness between him and myself. Once you are at Verrières, make friends with everyone, even the Liberals. I know that all the ladies will run after you.

'Do not go and quarrel with M. Valenod, nor crop his ears, as you once threatened; on the contrary, shew him every politeness. The essential thing is that it should be known throughout Verrières that you are going to Valenod's, or to some other house, for the children's education.

'That is what my husband will never stand. Should he resign himself to it, well, at least you will be living in Verrières, and I shall see you sometimes. My children, who are so fond of you, will go to see you. Great God! I feel that I love my children more, because they love you. What remorse! How is all this going to end? I am wandering.... Well, you understand what you must do; be gentle, polite, never contemptuous with these vulgar personages, I implore you on my knees: they are to be the arbiters of our destiny. Doubt not for a moment that my husband in dealing with you will conform to whatever *public opinion* may prescribe.

'It is you that are going to provide me with this anonymous letter; arm yourself with patience and a pair of scissors. Cut out of a book the words you will see below; paste them together, with water-glue, on the sheet of blue paper that I send you; it came to me from M. Valenod. Be prepared for

a search of your room; burn the pages of the book you mutil-
ate. If you do not find the words ready made, have the
patience to compose them letter by letter. To spare you
trouble, I have cut the anonymous letter short. Alas! If you
no longer love me, as I fear, how long mine must seem to
you!

ANONYMOUS LETTER

' "MADAME,

All your little goings on are known; but the persons to whose
interest it is to check them have been warned. From a lingering
affection for yourself, I beg you to detach yourself entirely from the
little peasant. If you have the wisdom to do this, your husband will
believe that the warning he has received was misleading, and he
will be left in his error. Bear in mind that I know your secret;
tremble, unhappy woman; henceforward you must tread a straight
path, driven by me."

'As soon as you have finished pasting together the words
that make up this letter (do you recognize the Governor's
style in it?) come out of your room, I shall meet you about
the house.

'I shall go to the village, and return with a troubled countenance; I shall indeed be greatly troubled. Great God! What
a risk I am running, and all because you *thought you detected*
an anonymous letter. Finally, with a woebegone face, I shall
give my husband this letter, which will have been handed to
me by a stranger. As for you, go for a walk in the direction
of the woods with the children, and do not return until dinner time.

'From the rocks above, you can see the tower of the
pigeoncote. If all goes well, I shall place a white handkerchief
there; if not, you will see nothing.

'Ungrateful wretch, will not your heart find out some way
of telling me that you love me, before starting on this walk?
Whatever may befall me, be certain of one thing: I should
not survive for a day a final parting. Ah! bad mother! These
are two idle words that I have written, dear Julien. I do not

feel them; I can think only of you at this moment, I have written them only so as not to be blamed by you. Now that I find myself brought to the point of losing you, what use is there in pretence? Yes, let my heart seem black as night to you, but let me not lie to the man whom I adore! I have been all too deceitful already in my life. Go to, I forgive you if you love me no longer. I have not time to read my letter through. It is a small thing in my eyes to pay with my life for the happy days which I have spent in your arms. You know that they will cost me more than life.'

CHAPTER TWENTY-ONE

CONVERSATION WITH A LORD AND MASTER

> Alas! our frailty is the cause, not we!
> For such as we are made of, such we be.
>
> *Twelfth Night.*

I T was with a childish pleasure that Julien spent an hour in pasting words together. As he left his room he came upon his pupils and their mother; she took the letter with a simplicity and courage, the calmness of which terrified him.

'Is the gum quite dry?' she asked him.

'Can this be the woman who was being driven mad by remorse?' he thought. 'What are her plans at this moment?' He was too proud to ask her; but never, perhaps, had she appealed to him more strongly.

'If things go amiss,' she went on with the same coolness, 'I shall be stripped of everything. Bury this store somewhere in the mountains; it may some day be my last resource.'

She handed him a glass-topped case, in red morocco, filled with gold and a few diamonds.

'Go now,' she said to him.

She embraced her children, the youngest of them twice over. Julien stood spellbound. She left him at a rapid pace and without looking at him again.

From the moment of his opening the anonymous letter, M. de Rênal's life had been a burden to him. He had not been so agitated since a duel that he had nearly had to fight in 1816, and, to do him justice, the prospect of receiving a bullet in his person would now have distressed him less. He

143

examined the letter from every angle. 'Is not this a woman's hand?' he asked himself. 'In that case, what woman can have written it?' He considered in turn all the women he knew at Verrières, without finding a definite object for his suspicions. Could a man have dictated the letter? If so, what man? Here again, a similar uncertainty; he had earned the jealousy and no doubt the hatred of the majority of the men he knew. 'I must consult my wife,' he said to himself, from force of habit, as he rose from the armchair in which he had collapsed.

No sooner had he risen than 'Good God!' he exclaimed, clapping his hand to his head, 'she is the one person whom I cannot trust; from this moment she is my enemy.' And tears of anger welled into his eyes.

It was a fitting reward for that barrenness of heart in which practical wisdom in the provinces is rooted, that the two men whom, at that moment, M. de Rênal most dreaded were his two most intimate friends.

'Apart from them, I have ten friends perhaps,' and he turned them over in his mind, calculating the exact amount of comfort that he would be able to derive from each. 'To all of them, to all of them,' he cried in his rage, 'my appalling misfortune will give the most intense pleasure.' Happily for him, he supposed himself to be greatly envied, and not without reason. Apart from his superb house in town on which the King of —— had just conferred everlasting honour by sleeping beneath its roof, he had made an admirable piece of work of his country house at Vergy. The front was painted white, and the windows adorned with handsome green shutters. He was comforted for a moment by the thought of this magnificence. The fact of the matter was that this mansion was visible from a distance of three or four leagues, to the great detriment of all the country houses or so-called *châteaux* of the neighbourhood, which had been allowed to retain the humble grey tones imparted to them by time.

M. de Rênal could reckon upon the tears and pity of one of his friends, the churchwarden of the parish; but he was an imbecile who shed tears at everything. This man was nevertheless his sole resource.

144

'What misfortune is comparable to mine?' he exclaimed angrily. 'What isolation!

'Is it possible,' this truly pitiable man asked himself, 'is it possible that, in my distress, I have not a single friend of whom to ask advice? For my mind is becoming unhinged, I can feel it! Ah, Falcoz! Ah, Ducros!' he cried bitterly. These were the names of two of his boyhood's friends whom he had alienated by his arrogance in 1814. They were not noble, and he had tried to alter the terms of equality on which they had been living all their lives.

One of them, Falcoz, a man of spirit and heart, a paper merchant at Verrières, had purchased a printing press in the chief town of the Department and had started a newspaper. The *Congregation* had determined to ruin him: his paper had been condemned, his printer's licence had been taken from him. In these unfortunate circumstances he ventured to write to M. de Rênal for the first time in ten years. The Mayor of Verrières felt it incumbent on him to reply in the Ancient Roman style: 'If the King's Minister did me the honour to consult me, I should say to him: "Ruin without compunction all provincial printers, and make printing a monopoly like the sale of tobacco."' This letter to an intimate friend which had set the whole of Verrières marvelling at the time, M. de Rênal now recalled, word for word, with horror. 'Who would have said that with my rank, my fortune, my Crosses, I should one day regret it?' It was in such transports of anger, now against himself, now against all around him, that he passed a night of anguish; but, fortunately, it did not occur to him to spy upon his wife.

'I am used to Louise,' he said to himself, 'she knows all my affairs; were I free to marry again to-morrow I could find no one fit to take her place.' Next, he sought relief in the idea that his wife was innocent; this point of view made it unnecessary for him to shew his strength of character, and was far more convenient; how many slandered wives have we not all seen!

'But what!' he suddenly exclaimed, pacing the floor with a convulsive step, 'am I to allow her, as though I were a man of straw, a mere ragamuffin, to make a mock of me with her lover? Is the whole of Verrières to be allowed to sneer at my complacency? What have they not said about Charmier?' (a notorious local cuckold) 'When he is mentioned, is there not a smile on every face? He is a good pleader, who is there that ever mentions his talent for public speaking? "Ah! Charmier!" is what they say; "Bernard's Charmier." They actually give him the name of the man that has disgraced him.

'Thank heaven,' said M. de Rênal at other moments, 'I have no daughter, and the manner in which I am going to punish their mother will not damage the careers of my children; I can surprise that young peasant with my wife, and kill the pair of them; in that event, the tragic outcome of my misfortune may perhaps make it less absurd.' This idea appealed to him: he worked it out in the fullest detail. 'The Penal Code is on my side, and, whatever happens, our *Congregation* and my friends on the jury will save me.' He examined his hunting knife, which had a keen blade; but the thought of bloodshed frightened him.

'I might thrash this insolent tutor black and blue and turn him from the house; but what a stir in Verrières and, indeed, throughout the Department! After the suppression of Falcoz's paper, when his editor came out of prison, I was instrumental in making him lose a place worth six hundred francs. They say that the scribbler has dared to shew his face again in Besançon, he may easily attack me, and so cunningly that it will be impossible to bring him to justice! That insolent fellow will insinuate in a thousand ways that he has been speaking the truth. A man of family, who respects his rank as I do, is always hated by plebeians. I shall see myself in those frightful Paris papers; my God! what degradation! To see the ancient name of Rênal plunged in the mire of ridicule. . . . If I ever travel, I shall have to change my name; what! give up this name which is my pride and my strength. What a crowning infamy!

'If I do not kill my wife, if I drive her from the house with ignominy, she has her aunt at Besançon, who will hand over

146

the whole of her fortune to her on the quiet. My wife will go and live in Paris with Julien; Verrières will hear of it, and I shall again be regarded as a dupe.' This unhappy man then perceived, from the failing light of his lamp, that day was beginning to break. He went to seek a breath of air in the garden. At that moment, he had almost made up his mind to create no scene, chiefly because a scene of that sort would fill his good friends at Verrières with joy.

His stroll in the garden calmed him somewhat. 'No,' he cried, 'I shall certainly not part with my wife, she is too useful to me.' He pictured to himself with horror what his house would be like without his wife; his sole female relative was the Marquise de R——, who was old, idiotic and evil-minded.

An idea of the greatest good sense occurred to him, but to put it into practice required a strength of character far exceeding the little that the poor man possessed. 'If I keep my wife,' he said to himself; 'I know my own nature; one day, when she taxes my patience, I shall reproach her with her offence. She is proud, we are bound to quarrel, and all this will happen before she has inherited her aunt's estate. And then, how they will all laugh at me! My wife loves her children, it will all come to them in the end. But I, I shall be the talk of Verrières. What, they will say, he couldn't even punish his wife! Would it not be better to stick to my suspicions and to verify nothing? Then I tie my own hands, I cannot afterwards reproach her with anything.'

A moment later M. de Rênal, his wounded vanity once more gaining the mastery, was laboriously recalling all the stories told in the billiard-room of the Casino or Noble Club of Verrières, when some fluent talker interrupted the pool to make merry at the expense of some cuckolded husband. How cruel, at that moment, those pleasantries seemed.

'God! Why is not my wife dead! Then I should be immune from ridicule. Why am I not a widower! I should go and spend six months in Paris in the best society.' After this momentary happiness caused by the idea of widowhood, his imagination returned to the methods of ascertaining the truth. Should he at midnight, after the whole household had gone to bed, sprinkle a few handfuls of bran outside the door of Julien's room? Next morning, at daybreak, he would see the footprints on it.

'But that would be no good,' he broke out angrily, 'that wretched Elisa would notice it, and it would be all over the house at once that I am jealous.'

In another story that circulated at the Casino, a husband had made certain of his plight by fastening a hair with a little wax so as to seal up the doors of his wife's room and her lover's.

After so many hours of vacillation, this method of obtaining enlightenment seemed to him decidedly the best, and he was thinking of adopting it, when at a bend in the path he came upon that wife whom he would have liked to see dead.

She was returning from the village. She had gone to hear mass in the church of Vergy. A tradition of extremely doubtful value in the eyes of the cold philosopher, but one in which she believed, made out that the little church now in use had been the chapel of the castle of the Lord of Vergy. This thought obsessed Madame de Rênal throughout the time which she had meant to pass in prayer in this church. She kept on picturing to herself her husband killing Julien during the chase, as though by accident, and afterwards, that evening, making her eat his heart.

'My fate,' she said to herself, 'depends on what he will think when he hears me. After these terrible moments, perhaps I shall not find another opportunity to speak to him. He is not a wise creature, swayed by reason. I might, if he were, with the aid of my own feeble wits, forecast what he would do or say. But my fate lies in my cunning, in the art of directing the thoughts of this whimsical creature, who becomes blind with anger and incapable of seeing things. Great God! I require talent, coolness, where am I to find them?'

She recovered her calm as though by magic on entering the garden and seeing her husband in the distance. The disorder of his hair and clothes shewed that he had not slept.

148

She handed him a letter which, though the seal was broken, was still folded. He, without opening it, gazed at his wife with madness in his eyes.

'Here is an abomination,' she said to him, 'which an evil looking man who claims to know you and that you owe him a debt of gratitude, handed to me as I came past the back of the lawyer's garden. One thing I must ask of you, and that is that you send back to his own people, and without delay, that Monsieur Julien.' Madame de Rênal made haste to utter this name, even beginning a little too soon perhaps, in order to rid herself of the fearful prospect of having to utter it.

She was filled with joy on beholding the joy that it gave her husband. From the fixed stare which he directed at her she realized that Julien had guessed aright. Instead of worrying about a very present trouble, 'what intelligence,' she thought to herself. 'What perfect tact! And in a young man still quite devoid of experience! To what heights will he not rise in time? Alas! Then his success will make him forget me.'

This little act of admiration of the man she adored completely restored her composure.

She congratulated herself on the step she had taken. 'I have proved myself not unworthy of Julien,' she said to herself, with a sweet and secret relish.

Without saying a word, for fear of committing himself, M. de Rênal examined this second anonymous letter composed, as the reader may remember, of printed words gummed upon a sheet of paper of a bluish tinge. 'They are making a fool of me in every way,' M. de Rênal said to himself, utterly worn out.

'Fresh insults to be looked into, and all owing to my wife!' He was on the point of deluging her with a stream of the coarsest invective; the thought of the fortune awaiting her at Besançon just stopped him. Overpowered by the necessity of venting his anger on something, he tore up the sheet on which this second anonymous letter was gummed, and strode rapidly away, feeling that he could not endure his wife's company. A minute later, he returned to her, already more calm.

'We must take action at once and dismiss Julien,' she

immediately began; 'after all he is only the son of a working man. You can compensate him with a few crowns, besides, he is clever and can easily find another place, with M. Valenod, for instance, or the Sub-Prefect Maugiron; they both have families. And so you will not be doing him any harm. . . .'

'You speak like the fool that you are,' cried M. de Rênal in a voice of thunder. 'How can one expect common sense of a woman? You never pay attention to what is reasonable; how should you have any knowledge? Your carelessness, your laziness leave you just enough activity to chase butterflies, feeble creatures which we are so unfortunate as to have in our households. . . .'

Madame de Rênal let him speak, and he spoke at length; he *passed his anger*, as they say in those parts.

'Sir,' she answered him finally, 'I speak as a woman whose honour, that is to say her most priceless possession, has been outraged.'

Madame de Rênal preserved an unalterable calm throughout the whole of this trying conversation, upon which depended the possibility of her continuing to live beneath the same roof as Julien. She sought out the ideas that seemed to her best fitted to guide her husband's blind anger. She had remained unmoved by all the insulting remarks that he had addressed to her, she did not hear them, she was thinking all the time of Julien. 'Will he be pleased with me?'

'This little peasant upon whom we have lavished every attention, including presents, may be innocent,' she said at length, 'but he is none the less the occasion of the first insult I have ever received. . . . Sir, when I read that abominable document, I vowed that either he or I should leave your roof.'

'Do you wish to create a scandal that will dishonour me and yourself as well? You'll be giving a fine treat to many people in Verrières.'

'That is true; they are all jealous of the state of prosperity to which your wise management has brought you, your family and the town. . . . Very well, I shall go and bid Julien ask you for leave to spend a month with that timber merchant in the mountains, a fit companion for that little workman.'

'Take care what you do,' put in M. de Rênal, calmly enough. 'The one thing I must insist on is that you do not speak to him. You would shew temper and make him cross with me; you know how touchy the little gentleman is.'

'That young man has no tact,' went on Madame de Rênal; 'he may be learned, you know about that, but at bottom he is nothing but a peasant. For my own part, I have never had any opinion of him since he refused to marry Elisa, it was a fortune ready made; and all because now and again she pays a secret visit to M. Valenod.'

'Ah!' said M. de Rênal, raising his eyebrows as far as they would go, 'what, did Julien tell you that?'

'No, not exactly; he has always spoken to me of the vocation that is calling him to the sacred ministry; but believe me, the first vocation for the lower orders is to find their daily bread. He made it fairly clear to me that he was not unaware of these secret visits.'

'And I, I, knew nothing about them!' cried M. de Rênal, all his fury returning, emphasizing every word. 'There are things going on in my house of which I know nothing.... What! There has been something between Elisa and Valenod?'

'Oh, that's an old story, my dear friend,' Madame de Rênal said laughing, 'and I daresay no harm was done. It was in the days when your good friend Valenod would not have been sorry to have it thought in Verrières that there was a little love—of a purely platonic sort—exchanged between him and me.'

'I had that idea at one time,' cried M. de Rênal striking his head in his fury as he advanced from one discovery to another, 'and you never said a word to me about it?'

'Was I to make trouble between two friends all for a little outburst of vanity on the part of our dear Governor? What woman is there in society to whom he has not addressed one or more letters, extremely witty and even a trifle gallant?'

'Has he written to you?'

'He writes frequently.'

'Shew me his letters this instant, I order you'; and M. de Rênal added six feet to his stature.

'I shall do nothing of the sort,' the answer came in a tone so gentle as to be almost indifferent, 'I shall let you see them some other day, when you are more yourself.'

'This very instant, damn it!' cried M. de Rênal, blind with rage, and yet happier than he had been at any time in the last twelve hours.

'Will you swear to me,' said Madame de Rênal solemnly, 'never to quarrel with the Governor of the Poorhouse over these letters?'

'Quarrel or no quarrel, I can take the foundlings away from him; but,' he continued, furiously, 'I want those letters this instant; where are they?'

'In a drawer in my desk; but you may be certain, I shall not give you the key of it.'

'I shall be able to force it,' he cried as he made off in the direction of his wife's room.

He did indeed break open with an iron bar a valuable mahogany writing desk, imported from Paris, which he used often to polish with the tail of his coat when he thought he detected a spot on its surface.

Madame de Rênal meanwhile had run up the hundred and twenty steps of the dovecote; she knotted the corner of a white handkerchief to one of the iron bars of the little window. She was the happiest of women. With tears in her eyes she gazed out at the wooded slopes of the mountain. 'Doubtless,' she said to herself, 'beneath one of those spreading beeches, Julien is watching for this glad signal.' For long she strained her ears, then cursed the monotonous drone of the grasshoppers and the twitter of the birds. But for those tiresome sounds, a cry of joy, issuing from among the rocks, might have reached her in her tower. Her ravening gaze devoured that immense slope of dusky verdure, unbroken as the surface of a meadow, that was formed by the treetops. 'How is it he has not the sense,' she asked herself with deep emotion, 'to think of some signal to tell me that his happiness is no less than mine?' She came down from the dovecote only when she began to be afraid that her husband might come up in search of her.

She found him foaming with rage. He was running through M. Valenod's anodyne sentences, that were little used to being read with such emotion.

Seizing a moment in which a lull in her husband's exclamations gave her a chance to make herself heard:

'I cannot get away from my original idea,' said Madame de Rênal, 'Julien ought to go for a holiday. Whatever talent he may have for Latin, he is nothing more, after all, than a peasant who is often coarse and wanting in tact; every day, thinking he is being polite, he plies me with extravagant compliments in the worst of taste, which he learns by heart from some novel....'

'He never reads any,' cried M. de Rênal; 'I am positive as to that. Do you suppose that I am a blind master who knows nothing of what goes on under his roof?'

'Very well, if he doesn't read those absurd compliments anywhere, he invents them, which is even worse. He will have spoken of me in that tone in Verrières; and, without going so far,' said Madame de Rênal, with the air of one making a discovery, 'he will have spoken like that before Elisa, which is just as though he had spoken to M. Valenod.'

'Ah!' cried M. de Rênal, making the table and the whole room shake with one of the stoutest blows that human fist ever gave, 'the anonymous letter in print and Valenod's letters were all on the same paper.'

'At last!' thought Madame de Rênal; she appeared thunderstruck by this discovery, and without having the courage to add a single word went and sat down on the divan, at the farther end of the room.

The battle was now won; she had her work cut out to prevent M. de Rênal from going and talking to the supposed author of the anonymous letter.

'How is it you do not feel that to make a scene, without sufficient proof, with M. Valenod would be the most deplorable error? If you are envied, Sir, who is to blame? Your own talents: your wise administration, the buildings you have erected with such good taste, the dowry I brought you, and above all the considerable fortune we may expect to inherit from my worthy aunt, a fortune the extent of which is vastly exaggerated, have made you the principal person in Verrières.'

'You forget my birth,' said M. de Rênal, with a faint smile.

'You are one of the most distinguished gentlemen in the province,' Madame de Rênal hastily added; 'if the King were free and could do justice to birth, you would doubtless be figuring in the House of Peers,' and so forth. 'And in this magnificent position do you seek to provide jealousy with food for comment?

'To speak to M. Valenod of his anonymous letter is to proclaim throughout Verrières, or rather in Besançon, throughout the Province, that this petty cit, admitted perhaps imprudently to the friendship of *a Rênal*, has found out a way to insult him. Did these letters which you have just discovered prove that I had responded to M. Valenod's overtures, then it would be for you to kill me, I should have deserved it a hundred times, but not to shew anger with him. Think that all your neighbours only await a pretext to be avenged for your superiority; think that in 1816 you were instrumental in securing certain arrests. That man who took refuge on your roof....'

'What I think is that you have neither respect nor affection for me,' shouted M. de Rênal with all the bitterness that such a memory aroused, 'and I have not been made a Peer!'

'I think, my friend,' put in Madame de Rênal with a smile, 'that I shall one day be richer than you, that I have been your companion for twelve years, and that on all these counts I ought to have a voice in your councils, especially in this business to-day. If you prefer Monsieur Julien to me,' she added with ill-concealed scorn, 'I am prepared to go and spend the winter with my aunt.'

This threat was uttered *with gladness*. It contained the firmness which seeks to cloak itself in courtesy; it determined M. de Rênal. But, obeying the provincial custom, he continued

154

to speak for a long time, harked back to every argument in turn; his wife allowed him to speak, there was still anger in his tone. At length, two hours of futile discourse wore out the strength of a man who had been helpless with rage all night. He determined upon the line of conduct which he was going to adopt towards M. Valenod, Julien, and even Elisa.

Once or twice, during this great scene, Madame de Rênal came within an ace of feeling a certain sympathy for the very real distress of this man who for ten years had been her friend. But our true passions are selfish. Moreover she was expecting every moment an avowal of the anonymous letter which he had received overnight, and this avowal never came. To gain complete confidence, Madame de Rênal required to know what ideas might have been suggested to the man upon whom her fate depended. For, in the country, husbands control public opinion. A husband who denounces his wife covers himself with ridicule, a thing that every day is becoming less dangerous in France; but his wife, if he does not supply her with money, declines to the position of a working woman at fifteen sous daily, and even then the virtuous souls have scruples about employing her.

An odalisque in the seraglio may love the Sultan with all her heart; he is all powerful, she has no hope of evading his authority by a succession of clever little tricks. The master's vengeance is terrible, bloody, but martial and noble: a dagger blow ends everything. It is with blows dealt by public contempt that a husband kills his wife in the nineteenth century; it is by shutting the doors of all the drawing-rooms in her face.

The sense of danger was keenly aroused in Madame de Rênal on her return to her own room; she was horrified by the disorder in which she found it. The locks of all her pretty little boxes had been broken; several planks in the floor had been torn up. 'He would have been without pity for me!' she told herself. 'To spoil so this floor of coloured parquet, of which he is so proud; when one of his children comes in with muddy shoes, he flushes with rage. And now it is ruined for ever!' The sight of this violence rapidly silenced the last reproaches with which she had been blaming herself for her too rapid victory.

Shortly before the dinner bell sounded, Julien returned with the children. At dessert, when the servants had left the room, Madame de Rênal said to him very drily,

'You expressed the desire to me to go and spend a fortnight at Verrières; M. de Rênal is kind enough to grant you leave. You can go as soon as you please. But, so that the children shall not waste any time, their lessons will be sent to you every day, for you to correct.'

'Certainly,' M. de Rênal added in a most bitter tone, 'I shall not allow you more than a week.'

Julien read in his features the uneasiness of a man in cruel torment.

'He has not yet come to a decision,' he said to his mistress, during a moment of solitude in the drawing-room.

Madame de Rênal informed him rapidly of all that she had done since the morning.

'The details to-night,' she added laughing.

'The perversity of woman!' thought Julien. 'What pleasure, what instinct leads them to betray us?

'I find you at once enlightened and blinded by your love,' he said to her with a certain coldness; 'your behaviour to-day has been admirable; but is there any prudence in our attempting to see each other to-night? This house is paved with enemies; think of the passionate hatred that Elisa has for me.'

'That hatred greatly resembles the passionate indifference that you must have for me.'

'Indifferent or not, I am bound to save you from a peril into which I have plunged you. If chance decrees that M. de Rênal speaks to Elisa, by a single word she may disclose everything to him. What is to prevent him from hiding outside my room, well armed. . . .'

'What! Lacking in courage even!' said Madame de Rênal, with all the pride of a woman of noble birth.

'I shall never sink so low as to speak of my courage,' said Julien coldly, 'that is mean. Let the world judge by my actions. But,' he went on, taking her hand, 'you cannot conceive how attached I am to you, and what a joy it is to me to be able to take leave of you before this cruel parting.'

156

CHAPTER TWENTY-TWO

MANNERS AND CUSTOMS IN 1830

Speech was given to man to enable him to conceal
his thoughts.

MALAGRIDA, S. J.

T HE first thing that Julien did on arriving in Verrières
was to reproach himself for his unfairness to Madame
de Rênal. 'I should have despised her as a foolish
woman if from weakness she had failed to bring off the scene
with M. de Rênal! She carried it through like a diplomat,
and my sympathies are with the loser, who is my enemy.
There is a streak of middle-class pettiness in my nature; my
vanity is hurt, because M. de Rênal is a man! That vast and
illustrious corporation to which I have the honour to belong;
I am a perfect fool.'

M. Chélan had refused the offers of hospitality which the
most respected Liberals of the place had vied with one
another in making him, when his deprivation drove him
from the presbytery. The pair of rooms which he had taken
were littered with his books. Julien, wishing to shew Verrières what it meant to be a priest, went and fetched from
his father's store a dozen planks of firwood, which he carried
on his back the whole length of the main street. He borrowed some tools from an old friend and had soon con-
structed a sort of bookcase in which he arranged M.
Chélan's library.

'I supposed you to have been corrupted by the vanity of
the world,' said the old man, shedding tears of joy; 'this

157

quite redeems the childishness of that dazzling guard of honour uniform which made you so many enemies.'

M. de Rênal had told Julien to put up in his house. No one had any suspicion of what had happened. On the third day after his arrival, there came up to his room no less a personage than the Sub-Prefect, M. de Maugiron. It was only after two solid hours of insipid tittle-tattle, and long jeremiads on the wickedness of men, on the lack of honesty in the people entrusted with the administration of public funds, on the dangers besetting poor France, etc., etc., that Julien saw him come at length to the purpose of his visit. They were already on the landing, and the poor tutor, on the verge of disgrace, was ushering out with all due respect the future Prefect of some fortunate Department, when it pleased the latter gentleman to occupy himself with Julien's career, to praise his moderation where his own interests were concerned, etc., etc. Finally M. de Maugiron, taking him in his arms in the most fatherly manner, suggested to him that he should leave M. de Rênal and enter the household of an official who had children to educate, and who, like King Philip, would thank heaven, not so much for having given him them as for having caused them to be born in the neighbourhood of M. Julien. Their tutor would receive a salary of eight hundred francs, payable not month by month, 'which is not noble,' said M. de Maugiron, but quarterly, and in advance to boot.

It was now the turn of Julien who, for an hour and a half, had been waiting impatiently for an opportunity to speak. His reply was perfect, and as long as a pastoral charge; it let everything be understood, and at the same time said nothing definite. A listener would have found in it at once respect for M. de Rênal, veneration for the people of Verrières and gratitude towards the illustrious Sub-Prefect. The said Sub-Prefect, astonished at finding a bigger Jesuit than himself, tried in vain to obtain something positive. Julien, overjoyed, seized the opportunity to try his skill and began his answer over again in different terms. Never did the most eloquent Minister, seeking to monopolize the last hours of a sitting when the Chamber seems inclined to wake up, say less in more words. As soon as M. de Maugiron had left him, Julien broke out in helpless laughter. To make the most of his Jesuitical bent, he wrote a letter of nine pages to M. de Rênal, in which he informed him of everything that had been said to him, and humbly asked his advice. 'Why, that rascal never even told me the name of the person who is making the offer! It will be M. Valenod, who sees in my banishment to Verrières the effect of his anonymous letter.'

His missive dispatched, Julien, as happy as a hunter who at six in the morning on a fine autumn day emerges upon a plain teeming with game, went out to seek the advice of M. Chélan. But before he arrived at the good curé's house, heaven, which was anxious to shower its blessings on him, threw him into the arms of M. Valenod, from whom he did not conceal the fact that his heart was torn; a penniless youth like himself was bound to devote himself entirely to the vocation which heaven had placed in his heart, but a vocation was not everything in this vile world. To be a worthy labourer in the Lord's vineyard, and not to be altogether unworthy of all one's learned fellow-labourers, one required education; one required to spend in the seminary at Besançon two very expensive years; it became indispensable, therefore—and, one might, in a certain sense, say, a duty—to save money, which was considerably easier with a salary of eight hundred francs paid quarterly, than with six hundred francs which melted away month by month. On the other hand, did not heaven, by placing him with the Rênal boys, and above all by inspiring in him a particular attachment to them, seem to indicate to him that it would be a mistake to abandon this form of education for another?...

Julien arrived at such a pitch of perfection in this kind of eloquence, which has taken the place of the swiftness of action of the Empire, that he ended by growing tired of the sound of his own voice.

Returning to the house he found one of M. Valenod's servants in full livery, who had been looking for him all over the town, with a note inviting him to dinner that very day.

159

Never had Julien set foot in the man's house; only a few days earlier, his chief thought was how he might give him a thorough good thrashing without subsequent action by the police. Although dinner was not to be until one o'clock, Julien thought it more respectful to present himself at half past twelve in the study of the Governor of the Poorhouse. He found him displaying his importance amid a mass of papers. His huge black whiskers, his enormous quantity of hair, his night-cap poised askew on the top of his head, his immense pipe, his embroidered slippers, the heavy gold chains slung across his chest in every direction, and all the equipment of a provincial financier, who imagines himself to be a ladies' man, made not the slightest impression upon Julien; he only thought all the more of the thrashing that he owed him.

He craved the honour of being presented to Madame Valenod; she was making her toilet and could not see him. To make up for this, he had the privilege of witnessing that of the Governor of the Poorhouse. They then proceeded to join Madame Valenod, who presented her children to him with tears in her eyes. This woman, one of the most important people in Verrières, had a huge masculine face, which she had plastered with rouge for this great ceremony. She displayed all the pathos of maternal feelings.

Julien thought of Madame de Rênal. His distrustful nature made him scarcely susceptible to any memories save those that are evoked by contrast, but such memories moved him to tears. This tendency was increased by the sight of the Governor's house. He was taken through it. Everything in it was sumptuous and new, and he was told the price of each article. But Julien felt that there was something mean about it, a taint of stolen money. Everyone, even the servants, wore a bold air that seemed to be fortifying them against contempt.

The collector of taxes, the receiver of customs, the chief constable and two or three other public officials arrived with their wives. They were followed by several wealthy Liberals. Dinner was announced. Julien, already in the worst of humours, suddenly reflected that on the other side of the dining-room wall there were wretched prisoners, whose rations of meat had perhaps been *squeezed* to purchase all this tasteless splendour with which his hosts sought to dazzle him.

'They are hungry perhaps at this moment,' he said to himself; his throat contracted, he found it impossible to eat and almost to speak. It was much worse a quarter of an hour later; they could hear in the distance a few snatches of a popular and, it must be admitted, not too refined song which one of the inmates was singing. M. Valenod glanced at one of his men in full livery, who left the room, and presently the sound of singing ceased. At that moment, a footman offered Julien some Rhine wine in a green glass, and Madame Valenod took care to inform him that this wine cost nine francs the bottle, direct from the grower. Julien, the green glass in his hand, said to M. Valenod:

'I don't hear that horrid song any more.'

'Gad! I should think not, indeed,' replied the Governor triumphantly. 'I've made the rascal shut up.'

This was too much for Julien; he had acquired the manners but had not yet the heart appropriate to his station. Despite all his hypocrisy, which he kept in such constant practice, he felt a large tear trickle down his cheek.

He tried to hide it with the green glass, but it was simply impossible for him to do honour to the Rhine wine. '*Stop the man singing!*' he murmured to himself, 'O my God, and Thou permittest it!'

Fortunately for him, no one noticed his ill-bred emotion. The collector of taxes had struck up a royalist ditty. During the clamour of the refrain, sung in chorus: 'There,' Julien's conscience warned him, 'you have the sordid fortune which you will achieve, and you will enjoy it only in these conditions and in such company as this! You will have a place worth perhaps twenty thousand francs, but it must be that while you gorge to repletion you stop the poor prisoner from singing; you will give dinner parties with the money you have filched from his miserable pittance, and during your dinner he will be more wretched still! O Napoleon! How pleasant it was in thy time to climb to fortune through the dangers of a battle; but meanly to intensify the sufferings of the wretched!'

I admit that the weakness which Julien displays in this monologue gives me a poor opinion of him. He would be a worthy colleague for those conspirators in yellow gloves, who profess to reform all the conditions of life in a great country, and would be horrified at having to undergo the slightest inconvenience themselves.

Julien was sharply recalled to his proper part. It was not that he might dream and say nothing that he had been invited to dine in such good company.

A retired calico printer, a corresponding member of the Academy of Besançon and of that of Uzès, was speaking to him, down the whole length of the table, inquiring whether all that was commonly reported as to his astonishing prowess in the study of the New Testament was true.

A profound silence fell instantly; a New Testament appeared as though by magic in the hands of the learned member of the two academies. Julien having answered in the affirmative, a few words in Latin were read out to him at random. He began to recite: his memory did not betray him, and this prodigy was admired with all the noisy energy of the end of a dinner. Julien studied the glowing faces of the women. Several of them were not ill looking. He had made out the wife of the collector who sang so well.

'Really, I am ashamed to go on speaking Latin so long before these ladies,' he said, looking at her. 'If M. Rubigneau' (this was the member of the two academies) 'will be so good as to read out any sentence in Latin, instead of going on with the Latin text, I shall endeavour to improvize a translation.'

This second test set the crown of glory on his achievement.

There were in the room a number of Liberals, men of means, but the happy fathers of children who were capable of winning bursaries, and in this capacity suddenly converted after the last Mission. Despite this brilliant stroke of policy, M. de Rênal had never consented to have them in his house. These worthy folk, who knew Julien only by reputation and from having seen him on horseback on the day of the King of ——'s visit, were his most vociferous admirers. 'When will these fools tire of listening to this Biblical language, of which they understand nothing?' he thought. On the contrary, this language amused them by its unfamiliarity; they laughed at it. But Julien had grown tired.

He rose gravely as six o'clock struck and mentioned a chapter of the new theology of Liguori, which he had to learn by heart in order to repeat it next day to M. Chélan. 'For my business,' he added pleasantly, 'is to make other people repeat lessons, and to repeat them myself.'

His audience laughed heartily and applauded; this is the kind of wit that goes down at Verrières. Julien was by this time on his feet, everyone else rose, regardless of decorum; such is the power of genius. Madame Valenod kept him for a quarter of an hour longer; he really must hear the children repeat their catechism; they made the most absurd mistakes which he alone noticed. He made no attempt to correct them. 'What ignorance of the first principles of religion,' he thought. At length he said good-bye and thought that he might escape; but the children must next attempt one of La Fontaine's Fables.

'That author is most immoral,' Julien said to Madame Valenod; 'in one of his Fables on Messire Jean Chouart, he has ventured to heap ridicule on all that is most venerable. He is strongly reproved by the best commentators.'

Before leaving the house Julien received four or five invitations to dinner. 'This young man does honour to the Department,' his fellow-guests, in great hilarity, were all exclaiming at once. They went so far as to speak of a pension voted out of the municipal funds, to enable him to continue his studies in Paris.

While this rash idea was making the dining-room ring, Julien had stolen away to the porch. 'Oh, what scum! What scum!' he murmured three or four times, as he treated himself to the pleasure of drinking in the fresh air.

He felt himself a thorough aristocrat for the moment, he who for long had been so shocked by the disdainful smile

163

and the haughty superiority which he found lurking behind all the compliments that were paid him at M. de Rênal's. He could not help feeling the extreme difference. 'Even if we forget,' he said to himself as he walked away, 'that the money has been stolen from the poor prisoners, and that they are forbidden to sing as well, would it ever occur to M. de Rênal to tell his guests the price of each bottle of wine that he offers them? And this M. Valenod, in going over the list of his property, which he does incessantly, cannot refer to his house, his land and all the rest of it, if his wife is present, without saying *your* house, *your* land.'

This lady, apparently so conscious of the joy of ownership, had just made an abominable scene, during dinner, with a servant who had broken a wineglass and *spoiled one of her sets*; and the servant had answered her with the most gross insolence.

'What a household!' thought Julien; 'if they were to give me half of all the money they steal, I wouldn't live among them. One fine day I should give myself away; I should be unable to keep back the contempt they inspire in me.'

He was obliged, nevertheless, obeying Madame de Rênal's orders, to attend several dinners of this sort; Julien was the fashion; people forgave him his uniform and the guard of honour, or rather that imprudent display was the true cause of his success. Soon, the only question discussed in Verrières was who would be successful in the struggle to secure the learned young man's services, M. de Rênal or the Governor of the Poorhouse. These two gentlemen formed with M. Maslon a triumvirate which for some years past had tyrannized over the town. People were jealous of the Mayor, the Liberals had grounds for complaint against him; but after all he was noble and created to fill a superior station, whereas M. Valenod's father had not left him an income of six hundred livres. He had been obliged to pass from the stage of being pitied for the shabby apple-green coat in which everybody remembered him in his younger days to that of being envied for his Norman horses, his gold chains, the clothes he ordered from Paris, in short, all his present prosperity.

In the welter of this world so new to Julien he thought he had discovered an honest man; this was a geometrician, was named Gros and was reckoned a Jacobin. Julien, having made a vow never to say anything except what he himself believed to be false, was obliged to make a shew of being suspicious of M. Gros. He received from Vergy large packets of exercises. He was advised to see much of his father, and complied with this painful necessity. In a word, he was quite redeeming his reputation, when one morning he was greatly surprised to find himself awakened by a pair of hands which were clapped over his eyes.

It was Madame de Rênal who had come in to town and, running upstairs four steps at a time and leaving her children occupied with a favourite rabbit that they had brought with them, had reached Julien's room a minute in advance of them. The moment was delicious but all too brief: Madame de Rênal had vanished when the children arrived with the rabbit, which they wanted to shew to their friend. Julien welcomed them all, including the rabbit. He seemed to be once more one of a family party; he felt that he loved these children, that it amused him to join in their chatter. He was amazed by the sweetness of their voices, the simplicity and nobility of their manners; he required to wash his imagination clean of all the vulgar behaviour, all the unpleasant thoughts the atmosphere of which he had to breathe at Verrières. There was always the dread of bankruptcy, wealth and poverty were always fighting for the upper hand. The people with whom he dined, in speaking of the joint on their table, made confidences humiliating to themselves, and nauseating to their hearers.

'You aristocrats, you have every reason to be proud,' he said to Madame de Rênal. And he told her of all the dinners he had endured.

'Why, so you are in the fashion!' And she laughed heartily at the thought of the rouge which Madame Valenod felt herself obliged to put on whenever she expected Julien. 'I believe she has designs on your heart,' she added.

Luncheon was a joy. The presence of the children, albeit

apparently a nuisance, increased as a matter of fact the general enjoyment. These poor children did not know how to express their delight at seeing Julien again. The servants had not failed to inform them that he was being offered two hundred francs more to 'bring up' the little Valenods.

In the middle of luncheon, Stanislas Xavier, still pale after his serious illness, suddenly asked his mother what was the value of his silver spoon and fork and of the mug out of which he was drinking.

'Why do you want to know?'

'I want to sell them to give the money to M. Julien, so that he shan't be a *dupe* to stay with us.'

Julien embraced him, the tears standing in his eyes. The mother wept outright, while Julien, who had taken Stanislas on his knees, explained to him that he must not use the word *dupe*, which, employed in that sense, was a servant's expression. Seeing the pleasure he was giving Madame de Rênal, he tried to explain, by picturesque examples, which amused the children, what was meant by a dupe.

'I understand,' said Stanislas, 'it's the crow who is silly and drops his cheese, which is picked up by the fox, who is a flatterer.'

Madame de Rênal, wild with joy, smothered her children in kisses, which she could hardly do without leaning slightly upon Julien.

Suddenly the door opened; it was M. de Rênal. His stern, angry face formed a strange contrast with the innocent gaiety which his presence banished. Madame de Rênal turned pale; she felt herself incapable of denying anything. Julien seized the opportunity and, speaking very loud, began to tell the Mayor the incident of the silver mug which Stanislas wanted to sell. He was sure that this story would be ill received. At the first word M. de Rênal frowned, from force of habit at the mere name of silver. 'The mention of that metal,' he would say, 'is always a preliminary to some call upon my purse.'

But here there was more than money at stake; there was an increase of his suspicions. The air of happiness which animated his family in his absence was not calculated to improve matters with a man dominated by so sensitive a vanity. When his wife praised the graceful and witty manner in which Julien imparted fresh ideas to his pupils:

'Yes, yes, I know, he is making me odious to my children; it is very easy for him to be a hundred times pleasanter to them than I, who am, after all, the master. Everything tends in these days to bring *lawful* authority into contempt. Unhappy France!'

Madame de Rênal did not stop to examine the implications of her husband's manner. She had just seen the possibility of spending twelve hours in Julien's company. She had any number of purchases to make in the town, and declared that she absolutely must dine in a tavern; in spite of anything her husband might say or do, she clung to her idea. The children were in ecstasies at the mere word *tavern*, which modern prudery finds such pleasure in pronouncing.

M. de Rênal left his wife in the first linendraper's shop that she entered, to go and pay some calls. He returned more gloomy than in the morning; he was convinced that the whole town was thinking about nothing but himself and Julien. As a matter of fact, no one had as yet allowed him to form any suspicion of the offensive element in the popular comments. Those that had been repeated to the Mayor had dealt exclusively with the question whether Julien would remain with him at six hundred francs or would accept the eight hundred francs offered by the Governor of the Poorhouse.

The said Governor, when he met M. de Rênal in society, gave him the cold shoulder. His behaviour was not without a certain subtlety; there is not much thoughtless action in the provinces: sensations are so infrequent there that people suppress them.

M. Valenod was what is called, a hundred leagues from Paris, a *faraud*; this is a species marked by coarseness and natural effrontery. His triumphant existence, since 1815, had confirmed him in his habits. He reigned, so to speak, at Verrières, under the orders of M. de Rênal; but being far more active, blushing at nothing, interfering in everything, ever-lastingly going about, writing, speaking, forgetting humili-ations, having no personal pretensions, he had succeeded in equalling the credit of his Mayor in the eyes of ecclesiastical authority. M. Valenod had as good as told the grocers of the place: 'Give me the two biggest fools among you'; the law-yers: 'Point me out the two most ignorant'; the officers of health: 'Let me have your two biggest rascals.' When he had collected the most shameless representatives of each profes-sion, he had said to them: 'Let us reign together.'

The manners of these men annoyed M. de Rênal. Vale-nod's coarse nature was offended by nothing, not even when the young abbé Maslon gave him the lie direct in public.

But, in the midst of this prosperity, M. Valenod was obliged to fortify himself by little insolences in points of detail against the harsh truths which he was well aware that everyone was entitled to address to him. His activity had multiplied since the alarms which M. Appert's visit had left in its wake. He had made three journeys to Besançon; he wrote several letters for each mail; he sent others by unknown messengers who came to his house at nightfall. He had been wrong perhaps in securing the deprivation of the old curé Chélan; for this vindictive action had made him be regarded, by several pious ladies of good birth, as a pro-foundly wicked man. Moreover this service rendered had placed him in the absolute power of the Grand Vicar de Frilair, from whom he received strange orders. He had reached this stage in his career when he yielded to the pleas-ure of writing an anonymous letter. To add to his embarrass-ment, his wife informed him that she wished to have Julien in the house; the idea appealed to her vanity.

In this situation, M. Valenod foresaw a final rupture with his former confederate M. de Rênal. The Mayor would address him in harsh language, which mattered little enough to him; but he might write to Besançon, or even to Paris. A cousin of some Minister or other might suddenly descend upon Verrières and take over the Governorship of the Poor-house. M. Valenod thought of making friends with the

Liberals; it was for this reason that several of them were invited to the dinner at which Julien recited. He would find powerful support there against the Mayor. But an election might come, and it went without saying that the Poorhouse and a vote for the wrong party were incompatible. The history of these tactics, admirably divined by Madame de Rênal, had been imparted to Julien while he gave her his arm to escort her from one shop to another, and little by little had carried them to the Cours de la Fidélité, where they spent some hours, almost as peaceful as the hours at Vergy.

At this period, M. Valenod was seeking to avoid a final rupture with his former chief, by himself adopting a bold air towards him. On the day of which we treat, this system proved successful, but increased the Mayor's ill humour.

Never can vanity, at grips with all the nastiest and shabbiest elements of a petty love of money, have plunged a man in a more wretched state than that in which M. de Rênal found himself, at the moment of his entering the tavern. Never, on the contrary, had his children been gayer or more joyful. The contrast goaded him to fury.

'I am not wanted in my own family, so far as I can see!' he said as he entered, in a tone which he sought to make imposing.

By way of reply, his wife drew him aside and explained to him the necessity of getting rid of Julien. The hours of happiness she had just enjoyed had given her back the ease and resolution necessary for carrying out the plan of conduct which she had been meditating for the last fortnight. What really and completely dismayed the poor Mayor of Verrières was that he knew that people joked publicly in the town at the expense of his attachment to *hard cash*: M. Valenod was as generous as a robber, whereas he had shewn himself in a prudent rather than a brilliant light in the last five or six subscription lists for the Confraternity of Saint Joseph, the Congregation of Our Lady, the Congregation of the Blessed Sacrament, and so forth.

Among the country gentlemen of Verrières and the neighbourhood, skilfully classified in the lists compiled by the collecting Brethren, according to the amount of their offerings, the name of M. de Rênal had more than once been seen figuring upon the lowest line. In vain might he protest that he *earned nothing*. The clergy allow no joking on that subject.

CHAPTER TWENTY-THREE
THE SORROWS OF AN OFFICIAL

Il piacere di alzar la testa tutto l'anno è ben pagato
da certi quarti d'ora che bisogna passar.

CASTI.

B UT let us leave this little man to his little fears; why
has he taken into his house a man of feeling, when
what he required was the soul of a flunkey? Why does
he not know how to select his servants? The ordinary procedure of the nineteenth century is that when a powerful and
noble personage encounters a man of feeling, he kills, exiles,
imprisons or so humiliates him that the other, like a fool,
dies of grief. In this instance it so happens that it is not yet
the man of feeling who suffers. The great misfortune of the
small towns of France and of elected governments, like that
of New York, is an inability to forget that there exist in the
world persons like M. de Rênal. In a town of twenty thousand inhabitants, these men form public opinion, and public
opinion is a terrible force in a country that has the Charter.
A man endowed with a noble soul, of generous instincts, who
would have been your friend did he not live a hundred
leagues away, judges you by the public opinion of your town,
which is formed by the fools whom chance has made noble,
rich and moderate. Woe to him who distinguishes himself!

Immediately after dinner, they set off again for Vergy; but,
two days later, Julien saw the whole family return to
Verrières.

An hour had not gone by before, greatly to his surprise,

he discovered that Madame de Rênal was making a mystery of something. She broke off her conversations with her husband as soon as he appeared, and seemed almost to wish him to go away. Julien did not wait to be told twice. He became cold and reserved; Madame de Rênal noticed this, and did not seek an explanation. 'Is she going to provide me with a successor?' thought Julien. 'Only the day before yesterday, she was so intimate with me! But they say that this is how great ladies behave. They are like kings, no one receives so much attention as the minister who, on going home, finds the letter announcing his dismissal.'

Julien remarked that in these conversations, which ceased abruptly on his approach, there was frequent mention of a big house belonging to the municipality of Verrières, old, but large and commodious, and situated opposite the church, in the most valuable quarter of the town. 'What connexion can there be between that house and a new lover?' Julien asked himself. In his distress of mind, he repeated to himself those charming lines of Francis I, which seemed to him new, because it was not a month since Madame de Rênal had taught them to him. At that time, by how many vows, by how many caresses had not each line been proved false!

> Souvent femme varie
> Bien fol est qui s'y fie.

M. de Rênal set off by post for Besançon. This journey was decided upon at two hours' notice, he seemed greatly troubled. On his return, he flung a large bundle wrapped in grey paper on the table.

'So much for that stupid business,' he said to his wife.

An hour later, Julien saw the bill-sticker carrying off this large bundle; he followed him hastily. 'I shall learn the secret at the first street corner.'

He waited impatiently behind the bill-sticker, who with his fat brush was slapping paste on the back of the bill. No sooner was it in its place than Julien's curiosity read on it the announcement in full detail of the sale by public auction of the lease of that large and old house which recurred so frequently in M. de Rênal's conversations with his wife. The assignation was announced for the following day at two o'clock, in the town hall, on the extinction of the third light. Julien was greatly disappointed; he considered the interval to be rather short: how could all the possible bidders come to know of the sale in time? But apart from this, the bill, which was dated a fortnight earlier and which he read from beginning to end in three different places, told him nothing.

He went to inspect the vacant house. The porter, who did not see him approach, was saying mysteriously to a friend:

'Bah! It's a waste of time. M. Maslon promised him he should have it for three hundred francs; and as the Mayor kicked, he was sent to the Bishop's Palace, by the Grand Vicar de Frilair.'

Julien's appearance on the scene seemed greatly to embarrass the two cronies, who did not say another word.

Julien did not fail to attend the auction. There was a crowd of people in an ill-lighted room; but everyone eyed his neighbours in a singular fashion. Every eye was fixed on a table, where Julien saw, on a pewter plate, three lighted candle-ends. The crier was shouting: 'Three hundred francs, gentlemen!'

'Three hundred francs! It is too bad!' one man murmured to another. Julien was standing between them. 'It is worth more than eight hundred; I am going to cover the bid.'

'It's cutting off your nose to spite your face. What are you going to gain by bringing M. Maslon, M. Valenod, the Bishop, his terrible Grand Vicar de Frilair and the whole of their gang down upon you?'

'Three hundred and twenty,' the other shouted.

'Stupid idiot!' retorted his neighbour. 'And here's one of the Mayor's spies,' he added pointing at Julien.

Julien turned sharply to rebuke him for this speech; but the two Franc-Comtois paid no attention to him. Their coolness restored his own. At this moment the last candle-end went out, and the drawling voice of the crier assigned the house for a lease of nine years to M. de Saint-Giraud, chief secretary at the Prefecture of ——, and for three hundred and thirty francs.

As soon as the Mayor had left the room, the discussion began.

'That's thirty francs Grogeot's imprudence has earned for the town,' said one.

'But M. de Saint-Giraud,' came the answer, 'will have his revenge on Grogeot, he will pass it on.'

'What a scandal,' said a stout man on Julien's left: 'a house for which I'd have given, myself, eight hundred francs as a factory, and then it would have been a bargain.'

'Bah!' replied a young Liberal manufacturer, 'isn't M. de Saint-Giraud one of the *Congregation*? Haven't his four children all got bursaries? Poor man! The town of Verrières is simply bound to increase his income with an allowance of five hundred francs; that is all.'

'And to think that the Mayor hasn't been able to stop it!' remarked a third. 'For he may be an ultra, if you like, but he's not a thief.'

'He's not a thief?' put in another; 'it's a regular thieves' kitchen. Everything goes into a common fund, and is divided up at the end of the year. But there's young Sorel; let us get away.'

Julien went home in the worst of tempers; he found Madame de Rênal greatly depressed.

'Have you come from the sale?' she said to him.

'Yes, Ma'am, where I had the honour to be taken for the Mayor's spy.'

'If he had taken my advice, he would have gone away somewhere.'

At that moment, M. de Rênal appeared; he was very sombre. Dinner was eaten in silence. M. de Rênal told Julien to accompany the children to Vergy; they travelled in unbroken gloom. Madame de Rênal tried to comfort her husband.

'Surely you are accustomed to it, my dear.'

That evening, they were seated in silence round the domestic hearth; the crackle of the blazing beech logs was their sole distraction. It was one of those moments of depression which are to be found in the most united families. One of the children uttered a joyful cry.

'There's the bell! The bell!'

'Egad, if it's M. de Saint-Giraud come to get hold of me, on the excuse of thanking me, I shall give him a piece of my mind; it's too bad. It's Valenod that he has to thank, and it is I who am compromised. What am I going to say if those pestilent Jacobin papers get hold of the story, and make me out a M. Nonante-Cinq?'[1]

A good-looking man, with bushy black whiskers, entered the room at this moment in the wake of the servant.

'M. le Maire, I am Signor Geronimo. Here is a letter which M. le Chevalier de Beauvaisis, attaché at the Embassy at Naples, gave me for you when I came away; it is only nine days ago,' Signor Geronimo added, with a sprightly air, looking at Madame de Rênal. 'Signor de Beauvaisis, your cousin, and my good friend, Madame, tells me that you know Italian.'

The good humour of the Neapolitan changed this dull evening into one that was extremely gay. Madame de Rênal insisted upon his taking supper. She turned the whole house upside down; she wished at all costs to distract Julien's thoughts from the description of him as a spy which twice in that day he had heard ringing in his ear. Signor Geronimo was a famous singer, a man used to good company, and at the same time the best of company himself, qualities which, in France, have almost ceased to be compatible. He sang after supper a little duet with Madame de Rênal. He told charming stories. At one o'clock in the morning the children protested when Julien proposed that they should go to bed.

'Just this story,' said the eldest.

'It is my own, Signorino,' replied Signor Geronimo. 'Eight years ago I was, like you, a young scholar in the Conser-

---

1 M. Marsan explains this allusion to a satire by Barthélemy at the expense of the Marseilles magistrate Mérindol, who in sentencing him to a fine had made use of the Common Southern expression 'Nonante-cinq' for 'Quatre-vingt-quinze.' C. K. S. M.

vatorio of Naples, by which I mean that I was your age; for I had not the honour to be the son of the eminent Mayor of the beautiful town of Verrières.'

This allusion drew a sigh from M. de Rênal, who looked at his wife.

'Signor Zingarelli,' went on the young singer, speaking with a slightly exaggerated accent which made the children burst out laughing, 'Signor Zingarelli is an exceedingly severe master. He is not loved at the Conservatorio; but he makes them act always as though they loved him. I escaped whenever I could; I used to go to the little theatre of San Carlino, where I used to hear music fit for the gods: but, O heavens, how was I to scrape together the eight soldi which were the price of admission to the pit? An enormous sum,' he said, looking at the children, and the children laughed again. 'Signor Giovannone, the Director of San Carlino, heard me sing. I was sixteen years old. "This boy is a treasure," he said.

' "Would you like me to engage you, my friend?" he said to me one day.

' "How much will you give me?"

' "Forty ducats a month." That, gentlemen, is one hundred and sixty francs. I seemed to see the heavens open.

' "But how," I said to Giovannone, "am I to persuade the strict Zingarelli to let me go?"

' "*Lascia fare a me.*" '

'Leave it to me!' cried the eldest of the children.

'Precisely, young Sir. Signor Giovannone said to me: "First of all, *caro*, a little agreement." I signed the paper: he gave me three ducats. I had never seen so much money. Then he told me what I must do.

'Next day, I demanded an interview with the terrible Signor Zingarelli. His old servant shewed me into the room.

' "What do you want with me, you scapegrace?" said Zingarelli.

' "*Maestro*," I told him, "I repent of my misdeeds; never again will I break out of the Conservatorio by climbing over the iron railings. I am going to study twice as hard."

' "If I were not afraid of spoiling the finest bass voice I

have ever heard, I should lock you up on bread and water for a fortnight, you scoundrel."

' "*Maestro*," I went on, "I am going to be a model to the whole school, *credete a me*. But I ask one favour of you, if anyone comes to ask for me to sing outside, refuse him. Please say that you cannot allow it."

' "And who do you suppose is going to ask for a good for nothing like you? Do you think I shall ever allow you to leave the Conservatorio? Do you wish to make a fool of me? Off with you, off with you!" he said, aiming a kick at my hind-quarters, "or it will be bread and water in a cell."

'An hour later, Signor Giovannone came to call on the Director.

' "I have come to ask you to make my fortune," he began, "let me have Geronimo. If he sings in my theatre this winter I marry my daughter."

' "What do you propose to do with the rascal?" Zingarelli asked him. "I won't allow it. You shan't have him; besides, even if I consented, he would never be willing to leave the Conservatorio; he's just told me so himself."

' "If his willingness is all that matters," said Giovannone gravely, producing my agreement from his pocket, "*carta canta!* Here is his signature."

'Immediately Zingarelli, furious, flew to the bell-rope: "Turn Geronimo out of the Conservatorio," he shouted, seething with rage. So out they turned me, I splitting my sides with laughter. That same evening, I sang the *aria del Moltiplico*. Pulcinella intends to marry, and counts up on his fingers the different things he will need for the house, and loses count afresh at every moment.'

'Oh, won't you, Sir, please sing us that air?' said Madame de Rênal.

Geronimo sang, and his audience all cried with laughter. Signor Geronimo did not go to bed until two in the morning, leaving the family enchanted with his good manners, his obliging nature and his gay spirits.

Next day M. and Madame de Rênal gave him the letters which he required for the French Court.

'And so, falsehood everywhere,' said Julien. 'There is Signor Geronimo on his way to London with a salary of sixty thousand francs. But for the cleverness of the Director of San Carlino, his divine voice might not have been known and admired for another ten years, perhaps.... Upon my soul, I would rather be a Geronimo than a Rênal. He is not so highly honoured in society, but he has not the humiliation of having to grant leases like that one to-day, and his is a merry life.'

One thing astonished Julien: the weeks of solitude spent at Verrières, in M. de Rênal's house, had been for him a time of happiness. He had encountered disgust and gloomy thoughts only at the dinners to which he had been invited; in that empty house, was he not free to read, write, meditate, undisturbed? He had not been aroused at every moment from his radiant dreams by the cruel necessity of studying the motions of a base soul, and that in order to deceive it by hypocritical words or actions.

'Could happiness be thus within my reach? ... The cost of such a life is nothing; I can, as I choose, marry Miss Elisa, or become Fouqué's partner.... But the traveller who has just climbed a steep mountain, sits down on the summit, and finds a perfect pleasure in resting. Would he be happy if he were forced to rest always?'

Madame de Rênal's mind was a prey to carking thoughts. In spite of her resolve to the contrary, she had revealed to Julien the whole business of the lease. 'So he will make me forget all my vows!' she thought.

She would have given her life without hesitation to save that of her husband, had she seen him in peril. Hers was one of those noble and romantic natures, for which to see the possibility of a generous action, and not to perform it gives rise to a remorse almost equal to that which one feels for a past crime. Nevertheless, there were dreadful days on which she could not banish the thought of the absolute happiness which she would enjoy, if, suddenly left a widow, she were free to marry Julien.

He loved her children far more than their father; in spite

of his strict discipline, he was adored by them. She was well aware that, if she married Julien, she would have to leave this Vergy whose leafy shade was so dear to her. She pictured herself living in Paris, continuing to provide her sons with that education at which everyone marvelled. Her children, she herself, Julien, all perfectly happy.

A strange effect of marriage, such as the nineteenth century has made it! The boredom of married life inevitably destroys love, when love has preceded marriage. And yet, as a philosopher has observed, it speedily brings about, among people who are rich enough not to have to work, an intense boredom with all quiet forms of enjoyment. And it is only dried up hearts, among women, that it does not predispose to love.

The philosopher's observation makes me excuse Madame de Rênal, but there was no excuse for her at Verrières, and the whole town, without her suspecting it, was exclusively occupied with the scandal of her love. Thanks to this great scandal, people that autumn were less bored than usual.

The autumn, the first weeks of winter had soon come and gone. It was time to leave the woods of Vergy. The high society of Verrières began to grow indignant that its anathemas were making so little impression upon M. de Rênal. In less than a week, certain grave personages who made up for their habitual solemnity by giving themselves the pleasure of fulfilling missions of this sort, implanted in him the most cruel suspicions, but without going beyond the most measured terms.

M. Valenod, who was playing a close game, had placed Elisa with a noble and highly respected family, which included five women. Elisa fearing, she said, that she might not find a place during the winter, had asked this family for only about two thirds of what she was receiving at the Mayor's. Of her own accord, the girl had the excellent idea of going to confess to the retired curé Chélan as well as to the new curé, so as to be able to give them both a detailed account of Julien's amours.

On the morning after his return, at six o'clock, the abbé Chélan sent for Julien:

'I ask you nothing,' he said to him; 'I beg you, and if need be order you to tell me nothing, I insist that within three days you leave either for the Seminary at Besançon or for the house of your friend Fouqué, who is still willing to provide a splendid career for you. I have foreseen and settled everything, but you must go, and not return to Verrières for a year.'

Julien made no answer; he was considering whether his honour ought to take offence at the arrangements which M. Chélan, who after all was not his father, had made for him.

'To-morrow at this hour I shall have the honour of seeing you again,' he said at length to the curé.

M. Chélan, who reckoned upon overcoming the young man by main force, spoke volubly. His attitude, his features composed in the utmost humility, Julien did not open his mouth.

At length he made his escape, and hastened to inform Madame de Rênal, whom he found in despair. Her husband had just been speaking to her with a certain frankness. The natural weakness of his character, seeking encouragement in the prospect of the inheritance from Besançon, had made him decide to regard her as entirely innocent. He had just confessed to her the strange condition in which he found public opinion at Verrières. The public were wrong, had been led astray by envious ill-wishers, but what was to be done?

Madame de Rênal had the momentary illusion that Julien might be able to accept M. Valenod's offer, and remain at Verrières. But she was no longer the simple, timid woman of the previous year; her fatal passion, her spells of remorse had enlightened her. Soon she had to bear the misery of proving to herself, while she listened to her husband, that a separation, at any rate for the time being, was now inevitable. 'Away from me, Julien will drift back into those ambitious projects that are so natural when one has nothing. And I, great God! I am so rich, and so powerless to secure my own happiness! He will forget me. Charming as he is, he will be loved, he will love. Ah, unhappy woman! Of what can I complain?

Heaven is just, I have not acquired merit by putting a stop to my crime; it blinds my judgment. It rested with me alone to win over Elisa with a bribe, nothing would have been easier. I did not take the trouble to reflect for a moment, the wild imaginings of love absorbed all my time. And now I perish.'

One thing struck Julien; as he conveyed to Madame de Rênal the terrible news of his departure, he was met with no selfish objection. Evidently she was making an effort not to cry.

'We require firmness, my friend.'

She cut off a lock of his hair.

'I do not know what is to become of me,' she said to him, 'but if I die, promise me that you will never forget my children. Far or near, try to make them grow up honourable men. If there is another revolution, all the nobles will be murdered, their father may emigrate, perhaps, because of that peasant who was killed upon a roof. Watch over the family.... Give me your hand. Farewell, my friend! These are our last moments together. This great sacrifice made, I hope that in public I shall have the courage to think of my reputation.'

Julien had been expecting despair. The simplicity of this farewell touched him.

'No, I do not accept your farewell thus. I shall go; they wish it; you wish it yourself. But, three days after my departure, I shall return to visit you by night.'

Madame de Rênal's existence was changed. So Julien really did love her since he had had the idea, of his own accord, of seeing her again. Her bitter grief changed into one of the keenest bursts of joy that she had ever felt in her life. Everything became easy to her. The certainty of seeing her lover again took from these last moments all their lacerating force. From that instant the conduct, like the features of Madame de Rênal was noble, firm, and perfectly conventional.

M. de Rênal presently returned; he was beside himself. For the first time he mentioned to his wife the anonymous letter which he had received two months earlier.

'I intend to take it to the Casino, to shew them all that it comes from that wretch Valenod, whom I picked up out of the gutter and made into one of the richest citizens of Verrières. I shall disgrace him publicly, and then fight him. It is going too far.'

'I might be left a widow, great God!' thought Madame de Rênal. But almost at the same instant she said to herself: 'If I do not prevent this duel, as I certainly can, I shall be my husband's murderess.'

Never before had she handled his vanity with so much skill. In less than two hours she made him see, always by the use of arguments that had occurred first to him, that he must shew himself friendlier than ever towards M. Valenod, and even take Elisa into the house again. Madame de Rênal required courage to make up her mind to set eyes on this girl, the cause of all her troubles. But the idea had come to her from Julien.

Finally, after having been set three or four times in the right direction, M. de Rênal arrived of his own accord at the idea (highly distressing, from the financial point of view) that the most unpleasant thing that could happen for himself was that Julien, amid the seething excitement and gossip of the whole of Verrières, should remain there as tutor to M. Valenod's children. It was obviously in Julien's interest to accept the offer made him by the Governor of the Poorhouse. It was essential however to M. de Rênal's fair fame that Julien should leave Verrières to enter the seminary at Besançon or at Dijon. But how was he to be made to agree, and after that how was he to maintain himself there?

M. de Rênal, seeing the imminence of a pecuniary sacrifice, was in greater despair than his wife. For her part, after this conversation, she was in the position of a man of feeling who, weary of life, has taken a dose of *stramonium*; he ceases to act, save, so to speak, automatically, and no longer takes an interest in anything. Thus Louis XIV on his deathbed was led to say: 'When I was king.' An admirable speech!

On the morrow, at break of day, M. de Rênal received an anonymous letter. It was couched in the most insulting style.

The coarsest words applicable to his position stared from every line. It was the work of some envious subordinate. This letter brought him back to the thought of fighting a duel with M. Valenod. Soon his courage had risen to the idea of an immediate execution of his design. He left the house unaccompanied, and went to the gunsmith's to procure a brace of pistols, which he told the man to load.

'After all,' he said to himself, 'should the drastic rule of the Emperor Napoleon be restored, I myself could not be charged with the misappropriation of a half-penny. At the most I have shut my eyes; but I have plenty of letters in my desk authorizing me to do so.'

Madame de Rênal was frightened by her husband's cold anger, it brought back to her mind the fatal thought of widowhood, which she found it so hard to banish. She shut herself up with him. For hours on end she pleaded with him in vain, the latest anonymous letter had determined him. At length she succeeded in transforming the courage required to strike M. Valenod into that required to offer Julien six hundred francs for his maintenance for one year in a Seminary. M. de Rênal, heaping a thousand curses on the day on which he had conceived the fatal idea of taking a tutor into his household, forgot the anonymous letter.

He found a grain of comfort in an idea which he did not communicate to his wife: by skilful handling, and by taking advantage of the young man's romantic ideas, he hoped to bind him, for a smaller sum, to refuse M. Valenod's offers.

Madame de Rênal found it far harder to prove to Julien that, if he sacrificed to her husband's convenience a post worth eight hundred francs, publicly offered him by the Governor of the Poorhouse, he might without blushing accept some compensation.

'But,' Julien continued to object, 'I have never had, even for a moment, the slightest thought of accepting that offer. You have made me too familiar with a life of refinement, the vulgarity of those people would kill me.'

Cruel necessity, with its hand of iron, bent Julien's will. His pride offered him the self-deception of accepting only as a loan the sum offered by the Mayor of Verrières, and giving him a note of hand promising repayment with interest after five years.

Madame de Rênal had still some thousands of francs hidden in the little cave in the mountains.

She offered him these, trembling, and feeling only too sure that they would be rejected with fury.

'Do you wish,' Julien asked her, 'to make the memory of our love abominable?'

At length Julien left Verrières. M. de Rênal was overjoyed; at the decisive moment of accepting money from him, this sacrifice proved to be too great for Julien. He refused pointblank. M. de Rênal fell upon his neck, with tears in his eyes. Julien having asked him for a testimonial to his character, he could not in his enthusiasm find terms laudatory enough to extol the young man's conduct. Our hero had saved up five louis, and intended to ask Fouqué for a similar amount.

He was greatly moved. But when he had gone a league from Verrières, where he was leaving such a treasure of love behind him, he thought only of the pleasure of seeing a capital, a great military centre like Besançon.

During this short parting of three days, Madame de Rênal was duped by one of love's most cruel illusions. Her life was tolerable enough, there was between her and the last extremes of misery this final meeting that she was still to have with Julien. She counted the hours, the minutes that divided her from it. Finally, during the night that followed the third day, she heard in the distance the signal arranged between them. Having surmounted a thousand perils, Julien appeared before her.

From that moment, she had but a single thought: 'I am looking at you now for the last time.' Far from responding to her lover's eagerness, she was like a barely animated corpse. If she forced herself to tell him that she loved him, it was with an awkward air that was almost a proof to the contrary. Nothing could take her mind from the cruel thought of eternal separation. The suspicious Julien fancied for a moment that she had already forgotten him. His hints at such a possibility were received only with huge tears that flowed in silence, and with a convulsive pressure of his hand.

'But, Great God! How do you expect me to believe you?' was Julien's reply to his mistress's chill protestations. 'You would shew a hundred times more of sincere affection to Madame Derville, to a mere acquaintance.'

Madame de Rênal, petrified, did not know how to answer.

'It would be impossible for a woman to be more wretched.... I hope I am going to die.... I feel my heart freezing....'

Such were the longest answers he was able to extract from her.

When the approach of day made his departure necessary, Madame de Rênal's tears ceased all at once. She saw him fasten a knotted cord to the window without saying a word, without returning his kisses. In vain might Julien say to her:

'At last we have reached the state for which you so longed. Henceforward you will live without remorse. At the slightest indisposition of one of your children, you will no longer see them already in the grave.'

'I am sorry you could not say good-bye to Stanislas,' she said to him coldly.

In the end, Julien was deeply impressed by the embraces, in which there was no warmth, of this living corpse; he could think of nothing else for some leagues. His spirit was crushed, and before crossing the pass, so long as he was able to see the steeple of Verrières church, he turned round often.

CHAPTER TWENTY-FOUR

A CAPITAL

> Que de bruit, que de gens affairés! que d'idées pour
> l'avenir dans une tête de vingt ans! quelle distraction
> pour l'amour!
>
> BARNAVE.

AT length he made out, on a distant mountain, a line of
dark walls; it was the citadel of Besançon. 'How
different for me,' he said with a sigh, 'if I were arriving in this noble fortress to be a sub-lieutenant in one of the
regiments entrusted with its defence!'

Besançon is not merely one of the most charming towns
in France, it abounds in men and women of feeling and
spirit. But Julien was only a young peasant and had no way
of approaching the distinguished people.

He had borrowed from Fouqué a layman's coat, and it
was in this attire that he crossed the drawbridges. His mind
full of the history of the siege of 1674, he was determined to
visit, before shutting himself up in the Seminary, the ramparts and the citadel. More than once, he was on the point
of being arrested by the sentries for making his way into
places from which the engineers of the garrison excluded the
public, in order to make a profit of twelve or fifteen francs
every year by the sale of the hay grown there.

The height of the walls, the depth of the moats, the awe-
inspiring appearance of the guns had occupied him for some
hours, when he happened to pass by the principal café, on
the boulevard. He stood speechless with admiration; albeit

he could read the word Café inscribed in huge letters over the two vast doors, he could not believe his eyes. He made an effort to master his timidity; he ventured to enter, and found himself in a hall thirty or forty feet long, the ceiling of which rose to a height of at least twenty feet. On this day of days everything wore an air of enchantment for him.

Two games of billiards were in progress. The waiters were calling out the scores; the players hurried round the tables through a crowd of onlookers. Streams of tobacco smoke, pouring from every mouth, enveloped them in a blue haze. The tall stature of these men, their rounded shoulders, their heavy gait, their bushy whiskers, the long frock coats that covered their bodies, all attracted Julien's attention. These noble sons of the ancient Bisontium conversed only in shouts; they gave themselves the air of tremendous warriors. Julien stood spellbound in admiration; he was thinking of the vastness and splendour of a great capital like Besançon. He felt that he could not possibly summon up courage to ask for a cup of coffee from one of those gentlemen with the proud gaze who were marking the score at billiards.

But the young lady behind the counter had remarked the charming appearance of this young country cousin, who, brought to a standstill three paces from the stove, hugging his little bundle under his arm, was studying the bust of the King, in gleaming white plaster. This young lady, a strapping Franc-Comtoise, extremely well made, and dressed in the style calculated to give tone to a café, had already said twice, in a low voice so modulated that only Julien should hear her: 'Sir! Sir!' Julien's gaze met that of a pair of the most tender blue eyes, and saw that it was himself who was being addressed.

He stepped briskly up to the counter and the pretty girl, as he might have advanced in the face of the enemy. As he executed this great movement, his bundle fell to the ground.

What pity will not our provincial inspire in the young scholars of Paris, who at fifteen, have already learned how to enter a café with so distinguished an air! But these children, so stylish at fifteen, at eighteen begin to turn *common*.

The passionate shyness which one meets in the provinces now and then overcomes itself, and then teaches its victim to desire. As he approached this beautiful girl who had deigned to speak to him, 'I must tell her the truth,' thought Julien, who was growing courageous by dint of his conquered shyness.

'Madame, I have come for the first time in my life to Besançon; I should like to have, and to pay for, a roll of bread and a cup of coffee.'

The girl smiled a little and then blushed; she feared, for this good-looking young man, the satirical attention and witticisms of the billiard players. He would be frightened and would never shew his face there again.

'Sit down here, near me,' she said, and pointed to a marble table, almost entirely hidden by the enormous mahogany counter which protruded into the room.

The young woman leaned over this counter, which gave her an opportunity to display a superb figure. Julien observed this; all his ideas altered. The pretty girl had just set before him a cup, some sugar and a roll of bread. She hesitated before calling to a waiter for coffee, realizing that on the arrival of the said waiter her private conversation with Julien would be at an end.

Julien, lost in thought, was comparing this fair and sprightly beauty with certain memories which often stirred him. The thought of the passion of which he had been the object took from him almost all his timidity. The pretty girl had only a moment; she read the expression in Julien's eyes.

'This pipe smoke makes you cough, come to breakfast to-morrow before eight o'clock; at that time, I am almost alone.'

'What is your name?' said Julien, with the caressing smile of happy timidity.

'Amanda Binet.'

'Will you permit me to send you, in an hour's time, a little parcel no bigger than this?'

The fair Amanda reflected for a while.

'I am watched: what you ask may compromise me; however, I am now going to write down my address upon a card, which you can attach to your parcel. Send it to me without fear.'

'My name is Julien Sorel,' said the young man. 'I have neither family nor friends in Besançon.'

'Ah! Now I understand,' she exclaimed joyfully, 'you have come for the law school?'

'Alas, no!' replied Julien; 'they are sending me to the Seminary.'

The most complete discouragement extinguished the light in Amanda's features; she called a waiter: she had the necessary courage now. The waiter poured out Julien's coffee, without looking at him.

Amanda was taking money at the counter; Julien prided himself on having ventured to speak to her: there was a dispute in progress at one of the billiard tables. The shouts and contradictions of the players, echoing through that vast hall, made a din which astonished Julien. Amanda was pensive and did not raise her eyes.

'If you like, Mademoiselle,' he said to her suddenly with assurance, 'I can say that I am your cousin.'

This little air of authority delighted Amanda. 'This is no good-for-nothing young fellow,' she thought. She said to him very quickly, without looking at him, for her eye was occupied in watching whether anyone were approaching the counter:

'I come from Genlis, near Dijon; say that you are from Genlis too, and my mother's cousin.'

'I shall not forget.'

'On Thursdays, at five o'clock, in summer, the young gentlemen from the Seminary come past the café here.'

'If you are thinking of me, when I pass, have a bunch of violets in your hand.'

Amanda gazed at him with an air of astonishment; this gaze changed Julien's courage into temerity; he blushed deeply, however, as he said to her:

'I feel that I love you with the most violent love.'

'Don't speak so loud, then,' she warned him with an air of alarm.

Julien thought of trying to recollect the language of an odd volume of the *Nouvelle Héloïse*, which he had found at Vergy. His memory served him well; he had been for ten minutes reciting the *Nouvelle Héloïse* to Miss Amanda, who was in ecstasies; he was delighted with his own courage, when suddenly the fair Franc-Comtoise assumed a glacial air. One of her admirers stood in the doorway of the café.

He came up to the counter, whistling and swaying his shoulders; he stared at Julien. For the moment, the latter's imagination, always flying to extremes, was filled entirely with thoughts of a duel. He turned deadly pale, thrust away his cup, assumed an air of assurance and studied his rival most attentively. While this rival's head was lowered as he familiarly poured himself out a glass of brandy upon the counter, with a glance Amanda ordered Julien to lower his gaze. He obeyed, and for a minute or two sat motionless in his place, pale, determined, and thinking only of what was going to happen; he was really fine at that moment. The rival had been astonished by Julien's eyes; his glass of brandy drained at a gulp, he said a few words to Amanda, thrust his hands into the side pockets of his ample coat, and made his way to one of the billiard tables, breathing loudly and staring at Julien. The latter sprang to his feet in a transport of rage; but did not know what action to take to be insulting. He laid down his little bundle and, with the most swaggering gait that he could assume, strode towards the billiard table.

In vain did prudence warn him: 'With a duel on the day of your arrival at Besançon, your career in the church is gone for ever.'

'What does that matter, it shall never be said that I quailed before an insult.'

Amanda observed his courage; it formed a charming contrast with the simplicity of his manners; in an instant, she preferred him to the big young man in the long coat. She rose, and, while appearing to be following with her eyes the movements of someone going by in the street, took her place swiftly between him and the billiard table.

'You are not to look askance at that gentleman; he is my brother-in-law.'

'What do I care? He looked at me.'

'Do you wish to get me into trouble? No doubt, he looked at you, perhaps he will even come up and speak to you. I have told him that you are one of my mother's family and that you have just come from Genlis. He is a Franc-Comtois and has never been farther than Dôle, on the road into Burgundy; so tell him whatever you like, don't be afraid.'

Julien continued to hesitate; she added rapidly, her barmaid's imagination supplying her with falsehoods in abundance:

'I dare say he did look at you, but it was when he was asking me who you were; he is a man who is rude with everyone, he didn't mean to insult you.'

Julien's eye followed the alleged brother-in-law; he saw him buy a number in the pool which was beginning at the farther of the two billiard tables. Julien heard his loud voice exclaim: 'I volunteer!' He passed nimbly behind Miss Amanda's back and took a step towards the billiard table. Amanda seized him by the arm.

'Come and pay me first,' she said to him.

'Quite right,' thought Julien; 'she is afraid I may leave without paying.' Amanda was as greatly agitated as himself, and had turned very red; she counted out his change as slowly as she could, repeating to him in a whisper as she did so:

'Leave the café this instant, or I shan't like you any more; I do like you, though, very much.'

Julien did indeed leave, but slowly. 'Is it not incumbent upon me,' he repeated to himself, 'to go and stare at that rude person in my turn, and breathe in his face?' This uncertainty detained him for an hour on the boulevard, outside the café; he watched to see if his man came out. He did not however appear, and Julien withdrew.

He had been but a few hours in Besançon, and already he had something to regret. The old Surgeon-Major had long ago, notwithstanding his gout, taught him a few lessons in fencing; this was all the science that Julien could place at the service of his anger. But this embarrassment would have been nothing if he had known how to pick a quarrel otherwise than by striking a blow; and, if they had come to fisticuffs, his rival, a giant of a man, would have beaten him and left him discomfited.

'For a poor devil like me,' thought Julien, 'without protectors and without money, there will be no great difference between a Seminary and a prison; I must leave my lay clothes in some inn, where I can put on my black coat. If I ever succeed in escaping from the Seminary for an hour or two, I can easily, in my lay clothes, see Miss Amanda again.' This was sound reasoning; but Julien, as he passed by all the inns in turn, had not the courage to enter any of them.

Finally, as he came again to the Hôtel des Ambassadeurs, his roving gaze met that of a stout woman, still reasonably young, with a high complexion, a happy and gay expression. He went up to her and told her his story.

'Certainly, my fine young priest,' the landlady of the Ambassadeurs said to him, 'I shall keep your lay clothes for you, indeed I will have them brushed regularly. In this weather, it is a mistake to leave a broadcloth coat lying.' She took a key and led him herself to a bedroom, advising him to write down a list of what he was leaving behind.

'Lord, how nice you look like that, M. l'abbé Sorel,' said the stout woman, when he came down to the kitchen. 'I am going to order you a good dinner; and,' she added in an undertone, 'it will only cost you twenty sous, instead of the fifty people generally pay; for you must be careful with your little purse.'

'I have ten louis,' retorted Julien with a certain note of pride.

'Oh, good Lord!' replied the good landlady in alarm, 'do not speak so loud; there are plenty of bad folk in Besançon. They will have that out of you in less than no time. Whatever you do, never go into the cafés, they are full of rogues.'

'Indeed!' said Julien, to whom this last statement gave food for thought.

'Never go anywhere except to me, I will give you your coffee. Bear in mind that you will always find a friend here and a good dinner for twenty sous; that's good enough for you, I hope. Go and sit down at the table, I am going to serve you myself.'

'I should not be able to eat,' Julien told her. 'I am too much excited, I am going to enter the Seminary as soon as I leave here.'

The good woman would not allow him to leave until she had stuffed his pockets with provisions. Finally Julien set out for the dread spot, the landlady from her doorstep pointing out the way.

CHAPTER TWENTY-FIVE

THE SEMINARY

Three hundred and thirty-six dinners at 83 centimes,
three hundred and thirty-six suppers at 38 centimes,
chocolate to such as are entitled to it; how much is
there to be made on the contract?

The VALENOD *of* BESANÇON.

H E saw from a distance the cross of gilded iron over
the door; he went towards it slowly; his legs seemed
to be giving way under him. 'So there is that hell
upon earth, from which I can never escape!' Finally he
decided to ring. The sound of the bell echoed as though in
a deserted place. After ten minutes, a pale man dressed in
black came and opened the door to him. Julien looked at
him and at once lowered his gaze. This porter had a singular
physiognomy. The prominent green pupils of his eyes were
convex as those of a cat's; the unwinking contours of his
eyelids proclaimed the impossibility of any human feeling;
his thin lips were stretched and curved over his protruding
teeth. And yet this physiognomy did not suggest a criminal
nature, so much as that entire insensibility which inspires far
greater terror in the young. The sole feeling that Julien's
rapid glance could discern in that long, smug face was a
profound contempt for every subject that might be mentioned to him, which did not refer to another and a better
world.

Julien raised his eyes with an effort, and in a voice which
the palpitation of his heart made tremulous explained that he

wished to speak to M. Pirard, the Director of the Seminary. Without a word, the man in black made a sign to him to follow. They climbed two flights of a wide staircase with a wooden baluster, the warped steps of which sloped at a downward angle from the wall, and seemed on the point of collapse. A small door, surmounted by a large graveyard cross of white wood painted black, yielded to pressure and the porter shewed him into a low and gloomy room, the whitewashed walls of which were adorned with two large pictures dark with age. There, Julien was left to himself; he was terrified, his heart throbbed violently; he would have liked to find the courage to weep. A deathly silence reigned throughout the building.

After a quarter of an hour, which seemed to him a day, the sinister porter reappeared on the threshold of a door at the other end of the room, and, without condescending to utter a word, beckoned to him to advance. He entered a room even larger than the first and very badly lighted. The walls of this room were whitewashed also; but they were bare of ornament. Only in a corner by the door, Julien noticed in passing a bed of white wood, two straw chairs and a little armchair made of planks of firwood without a cushion. At the other end of the room, near a small window with dingy panes, decked with neglected flowerpots, he saw a man seated at a table and dressed in a shabby cassock; he appeared to be in a rage, and was taking one after another from a pile of little sheets of paper which he spread out on his table after writing a few words on each. He did not observe Julien's presence. The latter remained motionless, standing in the middle of the room, where he had been left by the porter, who had gone out again shutting the door behind him.

Ten minutes passed in this fashion; the shabbily dressed man writing all the time. Julien's emotion and terror were such that he felt himself to be on the point of collapsing. A philosopher would have said, perhaps wrongly: 'It is the violent impression made by ugliness on a soul created to love what is beautiful.'

The man who was writing raised his head; Julien did not observe this for a moment, and indeed, after he had noticed it, still remained motionless, as though turned to stone by the terrible gaze that was fixed on him. Julien's swimming eyes could barely make out a long face covered all over with red spots, except on the forehead, which displayed a deathly pallor. Between the red cheeks and white forehead shone a pair of little black eyes calculated to inspire terror in the bravest heart. The vast expanse of his forehead was outlined by a mass of straight hair, as black as jet.

'Are you coming nearer, or not?' the man said at length impatiently.

Julien advanced with an uncertain step, and at length, ready to fall to the ground and paler than he had ever been in his life, came to a halt a few feet away from the little table of white wood covered with scraps of paper.

'Nearer,' said the man.

Julien advanced farther, stretching out his hand as though in search of something to lean upon.

'Your name?'

'Julien Sorel.'

'You are very late,' said the other, once more fastening upon him a terrible eye.

Julien could not endure this gaze; putting out his hand as though to support himself, he fell full length upon the floor.

The man rang a bell. Julien had lost only his sense of vision and the strength to move; he could hear footsteps approaching.

He was picked up and placed in the little armchair of white wood. He heard the terrible man say to the porter:

'An epileptic, evidently; I might have known it.'

When Julien was able to open his eyes, the man with the red face was again writing; the porter had vanished. 'I must have courage,' our hero told himself, 'and above all hide my feelings.' He felt a sharp pain at his heart. 'If I am taken ill, heaven knows what they will think of me.' At length the man stopped writing, and with a sidelong glance at Julien asked:

'Are you in a fit state to answer my questions?'

'Yes, Sir,' said Julien in a feeble voice.

'Ah! That is fortunate.'

The man in black had half risen and was impatiently seeking for a letter in the drawer of his table of firwood which opened with a creak. He found it, slowly resumed his seat, and once more gazing at Julien, with an air which seemed to wrest from him the little life that remained to him:

'You are recommended to me by M. Chélan, who was the best curé in the diocese, a good man if ever there was one, and my friend for the last thirty years.'

'Ah! It is M. Pirard that I have the honour to address,' said Julien in a feeble voice.

'So it seems,' said the Director of the Seminary, looking sourly at him.

The gleam in his little eyes brightened, followed by an involuntary jerk of the muscles round his mouth. It was the physiognomy of a tiger relishing in anticipation the pleasure of devouring its prey.

'Chélan's letter is short,' he said, as though speaking to himself. '*Intelligenti pauca*; in these days, one cannot write too little.' He read aloud:

' "I send you Julien Sorel, of this parish, whom I baptized nearly twenty years ago; his father is a wealthy carpenter but allows him nothing. Julien will be a noteworthy labourer in the Lord's vineyard. Memory, intelligence are not wanting, he has the power of reflexion. Will his vocation last? Is it sincere?"

'*Sincere!*' repeated the abbé Pirard with an air of surprise, gazing at Julien; but this time the abbé's gaze was less devoid of all trace of humanity. '*Sincere!*' he repeated, lowering his voice and returning to the letter:

' "I ask you for a bursary for Julien; he will qualify for it by undergoing the necessary examinations. I have taught him a little divinity, that old and sound divinity of Bossuet, Arnault, Fleury. If the young man is not to your liking, send him back to me; the Governor of our Poorhouse, whom you know well, offers him eight hundred francs to come as tutor to his children. Inwardly I am calm, thank God. I am growing accustomed to the terrible blow. *Vale et me ama.*" '

The abbé Pirard, relaxing the speed of his utterance as he came to the signature, breathed with a sigh the word 'Chélan.'

'He is calm,' he said; 'indeed, his virtue deserved that reward; God grant it to me, when my time comes!'

He looked upwards and made the sign of the Cross. At the sight of this holy symbol Julien felt a slackening of the profound horror which, from his entering the building, had frozen him.

'I have here three hundred and twenty-one aspirants for the holiest of callings,' the abbé Pirard said at length, in a severe but not hostile tone; 'only seven or eight have been recommended to me by men like the abbé Chélan; thus among the three hundred and twenty-one you will be the ninth. But my protection is neither favour nor weakness, it is an increase of precaution and severity against vice. Go and lock that door.'

Julien made an effort to walk and managed not to fall. He noticed that a little window, near the door by which he had entered, commanded a view of the country. He looked at the trees; the sight of them did him good, as though he had caught sight of old friends.

'*Loquerisne linguam latinam?* (Do you speak Latin?)' the abbé Pirard asked him as he returned.

'*Ita, pater optime* (Yes, excellent Father),' replied Julien, who was beginning to come to himself. Certainly nobody in the world had appeared to him less excellent than M. Pirard, during the last half-hour.

The conversation continued in Latin. The expression in the abbé's eyes grew gentler; Julien recovered a certain coolness. 'How weak I am,' he thought, 'to let myself be imposed upon by this shew of virtue! This man will be simply a rascal like M. Maslon'; and Julien congratulated himself on having hidden almost all his money in his boots.

The abbé Pirard examined Julien in theology, and was surprised by the extent of his knowledge. His astonishment increased when he questioned him more particularly on the Holy Scriptures. But when he came to questions touching the doctrine of the Fathers, he discovered that Julien barely knew the names of Saint Jerome, Saint Augustine, Saint Bonaventure, Saint Basil, etc., etc.

'In fact,' thought the abbé Pirard, 'here is another instance of that fatal tendency towards Protestantism which I have always had to rebuke in Chélan. A thorough, a too thorough acquaintance with the Holy Scriptures.'

(Julien had just spoken to him, without having been questioned on the subject, of the *true* date of authorship of Genesis, the Pentateuch, etc.)

'To what does all this endless discussion of the Holy Scriptures lead,' thought the abbé Pirard, 'if not to *private judgment*, that is to say to the most fearful Protestantism? And, in conjunction with this rash learning, nothing about the Fathers that can compensate for this tendency.'

But the astonishment of the Director of the Seminary knew no bounds when, questioning Julien as to the authority of the Pope, and expecting the maxims of the ancient Gallican church, he heard the young man repeat the whole of M. de Maistre's book.

'A strange man, Chélan,' thought the abbé Pirard; 'has he given him this book to teach him to laugh at it?'

In vain did he question Julien, trying to discover whether he seriously believed the doctrine of M. de Maistre. The young man could answer him only by rote. From this moment, Julien was really admirable, he felt that he was master of himself. After a prolonged examination it seemed to him that M. Pirard's severity towards him was no more than an affectation. Indeed, but for the rule of austere gravity which, for the last fifteen years, he had imposed on himself in dealing with his pupils in theology, the Director of the Seminary would have embraced Julien in the name of logic, such clarity, precision, and point did he find in the young man's answers.

'This is a bold and healthy mind,' he said to himself, 'but *corpus debile* (a frail body).

'Do you often fall like that?' he asked Julien in French, pointing with his finger to the floor.

'It was the first time in my life; the sight of the porter's face paralysed me,' Julien explained, colouring like a child.

The abbé Pirard almost smiled.

'Such is the effect of the vain pomps of this world; you are evidently accustomed to smiling faces, positive theatres of falsehood. The truth is austere, Sir. But is not our task here below austere also? You will have to see that your conscience is on its guard against this weakness: *Undue sensibility to vain outward charms.*

'Had you not been recommended to me,' said the abbé Pirard, returning with marked pleasure to the Latin tongue, 'had you not been recommended to me by a man such as the abbé Chélan, I should address you in the vain language of this world to which it appears that you are too well accustomed. The entire bursary for which you apply is, I may tell you, the hardest thing in the world to obtain. But the abbé Chélan has earned little, by fifty-six years of apostolic labours, if he cannot dispose of a bursary at the Seminary.'

After saying these words, the abbé Pirard advised Julien not to join any secret society or congregation without his consent.

'I give you my word of honour,' said Julien with the heart-felt warmth of an honest man.

The Director of the Seminary smiled for the first time.

'That expression is not in keeping here,' he told him; 'it is too suggestive of the vain honour of men of the world, which leads them into so many errors and often into crime. You owe me obedience in virtue of the seventeenth paragraph of the Bull *Unam Ecclesiam* of Saint Pius V. I am your ecclesiastical superior. In this house to hear, my dearly beloved son, is to obey. How much money have you?'

('Now we come to the point,' thought Julien, 'this is the reason of the "dearly beloved son."')

'Thirty-five francs, Father.'

'Keep a careful note of how you spend your money; you will have to account for it to me.'

This exhausting interview had lasted three hours. Julien was told to summon the porter.

'Put Julien Sorel in cell number 103,' the abbé Pirard told the man.

As a special favour, he was giving Julien a room to himself. 'Take up his trunk,' he added.

Julien lowered his eyes and saw his trunk staring him in the face; he had been looking at it for three hours and had never seen it.

On arriving at No. 103, which was a tiny room eight feet square on the highest floor of the building, Julien observed that it looked out towards the ramparts, beyond which one saw the smiling plain which the Doubs divides from the city.

'What a charming view!' exclaimed Julien; in speaking thus to himself he was not conscious of the feeling implied by his words. The violent sensations he had experienced in the short time that he had spent in Besançon had completely drained his strength. He sat down by the window on the solitary wooden chair that was in his cell, and at once fell into a profound slumber. He did not hear the supper bell, nor that for Benediction; he had been forgotten.

When the first rays of the sun awakened him next morning, he found himself lying upon the floor.

CHAPTER TWENTY-SIX

THE WORLD, OR WHAT THE RICH LACK

Je suis seul sur la terre, personne ne daigne penser à
moi. Tous ceux que je vois faire fortune ont une effron-
terie et une dureté de cœur que je ne me sens point.
Ils me naïssent à cause de ma bonté facile. Ah! bientôt
je mourrai, soit de faim, soit du malheur de voir les
hommes si durs.

YOUNG.[1]

H E made haste to brush his coat and to go downstairs;
he was late. An under-master rebuked him severely;
instead of seeking to excuse himself, Julien crossed
his arms on his breast:

'*Peccavi, pater optime,*' he said with a contrite air.

This was a most successful beginning. The sharp wits
among the seminarists saw that they had to deal with a man
who was not new to the game. The recreation hour came,
Julien saw himself the object of general curiosity. But they
found in him merely reserve and silence. Following the
maxims that he had laid down for himself, he regarded his
three hundred and twenty-one comrades as so many enemies; the most dangerous of all in his eyes was the abbé Pirard.

A few days later, Julien had to choose a confessor, he was
furnished with a list.

'Eh; Great God, for what do they take me?' he said to

1 I leave this motto in French as quoted by Stendhal, having failed to trace the
original passage, which may be from one of the works of Edward Young (1681–
1765). C. K. S. M.

202

himself. 'Do they suppose I can't take a hint?' And he chose the abbé Pirard.

Though he did not suspect it, this step was decisive. A little seminarist, still quite a boy, and a native of Verrières, who, from the first day, had declared himself his friend, informed him that if he had chosen M. Castanède, the vice-principal of the Seminary, he would perhaps have shewn greater prudence.

'The abbé Castanède is the enemy of M. Pirard, who is suspected of Jansenism'; the little seminarist added, whispering this information in his ear.

All the first steps taken by our hero who fancied himself so prudent were, like his choice of a confessor, foolish in the extreme. Led astray by all the presumption of an imaginative man, he mistook his intentions for facts, and thought himself a consummate hypocrite. His folly went the length of his reproaching himself for his successes in this art of the weak.

'Alas! It is my sole weapon! In another epoch, it would have been by speaking actions in the face of the enemy that I should have *earned my bread*.'

Julien, satisfied with his own conduct, looked around him; he found everywhere an appearance of the purest virtue.

Nine or ten of the seminarists lived in the odour of sanctity, and had visions like Saint Teresa and Saint Francis, when he received the Stigmata upon Monte Verna, in the Apennines. But this was a great secret which their friends kept to themselves. These poor young visionaries were almost always in the infirmary. Some hundred others combined with a robust faith an unwearying application. They worked until they made themselves ill, but without learning much. Two or three distinguished themselves by real talent, and, among these, one named Chazel; but Julien felt himself repelled by them, and they by him.

The rest of the three hundred and twenty-one seminarists were composed entirely of coarse creatures who were by no means certain that they understood the Latin words which they repeated all day long. Almost all of them were the sons of peasants, and preferred to earn their bread by reciting a few Latin words rather than by tilling the soil. It was after making this discovery, in the first few days, that Julien promised himself a rapid success. 'In every service, there is need of intelligent people, for after all there is work to be done,' he told himself. 'Under Napoleon, I should have been a serjeant; among these future curés, I shall be a Grand Vicar.

'All these poor devils,' he added, 'labourers from the cradle, have lived, until they came here, upon skim milk and black bread. In their cottages, they tasted meat only five or six times in a year. Like the Roman soldiers who found active service a holiday, these boorish peasants are enchanted by the luxuries of the Seminary.'

Julien never read anything in their lack-lustre eyes beyond the satisfaction of a bodily need after dinner, and the expectation of a bodily pleasure before the meal. Such were the people among whom he must distinguish himself; but what Julien did not know, what they refrained from telling him, was that to be at the top of the various classes of dogma, church history, etc., etc., which were studied in the Seminary, was nothing more in their eyes than a sin of *vainglory*. Since Voltaire, since Two Chamber government, which is at bottom only *distrust and private judgment*, and instils in the hearts of the people that fatal habit of *want of confidence*, the Church of France seems to have realized that books are its true enemies. It is heartfelt submission that is everything in its eyes. Success in studies, even in sacred studies, is suspect, and with good reason. What is to prevent the superior man from going over to the other side, like Sieyès or Grégoire? The trembling Church clings to the Pope as to her sole chance of salvation. The Pope alone can attempt to paralyse private judgment, and, by the pious pomps of the ceremonies of his court, make an impression upon the sick and listless minds of men and women of the world.

Having half mastered these several truths, which however all the words uttered in a Seminary tend to deny, Julien fell into a deep melancholy. He worked hard, and rapidly succeeded in learning things of great value to a priest, entirely false in his eyes, and in which he took no interest. He imagined that there was nothing else for him to do.

'Am I then forgotten by all the world?' he wondered. He little knew that M. Pirard had received and had flung in the fire several letters bearing the Dijon postmark, letters in which, despite the most conventional style and language, the most intense passion was apparent. Keen remorse seemed to be doing battle with this love. 'So much the better,' thought the abbé Pirard, 'at least it is not an irreligious woman that this young man has loved.'

One day, the abbé Pirard opened a letter which seemed to be half obliterated by tears, it was an eternal farewell. 'At last,' the writer informed Julien, 'heaven has granted me the grace of hating not the author of my fault, he will always be dearer to me than anything in the world, but my fault itself. The sacrifice is made, my friend. It is not without tears, as you see. The salvation of the beings to whom I am bound, and whom you have loved so dearly, has prevailed. A just but terrible God can no longer wreak vengeance upon them for their mother's crimes. Farewell, Julien, be just towards men.'

This ending to the letter was almost entirely illegible. The writer gave an address at Dijon, and at the same time hoped that Julien would never reply, or that at least he would confine himself to language which a woman restored to the ways of virtue could read without blushing.

Julien's melancholy, assisted by the indifferent food supplied to the Seminary by the contractor for dinners at 83 centimes a head, was beginning to have an effect on his health, when one morning Fouqué suddenly appeared in his room.

'At last I have found my way in. I have come five times to Besançon, honour bound, to see you. Always a barred door. I posted someone at the gate of the Seminary; why the devil do you never come out?'

'It is a test which I have set myself.'

'I find you greatly altered. At last I see you again. Two good five franc pieces have just taught me that I was no better than a fool not to have offered them on my first visit.'

The conversation between the friends was endless. Julien changed colour when Fouqué said to him:

205

'Have you heard, by the way? The mother of your pupils has become most devoutly religious.'

And he spoke with that detached air which makes so singular an impression on the passionate soul whose dearest interests the speaker unconsciously destroys.

'Yes, my friend, the most exalted strain of piety. They say that she makes pilgrimages. But, to the eternal shame of the abbé Maslon, who has been spying so long upon that poor M. Chélan, Madame de Rênal will have nothing to do with him. She goes to confession at Dijon or Besançon.'

'She comes to Besançon!' said Julien, his brow flushing.

'Quite often,' replied Fouqué with a questioning air.

'Have you any *Constitutionnels* on you?'

'What's that you say?' replied Fouqué.

'I ask you if you have any *Constitutionnels*?' Julien repeated, in a calmer tone. 'They are sold here for thirty sous a copy.'

'What! Liberals even in the Seminary!' cried Fouqué. 'Unhappy France!' he went on, copying the hypocritical tone and meek accents of the abbé Maslon.

This visit would have made a profound impression upon our hero, had not, the very next day, a remark addressed to him by that little seminarist from Verrières who seemed such a boy, led him to make an important discovery. Ever since he had been in the Seminary, Julien's conduct had been nothing but a succession of false steps. He laughed bitterly at himself.

As a matter of fact, the important actions of his life were wisely ordered; but he paid no attention to details, and the clever people in a Seminary look only at details. And so he passed already among his fellow students as a free thinker. He had been betrayed by any number of trifling actions.

In their eyes he was convicted of this appalling vice, *he thought, he judged for himself*, instead of blindly following *authority* and example. The abbé Pirard had been of no assistance to him; he had not once uttered a word to him apart from the tribunal of penitence, and even there he listened rather than spoke. It would have been very different had Julien chosen the abbé Castanède.

206

THE WORLD, OR WHAT THE RICH LACK

The moment that Julien became aware of his own folly, his interest revived. He wished to know the whole extent of the harm, and, with this object, emerged a little from that haughty and obstinate silence with which he repulsed his fellows. It was then that they took their revenge on him. His advances were received with a contempt which went the length of derision. He realized that since his entering the Seminary, not an hour had passed, especially during recreation, that had not borne some consequence for or against him, had not increased the number of his enemies, or won him the good will of some seminarist who was genuinely virtuous or a trifle less boorish than the rest. The damage to be repaired was immense, the task one of great difficulty. Thenceforward Julien's attention was constantly on the alert; it was a case of portraying himself in an entirely new character.

The control of his eyes, for instance, gave him a great deal of trouble. It is not without reason that in such places they are kept lowered. 'What was not my presumption at Verrières!' Julien said to himself, 'I imagined I was alive; I was only preparing myself for life; here I am at last in the world, as I shall find it until I have played out my part, surrounded by real enemies. What an immense difficulty,' he went on, 'is this incessant hypocrisy! It would put the labours of Hercules to shame. The Hercules of modern times is Sixtus V, who for fifteen years on end, by his modesty, deceived forty Cardinals, who had seen him proud and vigorous in his youth.

'So learning is really nothing here!' he told himself with scorn; 'progress in dogma, in sacred history, and the rest of it, count only in appearance. All that is said on that topic is intended to make fools like myself fall into the trap. Alas, my sole merit consisted in my rapid progress, in my faculty for grasping all that nonsense. Can it be that in their hearts they esteem it at its true value; judge of it as I do? And I was fool enough to be proud of myself! Those first places in class which I always obtain have served only to give me bad marks for the real places which we obtain when we leave the Seminary and in which we earn our living. Chazel, who knows far more than I, always puts into his compositions some piece of stupidity which sends him down to the fiftieth place; if he obtains the first, it is when he is not thinking. Ah! one word, a single word from M. Pirard, how useful it would have been to me!'

From the moment in which Julien's eyes were opened, the long exercises of ascetic piety, such as the Rosary five times weekly, the hymns to the Sacred Heart, etc., etc., which had seemed to him of such deadly dulness, became the most interesting actions of his life. Sternly criticising his own conduct, and seeking above all not to exaggerate his methods, Julien did not aspire from the first, like the seminarists who served as models to the rest, to perform at every moment some *significant* action, that is to say one which gave proof of some form of Christian perfection. In Seminaries, there is a way of eating a boiled egg which reveals the progress one has made in the godly life.

The reader, who is perhaps smiling, will please to remember all the mistakes made, in eating an egg, by the abbé Delille when invited to luncheon by a great lady of the Court of Louis XVI.

Julien sought at first to arrive at the *non culpa*, to wit, the state of the young seminarist whose gait, his way of moving his arms, eyes, etc., do not, it is true, indicate anything worldly, but do not yet shew the creature absorbed by the idea of the next life and the *absolute nullity* of this.

Everywhere Julien found inscribed in charcoal, on the walls of the passages, sentences like the following: 'What are sixty years of trial, set in the balance with an eternity of bliss or an eternity of boiling oil in hell!' He no longer despised them; he realized that he must have them always before his eyes. 'What shall I be doing all my life?' he said to himself; 'I shall be selling the faithful a place in heaven. How is that place to be made visible to them? By the difference between my exterior and that of a layman.'

After several months of application kept up at every moment, Julien still had the air of a *thinker*. His way of moving his eyes and opening his lips did not reveal an implicit faith ready to believe everything and to uphold everything, even by martyrdom. It was with anger that Julien saw himself surpassed in this respect by the most boorish peasants. They had good reasons for not having the air of thinkers.

What pains did he not take to arrive at that smug and narrow face, that expression of blind and fervent faith, which is so frequently to be found in the convents of Italy, and such perfect examples of which Guercino has bequeathed to us laymen in his paintings in churches.[1]

On the greatest festivals the seminarists were given sausages with pickled cabbage. Julien's neighbours at table had observed that he remained unmoved by this good fortune; it was one of his first crimes. His comrades saw in it an odious mark of the most stupid hypocrisy; nothing made him so many enemies. 'Look at that gentleman, look at that proud fellow,' they would say, 'pretending to despise our best ration, sausages with cabbage! The wretched conceit of the damned fellow!' He should have refrained as an act of penance from eating the whole of his portion, and should have made the sacrifice of saying to some friend, with reference to the pickled cabbage: 'What is there that man can offer to an All Powerful Being, if it be not *voluntary suffering*?'

Julien lacked the experience which makes it so easy for us to see things of this sort.

'Alas! The ignorance of these young peasants, my comrades, is a great advantage to them,' he would exclaim in moments of discouragement. 'When they arrive in the Seminary, the teacher has not to rid them of the appalling number of worldly thoughts which I brought with me, and which they read on my face, do what I will.'

Julien studied with an attention that bordered upon envy the more boorish of the young peasants who arrived at the Seminary. At the moment when they were stripped of their

---

1 For instance, in the Louvre, no.1130: 'Francis Duke of Aquitaine laying aside the crown and putting on a monastic habit.'

ratteen jackets to be garbed in the black cassock, their education was limited to an immense and unbounded respect for dry and liquid money, as the saying goes in the Franche-Comté.

It is the sacramental and heroic fashion of expressing the sublime idea of ready cash.

Happiness, for these seminarists, as for the heroes of Voltaire's tales, consists first and foremost in dining well. Julien discovered in almost all of them an innate respect for the man who wears a coat of *fine cloth*. This sentiment estimates *distributive justice*, as it is dealt out to us by our courts, at its true worth, indeed below its true worth. 'What is to be gained,' they would often say among themselves, 'by going to law with the big?'

'Big' is the word used in the valleys of the Jura to denote a rich man. One may imagine their respect for the richest party of all: the Government!

Not to smile respectfully at the mere name of the Prefect is reckoned, among the peasants of the Franche-Comté, an imprudence; and imprudence, among the poor, is promptly punished with want of bread.

After having been almost suffocated at first by his sense of scorn, Julien ended by feeling pity: it had often been the lot of the fathers of the majority of his comrades to come home on a winter evening to their cottages, and to find there no bread, no chestnuts, and no potatoes. 'Is it surprising then,' Julien asked himself, 'if the happy man, in their eyes, is first of all the man who has just eaten a good dinner, and after that he who possesses a good coat! My comrades have a definite vocation; that is to say, they see in the ecclesiastical calling a long continuation of this happiness: dining well and having a warm coat in winter.'

Julien happened to hear a young seminarist, endowed with imagination, say to his companion:

'Why should not I become Pope like Sixtus V, who was a swineherd?'

'They make none but Italians Popes,' replied the friend; 'but they'll draw lots among us, for sure, to fill places as

Grand Vicars and Canons, and perhaps Bishops. M. P——
the Bishop of Châlons, is the son of a cooper; that is my
father's trade.'

One day, in the middle of a lesson in dogma, the abbé
Pirard sent for Julien. The poor young fellow was delighted
to escape from the physical and moral atmosphere in which
he was plunged.

Julien found himself greeted by the Director in the manner
which had so frightened him on the day of his joining the
Seminary.

'Explain to me what I see written upon this playing card,'
he said to him, looking at him in such a way as to make him
wish that the earth would open and swallow him.

Julien read:

'Amanda Binet, at the Giraffe café, before eight o'clock.
Say you are from Genlis, and a cousin of my mother.'

Julien perceived the immensity of the danger; the abbé
Castanède's police had stolen the address from him.

'The day on which I came here,' he replied, gazing at the
abbé Pirard's forehead, for he could not face his terrible eye,
'I was trembling with fear: M. Chélan had told me that this
was a place full of tale-bearing and spite of all sorts; spying
and the accusation of one's comrades are encouraged here.
Such is the will of heaven, to shew life as it is to young
priests, and to inspire in them a disgust with the world and
its pomps.'

'And it is to me that you make these fine speeches'—the
abbé Pirard was furious. 'You young rascal!'

'At Verrières,' Julien went on calmly, 'my brothers used to
beat me when they had any reason to be jealous of me....'

'To the point! Get to the point!' cried M. Pirard, almost
beside himself.

Without being the least bit in the world intimidated, Julien
resumed his narrative.

'On the day of my coming to Besançon, about noon, I felt
hungry, I went into a café. My heart was filled with repugnance for so profane a spot; but I thought that my luncheon
would cost me less there than at an inn. A lady, who seemed

to be the mistress of the place, took pity on my raw looks. "Besançon is full of wicked people," she told me, "I am afraid for you, Sir. If you find yourself in any trouble, come to me, send a message to me before eight o'clock. If the porters at the Seminary refuse to take your message, say that you are my cousin, and come from Genlis...."'

'All this farrago will have to be investigated,' exclaimed the abbé Pirard who, unable to remain in one place, was striding up and down the room.

'You will go back to your cell!'

The abbé accompanied Julien and locked him in. He himself at once proceeded to examine his trunk, in the bottom of which the fatal card had been carefully concealed. Nothing was missing from the trunk, but several things had been disarranged; and yet the key never left his possession. 'How fortunate,' Julien said to himself, 'that during the time of my blindness I never made use of the permission to leave the building, which M. Castanède so frequently offered me with a generosity which I now understand. Perhaps I might have been so foolish as to change my clothes and pay the fair Amanda a visit, I should have been ruined. When they despaired of making any use of their information in that way, so as not to waste it they have used it to denounce me.'

A couple of hours later, the Director sent for him.

'You have not lied,' he said to him, looking at him less severely; 'but to keep such an address is an imprudence the serious nature of which you cannot conceive. Unhappy boy! In ten years, perhaps, it will redound to your hurt.'

CHAPTER TWENTY-SEVEN

FIRST EXPERIENCE OF LIFE

Le temps présent, grand Dieu! c'est l'arche du Seigneur. Malheur a qui y touche.

DIDEROT.

THE reader will kindly excuse our giving but few clear and precise details of this epoch in Julien's life. Not that we lack them, far from it; but perhaps the life he led in the Seminary is too black for the modest colouring which we have sought to preserve in these pages. People who have been made to suffer by certain things cannot be reminded of them without a horror which paralyses every other pleasure, even that to be found in reading a story.

Julien met with little success in his attempts at hypocrisy in action; he passed through moments of disgust and even of complete discouragement. He was utterly unsuccessful, and that moreover in a vile career. The slightest help from without would have sufficed to sustain his resolution, the difficulty to be overcome was not great; but he was alone, as lonely as a vessel abandoned in mid-ocean. 'And if I should succeed,' he said to himself; 'to have to spend my whole life in such evil company! Gluttons who think of nothing but the ham omelette they are going to devour at dinner, or men like the abbé Castanède, to whom no crime is too black! They will rise to power; but at what a price, great God!

'Man's will is powerful, I see it written everywhere; but is it sufficiently so to overcome such repulsion? The task of great men has always been easy; however terrible was their danger, it was beautiful in their eyes; and who but myself can realize the ugliness of all that surrounds me?'

This was the most trying moment in his life. It was so easy for him to enlist in one of the fine regiments that were stationed at Besançon! He might become a teacher of Latin; he wanted so little to keep himself alive! But then, no career, no future for his imagination: it was a living death. Here is a detailed account of one of his wretched days.

'My presumption has so often flattered itself upon my being different from the other young peasants! Well, I have lived long enough to see that difference breeds hatred,' he said to himself one morning. This great truth had just been revealed to him by one of his most annoying failures. He had laboured for a week to make himself agreeable to a student who lived in the odour of sanctity. He was walking with him in the courtyard, listening submissively to idiocies that sent him to sleep as he walked. Suddenly a storm broke, the thunder growled, and the saintly student exclaimed, thrusting him rudely away:

'Listen, each for himself in this world, I have no wish to be struck by lightning: God may blast you as an infidel, another Voltaire.'

His teeth clenched with rage and his eyes opened towards the sky furrowed by streaks of lightning: 'I should deserve to be submerged, were I to let myself sleep during the storm!' cried Julien. 'Let us attempt the conquest of some other drudge.'

The bell rang for the abbé Castanède's class of sacred history.

These young peasants who lived in such fear of the hard toil and poverty of their fathers, were taught that day by the abbé Castanède that that being so terrible in their eyes, the Government, had no real or legitimate power save what was delegated to it by God's Vicar on Earth.

'Render yourselves worthy of the Pope's bounties by the sanctity of your lives, by your obedience, be *like a rod in his hands*,' he went on, 'and you will attain to a superb position where you will be in supreme command, under no man's control; a permanent position, of which the Government pays one third of the emoluments, and the faithful, roused by your preaching, the other two thirds.'

On leaving his classroom, M. Castanède stopped in the courtyard among his students, who that day were most attentive.

'You may well say of a curé, each man gets what he deserves,' he said to the students who gathered round him. 'I myself have known mountain parishes where the fees came to more than those of many town curés. There was as much in money, not to speak of the fat capons, eggs, fresh butter, and endless little delicacies; and there the curé takes the first place without challenge: no good meal to which he is not invited, made much of,' etc.

No sooner had M. Castanède gone up to his own room, than the students divided into groups. Julien belonged to none of these; they drew away from him as from a tainted wether. In each of the groups, he saw a student toss a copper in the air, and if he guessed head or tail aright, his companions concluded that he would soon have one of these livings with fat fees.

Stories followed. One young priest, barely a year in orders, having presented a gelt rabbit to an old curé's servant, had got the curé to ask for him as his assistant, and a few months afterwards, for the curé had died almost immediately, had succeeded him in a good living. Another had managed to have his name put forward for the eventual succession to the curacy of a prosperous country town, by attending all the meals of the paralytic old curé and carving his chickens for him gracefully.

The seminarists, like young men in every profession, exaggerated the effect of these little stratagems when they were out of the ordinary and struck the imagination.

'I must,' thought Julien, 'take part in these conversations.' When they were not discussing sausages and rich livings, their talk ran on the worldly side of ecclesiastical teaching; the differences between Bishops and Prefects, mayors and curés. Julien saw lurking in their minds the idea of a second

God, but of a God far more to be feared and far more power-ful than the first; this second God was the Pope. It was said, but with lowered voice, and when the speaker was quite cer-tain of not being overheard by M. Pirard, that if the Pope did not take the trouble to appoint all the Prefects and all the mayors in France, it was because he had delegated the King of France for that duty, by naming him the Eldest Son of the Church.

It was about this time that Julien thought he might derive some benefit from his admiration for M. de Maistre's book on the Pope. He did, as a matter of fact, astonish his fellow-students; but this was a fresh misfortune. He annoyed them by expressing their opinions better than they could them-selves. M. Chélan had been a rash counsellor for Julien as he had been for himself. After training him to the habit of reasoning accurately and not letting himself be taken in by vain words, he had omitted to tell him that in a person of little repute this habit is a crime; for sound reasoning always gives offence.

Julien's fine speech was therefore only another crime against him. His companions, being compelled to think about him, succeeded in finding two words to express all the horror with which he filled them: they nicknamed him Martin Luther; 'chiefly,' they said, 'because of that infernal logic of which he is so proud.'

Several young seminarists had fresher complexions and might be reckoned better looking than Julien; but he had white hands, and could not hide certain habits of personal cleanliness. This distinction was none at all in the grim dwelling into which destiny had cast him. The unclean peas-ants among whom he lived declared that he had extremely lax morals. We are afraid to tire the reader by an account of our hero's endless mishaps. To take one instance, the more vigorous among his companions tried to make a practice of thrashing him; he was obliged to arm himself with a metal compass and to inform them, but only by signs, that he would use it. Signs cannot be represented, in a spy's report, so damningly as words.

CHAPTER TWENTY-EIGHT

A PROCESSION

Tous les cœurs étaient émus. La présence de Dieu
semblait descendue dans ces rues étroites et gothiques,
tendues de toutes parts, et bien sablées par les soins
des fidèles.

YOUNG.[1]

IN vain might Julien make himself small and foolish, he
could not give satisfaction, he was too different. 'And
yet,' he said to himself, 'all these Professors are men of
great discernment, and picked men, each of them one in a
thousand; how is it they do not like my humility?' One alone
seemed to him to be taking advantage of his readiness to
believe anything and to appear taken in by everything. This
was the abbé Chas-Bernard, Master of Ceremonies at the
Cathedral, where, for the last fifteen years, he had been kept
in hopes of a Canonry; in the meantime, he taught sacred
eloquence at the Seminary. In the period of his blindness,
this class was one of those in which Julien most regularly
came out at the top. The abbé Chas had been led by this to
shew a partiality for him, and, at the end of his class, would
gladly take his arm for a turn in the garden.

'What can his object be?' Julien asked himself. He found
with amazement that, for hours on end, the abbé talked to
him of the ornaments which the Cathedral possessed. It had

---

1 As in Chapter 26, I have left this motto in French. It seems, however, to be
taken from Arthur Young rather than Edward. C. K. S. M.

seventeen apparelled chasubles, apart from the vestments worn at requiems. They had great hopes of President de Rubempré's widow; this lady, who was ninety years old, had preserved for at least seventy of those years her wedding garments of superb Lyons stuffs, figured in gold. 'Just imagine, my friend,' said the abbé Chas coming to a standstill and opening his eyes wide, 'these stuffs stand by themselves, there is so much gold in them. It is the common opinion among the good people of Besançon that, under the Présidente's will, the treasury of the Cathedral will be enriched with more than ten chasubles, not to mention four or five copes for the greater feasts. I will go farther,' the abbé Chas added, lowering his voice. 'I have good reason to think that the Présidente will bequeath to us eight magnificent silver-gilt candlesticks, which are supposed to have been bought in Italy, by the Duke of Burgundy, Charles the Bold, whose favourite minister was an ancestor of hers.'

'But what is this man really aiming at behind all this frippery?' Julien wondered. 'This careful preparation has been going on for an age, and nothing comes of it. He must have singularly little faith in me! He is cleverer than any of the others, whose secret purposes one can see so plainly after a fortnight. I understand, this man's ambition has been in torment for fifteen years.'

One evening, in the middle of the armed drill, Julien was sent for by the abbé Pirard, who said to him:

'To-morrow is the festival of Corpus Domini. M. l'abbé Chas-Bernard requires you to help him to decorate the Cathedral; go and obey.'

The abbé Pirard called him back, and added, in a tone of compassion:

'It is for you to decide whether you wish to seize the opportunity of taking a stroll through the town.'

'*Incedo per ignes*,' replied Julien: which is to say, I am treading on dangerous ground.

Next morning at daybreak, Julien made his way to the Cathedral, walking with lowered eyes. The sight of the streets and the activity which was beginning to pervade the town did him good. On every side people were draping the fronts of their houses for the procession. All the time that he had spent in the Seminary seemed to him no more than an instant. His thoughts were at Vergy, and with that charming Amanda Binet, whom he might meet, for her café was but little out of his way. He saw in the distance the abbé Chas-Bernard, standing by the door of his beloved Cathedral; he was a large man with a joyful countenance and an open air. This morning he was triumphant: 'I have been waiting for you, my dear son,' he called out, as soon as he caught sight of Julien, 'you are welcome. Our labours this day will be long and hard, let us fortify ourselves with an early breakfast; the other we shall take at ten o'clock during high mass.'

'I desire, Sir,' Julien said to him with an air of gravity, 'not to be left alone for a moment; kindly observe,' he added, pointing to the clock above their heads, 'that I have arrived at one minute before five.'

'Ah! So you are afraid of those young rascals at the Seminary! It is too kind of you to give them a thought,' said the abbé Chas; 'is a road any the worse, because there are thorns in the hedges on either side of it? The traveller goes his way and leaves the wicked thorns to wither where they are. However, we must to work, my dear friend, to work.'

The abbé Chas had been right in saying that their labours would be hard. There had been a great funeral service in the Cathedral the day before; it had been impossible to make any preparations; they were obliged, therefore, in the course of the morning, to drape each of the gothic pillars which separate the nave from the aisles in a sort of jacket of red damask which rose to a height of thirty feet. The Bishop had ordered four upholsterers from Paris by mail coach, but these gentlemen could not do everything themselves, and so far from encouraging the awkward efforts of their Bisontine colleagues they increased their awkwardness by laughing at it.

Julien saw that he would have to go up the ladders himself, his agility stood him in good stead. He undertook to direct the local upholsterers in person. The abbé Chas was in ecstasies as he watched him spring from one ladder to

219

another. When all the pillars were hung with damask, the next thing was to go and place five enormous bunches of plumes on top of the great baldachino, over the high altar. A richly gilded wooden crown was supported on eight great twisted columns of Italian marble. But, in order to reach the centre of the baldachino, over the tabernacle, one had to step across an old wooden cornice, possibly worm-eaten, and forty feet from the ground.

The sight of this perilous ascent had extinguished the gaiety, so brilliant until then, of the Parisian upholsterers; they looked at it from beneath, discussed it volubly, and did not go up. Julien took possession of the bunches of plumes, and ran up the ladder. He arranged them admirably upon the ornament in the form of a crown in the centre of the baldachino. As he stepped down from the ladder, the abbé Chas-Bernard took him in his arms.

'*Optime!*' exclaimed the worthy priest, 'I shall tell Monseigneur of this.'

Their ten o'clock breakfast was a merry feast. Never had the abbé Chas seen his church looking so well.

'My dear disciple,' he said to Julien, 'my mother used to hire out chairs in this venerable fane, so that I was brought up in this great edifice. Robespierre's Terror ruined us; but, at eight years old, as I then was, I was already serving masses in private houses, and their owners gave me my dinner on mass days. No one could fold a chasuble better than I, the gold braid was never broken. Since the restoration of the Faith by Napoleon, it has been my happy lot to take charge of everything in this venerable mother church. On five days in the year, my eyes behold it decked out with these beautiful ornaments. But never has it been so resplendent, never have the damask strips been so well hung as they are to-day, have they clung so to the pillars.'

'At last, he is going to tell me his secret,' thought Julien, 'here he is talking to me of himself; he is beginning to expand.' But nothing imprudent was said by this man, evidently in an excited state. 'And yet he has worked hard, he is happy,' Julien said to himself, 'the good wine has not been spared. What a man! What an example for me! He takes the prize.' (This was a low expression which he had picked up from the old surgeon.)

When the Sanctus bell rang during high mass, Julien wished to put on a surplice so as to follow the Bishop in the superb procession.

'And the robbers, my friend, the robbers!' cried the abbé Chas, 'you forget them. The procession is going out; the church will be left empty; we must keep watch, you and I. We shall be fortunate if we lose only a couple of ells of that fine braid which goes round the base of the pillars. That is another gift from Madame de Rubempré; it comes from the famous Count, her great-grandfather; it is pure gold, my friend,' the abbé went on, whispering in his ear, and with an air of evident exaltation, 'nothing false about it! I entrust to you the inspection of the north aisle, do not stir from it. I keep for myself the south aisle and nave. Keep an eye on the confessionals; it is there that the robbers' women spies watch for the moment when our backs are turned.'

As he finished speaking, the quarter before twelve struck, at once the big bell began to toll. It was being pulled with all the ringers' might; the rich and solemn sound stirred Julien deeply. His imagination rose from the ground.

The odour of the incense and of the rose leaves strewn before the Blessed Sacrament by children dressed as little Saint Johns, intensified his excitement.

The sober note of the bell ought to have suggested to Julien only the thought of the work of a score of men earning fifty centimes, and assisted perhaps by fifteen or twenty of the faithful. He ought to have thought of the wear and tear of the ropes, of the timber, of the danger from the bell itself which fell every two hundred years, and to have planned some way of diminishing the wage of the ringers, or of paying them with some indulgence or other favour drawn from the spiritual treasury of the Church, with no strain upon her purse.

In place of these sage reflexions, Julien's soul, excited by these rich and virile sounds, was straying through imaginary space. Never will he make either a good priest or a great administrator. Souls that are moved thus are capable at most of producing an artist. Here Julien's presumption breaks out in the full light of day. Fifty, perhaps, of his fellow seminarists, made attentive to the realities of life by the public hatred and Jacobinism which, they are told, is lurking behind every hedge, on hearing the big bell of the Cathedral, would have thought only of the wages paid to the ringers. They would have applied the genius of a Barême to determine the question whether the degree of emotion aroused in the public was worth the money given to the ringers. Had Julien chosen to give his mind to the material interests of the Cathedral, his imagination flying beyond its goal would have thought of saving forty francs for the Chapter, and would have let slip the opportunity of avoiding an outlay of twenty-five centimes.

While, in the most perfect weather ever seen, the procession wound its way slowly through Besançon, and halted at the glittering stations which all the local authorities had vied with one another in erecting, the church remained wrapped in a profound silence. A suffused light, an agreeable coolness reigned in it; it was still balmy with the fragrance of flowers and incense.

The silence, the profound solitude, the coolness of the long aisles, made Julien's musings all the sweeter. He had no fear of being disturbed by the abbé Chas, who was occupied in another part of the building. His soul had almost quitted its mortal envelope, which was strolling at a slow pace along the north aisle committed to his charge. He was all the more at rest, since he was certain that there was nobody in the confessionals save a few devout women; he saw without observing.

His distraction was nevertheless half conquered by the sight of two women extremely well dressed who were kneeling, one of them in a confessional, the other, close beside her, upon a chair. He saw without observing them; at the same time, whether from a vague sense of his duty, or from admiration of the plain but noble attire of these ladies, he remarked that there was no priest in that confessional. 'It is strange,' he thought, 'that these beautiful ladies are not kneeling before some station, if they are religious; or placed in good seats in the front of some balcony, if they are fashionable. How well cut that gown is! What grace!' He slackened his pace in order to see their faces.

The one who was kneeling in the confessional turned her head slightly on hearing the sound of Julien's step amid the prevailing silence. All at once she gave a little cry, and fainted.

As her strength left her, this kneeling lady fell back; her friend, who was close at hand, hastened to the rescue. At the same time Julien caught sight of the shoulders of the lady who had fallen back. A rope of large seed pearls, well known to him, caught his eye. What was his state when he recognized the hair of Madame de Rênal! It was she. The lady who was trying to hold up her head, and to arrest her fall, was Madame Derville. Julien, beside himself with emotion, sprang forward; Madame de Rênal's fall would perhaps have brought down her friend if he had not supported them. He saw Madame de Rênal's head, pale, absolutely devoid of consciousness, drooping upon her shoulder. He helped Madame Derville to prop that charming head against the back of a straw chair; he was on his knees.

Madame Derville turned and recognized him.

'Fly, Sir, fly!' she said to him in accents of the most burning anger. 'On no account must she see you again. The sight of you must indeed fill her with horror, she was so happy before you came! Your behaviour is atrocious. Fly; be off with you, if you have any shame left.'

This speech was uttered with such authority, and Julien felt so weak at the moment, that he withdrew. 'She always hated me,' he said to himself, thinking of Madame Derville.

At that moment, the nasal chant of the leading priests in the procession rang through the church; the procession was returning. The abbé Chas-Bernard called repeatedly to Julien, who at first did not hear him: finally he came and led him by the arm from behind a pillar where Julien had taken refuge more dead than alive. He wished to present him to the Bishop.

'You are feeling unwell, my child,' said the abbé, seeing him so pale and almost unable to walk; 'you have been working too hard.' The abbé gave him his arm. 'Come, sit down here, on the sacristan's little stool, behind me; I shall screen you.' They were now by the side of the main door. 'Calm yourself, we have still a good twenty minutes before Monseigneur appears. Try to recover yourself; when he passes, I shall hold you up, for I am strong and vigorous, in spite of my age.'

But when the Bishop passed, Julien was so tremulous that the abbé Chas abandoned the idea of presenting him.

'Do not worry yourself about it,' he told him, 'I shall find another opportunity.'

That evening, he sent down to the chapel of the Seminary ten pounds of candles, saved, he said, by Julien's efforts and the rapidity with which he extinguished them. Nothing could have been farther from the truth. The poor boy was himself extinguished; he had not had a thought in his head after seeing Madame de Rênal.

CHAPTER TWENTY-NINE
THE FIRST STEP

Il a connu son siècle, il a connu son département, et
il est riche.

Le Précurseur.

JULIEN had not yet recovered from the profound abstraction in which the incident in the Cathedral had plunged him, when one morning the grim abbé Pirard sent for him.

'Here is M. l'abbé Chas-Bernard writing to me to commend you. I am quite satisfied with your conduct as a whole. You are extremely imprudent and indeed stupid, without shewing it; however, up to the present your heart is sound and even generous; your intellect is above the average. Taking you all in all, I see a spark in you which must not be neglected.

'After fifteen years of labour, I am on the eve of leaving this establishment: my crime is that of having allowed the seminarists to use their own judgment, and of having neither protected nor unmasked that secret society of which you have spoken to me at the stool of penitence. Before I go, I wish to do something for you; I should have acted two months ago, for you deserve it, but for the accusation based upon the address of Amanda Binet, which was found in your possession. I appoint you tutor in the New and Old Testaments.'

Julien, in a transport of gratitude, quite thought of falling on his knees and thanking God; but he yielded to a more genuine impulse. He went up to the abbé Pirard and took his hand, which he raised to his lips.

'What is this?' cried the Director in a tone of annoyance; but Julien's eyes were even more eloquent than his action.

The abbé Pirard gazed at him in astonishment, like a man who, in the course of long years, has fallen out of the way of meeting with delicate emotions. This attention pierced the Director's armour; his voice changed.

'Ah, well! Yes, my child, I am attached to you. Heaven knows that it is entirely against my will. I ought to be just, and to feel neither hatred nor love for anyone. Your career will be difficult. I see in you something that offends the common herd. Jealousy and calumny will pursue you. In whatever place Providence may set you, your companions will never set eyes on you without hating you; and if they pretend to love you, it will be in order to betray you the more surely. For this there is but one remedy: have recourse only to God, who has given you, to punish you for your presumption, this necessity of being hated; let your conduct be pure; that is the sole resource that I can see for you. If you hold fast to the truth with an invincible embrace, sooner or later your enemies will be put to confusion.'

It was so long since Julien had heard a friendly voice, that we must forgive him a weakness: he burst into tears. The abbé Pirard opened his arms to embrace him; the moment was very precious to them both.

Julien was wild with joy; this promotion was the first that he had obtained; the advantages were immense. In order to realize them, one must have been condemned to pass whole months without a moment's solitude, and in immediate contact with companions at best tiresome, and mostly intolerable. Their shouts alone would have been enough to create disorder in a sensitive organism. The boisterous joy of these peasants well fed and well dressed, could find expression, thought itself complete only when they were shouting with the full force of their lungs.

Now Julien dined by himself, or almost so, an hour later than the rest of the seminarists. He had a key to the garden, and might walk there at the hours when it was empty.

Greatly to his surprise, Julien noticed that they hated him

less; he had been expecting, on the contrary, an intensification of their hatred. That secret desire that no one should speak to him, which was all too apparent and had made him so many enemies, was no longer a sign of absurd pride. In the eyes of the coarse beings among whom he lived, it was a proper sense of his own dignity. Their hatred diminished perceptibly, especially among the youngest of his companions, now become his pupils, whom he treated with great courtesy. In course of time he had even supporters; it became bad form to call him Martin Luther.

But why speak of his friends, his enemies? It is all so ugly, and all the more ugly, the more accurately it is drawn from life. These are however the only teachers of ethics that the people have, and without them where should we be? Will the newspaper ever manage to take the place of the parish priest?

Since Julien's promotion, the Director of the Seminary made a point of never speaking to him except in the presence of witnesses. This was only prudent, in the master's interest as well as the pupil's; but more than anything else it was a *test*. The stern Jansenist Pirard's invariable principle was: 'Has a man any merit in your eyes? Place an obstacle in the way of everything that he desires, everything that he undertakes. If his merit be genuine, he will certainly be able to surmount or thrust aside your obstacles.'

It was the hunting season. Fouqué took it into his head to send to the Seminary a stag and a boar in the name of Julien's family. The dead animals were left lying in the passage, between kitchen and refectory. There all the seminarists saw them on their way to dinner. They aroused much interest. The boar, although stone dead, frightened the younger boys; they fingered his tusks. Nothing else was spoken of for a week.

This present, which classified Julien's family in the section of society that one must respect, dealt a mortal blow to jealousy. It was a form of superiority consecrated by fortune. Chazel and the most distinguished of the seminarists made overtures to him, and almost complained to him that he had not warned them of his parents' wealth, and had thus betrayed them into shewing a want of respect for money.

There was a conscription from which Julien was exempt in his capacity as a seminarist. This incident moved him deeply. 'And so there has passed now for ever the moment at which, twenty years ago, a heroic life would have begun for me!'

Walking by himself in the Seminary garden, he overheard a conversation between two masons who were at work upon the enclosing wall.

'Ah, well! One will have to go, here's another conscription.'

'In the *other man's* days, well and good! A stone mason became an officer, and became a general, that has been known.'

'Look what it's like now! Only the beggars go. A man with the *wherewithal* stays at home.'

'The man who is born poor stays poor, and that's all there is to it.'

'Tell me, now, is it true what people say, that the other is dead?' put in a third mason.

'It's the big ones who say that, don't you see? They were afraid of the other.'

'What a difference, how well everything went in his time! And to think that he was betrayed by his Marshals! There must always be a traitor somewhere!'

This conversation comforted Julien a little. As he walked away he repeated to himself with a sigh:

'The only King whose memory the people cherish still!'

The examinations came round. Julien answered the questions in a brilliant manner; he saw that Chazel himself was seeking to display the whole extent of his knowledge.

On the first day, the examiners appointed by the famous Grand Vicar de Frilair greatly resented having always to place first, or at the very most second on their list this Julien Sorel who had been pointed out to them as the Benjamin of the abbé Pirard. Wagers were made in the Seminary that in the aggregate list of the examinations, Julien would occupy the first place, a distinction that carried with it the honour of dining with the Bishop. But at the end of one session, in which the subject had been the Fathers of the Church, a skilful examiner, after questioning Julien upon Saint Jerome, and his passion for Cicero, began to speak of Horace, Virgil and other profane authors. Unknown to his companions, Julien had learned by heart a great number of passages from these authors. Carried away by his earlier successes, he forgot where he was and, at the repeated request of the examiner, recited and paraphrased with enthusiasm several odes of Horace. Having let him sink deeper and deeper for twenty minutes, suddenly the examiner's face changed, and he delivered a stinging rebuke to Julien for having wasted his time in these profane studies, and stuffed his head with useless if not criminal thoughts.

'I am a fool, Sir, and you are right,' said Julien with a modest air, as he saw the clever stratagem by which he had been taken in.

This ruse on the examiner's part was considered a dirty trick, even in the Seminary, though this did not prevent M. l'abbé de Frilair, that clever man, who had so ably organized the framework of the Bisontine *Congregation*, and whose reports to Paris made judges, prefect, and even the general officers of the garrison tremble, from setting, with his powerful hand, the number 198 against Julien's name. He was delighted thus to mortify his enemy, the Jansenist Pirard.

For the last ten years his great ambition had been to remove Pirard from control of the Seminary. That cleric, following in his own conduct the principles which he had outlined to Julien, was sincere, devout, innocent of intrigue, devoted to his duty. But heaven, in its wrath, had given him that splenetic temperament, bound to feel deeply insults and hatred. Not one of the affronts that were put upon him was lost upon his ardent spirit. He would have offered his resignation a hundred times, but he believed that he was of use in the post in which Providence had placed him. 'I prevent the spread of Jesuitry and idolatry,' he used to say to himself.

At the time of the examinations, it was perhaps two

months since he had spoken to Julien, and yet he was ill for a week, when, on receiving the official letter announcing the result of the competition, he saw the number 198 set against the name of that pupil whom he regarded as the glory of his establishment. The only consolation for this stern character was to concentrate upon Julien all the vigilance at his command. He was delighted to find in him neither anger nor thoughts of revenge, nor discouragement.

Some weeks later, Julien shuddered on receiving a letter; it bore the Paris postmark. 'At last,' he thought, 'Madame de Rênal has remembered her promises.' A gentleman who signed himself Paul Sorel, and professed to be related to him, sent him a bill of exchange for five hundred francs. The writer added that if Julien continued to study with success the best Latin authors, a similar sum would be sent to him every year.

'It is she, it is her bounty!' Julien said to himself with emotion, 'she wishes to comfort me; but why is there not one word of affection?'

He was mistaken with regard to the letter; Madame de Rênal, under the influence of her friend Madame Derville, was entirely absorbed in her own profound remorse. In spite of herself, she often thought of the strange creature whose coming into her life had so upset it, but she would never have dreamed of writing to him.

If we spoke the language of the Seminary, we might see a miracle in this windfall of five hundred francs, and say that it was M. de Frilair himself that heaven had employed to make this gift to Julien.

Twelve years earlier, M. l'abbé de Frilair had arrived at Besançon with the lightest of portmanteaux, which, the story went, contained his entire fortune. He now found himself one of the wealthiest landowners in the Department. In the course of his growing prosperity he had purchased one half of an estate of which the other half passed by inheritance to M. de La Mole. Hence a great lawsuit between these worthies.

Despite his brilliant existence in Paris, and the posts which he held at court, the Marquis de La Mole felt that it was dangerous to fight down at Besançon against a Grand Vicar who was reputed to make and unmake Prefects. Instead of asking for a gratuity of fifty thousand francs, disguised under some head or other that would pass in the budget, and allowing M. de Frilair to win this pettifogging action for fifty thousand francs, the Marquis took offence. He believed that he had a case: a fine reason!

For, if we may be so bold as to say it: what judge is there who has not a son, or at least a cousin to help on in the world?

To enlighten the less clear-sighted, a week after the first judgment that he obtained, M. l'abbé de Frilair took the Bishop's carriage, and went in person to convey the Cross of the Legion of Honour to his counsel. M. de La Mole, somewhat dismayed by the bold front assumed by the other side, and feeling that his own counsel were weakening, asked the advice of the abbé Chélan, who put him in touch with M. Pirard.

At the date of our story they had been corresponding thus for some years. The abbé Pirard dashed into the business with all the force of his passionate nature. In constant communication with the Marquis's counsel, he studied his case, and finding him to be in the right, openly declared himself a partisan of the Marquis de La Mole against the all powerful Grand Vicar. The latter was furious at such insolence, and coming from a little Jansenist to boot!

'You see what these court nobles are worth who claim to have such power!' the abbé de Frilair would say to his intimates; 'M. de La Mole has not sent so much as a wretched Cross to his agent at Besançon, and is going to allow him to be deprived of his post without a murmur. And yet, my friends write to me, this noble peer never allows a week to pass without going to shew off his blue riband in the drawing-room of the Keeper of the Seals, for what that is worth.'

In spite of all M. Pirard's activity, and albeit M. de La Mole was always on the best of terms with the Minister of Justice and still more with his officials, all that he had been able to achieve, after six years of constant effort, was to avoid actually losing his case.

In ceaseless correspondence with the abbé Pirard, over an affair which they both pursued with passion, the Marquis came in time to appreciate the abbé's type of mind. Gradually, despite the immense gulf between their social positions, their correspondence took on a tone of friendship. The abbé Pirard told the Marquis that his enemies were seeking to oblige him, by their insults, to offer his resignation. In the anger which he felt at the infamous stratagem (according to him) employed against Julien, he related the latter's story to the Marquis.

Although extremely rich, this great nobleman was not in the least a miser. He had never once been able to make the abbé Pirard accept so much as the cost of postage occasioned by the lawsuit. He took the opportunity to send five hundred francs to the abbé's favourite pupil.

M. de La Mole took the trouble to write the covering letter with his own hand. This set him thinking of the abbé.

One day the latter received a short note in which he was requested to call at once, upon urgent business, at an inn on the outskirts of Besançon. There he found M. de La Mole's steward.

'M. le Marquis has instructed me to bring you his carriage,' he was informed. 'He hopes that after you have read this letter, you will find it convenient to start for Paris, in four or five days from now. I am going to employ the time which you will be so kind as to indicate to me in visiting the estates of M. le Marquis in the Franche-Comté. After which, on whatever day suits you, we shall start for Paris.'

The letter was brief:

'Rid yourself, my dear Sir, of all these provincial bickerings, come and breathe a calmer air in Paris. I am sending you my carriage, which has orders to await your decision for four days. I shall wait for you myself, in Paris, until Tuesday. It requires only the word yes, from you, Sir, to make me accept in your name one of the best livings in the neighbourhood of Paris. The wealthiest of your future parishioners has never set eyes on you, but is devoted to you more warmly than you can suppose; he is the Marquis de La Mole.'

Without knowing it, the stern abbé Pirard loved this Seminary, peopled with his enemies, to which, for fifteen years, he had devoted all his thoughts. M. de La Mole's letter was to him like the sudden appearance of a surgeon with the duty of performing a painful but necessary operation. His dismissal was certain. He gave the steward an appointment, in three days' time.

For the next forty-eight hours, he was in a fever of uncertainty. Finally, he wrote to M. de La Mole and composed, for the Bishop's benefit, a letter, a masterpiece of ecclesiastical diction, though a trifle long. It would have been difficult to find language more irreproachable, or breathing a more sincere respect. And yet this letter, intended to give M. de Frilair a trying hour with his patron, enumerated all the serious grounds for complaint and descended to the sordid little pinpricks which, after he had borne them, with resignation, for six years, were forcing the abbé Pirard to leave the diocese.

They stole the wood from his shed, they poisoned his dog, etc., etc.

This letter written, he sent to awaken Julien who, at eight o'clock in the evening, was already asleep, as were all the seminarists.

'You know where the Bishop's Palace is?' he said to him in the best Latin; 'take this letter to Monseigneur. I shall not attempt to conceal from you that I am sending you amongst wolves. Be all eyes and ears. No prevarication in your answers; but remember that the man who is questioning you would perhaps take a real delight in trying to harm you. I am glad, my child, to give you this experience before I leave you, for I do not conceal from you that the letter which you are taking contains my resignation.'

Julien did not move; he was fond of the abbé Pirard. In vain might prudence warn him:

'After this worthy man's departure, the Sacred Heart party will degrade and perhaps even expel me.'

He could not think about himself. What embarrassed him was a sentence which he wished to cast in a polite form, but really he was incapable of using his mind.

'Well, my friend, aren't you going?'

'You see, Sir, they say,' Julien began timidly, 'that during your long administration here, you have never put anything aside. I have six hundred francs.'

Tears prevented him from continuing.

'That too will be noticed,' said the ex-Director of the Seminary coldly. 'Go to the Palace, it is getting late.'

As luck would have it, that evening M. l'abbé de Frilair was in attendance in the Bishop's parlour; Monseigneur was dining at the Prefecture. So that it was to M. de Frilair himself that Julien gave the letter, but he did not know who he was.

Julien saw with astonishment that this priest boldly opened the letter addressed to the Bishop. The fine features of the Grand Vicar soon revealed a surprise mingled with keen pleasure, and his gravity increased. While he was reading, Julien, struck by his good looks, had time to examine him. It was a face that would have had more gravity but for the extreme subtlety that appeared in certain of its features, and would actually have suggested dishonesty, if the owner of that handsome face had ceased for a moment to control it. The nose, which was extremely prominent, formed an unbroken and perfectly straight line, and gave unfortunately to a profile that otherwise was most distinguished, an irremediable resemblance to the mask of a fox. In addition, this abbé who seemed so greatly interested in M. Pirard's resignation, was dressed with an elegance that greatly pleased Julien, who had never seen its like on any other priest.

It was only afterwards that Julien learned what was the abbé de Frilair's special talent. He knew how to amuse his Bishop, a pleasant old man, made to live in Paris, who regarded Besançon as a place of exile. This Bishop was extremely short-sighted, and passionately fond of fish. The abbé de Frilair used to remove the bones from the fish that was set before Monseigneur.

Julien was silently watching the abbé as he read over again the letter of resignation, when suddenly the door burst open. A lackey, richly attired, passed rapidly through the room. Julien had barely time to turn towards the door; he saw a little old man, wearing a pectoral cross. He fell on his knees: the Bishop bestowed a kind smile upon him as he passed through the room. The handsome abbé followed him, and Julien was left alone in this parlour, the pious magnificence of which he could now admire at his leisure.

The Bishop of Besançon, a man of character, tried, but not crushed by the long hardships of the Emigration, was more than seventy-five, and cared infinitely little about what might happen in the next ten years.

'Who is that clever looking seminarist, whom I seemed to see as I passed?' said the Bishop. 'Ought they not, by my orders, to be in their beds at this hour?'

'This one is quite wide awake, I assure you, Monseigneur, and he brings great news: the resignation of the only Jansenist left in your diocese. That terrible abbé Pirard understands at last the meaning of a hint.'

'Well,' said the Bishop with a roguish smile, 'I defy you to fill his place with a man of his quality. And to shew you the value of the man, I invite him to dine with me to-morrow.'

The Grand Vicar wished to insinuate a few words as to the choice of a successor. The prelate, little disposed to discuss business, said to him:

'Before we put in the next man, let us try to discover why this one is going. Fetch me in that seminarist, the truth is to be found in the mouths of babes.'

Julien was summoned: 'I shall find myself trapped between two inquisitors,' he thought. Never had he felt more courageous.

At the moment of his entering the room, two tall valets, better dressed than M. Valenod himself, were disrobing Monseigneur. The prelate, before coming to the subject of M. Pirard, thought fit to question Julien about his studies. He touched upon dogma, and was amazed. Presently he turned to the Humanities, Virgil, Horace, Cicero. 'Those names,' thought Julien, 'earned me my number 198. I have nothing more to lose, let us try to shine.' He was successful; the prelate, an excellent humanist himself, was enchanted.

At dinner at the Prefecture, a girl, deservedly famous, had recited the poem of *La Madeleine*.[1] He was in the mood for literary conversation, and at once forgot the abbé Pirard and everything else, in discussing with the seminarist the important question, whether Horace had been rich or poor. The prelate quoted a number of odes, but at times his memory began to fail him, and immediately Julien would recite the entire ode, with a modest air; what struck the Bishop was that Julien never departed from the tone of the conversation; he said his twenty or thirty Latin verses as he would have spoken of what was going on in his Seminary. A long discussion followed of Virgil and Cicero. At length the prelate could not refrain from paying the young seminarist a compliment.

'It would be impossible to have studied to better advantage.'

'Monseigneur,' said Julien, 'your Seminary can furnish you with one hundred and ninety-seven subjects far less unworthy of your esteemed approval.'

'How so?' said the prelate, astonished at this figure.

'I can support with official proof what I have the honour to say before Monseigneur.

'At the annual examination of the Seminary, answering questions upon these very subjects which have earned me, at this moment, Monseigneur's approval, I received the number 198.'

'Ah! This is the abbé Pirard's Benjamin,' exclaimed the Bishop, with a laugh, and with a glance at M. de Frilair; 'we ought to have expected this; but it is all in fair play. Is it not the case, my friend,' he went on, turning to Julien, 'that they waked you from your sleep to send you here?'

'Yes, Monseigneur. I have never left the Seminary alone in my life but once, to go and help M. l'abbé Chas-Bernard to decorate the Cathedral, on the feast of Corpus Domini.'

---

1 A poem by Delphine Gay.

'*Optime*,' said the Bishop; 'what, it was you that shewed such great courage, by placing the bunches of plumes on the baldachino? They make me shudder every year; I am always afraid of their costing me a man's life. My friend, you will go far; but I do not wish to cut short your career, which will be brilliant, by letting you die of hunger.'

And, on an order from the Bishop, the servants brought in biscuits and Malaga wine, to which Julien did honour, and even more so than abbé Frilair, who knew that his Bishop liked to see him eat cheerfully and with a good appetite.

The prelate, growing more and more pleased with the close of his evening, spoke for a moment of ecclesiastical history. He saw that Julien did not understand. He then passed to the moral conditions of the Roman Empire, under the Emperors of the Age of Constantine. The last days of paganism were accompanied by that state of uneasiness and doubt which, in the nineteenth century, is disturbing sad and weary minds. Monseigneur remarked that Julien seemed hardly to know even the name of Tacitus.

Julien replied with candour, to the astonishment of his Bishop, that this author was not to be found in the library of the Seminary.

'I am really delighted to hear it,' said the Bishop merrily. 'You relieve me of a difficulty; for the last ten minutes, I have been trying to think of a way of thanking you for the pleasant evening which you have given me, and certainly in a most unexpected manner. Although the gift is scarcely canonical, I should like to give you a set of Tacitus.'

The prelate sent for eight volumes handsomely bound, and insisted upon writing with his own hand, on the title page of the first, a Latin inscription to Julien Sorel. The Bishop prided himself on his fine Latinity; he ended by saying to him, in a serious tone, completely at variance with his tone throughout the rest of the conversation:

'Young man, *if you are wise*, you shall one day have the best living in my diocese, and not a hundred leagues from my episcopal Palace; but you must be *wise*.'

Julien, burdened with his volumes, left the Palace, in great bewilderment, as midnight was striking.

Monseigneur had not said a word to him about the abbé Pirard. Julien was astonished most of all by the extreme politeness shewn him by the Bishop. He had never imagined such an urbanity of form, combined with so natural an air of dignity. He was greatly struck by the contrast when he set eyes once more on the sombre abbé Pirard, who awaited him with growing impatience.

'*Quid tibi dixerunt?* (What did they say to you?)' he shouted at the top of his voice, the moment Julien came within sight.

Then, as Julien found some difficulty in translating the Bishop's conversation into Latin:

'Speak French, and repeat to me Monseigneur's own words, without adding or omitting anything,' said the ex-Director of the Seminary, in his harsh tone and profoundly inelegant manner.

'What a strange present for a Bishop to make to a young seminarist,' he said as he turned the pages of the sumptuous Tacitus, the gilded edges of which seemed to fill him with horror.

Two o'clock was striking when, after a detailed report of everything, he allowed his favourite pupil to retire to his own room.

'Leave me the first volume of your Tacitus, which contains the Bishop's inscription,' he said to him. 'That line of Latin will be your lightning conductor in this place, when I have gone.

'*Erit tibi, fili mi, successor meus tanquam leo quaerens quem devoret.* (My successor will be to you, my son, as a lion seeking whom he may devour.)'

On the following morning, Julien detected something strange in the manner in which his companions addressed him. This made him all the more reserved. 'Here,' he thought, 'we have the effect of M. Pirard's resignation. It is known throughout the place, and I am supposed to be his favourite. There must be an insult behind this attitude'; but he could not discover it. There was, on the contrary, an

238

absence of hatred in the eyes of all whom he encountered in the dormitories. 'What can this mean? It is doubtless a trap, we are playing a close game.' At length the young seminarist from Verrières said to him with a laugh: '*Cornelii Taciti opera omnia.*'

At this speech, which was overheard, all the rest seemed to vie with one another in congratulating Julien, not only upon the magnificent present which he had received from Monseigneur, but also upon the two hours of conversation with which he had been honoured. It was common knowledge, down to the most trifling details. From this moment, there was no more jealousy; everyone paid court to him most humbly; the abbé Castanède who, only yesterday, had treated him with the utmost insolence, came to take him by the arm and invited him to luncheon.

Owing to a weakness in Julien's character, the insolence of these coarse creatures had greatly distressed him; their servility caused him disgust and no pleasure.

Towards midday, the abbé Pirard took leave of his pupils, not without first delivering a severe allocution. 'Do you seek the honours of this world,' he said to them, 'all social advantages, the pleasure of commanding men, that of defying the laws and of being insolent to all men with impunity? Or indeed do you seek your eternal salvation? The most ignorant among you have only to open their eyes to distinguish between the two paths.'

No sooner had he left than the devotees of the Sacred Heart of Jesus went to chant a *Te Deum* in the chapel. Nobody in the Seminary took the late Director's allocution seriously. 'He is very cross at being dismissed,' was what might be heard on all sides. Not one seminarist was simple enough to believe in the voluntary resignation of a post which provided so many opportunities for dealing with the big contractors.

The abbé Pirard took up his abode in the best inn in Besançon; and on the pretext of some imaginary private affairs, proposed to spend a couple of days there.

The Bishop invited him to dinner, and, to tease his Grand Vicar de Frilair, endeavoured to make him shine. They had reached the dessert when there arrived from Paris the strange tidings that the abbé Pirard was appointed to the splendid living of N——, within four leagues of the capital. The worthy prelate congratulated him sincerely. He saw in the whole affair a well played game which put him in a good humour and gave him the highest opinion of the abbé's talents. He bestowed upon him a magnificent certificate in Latin, and silenced the abbé de Frilair, who ventured to make remonstrances.

That evening, Monseigneur carried his admiration to the drawing-room of the Marquise de Rubempré. It was a great piece of news for the select society of Besançon; people were lost in conjectures as to the meaning of this extraordinary favour. They saw the abbé Pirard a Bishop already. The sharper wits supposed M. de La Mole to have become a Minister, and allowed themselves that evening to smile at the imperious airs which M. l'abbé de Frilair assumed in society.

Next morning, the abbé Pirard was almost followed through the streets, and the tradesmen came out to their shop-doors when he went to beg an audience of the Marquis's judges. For the first time, he was received by them with civility. The stern Jansenist, indignant at everything that he saw around him, spent a long time at work with the counsel whom he had chosen for the Marquis de La Mole, and then left for Paris. He was so foolish as to say to two or three lifelong friends who escorted him to the carriage and stood admiring its heraldic blason, that after governing the Seminary for fifteen years he was leaving Besançon with five hundred and twenty francs in savings. These friends embraced him with tears in their eyes, and then said to one another: 'The good abbé might have spared himself that lie, it is really too absurd.'

The common herd, blinded by love of money, were not fitted to understand that it was in his sincerity that the abbé Pirard had found the strength to fight single-handed for six years against Marie Alacoque, the Sacred Heart of Jesus, the Jesuits and his Bishop.

CHAPTER THIRTY

AMBITION

There is only one true nobility left; namely, the title
of Duke; Marquis is absurd, at the word Duke one
turns one's head.

The Edinburgh Review.[1]

THE abbé was astonished by the noble air and almost
gay tone of the Marquis. Nevertheless this future
Minister received him without any of those little
mannerisms of a great gentleman, outwardly so polite, but
so impertinent to him who understands them. It would have
been a waste of time, and the Marquis was so far immersed
in public business as to have no time to waste.

For six months he had been intriguing to make both King
and nation accept a certain Ministry, which, as a mark of
gratitude, would make him a Duke.

The Marquis had appealed in vain, year after year, to his
lawyer at Besançon for a clear and definite report on his
lawsuits in the Franche-Comté. How was the eminent lawyer
to explain them to him, if he did not understand them
himself?

The little slip of paper which the abbé gave him explained
everything.

'My dear abbé,' said the Marquis, after polishing off in
less than five minutes all the polite formulas and personal

1 I have translated this motto, which is quoted in French by Stendhal, but have
not been able to find the original passage in the *Edinburgh Review*. C. K. S. M.

241

inquiries, 'my dear abbé, in the midst of my supposed prosperity, I lack the time to occupy myself seriously with two
little matters which nevertheless are of considerable importance: my family and my affairs. I take the greatest interest
in the fortunes of my house, I may carry it far; I look after
my pleasures, and that is what must come before everything
else, at least in my eyes,' he went on, noticing the astonishment in the eyes of the abbé Pirard. Although a man of sense,
the abbé was amazed to see an old man talking so openly of
his pleasures.

'Work does no doubt exist in Paris,' the great nobleman
continued, 'but perched in the attics; and as soon as I come
in contact with a man, he takes an apartment on the second
floor, and his wife starts a *day*; consequently, no more work,
no effort except to be or to appear to be a man of fashion.
That is their sole interest once they are provided with bread.

'For my lawsuits, to be strictly accurate, and also for each
lawsuit separately, I have lawyers who work themselves to
death; one of them died of consumption, the day before yesterday. But, for my affairs in general, would you believe, Sir,
that for the last three years I have given up hope of finding
a man who, while he is writing for me, will deign to think a
little seriously of what he is doing. However, all this is only
a preamble.

'I respect you, and, I would venture to add, although we
meet for the first time, I like you. Will you be my secretary,
with a salary of eight thousand francs, or indeed twice that
sum? I shall gain even more, I assure you; and I shall make
it my business to keep your fine living for you, for the day
on which we cease to agree.'

The abbé declined, but towards the end of the conversation, the sight of the Marquis's genuine embarrassment suggested an idea to him.

'I have left down in my Seminary,' he said to the Marquis,
'a poor young man who, if I be not mistaken, is going to be
brutally persecuted. If he were only a simple religious he
would be already *in pace*.

'At present this young man knows only Latin and the Holy

Scriptures; but it is by no means impossible that one day he may display great talent, either for preaching or for the guidance of souls. I do not know what he will do; but he has the sacred fire, he may go far. I intended to give him to our Bishop, should one ever be sent to us who had something of your way of looking at men and affairs.'

'What is your young man's origin?' said the Marquis.

'He is said to be the son of a carpenter in our mountains, but I am inclined to believe that he is the natural son of some rich man. I have seen him receive an anonymous or pseudonymous letter containing a bill of exchange for five hundred francs.'

'Ah! It is Julien Sorel,' said the Marquis.

'How do you know his name?' asked the astonished abbé; and, as he was blushing at his own question:

'That is what I am not going to tell you,' replied the Marquis.

'Very well!' the abbé went on, 'you might try making him your secretary, he has energy, and judgment; in short, it is an experiment worth trying.'

'Why not?' said the Marquis; 'but would he be the sort of man to let his palm be greased by the Prefect of Police or by anyone else, to play the spy on me? That is my only objection.'

Receiving favourable assurances from the abbé Pirard, the Marquis produced a note for one thousand francs:

'Send this to Julien Sorel for his journey; tell him to come to me.'

'Life in Paris must surely, M. le Marquis, have created this illusion in your mind; you are unaware, because you occupy an exalted social position, of the tyranny that weighs upon us poor provincials, and especially upon priests who are not on good terms with the Jesuits. They will never allow Julien Sorel to leave, they will manage to cover themselves with the cleverest excuses, they will reply that he is ill, letters will have gone astray in the post,' etc., etc.

'One of these days I shall procure a letter from the Minister to the Bishop,' said the Marquis.

'I was forgetting one thing,' said the abbé: 'this young man, although of quite humble birth, has a proud heart, he will be of no use to you in your business if his pride is offended; you will only make him stupid.'

'I like that,' said the Marquis, 'I shall make him my son's companion, will that do?'

Some time after this, Julien received a letter in an unknown hand and bearing the postmark of Châlon, and found a draft upon a merchant in Besançon and instructions to proceed to Paris without delay. The letter was signed with an assumed name, but as he opened it Julien trembled: a great blot of ink had dropped full upon the thirteenth word.[1] It was the signal arranged between him and the abbé Pirard.

Within an hour, Julien was summoned to the Bishop's Palace, where he found himself greeted with a wholly fatherly welcome. Interspersed with quotations from Horace, Monseigneur paid him, with regard to the exalted destiny that awaited him in Paris, a number of very neat compliments, which required an explanation if he were to express his thanks. Julien could say nothing, chiefly because he knew nothing, and Monseigneur shewed a high regard for him. One of the minor clergy of the Palace wrote to the Mayor who made haste to appear in person bringing a passport already signed, but with a blank space for the name of the traveller.

Before midnight, Julien was with Fouqué, whose sober mind was more astonished than delighted by the future which seemed to be in store for his friend.

'The end of it will be,' said this Liberal elector, 'a post under Government, which will oblige you to take some action that will be pilloried in the newspapers. It will be through your disgrace that I shall have news of you. Remember that, even financially speaking, it is better to earn one hundred louis in an honest trade in timber, where you are

1 Originally this passage read: 'A leaf from a tree had fallen out at his feet.' In correcting a copy of the first edition, Stendhal added the marginal note: 'The spy who opened the letter might fail to replace the leaf.' C. K. S. M.

your own master, than to receive four thousand francs from a Government, were it that of King Solomon himself.'

Julien saw no more in this than the pettiness of a rustic mind. He was at last going to appear on the stage of great events. He preferred less certainty and greater chances. In his heart there was no longer the slightest fear of dying of hunger. The good fortune of going to Paris, which he peopled in his imagination with men of intelligence, great intriguers, great hypocrites, but as courteous as the Bishop of Besançon and the Bishop of Agde, eclipsed everything else in his eyes. He represented himself humbly to his friend as deprived of his free will by the abbé Pirard's letter.

Towards noon on the following day he arrived in Verrières the happiest of men, he reckoned upon seeing Madame de Rênal again. He went first of all to his original protector, the good abbé Chélan. He met with a stern reception.

'Do you consider that you are under any obligation to me?' said M. Chélan, without acknowledging his greeting. 'You will take luncheon with me, meanwhile another horse will be hired for you, and you will leave Verrières, *without seeing anyone.*'

'To hear is to obey,' replied Julien, with the prim face of a seminarist; and there was no further discussion save of theology and Latin scholarship.

He mounted his horse, rode a league, after which, coming upon a wood, with no one to see him enter it, he hid himself there. At sunset he sent back the horse by a peasant to the nearest gate of the town. Later on, he entered the house of a vine-dresser who agreed to sell him a ladder, and to go with him, carrying the ladder, to the little wood that overhung the Cours de la Fidélité, in Verrières.

'We are a poor conscript deserting—or a smuggler,' said the peasant, as he took leave of him, 'but what do I care? My ladder is well paid for, and I myself have had to pass some awkward moments in my life.'

The night was very dark. About one o'clock in the morning, Julien, carrying his ladder, made his way into Verrières. He climbed down as soon as he could into the bed of the torrent, which ran through M. de Rênal's magnificent gardens at a depth of ten feet, and confined between walls. Julien climbed up easily by his ladder. 'What sort of greeting will the watch-dogs give me?' he wondered. 'That is the whole question.' The dogs barked, and rushed towards him; but he whistled softly, and they came and fawned upon him.

Then climbing from terrace to terrace, although all the gates were shut, he had no difficulty in arriving immediately beneath the window of Madame de Rênal's bedroom, which, on the garden side, was no more than nine or ten feet above the ground.

There was in the shutters a small opening in the shape of a heart, which Julien knew well. To his great dismay, this little opening was not lighted by the glimmer of a nightlight within.

'Great God!' he said to himself; 'to-night, of all nights, this room is not occupied by Madame de Rênal! Where can she be sleeping? The family are at Verrières, since I found the dogs here; but I may in this room, without a light, come upon M. de Rênal himself or a stranger, and then what a scandal!'

The most prudent course was to retire; but the idea filled Julien with horror. 'If it is a stranger, I shall make off as fast as my legs will carry me, leaving my ladder behind; but if it is she, what sort of welcome awaits me? She is steeped in repentance and the most extreme piety, I may be sure of that; but after all, she has still some memory of me, since she has just written to me.' With this argument he made up his mind.

His heart trembling, but determined nevertheless to see her or to perish, he flung a handful of gravel against the shutter; no reply. He placed his ladder against the wall by the side of the window and tapped himself on the shutter, softly at first then more loudly. 'Dark as it is, they may fire a gun at me,' thought Julien. This thought reduced his mad undertaking to a question of physical courage.

'This room is unoccupied to-night,' he thought, 'or else whoever it is that is sleeping here is awake by this time. So there is no need for any further precaution here; all I need think of is not making myself heard by the people who are sleeping in the other rooms.'

He stepped down, placed his ladder against one of the shutters, climbed up again and passing his hand through the heart-shaped opening, was fortunate in finding almost at once the wire fastened to the latch that closed the shutter. He pulled this wire; it was with an unspeakable joy that he felt that the shutter was no longer closed and was yielding to his efforts. 'I must open it little by little and let her recognize my voice.' He opened the shutter sufficiently to pass his head through the gap, repeating in a whisper: '*It is a friend.*'

He made certain, by applying his ear, that nothing broke the profound silence in the room. But decidedly, there was no nightlight, even half extinguished, on the hearth; this was indeed a bad sign.

'Beware of a gunshot!' He thought for a moment; then, with one finger, ventured to tap the pane: no response; he tapped more loudly. 'Even if I break the glass, I must settle this business.' As he was knocking hard, he thought he could just make out, in the pitch darkness, something like a white phantom coming across the room. In a moment, there was no doubt about it, he did see a phantom which seemed to be advancing with extreme slowness. Suddenly he saw a cheek pressed to the pane to which his eye was applied.

He shuddered, and recoiled slightly. But the night was so dark that, even at this close range, he could not make out whether it was Madame de Rênal. He feared an instinctive cry of alarm; already he could hear the dogs prowling with muttered growls round the foot of his ladder. 'It is I,' he repeated, quite loudly, 'a friend.' No answer; the white phantom had vanished. 'For pity's sake, open the window. I must speak to you, I am too wretched!' and he knocked until the window nearly broke.

A little sharp sound was heard; the catch of the window gave way; he pushed it open and sprang lightly into the room.

The white phantom moved away; he seized it by the arms;

247

it was a woman. All his ideas of courage melted. 'If it is she, what will she say to me?' What was his state when he realized from a faint cry that it was Madame de Rênal.

He gathered her in his arms; she trembled, and had barely the strength to repulse him.

'Wretch! What are you doing?'

Scarcely could her tremulous voice articulate the words. Julien saw that she was genuinely angry.

'I have come to see you after fourteen months of a cruel parting.'

'Go, leave me this instant. Ah! M. Chélan, why did you forbid me to write to him? I should have prevented this horror.' She thrust him from her with a force that was indeed extraordinary. 'I repent of my crime; heaven has deigned to enlighten me,' she repeated in a stifled voice. 'Go! Fly!'

'After fourteen months of misery, I shall certainly not leave you until I have spoken to you. I wish to know all that you have been doing. Ah! I have loved you well enough to deserve this confidence. . . . I wish to know all.'

In spite of herself Madame de Rênal felt this tone of authority exert its influence over her heart.

Julien, who was holding her in a passionate embrace, and resisting her efforts to liberate herself, ceased to press her in his arms. This relaxation helped to reassure Madame de Rênal.

'I am going to draw up the ladder,' he said, 'so that it may not compromise us if one of the servants, awakened by the noise, goes the rounds.'

'Ah! Leave me, leave me rather,' the answer came with unfeigned anger. 'What do men matter to me? It is God that sees the terrible wrong you are doing me, and will punish me for it. You are taking a cowardly advantage of the regard that I once felt for you, but no longer feel. Do you hear, Master Julien?'

He drew up the ladder very slowly, so as not to make any noise.

'Is your husband in town?' he asked, not to defy her, but from force of habit.

'Do not speak to me so, for pity's sake, or I shall call my husband. I am all too guilty already of not having sent you away, at any cost. I pity you,' she told him, seeking to wound his pride which she knew to be so irritable.

Her use of the plural pronoun, that abrupt method of breaking so tender a bond, and one upon which he still reckoned, roused Julien's amorous transport to a frenzy.

'What! Is it possible that you no longer love me!' he said to her, in those accents of the heart to which it is so difficult to listen unmoved.

She made no reply; as for him, he was weeping bitter tears.

Really, he had no longer the strength to speak.

'And so I am completely forgotten by the one person who has ever loved me! What use to live any longer?' All his courage had left him as soon as he no longer had to fear the danger of encountering a man; everything had vanished from his heart, save love.

He wept for a long time in silence. She could hear the sound of his sobs. He took her hand, she tried to withdraw it; and yet, after a few almost convulsive movements she let him keep it. The darkness was intense; they found themselves both seated upon Madame de Rênal's bed.

'What a difference from the state of things fourteen months ago!' thought Julien, and his flow of tears increased. 'So absence unfailingly destroys all human feelings! The best thing will be for me to go!

'Be so kind as to tell me what has happened to you,' Julien said at length, in a voice almost stifled by emotion.

'There can be no doubt,' replied Madame de Rênal in a harsh voice, the tone of which offered a cutting reproach to Julien, 'my misdeeds were known in the town, at the time of your departure. You were so imprudent in your behaviour. Some time later, when I was in despair, the respectable M. Chélan came to see me. It was in vain that, for a long time, he sought to obtain a confession. One day, the idea occurred to him to take me into that church at Dijon in which I made my first Communion. There, he ventured to broach the subject. . . .' Madame de Rênal's speech was interrupted by her tears. 'What a shameful moment! I confessed all. That worthy man was kind enough not to heap on me the weight of his indignation: he shared my distress. At that time I was writing you day after day letters which I dared not send you; I concealed them carefully, and when I was too wretched used to shut myself up in my room and read over my own letters.

'At length, M. Chélan persuaded me to hand them over to him. . . . Some of them, written with a little more prudence than the rest, had been sent to you; never once did you answer me.'

'Never, I swear to you, did I receive any letter from you at the Seminary.'

'Great God! who can have intercepted them?'

'Imagine my grief; until the day when I saw you in the Cathedral, I did not know whether you were still alive.'

'God in His mercy made me understand how greatly I was sinning against Him, against my children, against my husband,' replied Madame de Rênal. 'He has never loved me as I believed then that you loved me. . . .'

Julien flung himself into her arms, without any definite intention but with entire lack of self-control. But Madame de Rênal thrust him from her, and continued quite firmly:

'My respectable friend M. Chélan made me realize that, in marrying M. de Rênal, I had pledged all my affections to him, even those of which I was still ignorant, which I had never felt before a certain fatal intimacy. . . . Since the great sacrifice of those letters, which were so precious to me, my life has flowed on, if not happily, at any rate quietly enough. Do not disturb it any more; be a friend to me . . . the best of friends.' Julien covered her hands with kisses; she could feel that he was still crying. 'Do not cry, you distress me so. . . . Tell me, it is your turn now, all that you have been doing.' Julien was unable to speak. 'I wish to know what sort of life you led at the Seminary,' she repeated, 'then you shall go.'

Without a thought of what he was telling her, Julien spoke of the endless intrigues and jealousies which he had encountered at first, then of his more peaceful life after he was appointed tutor.

'It was then,' he added, 'that after a long silence, which was doubtless intended to make me understand what I see only too clearly now, that you no longer love me, and that I had become as nothing to you. . . .'

Madame de Rênal gripped his hands. 'It was then that you sent me a sum of five hundred francs.'

'Never,' said Madame de Rênal.

'It was a letter postmarked *Paris* and signed Paul Sorel, to avoid all suspicion.'

A short discussion followed as to the possible source of this letter. The atmosphere began to change. Unconsciously, Madame de Rênal and Julien had departed from their solemn tone; they had returned to that of a tender intimacy. They could not see each other, so intense was the darkness, but the sound of their voices told all. Julien slipped his arm round the waist of his mistress; this movement was highly dangerous. She tried to remove Julien's arm, whereupon he, with a certain adroitness, distracted her attention by an interesting point in his narrative. The arm was then forgotten, and remained in the position that it had occupied.

After abundant conjectures as to the source of the letter with the five hundred francs, Julien had resumed his narrative; he became rather more his own master in speaking of his past life which, in comparison with what was happening to him at that moment, interested him so little. His attention was wholly concentrated on the manner in which his visit was to end. 'You must leave me,' she kept on telling him, in a curt tone.

'What a disgrace for me if I am shewn the door! The remorse will be enough to poison my whole life,' he said to himself, 'she will never write to me. God knows when I shall return to this place!' From that moment, all the element of heavenly bliss in Julien's situation vanished rapidly from his heart. Seated by the side of a woman whom he adored, clasping her almost in his arms, in this room in which he had been so happy, plunged in a black darkness, perfectly well aware that for the last minute she had been crying, feeling, from the movement of her bosom, that she was convulsed

251

with sobs, he unfortunately became a frigid politician, almost as calculating and as frigid as when, in the courtyard of the Seminary, he saw himself made the butt of some malicious joke by one of his companions stronger than himself. Julien spun out his story, and spoke of the wretched life he had led since leaving Verrières. 'And so,' Madame de Rênal said to herself, 'after a year's absence, almost without a single token of remembrance, while I was forgetting him, his mind was entirely taken up with the happy days he had enjoyed at Vergy.' Her sobs increased in violence. Julien saw that his story had been successful. He realized that he must now try his last weapon: he came abruptly to the letter that he had just received from Paris.

'I have taken leave of Monseigneur, the Bishop.'

'What! You are not returning to Besançon! You are leaving us for ever?'

'Yes,' replied Julien, in a resolute tone; 'yes, I am abandoning the place where I am forgotten even by her whom I have most dearly loved in all my life, and I am leaving it never to set eyes on it again. I am going to Paris....'

'You are going to Paris!' Madame de Rênal exclaimed quite aloud.

Her voice was almost stifled by her tears, and shewed the intensity of her grief. Julien had need of this encouragement; he was going to attempt a course which might decide everything against him; and before this exclamation, seeing no light, he was absolutely ignorant of the effect that he was producing. He hesitated no longer; the fear of remorse gave him complete command of himself; he added coldly as he rose to his feet:

'Yes, Madame, I leave you for ever, may you be happy; farewell.'

He took a few steps towards the window; he was already opening it. Madame de Rênal sprang after him. He felt her head droop on his shoulder, and that she was clasping him in her arms, pressing her cheek to his.

Thus, after three hours of conversation, Julien obtained what he had so passionately desired during the first two. Had they come a little earlier, this return to tender sentiments, the eclipse of remorse in Madame de Rênal would have been a divine happiness; obtained thus by artifice, they were no more than a formal triumph. Julien positively insisted, against the entreaties of his mistress, upon lighting the nightlight.

'Do you then wish me,' he asked her, 'to retain no memory of having seen you? The love that is doubtless glowing in those charming eyes, shall it then be lost to me? Shall the whiteness of that lovely hand be invisible to me? Think that I am leaving you for a very long time perhaps!'

'This is shocking,' Madame de Rênal said to herself, but she could refuse nothing to this idea of lifelong separation, which made her dissolve in tears. Dawn was beginning to paint in clear hues the outline of the fir trees on the mountain to the east of Verrières. Instead of going away, Julien, drunken with pleasure, asked Madame de Rênal to let him spend the whole day hidden in her room, and not to leave until the following night.

'And why not?' was her answer. 'This fatal relapse destroys all my self-esteem, and dooms me to lifelong misery,' and she pressed him rapturously to her heart. 'My husband is no longer the same, he has suspicions; he believes that I have been fooling him throughout this affair, and is in the worst of tempers with me. If he hears the least sound I am lost, he will drive me from the house like the wretch that I am.'

'Ah! There I can hear the voice of M. Chélan,' said Julien; 'you would not have spoken to me like that before my cruel departure for the Seminary; you loved me then!'

Julien was rewarded for the coolness with which he had uttered this speech; he saw his mistress at once forget the danger in which the proximity of her husband involved her, to think of the far greater danger of seeing Julien doubtful of her love for him. The daylight was rapidly increasing and now flooded the room; Julien recovered all the exquisite sensations of pride when he was once more able to see in his arms and almost at his feet this charming woman, the only woman that he had ever loved, who, a few hours earlier, had been entirely wrapped up in the fear of a terrible God and in devotion to duty. Resolutions fortified by a year of constancy had not been able to hold out against his boldness.

Presently they heard a sound in the house; a consideration to which she had not given a thought now disturbed Madame de Rênal.

'That wicked Elisa will be coming into the room, what are we to do with that enormous ladder?' she said to her lover; 'where are we to hide it? I am going to take it up to the loft,' she suddenly exclaimed, with a sort of joviality.

'There, that is the face I remember,' said the delighted Julien. 'But you will have to go through the man's room.'

'I shall leave the ladder in the corridor, call the man and send him on an errand.'

'Remember to have some excuse ready in case the man notices the ladder when he passes it in the passage.'

'Yes, my angel,' said Madame de Rênal as she gave him a kiss. 'And you, remember to hide yourself quickly under the bed if Elisa comes into the room while I am away.'

Julien was amazed at this sudden gaiety. 'And so,' hc thought, 'the approach of physical danger, so far from disturbing her, restores her gaiety because she forgets her remorse! Indeed a superior woman! Ah! There is a heart in which it is glorious to reign!' Julien was in ecstasies.

Madame de Rênal took the ladder; plainly it was too heavy for her. Julien went to her assistance; he was admiring that elegant figure, which suggested anything rather than strength, when suddenly, without help, she grasped the ladder and picked it up as she might have picked up a chair. She carried it swiftly to the corridor on the third storey, where she laid it down by the wall. She called the man-servant, and, to give him time to put on his clothes, went up to the dovecote. Five minutes later, when she returned to the corridor, the ladder was no more to be seen. What had become of it? Had Julien been out of the house, the danger would have been nothing. But, at that moment, if her husband saw the ladder! The consequences might be appalling. Madame de Rênal ran up and down the house. At last she discovered the ladder under the roof, where the man had taken and in fact hidden it himself. This in itself was strange, and at another time would have alarmed her.

'What does it matter to me,' she thought, 'what may happen in twenty-four hours from now, when Julien will have gone? Will not everything then be to me horror and remorse?'

She had a sort of vague idea that she ought to take her life, but what did that matter? After a parting which she had supposed to be for ever, he was restored to her, she saw him again, and what he had done in making his way to her gave proof of such a wealth of love!

In telling Julien of the incident of the ladder:

'What shall I say to my husband,' she asked him, 'if the man tells him how he found the ladder?' She meditated for a moment. 'It will take them twenty-four hours to discover the peasant who sold it to you'; and flinging herself into Julien's arms and clasping him in a convulsive embrace: 'Ah! to die, to die like this!' she cried as she covered him with kisses; 'but I must not let you die of hunger,' she added with a laugh.

'Come; first of all, I am going to hide you in Madame Derville's room, which is always kept locked.' She kept watch at the end of the corridor and Julien slipped from door to door. 'Remember not to answer, if anyone knocks,' she reminded him as she turned the key outside; 'anyhow, it would only be the children playing.'

'Make them go into the garden, below the window,' said Julien, 'so that I may have the pleasure of seeing them, make them speak.'

'Yes, yes,' cried Madame de Rênal as she left him.

She returned presently with oranges, biscuits, a bottle of Malaga; she had found it impossible to purloin any bread.

'What is your husband doing?' said Julien.

'He is writing down notes of the deals he proposes to do with some peasants.'

But eight o'clock had struck, the house was full of noise. If Madame de Rênal were not to be seen, people would begin

searching everywhere for her; she was obliged to leave him.
Presently she returned, in defiance of all the rules of prudence, to bring him a cup of coffee; she was afraid of his
dying of hunger. After luncheon she managed to shepherd
the children underneath the window of Madame Derville's
room. He found that they had grown considerably, but they
had acquired a common air, or else his ideas had changed.
Madame de Rênal spoke to them of Julien. The eldest replied
with affection and regret for his former tutor, but it appeared
that the two younger had almost forgotten him.

M. de Rênal did not leave the house that morning; he
was incessantly going up and downstairs, engaged in striking
bargains with certain peasants, to whom he was selling his
potato crop. Until dinner time, Madame de Rênal had not
a moment to spare for her prisoner. When dinner was on
the table, it occurred to her to steal a plateful of hot soup
for him. As she silently approached the door of the room in
which he was, carrying the plate carefully, she found herself
face to face with the servant who had hidden the ladder that
morning. At the moment, he too was coming silently along
the corridor, as though listening. Probably Julien had forgotten to tread softly. The servant made off in some confusion.
Madame de Rênal went boldly into Julien's room; her
account of the incident made him shudder.

'You are afraid'; she said to him; 'and I, I would brave all
the dangers in the world without a tremor. I fear one thing
only, that is the moment when I shall be left alone after you
have gone,' and she ran from the room.

'Ah!' thought Julien, greatly excited, 'remorse is the only
danger that sublime soul dreads!'

Night came at last. M. de Rênal went to the Casino.

His wife had announced a severe headache, she retired to
her room, made haste to dismiss Elisa, and speedily rose from
her bed to open the door to Julien.

It so happened that he really was faint with hunger.
Madame de Rênal went to the pantry to look for bread.
Julien heard a loud cry. She returned and told him that on
entering the dark pantry, making her way to a cupboard in

which the bread was kept, and stretching out her hand, she
had touched a woman's arm. It was Elisa who had uttered
the cry which Julien had heard.

'What was she doing there?'

'She was stealing sweets, or possibly spying on us,' said
Madame de Rênal with complete indifference. 'But fortunately I have found a pie and a big loaf.'

'And what have you got there?' said Julien, pointing to the
pockets of her apron.

Madame de Rênal had forgotten that, ever since dinner,
they had been filled with bread.

Julien clasped her in his arms with the keenest passion;
never had she seemed to him so beautiful. 'Even in Paris,'
he told himself vaguely, 'I shall not be able to find a nobler
character.' She had all the awkwardness of a woman little
accustomed to attentions of this sort, and at the same time
the true courage of a person who fears only dangers of
another kind and far more terrible.

While Julien was devouring his supper with a keen appetite, and his mistress was playfully apologizing for the simplicity of the repast, for she had a horror of serious speech, the
door of the room was all at once shaken violently. It was M.
de Rênal.

'Why have you locked yourself in?' he shouted to her.

Julien had just time to slip beneath the sofa.

'What! You are fully dressed,' said M. de Rênal, as he
entered; 'you are having supper, and you have locked your
door?'

On any ordinary day, this question, put with all the brutal-
ity of a husband, would have troubled Madame de Rênal,
but she felt that her husband had only to lower his eyes a
little to catch sight of Julien; for M. de Rênal had flung himself upon the chair on which Julien had been sitting a
moment earlier, facing the sofa.

Her headache served as an excuse for everything. While
in his turn her husband was giving her a long and detailed
account of the pool he had won in the billiard room of the
Casino, 'a pool of nineteen francs, begad!' he added, she saw

lying on a chair before their eyes, and within a few feet of them, Julien's hat. Cooler than ever, she began to undress, and, choosing her moment, passed swiftly behind her husband and flung a garment over the chair with the hat on it.

At length M. de Rênal left her. She begged Julien to begin over again the story of his life in the Seminary: 'Yesterday I was not listening to you, I was thinking, while you were speaking, only of how I was to summon up courage to send you away.'

She was the embodiment of imprudence. They spoke very loud; and it might have been two o'clock in the morning when they were interrupted by a violent blow on the door. It was M. de Rênal again:

'Let me in at once, there are burglars in the house!' he said, 'Saint-Jean found their ladder this morning.'

'This is the end of everything,' cried Madame de Rênal, throwing herself into Julien's arms. 'He is going to kill us both, he does not believe in the burglars; I am going to die in your arms, more fortunate in my death than I have been in my life.' She made no answer to her husband, who was waiting angrily outside, she was holding Julien in a passionate embrace.

'Save Stanislas's mother,' he said to her with an air of command. 'I am going to jump down into the courtyard from the window of the closet, and escape through the garden, the dogs know me. Make a bundle of my clothes and throw it down into the garden as soon as you can. Meanwhile, let him break the door in. And whatever you do, no confession, I forbid it, suspicion is better than certainty.'

'You will kill yourself, jumping down,' was her sole reply and her sole anxiety.

She went with him to the window of the closet; she then took such time as she required to conceal his garments. Finally she opened the door to her husband, who was boiling with rage. He searched the bedroom, the closet, without uttering a word, and then vanished. Julien's clothes were thrown down to him, he caught them and ran quickly down the garden towards the Doubs.

As he ran, he heard a bullet whistle past him, and simultaneously the sound of a gun being fired.

'That is not M. de Rênal,' he decided, 'he is not a good enough shot.' The dogs were running by his side in silence, a second shot apparently shattered the paw of one dog, for it began to emit lamentable howls. Julien jumped the wall of a terrace, proceeded fifty yards under cover, then continued his flight in a different direction. He heard voices calling to him, and could distinctly see the servant, his enemy, fire a gun; a farmer also came and shot at him from the other side of the garden, but by this time Julien had reached the bank of the Doubs, where he put on his clothes.

An hour later, he was a league from Verrières, on the road to Geneva. 'If there is any suspicion,' thought Julien, 'it is on the Paris road that they will look for me.'

VOLUME TWO

She is not pretty, she wears no rouge.
SAINTE-BEUVE

CHAPTER THIRTY-ONE
COUNTRY PLEASURES

O rus, quando ego te aspiciam!
HORACE.

'THE gentleman is waiting, surely, for the mail-coach for Paris?' he was asked by the landlord of an inn at which he stopped to break his fast.

'To-day or to-morrow, it is all the same to me,' said Julien.

The coach arrived while he was feigning indifference. There were two places vacant.

'What! It is you, my poor Falcoz,' said the traveller, who had come from the direction of Geneva to him who now entered the coach with Julien.

'I thought you had settled in the neighbourhood of Lyons,' said Falcoz, 'in a charming valley by the Rhone.'

'Settled, indeed! I am running away.'

'What! Running away? You, Saint-Giraud! With that honest face of yours, have you committed a crime?' said Falcoz, with a laugh.

'Upon my soul, not far off it. I am running away from the abominable life one leads in the country. I love the shade of the woods and the quiet of the fields, as you know; you have often accused me of being romantic. The one thing I never wished to hear mentioned was politics, and politics pursue me everywhere.'

'But to what party do you belong?'

'To none, and that is what has been fatal to me. These are all my politics: I enjoy music, and painting; a good book is an event in my life; I shall soon be four and forty. How many years have I to live? Fifteen, twenty, thirty, perhaps, at the most. Very well; I hold that in thirty years from now, our Ministers will be a little more able, but otherwise just as good fellows as we have to-day. The history of England serves as a mirror to shew me our future. There will always be a King who seeks to extend his prerogative; the ambition to enter Parliament, the glory and the hundreds of thousands of francs amassed by Mirabeau will always keep our wealthy provincials awake at night: they will call that being Liberal and loving the people. The desire to become a Peer or a Gentleman in Waiting will always possess the Ultras. On board the Ship of State, everyone will wish to be at the helm, for the post is well paid. Will there never be a little corner anywhere for the mere passenger?'

'Why, of course, and a very pleasant one, too, for a man of your peaceful nature. Is it the last election that is driving you from your district?'

'My trouble dates from farther back. I was, four years ago, forty years old, and had five hundred thousand francs, I am four years older now, and have probably fifty thousand less, which I shall lose by the sale of my place, Monfleury, by the Rhone, a superb position.

'In Paris, I was tired of that perpetual play-acting, to which one is driven by what you call nineteenth century civilisation. I felt a longing for human fellowship and simplicity. I bought a piece of land in the mountains by the Rhone, the most beautiful spot in the world.

'The vicar of the village and the neighbouring squires made much of me for the first six months; I had them to dine; I had left Paris, I told them, so as never to mention or to hear of politics again. You see, I subscribe to no newspaper. The fewer letters the postman brings me, the happier I am.

'This was not what the vicar wanted; presently I was besieged with endless indiscreet requests, intrigues, and so forth. I wished to give two or three hundred francs every year to the poor, they pestered me for them on behalf of pious associations; Saint Joseph, Our Lady, and so forth. I refused: then I came in for endless insults. I was foolish enough to shew annoyance. I could no longer leave the house in the morning to go and enjoy the beauty of our mountain scenery, without meeting some bore who would interrupt my thoughts with an unpleasant reminder of my fellow men and their evil ways. In the Rogation-tide processions, for instance, the chanting in which I like (it is probably a Greek melody), they no longer bless my fields, because, the vicar says, they belong to an unbeliever. A pious old peasant woman's cow dies, she says that it is because there is a pond close by which belongs to me, the unbeliever, a philosopher from Paris, and a week later I find all my fish floating on the water, poisoned with lime. I am surrounded by trickery in every form. The justice of the peace, an honest man, but afraid of losing his place, always decides against me. The peace of the fields is hell to me. As soon as they saw me abandoned by the vicar, head of the village *Congregation*, and not supported by the retired captain, head of the Liberals, they all fell upon me, even the mason who had been living upon me for a year, even the wheelwright, who tried to rob me with the utmost impunity, when he mended my ploughs.

'In order to have some footing and to win a few at least of my lawsuits, I turned Liberal; but, as you were saying, those damned elections came, they asked me for my vote. . . .'

'For a stranger?'

'Not a bit of it, for a man I know only too well. I refused, a fearful imprudence! From that moment, I had the Liberals on top of me as well, my position became intolerable. I believe that if it had ever entered the vicar's head to accuse me of having murdered my servant, there would have been a score of witnesses from both parties, ready to swear that they had seen me commit the crime.'

'You wish to live in the country without ministering to your neighbours' passions, without even listening to their gossip. What a mistake!'

'I have made amends for it now. Monfleury is for sale. I shall lose fifty thousand francs, if I must, but I am overjoyed,

265

I am leaving that hell of hypocrisy and malice. I am going to seek solitude and rustic peace in the one place in France where they exist, in a fourth-floor apartment, overlooking the Champs-Elysées. And yet I am just thinking whether I shall not begin my political career, in the Roule quarter, by presenting the blessed bread in the parish church.'

'None of that would have happened to you under Bonaparte,' said Falcoz, his eyes shining with anger and regret.

'That's all very well, but why couldn't he keep going, your Bonaparte? Everything that I suffer from to-day is his doing.'

Here Julien began to listen with increased attention. He had realised from the first that the Bonapartist Falcoz was the early playmate of M. de Rênal, repudiated by him in 1816, while the philosopher Saint-Giraud must be a brother of that chief clerk in the Prefecture of ——, who knew how to have municipal property knocked down to him on easy terms.

'And all that has been your Bonaparte's doing,' Saint-Giraud continued: 'An honest man, harmless if ever there was one, forty years old and with five hundred thousand francs, can't settle down in the country and find peace there. Bonaparte's priests and nobles drive him out again.'

'Ah! You must not speak evil of him,' cried Falcoz, 'never has France stood so high in the esteem of foreign nations as during the thirteen years of his reign. In those days, everything that was done had greatness in it.'

'Your Emperor, may the devil fly away with him,' went on the man of four and forty, 'was great only upon his battle-fields, and when he restored our financial balance in 1802. What was the meaning of all his conduct after that? With his chamberlains and his pomp and his receptions at the Tuileries, he simply furnished a new edition of all the stuff and nonsense of the monarchy. It was a corrected edition, it might have served for a century or two. The nobles and priests preferred to return to the old edition, but they have not the iron hand that they need to bring it before the public.'

'Listen to the old printer talking!'

'Who is it that is turning me off my land?' went on the printer with heat. 'The priests, whom Napoleon brought back with his Concordat, instead of treating them as the State treats doctors, lawyers, astronomers, of regarding them merely as citizens, without inquiring into the trade by which they earn their living. Would there be these insolent gentlemen to-day if your Bonaparte had not created barons and counts? No, the fashion had passed. Next to the priests, it is the minor country nobles that have annoyed me most, and forced me to turn Liberal.'

The discussion was endless, this theme will occupy the minds and tongues of France for the next half-century. As Saint-Giraud kept on repeating that it was impossible to live in the provinces, Julien timidly cited the example of M. de Rênal.

'Egad, young man, you're a good one!' cried Falcoz, 'he has turned himself into a hammer so as not to be made the anvil, and a terrible hammer at that. But I can see him cut out by Valenod. Do you know that rascal? He's the real article. What will your M. de Rênal say when he finds himself turned out of office one of these fine days, and Valenod filling his place?'

'He will be left to meditate on his crimes,' said Saint-Giraud. 'So you know Verrières, young man, do you? Very good! Bonaparte, whom heaven confound, made possible the reign of the Rênals and Chélans, which has paved the way for the reign of the Valenods and Maslons.'

This talk of shady politics astonished Julien, and took his thoughts from his dreams of sensual bliss.

He was little impressed by the first view of Paris seen in the distance. His fantastic imaginings of the future in store for him had to do battle with the still vivid memory of the twenty-four hours which he had just spent at Verrières. He made a vow that he would never abandon his mistress's children, but would give up everything to protect them, should the impertinences of the priests give us a Republic and lead to persecutions of the nobility.

What would have happened to him on the night of his

arrival at Verrières if, at the moment when he placed his ladder against Madame de Rênal's bedroom window, he had found that room occupied by a stranger, or by M. de Rênal?

But also what bliss in those first few hours, when his mistress really wished to send him away, and he pleaded his cause, seated by her side in the darkness! A mind like Julien's is pursued by such memories for a lifetime. The rest of their meeting had already merged into the first phases of their love, fourteen months earlier.

Julien was awakened from his profound abstraction by the stopping of the carriage. They had driven into the courtyard of the posthouse in the rue Jean-Jacques Rousseau. 'I wish to go to the Malmaison,' he told the driver of a passing cabriolet.

'At this time of night, Sir? What to do?'

'What business is it of yours? Drive on.'

True passion thinks only of itself. That, it seems to me, is why the passions are so absurd in Paris, where one's neighbour always insists upon one's thinking largely of him. I shall not describe Julien's transports at Malmaison. He wept. What! In spite of the ugly white walls set up this year, which divide the park in pieces? Yes, sir; for Julien, as for posterity, there was no distinction between Arcole, Saint Helena and Malmaison.

That evening, Julien hesitated for long before entering the playhouse; he had strange ideas as to that sink of iniquity.

An intense distrust prevented him from admiring the Paris of to-day, he was moved only by the monuments bequeathed by his hero.

'So here I am in the centre of intrigue and hypocrisy! This is where the Abbé de Frilair's protectors reign.'

On the evening of the third day, curiosity prevailed over his plan of seeing everything before calling upon the Abbé Pirard. The said abbé explained to him, in a frigid tone, the sort of life that awaited him at M. de La Mole's.

'If after a few months you are of no use to him, you will return to the Seminary, but by the front door. You are going to lodge with the Marquis, one of the greatest noblemen in

France. You will dress in black, but like a layman in mourning, not like a churchman. I require that, thrice weekly, you pursue your theological studies in a Seminary, where I shall introduce you. Each day, at noon, you will take your place in the library of the Marquis, who intends to employ you in writing letters with reference to lawsuits and other business. The Marquis notes down, in a word or two, upon the margin of each letter that he receives, a summary of the answer that it requires. I have undertaken that, by the end of three months, you will have learned to compose these answers to such effect that, of every twelve which you present to the Marquis for his signature, he will be able to sign eight or nine. In the evening, at eight o'clock, you will put his papers in order, and at ten you will be free.

'It may happen,' the Abbé Pirard continued, 'that some old lady or some man of persuasive speech will hint to you the prospect of immense advantages, or quite plainly offer you money to let him see the letters received by the Marquis....'

'Oh, Sir!' cried Julien, blushing.

'It is strange,' said the abbé with a bitter smile, 'that, poor as you are, and after a year of Seminary, you still retain these virtuous indignations. You must indeed have been blind!

'Can it be his blood coming out?' murmured the abbé, as though putting the question to himself. 'The strange thing is,' he added, looking at Julien, 'that the Marquis knows you.... How, I cannot say. He is giving you, to begin with, a salary of one hundred louis. He is a man who acts only from caprice, that is his weakness; he will outdo you in puerilities. If he is pleased with you, your salary may rise in time to eight thousand francs.

'But you must be well aware,' the abbé went on in a harsh tone, 'that he is not giving you all this money for your handsome face. You will have to be of use to him. If I were in your position, I should speak as little as possible, and above all, never speak of matters of which I know nothing.

'Ah!' said the abbé, 'I have been making inquiries on your behalf; I was forgetting M. de La Mole's family. He has two

269

children, a daughter, and a son of nineteen, the last word in elegance, a mad fellow, who never knows at one minute what he will be doing the next. He has spirit, and courage; he has fought in Spain. The Marquis hopes, I cannot say why, that you will become friends with the young Comte Norbert. I have said that you are a great Latin scholar, perhaps he reckons upon your teaching his son a few ready-made phrases, upon Cicero and Virgil.

'In your place, I should never allow this fine young man to make free with me; and, before yielding to his overtures, which will be perfectly civil, but slightly marred by irony, I should make him repeat them at least twice.

'I shall not conceal from you that the young Comte de La Mole is bound to look down upon you at first, because of your humble birth. He is the direct descendant of a courtier, who had the honour to have his head cut off on the Place de Grève, on the 26th of April, 1574, for a political intrigue. As for you, you are the son of a carpenter at Verrières, and moreover, you are in his father's pay. Weigh these differences carefully, and study the history of this family in Moreri; all the flatterers who dine at their table make from time to time what they call delicate allusions to it.

'Take care how you respond to the pleasantries of M. le Comte Norbert de La Mole, Squadron Commander of Hussars and a future Peer of France, and do not come and complain to me afterwards.'

'It seems to me,' said Julien, blushing deeply, 'that I ought not even to answer a man who looks down upon me.'

'You have no idea of this form of contempt; it will reveal itself only in exaggerated compliments. If you were a fool, you might let yourself be taken in by them; if you wished to succeed, you ought to let yourself be taken in.'

'On the day when all this ceases to agree with me,' said Julien, 'shall I be considered ungrateful if I return to my little cell, number 103?'

'No doubt,' replied the abbé, 'all the sycophants of the house will slander you, but then I shall appear. *Adsum qui feci*. I shall say that it was from me that the decision came.'

Julien was dismayed by the bitter and almost malicious tone which he remarked in M. Pirard; this tone completely spoiled his last utterance.

The fact was that the abbé felt a scruple of conscience about loving Julien, and it was with a sort of religious terror that he was thus directly interfering with the destiny of another man.

'You will also see,' he continued, with the same ill grace, and as though in the performance of a painful duty, 'you will see Madame la Marquise de La Mole. She is a tall, fair woman, pious, proud, perfectly civil and even more insignificant. She is a daughter of the old Duc de Chaulnes, so famous for his aristocratic prejudices. This great lady is a sort of compendium, in high relief, of all that makes up the character of the women of her rank. She makes it no secret that to have had ancestors who went to the Crusades is the sole advantage to which she attaches any importance. Money comes only a long way after: does that surprise you? We are no longer in the country, my friend.

'You will find in her drawing-room many great noblemen speaking of our Princes in a tone of singular disrespect. As for Madame de La Mole, she lowers her voice in respect whenever she names a Prince, let alone a Princess. I should not advise you to say in her hearing that Philip II or Henry VIII was a monster. They were KINGS, and that gives them an inalienable right to the respect of everyone, and above all to the respect of creatures without birth, like you and me. However,' M. Pirard added, 'we are priests, for she will take you for one; on that footing, she regards us as lackeys necessary to her salvation.'

'Sir,' said Julien, 'it seems to me that I shall not remain long in Paris.'

'As you please; but observe that there is no hope of success, for a man of our cloth, except through the great nobles. With that indefinable element (at least, I cannot define it), which there is in your character, if you do not succeed you will be persecuted; there is no middle way for you. Do not abuse your position. People see that you are not pleased when they

271

speak to you; in a social environment like this, you are doomed to misfortune, if you do not succeed in winning respect.

'What would have become of you at Besançon, but for this caprice on the part of the Marquis de La Mole? One day, you will appreciate all the singularity of what he is doing for you, and, if you are not a monster, you will feel eternal gratitude to him and his family. How many poor abbés, cleverer men than you, have lived for years in Paris, upon the fifteen sous for their mass and the ten sous for their lectures in the Sorbonne!... Remember what I told you, last winter, of the early years of that wretch, Cardinal Dubois. Are you, by any chance, so proud as to imagine that you have more talent than he?

'I, for example, a peaceable and insignificant man, expected to end my days in my Seminary; I was childish enough to have grown attached to it. Very well! I was going to be turned out when I offered my resignation. Do you know what was the extent of my fortune? I had five hundred and twenty francs of capital, neither more nor less; not a friend, at most two or three acquaintances. M. de La Mole, whom I had never seen, saved me from disaster; he had only to say the word, and I was given a living in which all my parishioners are people in easy circumstances, above the common vices, and the stipend fills me with shame, so far out of proportion is it to my work. I have spoken to you at this length only to put a little ballast into that head of yours.

'One word more; it is my misfortune to have a hasty temper; it is possible that you and I may cease to speak to one another.

'If the arrogance of the Marquise, or the mischievous pranks of her son, make the house definitely insupportable to you, I advise you to finish your studies in some Seminary thirty leagues from Paris, and in the North, rather than in the South. You will find in the North more civilisation and fewer injustices; and,' he added, lowering his voice, 'I must admit it, the proximity of the Parisian newspapers makes the petty tyrants afraid.

'If we continue to find pleasure in each other's company, and the Marquis's household does not agree with you, I offer you a place as my vicar, and shall divide the revenues of this living with you equally. I owe you this and more,' he added, cutting short Julien's expressions of gratitude, 'for the singular offer which you made me at Besançon. If, instead of five hundred and twenty francs, I had had nothing, you would have saved me.'

The cruel tone had gone from the abbé's voice. To his great confusion, Julien felt the tears start to his eyes; he was longing to fling himself into the arms of his friend: he could not resist saying to him, with the most manly air that he was capable of affecting:

'I have been hated by my father from the cradle; it was one of my great misfortunes; but I shall no longer complain of fortune. I have found another father in you, Sir.'

'Good, good,' said the abbé, with embarrassment; then remembering most opportunely a phrase from the vocabulary of a Director of a Seminary: 'You must never say fortune, my child, always say Providence.'

The cab stopped; the driver lifted the bronze knocker on an immense door. It was the Hôtel de La Mole; and, so that the passer-by might be left in no doubt of this, the words were to be read on a slab of black marble over the door.

This affectation was not to Julien's liking. 'They are so afraid of the Jacobins! They see a Robespierre and his tumbril behind every hedge; often they make one die with laughing, and they advertise their house like this so that the mob shall know it in the event of a rising, and sack it.' He communicated what was in his mind to the Abbé Pirard.

'Ah! Poor boy, you will soon be my vicar. What an appalling idea to come into your head!'

'I can think of nothing more simple,' said Julien.

The gravity of the porter and above all the cleanness of the courtyard had filled him with admiration. The sun was shining brightly.

'What magnificent architecture,' he said to his friend. It was one of the typical town houses, with their lifeless fronts, of the Faubourg Saint-Germain, built about the date of Voltaire's death. Never have the fashionable and the beautiful been such worlds apart.

CHAPTER THIRTY-TWO

FIRST APPEARANCE IN SOCIETY

Absurd and touching memory: one's first appearance,
at eighteen, alone and unsupported, in a drawing-room!
A glance from a woman was enough to terrify me. The
more I tried to shine, the more awkward I became.
I formed the most false ideas of everything; either I
surrendered myself for no reason, or I saw an enemy
in a man because he had looked at me with a serious
expression. But then, amid all the fearful sufferings of
my shyness, how fine was a fine day!

KANT.

JULIEN stopped in confusion in the middle of the
courtyard.

'Do assume a reasonable air,' said the Abbé Pirard;
'you take hold of horrible ideas, and you are only a boy!
Where is the *nil mirari* of Horace?' (That is: no enthusiasm.)
'Reflect that this tribe of flunkeys, seeing you established here,
will try to make a fool of you; they will regard you as an
equal, unjustly set over them. Beneath a shew of good nature,
of good advice, of a wish to guide you, they will try to catch
you out in some stupid blunder.'

'I defy them to do so,' said Julien, biting his lip; and he
recovered all his former distrust.

The drawing-rooms through which our friends passed on
the first floor, before coming to the Marquis's study, would
have seemed to you, gentle reader, as depressing as they were
magnificent. Had you been made a present of them as they
stood, you would have refused to live in them; they are the

275

native heath of boredom and dreary argument. They doubled Julien's enchantment. 'How can anyone be unhappy,' he thought, 'who lives in so splendid a residence?'

Finally, our friends came to the ugliest of the rooms in this superb suite: the daylight barely entered it; here, they found a wizened little man with a keen eye and a fair periwig. The abbé turned to Julien, whom he presented. It was the Marquis. Julien had great difficulty in recognising him, so civil did he find him. This was no longer the great nobleman, so haughty in his mien, of the Abbey of Bray-le-Haut. It seemed to Julien that there was far too much hair in his wig. Thanks to this impression, he was not in the least intimidated. The descendant of Henri III's friend struck him at first as cutting but a poor figure. He was very thin and greatly agitated. But he soon remarked that the Marquis shewed a courtesy even more agreeable to the person he was addressing than that of the Bishop of Besançon himself. The audience did not occupy three minutes. As they left the room, the abbé said to Julien:

'You looked at the Marquis as you would have looked at a picture. I am no expert in what these people call politeness, soon you will know more about it than I; still, the boldness of your stare seemed to me to be scarcely polite.'

They had returned to their vehicle; the driver stopped by the boulevard; the abbé led Julien through a series of spacious saloons. Julien remarked that they were unfurnished. He was looking at a magnificent gilt clock, representing a subject that in his opinion was highly indecent, when a most elegant gentleman approached them with an affable expression. Julien made him a slight bow.

The gentleman smiled and laid a hand on his shoulder. Julien quivered and sprang back. He was flushed with anger. The Abbé Pirard, for all his gravity, laughed till the tears ran down his cheeks. The gentleman was a tailor.

'I leave you at liberty for two days,' the abbé told him as they emerged; 'it is not until then that you can be presented to Madame de La Mole. Most people would protect you like a young girl, in these first moments of your sojourn in this modern Babylon. Ruin yourself at once, if you are to be ruined, and I shall be rid of the weakness I shew in caring for you. The day after to-morrow, in the morning, this tailor will bring you two coats; you will give five francs to the boy who tries them on you. Otherwise, do not let these Parisians hear the sound of your voice. If you utter a word, they will find a way of making you look foolish. That is their talent. The day after to-morrow, be at my house at midday.... Run along, ruin yourself.... I was forgetting, go and order boots, shirts, a hat at these addresses.'

Julien studied the handwriting of the addresses.

'That is the Marquis's hand,' said the abbé, 'he is an active man who provides for everything, and would rather do a thing himself than order it to be done. He is taking you into his household so that you may save him trouble of this sort. Will you have sufficient intelligence to carry out all the orders that this quick-witted man will suggest to you in a few words? The future will shew: have a care!'

Julien, without uttering a word, made his way into the shops indicated on the list of addresses; he observed that he was greeted there with respect, and the bootmaker, in entering his name in his books, wrote 'M. Julien de Sorel.'

In the Cemetery of Père-Lachaise a gentleman who seemed highly obliging, and even more Liberal in his speech, offered to guide Julien to the tomb of Marshal Ney, from which a wise administration has withheld the honour of an epitaph. But, after parting from this Liberal, who, with tears in his eyes, almost clasped him to his bosom, Julien had no longer a watch. It was enriched by this experience that, two days later, at noon, he presented himself before the Abbé Pirard, who studied him attentively.

'You are perhaps going to become a fop,' the abbé said to him, with a severe expression. Julien had the appearance of an extremely young man, in deep mourning; he did, as a matter of fact, look quite well, but the good abbé was himself too provincial to notice that Julien had still that swing of the shoulders which in the provinces betokens at once elegance and importance. On seeing Julien, the Marquis considered his graces in a light so different from that of the good abbé that he said to him:

277

'Should you have any objection to M. Sorel's taking dancing-lessons?'

The abbé remained petrified.

'No,' he replied, at length, 'Julien is not a priest.'

The Marquis, mounting two steps at a time by a little secret stair, conducted our hero personally to a neat attic which overlooked the huge garden of the house. He asked him how many shirts he had ordered from the hosier.

'Two,' replied Julien, dismayed at seeing so great a gentleman descend to these details.

'Very good,' said the Marquis, with a serious air, and an imperative, curt note in his voice, which set Julien thinking: 'very good! Order yourself two and twenty more. Here is your first quarter's salary.'

As they came down from the attic, the Marquis summoned an elderly man: 'Arsène,' he said to him, 'you will look after M. Sorel.' A few minutes later, Julien found himself alone in a magnificent library: it was an exquisite moment. So as not to be taken by surprise in his emotion, he went and hid himself in a little dark corner; from which he gazed with rapture at the glittering backs of the books. 'I can read all of those,' he told himself. 'And how should I fail to be happy here? M. de Rênal would have thought himself disgraced for ever by doing the hundredth part of what the Marquis de La Mole has just done for me.

'But first of all, we must copy the letters.' This task ended, Julien ventured towards the shelves; he almost went mad with joy on finding an edition of Voltaire. He ran and opened the door of the library so as not to be caught. He then gave himself the pleasure of opening each of the eighty volumes in turn. They were magnificently bound, a triumph of the best craftsman in London. This was more than was needed to carry Julien's admiration beyond all bounds.

An hour later, the Marquis entered the room, examined the copies, and was surprised to see that Julien wrote *cela* with a double *l, cella*. 'So all that the abbé has been telling me of his learning is simply a tale!' The Marquis, greatly discouraged, said to him gently:

'You are not certain of your spelling?'

'That is true,' said Julien, without the least thought of the harm he was doing himself; he was moved by the Marquis's kindness, which made him think of M. de Rênal's savage tone.

'It is all a waste of time, this experiment with a little Franc-Comtois priest,' thought the Marquis; 'but I did so want a trustworthy man.

'*Cela* has only one *l*,' the Marquis told him; 'when you have finished your copies, take the dictionary and look out all the words of which you are not certain.'

At six o'clock the Marquis sent for him; he looked with evident dismay at Julien's boots: 'I am to blame. I forgot to tell you that every evening at half-past five you must dress.'

Julien looked at him without understanding him.

'I mean put on stockings. Arsène will remind you; to-day I shall make your apologies.'

So saying, M. de La Mole ushered Julien into a drawing-room resplendent with gilding. On similar occasions, M. de Rênal never failed to increase his pace so that he might have the satisfaction of going first through the door.

The effect of his old employer's petty vanity was that Julien now trod upon the Marquis's heels, and caused him considerable pain, owing to his gout. 'Ah! He is even more of a fool than I thought,' the Marquis said to himself. He presented him to a woman of tall stature and imposing aspect. It was the Marquise. Julien decided that she had an impertinent air, which reminded him a little of Madame de Maugiron, the Sub-Prefect's wife of the Verrières district, when she attended the Saint Charles's day dinner. Being somewhat embarrassed by the extreme splendour of the room, Julien did not hear what M. de La Mole was saying. The Marquise barely deigned to glance at him. There were several men in the room, among whom Julien recognised with unspeakable delight the young Bishop of Agde, who had condescended to say a few words to him once at the ceremony at Bray-le-Haut. The young prelate was doubtless alarmed by the tender gaze which Julien, in his timidity, fastened upon him, and made no effort to recognise this provincial.

The men assembled in this drawing-room seemed to Julien to be somehow melancholy and constrained; people speak low in Paris, and do not exaggerate trifling matters.

A handsome young man, wearing moustaches, very pale and slender, entered the room at about half-past six; he had an extremely small head.

'You always keep us waiting,' said the Marquise, as he kissed her hand.

Julien gathered that this was the Comte de La Mole. He found him charming from the first.

'Is it possible,' he said to himself, 'that this is the man whose offensive pleasantries are going to drive me from this house?'

By dint of a survey of Comte Norbert's person, Julien discovered that he was wearing boots and spurs; 'and I ought to be wearing shoes, evidently as his inferior.' They sat down to table. Julien heard the Marquise utter a word of rebuke, slightly raising her voice. Almost at the same moment he noticed a young person extremely fair and very comely, who was taking her place opposite to him. She did not attract him at all; on studying her attentively, however, he thought that he had never seen such fine eyes; but they hinted at great coldness of heart. Later, Julien decided that they expressed a boredom which studies other people but keeps on reminding itself that it is one's duty to be imposing. 'Madame de Rênal, too, had the most beautiful eyes,' he said to himself; 'people used to compliment her on them; but they had nothing in common with these.' Julien had not enough experience to discern that it was the fire of wit that shone from time to time in the eyes of Mademoiselle Mathilde, for so he heard her named. When Madame de Rênal's eyes became animated, it was with the fire of her passions, or was due to a righteous indignation upon hearing of some wicked action. Towards the end of dinner, Julien found the right word to describe the type of beauty exemplified by the eyes of Mademoiselle de La Mole: 'They are scintillating,' he said to himself. Otherwise, she bore a painful resemblance to her mother, whom he disliked more and more, and he ceased to look at her. Comte Norbert, on the other hand, struck him as admirable in every respect. Julien was so captivated, that it never entered his head to be jealous of him and to hate him, because he was richer and nobler than himself.

Julien thought that the Marquis appeared bored.

During the second course, he said to his son:

'Norbert, I must ask you to look after M. Julien Sorel, whom I have just taken upon my staff, and intend to make a man of, if that (*cella*) can be done.

'He is my secretary,' the Marquis added to his neighbour, 'and he spells *cela* with a double *l*.'

Everyone looked at Julien, who gave Norbert a slightly exaggerated bow; but on the whole, they were satisfied with his appearance.

The Marquis must have spoken of the kind of education that Julien had received, for one of the guests tackled him upon Horace: 'It was precisely in discussing Horace that I was successful with the Bishop of Besançon,' Julien said to himself, 'evidently he is the only author they know.' From that moment he was master of himself. This change was made easy by his having just decided that Mademoiselle de La Mole would never be a woman in his eyes. Since his Seminary days he defied men to do their worst, and refused to be intimidated by them. He would have enjoyed perfect self-possession, had the dining-room been furnished with less magnificence. It was, as a matter of fact, a pair of mirrors, each of them eight feet high, in which he caught sight now and then of his challenger as he spoke of Horace, that still continued to overawe him. His sentences were not unduly long for a provincial. He had fine eyes, the sparkle in which was enhanced by his tremulous, or, when he had made a good answer, his happy shyness. This sort of examination made a serious dinner-party quite interesting. The Marquis made a sign to the other speaker to press Julien hard. 'Can it be possible that he does know something?' he thought.

Julien found fresh ideas as he answered, and lost enough of his shyness not, indeed, to display wit, a thing impossible to a person ignorant of the language that is spoken in Paris, but he had original ideas, albeit expressed without grace-fulness or appropriateness, and it could be seen that he had a thorough knowledge of Latin.

His adversary was a member of the Academy of Inscriptions, who, nevertheless, knew Latin; he found in Julien an excellent humanist, lost all fear of making him blush, and really did seek to embarrass him. In the heat of the duel, Julien at length forgot the magnificent decoration of the dining-room, and began to express ideas with regard to the Latin poets, which the other had never read in any book. Being an honest man, he gave the credit for them to the young secretary. Fortunately, the discussion turned to the question whether Horace had been poor or rich: an amiable person, sensual and easy-going, making poetry for his own amusement, like Chapelle, the friend of Molière and La Fontaine; or a poor devil of a Poet Laureate attached to the court and composing odes for the King's Birthday, like Southey, the traducer of Lord Byron. They spoke of the state of society under Augustus and under George IV; in both epochs the aristocracy was all-powerful! but in Rome it saw its power wrested from it by Mæcenas, who was a mere knight; and in England it had reduced George IV more or less to the position of a Doge of Venice. This discussion seemed to draw the Marquis out of the state of torpor in which his boredom had kept him plunged at the beginning of dinner.

Julien could make nothing of all these modern names, such as Southey, Lord Byron, George IV, which he now heard for the first time. But no one could fail to observe that whenever there was any question of historical events at Rome, a knowledge of which might be derived from the works of Horace, Martial, Tacitus, etc., he had an unchallengeable superiority. Julien appropriated without a scruple a number of ideas which he had acquired from the Bishop of Besançon, during the famous discussion he had had with that prelate; these proved to be not the least acceptable.

When the party tired of discussing poets, the Marquise, who made it a rule to admire anything that amused her husband, condescended to glance at Julien. 'The awkward manners of this young cleric may perhaps be concealing a learned man,' the Academician, who was sitting near her, said to the Marquise; and Julien overheard something of what he was saying. Ready-made phrases were quite to the taste of his hostess; she adopted this description of Julien, and was glad that she had invited the Academician to dine, 'He amuses M. de La Mole,' she thought.

CHAPTER THIRTY-THREE

FIRST STEPS

That immense valley filled with brilliant lights and
with all those thousands of people dazzles my sight.
Not one of them knows me, all are superior to me. My
head reels.

Poemi dell' avvocato REINA.

EARLY in the morning of the following day, Julien was
copying letters in the library, when Mademoiselle
Mathilde entered by a little private door, cleverly concealed with shelves of dummy books. While Julien was
admiring this device, Mademoiselle Mathilde appeared
greatly surprised and distinctly annoyed to see him there.
Julien decided that her curl-papers gave her a hard, haughty,
almost masculine air. Mademoiselle de La Mole had a secret
habit of stealing books from her father's library, undetected.
Julien's presence frustrated her expedition that morning,
which annoyed her all the more as she had come to secure
the second volume of Voltaire's *Princesse de Babylone*, a fitting
complement to an eminently monarchical and religious education, a triumph on the part of the Sacré-Cœur! This poor
girl, at nineteen, already required the spice of wit to make
her interested in a novel.

Comte Norbert appeared in the library about three
o'clock; he had come to study a newspaper, in order to be
able to talk politics that evening, and was quite pleased to
find Julien, whose existence he had forgotten. He was charming to him, and offered to lend him a horse.

'My father lets us take a holiday until dinner.'

Julien appreciated this *us*, and thought it charming.

'Heavens, Monsieur le Comte,' said Julien, 'if it were a question of felling an eighty-foot tree, trimming it and sawing it into planks, I venture to say that I should manage it well enough; but riding a horse is a thing I haven't done six times in my life.'

'Well, this will be the seventh,' said Norbert.

Privately, Julien remembered the entry of the King of —— into Verrières and imagined himself a superior horseman. But, on their way back from the Bois de Boulogne, in the very middle of the Rue du Bac, he fell off, while trying to avoid a passing cab, and covered himself in mud. It was fortunate for him that he had a change of clothes. At the dinner the Marquis, wishing to include him in the conversation, asked him about his ride; Norbert made haste to reply in generous language.

'Monsieur le Comte is too kind to me,' put in Julien. 'I thank him for it, and fully appreciate his kindness. He has been so good as to give me the quietest and handsomest of horses; but after all he could not glue me on to it, and, that being so, I fell off right in the middle of that very long street near the bridge.'

Mademoiselle Mathilde tried in vain to stifle a peal of laughter; finally indiscretion prevailed and she begged for details. Julien emerged from the difficulty with great simplicity; he had an unconscious grace.

'I augur well of this little priest,' the Marquis said to the Academician; 'a simple countryman in such a scrape! Such a thing was never yet seen and never will be seen; in addition to which he relates his misadventure before the *ladies*!'

Julien set his listeners so thoroughly at ease over his mishap that at the end of dinner, when the general conversation had taken another turn, Mademoiselle Mathilde began to ply her brother with questions as to the details of the distressing event. As her inquiry continued, and as Julien more than once caught her eye, he ventured to reply directly, although he had not been questioned, and all three ended in laughter, just like three young peasants from a village in the heart of a forest.

On the following day Julien attended two lectures on theology, and then returned to transcribe a score of letters. He found ensconced by his own place in the library a young man dressed with great neatness, but his general appearance was ignominious and his expression one of envy.

The Marquis entered.

'What are you doing here, Monsieur Tanbeau?' he asked the newcomer in a severe tone.

'I thought,' the young man began with a servile smile.

'No, Sir, you *did not think*. This is an attempt, but it is an unfortunate one.'

Young Tanbeau rose in a fury and left the room. He was a nephew of the Academician, Madame de La Mole's friend, and was intended for a literary career. The Academician had persuaded the Marquis to take him as a secretary. Tanbeau, who worked in a room apart, having heard of the favour that was being bestowed upon Julien, was anxious to share it, and that morning had come and set up his desk in the library.

At four o'clock, Julien ventured, after some hesitation, to seek out Comte Norbert. This young gentleman was going out riding, and was somewhat embarrassed, for his manners were perfect.

'I think,' he said to Julien, 'that presently you might go to the riding school; and after a few weeks I shall be delighted to ride with you.'

'I wished to have the honour of thanking you for all your kindness to me; pray believe, Sir,' Julien, added with a most serious air, 'that I am fully conscious of all that I owe you. If your horse is not injured as a result of my clumsiness yesterday, and if it is free, I should like to ride it to-day.'

'Faith, my dear Sorel, on your own head be it! Assume that I have raised all the objections that prudence demands; the fact is that it is four o'clock, we have no time to lose.'

After he was in the saddle:

'What must one do, not to fall off?' Julien asked the young Comte.

'All sorts of things,' replied Norbert with a shout of laughter: 'for instance, sit well back.'

Julien began to trot. They were crossing the Place Louis XVI.

'Ah! Young hothead, there are too many carriages here, and with careless drivers too. Once you are on the ground, their tilburys will go bowling over you; they are not going to risk hurting their horses' mouths by pulling up short.'

A score of times Norbert saw Julien on the point of falling; but at last their ride ended without mishap. On their return, the young Comte said to his sister:

'Let me introduce a regular dare-devil.'

At dinner, speaking to his father, down the length of the table, he did justice to Julien's courage; it was all that one could praise in his method of riding. During the day the young Comte had heard the men who were grooming the horses in the yard make Julien's fall an excuse for the most outrageous mockery of him.

In spite of all this kindness, Julien soon felt himself completely isolated among this family. All their customs seemed strange to him, and he was always making mistakes. His blunders were the delight of the footmen.

The Abbé Pirard had gone off to his living. 'If Julien is a frail reed, let him perish; if he is a man of courage, let him make his way by himself,' he thought.

CHAPTER THIRTY-FOUR
THE HÔTEL DE LA MOLE

Que fait-il ici? s'y plairait-il? penserait-il y plaire?
RONSARD.

IF everything seemed strange to Julien, in the noble drawing-room of the Hôtel de La Mole, the young man himself, pale and dressed in black, seemed in turn highly singular to those who deigned to notice him. Madame de La Mole suggested that her husband should send him away on business upon days when certain personages were coming to dine.

'I should like to carry through the experiment,' replied the Marquis. 'The Abbé Pirard maintains that we do wrong to crush the self-respect of the people we admit into our households. *One can lean only upon what resists*, etc. There is nothing wrong with this fellow except his uncouth appearance; he might be deaf and dumb.'

'If I am to keep my bearings, I must,' Julien said to himself, 'write down the names and a few words as to the character of the people I see appear in this drawing-room.'

At the head of his list he placed five or six friends of the family who paid a desperate court to him, supposing him to be protected by some caprice of the Marquis. These were poor devils, more or less spiritless; but, it must be said in praise of men of this class as they are to be found to-day in the drawing-rooms of the nobility, they were not equally spiritless to all comers. Some of them would have let themselves be abused by the Marquis, and yet would have revolted

288

against a harsh word addressed to them by Madame de La Mole.

There was too much pride, there was too much boredom in the character of both host and hostess; they were too much in the habit of insulting people for their own distraction, to be able to expect any true friends. But, except on wet days, and in their moments of furious boredom, which were rare, they were never to be found wanting in politeness.

If the five or six flatterers who treated Julien with such fatherly affection had deserted the Hôtel de La Mole, the Marquise would have been left to long hours of solitude; and, in the eyes of women of her rank, solitude is a dreadful thing: it is the badge of disgrace.

The Marquis behaved admirably to his wife; he saw to it that her drawing-room was adequately filled; not with peers, he found his new colleagues scarcely noble enough to come to his house as friends, nor entertaining enough to be admitted as subordinates.

It was not until much later that Julien discovered these secrets. The political questions which form the chief topic in middle-class houses are never mentioned in houses like that of the Marquis, save in times of trouble.

So powerful still, even in this age of boredom, are the dictates of the need of amusement, that even on the evenings of dinner-parties, as soon as the Marquis had left the drawing-room, everyone else fled. So long as you did not speak lightly of God, or of the clergy, or of the King, or of the men in power, or of the artists patronised by the court, or of anything established; so long as you did not say anything good of Béranger, or of the opposition press, or of Voltaire, or of Rousseau, or of anything that allowed itself the liberty of a little freedom of speech; so long, above all, as you did not talk politics, you could discuss anything you pleased with freedom.

There is no income of a hundred thousand crowns, no blue riband that can prevail against a drawing-room so constituted. The smallest living idea seemed an outrage. Despite good tone, perfect manners, the desire to be agreeable, boredom was written upon every brow. The young men who came to pay their respects, afraid to speak of anything that might lead to their being suspected of thinking, afraid to reveal some forbidden reading, became silent after a few elegantly phrased sentences on Rossini and the weather.

Julien observed that the conversation was usually kept going by two Viscounts and five Barons whom M. de La Mole had known during the emigration. These gentlemen enjoyed incomes of from six to eight thousand livres; four of them swore by the *Quotidienne*, and three by the *Gazette de France*. One of them had some new story to tell every day of the Château, in which the word 'admirable' was lavishly used. Julien remarked that this man wore five Crosses, whereas the others, as a rule, had no more than three.

On the other hand, you saw in the ante-room ten footmen in livery, and all through the evening you had ices or tea every quarter of an hour; and, at midnight, a sort of supper with champagne.

It was for this reason that Julien sometimes remained to the end; otherwise, he failed to understand how anyone could listen seriously to the ordinary conversation of this drawing-room, so magnificently gilded. Now and again he would watch the speakers, to see whether they themselves were not laughing at what they were saying. 'My M. de Maistre, whom I know by heart, has said things a hundred times better,' he thought; 'and even he is extremely boring.'

Julien was not the only one to be aware of the mental stagnation. Some consoled themselves by taking quantities of ices; the others with the pleasure of being able to say for the rest of the evening: 'I have just come from the Hôtel de La Mole, where I heard that Russia,' etc., etc.

Julien learned, from one of the flatterers, that less than six months ago Madame de La Mole had rewarded an assiduity that had lasted for more than twenty years by securing a Prefecture for poor Baron Le Bourguignon, who had been a Sub-Prefect ever since the Restoration.

This great event had rekindled the zeal of these gentlemen; the least thing might have offended them before, now they were no longer offended by anything. It was rare that the incivility was direct, but Julien had already overheard at table two or three brief little passages between the Marquis and his wife, wounding to those who were placed near them. These noble personages did not conceal their sincere contempt for every one that was not the offspring of people who *rode in the King's carriages.* Julien observed that the word *Crusade* was the only one that brought to their faces an expression of intense seriousness, blended with respect. Their ordinary respect had always a shade of condescension.

In the midst of this magnificence and this boredom, Julien was interested in nothing but M. de La Mole; he listened with pleasure one day to his protestations that he was in no way responsible for the promotion of that poor Le Bourguignon. This was a delicate attention to the Marquise: Julien had learned the truth from the Abbé Pirard.

One morning when the abbé was working with Julien, in the Marquis's library, on the endless litigation with Frilair:

'Sir,' said Julien suddenly, 'is dining every evening with Madame la Marquise one of my duties, or is it a favour that they shew me?'

'It is a signal honour!' replied the abbé, greatly shocked. 'M. N——, the Academician, who has been paying assiduous court for the last fifteen years, has never been able to obtain it for his nephew M. Tanbeau.'

'It is to me, Sir, the most tedious part of my employment. I was less bored at the Seminary. I see even Mademoiselle de La Mole yawn at times, although she must be accustomed to the pretty speeches of the friends of the family. I am afraid of falling asleep. Please be so good as to obtain leave for me to go and dine for forty sous in some obscure inn.'

The abbé, a regular *parvenu*, was highly sensible of the honour of dining with a great nobleman. While he was endeavouring to make Julien understand what he felt, a slight sound made them turn their heads. Julien saw Mademoiselle de La Mole who was listening. He blushed. She had come in search of a book and had heard everything; she felt a certain respect for Julien. 'This fellow was not born on his knees,' she thought, 'like that old abbé. Heavens! How ugly he is.'

At dinner, Julien dared not look at Mademoiselle de La Mole, but she was so kind as to speak to him. That evening, they expected a large party; she made him promise to remain. Girls in Paris do not care for men of a certain age, especially when they are not well dressed. Julien did not require much sagacity to perceive that M. Le Bourguignon's colleagues, who remained in the drawing-room, had the honour to be the customary butt of Mademoiselle de La Mole's wit. That evening, whether with deliberate affectation or not, she was cruel in her treatment of the bores.

Mademoiselle de La Mole was the centre of a little group that assembled almost every evening behind the Marquise's immense armchair. There, you would find the Marquis de Croisenois, the Comte de Caylus, the Vicomte de Luz and two or three other young officers, friends of Norbert or his sister. These gentlemen sat upon a large blue sofa. At the end of the sofa, opposite to that occupied by the brilliant Mathilde, Julien was silently installed upon a little cane-bottomed chair with a low seat. This modest post was the envy of all the flatterers; Norbert kept his father's young secretary in countenance by addressing him or uttering his name once or twice in the course of the evening. On this occasion, Mademoiselle de La Mole asked him what might be the height of the mountain on which the citadel of Besançon stood. Julien could not for the life of him have said whether this mountain was higher or lower than Montmartre. Often he laughed heartily at what was being said in the little group; but he felt himself incapable of thinking of anything similar to say. It was like a foreign language which he could understand and admire, but was unable to speak.

Mathilde's friends were that evening in a state of constant hostility towards the people who kept arriving in this splendid drawing-room. The friends of the family had the preference at first, being better known. One can imagine whether Julien was attentive; everything interested him, both the things themselves, and the way they were made to seem ridiculous.

'Ah! Here comes M. Descoulis,' said Mathilde; 'he has left off his wig; can he be hoping to secure a Prefecture by his genius? He is exposing that bald brow which he says is filled with lofty thoughts.'

'He is a man who knows the whole world,' said the Marquis de Croisenois; 'he comes to my uncle, the Cardinal's, too. He is capable of cultivating a lie with each of his friends, for years on end, and he has two or three hundred friends. He knows how to foster friendship, that is his talent. You ought to see him, covered in mud, at the door of a friend's house, at seven o'clock on a winter morning.

'He hatches a quarrel, now and again, and writes seven or eight letters to keep up the quarrel. Then he is reconciled, and produces seven or eight letters for the transports of affection. But it is in the frank and sincere expansion of an honest man who can keep nothing on his conscience that he shines most. This is his favourite device when he has some favour to ask. One of my uncle's Grand Vicars is perfect when he relates the life of M. Descoulis since the Restoration. I shall bring him to see you.'

'Bah! I shouldn't listen to that talk; it is the professional jealousy of small-minded people,' said the Comte de Caylus.

'M. Descoulis will have a name in history,' the Marquis went on; 'he made the Restoration with the Abbé de Pradt and M. Talleyrand and Pozzo di Borgo.'

'That man has handled millions,' said Norbert, 'and I cannot conceive why he comes here to swallow my father's epigrams, which are often appalling. "How many times have you betrayed your friends, my dear Descoulis?" he shouted at him the other day, down the whole length of the table.'

'But is it true that he has betrayed people?' said Mademoiselle de La Mole. 'Who is there that has not?'

'What!' said the Comte de Caylus to Norbert, 'you have M. Sainclair here, the notorious Liberal; what the devil can he have come for? I must go over to him, and talk to him, and make him talk; they say he is so clever.'

'But how can your mother have him in the house?' said

M. de Croisenois. 'His ideas are so extravagant, so enthusiastic, so independent....'

'Look,' said Mademoiselle de La Mole, 'there is your independent man, bowing to the ground before M. Descoulis, and seizing his hand. I almost thought he was going to raise it to his lips.'

'Descoulis must stand better with the authorities than we thought,' put in M. de Croisenois.

'Sainclair comes here to get into the Academy,' said Norbert; 'look how he is bowing to Baron L——, Croisenois.'

'He would be less servile if he went on his knees,' put in M. de Luz.

'My dear Sorel,' said Norbert, 'you who are a man of brains, but have just come down from your mountains, see that you never bow to people as that great poet does, not even to God Almighty.'

'Ah! Here comes a man of brains if you like, M. le Baron Bâton,' said Mademoiselle de La Mole, imitating the voice of the footman who had just announced him.

'I think even your servants laugh at him. What a name, Baron Bâton!' said M. de Caylus.

' "What's in a name?" as he said to us the other day,' retorted Mathilde. ' "Imagine the Duc de Bouillon announced for the first time. All the public needs, in my case, is to have grown accustomed to it." '

Julien quitted the circle round the sofa. Still but little sensible of the charming subtleties of a light-handed mockery, if he were to laugh at a witticism, he required that it should be founded on reason. He could see nothing in the talk of these young men, but the tone of general depreciation, and this shocked him. His provincial or English prudery went so far as to detect envy in it, wherein he was certainly mistaken.

'Comte Norbert,' he said to himself, 'whom I have seen make three rough copies of a letter of twenty lines to his Colonel, would be very glad to have written a single page in his life like those of M. Sainclair.'

Passing unperceived owing to his lack of importance, Julien approached several groups in turn; he was following

Baron Bâton at a distance, and wished to hear him talk. This man of such intelligence wore a troubled air, and Julien saw him recover himself a little only when he had hit upon three or four sparkling sentences. It seemed to Julien that this kind of wit required ample room to develop itself.

The Baron could not produce epigrams; he required at least four sentences of six lines each to be brilliant.

'This learned man is not talking,' said some one behind Julien's back. He turned round and flushed with pleasure when he heard the name of Comte Chalvet. This was the cleverest man of the day. Julien had often come upon his name in the *Mémorial de Sainte-Hélène* and in the fragments of history dictated by Napoleon. Comte Chalvet was curt in his speech; his remarks were flashes of lightning, accurate, keen, profound. If he spoke of any public matter, immediately one saw the discussion reach a fresh stage. He brought facts to bear on it, it was a pleasure to listen to him. In politics, however, he was a brazen cynic.

'I am independent, myself,' he was saying to a gentleman wearing three decorations, whom he was apparently quizzing. 'Why should I be expected to hold the same opinion to-day that I held six weeks ago? If I did, I should be a slave to my opinion.'

Four grave young men who stood round him made grimaces at this; these gentlemen do not care for the flippant style. The Comte saw that he had gone too far. Fortunately he caught sight of the honest M. Balland, a *tartufe* of honesty. The Comte began talking to him: people gathered round them, guessing that poor Balland was going to be scarified. By dint of morals and morality, although horribly ugly, and after early struggles with the world which it would be hard to describe, M. Balland had married an extremely rich wife, who died; then a second extremely rich wife, who was never seen in society. He enjoyed in all humility an income of sixty thousand livres, and had flatterers of his own. Comte Chalvet spoke to him of all this, without pity. Presently they were surrounded by a circle of thirty people. Everyone smiled, even the grave young men, the hope of the age.

'Why does he come to M. de La Mole's, where he is obviously made a butt?' thought Julien. He went across to the Abbé Pirard, to ask him.

M. Balland left the room.

'Good!' said Norbert, 'there's one of my father's spies gone; that leaves only the little cripple Napier.'

'Can that be the clue to the riddle?' thought Julien. 'But, in that case, why does the Marquis invite M. Balland?'

The stern Abbé Pirard was making faces in a corner of the room, as he heard fresh names announced.

'Why, it is a den,' he said, like Basilio, 'I see none but villains enter.'

The fact was that the stern abbé did not recognise the distinguishing marks of good society. But, from his Jansenist friends, he had a very accurate notion of the men who make their way into drawing-rooms only by their extreme cleverness in the service of all parties, or by a fortune of notorious origin. For some minutes, that evening, he replied from the abundance of his heart to Julien's eager questions, then cut himself short, distressed to find himself speaking ill of everyone, and imputing it to himself as a sin. Being choleric and a Jansenist, and regarding Christian charity as a duty, his life in society was a perpetual conflict.

'How frightful that Abbé Pirard looks!' Mademoiselle de La Mole was saying, as Julien returned to the sofa.

Julien felt a sting of irritation, and yet she was right. M. Pirard was beyond question the most honest man in the room, but his blotched face, distorted by the pangs of conscience, made him hideous at the moment. 'Never judge by appearances after this,' thought Julien; 'it is at the moment when the abbé's scruples are reproaching him with some peccadillo that he looks terrible; whereas on the face of that Napier, whom everyone knows to be a spy, one sees a pure and tranquil happiness.' The Abbé Pirard had nevertheless made a great concession to his party; he had engaged a valet, and was quite well dressed.

Julien remarked a singular occurrence in the drawing-room: this was a general movement of all eyes towards the door, with a lull in the conversation. A footman announced the famous Baron de Tolly, to whom the recent elections had attracted universal attention. Julien moved forward and had an excellent view of him. The Baron was returning officer in a certain constituency: he had had the bright idea of making away with the little slips of paper bearing the votes of one of the parties. But, to compensate for this, he duly replaced them with other little slips of paper bearing a name of which he himself approved. This decisive manœuvre was observed by some of the electors, who lost no time in presenting their compliments to Baron de Tolly. The worthy man was still pale after his great excitement. Evil tongues had uttered the word *galleys*. M. de La Mole received him coldly. The poor Baron hurriedly made his escape.

'If he leaves us so soon, it must be to go to M. Comte's,'[1] said Comte Chalvet; and the others laughed.

Amid a crowd of great noblemen who remained silent, and of intriguers, mostly disreputable, but all of them clever fellows, who arrived one after another that evening, in M. de La Mole's drawing-room (people were speaking of him for a vacant Ministry), young Tanbeau was winning his spurs. If he had not yet acquired any fineness of perception, he made up for the deficiency, as we shall see, by the vigour of his language.

'Why not sentence the man to ten years' imprisonment?' he was saying at the moment when Julien joined his group; 'it is in a dungeon underground that we ought to keep reptiles shut up; they must be made to die in the dark, otherwise their venom spreads and becomes more dangerous. What is the good of fining him a thousand crowns? He is poor, very well, all the better; but his party will pay the fine for him. It should have been a fine of five hundred francs and ten years in a dungeon.'

'Good God! Who can the monster be that they are discussing?' thought Julien, marvelling at his colleague's vehement tone and stilted gestures. The thin, drawn little face of

1 A celebrated conjurer of the day.

the Academician's favourite nephew was hideous as he spoke. Julien soon learned that the person in question was the greatest poet of the day.[1]

'Ah, monster!' exclaimed Julien, half aloud, and generous tears sprang to his eyes. 'Ah, little wretch, I shall make you eat those words.

'And yet these,' he thought, 'are the waifs and strays of the party of which the Marquis is one of the leaders! And that illustrious man whom he is slandering, how many Crosses, how many sinecures might he not have collected, if he had sold himself, I do not say to the lifeless Ministry of M. de Nerval, but to one of those passably honest Ministers whom we have seen succeed one another in office?'

The Abbé Pirard beckoned to Julien; M. de La Mole had just been saying something to him. But when Julien, who at the moment was listening, with lowered gaze, to the lamentations of a Bishop, was free to move, and able to join his friend, he found him monopolised by that abominable young Tanbeau. The little monster loathed him as the source of the favour that Julien enjoyed, and had come to pay court to him.

'When will death rid us of that old mass of corruption?' It was in these terms, with Biblical emphasis, that the little man of letters was speaking at that moment of the eminent Lord Holland. His chief merit was a thorough knowledge of the biography of living men, and he had just been making a rapid survey of all those who might aspire to positions of influence under the new King of England.

The Abbé Pirard moved into an adjoining room; Julien followed him.

'The Marquis does not like scribblers, I warn you; it is his one antipathy. Know Latin, Greek if you can, the History of the Egyptians, of the Persians, and so forth; he will honour you and protect you as a scholar. But do not go and write a single page in French, especially upon grave subjects, that

1 Béranger, sentenced in December, 1828, to imprisonment and a fine of 10,000 francs. C. K. S. M.

298

are above your position in society; he would call you a scribbler, and would take a dislike to you. What, living in a great nobleman's mansion, don't you know the Duc de Castries's saying about d'Alembert and Rousseau: "That sort of fellow wishes to argue about everything, and has not a thousand crowns a year?"'

'Everything becomes known,' thought Julien, 'here as in the Seminary.' He had written nine or ten pages with distinct emphasis: they were a sort of historical eulogy of the old Surgeon-Major, who, he said, had made a man of him. 'And that little copy-book,' Julien said to himself, 'has always been kept under lock and key.' He went upstairs, burned his manuscript and returned to the drawing-room. The brilliant rogues had departed, there remained only the stars and ribands.

Round the table, which the servants had just brought in already laid, were seated seven or eight ladies, extremely noble, extremely religious, extremely affected, between thirty and thirty-five years of age. The brilliant wife of Marshal de Fervaques entered the room, apologising for the lateness of the hour. It was after midnight; she took her place next to the Marquise. Julien was deeply stirred; her eyes and her expression reminded him of Madame de Rênal.

The group round Mademoiselle de La Mole was still numerous. She and her friends were engaged in making fun of the unfortunate Comte de Thaler. This was the only son of the famous Jew, celebrated for the riches that he had acquired by lending money to Kings to make war on the common people. The Jew had recently died leaving his son a monthly income of one hundred thousand crowns, and a name that, alas, was only too well known! This singular position required either simplicity of character or great determination.

Unfortunately, the Comte was nothing but a good fellow, adorned with all sorts of pretensions inspired in him one by one by the voice of his flatterers.

M. de Caylus asserted that he had been credited with the determination to propose for the hand of Mademoiselle de La Mole (to whom the Marquis de Croisenois, who was heir to a Dukedom with an income of one hundred thousand livres, was paying court).

'Ah! Don't accuse him of having any determination,' Norbert pleaded compassionately.

What this poor Comte de Thaler most lacked was, perhaps, the power to determine anything. In this respect, he would have made an excellent King. Taking advice incessantly from everybody, he had not the courage to follow out any suggestion to the end.

His features would have been enough by themselves, said Mademoiselle de La Mole, to fill her with everlasting joy. His face was a curious blend of uneasiness and disappointment; but from time to time one could make out quite plainly bursts of self-importance, combined with that cutting tone which the wealthiest man in France ought to adopt, especially when he is by no means bad looking, and is not yet thirty-six. 'He is timidly insolent,' said M. de Croisenois. The Comte de Caylus, Norbert and two or three young men with moustaches made fun of him to their hearts' content, without his guessing it, and finally sent him away as one o'clock struck.

'Is it your famous pair of arabs that you are keeping waiting in this weather?' Norbert asked him.

'No, I have a new pair that cost much less,' replied M. de Thaler. 'The near horse cost me five thousand francs, and the off horse is only worth a hundred louis; but I must have you understand that he is only brought out at night. The fact is that he trots perfectly with the other.'

Norbert's remark made the Comte think that it befitted a man in his position to have a passion for horses, and that he ought not to allow his to stand in the rain. He left, and the other gentlemen took their leave immediately, laughing at him as they went.

'And so,' thought Julien, as he heard the sound of their laughter on the staircase, 'I have been allowed to see the opposite extreme to my own position! I have not an income of twenty louis, and I have found myself rubbing shoulders with a man who has an income of twenty louis an hour, and they laughed at him.... A sight like that cures one of envy.'

CHAPTER THIRTY-FIVE

SENSIBILITY AND A PIOUS LADY

> Une idée un peu vive a l'air d'une grossièreté, tant
> on y est accoutumé aux mots sans relief. Malheur à qui
> invente en parlant!
>
> FAUBLAS.

AFTER many months of trial, this is the stage that Julien had reached on the day when the steward of the household paid him his third quarter's salary. M. de La Mole had set him to study the management of his estates in Brittany and Normandy. Julien made frequent journeys to those parts. His principal duty was to take charge of the correspondence relative to the famous lawsuit with the Abbé de Frilair. M. Pirard had given him the necessary instructions.

From the brief notes which the Marquis used to scribble on the margins of the papers of all kinds that came to him, Julien composed letters almost all of which were signed.

At the school of theology, his teachers complained of his lack of industry, but regarded him none the less as one of their most distinguished pupils. These several labours, taken up with all the ardour of a chafed ambition, had soon robbed Julien of the fresh complexion he had brought with him from the country. His pallor was a merit in the eyes of the young seminarists his companions; he found them much less irritating, much less inclined to fall upon their knees before a coin of the realm than those at Besançon; they, for their part, supposed him to be consumptive. The Marquis had given him a horse.

Afraid of their seeing him when he was out riding, Julien had told them that this exercise had been ordered him by the doctors. The Abbé Pirard had taken him to a number of Jansenist houses. Julien was astonished; the idea of religion was inseparably linked in his mind with that of hypocrisy, and the hope of making money. He admired these devout and stern men who took no interest in the budget. Several of the Jansenists had formed an affection for him and gave him advice. A new world opened before him. He met among the Jansenists a certain Conte Altamira, a man six feet in height, a Liberal under sentence of death in his own country, and a devout Catholic. This strange incongruity, religion wedded to a love of freedom, impressed him.

Julien was out of favour with the young Count. Norbert had found that he replied with too much warmth to the pleasantries of certain of his friends. Julien after being guilty once or twice of a breach of good manners, had pledged himself never to address another word to Mademoiselle Mathilde. They were always perfectly civil to him at the Hôtel de La Mole; but he felt that he had fallen in their esteem. His provincial common sense explained this change in the words of the popular proverb: 'familiarity breeds contempt.'

Perhaps his perception was now a little clearer than at first, or else the first fascination produced by the urbanity of Paris had ceased.

As soon as he stopped working, he fell into the clutches of a deadly boredom; this was the withering effect of the politeness, admirable in itself, but so measured, so perfectly graduated according to one's position, which is a mark of high society. A heart that is at all sensitive discerns the artificiality.

No doubt, provincials may be accused of a trace of vulgarity, or of a want of politeness; but they do shew a little warmth in answering one. Never, in the Hôtel de La Mole, was Julien's self-esteem wounded; but often, at the end of the day, as he took his candlestick in the ante-room, he felt inclined to weep. In the provinces, a waiter in a café takes

302

an interest in you if you meet with some accident on entering his café; but if that accident involves anything capable of wounding your vanity, then, in condoling with you, he will repeat again and again the word that makes you wince. In Paris they are so considerate as to turn their backs to laugh at you, but you will always remain a stranger.

We pass without comment over a multitude of minor adventures which would have brought Julien into ridicule had he not been in a sense beneath ridicule. An insane self-consciousness made him commit thousands of blunders. All his pleasures were forms of precaution; he practised with his pistol every day, and was numbered among the more promising pupils of the most famous fencing masters. Whenever he had a moment to spare, instead of spending it with a book as at one time, he would dash to the riding school and ask for the most vicious horses. In his outings with the riding master, he was almost invariably thrown.

The Marquis found him useful owing to his persistent hard work, his reticence and his intelligence, and, by degrees, entrusted him with the handling of all his business that was at all complicated. In those moments in which his lofty ambition allowed him some relaxation, the Marquis did his business with sagacity; being in a position to hear all the latest news, he speculated with success. He bought houses, timber; but he took offence easily. He gave away hundreds of louis and went to law over hundreds of francs. Rich men with big ideas seek amusement and not results from their private undertakings. The Marquis needed a chief of staff who would put into an easily intelligible order all his financial affairs.

Madame de La Mole, albeit of so restrained a character, would sometimes make fun of Julien. The *unexpected*, an outcome of sensibility, horrifies great ladies; it is a direct challenge to all the conventions. On two or three occasions the Marquis took his part: 'If he is absurd in your drawing-room, in his own office he reigns supreme.' Julien, for his part, thought he could divine the Marquise's secret. She deigned to take an interest in everything as soon as her servants announced the Baron de La Joumate. This was a chilly

303

creature, with expressionless features. He was small, thin, ugly, very well dressed, he spent all his time at the Château, and, as a rule, had nothing to say about anything. His speech revealed his mind. Madame de La Mole would have been passionately happy, for the first time in her life, if she could have secured him as a husband for her daughter.

CHAPTER THIRTY-SIX

PRONUNCIATION

Leur haute mission est de juger avec calme les petits
événements de la vie journalière des peuples. Leur
sagesse doit prévenir les grandes colères pour les petites
causes, ou pour des événements que la voix de la
renommée transfigure en les portant au loin.

GRATIUS.

FOR a newcomer, who, out of pride, never asked any
questions, Julien managed to avoid any serious pitfall.
One day, when he had been driven into a café in the
Rue Saint-Honoré by a sudden shower, a tall man in a bea-
ver coat, surprised at his gloomy stare, began to stare back
at him exactly as Mademoiselle Amanda's lover had stared
at him, long before, at Besançon.

Julien had too often reproached himself for having allowed
the former insult to pass unpunished to tolerate this stare.
He demanded an explanation, the man in the greatcoat at
once began to abuse him in the the foulest terms: everyone
in the café gathered round them; the passers-by stopped outside the door. With provincial caution, Julien always carried
a brace of pocket pistols; his hand gripped one of these in
his pocket with a convulsive movement. Better counsels prevailed, however, and he confined himself to repeating with
clockwork regularity: 'Sir, your address? I scorn you.'

The persistence with which he clung to these six words
began to impress the crowd.

'Gad, that other fellow who goes on talking by himself

305

ought to give him his address.' The man in the greatcoat, hearing this opinion freely vented, flung a handful of visiting cards in Julien's face. Fortunately, none of them hit him, he had vowed that he would use his pistol only in the event of his being touched. The man went away, not without turning round from time to time to shake his fist at Julien and to shout abuse.

Julien found himself bathed in sweat. 'So it lies within the power of the lowest of mankind to work me up like this!' he said angrily to himself. 'How am I to destroy this humiliating sensibility?'

He would have liked to be able to fight at once. But he was stopped by a difficulty. In all this great city of Paris, where was he to find a second? He had made the acquaintance of a number of men; but all of them, after six weeks or so, had drifted away from him. 'I am unsociable, and here I am cruelly punished for it,' he thought. Finally, it occurred to him to apply to a retired Lieutenant of the 96th named Liéven, a poor devil with whom he used often to fence. Julien was frank with him.

'I shall be glad to be your second,' said Liéven, 'but upon one condition: if you do not hit your man, you shall fight with me, there and then.'

'Agreed,' said Julien, with an enthusiastic handclasp; and they went to find M. C. de Beauvoisis at the address indicated upon his cards, in the heart of the Faubourg Saint-Germain.

It was seven o'clock in the morning. It was only when he sent in his name that it occurred to Julien that this might be Madame de Rênal's young relative, formerly attached to the Embassy at Rome or Naples, who had given the singer Geronimo a letter of introduction.

Julien had handed to a tall footman one of the cards flung at him the day before, together with one of his own.

He was kept waiting, with his second, for fully three quarters of an hour; finally they were shewn into an admirably furnished apartment. They found a tall young man, in an orange and white dressing-gown, got up like a doll; his features exemplified the perfection and the insignificance of Grecian beauty. His head, remarkably narrow, was crowned with a pyramid of the most beautiful golden locks. These were curled with scrupulous care, not a hair stood out from the rest. 'It is to have his hair curled like that,' thought the Lieutenant of the 96th, 'that this damned idiot has been keeping us waiting.' His striped dressing-gown, his morning trousers, everything, down to his embroidered slippers, was correct and marvellously well cared for. His features, noble and vacuous, betokened a propriety and paucity of ideas, the ideal of the well-meaning man, a horror of the unexpected and of ridicule, an abundance of gravity.

Julien, to whom his Lieutenant of the 96th had explained that to keep him waiting so long, after rudely flinging his card in his face, was an additional insult, strode boldly into M. de Beauvoisis's presence. It was his intention to be insolent, but he wished at the same time to shew his good breeding.

He was so much impressed by M. de Beauvoisis's gentle manners, by his air at once formal, important and self-satisfied, by the admirable elegance of his surroundings, that in a twinkling all thought of being insolent forsook him. This was not his man of the day before. So great was his astonishment at finding so distinguished a person in place of the vulgar fellow he had met in the café, that he could not think of a single word to say. He presented one of the cards that had been flung at him:

'This is my name,' said the man of fashion, in whom Julien's black coat, at seven o'clock in the morning, inspired but scant respect; 'but I do not understand, the honour....'

His way of pronouncing these last words restored some of Julien's ill humour.

'I have come to fight with you, Sir,' and he rapidly explained the situation.

M. Charles de Beauvoisis, after giving it careful thought, was quite satisfied with the cut of Julien's black coat. 'By Staub, clearly,' he said to himself, listening to him in silence; 'that waistcoat is in good taste, the boots are right; but, on the other hand, that black coat in the early morning! ... It will be to stop the bullet,' thought the Chevalier de Beauvoisis.

As soon as he had furnished himself with this explanation, he reverted to a perfect politeness, and addressed Julien almost as an equal. The discussion lasted for some time, it was a delicate matter; but in the end Julien could not reject the evidence of his own eyes. The well-bred young man whom he saw before him bore no resemblance whatsoever to the rude person who, the day before, had insulted him.

Julien felt an invincible reluctance to go away, he prolonged the explanation. He observed the self-sufficiency of the Chevalier de Beauvoisis, for such was the style that he had adopted in referring to himself, shocked at Julien's addressing him as Monsieur, pure and simple.

He admired the other's gravity, blended with a certain modest fatuity but never discarded for a single instant. He was astonished by the curious way in which his tongue moved as he enunciated his words.... But after all, in all this, there was not the slightest reason to pick a quarrel with him.

The young diplomat offered to fight with great courtesy, but the ex-Lieutenant of the 96th, who had been sitting for an hour with his legs apart, his hands on his hips and his arms akimbo, decided that his friend, M. Sorel, was not the sort of person to pick a quarrel, in the German fashion, with another man, because that man's visiting cards had been stolen.

Julien left the house in the worst of tempers. The Chevalier de Beauvoisis's carriage was waiting for him in the courtyard, in front of the steps; as it happened, Julien raised his eyes and recognised his man of the previous day in the coachman.

Seeing him, grasping him by the skirts of his coat, pulling him down from his box and belabouring him with his whip, were the work of a moment. Two lackeys tried to defend their fellow; Julien received a pummelling: immediately he drew one of his pocket pistols and fired at them; they took to their heels. It was all over in a minute.

The Chevalier de Beauvoisis came slowly downstairs with

308

the most charming gravity, repeating in the accents of a great nobleman: 'What's this? What's this?' His curiosity was evidently aroused, but his diplomatic importance did not allow him to shew any sign of interest. When he learned what the matter was, a lofty pride still struggled in his features against the slightly playful coolness which ought never to be absent from the face of a diplomat.

The Lieutenant of the 96th realised that M. de Beauvoisis was anxious to fight; he wished also, diplomatically enough, to preserve for his friend the advantages of the initiative. 'This time,' he cried, 'there are grounds for a duel!' 'I should think so,' replied the diplomat.

'I dismiss that rascal,' he said to his servants; 'some one else must drive.' They opened the carriage door: the Chevalier insisted that Julien and his second should get in before him. They went to find a friend of M. de Beauvoisis, who suggested a quiet spot. The conversation as they drove to it was perfect. The only odd thing was the diplomat in undress.

'These gentlemen, although of the highest nobility,' thought Julien, 'are not in the least boring like the people who come to dine with M. de La Mole; and I can see why,' he added a moment later, 'they are not ashamed to be indecent.' They were speaking of the dancers whom the public had applauded in a ballet of the previous evening. The gentlemen made allusions to spicy anecdotes of which Julien and his second, the Lieutenant of the 96th, were entirely ignorant. Julien did not make the mistake of pretending to know them; he admitted his ignorance with good grace. This frankness found favour with the Chevalier's friend; he repeated the anecdotes to him in full detail, and extremely well.

One thing astonished Julien vastly. A station which was being erected in the middle of the street for the Corpus Christi procession, held up the carriage for a moment. The gentlemen indulged in a number of pleasantries; the curé, according to them, was the son of an Archbishop. Never, in the house of the Marquis de La Mole, who hoped to become a Duke, would anyone have dared to say such a thing.

The duel was over in an instant: Julien received a bullet

309

in his arm; they bound it up for him with handkerchiefs; these were soaked in brandy, and the Chevalier de Beauvoisis asked Julien most politely to allow him to take him home, in the carriage that had brought them. When Julien gave his address as the Hôtel de La Mole, the young diplomat and his friend exchanged glances. Julien's cab was waiting, but he found these gentlemen's conversation infinitely more amusing than that of the worthy Lieutenant of the 96th.

'Good God! A duel, is that all?' thought Julien. 'How fortunate I was to come across that coachman again! What a misfortune, if I had had to endure that insult a second time in a café!' The amusing conversation had scarcely been interrupted. Julien now understood that the affectation of a diplomat does serve some purpose.

'So dulness is by no means inherent,' he said to himself, 'in a conversation between people of high birth! These men make fun of the Corpus Christi procession, they venture to repeat highly scabrous anecdotes, and with picturesque details. Positively the only thing lacking to them is judgment in politics, and this deficiency is more than made up for by the charm of their tone and the perfect aptness of their expressions.' Julien felt himself keenly attracted to them. 'How glad I should be to see them often!'

No sooner had they parted than the Chevalier de Beauvoisis hastened in search of information: what he heard was by no means promising.

He was extremely curious to know his man better; could he with decency call upon him? The scanty information he managed to obtain was not of an encouraging nature.

'This is frightful!' he said to his second. 'It is impossible for me to admit that I have fought a duel with a mere secretary of M. de La Mole, and that because I have been robbed of my visiting cards by a coachman.'

'Certainly the whole story leaves one exposed to ridicule.'

That evening, the Chevalier de Beauvoisis spread the report everywhere that this M. Sorel, who incidentally was a perfectly charming young man, was the natural son of an intimate friend of the Marquis de La Mole. The rumour passed without difficulty. As soon as it was established, the young diplomat and his friend deigned to pay Julien several visits, during the fortnight for which he was confined to his room. Julien confessed to them that he had never in his life been to the Opera.

'This is terrible,' they told him, 'where else does one go? Your first outing must be to the *Comte Ory*.'

At the Opera, the Chevalier de Beauvoisis presented him to the famous singer Geronimo, who was enjoying an immense success that season.

Julien almost paid court to the Chevalier; his blend of self-respect, mysterious importance and boyish fatuity enchanted him. For instance, the Chevalier stammered slightly because he had the honour to be frequently in the company of a great nobleman who suffered from that infirmity. Never had Julien seen combined in a single person the absurdity which keeps one amused and the perfection of manners which a poor provincial must seek to copy.

He was seen at the Opera with the Chevalier de Beauvoisis; their association caused his name to be mentioned.

'Well, Sir!' M. de La Mole said to him one day, 'and so you are the natural son of a rich gentleman of the Franche-Comté, my intimate friend!'

The Marquis cut Julien short when he tried to protest that he had in no way helped to give currency to this rumour.

'M. de Beauvoisis did not wish to have fought a duel with a carpenter's son.'

'I know, I know,' said M. de La Mole; 'it rests with me now to give consistency to the story, which suits me. But I have one favour to ask you, which will cost you no more than half an hour of your time: every Opera evening, at half-past eleven, go and stand in the vestibule when the people of fashion are coming out. I still notice in you at times provincial mannerisms, you must get rid of them; besides, it can do you no harm to know, at least by sight, important personages to whom I may one day have occasion to send you. Call at the box office to have yourself identified; they have placed your name on the list.'

CHAPTER THIRTY-SEVEN

AN ATTACK OF GOUT

And I received promotion, not on my own merits,
but because my master had the gout.

BERTOLOTTI.

THE reader is perhaps surprised at this free and almost
friendly tone; we have forgotten to say that for six
weeks the Marquis had been confined to the house
by an attack of gout.

Mademoiselle de La Mole and her mother were at Hyères,
with the Marquise's mother. Comte Norbert saw his father
only for brief moments; they were on the best of terms, but
had nothing to say to one another. M. de La Mole, reduced
to Julien's company, was astonished to find him endowed
with ideas. He made him read the newspapers aloud. Soon
the young secretary was able to select the interesting passages. There was a new paper which the Marquis abhorred;
he had vowed that he would never read it, and spoke of it
every day. Julien laughed, and marvelled at the feebleness of
the resistance offered to an idea by those in power. This
weakness in the Marquis restored to him all the coolness
which he was in danger of losing after a number of evenings
spent in the private society of so great a nobleman. The Marquis, out of patience with the times, made Julien read him
Livy; the translation improvised from the Latin text
amused him.

One day the Marquis said, with that tone of over-elaborate
politeness, which often tried Julien's patience:

'Allow me, my dear Sorel, to make you the present of a blue coat: when it suits you to put it on and to pay me a visit, you will be, in my eyes, the younger brother of the Comte de Retz, that is to say, the son of my old friend the Duke.'

Julien was somewhat in the dark as to what was happening; that evening he ventured to pay a visit in his blue coat. The Marquis treated him as an equal. Julien had a heart capable of appreciating true politeness, but he had no idea of the finer shades. He would have sworn, before this caprice of the Marquis, that it would be impossible to be received by him with greater deference. 'What a marvellous talent!' Julien said to himself; when he rose to go, the Marquis apologised for not being able to see him to the door on account of his gout.

Julien was obsessed by this strange idea: 'Can he be laughing at me?' he wondered. He went to seek the advice of the Abbé Pirard, who, less courteous than the Marquis, answered him only with a whistle and changed the subject. The following morning Julien appeared before the Marquis, in a black coat, with his portfolio and the letters to be signed. He was received in the old manner. That evening, in his blue coat, it was with an entirely different tone and one in every way as polite as the evening before.

'Since you appear to find some interest in the visits which you are so kind as to pay to a poor, suffering old man,' the Marquis said to him, 'you must speak to him of all the little incidents in your life, but openly, and without thinking of anything but how to relate them clearly and in an amusing fashion. For one must have amusement,' the Marquis went on; 'that is the only real thing in life. A man cannot save my life on a battle-field every day, nor can he make me every day the present of a million; but if I had Rivarol here, by my couch, every day, he would relieve me of an hour of pain and boredom. I saw a great deal of him at Hamburg, during the Emigration.'

And the Marquis told Julien stories of Rivarol among the Hamburgers, who would club together in fours to elucidate the point of a witty saying.

M. de La Mole, reduced to the society of this young cleric, sought to enliven him. He stung Julien's pride. Since he was asked for the truth, Julien determined to tell his whole story; but with the suppression of two things: his fanatical admiration for a name which made the Marquis furious, and his entire unbelief, which hardly became a future curé. His little affair with the Chevalier de Beauvoisis arrived most opportunely. The Marquis laughed till he cried at the scene in the café in the Rue Saint-Honoré, with the coachman who covered him with foul abuse. It was a period of perfect frankness in the relations between employer and protégé.

M. de La Mole became interested in this singular character. At first, he played with Julien's absurdities, for his own entertainment; soon he found it more interesting to correct, in the gentlest manner, the young man's mistaken view of life. 'Most provincials who come to Paris admire everything,' thought the Marquis; 'this fellow hates everything. They have too much sentiment, he has not enough, and fools take him for a fool.'

The attack of gout was prolonged by the wintry weather and lasted for some months.

'One becomes attached to a fine spaniel,' the Marquis told himself; 'why am I so ashamed of becoming attached to this young cleric? He is original. I treat him like a son; well, what harm is there in that! This fancy, if it lasts, will cost me a diamond worth five hundred louis in my will.'

Once the Marquis had realised the firm character of his protégé, he entrusted him with some fresh piece of business every day.

Julien noticed with alarm that this great nobleman would occasionally give him contradictory instructions with regard to the same matter.

This was liable to land him in serious trouble. Julien, when he came to work with the Marquis, invariably brought a diary in which he wrote down his instructions, and the Marquis initialed them. Julien had engaged a clerk who copied out the instructions relative to each piece of business in a special book. In this book were kept also copies of all letters.

This idea seemed at first the most ridiculous and tiresome thing imaginable. But, in less than two months, the Marquis realised its advantages. Julien suggested engaging a clerk from a bank, who should keep an account by double entry of all the revenue from and expenditure on the estates of which he himself had charge.

These measures so enlightened the Marquis as to his own financial position that he was able to give himself the pleasure of embarking on two or three fresh speculations without the assistance of his broker, who had been robbing him.

'Take three thousand francs for yourself,' he said, one day to his young minister.

'But, Sir, my conduct may be criticised.'

'What do you want, then?' replied the Marquis, with irritation.

'I want you to be so kind as to make a formal agreement, and to write it down yourself in the book; the agreement will award me a sum of three thousand francs. Besides, it was M. l'Abbé Pirard who first thought of all this book-keeping.' The Marquis, with the bored expression of the Marquis de Moncade, listening to M. Poisson, his steward, reading his accounts, wrote out his instructions.

In the evening, when Julien appeared in his blue coat, there was never any talk of business. The Marquis's kindness was so flattering to our hero's easily wounded vanity that presently, in spite of himself, he felt a sort of attachment to this genial old man. Not that Julien was sensitive, as the word is understood in Paris; but he was not a monster, and no one, since the death of the old Surgeon-Major, had spoken to him so kindly. He remarked with astonishment that the Marquis shewed a polite consideration for his self-esteem which he had never received from the old surgeon. Finally he realised that the surgeon had been prouder of his Cross than the Marquis was of his Blue Riband. The Marquis was the son of a great nobleman.

One day, at the end of a morning interview, in his black coat, and for the discussion of business, Julien amused the Marquis, who kept him for a couple of hours, and positively insisted upon giving him a handful of bank notes which his broker had just brought him from the Bourse.

'I hope, Monsieur le Marquis, not to be wanting in the profound respect which I owe you if I ask you to allow me to say something.'

'Speak, my friend.'

'Will Monsieur le Marquis be graciously pleased to let me decline this gift. It is not to the man in black that it is offered, and it would at once put an end to the liberties which he is so kind as to tolerate from the man in blue.' He bowed most respectfully, and left the room without looking round.

This attitude amused the Marquis, who reported it that evening to the Abbé Pirard.

'There is something that I must at last confess to you, my dear Abbé. I know the truth about Julien's birth, and I authorise you not to keep this confidence secret.

'His behaviour this morning was noble,' thought the Marquis, 'and I shall ennoble him.'

Some time after this, the Marquis was at length able to leave his room.

'Go and spend a couple of months in London,' he told Julien. 'The special couriers and other messengers will bring you the letters I receive, with my notes. You will write the replies and send them to me, enclosing each letter with its reply. I have calculated that the delay will not amount to more than five days.'

As he travelled post along the road to Calais, Julien thought with amazement of the futility of the alleged business on which he was being sent.

We shall not describe the feeling of horror, almost of hatred, with which he set foot on English soil. The reader is aware of his insane passion for Bonaparte. He saw in every officer a Sir Hudson Lowe, in every nobleman a Lord Bathurst, ordering the atrocities of Saint Helena, and receiving his reward in ten years of office.

In London he at last made acquaintance with the extremes of fatuity. He made friends with some young Russian gentlemen who initiated him.

'You are predestined, my dear Sorel,' they told him, 'you are endowed by nature with that cold expression *a thousand leagues from the sensation of the moment*, which we try so hard to assume.'

'You have not understood our age,' Prince Korasoff said to him; '*always do the opposite to what people expect of you*. That, upon my honour, is the only religion of the day. Do not be either foolish or affected, for then people will expect foolishness and affectations, and you will not be obeying the rule.'

Julien covered himself with glory one day in the drawing-room of the Duke of Fitz-Fulke, who had invited him to dine, with Prince Korasoff. The party were kept waiting for an hour. The way in which Julien comported himself amid the score of persons who stood waiting is still quoted by the young Secretaries of Embassy in London. His expression was inimitable.

He was anxious to meet, notwithstanding the sneers of his friends the dandies, the celebrated Philip Vane, the one philosopher that England has produced since Locke. He found him completing his seventh year in prison. 'The aristocracy does not take things lightly in this country,' thought Julien; 'in addition to all this, Vane is disgraced, abused,' etc.

Julien found him good company; the fury of the aristocracy kept him amused. 'There,' Julien said to himself, as he left the prison, 'is the one cheerful man that I have met in England.'

'The idea of most use to tyrants is that of God,' Vane had said to him.

We suppress the rest of the philosopher's system as being cynical.

On his return: 'What amusing idea have you brought me from England?' M. de La Mole asked him. He remained silent. 'What idea have you brought, amusing or not?' the Marquis went on, sharply.

'First of all,' said Julien, 'the wisest man in England is mad for an hour daily; he is visited by the demon of suicide, who is the national deity.

'Secondly, intelligence and genius forfeit twenty-five per cent of their value on landing in England.

'Thirdly, nothing in the world is so beautiful, admirable, moving as the English countryside.'

'Now, it is my turn,' said the Marquis.

'First of all, what made you say, at the ball at the Russian Embassy, that there are in France three hundred thousand young men of five and twenty who are passionately anxious for war? Do you think that that is quite polite to the Crowned Heads?'

'One never knows what to say in speaking to our great diplomats,' said Julien. 'They have a mania for starting serious discussions. If one confines oneself to the commonplaces of the newspapers, one is reckoned a fool. If one allows oneself to say something true and novel, they are astonished, they do not know how to answer, and next morning, at seven o'clock, they send word to one by the First Secretary, that one has been impolite.'

'Not bad,' said the Marquis, with a laugh. 'I wager, however, Master Philosopher, that you have not discovered what you went to England to do.'

'Pardon me,' replied Julien; 'I went there to dine once a week with His Majesty's Ambassador, who is the most courteous of men.'

'You went to secure the Cross which is lying there,' the Marquis told him. 'I do not wish to make you lay aside your black coat, and I have grown accustomed to the more amusing tone which I have adopted with the man in blue. Until further orders, understand this: when I see this Cross, you are the younger son of my friend the Duc de Retz, who, without knowing it, has been for the last six months employed in diplomacy. Observe,' added the Marquis, with a highly serious air, cutting short Julien's expressions of gratitude, 'that I do not on any account wish you to rise above your station. That is always a mistake, and a misfortune both for patron and for protégé. When my lawsuits bore you, or when you no longer suit me, I shall ask for a good living for you, like that of our friend the Abbé Pirard, and *nothing more*,' the Marquis added, in the driest of tones.

This Cross set Julien's pride at rest; he began to talk far

more freely. He felt himself less frequently insulted and made a butt by those remarks, susceptible of some scarcely polite interpretation, which, in the course of an animated conversation, may fall from the lips of anyone.

His Cross was the cause of an unexpected visit; this was from M. le Baron de Valenod, who came to Paris to thank the Minister for his Barony and to come to an understanding with him. He was going to be appointed Mayor of Verrières on the deposition of M. de Rênal.

Julien was consumed with silent laughter when M. de Valenod gave him to understand that it had just been discovered that M. de Rênal was a Jacobin. The fact was that, in a new election which was in preparation, the new Baron was the ministerial candidate, and in the combined constituency of the Department, which in reality was strongly Ultra, it was M. de Rênal who was being put forward by the Liberals.

It was in vain that Julien tried to learn something of Madame de Rênal; the Baron appeared to remember their former rivalry, and was impenetrable. He ended by asking Julien for his father's vote at the coming election. Julien promised to write.

'You ought, Monsieur le Chevalier, to introduce me to M. le Marquis de La Mole.'

'Indeed, so *I ought*,' thought Julien; 'but a rascal like this!'

'To be frank,' he replied, 'I am too humble a person in the Hôtel de La Mole to take it upon me to introduce anyone.'

Julien told the Marquis everything: that evening he informed him of Valenod's pretension, and gave an account of his life and actions since 1814.

'Not only,' M. de La Mole replied, with a serious air, 'will you introduce the new Baron to me to-morrow, but I shall invite him to dine the day after. He will be one of our new Prefects.'

'In that case,' retorted Julien coldly, 'I request the post of Governor of the Poorhouse for my father.'

'Excellent,' said the Marquis, recovering his gaiety; 'granted; I was expecting a sermon. You are growing up.'

M. de Valenod informed Julien that the keeper of the

lottery office at Verrières had just died; Julien thought it amusing to bestow this place upon M. de Cholin, the old imbecile whose petition he had picked up in the room occupied there by M. de La Mole. The Marquis laughed heartily at the petition which Julien recited as he made him sign the letter applying for this post to the Minister of Finance.

No sooner had M. de Cholin been appointed than Julien learned that this post had been requested by the Deputies of the Department for M. Gros, the celebrated geometrician: this noble-hearted man had an income of only fourteen hundred francs, and every year had been lending six hundred francs to the late holder of the post, to help him to bring up his family.

Julien was astonished at the effect of what he had done. 'This family of the dead man, what are they living on now?' The thought of this wrung his heart. 'It is nothing,' he told himself; 'I must be prepared for many other acts of injustice, if I am to succeed, and, what is more, must know how to conceal them, under a cloak of fine sentimental words: poor M. Gros! It is he that deserved the Cross, it is I that have it, and I must act according to the wishes of the Government that has given it to me.'

CHAPTER THIRTY-EIGHT

WHAT IS THE DECORATION THAT CONFERS DISTINCTION?

Your water does not refresh me, said the thirsty
genie. Yet it is the coolest well in all the Diar Bekir.

PELLICO.

O NE day Julien returned from the charming property
of Villequier, on the bank of the Seine, in which M.
de La Mole took a special interest because, of all his
estates, it was the only one that had belonged to the celebrated Boniface de La Mole. He found at the Hôtel the Marquise and her daughter, who had returned from Hyères.

Julien was now a dandy and understood the art of life
in Paris. He greeted Mademoiselle de La Mole with perfect
coolness. He appeared to remember nothing of the time
when she asked him so gaily to tell her all about his way of
falling gracefully from his horse.

Mademoiselle de La Mole found him taller and paler.
There was no longer anything provincial about his figure or
his attire; not so with his conversation: this was still perceptibly too serious, too positive. In spite of these sober qualities,
and thanks to his pride, it conveyed no sense of inferiority;
one felt merely that he still regarded too many things as
important. But one saw that he was a man who would stand
by his word.

'He is wanting in lightness of touch, but not in intelligence,' Mademoiselle de La Mole said to her father, as she
teased him over the Cross he had given Julien. 'My brother

321

has been asking you for it for the last eighteen months, and he is a La Mole!'

'Yes; but Julien has novelty. That has never been the case with the La Mole you mention.'

M. le Duc de Retz was announced.

Mathilde felt herself seized by an irresistible desire to yawn; the sight of the man brought to her mind the antique decorations and the old frequenters of the paternal drawing-room. She formed an entirely boring picture of the life she was going to resume in Paris. And yet at Hyères she had longed for Paris.

'To think that I am nineteen!' she reflected: 'it is the age of happiness, according to all those gilt-edged idiots.' She looked at nine or ten volumes of recent poetry that had accumulated, during her absence in Provence, on the drawing-room table. It was her misfortune to have more intelligence than MM. de Croisenois, de Caylus, de Luz, and the rest of her friends. She could imagine everything that they would say to her about the beautiful sky in Provence, poetry, the south, etc., etc.

Those lovely eyes, in which was revealed the most profound boredom, and, what was worse still, a despair of finding any pleasure, came to rest upon Julien. At any rate, he was not exactly like all the rest.

'Monsieur Sorel,' she said in that short, sharp voice, with nothing feminine about it, which is used by young women of the highest rank, 'Monsieur Sorel, are you coming to M. de Retz's ball to-night?'

'Mademoiselle, I have not had the honour to be presented to M. le Duc.' (One would have said that these words and the title burned the lips of the proud provincial.)

'He has asked my brother to bring you; and, if you came, you could tell me all about Villequier; there is some talk of our going there in the spring. I should like to know whether the house is habitable, and if the country round it is as pretty as people say. There are so many undeserved reputations!'

Julien made no reply.

'Come to the ball with my brother,' she added, in the driest of tones.

Julien made a respectful bow. 'So, even in the middle of a ball, I must render accounts to all the members of the family. Am I not paid to be their man of business?' In his ill humour, he added: 'Heaven only knows whether what I tell the daughter may not upset the plans of her father, and brother, and mother! It is just like the court of a Sovereign Prince. One is expected to be a complete nonentity, and at the same time give no one any grounds for complaint.

'How I dislike that great girl!' he thought, as he watched Mademoiselle de La Mole cross the room, her mother having called her to introduce her to a number of women visitors. 'She overdoes all the fashions, her gown is falling off her shoulders ... she is even paler than when she went away.... What colourless hair, if that is what they call golden! You would say the light shone through it. How arrogant her way of bowing, of looking at people! What regal gestures!'

Mademoiselle de La Mole had called her brother back, as he was leaving the room.

Comte Norbert came up to Julien:

'My dear Sorel,' he began, 'where would you like me to call for you at midnight for M. de Retz's ball? He told me particularly to bring you.'

'I know to whom I am indebted for such kindness,' replied Julien, bowing to the ground.

His ill humour, having no fault to find with the tone of politeness, indeed of personal interest, in which Norbert had addressed him, vented itself upon the reply which he himself had made to this friendly speech. He detected a trace of servility in it.

That night, on arriving at the ball, he was struck by the magnificence of the Hôtel de Retz. The courtyard was covered with an immense crimson awning patterned with golden stars: nothing could have been more elegant. Beneath this awning, the court was transformed into a grove of orange trees and oleanders in blossom. As their tubs had been carefully buried at a sufficient depth, these oleanders and orange trees seemed to be springing from the ground. The carriage drive had been sprinkled with sand.

The general effect seemed extraordinary to our provincial. He had no idea that such magnificence could exist; in an instant his imagination had taken wings and flown a thousand leagues away from ill humour. In the carriage, on their way to the ball, Norbert had been happy, and he had seen everything in dark colours; as soon as they entered the courtyard their moods were reversed.

Norbert was conscious only of certain details, which, in the midst of all this magnificence, had been overlooked. He reckoned up the cost of everything, and as he arrived at a high total, Julien remarked that he appeared almost jealous of the outlay and began to sulk.

As for Julien, he arrived spellbound with admiration, and almost timid with excess of emotion in the first of the saloons in which the company were dancing. Everyone was making for the door of the second room, and the throng was so great that he found it impossible to move. This great saloon was decorated to represent the Alhambra of Granada.

'She is the belle of the ball, no doubt about it,' said a young man with moustaches, whose shoulder dug into Julien's chest.

'Mademoiselle Fourmont, who has been the reigning beauty all winter,' his companion rejoined, 'sees that she must now take the second place: look how strangely she is frowning.'

'Indeed she is hoisting all her canvas to attract. Look, look at that gracious smile as soon as she steps into the middle in that country dance. It is inimitable, upon my honour.'

'Mademoiselle de La Mole has the air of being in full control of the pleasure she derives from her triumph, of which she is very well aware. One would say that she was afraid of attracting whoever speaks to her.'

'Precisely! That is the art of seduction.'

Julien was making vain efforts to catch a glimpse of this seductive woman; seven or eight men taller than himself prevented him from seeing her.

'There is a good deal of coquetry in that noble reserve,' went on the young man with the moustaches.

'And those big blue eyes which droop so slowly just at the moment when one would say they were going to give her away,' his companion added. 'Faith, she's a past master.'

'Look how common the fair Fourmont appears beside her,' said a third.

'That air of reserve is as much as to say: "How charming I should make myself to you, if you were the man that was worthy of me." '

'And who could be worthy of the sublime Mathilde?' said the first: 'Some reigning Prince, handsome, clever, well made, a hero in battle, and aged twenty at the most.'

'The natural son of the Emperor of Russia, for whom, on the occasion of such a marriage, a Kingdom would be created; or simply the Comte de Thaler, with his air of a peasant in his Sunday clothes....'

The passage was now cleared, Julien was free to enter.

'Since she appears so remarkable in the eyes of these puppets, it is worth my while to study her,' he thought. 'I shall understand what perfection means to these people.'

As he was trying to catch her eye, Mathilde looked at him. 'Duty calls me,' Julien said to himself, but his resentment was now confined to his expression. Curiosity made him step forward with a pleasure which the low cut of the gown on Mathilde's shoulders rapidly enhanced, in a manner, it must be admitted, by no means flattering to his self-esteem. 'Her beauty has the charm of youth,' he thought. Five or six young men, among whom Julien recognised those whom he had heard talking in the doorway, stood between her and him.

'You can tell me, Sir, as you have been here all the winter,' she said to him, 'is it not true that this is the prettiest ball of the season?' He made no answer.

'This Coulon quadrille seems to me admirable; and the ladies are dancing it quite perfectly.' The young men turned round to see who the fortunate person was who was being thus pressed for an answer. It was not encouraging.

'I should hardly be a good judge, Mademoiselle; I spend my time writing: this is the first ball on such a scale that I have seen.'

The moustached young men were shocked.

'You are a sage, Monsieur Sorel,' she went on with a more marked interest; 'you look upon all these balls, all these parties, like a philosopher, like a Jean-Jacques Rousseau. These follies surprise you without tempting you.'

A chance word had stifled Julien's imagination and banished every illusion from his heart. His lips assumed an expression of disdain that was perhaps slightly exaggerated.

'Jean-Jacques Rousseau,' he replied, 'is nothing but a fool in my eyes when he takes it upon himself to criticise society; he did not understand it, and approached it with the heart of an upstart flunkey.'

'He wrote the *Contrat Social*,' said Mathilde in a tone of veneration.

'For all his preaching a Republic and the overthrow of monarchical titles, the upstart is mad with joy if a Duke alters the course of his after-dinner stroll to accompany one of his friends.'

'Ah, yes! The Duc de Luxembourg at Montmorency accompanies a M. Coindet on the road to Paris,' replied Mademoiselle de La Mole with the impetuous delight of a first enjoyment of pedantry. She was overjoyed at her own learning, almost like the Academician who discovered the existence of King Feretrius. Julien's eye remained penetrating and stern. Mathilde had felt a momentary enthusiasm; her partner's coldness disconcerted her profoundly. She was all the more astonished inasmuch as it was she who was in the habit of producing this effect upon other people.

At that moment, the Marquis de Croisenois advanced eagerly towards Mademoiselle de La Mole. He stopped for a moment within a few feet of her, unable to approach her on account of the crowd. He looked at her, with a smile at the obstacle. The young Marquise de Rouvray was close beside him; she was a cousin of Mathilde. She gave her arm to her husband, who had been married for only a fortnight. The Marquis de Rouvray, who was quite young also, shewed all that fatuous love which seizes a man, who having made a 'suitable' marriage entirely arranged by the family lawyers, finds that he has a perfectly charming spouse. M. de Rouvray would be a Duke on the death of an uncle of advanced years.

While the Marquis de Croisenois, unable to penetrate the throng, stood gazing at Mathilde with a smiling air, she allowed her large, sky-blue eyes to rest upon him and his neighbours. 'What could be duller,' she said to herself, 'than all that group! Look at Croisenois who hopes to marry me; he is nice and polite, he has perfect manners like M. de Rouvray. If they did not bore me, these gentlemen would be quite charming. He, too, will come to balls with me with that smug, satisfied air. A year after we are married, my carriage, my horses, my gowns, my country house twenty leagues from Paris, everything will be as perfect as possible, just what is needed to make an upstart burst with envy, a Comtesse de Roiville for instance; and after that? . . .'

Mathilde let her mind drift into the future. The Marquis de Croisenois succeeded in reaching her, and spoke to her, but she dreamed on without listening. The sound of his voice was lost in the hubbub of the ball. Her eye mechanically followed Julien, who had moved away with a respectful, but proud and discontented air. She saw in a corner, aloof from the moving crowd, Conte Altamira, who was under sentence of death in his own country, as the reader already knows. Under Louis XIV, a lady of his family had married a Prince de Conti; this antecedent protected him to some extent from the police of the Congregation.

'I can see nothing but a sentence of death that distinguishes a man,' thought Mathilde: 'it is the only thing that is not to be bought.

'Ah! There is a witty saying that I have wasted on myself! What a pity that it did not occur to me when I could have made the most of it!' Mathilde had too much taste to lead up in conversation to a witticism prepared beforehand; but she had also too much vanity not to be delighted with her own wit. An air of happiness succeeded the appearance of boredom in her face. The Marquis de Croisenois, who was still addressing her, thought he saw a chance of success, and doubled his loquacity.

'What fault would anyone have to find with my remark?' Mathilde asked herself. 'I should answer my critic: "A title of Baron, or Viscount, that can be bought; a Cross, that is given; my brother has just had one, what has he ever done? A step in promotion, that is obtained. Ten years of garrison duty, or a relative as Minister for War, and one becomes a squadron-commander, like Norbert. A great fortune! That is still the most difficult thing to secure, and therefore the most meritorious. Now is not that odd? It is just the opposite to what all the books say.... Well, to secure a fortune, one marries M. Rothschild's daughter."

'My remark is really subtle. A death sentence is still the only thing for which no one has ever thought of asking.

'Do you know Conte Altamira?' she asked M. de Croisenois.

She had the air of having come back to earth from so remote an abstraction, and this question bore so little relation to all that the poor Marquis had been saying to her for the last five minutes, that his friendly feelings were somewhat disconcerted. He was, however, a man of ready wit, and highly esteemed in that capacity.

'Mathilde is certainly odd,' he thought; 'it is a drawback, but she gives her husband such a splendid social position! I cannot think how the Marquis de La Mole manages it; he is on intimate terms with all the best people of every colour, he is a man who cannot fall. Besides, this oddity in Mathilde may pass for genius. Given noble birth and an ample fortune, genius is not to be laughed at, and then, what distinction! She has such a command, too, when she pleases, of that combination of wit, character and aptness, which makes conversation perfect....' As it is hard to do two things well at the same time, the Marquis answered Mathilde with a vacant air, and as though repeating a lesson:

'Who does not know poor Altamira?' and he told her the story of the absurd, abortive conspiracy.

'Most absurd!' said Mathilde, as though speaking to herself, 'but he has done something. I wish to see a man; bring him to me,' she said to the Marquis, who was deeply shocked.

WHAT CONFERS DISTINCTION

Conte Altamira was one of the most openly professed admirers of the haughty and almost impertinent air of Mademoiselle de La Mole; she was, according to him, one of the loveliest creatures in Paris.

'How beautiful she would be on a throne!' he said to M. de Croisenois, and made no difficulty about allowing himself to be led to her.

There are not wanting in society people who seek to establish the principle that nothing is in such bad tone as a conspiracy; it reeks of Jacobinism. And what can be more vile than an unsuccessful Jacobin?

Mathilde's glance derided Altamira's Liberalism to M. de Croisenois, but she listened to him with pleasure.

'A conspirator at a ball, it is a charming contrast,' she thought. In this conspirator, with his black moustaches, she detected a resemblance to a lion in repose; but she soon found that his mind had but one attitude: *utility, admiration for utility.*

Excepting only what might bring to his country Two Chamber government, the young Count felt that nothing was worthy of his attention. He parted from Mathilde, the most attractive person at the ball, with pleasure because he had seen a Peruvian General enter the room.

Despairing of Europe, poor Altamira had been reduced to hoping that, when the States of South America became strong and powerful, they might restore to Europe the freedom which Mirabeau had sent to them.[1]

A swarm of young men with moustaches had gathered round Mathilde. She had seen quite well that Altamira was not attracted, and felt piqued by his desertion of her; she saw his dark eye gleam as he spoke to the Peruvian General. Mademoiselle de La Mole studied the young Frenchmen with that profound seriousness which none of her rivals was able to

[1] This page, written on July 25, 1830, was printed on August 4. (*Publisher's note.*) It was an order of July 25, 1830, dissolving the Chamber, which provoked the Revolution of the following days, the abdication of Charles X, and the accession of Louis-Philippe. C. K. S. M.

imitate. 'Which of them,' she thought, 'could ever be sentenced to death, even allowing him the most favourable conditions?'

This singular gaze flattered those who had little intelligence, but disturbed the rest. They feared the explosion of some pointed witticism which it would be difficult to answer.

'Good birth gives a man a hundred qualities the absence of which would offend me: I see that in Julien's case,' thought Mathilde; 'but it destroys those qualities of the spirit which make people be sentenced to death.'

At that moment someone remarked in her hearing: 'That Conte Altamira is the second son of the Principe di San Nazaro-Pimentel; it was a Pimentel who attempted to save Conradin, beheaded in 1268. They are one of the noblest families of Naples.'

'There,' Mathilde said to herself, 'is an excellent proof of my maxim: Good birth destroys the strength of character without which people do not incur sentences of death. I seem fated to go wrong this evening. Since I am only a woman like any other, well, I must dance.' She yielded to the persistence of the Marquis de Croisenois, who for the last hour had been pleading for a galop. To distract her thoughts from her philosophical failure, Mathilde chose to be perfectly bewitching; M. de Croisenois was in ecstasies.

But not the dance, nor the desire to please one of the handsomest men at court, nothing could distract Mathilde. She could not possibly have enjoyed a greater triumph. She was the queen of the ball, she knew it, but she remained cold.

'What a colourless life I shall lead with a creature like Croisenois,' she said to herself, as he led her back to her place an hour later. . . . 'What pleasure can there be for me,' she went on sadly, 'if after an absence of six months, I do not find any in a ball which is the envy of all the women in Paris? And moreover I am surrounded by the homage of a society which could not conceivably be more select. There is no plebeian element here except a few peers and a Julien or two perhaps. And yet,' she added, with a growing melancholy, 'what advantages has not fate bestowed on me! Birth, wealth, youth! Everything, alas, but happiness.

'The most dubious of my advantages are those of which they have been telling me all evening. Wit, I know I have, for obviously I frighten them all. If they venture to broach a serious subject, after five minutes of conversation they all arrive out of breath, and as though making a great discovery, at something which I have been repeating to them for the last hour. I am beautiful, I have that advantage for which Madame de Staël would have sacrificed everything, and yet the fact remains that I am dying of boredom. Is there any reason why I should be less bored when I have changed my name to that of the Marquis de Croisenois?

'But, Lord!' she added, almost in tears, 'is he not a perfect man? He is the masterpiece of the education of the age; one cannot look at him without his thinking of something pleasant, and even clever, to say to one; he is brave.... But that Sorel is a strange fellow,' she said to herself, and the look of gloom in her eye gave place to a look of anger. 'I told him that I had something to say to him, and he does not condescend to return!'

CHAPTER THIRTY-NINE

THE BALL

The splendour of the dresses, the blaze of the
candles, the perfumes; all those rounded arms, and fine
shoulders; bouquets, the sound of Rossini's music,
pictures by Ciceri! I am beside myself!

Travels of Uzeri.

'You are feeling cross,' the Marquise de La Mole said
to her; 'I warn you, that is not good manners at
a ball.'

'It is only a headache,' replied Mathilde contemptuously,
'it is too hot in here.'

At that moment, as though to corroborate Mademoiselle
de La Mole, the old Baron de Tolly fainted and fell to the
ground; he had to be carried out. There was talk of apoplexy,
it was a disagreeable incident.

Mathilde did not give it a thought. It was one of her definite habits never to look at an old man or at anyone known
to be given to talking about sad things.

She danced to escape the conversation about the apoplexy,
which indeed was nothing of the sort, for a day or two later
the Baron reappeared.

'But M. Sorel does not appear,' she said to herself again
after she had finished dancing. She was almost searching for
him with her eyes when she caught sight of him in another
room. Strange to say, he seemed to have shed the tone of
impassive coldness which was so natural to him; he had no
longer the air of an Englishman.

'He is talking to Conte Altamira, my condemned man!' Mathilde said to herself. 'His eye is ablaze with a sombre fire; he has the air of a Prince in disguise; the arrogance of his gaze has increased.'

Julien was coming towards the spot where she was, still talking to Altamira; she looked fixedly at him, studying his features in search of those lofty qualities which may entitle a man to the honour of being sentenced to death.

As he passed by her:

'Yes,' he was saying to Conte Altamira, 'Danton was a man!'

'Oh, heavens! Is he to be another Danton,' thought Mathilde; 'but he has such a noble face, and that Danton was so horribly ugly, a butcher, I fancy.' Julien was still quite near her, she had no hesitation in calling to him; she was conscious and proud of asking a question that was extraordinary, coming from a girl.

'Was not Danton a butcher?' she asked him.

'Yes, in the eyes of certain people,' Julien answered her with an expression of the most ill-concealed scorn, his eye still ablaze from his conversation with Altamira, 'but unfortunately for people of birth, he was a lawyer at Méry-sur-Seine; that is to say, Mademoiselle,' he went on with an air of sarcasm, 'that he began life like several of the Peers whom I see here this evening. It is true that Danton had an enormous disadvantage in the eyes of beauty: he was extremely ugly.'

The last words were uttered rapidly, with an extraordinary and certainly far from courteous air.

Julien waited for a moment, bowing slightly from the waist and with an arrogantly humble air. He seemed to be saying: 'I am paid to answer you, and I live upon my pay.' He did not deign to raise his eyes to her face. She, with her fine eyes opened extraordinarily wide and fastened upon him, seemed like his slave. At length, as the silence continued, he looked at her as a servant looks at his master, when receiving orders. Although his eyes looked full into those of Mathilde, still fastened upon him with a strange gaze, he withdrew with marked alacrity.

'That he, who really is so handsome,' Mathilde said to herself at length, awakening from her dreams, 'should pay such a tribute to ugliness! Never a thought of himself! He is not like Caylus or Croisenois. This Sorel has something of the air my father adopts when he is playing the Napoleon, at a ball.' She had entirely forgotten Danton. 'No doubt about it, I am bored this evening.' She seized her brother by the arm, and, greatly to his disgust, forced him to take her for a tour of the rooms. The idea occurred to her of following the condemned man's conversation with Julien.

The crowd was immense. She suceeded, however, in overtaking them at the moment when, just in front of her, Altamira had stopped by a tray of ices to help himself. He was talking to Julien, half turning towards him. He saw an arm in a braided sleeve stretched out to take an ice from the same tray. The gold lace seemed to attract his attention; he turned round bodily to see whose this arm was. Immediately his black eyes, so noble and unaffected, assumed a slight expression of scorn.

'You see that man,' he murmured to Julien; 'he is the Principe d'Araceli, the —— Ambassador. This morning he applied for my extradition to your French Foreign Minister, M. de Nerval. Look, there he is over there, playing whist. M. de Nerval is quite ready to give me up, for we gave you back two or three conspirators in 1816. If they surrender me to my King I shall be hanged within twenty-four hours. And it will be one of those pretty gentlemen with moustaches who will seize me.'

'The wretches!' exclaimed Julien, half aloud.

Mathilde did not lose a syllable of their conversation. Her boredom had vanished.

'Not such wretches as all that,' replied Conte Altamira. 'I have spoken to you of myself to impress you with a real instance. Look at Principe d'Araceli; every five minutes he casts a glance at his Golden Fleece; he cannot get over the pleasure of seeing that gewgaw on his breast. The poor man is really nothing worse than an anachronism. A hundred years ago, the Golden Fleece was a signal honour, but then it would have been far above his head. To-day, among people of breeding, one must be an Araceli to be thrilled by it. He would have hanged a whole town to obtain it.'

'Was that the price he paid for it?' said Julien, with anxiety.

'Not exactly,' replied Altamira coldly; 'he perhaps had some thirty wealthy landowners of his country, who were supposed to be Liberals, flung into the river.'

'What a monster!' said Julien again.

Mademoiselle de La Mole, leaning forward with the keenest interest, was so close to him that her beautiful hair almost brushed his shoulder.

'You are very young!' replied Altamira. 'I told you that I have a married sister in Provence; she is still pretty, good, gentle; she is an excellent mother, faithful to all her duties, pious without bigotry.'

'What is he leading up to?' thought Mademoiselle de La Mole.

'She is happy,' Conte Altamira continued; 'she was happy in 1815. At that time I was in hiding there, on her property near Antibes; well, as soon as she heard of the execution of Marshal Ney, she began to dance!'

'Is it possible?' said the horrified Julien.

'It is the party spirit,' replied Altamira. 'There are no longer any genuine passions in the nineteenth century; that is why people are so bored in France. We commit the greatest cruelties, but without cruelty.'

'All the worse!' said Julien; 'at least, when we commit crimes, we should commit them with pleasure: that is the only good thing about them, and the only excuse that can in any way justify them.'

Mademoiselle de La Mole, entirely forgetting what she owed to herself, had placed herself almost bodily between Altamira and Julien. Her brother, upon whose arm she leaned, being accustomed to obey her, was looking about the room, and, to keep himself in countenance, pretending to be held up by the crowd.

'You are right,' said Altamira; 'we do everything without

335

pleasure and without remembering it afterwards, even our crimes. I can point out to you at this ball ten men, perhaps, who will be damned as murderers. They have forgotten it, and the world also.[1]

'Many of them are moved to tears if their dog breaks its paw. At Père-Lachaise, when people strew flowers on their graves, as you so charmingly say in Paris, we are told that they combined all the virtues of the knights of old, and we hear of the great deeds of their ancestor who lived in the days of Henri IV. If, despite the good offices of Principe d'Araceli, I am not hanged, and if I ever come to enjoy my fortune in Paris, I hope to invite you to dine with nine or ten murderers who are honoured and feel no remorse.

'You and I, at that dinner, will be the only two whose hands are free from blood, but I shall be despised and almost hated, as a bloody and Jacobinical monster, and you will simply be despised as a plebeian who has thrust his way into good society.'

'Nothing could be more true,' said Mademoiselle de La Mole.

Altamira looked at her in astonishment; Julien did not deign to look at her.

'Note that the revolution at the head of which I found myself,' Conte Altamira went on, 'was unsuccessful, solely because I would not cut off three heads, and distribute among our supporters seven or eight millions which happened to be in a safe of which I held the key. My King, who is now burning to have me hanged, and who, before the revolt, used to address me as *tu*, would have given me the Grand Cordon of his Order if I had cut off those three heads and distributed the money in those safes: for then I should have scored at least a partial success, and my country would have had a Charter of sorts.... Such is the way of the world, it is a game of chess.'

'Then,' replied Julien, his eyes ablaze, 'you did not know the game; now....'

---

1 'A malcontent is speaking.' (Note by Molière to *Tartufe*.)

'I should cut off the heads, you mean, and I should not be a Girondin as you gave me to understand the other day? I will answer you,' said Altamira sadly, 'when you have killed a man in a duel, and that is a great deal less unpleasant than having him put to death by a headsman.'

'Faith!' said Julien, 'the end justifies the means; if, instead of being a mere atom, I had any power, I would hang three men to save the lives of four.'

His eyes expressed the fire of conscience and a contempt for the vain judgments of men; they met those of Mademoiselle de La Mole who stood close beside him, and this contempt, instead of changing into an air of gracious civility, seemed to intensify.

It shocked her profoundly; but it no longer lay in her power to forget Julien; she moved indifferently away, taking her brother with her.

'I must take some punch, and dance a great deal,' she said to herself, 'I intend to take the best that is going, and to create an effect at all costs. Good, here comes that master of impertinence, the Comte de Fervaques.' She accepted his invitation; they danced. 'It remains to be seen,' she thought, 'which of us will be the more impertinent, but, to get the full enjoyment out of him, I must make him talk.' Presently all the rest of the country dance became a pure formality. No one was willing to miss any of Mathilde's piquant repartees. M. de Fervaques grew troubled, and, being able to think of nothing but elegant phrases, in place of ideas, began to smirk; Mathilde, who was out of temper, treated him cruelly, and made an enemy of him. She danced until daybreak, and finally went home horribly tired. But, in the carriage, the little strength that remained to her was still employed in making her melancholy and wretched. She had been scorned by Julien, and was unable to scorn him.

Julien was on a pinnacle of happiness. Carried away unconsciously by the music, the flowers, the beautiful women, the general elegance, and, most of all, by his own imagination, which dreamed of distinctions for himself and of liberty for mankind:

'What a fine ball!' he said to the Conte, 'nothing is lacking.'

'Thought is lacking,' replied Altamira.

And his features betrayed that contempt which is all the more striking because one sees that politeness makes it a duty to conceal it.

'You are here, Monsieur le Comte. Is not that thought, and actively conspiring, too?'

'I am here because of my name. But they hate thought in your drawing-rooms. It must never rise above the level of a comic song: then it is rewarded. But the man who thinks, if he shews energy and novelty in his sallies, you call a *cynic*. Is not that the name that one of your judges bestowed upon Courier? You put him in prison, and Béranger also. Everything that is of any value among you, intellectually, the Congregation flings to the criminal police; and society applauds.

'The truth is that your antiquated society values conventionality above everything. . . . You will never rise higher than martial gallantry; you will have Murats, but never a Washington. I can see nothing in France but vanity. A man who thinks of things as he speaks may easily say something rash, and his host then imagines himself insulted.'

At this point, the Conte's carriage, which was taking Julien home, stopped at the Hôtel de La Mole. Julien was in love with his conspirator. Altamira had paid him a handsome compliment, evidently springing from a profound conviction: 'You have not the French frivolity, and you understand the principle of *utility*.' It so happened that, only two evenings before, Julien had seen *Marino Faliero*, a tragedy by M. Casimir Delavigne.

'Has not Israel Bertuccio, a humble carpenter in the arsenal, more character than all those Venetian nobles?' our rebellious plebeian asked himself; 'and yet they are men whose noble descent can be proved as far back as the year 700, a century before Charlemagne; whereas the bluest blood at M. de Retz's ball to-night does not go farther back, and that only by a hop, skip and jump, than the thirteenth century. Very well! Among those Venetian nobles, so great by

338

birth, but so etiolated, so colourless in character, it is Israel
Bertuccio that one remembers.

'A conspiracy wipes out all the titles conferred by social
caprice. In those conditions, a man springs at once to the
rank which his manner of facing death assigns to him. The
mind itself loses some of its authority....

'What would Danton be to-day, in this age of Valenods
and Rênals? Not even a Deputy Crown Prosecutor....

'What am I saying? He would have sold himself to the
Congregation; he would be a Minister, for after all the great
Danton did steal. Mirabeau, too, sold himself. Napoleon
stole millions in Italy, otherwise he would have been brought
to a standstill by poverty, like Pichegru. Only La Fayette
never stole. Must one steal, must one sell oneself?' Julien
wondered. The question arrested the flow of his imagination.
He spent the rest of the night reading the history of the
Revolution.

Next day, as he copied his letters in the library, he could
still think of nothing but Conte Altamira's conversation.

'It is quite true,' he said to himself, after a long spell of
absorption; 'if those Spanish Liberals had compromised the
people by a few crimes, they would not have been swept
away so easily. They were conceited, chattering boys ... like
myself!' Julien suddenly cried, as though awaking with a
bound.

'What difficult thing have I ever done that gives me the
right to judge poor devils who, after all, once in their lives,
have dared, have begun to act? I am like a man who, on
rising from table, exclaims: "To-morrow I shall not dine; that
will not prevent me from feeling strong and brisk as I do to-
day." How can I tell what people feel in the middle of a great
action? For after all these things are not as easy as firing a
pistol.' These lofty thoughts were interrupted by the sudden
arrival of Mademoiselle de La Mole, who at this moment
entered the library. He was so excited by his admiration for
the great qualities of Danton, Mirabeau, Carnot, who had
contrived not to be crushed, that his eyes rested upon
Mademoiselle de La Mole, but without his thinking of her,

without his greeting her, almost without his seeing her. When at length his great staring eyes became aware of her presence, the light died out in them. Mademoiselle de La Mole remarked this with a feeling of bitterness.

In vain did she ask him for a volume of Vély's *Histoire de France*, which stood on the highest shelf, so that Julien was obliged to fetch the longer of the two ladders. He brought the ladder; he found the volume, he handed it to her, still without being able to think of her. As he carried back the ladder, in his preoccupation, his elbow struck one of the glass panes protecting the shelves; the sound of the splinters falling on the floor at length aroused him. He hastened to make his apology to Mademoiselle de La Mole; he tried to be polite, but he was nothing more. Mathilde saw quite plainly that she had disturbed him, that he would have preferred to dream of what had been occupying his mind before her entry, rather than to talk to her. After a long glance at him, she slowly left the room. Julien watched her as she went. He enjoyed the contrast between the simplicity of the attire she was now wearing and her sumptuous magnificence overnight. The difference in her physiognomy was hardly less striking. This girl, so haughty at the Duc de Retz's ball, had at this moment almost a suppliant look. 'Really,' Julien told himself, 'that black gown shews off the beauty of her figure better than anything; but why is she in mourning?

'If I ask anyone the reason of this mourning, I shall only make myself appear a fool as usual.' Julien had quite come to earth from the soaring flight of his enthusiasm. 'I must read over all the letters I have written to-day; Heaven knows how many missing words and blunders I shall find.' As he was reading with forced attention the first of these letters, he heard close beside him the rustle of a silken gown; he turned sharply round; Mademoiselle de La Mole was standing by his table, and smiling. This second interruption made Julien lose his temper.

As for Mathilde, she had just become vividly aware that she meant nothing to this young man; her smile was intended to cover her embarrassment, and proved successful.

340

'Evidently, you are thinking about something that is extremely interesting, Monsieur Sorel. Is it by any chance some curious anecdote of the conspiracy that has sent the Conte Altamira here to Paris? Tell me what it is? I am burning to know; I shall be discreet, I swear to you!' This last sentence astonished her as she uttered it. What, she was pleading with a subordinate! Her embarrassment grew, she adopted a light manner:

'What can suddenly have turned you, who are ordinarily so cold, into an inspired creature, a sort of Michelangelo prophet?'

This bold and indiscreet question, cutting Julien to the quick, revived all his passion.

'Was Danton justified in stealing?' he said to her sharply, and with an air that grew more and more savage. 'The Revolutionaries of Piedmont, of Spain, ought they to have compromised the people by crimes? To have given away, even to men without merit, all the commands in the army, all the Crosses? Would not the men who wore those Crosses have had reason to fear a Restoration of their King? Ought they to have let the Treasury in Turin be pillaged? In a word, Mademoiselle,' he said, as he came towards her with a terrible air, 'ought the man who seeks to banish ignorance and crime from the earth to pass like a whirlwind and do evil as though blindly?'

Mathilde was afraid, she could not meet his gaze, and recoiled a little. She looked at him for a moment; then, ashamed of her fear, with a light step left the library.

CHAPTER FORTY

QUEEN MARGUERITE

Love! In what folly do you not contrive to make us
find pleasure?

Letters of a Portuguese Nun.

JULIEN read over his letters. When the dinner bell
sounded: 'How ridiculous I must have appeared in the
eyes of that Parisian doll!' he said to himself; 'what madness to tell her what was really in my thoughts! And yet
perhaps not so very mad. The truth on this occasion was
worthy of me.

'Why, too, come and cross-examine me on private matters? Her question was indiscreet. She forgot herself. My
thoughts on Danton form no part of the sacrifice for which
her father pays me.'

On reaching the dining-room, Julien was distracted from
his ill humour by Mademoiselle de La Mole's deep mourning, which was all the more striking since none of the rest of
the family was in black.

After dinner, he found himself entirely recovered from the
fit of enthusiasm which had possessed him all day. Fortunately, the Academician who knew Latin was present at dinner. 'There is the man who will be least contemptuous of
me, if, as I suppose, my question about Mademoiselle de La
Mole's mourning should prove a blunder.'

Mathilde was looking at him with a singular expression.
'There we have an instance of the coquetry of the women of
these parts, just as Madame de Rênal described it to me,'

Julien told himself. 'I was not agreeable to her this morning, I did not yield to her impulse for conversation. My value has increased in her eyes. No doubt the devil loses no opportunity there. Later on, her proud scorn will find out a way of avenging itself. Let her do her worst. How different from the woman I have lost! What natural charm! What simplicity! I knew what was in her mind before she did; I could see her thoughts take shape; I had no competitor, in her heart, but the fear of losing her children; it was a reasonable and natural affection, indeed it was pleasant for me who felt the same fear. I was a fool. The ideas that I had formed of Paris prevented me from appreciating that sublime woman.

'What a difference, great God! And what do I find here? A sere and haughty vanity, all the refinements of self-esteem and nothing more.'

The party left the table. 'I must not let my Academician be intercepted,' said Julien. He went up to him as they were moving into the garden, assumed a meek, submissive air, and sympathised with his rage at the success of *Hernani*.

'If only we lived in the days of *lettres de cachet*!' he said.

'Ah, then he would never have dared,' cried the Academician, with a gesture worthy of Talma.

In speaking of a flower, Julien quoted a line or two from Virgil's *Georgics*, and decided that nothing came up to the poetry of the Abbé Delille. In short, he flattered the Academician in every possible way. After which, with an air of the utmost indifference: 'I suppose,' he said to him, 'that Mademoiselle de La Mole has received a legacy from some uncle for whom she is in mourning.'

'What! You live in the house,' said the Academician, coming to a standstill, 'and you don't know her mania? Indeed, it is strange that her mother allows such things; but, between you and me, it is not exactly by strength of character that they shine in this family. Mademoiselle Mathilde has enough for them all, and leads them by the nose. To-day is the 30th of April!' and the Academician broke off, looking at Julien, with an air of connivance. Julien smiled as intelligently as he was able.

343

'What connexion can there be between leading a whole household by the nose, wearing black and the 30th of April?' he asked himself. 'I must be even stupider than I thought.

'I must confess to you,' he said to the Academician, and his eye continued the question.

'Let us take a turn in the garden,' said the Academician, delighted to see this chance of delivering a long and formal speech. 'What! Is it really possible that you do not know what happened on the 30th of April, 1574?'

'Where?' asked Julien, in surprise.

'On the Place de Grève.'

Julien was so surprised that this name did not enlighten him. His curiosity, the prospect of a tragic interest, so attuned to his nature, gave him those sparkling eyes which a story-teller so loves to see in his audience. The Academician, delighted to find a virgin ear, related at full length to Julien how, on the 30th of April, 1574, the handsomest young man of his age, Boniface de La Mole, and Annibal de Coconasso, a Piedmontese gentleman, his friend, had been beheaded on the Place de Grève. 'La Mole was the adored lover of Queen Marguerite of Navarre; and observe,' the Academician added, 'that Mademoiselle de La Mole is named *Mathilde-Marguerite*. La Mole was at the same time the favourite of the Duc d'Alençon and an intimate friend of the King of Navarre, afterwards Henri IV, the husband of his mistress. On Shrove Tuesday in this year, 1574, the Court happened to be at Saint-Germain, with the unfortunate King Charles IX, who was on his deathbed. La Mole wished to carry off the Princes, his friends, whom Queen Catherine de' Medici was keeping as prisoners with the Court. He brought up two hundred horsemen under the walls of Saint-Germain, the Duc d'Alençon took fright, and La Mole was sent to the scaffold.

'But what appeals to Mademoiselle Mathilde, as she told me herself, seven or eight years ago, when she was only twelve, for she has a head, such a head!...' and the Academician raised his eyes to heaven. 'What impresses her in this political catastrophe is that Queen Marguerite of Navarre, who had waited concealed in a house on the Place de Grève,

344

made bold to ask the executioner for her lover's head. And the following night, at midnight, she took the head in her carriage, and went to bury it with her own hands in a chapel which stood at the foot of the hill of Montmartre.'

'Is it possible?' exclaimed Julien, deeply touched.

'Mademoiselle Mathilde despises her brother because, as you see, he thinks nothing of all this ancient history, and never goes into mourning on the 30th of April. It is since this famous execution, and to recall the intimate friendship between La Mole and Coconasso, which Coconasso, being as he was an Italian, was named Annibal, that all the men of this family have borne that name. And,' the Academician went on, lowering his voice, 'this Coconasso was, on the authority of Charles IX, himself, one of the bloodiest assassins on the 24th of August, 1572. But how is it possible, my dear Sorel, that you are ignorant of these matters, you, who are an inmate of the house?'

'Then that is why twice, during the dinner, Mademoiselle de La Mole addressed her brother as Annibal. I thought I had not heard aright.'

'It was a reproach. It is strange that the Marquise permits such folly.... That great girl's husband will see some fine doings!'

This expression was followed by five or six satirical phrases. The joy at thus revealing an intimate secret that shone in the Academician's eyes shocked Julien. 'What are we but a pair of servants engaged in slandering our employers?' he thought. 'But nothing ought to surprise me that is done by this academic gentleman.'

One day Julien had caught him on his knees before the Marquise de La Mole; he was begging her for a tobacco licence for a nephew in the country. That night, he gathered from a little maid of Mademoiselle de La Mole, who was making love to him, as Elisa had done in the past, that her mistress's mourning was by no means put on to attract attention. This eccentricity was an intimate part of her nature. She really loved this La Mole, the favoured lover of the most brilliant Queen of her age, who had died for having sought

345

to set his friends at liberty. And what friends! The First Prince of the Blood and Henri IV.

Accustomed to the perfect naturalness that shone through the whole of Madame de Rênal's conduct, Julien saw nothing but affectation in all the women of Paris, and even without feeling disposed to melancholy, could think of nothing to say to them. Mademoiselle de La Mole was the exception.

He began no longer to mistake for hardness of heart the kind of beauty that goes with nobility of bearing. He had long conversations with Mademoiselle de La Mole, who in the fine spring weather would stroll with him in the garden, past the open windows of the drawing-room. She told him one day that she was reading d'Aubigné's *History*, and Brantôme. 'A strange choice,' thought Julien, 'and the Marquise does not allow her to read the novels of Walter Scott!'

One day she related to him, with that glow of pleasure in her eyes which proves the sincerity of the speaker's admiration, the feat of a young woman in the reign of Henri III, which she had just discovered in the *Mémoires de l'Etoile*: Finding that her husband was unfaithful, she had stabbed him.

Julien's self-esteem was flattered. A person surrounded by such deference, one who, according to the Academician, was the leader of the household, deigned to address him in a tone which might almost be regarded as friendly. 'I was mistaken,' was his next thought; 'this is not familiarity, I am only the listener to a tragic story, it is the need to speak. I am regarded as learned by this family. I shall go and read Brantôme, d'Aubigné, l'Etoile. I shall be able to challenge some of the anecdotes which Mademoiselle de La Mole cites to me. I must emerge from this part of a passive listener.'

In course of time his conversations with this girl, whose manner was at once so imposing and so easy, became more interesting. He forgot his melancholy part as a plebeian in revolt. He found her learned and indeed rational. Her opinions in the garden differed widely from those which she maintained in the drawing-room. At times she displayed with him an enthusiasm and a frankness which formed a perfect contrast with her normal manner, so haughty and cold.

'The Wars of the League are the heroic age of France,' she said to him one day, her eyes aflame with intellect and enthusiasm. 'Then everyone fought to secure a definite object which he desired in order to make his party triumph, and not merely to win a stupid Cross as in the days of your Emperor. You must agree that there was less egoism and pettiness. I love that period.'

'And Boniface de La Mole was its hero,' he said to her.

'At any rate he was loved as it is perhaps pleasant to be loved. What woman alive to-day would not be horrified to touch the head of her decapitated lover?'

Madame de La Mole called her daughter indoors. Hypocrisy, to be effective, must be concealed; and Julien, as we see, had taken Mademoiselle de La Mole partly into his confidence as to his admiration for Napoleon.

'That is the immense advantage which they have over us,' he said to himself, when left alone in the garden. 'The history of their ancestors raises them above vulgar sentiments, and they have not always to be thinking of their daily bread! What a wretched state of things!' he added bitterly. 'I am not worthy to discuss these serious matters. I take a wrong view of them, probably. My life is nothing more than a sequence of hypocrisies, because I have not an income of a thousand francs with which to buy my bread.'

'What are you dreaming of, Sir?' Mathilde asked him. There was a note of intimacy in her question, and she had come back running and was quite out of breath in her eagerness to be with him.

Julien was tired of self-suppression. In a moment of pride, he told her frankly what he was thinking. He blushed deeply when speaking of his poverty to a person who was so rich. He sought to make it quite clear by his proud tone that he asked for nothing. Never had he seemed so handsome to Mathilde; she found in him an expression of sensibility and frankness which he often lacked.

Less than a month later, Julien was strolling pensively in the garden of the Hôtel de La Mole; but his features no longer shewed the harshness, as of a surly philosopher, which

347

the constant sense of his own inferiority impressed on them. He had just come from the door of the drawing-room to which he had escorted Mademoiselle de La Mole, who pretended that she had hurt her foot when running with her brother.

'She leaned upon my arm in the strangest fashion!' Julien said to himself. 'Am I a fool, or can it be true that she has a liking for me? She listens to me so meekly even when I confess to her all the sufferings of my pride! She, who is so haughty with everyone else! They would be greatly surprised in the drawing-room if they saw her looking like that. There is no doubt about it, she never assumes that meek, friendly air with anyone but myself.'

Julien tried not to exaggerate this singular friendship. He compared it himself to an armed neutrality. Day by day, when they met, before resuming the almost intimate tone of the day before, they almost asked themselves: 'Are we friends to-day, or enemies?' In the first words they exchanged, the matter counted for nothing. On either side they paid attention only to the form. Julien had realised that, were he once to allow himself to be insulted with impunity by this haughty girl, all was lost. 'If I must quarrel, is it not to my advantage to do so from the first, in defending the lawful rights of my pride, rather than in repelling the marks of contempt that must quickly follow the slightest surrender of what I owe to my personal dignity?'

Several times, on days of mutual discord, Mathilde tried to adopt with him the tone of a great lady; she employed a rare skill in these attempts, but Julien repulsed them rudely.

One day he interrupted her suddenly: 'Has Mademoiselle de La Mole some order to give to her father's secretary?' he asked her; 'he is obliged to listen to her orders and to carry them out with respect; but apart from that, he has not one word to say to her. He certainly is not paid to communicate his thoughts to her.'

This state of affairs, and the singular doubts which Julien felt, banished the boredom which he had found during the first months in that drawing-room, in which, for all its magnificence, people were afraid of everything, and it was not thought proper to treat any subject lightly.

'It would be amusing if she loved me! Whether she loves me or not,' Julien went on, 'I have as my intimate confidant an intelligent girl, before whom I see the whole household tremble, and most of all the Marquis de Croisenois. That young man who is so polished, so gentle, so brave, who combines in his own person all the advantages of birth and fortune, any one of which would set my heart so at ease! He is madly in love with her, that is to say as much in love as a Parisian can be in love, he is going to marry her. Think of all the letters M. de La Mole has made me write to the two lawyers arranging the contract! And I who see myself every morning so subordinate, pen in hand, two hours later, here in the garden, I triumph over so attractive a young man: for after all, her preference is striking, direct. Perhaps, too, she hates the idea of him as a future husband. She is proud enough for that. In that case, the favour she shews me, I obtain on the footing of a confidential servant!

'But no, either I am mad, or she is making love to me; the more I shew myself cold and respectful towards her, the more she seeks me out. That might be deliberate, an affectation; but I see her eyes become animated when I appear unexpectedly. Are the women of Paris capable of pretending to such an extent? What does it matter! I have appearances on my side, let us make the most of them. My God, how handsome she is! How I admire her great blue eyes, seen at close range, and looking at me as they often do! What a difference between this spring and the last, when I was living in misery, keeping myself alive by my strength of character, surrounded by those three hundred dirty and evil-minded hypocrites! I was almost as evil as they.'

In moments of depression: 'That girl is making a fool of me,' Julien would think. 'She is plotting with her brother to mystify me. But she seems so to despise her brother's want of energy! He is brave, and there is no more to be said, she tells me. And even then, brave in facing the swords of the Spaniards. In Paris everything alarms him, he sees every-

349

where the danger of ridicule. He has not an idea which ventures to depart from the fashion. It is always I who am obliged to take up her defence. A girl of nineteen! At that age can a girl be faithful at every moment of the day to the code of hypocrisy that she has laid down for herself?

'On the other hand, when Mademoiselle de La Mole fastens her great blue eyes on me with a certain strange expression, Comte Norbert always moves away. That seems to me suspicious; ought he not to be annoyed at his sister's singling out a *domestic* of their household? For I have heard the Duc de Chaulnes use that term of me.' At this memory anger obliterated every other feeling. 'Is it only the love of old-fashioned speech in that ducal maniac?

'Anyhow, she is pretty!' Julien went on, with the glare of a tiger. 'I will have her, I shall then depart and woe to him that impedes me in my flight!'

This plan became Julien's sole occupation; he could no longer give a thought to anything else. His days passed like hours.

At all hours of the day, when he sought to occupy his mind with some serious business, his thoughts would drift into a profound meditation, and he would come to himself a quarter of an hour later, his heart throbbing with ambition, his head confused, and dreaming of this one idea: 'Does she love me?'

CHAPTER FORTY-ONE
THE TYRANNY OF A GIRL

J'admire sa beauté, mais je crains son esprit.
                                    MÉRIMÉE.

HAD Julien devoted to the consideration of what went on in the drawing-room the time which he spent in exaggerating Mathilde's beauty, or in lashing himself into a fury at the aloofness natural to her family, whom she was forgetting in his company, he would have understood in what her despotic power over everyone round about her consisted. Whenever anyone earned Mademoiselle de La Mole's displeasure, she knew how to punish him by a witticism so calculated, so well chosen, apparently so harmless, so aptly launched, that the wound it left deepened the more he thought of it. In time she became deadly to wounded vanity. As she attached no importance to many things that were the object of serious ambition with the rest of her family, she always appeared cool in their eyes. The drawing-rooms of the nobility are pleasant things to mention after one has left them, but that is all. Complete insignificance, above all the *common* utterances with which even hypocrisy is met, end by exhausting our patience with their cloying sweetness. Bare politeness is something in itself only for the first few days. Julien experienced this; after the first enchantment, the first bewilderment. 'Politeness,' he said to himself, 'is nothing more than the absence of the irritation which would come from bad manners.' Mathilde was frequently bored, perhaps she would have been bored in any circum-

351

stances. At such times to sharpen the point of an epigram was for her a distraction and a real pleasure.

It was perhaps in order to have victims slightly more amusing than her distinguished relatives, the Academician and the five or six other inferiors who formed their court, that she had given grounds for hope to the Marquis de Croisenois, the Comte de Caylus and two or three other young men of the highest distinction. They were nothing more to her than fresh subjects for epigram.

We confess with sorrow, for we are fond of Mathilde, that she had received letters from several of their number, and had occasionally answered them. We hasten to add that this character in our story forms an exception to the habits of the age. It is not, generally speaking, with want of prudence that one can reproach the pupils of the noble Convent of the Sacré-Cœur.

One day the Marquis de Croisenois returned to Mathilde a distinctly compromising letter which she had written him the day before. He thought that by this sign of extreme prudence he was greatly strengthening his position. But imprudence was what Mathilde enjoyed in her correspondence. It was her chief pleasure to play with fire. She did not speak to him again for six weeks.

She amused herself with the letters of these young men; but, according to her, they were all alike. It was always the most profound, the most melancholy passion.

'They are all the same perfect gentlemen, ready to set off for Palestine,' she said to her cousin. 'Can you think of anything more insipid? Think that this is the sort of letter that I am going to receive for the rest of my life! These letters can only change every twenty years, according to the kind of occupation that is in fashion. They must have been less colourless in the days of the Empire. Then all these young men in society had seen or performed actions in which there was *real* greatness. The Duc de N——, my uncle, fought at Wagram.'

'What intelligence is required to wield a sabre? And when that has happened to them, they talk about it so often!' said Mademoiselle de Sainte-Hérédité, Mathilde's cousin.

'Oh, well, those stories amuse me. To have been in a *real* battle, one of Napoleon's battles, in which ten thousand soldiers were killed, is a proof of courage. Exposing oneself to danger elevates the soul, and saves it from the boredom in which all my poor adorers seem to be plunged; and it is contagious, that boredom. Which of them ever dreams of doing anything out of the common? They seek to win my hand, a fine enterprise! I am rich, and my father will help on his son-in-law. Oh, if only he could find one who was at all amusing!'

Mathilde's vivid, picturesque point of view affected her speech, as we can see. Often something she said jarred on the refined nerves of her highly polished friends. They would almost have admitted, had she been less in the fashion, that there was something in her language a little too highly coloured for feminine delicacy.

She, on her part, was most unjust to the handsome cavaliers who throng the Bois de Boulogne. She looked towards the future, not with terror, that would have been too strong a feeling, but with a disgust very rare at her age.

What had she left to desire? Fortune, noble birth, wit, beauty, or so it was said, and she believed, all had been heaped upon her by the hand of chance.

Such were the thoughts of the most envied heiress of the Faubourg Saint-Germain, when she began to find pleasure in strolling with Julien. She was amazed at his pride; she admired the cunning of this little plebeian. 'He will manage to get himself made a Bishop like the Abbé Maury,' she said to herself.

Presently the sincere and unfeigned resistance, with which our hero received a number of her ideas, began to occupy her mind; she thought about him; she reported to her cousin the pettiest details of their conversations, and found that she could never succeed in displaying them in every aspect.

Suddenly an idea dawned upon her: 'I have the good fortune to be in love,' she told herself one day, with an indescribable transport of joy. 'I am in love, I am in love, it is quite clear! At my age, a young girl, beautiful, clever, where can she find sensations, if not in love? I may do what I like, I shall never feel any love for Croisenois, Caylus, *e tutti quanti.* They are perfect, too perfect perhaps; in short, they bore me.'

She turned over in her mind all the descriptions of passion which she had read in *Manon Lescaut,* the *Nouvelle Héloïse,* the *Letters of a Portuguese Nun,* and so forth. There was no question, of course, of anything but a grand passion; mere fleeting affection was unworthy of a girl of her age and birth. She bestowed the name of love only upon that heroic sentiment which was to be found in France in the days of Henri III and Bassompierre. That love never basely succumbed to obstacles; far from it, it caused great deeds to be done. 'What a misfortune for me that there is not a real Court like that of Catherine de' Medici or Louis XIII! I feel that I am equal to everything that is most daring and great. What should I not do with a King who was a man of feeling, like Louis XIII, sighing at my feet! I should lead him to the Vendée, as Baron de Tolly is always saying, and from there he would reconquer his Kingdom; then no more talk of a Charter ... and Julien would aid me. What is it that he lacks? A name and a fortune. He would make a name for himself, he would acquire a fortune.

'The Marquis de Croisenois lacks nothing, and all his life long he will be merely a Duke half Ultra, half Liberal, an undecided creature speaking when action is required, always holding back from extremes, and *consequently finding himself everywhere in the second rank.*

'Where is the great action which is not *an extreme* at the moment in which one undertakes it? It is when it is accomplished that it seems possible to creatures of common clay. Yes, it is love with all its miracles that is going to reign in my heart; I feel it by the fire that is animating me. Heaven owed me this favour. Not in vain will it have heaped every advantage upon a single head. My happiness will be worthy of myself. Each of my days will not coldly resemble the day before. There is already something grand and audacious in daring to love a man placed so far beneath me in social position. Let me see: will he continue to deserve me? At the first sign of weakness that I observe in him, I abandon him. A girl of my birth, and with the chivalrous character which they are so kind as to attribute to me' (this was one of her father's sayings) 'ought not to behave like a fool.

'Is not that the part that I should be playing if I loved the Marquis de Croisenois? It would be simply a repetition of the happiness of my cousins, whom I despise so utterly. I know beforehand everything that the poor Marquis would say to me, all that I should have to say to him in reply. What is the use of a love that makes one yawn? One might as well take to religion. I should have a scene at the signing of my marriage contract like my youngest cousin, with the noble relatives shedding tears, provided they were not made angry by a final condition inserted in the contract the day before by the solicitor to the other party.'

CHAPTER FORTY-TWO

ANOTHER DANTON

Le besoin d'anxiété, tel était le caractère de la belle
Marguerite de Valois, ma tante, que bientôt épousa le
roi de Navarre, que nous voyons de présent régner en
France sous le nom de Henry IV. Le besoin de jouer
formait tout le secret du caractère de cette princesse
aimable; de là ses brouilles et ses raccommodements
avec ses frères dès l'âge de seize ans. Or que peut jouer
une jeune fille? Ce qu'elle a de plus précieux: sa réputa-
tion, la considération de toute sa vie.

> *Mémoires du duc d'*ANGOULÊME.
> *fils naturel de Charles IX.*

'WITH Julien and me there is no contract to be
signed, no lawyer for the civil ceremony; everything is heroic, everything will be left to chance.
But for nobility, which he lacks, it is the love of Marguerite
de Valois for young La Mole, the most distinguished man of
his time. Is it my fault if the young men at Court are such
ardent devotees of the *Conventions,* and turn pale at the mere
thought of any adventure that is slightly out of the common?
A little expedition to Greece or Africa is to them the height
of audacity, and even then they can only go in a troop. As
soon as they find themselves alone, they become afraid, not
of Bedouin spears, but of ridicule, and that drives them
mad.

'My little Julien, on the contrary, will only act alone.
Never, in that privileged being, is there the slightest thought

356

of seeking the approval and support of others! He despises other people, that is why I do not despise him.

'If, with his poverty, Julien had been noble, my love would be nothing more than a piece of vulgar folly, an unfortunate marriage; I should not object to that; it would lack that element which characterises great passion: the immensity of the difficulty to be overcome and the dark uncertainty of the issue.'

Mademoiselle de La Mole was so absorbed in these fine speculations that next day, quite unintentionally, she sang Julien's praises to the Marquis de Croisenois and her brother. Her eloquence went so far that they became annoyed.

'Beware of that young man, who has so much energy,' her brother cried; 'if the Revolution begins again, he will have us all guillotined.'

She made no answer, and hastened to tease her brother and the Marquis de Croisenois over the fear that energy inspired in them. It was nothing more, really, than the fear of meeting something unexpected, the fear of being brought up short in presence of the unexpected. . . .

'Still, gentlemen, still the fear of ridicule, a monster which, unfortunately, died in 1816.'

'There can be no more ridicule,' M. de La Mole used to say, 'in a country where there are two Parties.'

His daughter had assimilated this idea.

'And so, gentlemen,' she told Julien's enemies, 'you will be haunted by fear all your lives, and afterwards people will say of you:

' "It was not a wolf, it was only a shadow." '

Mathilde soon left them. Her brother's remark filled her with horror; it greatly disturbed her; but after sleeping on it, she interpreted it as the highest possible praise.

'In this age, when all energy is dead, his energy makes them afraid. I shall tell him what my brother said. I wish to see what answer he will make. But I shall choose a moment when his eyes are glowing. Then he cannot lie to me.

'Another Danton?' she went on after a long, vague spell of musing. 'Very well! Let us suppose that the Revolution has begun. What parts would Croisenois and my brother play? It is all prescribed for them: sublime resignation. They would be heroic sheep, allowing their throats to be cut without a word. Their sole fear when dying would still be of committing a breach of taste. My little Julien would blow out the brains of the Jacobin who came to arrest him, if he had the slightest hope of escaping. He, at least, has no fear of bad taste.'

These last words made her pensive again; they revived painful memories, and destroyed all her courage. They reminded her of the witticisms of MM. de Caylus, de Croisenois, de Luz, and her brother. These gentlemen were unanimous in accusing Julien of a *priestly* air, humble and hypocritical.

'But,' she went on, suddenly, her eye sparkling with joy, 'by the bitterness and the frequency of their sarcasms, they prove, in spite of themselves, that he is the most distinguished man that we have seen this winter. What do his faults, his absurdities matter? He has greatness, and they are shocked by it, they who in other respects are so kind and indulgent. He knows well that he is poor, and that he has studied to become a priest; they are squadron commanders, and have no need of study; it is a more comfortable life.

'In spite of all the drawbacks of his eternal black coat, and of that priestly face, which he is obliged to assume, poor boy, if he is not to die of hunger, his merit alarms them, nothing could be clearer. And that priestly expression, he no longer wears it when we have been for a few moments by ourselves. Besides, when these gentlemen say anything which they consider clever and startling, is not their first glance always at Julien? I have noticed that distinctly. And yet they know quite well that he never speaks to them, unless he is asked a question. It is only myself that he addresses. He thinks that I have a lofty nature. He replies to their objections only so far as politeness requires. He becomes respectful at once. With me, he will discuss things for hours on end, he is not sure of his own ideas if I offer the slightest objection. After all, all this winter we have not heard a shot fired; the only possible way to attract attention has been by one's talk. Well, my father, a superior man, and one who will greatly advance the fortunes of our family, respects Julien. All the rest hate him, no one despises him, except my mother's religious friends.'

The Comte de Caylus had or pretended to have a great passion for horses; he spent all his time in his stables, and often took his luncheon there. This great passion, combined with his habit of never laughing, had won him a great esteem among his friends: he was the 'strong man' of their little circle.

As soon as it had assembled next day behind Madame de La Mole's armchair, Julien not being present, M. de Caylus, supported by Croisenois and Norbert, launched a violent attack upon the good opinion Mathilde had of Julien, without any reason and almost as soon as he saw Mademoiselle de La Mole. She detected this stratagem a mile off, and was charmed by it.

'There they are all in league,' she said to herself, 'against a man who has not ten louis to his name, and can answer them only when he is questioned. They are afraid of him in his black coat. What would he be with epaulettes?'

Never had she been so brilliant. At the first onslaught, she covered Caylus and his allies with witty sarcasm. When the fire of these brilliant officers' pleasantries was extinguished:

'To-morrow some country bumpkin from the mountains of the Franche-Comté,' she said to M. de Caylus, 'has only to discover that Julien is his natural son, and give him a name and a few thousand francs, and in six weeks he will have grown moustaches like yourselves, gentlemen; in six months he will be an officer of hussars like yourselves, gentlemen. And then the greatness of his character will no longer be a joke. I can see you reduced, My Lord Duke-to-be, to that old and worthless plea: the superiority of the nobility of the Court to the provincial nobility. But what defence have you left if I choose to take an extreme case, if I am so unkind as to make Julien's father a Spanish Duke, a prisoner of war at Besançon in Napoleon's time, who, from a scruple of conscience, acknowledges him on his deathbed?'

All these assumptions of a birth out of wedlock were regarded by MM. de Caylus and de Croisenois as in distinctly bad taste. This was all that they saw in Mathilde's argument.

Obedient as Norbert was, his sister's meaning was so unmistakable that he assumed an air of gravity, little in keeping, it must be confessed, with his genial, smiling features. He ventured to say a few words:

'Are you unwell, dear?' Mathilde answered him with a mock-serious expression. 'You must be feeling very ill to reply to a joke with a sermon.

'A sermon, from you! Are you thinking of asking to be made a Prefect?'

Mathilde very soon forgot the annoyance of the Comte de Caylus, Norbert's ill humour and the silent despair of M. de Croisenois. She had to make up her mind over a desperate idea which had taken possession of her.

'Julien is quite sincere with me,' she told herself; 'at his age, in an inferior state of fortune, wretched as an astounding ambition makes him, he needs a woman friend. I can be that friend; but I see no sign in him of love. With the audacity of his nature, he would have spoken to me of his love.'

This uncertainty, this inward discussion, which, from now onwards, occupied every moment of Mathilde's life, and in support of which, whenever Julien addressed her, she found fresh arguments, completely banished those periods of depression to which she was so liable.

The daughter of a man of intelligence who might become a Minister, and restore their forests to the Clergy, Mademoiselle de La Mole had been, in the Convent of the Sacré-Cœur, the object of the most extravagant flatteries. The harm done in this way can never be effaced. They had persuaded her that, in view of all her advantages of birth, fortune, etc., she ought to be happier than other girls. This is the source of the boredom from which princes suffer, and of all their follies.

Mathilde had not been immune to the fatal influence of this idea. However intelligent a girl may be, she cannot be on her guard for ten years against the flattery of an entire convent, especially when it appears to be so well founded.

From the moment in which she decided that she was in love with Julien, she was no longer bored. Every day she congratulated herself on the decision she had made to indulge in a grand passion. 'This amusement has its dangers,' she thought. 'All the better! A thousand times better!

'Without a grand passion, I was languishing with boredom at the best moment in a girl's life, between sixteen and twenty. I have already wasted my best years; with no pleasure but to listen to the nonsense talked by my mother's friends, who at Coblenz, in 1792, were not quite, one gathers, so strict in their conduct, as they are to-day in speech.'

It was while Mathilde was still devoured by this great uncertainty that Julien was unable to understand the gaze which she kept fastened upon him. He did indeed find an increased coldness in Comte Norbert's manner, and a stiffening of pride in that of MM. de Caylus, de Luz and de Croisenois. He was used to it. This discomfiture befell him at times after an evening in which he had shone more brightly than befitted his position. But for the special welcome which Mathilde extended to him, and the curiosity which the whole scene inspired in him, he would have refrained from following into the garden these brilliant young men with the moustaches, when after dinner they escorted Mademoiselle de La Mole.

'Yes, I cannot possibly blind myself to the fact,' thought Julien, 'Mademoiselle de La Mole keeps looking at me in a strange fashion. But, even when her beautiful blue eyes seem to gaze at me with least restraint, I can always read in them a cold, malevolent scrutiny. Is it possible that this is love? How different from the look in Madame de Rênal's eyes.'

One evening after dinner, Julien, who had gone with M. de La Mole to his study, came rapidly out to the garden. As he walked boldly up to the group round Mathilde, he overheard a few words uttered in a loud voice. She was teasing her brother. Julien heard his own name uttered distinctly twice. He appeared; a profound silence at once fell, and vain efforts were made to break it. Mademoiselle de La Mole and her brother were too much excited to think of another topic of conversation. MM. de Caylus, de Croisenois, de Luz and another of their friends met Julien with an icy coldness. He withdrew.

CHAPTER FORTY-THREE

A PLOT

Disconnected remarks, chance meetings turn into proofs of the utmost clarity in the eyes of the imaginative man, if he has any fire in his heart.

SCHILLER.

ON the following day he again surprised Norbert and his sister, who were talking about him. On his arrival, a deathly silence fell, as on the day before. His suspicions knew no bounds. 'Can these charming young people be planning to make a fool of me? I must own, that is far more probable, far more natural than a pretended passion on the part of Mademoiselle de La Mole, for a poor devil of a secretary. For one thing, do these people have passions? Mystification is their specialty. They are jealous of my wretched little superiority in language. Being jealous, that is another of their weaknesses. That explains everything. Mademoiselle de La Mole hopes to persuade me that she is singling me out, simply to offer me as a spectacle to her intended.'

This cruel suspicion completely changed Julien's moral attitude. The idea encountered in his heart a germ of love which it had no difficulty in destroying. This love was founded only upon Mathilde's rare beauty, or rather upon her regal manner and her admirable style in dress. In this respect Julien was still an upstart. A beautiful woman of fashion is, we are assured, the sight that most astonishes a clever man of peasant origin when he arrives amid the higher ranks of society. It was certainly not Mathilde's character that had set Julien dreaming for days past. He had enough sense to grasp that he knew nothing about her character. Everything that he saw of it might be only a pretence.

For instance, Mathilde would not for anything in the world have failed to hear mass on a Sunday; almost every day she went to church with her mother. If, in the drawing-room of the Hôtel de La Mole, some impudent fellow forgot where he was and allowed himself to make the remotest allusion to some jest aimed at the real or supposed interests of Throne or Altar, Mathilde would at once assume an icy severity. Her glance, which was so sparkling, took on all the expressionless pride of an old family portrait.

But Julien knew for certain that she always had in her room one or two of the most philosophical works of Voltaire. He himself frequently abstracted a volume or two of the handsome edition so magnificently bound. By slightly separating the other volumes on the shelf, he concealed the absence of the volume he was taking away; but soon he discovered that someone else was reading Voltaire. He had recourse to a trick of the Seminary, he placed some little pieces of horsehair across the volumes which he supposed might interest Mademoiselle de La Mole. They vanished for weeks at a time.

M. de La Mole, losing patience with his bookseller, who kept sending him all the sham *Memoirs*, gave Julien orders to buy every new book that was at all sensational. But, so that the poison might not spread through the household, the secretary was instructed to place these books in a little bookcase that stood in the Marquis's own room. He soon acquired the certainty that if any of these books were hostile to the interests of Throne and Altar, they were not long in vanishing. It was certainly not Norbert that was reading them.

Julien, exaggerating the importance of this discovery, credited Mademoiselle de La Mole with a Machiavellian duplicity. This feigned criminality was a charm in his eyes, almost the only moral charm that she possessed. The tediousness of hypocrisy and virtuous conversation drove him to this excess.

He excited his imagination rather than let himself be carried away by love.

It was after he had lost himself in dreams of the elegance of Mademoiselle de La Mole's figure, the excellent taste of her toilet, the whiteness of her hand, the beauty of her arm, the *disinvoltura* of all her movements, that he found himself in love. Then, to complete her charm, he imagined her to be a Catherine de' Medici. Nothing was too profound or too criminal for the character that he assigned to her. It was the ideal of the Maslons, the Frilairs and Castanèdes whom he had admired in his younger days. It was, in short, the ideal, to him, of Paris.

Was ever anything so absurd as to imagine profundity or criminality in the Parisian character?

'It is possible that this trio may be making a fool of me,' he thought. The reader has learned very little of Julien's nature if he has not already seen the sombre, frigid expression that he assumed when his eyes met those of Mathilde. A bitter irony repulsed the assurances of friendship with which Mademoiselle de La Mole in astonishment ventured on two or three occasions, to try him.

Piqued by his sudden eccentricity, the heart of this girl, naturally cold, bored, responsive to intelligence, became as passionate as it was in her nature to be. But there was also a great deal of pride in Mathilde's nature, and the birth of a sentiment which made all her happiness dependent upon another was attended by a sombre melancholy.

Julien had made sufficient progress since his arrival in Paris to discern that this was not the barren melancholy of boredom. Instead of being eager, as in the past, for parties, shews and distractions of every kind, she avoided them.

Music performed by French singers bored Mathilde to death, and yet Julien, who made it his duty to be present at the close of the Opera, observed that she made her friends take her there as often as possible. He thought he could detect that she had lost a little of the perfect balance which shone in all her actions. She would sometimes reply to her friends with witticisms that were offensive in their pointed emphasis. It seemed to him that she had taken a dislike to the Marquis de Croisenois. 'That young man must have a furious passion for money, not to go off and leave a girl like that, however rich she may be!' thought Julien. As for himself, indignant at the insults offered to masculine dignity, his coldness towards her increased. Often he went the length of replying with positive discourtesy.

However determined he might be not to be taken in by the signs of interest shewn by Mathilde, they were so evident on certain days, and Julien, from whose eyes the scales were beginning to fall, found her so attractive, that he was at times embarrassed by them.

'The skill and forbearance of these young men of fashion will end by triumphing over my want of experience,' he told himself; 'I must go away, and put an end to all this.' The Marquis had recently entrusted to him the management of a number of small properties and houses which he owned in lower Languedoc. A visit to the place became necessary: M. de La Mole gave a reluctant consent. Except in matters of high ambition, Julien had become his second self.

'When all is said and done, they have not managed to catch me,' Julien told himself as he prepared for his departure. 'Whether the jokes which Mademoiselle de La Mole makes at the expense of these gentlemen be real, or only intended to inspire me with confidence, I have been amused by them.

'If there is no conspiracy against the carpenter's son, Mademoiselle de La Mole is inexplicable, but she is just as much so to the Marquis de Croisenois as to me. Yesterday, for instance, her ill humour was quite genuine, and I had the pleasure of seeing discomfited in my favour a young man as noble and rich as I am penniless and plebeian. That is my finest triumph. It will keep me in good spirits in my postchaise, as I scour the plains of Languedoc.'

He had kept his departure secret, but Mathilde knew better than he that he was leaving Paris next day, and for a long time. She pleaded a splitting headache, which was made worse by the close atmosphere of the drawing-room. She walked for hours in the garden, and so pursued with her mordant pleasantries Norbert, the Marquis de Croisenois, Caylus, de Luz and various other young men who had dined at the Hôtel de La Mole, that she forced them to take their leave. She looked at Julien in a strange fashion.

'This look is perhaps a piece of play-acting,' thought he; 'but her quick breathing, all that emotion! Bah!' he said to himself, 'who am I to judge of these matters? This is an example of the most consummate, the most artificial behaviour to be found among the women of Paris. That quick breathing, which so nearly proved too much for me, she will have learned from Léontine Fay, whom she admires so.'

They were now left alone; the conversation was plainly languishing. 'No! Julien has no feeling for me,' Mathilde told herself with genuine distress.

As he took leave of her, she clutched his arm violently:

'You will receive a letter from me this evening,' she told him in a voice so strained as to be barely audible.

This had an immediate effect on Julien.

'My father,' she went on, 'has a most natural regard for the services that you render him. You *must not* go to-morrow; find some excuse.' And she ran from the garden.

Her figure was charming. It would have been impossible to have a prettier foot, she ran with a grace that enchanted Julien; but guess what was his second thought when she had quite vanished. He was offended by the tone of command in which she had uttered the words, *you must*. Similarly Louis XV, as he breathed his last, was keenly annoyed by the words *you must* awkwardly employed by his Chief Physician, and yet Louis XV was no upstart.

An hour later, a footman handed Julien a letter; it was nothing less than a declaration of love.

'The style is not unduly affected,' he said to himself, seeking by literary observations to contain the joy that was contorting his features and forcing him to laugh in spite of himself.

'And so I,' he suddenly exclaimed, his excitement being too strong to be held in check, 'I, a poor peasant, have received a declaration of love from a great lady!

'As for myself, I have not done badly,' he went on, controlling his joy as far as was possible. 'I have succeeded in preserving the dignity of my character. I have never said that I was in love.' He began to study the shapes of her letters; Mademoiselle de La Mole wrote in a charming little English hand. He required some physical occupation to take his mind from a joy which was bordering on delirium.

'Your departure obliges me to speak.... It would be beyond my endurance not to see you any more.'

A sudden thought occurred to strike Julien as a discovery, interrupt the examination that he was making of Mathilde's letter, and intensify his joy. 'I am preferred to the Marquis de Croisenois,' he cried, 'I, who never say anything that is not serious! And he is so handsome! He wears moustaches, a charming uniform; he always manages to say, just at the right moment, something witty and clever.'

It was an exquisite moment for Julien; he roamed about the garden, mad with happiness.

Later, he went upstairs to his office, and sent in his name to the Marquis de La Mole, who fortunately had not gone out. He had no difficulty in proving to him, by shewing him various marked papers that had arrived from Normandy, that the requirements of his employer's lawsuits there obliged him to postpone his departure for Languedoc.

'I am very glad you are not going,' the Marquis said to him, when they had finished their business, '*I like to see you.*' Julien left the room; this speech disturbed him.

'And I am going to seduce his daughter! To render impossible, perhaps, that marriage with the Marquis de Croisenois, which is the bright spot in his future: if he is not made Duke, at least his daughter will be entitled to a *tabouret.*' Julien thought of starting for Languedoc in spite of Mathilde's letter, in spite of the explanation he had given the Marquis. This virtuous impulse soon faded.

'How generous I am,' he said to himself; 'I, a plebeian, to feel pity for a family of such high rank! I, whom the Duc de Chaulnes calls a domestic! How does the Marquis increase his vast fortune? By selling national securities, when he hears at the Château that there is to be the threat of a *Coup d'État* next day. And I, cast down to the humblest rank by a step-motherly Providence, I, whom Providence has endowed with a noble heart and not a thousand francs of income, that is to say not enough for my daily bread, *literally speaking, not enough for my daily bread*; am I to refuse a pleasure that is offered me? A limpid spring which wells up to quench my thirst in the burning desert of mediocrity over which I trace my painful course! Faith, I am no such fool; everyone for himself in this desert of selfishness which is called life.'

And he reminded himself of several disdainful glances aimed at him by Madame de La Mole, and especially by the *ladies*, her friends.

The pleasure of triumphing over the Marquis de Croi-senois completed the rout of this lingering trace of virtue.

'How I should love to make him angry!' said Julien; 'with what assurance would I now thrust at him with my sword.' And he struck a sweeping blow at the air, 'Until now, I was a smug, basely profiting by a trace of courage. After this letter, I am his equal.

'Yes,' he said to himself with an infinite delight, dwelling on the words, 'our merits, the Marquis's and mine, have been weighed, and the poor carpenter from the Jura wins the day.

'Good!' he cried, 'here is the signature to my reply ready found. Do not go and imagine, Mademoiselle de La Mole, that I am forgetting my station. I shall make you realise and feel that it is for the son of a carpenter that you are betraying a descendant of the famous Guy de Croisenois, who followed Saint Louis on his Crusade.'

Julien was unable to contain his joy. He was obliged to go down to the garden. His room, in which he had locked himself up, seemed too confined a space for him to breathe in.

'I, a poor peasant from the Jura,' he kept on repeating. 'I, condemned always to wear this dismal black coat Alas, twenty years ago, I should have worn uniform like them! In those days a man of my sort was either killed, or *a General at six and thirty*.' The letter, which he kept tightly clasped in his hand, gave him the bearing and pose of a hero. 'Nowadays, it is true, with the said black coat, at the age of forty, a man has emoluments of one hundred thousand francs and the Blue Riband, like the Bishop of Beauvais.

'Oh, well!' he said to himself, laughing like Mephistopheles, 'I have more sense than they; I know how to choose the uniform of my generation.' And he felt an intensification of his ambition and of his attachment to the clerical habit. 'How many Cardinals have there been of humbler birth than mine, who have risen to positions of government! My fellow-countryman Granvelle, for instance.'[1]

Gradually Julien's agitation subsided; prudence rose to the surface. He said to himself, like his master Tartufe, whose part he knew by heart:

> 'I might suppose these words an honest artifice ...
> Nay, I shall not believe so flattering a speech
> Unless some favour shewn by her for whom I sigh
> Assure me that they mean all that they might imply.'
> *(Tartufe, Act iv, Scene v.)*

'Tartufe also was ruined by a woman, and he was as good a man as most.... My answer may be shewn ... a mishap for which we find this remedy,' he went on, pronouncing each word slowly, and in accents of restrained ferocity, 'we begin it by quoting the strongest expressions from the letter of the sublime Mathilde.

'Yes, but then four of M. de Croisenois's flunkeys will spring upon me, and tear the original from me.

'No, for I am well armed, and am accustomed, as they know, to firing on flunkeys.

'Very well! Say, one of them has some courage; he springs upon me. He has been promised a hundred napoleons. I kill or injure him, all the better, that is what they want. I am flung into prison with all the forms of law; I appear in the police court, and they send me, with all justice and equity on the judges' part, to keep MM. Fontan and Magalon com-

1 Antoine de Granvelle, born at Besançon in 1517, was Minister to Charles V and Philip II and Governor of the Netherlands. C. K. S. M.

pany at Poissy. There, I lie upon straw with four hundred poor wretches, pell-mell. . . . And I am to feel some pity for these people,' he cried, springing impetuously to his feet. 'What pity do they shew for the Third Estate when they have us in their power?' These words were the dying breath of his gratitude to M. de La Mole which, in spite of himself, had tormented him until then.

'Not so fast, my fine gentlemen, I understand this little stroke of Machiavellianism; the Abbé Maslon or M. Castanède of the Seminary could not have been more clever. You rob me of my *incitement*, the letter, and I become the second volume of Colonel Caron at Colmar.

'One moment, gentlemen, I am going to send the fatal letter in a carefully sealed packet to the custody of M. l'Abbé Pirard. He is an honest man, a Jansenist, and as such out of reach of the temptations of the Budget. Yes, but he opens letters . . . it is to Fouqué that I must send this one.'

It must be admitted the glare in Julien's eyes was ghastly, his expression hideous; it was eloquent of unmitigated crime. He was an unhappy man at war with the whole of society.

'*To arms!*' cried Julien. And he sprang with one bound down the steps that led from the house. He entered the letter-writer's booth at the street corner; the man was alarmed. 'Copy this,' said Julien, giving him Mademoiselle de La Mole's letter.

While the writer was thus engaged, he himself wrote to Fouqué; he begged him to keep for him a precious article. 'But,' he said to himself, laying down his pen, 'the secret room in the post office will open my letter, and give you back the one you seek; no, gentlemen.' He went and bought an enormous Bible from a Protestant bookseller, skilfully concealed Mathilde's letter in the boards, had it packed up with his own letter, and his parcel went off by the mail, addressed to one of Fouqué's workmen, whose name was unknown to anybody in Paris.

This done, he returned joyful and brisk to the Hôtel de La Mole. 'It is *our turn*, now,' he exclaimed, as he locked himself into his room, and flung off his coat:

'What, Mademoiselle,' he wrote to Mathilde, 'it is Mademoiselle de La Mole who, by the hand of Arsène, her father's servant, transmits a letter couched in too seductive terms to a poor carpenter from the Jura, doubtless to play a trick upon his simplicity. . . .' And he transcribed the most unequivocal sentences from the letter he had received.

His own would have done credit to the diplomatic prudence of M. le Chevalier de Beauvoisis. It was still only ten o'clock; Julien, intoxicated with happiness and with the sense of his own power, so novel to a poor devil like himself, went off to the Italian opera. He heard his friend Geronimo sing. Never had music raised him to so high a pitch. He was a god.[1]

---

[1] Esprit per, pré. gui II.A.30. (*Note by Stendhal.*)

CHAPTER FORTY-FOUR

A GIRL'S THOUGHTS

Que de perplexités! Que de nuits passées sans som-
meil! Grand Dieu! Vais-je me rendre méprisable? Il
méprisera lui-même. Mais il part, il s'éloigne.

ALFRED DE MUSSET.

I T was not without an inward struggle that Mathilde had
brought herself to write. Whatever might have been the
beginning of her interest in Julien, it soon overcame the
pride which, ever since she had been aware of herself, had
reigned alone in her heart. That cold and haughty spirit was
carried away for the first time by a passionate sentiment. But
if this overcame her pride, it was still faithful to the habits
bred of pride. Two months of struggle and of novel sensations
had so to speak altered her whole moral nature.

Mathilde thought she had happiness in sight. This prospect, irresistible to a courageous spirit combined with a
superior intellect, had to make a long fight against dignity
and every sentiment of common duty. One day she entered
her mother's room, at seven o'clock in the morning, begging
her for leave to retire to Villequier. The Marquise did not
even deign to answer her, and recommended her to go back
to her bed. This was the last effort made by plain sense and
the deference paid to accepted ideas.

The fear of wrongdoing and of shocking the ideas held as
sacred by the Caylus, the de Luz, the Croisenois, had little
or no hold over her; such creatures as they did not seem to
her to be made to understand her; she would have consulted

them had it been a question of buying a carriage or an estate. Her real terror was that Julien might be displeased with her.

'Perhaps, too, he has only the outward appearance of a superior person.'

She abhorred want of character, it was her sole objection to the handsome young men among whom she lived. The more gracefully they mocked at everything which departed from the fashion, or which followed it wrongly when intending to follow it, the more they condemned themselves in her eyes.

They were brave, and that was all. 'And besides, how are they brave?' she asked herself: 'in a duel. But the duel is nothing more now than a formality. Everything is known beforehand, even what a man is to say when he falls. Lying on the grass, his hand on his heart, he must extend a handsome pardon to his adversary and leave a message for a fair one who is often imaginary, or who goes to a ball on the day of his death, for fear of arousing suspicion.

'A man will face danger at the head of a squadron all glittering with steel, but a danger that is solitary, strange, sudden, truly ugly?'

'Alas!' said Mathilde, 'it was at the Court of Henri III that one found men great by character as well as by birth! Ah, if Julien had served at Jarnac or at Moncontour, I should no longer be in doubt. In those days of strength and prowess, Frenchmen were not mere dolls. The day of battle was almost the day of least perplexity.

'Their life was not imprisoned like an Egyptian mummy, within an envelope always common to them all, always the same. Yes,' she went on, 'there was more true courage in crossing the town alone at eleven o'clock at night, after leaving the Hôtel de Soissons, occupied by Catherine de' Medici, than there is to-day in dashing to Algiers. A man's life was a succession of hazards. Nowadays civilisation and the Prefect of Police have banished hazard, there is no room for the unexpected. If it appears in our ideas, there are not epigrams enough to cope with it; if it appears in events, no act of cowardice is too great for our fear. Whatever folly our fear makes us commit is excused us. Degenerate and boring age! What would Boniface de La Mole have said if, raising his severed head from the tomb he had seen, in 1793, seventeen of his descendants allow themselves to be penned like sheep, to be guillotined a day or two later? Their death was certain, but it would have been in bad form to defend themselves and at least kill a Jacobin or two. Ah! In the heroic age of France, in the days of Boniface de La Mole, Julien would have been the squadron commander, and my brother the young priest, properly behaved, with wisdom in his eyes and reason on his lips.'

A few months since, Mathilde had despaired of meeting anyone a little different from the common pattern. She had found a certain happiness in allowing herself to write to various young men of fashion. This act of boldness, so unconventional, so imprudent in a young girl, might dishonour her in the eyes of M. de Croisenois, of his father, the Duc de Chaulnes, and of the whole house of Chaulnes, who, seeing the projected marriage broken off, would wish to know the reason. At that time, on the night after she had written one of these letters, Mathilde was unable to sleep. But these letters were mere replies.

Now she had ventured to say that she was in love. She had written *first* (what a terrible word!) to a man in the lowest rank of society.

This circumstance assured her, in the event of discovery, eternal disgrace. Which of the women who came to see her mother would dare to take her part? What polite expression could be put into their mouths to lessen the shock of the fearful contempt of the drawing-rooms?

And even to speak to a man was fearful, but to write! 'There are things which one does not write,' Napoleon exclaimed when he heard of the surrender of Baylen. And it was Julien who had told her of this saying! As though teaching her a lesson in advance.

But all this was still nothing, Mathilde's anguish had other causes. Oblivious of the horrible effect upon society, of the ineradicable blot, the universal contempt, for she was outraging her caste, Mathilde was writing to a person of a very different nature from the Croisenois, the de Luz, the Caylus.

The depth, the *strangeness* of Julien's character had alarmed her, even when she was forming an ordinary relation with him. And she was going to make him her lover, possibly her master!

'What claims will he not assert, if ever he is in a position to do as he likes with me? Very well! I shall say to myself like Medea: "*Midst all these perils, I have still* MYSELF."'

Julien had no reverence for nobility of blood, she understood. Worse, still, perhaps, he felt no love for her!

In these final moments of tormenting doubts, she was visited by ideas of feminine pride. 'Everything ought to be strange in the lot of a girl like myself,' cried Mathilde, with impatience. And so the pride that had been inculcated in her from her cradle began to fight against her virtue. It was at this point that Julien's threatened departure came to precipitate her fall.

(Such characters are fortunately quite rare.)

Late that night, Julien was malicious enough to have an extremely heavy trunk carried down to the porter's lodge; to carry it, he summoned the footman who was courting Mademoiselle de La Mole's maid. 'This device may lead to no result,' he said to himself, 'but if it proves successful, she will think that I have gone.' He went to sleep, highly delighted with his trick. Mathilde never closed an eye.

Next morning, at a very early hour, Julien left the house unobserved, but returned before eight o'clock.

No sooner was he in the library than Mademoiselle de La Mole appeared on the threshold. He handed her his answer. He thought that it was incumbent upon him to speak to her; this, at least, was the most polite course, but Mademoiselle de La Mole would not listen to him and vanished. Julien was overjoyed, he had not known what to say to her.

'If all this is not a trick arranged with Comte Norbert, plainly it must have been my frigid glance that has kindled the freakish love which this girl of noble birth has taken it into her head to feel for me. I should be a little too much of a fool if I ever allowed myself to be drawn into feeling any attraction towards the great flaxen doll.' This piece of reasoning left him more cold and calculating than he had ever been in his life.

'In the battle that is preparing,' he went on, 'pride of birth will be like a high hill, forming a military position between her and myself. It is there that we must manœuvre. I have done wrong to remain in Paris; this postponement of my departure cheapens me, and exposes my flank if all this is only a game. What danger was there in my going? I was fooling them, if they are fooling me. If her interest in me has any reality, I was increasing that interest an hundredfold.'

Mademoiselle de La Mole's letter had so flattered Julien's vanity that, while he laughed at what was happening to him, he had forgotten to think seriously of the advantages of departure.

It was a weakness of his character to be extremely sensitive to his own faults. He was extremely annoyed at this instance of his weakness, and had almost ceased to think of the incredible victory which had preceded this slight check when, about nine o'clock, Mademoiselle de La Mole appeared on the threshold of the library, flung him a letter, and fled.

'It appears that this is to be a romance told in letters,' he said, as he picked this one up. 'The enemy makes a false move, now I am going to bring coldness and virtue into play.'

The letter called for a definite answer with an arrogance which increased his inward gaiety. He gave himself the pleasure of mystifying, for the space of two pages, the people who might wish to make a fool of him, and it was with a fresh pleasantry that he announced, towards the end of his reply, his decision to depart on the following morning.

This letter finished: 'The garden can serve me as a post office,' he thought, and made his way there. He looked up at the window of Mademoiselle de La Mole's room.

It was on the first floor, next to her mother's apartment, but there was a spacious mezzanine beneath.

This first floor stood so high, that, as he advanced beneath the lime-alley, letter in hand, Julien could not be seen from

Mademoiselle de La Mole's window. The vault formed by the limes, which were admirably pleached, intercepted the view. 'But what is this!' Julien said to himself, angrily, 'another imprudence! If they have decided to make a fool of me, to let myself be seen with a letter in my hand, is to play the enemy's game.'

Norbert's room was immediately above his sister's, and if Julien emerged from the alley formed by the pleached branches of the limes, the Count and his friends would be able to follow his every movement.

Mademoiselle de La Mole appeared behind her closed window; he half shewed her his letter; she bowed her head. At once Julien ran up to his own room, and happened to meet, on the main staircase, the fair Mathilde, who snatched the letter with perfect composure and laughing eyes.

'What passion there was in the eyes of that poor Madame de Rênal,' Julien said to himself, 'when, even after six months of intimate relations, she ventured to receive a letter from me! Never once, I am sure, did she look at me with a laugh in her eyes.'

He did not express to himself so clearly the rest of his comment; was he ashamed of the futility of his motives? 'But also what a difference,' his thoughts added, 'in the elegance of her morning gown, in the elegance of her whole appearance! On catching sight of Mademoiselle de La Mole thirty yards off, a man of taste could tell the rank that she occupies in society. That is what one may call an explicit merit.'

Still playing with his theme, Julien did not yet confess to himself the whole of his thoughts; Madame de Rênal had had no Marquis de Croisenois to sacrifice to him. He had had as a rival only that ignoble Sub-Prefect M. Charcot, who had assumed the name of Maugiron, because the Maugirons were extinct.

At five o'clock, Julien received a third letter; it was flung at him from the library door. Mademoiselle de La Mole again fled. 'What a mania for writing,' he said to himself with a laugh, 'when it is so easy for us to talk! The enemy wishes to have my letters, that is clear, and plenty of them!'

He was in no haste to open this last. 'More elegant phrases,' he thought; but he turned pale as he read it. It consisted of eight lines only.

'I have to speak to you: I must speak to you, to-night; when one o'clock strikes, be in the garden. Take the gardener's long ladder from beside the well; place it against my window and come up to my room. There is a moon: no matter.'

379

CHAPTER FORTY-FIVE

IS IT A PLOT?

Ah! How cruel is the interval between the conception
of a great project and its execution! What vain terrors!
What irresolutions! Life is at stake. Far more than
life—honour!

SCHILLER.

'THIS is becoming serious,' thought Julien ... 'and a
little too obvious,' he added, after a moment's
reflexion. 'Why! This pretty young beauty can speak
to me in the library with a freedom which, thank heaven, is
unrestricted; the Marquis, for fear of my bothering him with
accounts, never comes there. Why! M. de La Mole and
Comte Norbert, the only people who ever shew their faces
here, are absent almost all day; it is easy to watch for the
moment of their return to the house, and the sublime
Mathilde, for whose hand a Sovereign Prince would not be
too noble, wishes me to commit an act of abominable
imprudence!

'It is clear, they wish to ruin me, or to make a fool of me,
at least. First of all, they sought to ruin me by my letters;
these proved cautious; very well, now they require an action
that shall be as clear as daylight. These pretty little gentlemen think me too simple or too conceited. The devil! With
the brightest moon you ever saw, to climb up by a ladder to
a first floor, five and twenty feet from the ground! They will
have plenty of time to see me, even from the neighbouring
houses. I shall be a fine sight on my ladder!' Julien went up

to his room and began to pack his trunk, whistling as he did so. He had made up his mind to go, and not even to answer the letter.

But this sage resolution gave him no peace of heart. 'If, by any chance,' he said to himself, suddenly, his trunk packed and shut, 'Mathilde were sincere! Then I shall be cutting in her eyes the most perfect figure of a coward. I have no birth, so I require great qualities, ready on demand, with no flattering suppositions, qualities proved by eloquent deeds....'

He spent a quarter of an hour pacing the floor of his room. 'What use in denying it?' he asked himself, at length; 'I shall be a coward in her eyes. I lose not only the most brilliant young person in high society, as everyone was saying at M. le Duc de Retz's ball, but, furthermore, the heavenly pleasure of seeing her throw over for me the Marquis de Croisenois, the son of a Duke, and a future Duke himself. A charming young man who has all the qualities that I lack: a ready wit, birth, fortune....

'This remorse will pursue me all my life, not for her, there are heaps of mistresses, "but only one honour," as old Don Diego says, and here I am clearly and plainly recoiling from the first peril that comes my way; for that duel with M. de Beauvoisis was a mere joke. This is quite different. I may be shot point-blank by a servant, but that is the least danger; I may forfeit my honour.

'This is becoming serious, my boy,' he went on, with a Gascon gaiety and accent. '*Honur* is at stake. A poor devil kept down by fate in my lowly station will never find such an opportunity again; I shall have adventures, but tawdry ones....'

He reflected at length, he paced the room with a hurried step, stopping short now and again. There stood in his room a magnificent bust in marble of Cardinal Richelieu, which persistently caught his eye. This bust, as the light of his lamp fell upon it, appeared to be gazing at him sternly, as though reproaching him for the want of that audacity which ought to be so natural to the French character. 'In thy time, great man, should I have hesitated?

381

'At the worst,' Julien told himself finally, 'let us suppose that all this is a plot, it is a very dark one, and highly compromising for a young girl. They know that I am not the man to keep silent. They will therefore have to kill me. That was all very well in 1574, in the days of Boniface de La Mole, but the La Mole of to-day would never dare. These people are not the same now. Mademoiselle de La Mole is so envied! Four hundred drawing-rooms would echo with her disgrace next day, and with what rejoicing!

'The servants chatter among themselves of the marked preference that is shewn me; I know it, I have heard them....

'On the other hand, her letters! ... They may suppose that I have them on me. They surprise me in her room, and take them from me. I shall have two, three, four, any number of men to deal with. But these men, where will they collect them? Where is one to find discreet agents in Paris? They are afraid of the law.... Gad! It will be the Caylus and Croisenois and de Luz themselves. The thought of that moment, and the foolish figure I shall cut there among them will be what has tempted them. Beware the fate of Abelard, Master Secretary!

'Begad, then, gentlemen, you shall bear the mark of my fists, I shall strike at your faces, like Cæsar's soldiers at Pharsalia.... As for the letters, I can put them in a safe place.'

Julien made copies of the two last, concealed them in a volume of the fine Voltaire from the library, and went himself with the originals to the post.

When he returned: 'Into what madness am I rushing!' he said to himself with surprise and terror. He had been a quarter of an hour without considering his action of the coming night in all its aspects.

'But, if I refuse, I must despise myself ever afterwards. All my life long, that action will be a matter for doubt to me, and such a doubt is the most bitter agony. Have I not felt it over Amanda's lover? I believe that I should find it easier to forgive myself what was clearly a crime; once I had confessed it, I should cease to think about it.

IS IT A PLOT?

'What! An incredible stroke of fortune takes me from the common herd to set me in rivalry with a man bearing one of the best names in France, and I myself, with a light heart, am to declare myself his inferior! Indeed, there is a strain of cowardice in not going. That word settles everything,' cried Julien, springing to his feet ... 'besides, she is a real beauty!

'If this is not treachery, how foolishly she is behaving for me!... If it is a mystification, begad, gentlemen, it rests with me to turn the jest to earnest, and so I shall.

'But if they pinion my arms, the moment I enter the room; they may have set some diabolical machine there ready for me!

'It is like a duel,' he told himself with a laugh, 'there is a parry for every thrust, my fencing master says, but the Almighty, who likes things to end, makes one of the fighters forget to parry. Anyhow, here is what will answer them'; he drew his pocket pistols; and, albeit they were fully charged, renewed the primings.

There were still many hours to wait; in order to have something to do, Julien wrote to Fouqué: 'My friend, open the enclosed letter only in case of accident, if you hear it said that something strange has befallen me. Then, erase the proper names from the manuscript that I am sending you, and make eight copies of it which you will send to the newspapers of Marseilles, Bordeaux, Lyons, Brussels, etc.; ten days later, have the manuscript printed, send the first copy to M. le Marquis de La Mole, and a fortnight after that, scatter the other copies by night about the streets of Verrières.'

This brief exonerating memoir, arranged in the form of a tale, which Fouqué was to open only in case of accident, Julien made as little compromising as possible to Mademoiselle de La Mole, but, nevertheless, it described his position very accurately.

He had just sealed his packet when the dinner-bell rang; it made his heart beat violently. His imagination, preoccupied with the narrative which he had just composed, was a prey to all sorts of tragic presentiment. He had seen himself

383

seized by servants, garrotted, carried down to a cellar with a gag in his mouth. There, one of them kept a close watch over him, and if the honour of the noble family required that the adventure should have a tragic ending, it was easy to end everything with one of those poisons which leave no trace; then, they would say that he had died a natural death, and would take his dead body back to his room.

Carried away by his own story like a dramatic author, Julien was really afraid when he entered the dining-room. He looked at all the servants in full livery. He studied their expressions. 'Which of them have been chosen for to-night's expedition?' he asked himself. 'In this family, the memories of the Court of Henri III are so present, so often recalled, that, when they think themselves outraged, they will shew more decision than other people of their rank.' He looked at Mademoiselle de La Mole in order to read in her eyes what were the plans of her family; she was pale, and had, he thought, quite a mediæval appearance. Never had he observed such an air of grandeur in her, she was truly beautiful and imposing. He almost fell in love with her. '*Pallida morte futura*,' he told himself, 'her pallor betokens that something serious is afoot.'

In vain, after dinner, did he prolong his stroll in the garden, Mademoiselle de La Mole did not come out. Conversation with her would, at that moment, have relieved his heart of a great burden.

Why not confess it? He was afraid. As he was determined to act, he abandoned himself to this sentiment without shame. 'Provided that at the moment of action, I find the courage that I require,' he said to himself, 'what does it matter how I may be feeling now?' He went to reconnoitre the position and to try the weight of the ladder.

'It is an instrument,' he said to himself, with a laugh, 'which it is written in my destiny that I am to use! Here as at Verrières. What a difference! Then,' he continued with a sigh, 'I was not obliged to be suspicious of the person for whose sake I was exposing myself. What a difference, too, in the danger!

IS IT A PLOT?

'I might have been killed in M. de Rênal's gardens without any harm to my reputation. It would have been easy to make my death unaccountable. Here, what abominable tales will they not bandy about in the drawing-rooms of the Hôtel de Chaulnes, the Hôtel de Caylus, the Hôtel de Retz, and in short everywhere? I shall be handed down to posterity as a monster.

'For two or three years,' he added, laughing at himself. But the thought of this overwhelmed him. 'And I, who is going to justify me? Supposing that Fouqué prints my posthumous pamphlet, it will be only an infamy the more. What! I am received in a house, and in payment for the hospitality I receive there, the kindness that is showered upon me, I print a pamphlet reporting all that goes on in the house! I attack the honour of its women! Ah, a thousand times rather, let us be trapped!'

It was a terrible evening.

CHAPTER FORTY-SIX

ONE O'CLOCK IN THE MORNING

> Ce jardin était fort grand, dessiné depuis peu d'an-
> nées avec un goût parfait. Mais les arbres avaient figuré
> dans le fameux Pré-aux-Clercs, si célèbre du temps de
> Henri III, ils avaient plus d'un siècle. On y trouvait
> quelque chose de champêtre.
>
> MASSINGER[1]

H E was on the point of countermanding his instructions to Fouqué when the clock struck eleven. He
came out of his bedroom and shut the door behind
him, turning the key noisily in the lock, as though he were
locking himself in. He prowled round the house to see what
was afoot everywhere, especially in the attics on the fourth
floor, where the servants slept. There was nothing unusual.
One of Madame de La Mole's maids was giving a party, the
servants were merrily imbibing punch. 'The men who are
laughing like that,' thought Julien, 'cannot have been
detailed for the midnight encounter, they would be more
serious.'

Finally he took his stand in a dark corner of the garden.
'If their plan is to avoid the notice of the servants of the
house, they will make the men they have hired to seize me
come in over the garden wall.

'If M. de Croisenois is taking all this calmly, he must feel

1 I have left this motto untranslated, as the attribution to Massinger seems to
be entirely fantastic. C. K. S. M.

that it will be less compromising for the young person whom he intends to marry to have me seized before the moment when I shall have entered her room.'

He made an extremely careful military reconnaissance. 'My honour is at stake,' he thought; 'if I make some blunder, it will be no excuse in my own eyes to say to myself: "I never thought of that."'

The sky was maddeningly clear. About eleven o'clock the moon had risen, at half-past twelve it lighted the whole garden front of the house.

'She is mad,' Julien said to himself; when one o'clock struck, there was still a light in Comte Norbert's windows. Never in his life had Julien been so much afraid, he saw only the dangers of the enterprise, and felt not the least enthusiasm.

He went to fetch the huge ladder, waited five minutes, to allow time for a countermand, and at five minutes past one placed the ladder against Mathilde's window. He climbed quietly, pistol in hand, astonished not to find himself attacked. As he reached the window, she opened it silently:

'Here you are, Sir,' Mathilde said to him with deep emotion; 'I have been following your movements for the last hour.'

Julien was greatly embarrassed, he did not know how to behave, he did not feel the least vestige of love. In his embarrassment, he decided that he must shew courage, he attempted to embrace Mathilde.

'Fie, Sir!' she said, and thrust him from her.

Greatly relieved at this repulse, he hastened to cast an eye round the room: the moonlight was so brilliant that the shadows which it formed in Mademoiselle de La Mole's room were black. 'There may easily be men concealed there without my seeing them,' he thought.

'What have you in the side pocket of your coat?' Mathilde asked him, delighted at finding a topic of conversation. She was strangely ill at ease; all the feelings of reserve and timidity, so natural to a young girl of good family, had resumed their sway and were keeping her on tenter-hooks.

'I have all sorts of weapons and pistols,' replied Julien, no less pleased at having something to say.

'You must let down the ladder,' said Mathilde.

'It is huge, and may break the windows of the room below, or of the mezzanine.'

'It must not break the windows,' Mathilde went on, trying in vain to adopt the tone of ordinary conversation; 'you might, it seems to me, let the ladder down by means of a cord tied to the top rung. I always keep a supply of cords by me.'

'And this is a woman in love!' thought Julien, 'she dares to say that she loves! Such coolness, such sagacity in her precautions make it plain to me that I am not triumphing over M. de Croisenois, as I foolishly imagined; but am simply becoming his successor. After all, what does it matter? I am not in love! I triumph over the Marquis in this sense, that he will be greatly annoyed at having a successor, and still more annoyed that his successor should be myself. How arrogantly he stared at me last night in the Café Tortoni, pretending not to know me! How savagely he bowed to me afterwards, when he could no longer avoid it!'

Julien had fastened the cord to the highest rung of the ladder, he now let it down gently, leaning far out over the balcony so as to see that it did not touch the windows. 'A fine moment for killing me,' he thought, 'if there is anyone hidden in Mathilde's room'; but a profound silence continued to reign everywhere.

The head of the ladder touched the ground. Julien succeeded in concealing it in the bed of exotic flowers that ran beneath the wall.

'What will my mother say,' said Mathilde, 'when she sees her beautiful plants all ruined! You must throw down the cord,' she went on, with perfect calm. 'If it were seen running up to the balcony, it would be difficult to explain its presence.'

'And how me gwine get way?' asked Julien, in a playful tone, imitating the Creole speech. (One of the maids in the house was a native of San Domingo.)

'You get way by the door,' said Mathilde, delighted at this solution.

'Ah! How worthy this man is of all my love,' she thought.

Julien had just let the cord drop into the garden; Mathilde gripped him by the arm. He thought he was being seized by an enemy, and turned sharply round drawing a dagger. She thought she had heard a window being opened. They stood motionless, without breathing. The moon shone full upon them. As the sound was not repeated, there was no further cause for alarm.

Then their embarrassment began again, and was great on both sides. Julien made sure that the door was fastened with all its bolts; he even thought of looking under the bed, but dared not; they might have hidden a footman or two there. Finally, the fear of a subsequent reproach from his prudence made him look.

Mathilde had succumbed to all the agonies of extreme shyness. She felt a horror of her position.

'What have you done with my letters?' she said, at length.

'What a fine opportunity to discomfit these gentlemen, if they are listening, and so avoid the conflict!' thought Julien.

'The first is hidden in a stout Protestant Bible which last night's mail has carried far from here.'

He spoke very distinctly as he entered into these details, and in such a way as to be overheard by anyone who might be concealed in two great mahogany wardrobes which he had not dared to examine.

'The other two are in the post, and are going the same way as the first.'

'Good Lord! But why all these precautions?' said Mathilde, with astonishment.

'Is there any reason why I should lie to her?' thought Julien; and he confessed to her all his suspicions.

'So that accounts for the coldness of thy letters!' cried Mathilde, in accents rather of frenzy than of affection.

Julien did not observe her change of tone. This use of the singular pronoun made him lose his head, or at least his suspicions vanished; he felt himself raised in his own estimation; he ventured to clasp in his arms this girl who was so beautiful and inspired such respect in him. He was only half repulsed.

He had recourse to his memory, as once before, long ago, at Besançon with Amanda Binet, and repeated several of the finest passages from the *Nouvelle Héloïse.*

'Thou hast a man's heart,' she replied, without paying much attention to what he was saying; 'I wished to test thy bravery, I admit. Thy first suspicions and thy determination to come shew thee to be even more intrepid than I supposed.'

Mathilde made an effort to use the more intimate form; she was evidently more attentive to this unusual way of speaking than to what she was saying. This use of the singular form, stripped of the tone of affection, ceased, after a moment, to afford Julien any pleasure, he was astonished at the absence of happiness; finally, in order to feel it, he had recourse to his reason. He saw himself highly esteemed by this girl who was so proud, and never bestowed unrestricted praise; by this line of reasoning he arrived at a gratification of his self-esteem.

This was not, it is true, that spiritual ecstasy which he had found at times in the company of Madame de Rênal. What a difference, great God! There was nothing tender in his sentiments at this first moment. What he felt was the keenest gratification of his ambition, and Julien was above all things ambitious. He spoke again of the people he suspected and of the precautions he had contrived. As he spoke he was thinking of how best to profit by his victory.

Mathilde, who was still greatly embarrassed and had the air of one appalled by what she had done, seemed enchanted at finding a topic of conversation. They discussed how they should meet again. Julien employed to the full the intelligence and daring of which he furnished fresh proofs in the course of this discussion. They had some extremely sharp-sighted people against them, young Tanbeau was certainly a spy, but Mathilde and he were not altogether incompetent either.

What could be easier than to meet in the library, and arrange everything?

'I can appear, without arousing suspicion, in any part of the house, I could almost appear in Madame de La Mole's bedroom.' It was absolutely necessary to pass through this room to reach her daughter's. If Mathilde preferred that he should always come by a ladder, it was with a heart wild with joy that he would expose himself to this slight risk.

As she listened to him speaking, Mathilde was shocked by his air of triumph. 'He is my master, then!' she told herself. Already she was devoured by remorse. Her reason felt a horror of the signal act of folly which she had just committed. Had it been possible, she would have destroyed herself and Julien. Whenever, for an instant, the strength of her will made her remorse silent, feelings of shyness and outraged modesty made her extremely wretched. She had never for a moment anticipated the dreadful plight in which she now found herself.

'I must speak to him, though,' she said to herself, finally, 'that is laid down in the rules, one speaks to one's lover.' And then, as though performing a duty, and with a tenderness that was evident rather in the words that she used than in the sound of her voice, she told him of the various decisions to which she had come with regard to him during the last few days.

She had made up her mind that if he ventured to come to her with the aid of the gardener's ladder, as she had bidden him, she would give herself to him. But never were things so tender said in a colder and more formal tone. So far, their intercourse was ice-bound. It was enough to make one hate the thought of love. What a moral lesson for a rash young woman! Is it worth her while to wreck her future for such a moment?

After prolonged uncertainties, which might have appeared to a superficial observer to be due to the most decided hatred, so hard was it for the feeling of self-respect which a woman owes to herself, to yield to so masterful a will, Mathilde finally became his mistress.

To tell the truth, their transports were somewhat deliberate. Passionate love was far more a model which they were imitating than a reality with them.

Mademoiselle de La Mole believed that she was performing a duty towards herself and towards her lover. 'The

391

poor boy,' she told herself, 'has been the last word in daring, he deserves to be made happy, or else I am wanting in character.' But she would gladly have redeemed at the cost of an eternity of suffering the cruel necessity to which she found herself committed.

In spite of the violent effort that she had to make to control herself, she retained entire command of her speech.

No regret, no reproach came to mar this night which seemed odd rather than happy to Julien. What a difference, great God, from his last visit, of twenty-four hours, to Verrières! 'These fine Paris manners have found out the secret of spoiling everything, even love,' he said to himself with an extreme disregard of justice.

He abandoned himself to these reflexions, standing upright in one of the great mahogany wardrobes into which he had been thrust at the first sound heard from the next room, which was Madame de La Mole's bedroom. Mathilde accompanied her mother to mass, the maids left the apartment, and Julien made his escape before they returned to complete their labours.

He mounted his horse and made at a leisurely pace for the most solitary recesses of the forest of Meudon. He was still more surprised than happy. The happiness which, from time to time, came flooding into his heart, was akin to that of a young Second Lieutenant who, after some astounding action, has just been promoted Colonel by the Commander in Chief; he felt himself carried to an immense height. Everything that had been above him the day before was now on his level or far beneath him. Gradually Julien's happiness increased as he put the miles behind him.

If there was nothing tender in his heart, it was because, strange as it may appear, Mathilde, throughout the whole of her conduct with him, had been performing a duty. There was nothing unforeseen for her in all the events of this night but the misery and shame which she had found in the place of those divine transports of which we read in novels.

'Can I have been mistaken? Am I not in love with him?' she asked herself.

CHAPTER FORTY-SEVEN

AN OLD SWORD

I now mean to be serious:—it is time,
  Since laughter nowadays is deem'd too serious.
A jest at Vice by Virtue's call'd a crime.
Don Juan, XIII.

S HE did not appear at all at dinner. In the evening she came to the drawing-room for a moment, but did not look at Julien. This behaviour seemed to him strange; 'but,' he thought, 'I must confess, I know the ways of good society only from the actions of their daily life which I have seen them perform a hundred times; she will give me some good reason for all this.' At the same time, urged by the most intense curiosity, he studied the expression on Mathilde's features; he could not conceal from himself that she had a sharp and malevolent air. Evidently this was not the same woman who, the night before, had felt or pretended to feel transports of joy too excessive to be genuine.

Next day, and the day after, the same coldness on her part; she never once looked at him, she seemed unaware of his existence. Julien, devoured by the keenest anxiety, was a thousand leagues from the feeling of triumph which alone had animated him on the first day. 'Can it, by any chance,' he asked himself, 'be a return to the path of virtue?' But that was a very middle-class expression to use of the proud Mathilde.

'In the ordinary situations of life she has no belief in religion,' thought Julien; 'she values it as being useful to the interests of her caste.

393

'But simply from feminine delicacy may she not be bitterly reproaching herself with the irreparable mistake that she has made?' Julien assumed that he was her first lover.

'But,' he said to himself at other moments, 'one must admit that there is nothing artless, simple, tender, in her attitude; never have I seen her looking so like a queen who has just stepped down from her throne. Can she despise me? It would be like her to reproach herself with what she has done for me, solely on account of my humble birth.'

While Julien, steeped in the prejudices he had derived from books and from memories of Verrières, was pursuing the chimera of a tender mistress who never gives a thought to her own existence the moment she has gratified the desires of her lover, Mathilde in her vanity was furious with him.

As she had ceased to be bored for the last two months, she was no longer afraid of boredom; so, albeit he could not for a moment suspect it, Julien was deprived of his strongest advantage.

'So I have given myself a master!' Mademoiselle de La Mole was saying to herself, angrily pacing the floor of her room. 'He may be the soul of honour; but if I goad his vanity to extremes, he will have his revenge by making public the nature of our relations.' This is the curse of our age, even the strangest aberrations are no cure for boredom. Julien was Mathilde's first lover, and at this epoch in life, which gives certain tender illusions to even the most sterile hearts, she was a prey to the bitterest reflexions.

'He has an immense power over me, since he reigns by terror and can inflict a fearful punishment on me if I drive him to extremes.' This idea, by itself, was enough to provoke Mathilde to insult him, for courage was the fundamental quality in her character. Nothing was capable of giving her any excitement and of curing her of an ever-present tendency to boredom, but the idea that she was playing heads or tails with her whole existence.

On the third day, as Mademoiselle de La Mole persisted in not looking at him, Julien followed her after dinner, to her evident annoyance, into the billiard room.

'Well, Sir; you must imagine yourself to have acquired some very powerful hold over me,' she said to him, with ill-controlled rage, 'since in opposition to my clearly expressed wishes, you insist on speaking to me? Are you aware that nobody in the world has ever been so presumptuous?'

Nothing could be more entertaining than the dialogue between these young lovers; unconsciously they were animated by a mutual sentiment of the keenest hatred. As neither of them had a consistent nature, as moreover they were used to the ways of good society, it was not long before they both declared in plain terms that they had quarrelled for ever.

'I swear to you eternal secrecy,' said Julien; 'I would even add that I will never address a word to you again, were it not that your reputation might be injured by too marked a change.' He bowed with the utmost respect and left her.

He performed without undue difficulty what he regarded as a duty; he was far from imagining himself to be deeply in love with Mademoiselle de La Mole. No doubt he had not been in love with her three days earlier, when he had been concealed in the great mahogany wardrobe. But everything changed rapidly in his heart from the moment when he saw himself parted from her for ever.

His pitiless memory set to work reminding him of the slightest incidents of that night which in reality had left him so cold.

On the second night after their vow of eternal separation, Julien nearly went mad when he found himself forced to admit that he was in love with Mademoiselle de La Mole.

A ghastly conflict followed this discovery: all his feelings were thrown into confusion.

A week later, instead of being haughty with M. de Croisenois, he could almost have burst into tears and embraced him.

The force of continued unhappiness gave him a glimmer of common sense; he decided to set off for Languedoc, packed his trunk and went to the posting house.

He almost fainted when, on reaching the coach office, he

was informed that, by mere chance, there was a place vacant next day in the Toulouse mail. He engaged it and returned to the Hôtel de La Mole to warn the Marquis of his departure.

M. de La Mole had gone out. More dead than alive, Julien went to wait for him in the library. What were his feelings on finding Mademoiselle de La Mole there?

On seeing him appear, she assumed an air of malevolence which it was impossible for him to misinterpret.

Carried away by his misery, dazed by surprise, Julien was weak enough to say to her, in the tenderest of tones and one that sprang from the heart: 'Then, you no longer love me?'

'I am horrified at having given myself to the first comer,' said Mathilde, weeping with rage at herself.

'*To the first comer!*' cried Julien, and he snatched up an old mediæval sword which was kept in the library as a curiosity.

His grief, which he had believed to be intense at the moment of his speaking to Mademoiselle de La Mole, had now been increased an hundredfold by the tears of shame which he saw her shed. He would have been the happiest of men had it been possible to kill her.

Just as he had drawn the sword, with some difficulty, from its antiquated scabbard, Mathilde, delighted by so novel a sensation, advanced proudly towards him; her tears had ceased to flow.

The thought of the Marquis de La Mole, his benefactor, arose vividly in Julien's mind. 'I should be killing his daughter!' he said to himself; 'how horrible!' He made as though to fling away the sword. 'Certainly,' he thought, 'she will now burst out laughing at the sight of this melodramatic gesture': thanks to this consideration, he entirely regained his self-possession. He examined the blade of the old sword with curiosity, and as though he were looking for a spot of rust, then replaced it in its scabbard, and with the utmost calm hung it up on the nail of gilded bronze from which he had taken it.

This series of actions, very deliberate towards the end,

occupied fully a minute; Mademoiselle de La Mole gazed at him in astonishment. 'So I have been within an inch of being killed by my lover!' she said to herself.

This thought carried her back to the bravest days of the age of Charles IX and Henri III.

She stood motionless before Julien who had now replaced the sword, she gazed at him with eyes in which the light of hatred no longer shone. It must be admitted that she was very attractive at that moment, certainly no woman had ever borne less resemblance to a *Parisian doll* (this label expressed Julien's chief objection to the women of that city).

'I am going to fall back into a fondness for him,' thought Mathilde; 'and then at once he would suppose himself to be my lord and master, after a relapse, and at the very moment when I have just spoken to him so firmly.' She fled.

'My God! How beautiful she is!' said Julien, as he watched her run from the room: 'that is the creature who flung herself into my arms with such frenzy not a fortnight ago.... And those moments will never come again! And it is my fault! And, at the moment of so extraordinary an action, and one that concerned me so closely, I was not conscious of it! ... I must admit that I was born with a very dull and unhappy nature.'

The Marquis appeared; Julien made haste to inform him of his departure.

'For where?' said M. de La Mole.

'For Languedoc.'

'No, if you please, you are reserved for a higher destiny; if you go anywhere, it will be to the North.... Indeed, in military parlance, I confine you to your quarters. You will oblige me by never being absent for more than two or three hours, I may need you at any moment.'

Julien bowed, and withdrew without uttering a word, leaving the Marquis greatly astonished; he was incapable of speech, and shut himself up in his room. There, he was free to exaggerate all the iniquity of his lot.

'And so,' he thought, 'I cannot even go away! God knows for how many days the Marquis is going to keep me in Paris;

great God! What is to become of me? And not a friend that I can consult; the Abbé Pirard would not let me finish my first sentence, Conte Altamira, to distract me, would offer to enlist me in some conspiracy.

'And meanwhile I am mad, I feel it; I am mad!

'Who can guide me, what is to become of me?'

CHAPTER FORTY-EIGHT

PAINFUL MOMENTS

And she admits it to me! She goes into the minutest
details! Her lovely eye fixed on mine reveals the love
that she feels for another!

SCHILLER.

MADEMOISELLE DE LA MOLE, in an ecstasy, could
think only of the felicity of having come within an
inch of being killed. She went so far as to say to
herself: 'He is worthy to be my master, since he has been on
the point of killing me. How many of the good-looking young
men in society would one have to fuse together to arrive at
such an impulse of passion?

'One must admit that he did look handsome when he
climbed on the chair, to replace the sword, precisely in the
picturesque position which the upholsterer had chosen for it!
After all, I was not such a fool to fall in love with him.'

At that moment, had any honourable way of renewing
their relations presented itself, she would have seized it with
pleasure. Julien, locked and double-locked in his room, was
a prey to the most violent despair. In the height of his folly,
he thought of flinging himself at her feet. If, instead of
remaining hidden in a remote corner, he had wandered
through the house and into the garden, so as to be within
reach of any opportunity, he might perhaps in a single instant have converted his fearful misery into the keenest
happiness.

But the adroitness with the want of which we are

399

reproaching him would have debarred the sublime impulse of seizing the sword which, at that moment, made him appear so handsome in the eyes of Mademoiselle de La Mole. This caprice, which told in Julien's favour, lasted for the rest of the day; Mathilde formed a charming impression of the brief moments during which she had loved him, and looked back on them with regret.

'Actually,' she said to herself, 'my passion for that poor boy lasted, in his eyes, only from one o'clock in the morning, when I saw him arrive by his ladder, with all his pistols in the side pocket of his coat, until nine. It was at a quarter past nine, when hearing mass at Sainte Valère, that it first occurred to me that he would imagine himself to be my master, and might try to make me obey him by force of terror.'

After dinner, Mademoiselle de La Mole, far from avoiding Julien, spoke to him, and almost ordered him to accompany her to the garden; he obeyed. This proved too much for her self-control. Mathilde yielded, almost unconsciously, to the love which she began to feel for him. She found an intense pleasure in strolling by his side, it was with curiosity that she gazed at his hands which that morning had seized the sword to kill her.

Still after such an action, after all that had passed, there could no longer be any question of their conversing on the same terms as before.

Gradually Mathilde began to talk to him with an intimate confidence of the state of her heart. She found a strange delight in this kind of conversation; she proceeded to tell him in detail of the fleeting impulses of enthusiasm which she had felt, first for M. de Croisenois, afterwards for M. de Caylus....

'What! For M. de Caylus as well!' cried Julien; and all the bitter jealousy of a past jilted lover was made manifest in his words. Mathilde received them in that light, and was not offended.

She continued to torture Julien, detailing her past feelings in the most picturesque fashion, and in accents of the most absolute sincerity. He saw that she was describing what was present before her eyes. He had the grief of remarking that as she spoke she made fresh discoveries in her own heart.

The agony of jealousy can go no farther.

The suspicion that a rival is loved is painful enough already, but to have the love that he inspires in her confessed to one in detail by the woman whom one adores is without doubt the acme of suffering.

Oh, how she punished, at that moment, the impulse of pride which had led Julien to set himself above all the Caylus and Croisenois! With what an intense and heartfelt misery he now exaggerated their most trivial advantages! With what ardent sincerity he now despised himself!

Mathilde seemed to him a creature more than divine, language fails to express the intensity of his admiration. As he walked by her side, he cast furtive glances at her hands, her arms, her regal bearing. He was on the point of falling at her feet, crushed with love and misery, and crying: 'Pity!'

'And this creature who is so lovely, so superior to all the rest, who has once loved me, it is M. de Caylus whom, no doubt, she will presently be loving!'

Julien could not doubt Mademoiselle de La Mole's sincerity; the accent of truth was all too evident in everything that she said. That absolutely nothing might be wanting to complete his misery, there were moments when, by dint of occupying her mind with the sentiments which she had at one time felt for M. de Caylus, Mathilde was led to speak of him as though she loved him still. Certainly there was love in her accents, Julien could see it plainly.

Had his bosom been flooded with a mass of molten lead, he would have suffered less. How, arrived at this extreme pitch of misery, was the poor boy to guess that it was because she was talking to him that Mademoiselle de La Mole found such pleasure in recalling all the niceties of love that she had felt in the past for M. de Caylus or M. de Croisenois?

No words could express Julien's torments. He was listening to the detailed confidences of the love felt for others in that same lime walk where, so few days since, he had waited for one o'clock to strike before making his way into her room.

Human nature is incapable of enduring misery at a higher pitch than this.

This kind of cruel intimacy lasted for a whole week. Mathilde now appeared to seek, now did not shun opportunities of speaking to him; and the subject of conversation, to which they seemed both to return with a sort of torturing pleasure, was the recital of the sentiments that she had felt for others; she recounted to him the letters that she had written, told him the very words of them, repeated whole sentences. On the final days she seemed to be studying Julien with a sort of malignant delight. His sufferings were a source of keen enjoyment to her; she saw in them her tyrant's weakness, she could permit herself, therefore, to love him.

We can see that Julien had no experience of life, he had not even read any novels; if he had been a little less awkward, and had said with a certain coldness to this girl, whom he so adored and who made him such strange confidences: 'Admit that though I am not the equal of all these gentlemen, it is still myself that you love....'

Perhaps she would have been glad to have her secret guessed; at any rate his success would have depended entirely upon the grace with which Julien expressed this idea, and the moment that he chose. However that might be, he came out well, and with advantage to himself, from a situation which was tending to become montonous in Mathilde's eyes.

'And you no longer love me, me who adore you!' Julien said to her one day, after a prolonged stroll, desperate with love and misery. It was almost the worst blunder that he could have made.

This speech destroyed in an instant all the pleasure that Mademoiselle de La Mole found in speaking to him of the state of her heart. She was beginning to feel astonished that after what had happened he did not take offence at her confidences, she was on the point of imagining, at the moment when he made this foolish speech, that perhaps he no longer loved her. 'Pride has doubtless quenched his love,' she said to herself. 'He is not the man to see himself set with impunity beneath creatures like Caylus, de Luz, Croisenois, who he admits are so far his superiors. No, I shall never see him at my feet again!'

On the preceding days, in the artlessness of his misery, Julien had paid a glowing tribute to the brilliant qualities of these gentlemen; he went so far as to exaggerate them. This change of attitude had by no means escaped the notice of Mademoiselle de La Mole; it had surprised her. Julien's frenzied soul, in praising a rival whom he believed to be loved, sympathised with that rival in his good fortune.

This speech, so frank but so stupid, altered the whole situation in an instant: Mathilde, certain of being loved, despised him completely.

She was strolling with him at the moment of this unfortunate utterance; she left him, and her final glance was expressive of the most bitter scorn. Returning to the drawing-room, for the rest of the evening she never looked at him again. Next day, this scorn of him had entire possession of her heart; there was no longer any question of the impulse which, for a whole week, had made her find such pleasure in treating Julien as her most intimate friend; the sight of him was repulsive to her. Mathilde's feeling soon reached the point of disgust; no words could express the intensity of the scorn that she felt when her eyes happened to fall on him.

Julien had understood nothing of all that had been happening in Mathilde's heart, but his far-seeing vanity discerned her scorn. He had the good sense to appear in her presence as rarely as possible, and never looked her in the face.

But it was not without a mortal anguish that he deprived himself to some extent of her company. He thought he could feel that his misery was thereby actually increased. 'The courage of a man's heart can go no farther,' he told himself. He spent all his time at a little window in the attics of the house; the shutters were carefully closed, and from there, at least, he could catch a glimpse of Mademoiselle de La Mole at the moment when she appeared in the garden.

What were his feelings when, after dinner, he saw her strolling with M. de Caylus, M. de Luz or any of the others for whom she had avowed some slight amorous inclination in the past?

Julien had had no idea of such an intensity of misery; he was on the point of crying aloud; that resolute heart was at last reduced to utter helplessness.

Any thought that was not of Mademoiselle de La Mole had become odious to him; he was incapable of writing the most simple letters.

'You are crazy,' the Marquis said to him one morning. Julien, trembling with fear of a disclosure, pleaded illness and managed to make himself believed. Fortunately for him, M. de La Mole rallied him at dinner over his coming journey: Mathilde gathered that it might be prolonged. For several days now Julien had been avoiding her, and the brilliant young men who had everything that was lacking in this creature so pale and sombre, once loved by her, had no longer the power to distract her from her dreams.

'An ordinary girl,' she said to herself, 'would have sought for the man of her choice among the young fellows who attract every eye in a drawing-room; but one of the characteristics of genius is not to let its thoughts move in the rut traced by the common herd.

'As the partner of such a man as Julien, who lacks nothing but the fortune which I possess, I shall continue to attract attention, I shall by no means pass unperceived through life. So far from incessantly dreading a Revolution like my cousins, who, in their fear of the people, dare not scold a postilion who drives them badly, I shall be certain of playing a part and a great part, for the man of my choice has character and an unbounded ambition. What does he lack? Friends? Money? I can give him all that.' But in her thoughts she was inclined to treat Julien rather as an inferior whose fortune one makes when and as one pleases and of whose love one does not even allow oneself to doubt.

CHAPTER FORTY-NINE

THE OPERA BOUFFE

O how this spring of love resembleth
The uncertain glory of an April day;
Which now shews all the beauty of the sun,
And by and by a cloud takes all away!
                              SHAKESPEARE.

OCCUPIED with thoughts of the future and of the singular part which she hoped to play, Mathilde soon came to look back with regret upon the dry, metaphysical discussions which she had often held with Julien. Wearied with keeping her thoughts on so high a plane, sometimes also she would sigh for the moments of happiness which she had found in his company; these memories were not untouched by remorse, which at certain moments overwhelmed her.

'But if one has a weakness,' she said to herself, 'it is incumbent upon a girl like myself to forget her duties only for a man of merit; people will not be able to say that it was his handsome moustaches or his elegant seat on a horse that seduced me, but his profound discussions of the future in store for France, his ideas as to the resemblance the events that are going to burst upon us may bear to the Revolution of 1688 in England. I have been seduced,' she answered the voice of remorse, 'I am a weak woman, but at least I have not been led astray like a puppet by outward advantages.

'If there be a Revolution, why should not Julien Sorel play the part of Roland, and I that of Madame Roland? I prefer

405

that to the part of Madame de Staël: immoral conduct will be an obstacle in our time. Certainly they shall not reproach me with a second lapse; I should die of shame.'

Mathilde's meditations were not all as grave, it must be admitted, as the thoughts we have just transcribed.

She kept a stealthy watch upon Julien, she found a charming grace in his most trivial actions.

'No doubt,' she said to herself, 'I have succeeded in destroying every idea in his mind that he has certain rights.

'The air of misery and profound passion with which the poor boy addressed those words of love to me, in the garden, a week ago, is proof positive; I must confess that it was extraordinary in me to be vexed by a speech so fervent with respect and passion. Am I not his wife? That speech was only natural, and, I am bound to say, quite agreeable. Julien still loved me after endless conversations, in which I had spoken to him, and with great cruelty, I admit, only of the feelings of love which the boredom of the life I lead had inspired in me for the young men in society of whom he is so jealous. Ah, if he knew how little danger there is in them for himself! What pale and lifeless copies they seem to me when compared with him, all made to the same pattern.'

As she made these reflexions, Mathilde, to keep herself in countenance in the eyes of her mother who was looking at her, was tracing lines with a pencil at random on a page of her album. One of the profiles as she finished it startled and delighted her: it bore a striking resemblance to Julien. 'It is the voice of heaven! This is one of the miracles of love,' she cried in a transport, 'quite unconsciously I have drawn his portrait.'

She fled to her room, locked herself in, took a paintbox, set to work, tried seriously to make a portrait of Julien, but could not succeed; the profile drawn at random was still the best likeness. Mathilde was enchanted; she saw in it a clear proof of her grand passion.

She did not lay aside her album until late in the evening, when the Marquise sent for her to go to the Italian opera. She had only one idea, to catch Julien's eye, so as to make her mother invite him to join them.

He did not appear; the ladies had only the most common-place people in their box. During the whole of the first act of the opera, Mathilde sat dreaming of the man whom she loved with transports of the most intense passion; but in the second act a maxim of love sung, it must be admitted, to a melody worthy of Cimarosa, penetrated her heart. The heroine of the opera said: 'I must be punished for all the adoration that I feel for him, it is loving him too well!'

The moment she had heard this sublime *cantilena*, everything that existed in the world vanished from Mathilde's ken. People spoke to her; she did not answer; her mother scolded her, it was all she could do to look at her. Her ecstasy reached a state of exaltation and passion comparable to the most violent emotions that, during the last few days, Julien had felt for her. The *cantilena*, divinely graceful, to which was sung the maxim that seemed to her to bear so striking an application to her own situation, occupied every moment in which she was not thinking directly of Julien. Thanks to her love of music, she became that evening as Madame de Rênal invariably was when thinking of him. Love born in the brain is more spirited, doubtless, than true love, but it has only flashes of enthusiasm; it knows itself too well, it criticises itself incessantly; so far from banishing thought, it is itself reared only upon a structure of thought.

On her return home, in spite of anything that Madame de La Mole might say, Mathilde alleged an attack of fever, and spent part of the night playing over the *cantilena* on her piano. She sang the words of the famous *aria* which had charmed her:

> Devo punirmi, devo punirmi,
> Se troppo amai.

The result of this night of madness was that she imagined herself to have succeeded in conquering her love. (This page will damage the unfortunate author in more ways than one. The frigid hearts will accuse it of indecency. It does not offer the insult to the young persons who shine in the drawing-rooms of Paris, of supposing that a single one of their number

is susceptible to the mad impulses which degrade the character of Mathilde. This character is wholly imaginary, and is
indeed imagined quite apart from the social customs which
among all the ages will assure so distinguished a place to the
civilisation of the nineteenth century.

It is certainly not prudence that is lacking in the young
ladies who have been the ornament of the balls this winter.

Nor do I think that one can accuse them of unduly despising a brilliant fortune, horses, fine properties, and everything
that ensures an agreeable position in society. So far from
their seeing nothing but boredom in all these advantages,
they are as a rule the object of their most constant desires,
and if there is any passion in their hearts it is for them.

Neither is it love that provides for the welfare of young
men endowed with a certain amount of talent like Julien;
they attach themselves inseparably to a certain set, and when
the set 'arrives', all the good things of society rain upon them.
Woe to the student who belongs to no set, even his minute
and far from certain successes will be made a reproach to
him, and the higher virtue will triumph over him as it robs
him. Ah, Sir, a novel is a mirror carried along a high road.
At one moment it reflects to your vision the azure skies, at
another the mire of the puddles at your feet. And the man
who carries this mirror in his pack will be accused by you of
being immoral! His mirror shews the mire, and you blame
the mirror! Rather blame that high road upon which the
puddle lies, still more the inspector of roads who allows the
water to gather and the puddle to form.

Now that it is quite understood that the character of
Mathilde is impossible in our age, no less prudent than virtuous, I am less afraid of causing annoyance by continuing the
account of the follies of this charming girl.)

Throughout the whole of the day that followed she looked
out for opportunities to assure herself that she had indeed
conquered her insane passion. Her main object was to dis-
please Julien in every way; but none of her movements
passed unperceived by him.

Julien was too wretched and above all, too greatly agitated, to interpret so complicated a stratagem of passion, still less could he discern all the promise that it held out to himself: he fell a victim to it; never perhaps had his misery been so intense. His actions were so little under the control of his mind that if some morose philosopher had said to him: 'Seek to take advantage rapidly of a disposition which for the moment is favourable to you; in this sort of brain-fed love, which we see in Paris, the same state of mind cannot continue for more than a couple of days,' he would not have understood. But, excited as he might be, Julien had a sense of honour. His first duty was discretion; so much he did understand. To ask for advice, to relate his agony to the first comer would have been a happiness comparable to that of the wretch who, crossing a burning desert, receives from the sky a draught of ice-cold water. He was aware of the danger, he was afraid of answering with a torrent of tears the indiscreet person who should question him; he closeted himself in his room.

He saw Mathilde strolling late and long in the garden; when at length she had left it, he went down there; he made his way to a rose tree from which she had plucked a rose.

The night was dark, he could indulge the full extent of his misery without fear of being seen. It was evident to him that Mademoiselle de La Mole was in love with one of those young officers to whom she had been chattering so gaily. He himself had been loved by her, but she had seen how slight were his merits.

'And indeed, they are slight!' Julien told himself with entire conviction; 'I am, when all is said, a very dull creature, very common, very tedious to others, quite insupportable to myself.' He was sick to death of all his own good qualities, of all the things that he had loved with enthusiasm; and in this state of *inverted imagination* he set to work to criticise life with his imagination. This is an error that stamps a superior person.

More than once the idea of suicide occurred to him; this image was full of charm, it was like a delicious rest; it was the glass of ice-cold water offered to the wretch who, in the desert, is dying of thirst and heat.

'My death will increase the scorn that she feels for me!' he exclaimed. 'What a memory I shall leave behind me!'

Fallen into the nethermost abyss of misery, a human being has no resource left but courage. Julien had not wisdom enough to say to himself: 'I must venture all'; but as, that evening, he looked up at the window of Mathilde's room, he could see through the shutters that she was putting out her light: he pictured to himself that charming room which he had seen, alas, once only in his life. His imagination went no farther.

One o'clock struck; from hearing the note of the bell to saying to himself: 'I am going up by the ladder,' did not take a moment.

This was a flash of genius, cogent reasons followed in abundance. 'Can I possibly be more wretched?' he asked himself. He ran to the ladder, the gardener had made it fast with a chain. With the hammer of one of his pocket pistols, which he broke, Julien, animated for the moment by a super-human force, wrenched open one of the iron links of the chain which bound the ladder; in a few minutes it was free, and he had placed it against Mathilde's window.

'She will be angry, will heap contempt upon me, what of that? I give her a kiss, a final kiss, I go up to my room and kill myself ...; my lips will have touched her cheek before I die!'

He flew up the ladder, tapped at the shutter; a moment later Mathilde heard him, she tried to open the shutter, the ladder kept it closed: Julien clung to the iron latch intended to hold the shutter open, and, risking a thousand falls, gave the ladder a violent shake, and displaced it a little. Mathilde was able to open the shutter.

He flung himself into the room more dead than alive:

'So it is thou!' she said, and fell into his arms....

*   *   *

What words can describe the intensity of Julien's happiness? Mathilde's was almost as great.

She spoke to him against herself, she accused herself to him.

'Punish me for my atrocious pride,' she said to him, squeezing him in her arms as though to strangle him; 'thou art my master, I am thy slave, I must beg pardon upon my knees for having sought to rebel.' She slipped from his embrace to fall at his feet. 'Yes, thou art my master,' she said again, intoxicated with love and joy; 'reign over me for ever, punish thy slave severely when she seeks to rebel.'

In another moment she had torn herself from his arms, lighted the candle, and Julien had all the difficulty in the world in preventing her from cutting off all one side of her hair.

'I wish to remind myself,' she told him, 'that I am thy servant: should my accursed pride ever make me forget it, shew me these locks and say: "There is no question now of love, we are not concerned with the emotion that your heart may be feeling at this moment, you have sworn to obey, obey upon your honour."'

But it is wiser to suppress the description of so wild a felicity.

Julien's chivalry was as great as his happiness; 'I must go down now by the ladder,' he said to Mathilde, when he saw the dawn appear over the distant chimneys to the east, beyond the gardens. 'The sacrifice that I am imposing on myself is worthy of you, I am depriving myself of some hours of the most astounding happiness that a human soul can enjoy, it is a sacrifice that I am offering to your reputation: if you know my heart you appreciate the effort that I have to make. Will you always be to me what you are at this moment? But the voice of honour speaks, it is enough. Let me tell you that, since our first meeting, suspicion has not been directed only against robbers. M. de La Mole has set a watch in the garden. M. de Croisenois is surrounded by spies, we know what he is doing night by night....'

'Poor boy,' cried Mathilde with a shout of laughter. Her mother and one of the maids were aroused: immediately they called to her through the door. Julien looked at her, she turned pale as she scolded the maid, and did not condescend to speak to her mother.

'But if it should occur to them to open the window, they will see the ladder!' Julien said to her.

He clasped her once more in his arms, sprang on to the ladder and slid rather than climbed down it; in a moment he was on the ground.

Three seconds later the ladder was under the lime alley, and Mathilde's honour was saved. Julien, on recovering his senses, found himself bleeding copiously and half naked: he had cut himself in his headlong descent.

The intensity of his happiness had restored all the energy of his nature: had a score of men appeared before him, to attack them single-handed would, at that moment, have been but a pleasure the more. Fortunately, his martial valour was not put to the proof: he laid down the ladder in its accustomed place; he replaced the chain that fastened it; he did not forget to come back and obliterate the print which the ladder had left in the border of exotic flowers beneath Mathilde's window.

As in the darkness he explored the loose earth with his hand, to make sure that the mark was entirely obliterated, he felt something drop on his hand; it was a whole side of Mathilde's hair which she had clipped and threw down to him.

She was at her window.

'See what thy servant sends thee,' she said in audible tones, 'it is the sign of eternal obedience. I renounce the exercise of my own reason; be thou my master.'

Julien, overcome, was on the point of fetching back the ladder and mounting again to her room. Finally reason prevailed.

To enter the house from the garden was by no means easy. He succeeded in forcing the door of a cellar; once in the house he was obliged to break open, as silently as possible, the door of his own room. In his confusion he had left everything behind, including the key, which was in the pocket of his coat. 'Let us hope,' he thought, 'that she will remember to hide all that *corpus delicti*!'

Finally exhaustion overpowered happiness, and, as the sun rose, he fell into a profound slumber.

The luncheon bell just succeeded in waking him, he made his appearance in the dining-room. Shortly afterwards, Mathilde entered the room. Julien's pride tasted a momentary joy when he saw the love that glowed in the eyes of this beautiful creature, surrounded by every mark of deference; but soon his prudence found an occasion for alarm.

On the pretext of not having had time to dress her hair properly, Mathilde had so arranged it that Julien could see at a glance the whole extent of the sacrifice that she had made for him in clipping her locks that night. If anything could have spoiled so lovely a head, Mathilde would have succeeded in spoiling hers; all one side of those beautiful pale golden locks were cropped unevenly to within half an inch of her scalp.

At luncheon, Mathilde's whole behaviour was in keeping with this original imprudence. You would have said that she was deliberately trying to let everyone see the insane passion that she had for Julien. Fortunately, that day, M. de La Mole and the Marquise were greatly taken up with a list of forthcoming promotions to the Blue Riband, in which the name of M. de Chaulnes had not been included. Towards the end of the meal, Mathilde in talking to Julien addressed him as 'my master.' He coloured to the whites of his eyes.

Whether by accident or by the express design of Madame de La Mole, Mathilde was not left alone for an instant that day. In the evening, however, as she passed from the dining-room to the drawing-room, she found an opportunity of saying to Julien:

'All my plans are upset. You are not to think that it is my doing: Mamma has just decided that one of her maids is to sleep in my room.'

The day passed like lightning; Julien was on the highest pinnacle of happiness. By seven o'clock next morning he was installed in the library; he hoped that Mademoiselle de La Mole would design to appear there; he had written her an endless letter.

He did not see her until several hours had passed, at luncheon. Her head was dressed on this occasion with the greatest pains; a marvellous art had been employed to conceal the gap left by the clipped locks. She looked once or twice at Julien, but with polite, calm eyes; there was no longer any question of her calling him 'my master.'

Julien could not breathe for astonishment.... Mathilde found fault with herself for almost everything that she had done for him.

On mature reflexion, she had decided that he was a creature, if not altogether common, at any rate not sufficiently conspicuous to deserve all the strange follies which she had ventured to commit for him. On the whole, she no longer thought of love; she was tired of love that day.

As for Julien, the emotions of his heart were those of a boy of sixteen. Harrowing doubt, bewilderment, despair, seized upon him by turns during this luncheon, which seemed to him to be everlasting.

As soon as he could decently rise from table, he flew rather than ran to the stable, saddled his horse himself and was off at a gallop; he was afraid of disgracing himself by some sign of weakness. 'I must kill my heart by physical exhaustion,' he said to himself as he galloped through the woods of Meudon. 'What have I done, what have I said to deserve such disgrace?

'I must do nothing, say nothing to-day,' he decided as he returned to the house, 'be dead in body as I am in spirit. Julien no longer lives, it is his corpse that is still stirring.'

CHAPTER FIFTY
THE JAPANESE VASE

His heart does not at first realise the whole extent of
his misery: he is more disturbed than moved. But in
proportion as his reason returns, he feels the depth of
his misfortune. All the pleasures in life are as nothing
to him, he can feel only the sharp points of the despair
that is rending him. But what is the good of speaking
of physical pain? What pain felt by the body alone is
comparable to this?

JEAN-PAUL.

THE dinner bell rang, Julien had barely time to dress;
he found Mathilde in the drawing-room urging her
brother and M. de Croisenois not to go and spend
the evening with Madame la Maréchale de Fervaques.

She could hardly have been more seductive and charming
with them. After dinner they were joined by M. de Luz, M.
de Caylus and several of their friends. One would have said
that Mademoiselle de La Mole had resumed, together with
the observance of sisterly affection, that of the strictest conventions. Although the weather that evening was charming,
she insisted that they should not go out to the garden; she
was determined not to be lured away from the armchair in
which Madame de La Mole was enthroned. The blue sofa
was the centre of the group, as in winter.

Mathilde was out of humour with the garden, or at least
it seemed to her to be utterly boring: it was associated with
the memory of Julien.

Misery destroys judgment. Our hero made the blunder of

415

clinging to that little cane chair which in the past had witnessed such brilliant triumphs. This evening, nobody spoke to him; his presence passed as though unperceived or worse. Those of Mademoiselle de La Mole's friends who were seated near him at the end of the sofa made an affectation of turning their backs on him, or so he thought.

'It is a courtier's disgrace,' he concluded. He decided to study for a moment the people who were trying to crush him with their disdain.

M. de Luz's uncle held an important post in the King's Household, the consequence of which was that this gallant officer opened his conversation with each fresh arrival with the following interesting detail: His uncle had set off at seven o'clock for Saint-Cloud, and expected to spend the night there. This piece of news was introduced in the most casual manner, but it never failed to come out.

Upon observing M. de Croisenois with the severe eye of misery, Julien remarked the enormous influence which this worthy and amiable young man attributed to occult causes. So much so that he became moody and cross if he heard an event of any importance set down to a simple and quite natural cause. 'There is a trace of madness there,' Julien told himself. 'This character bears a striking resemblance to that of the Emperor Alexander, as Prince Korasoff described him to me.' During the first year of his stay in Paris, poor Julien, coming fresh from the Seminary, dazzled by the graces, so novel to him, of all these agreeable young men, could do nothing but admire them. Their true character was only now beginning to outline itself before his eyes.

'I am playing an undignified part here,' he suddenly decided. The next thing was how to leave his little cane chair in a fashion that should not be too awkward. He tried to think of one, he called for something original upon an imagination that was fully occupied elsewhere. He was obliged to draw upon his memory, which, it must be confessed, was by no means rich in resources of this order; the boy was still a thorough novice, so that his awkwardness was complete and attracted everyone's attention when he rose to leave the drawing-room. Misery was all too evident in his whole deportment. He had been playing the part for three quarters of an hour of a troublesome inferior from whom people do not take the trouble to conceal what they think of him.

The critical observations which he had been making at the expense of his rivals prevented him, however, from taking his misfortune too seriously; he retained, to give support to his pride, the memory of what had occurred the night before last. 'Whatever the thousand advantages they may have over me,' he thought as he went into the garden by himself, 'Mathilde has not been to any of them what, on two occasions in my life, she has deigned to be to me.'

His sagacity went no farther. He failed entirely to understand the character of the singular person whom chance had now made absolute mistress of his whole happiness.

He devoted the next day to killing himself and his horse with exhaustion. He made no further attempt, that evening, to approach the blue sofa to which Mathilde remained faithful. He remarked that Comte Norbert did not so much as deign to look at him when they met in the house. 'He must be making an extraordinary effort,' he thought, 'he who is naturally so polite.'

For Julien, sleep would have meant happiness. Despite his bodily exhaustion, memories of a too seductive kind began to invade his whole imagination. He had not the intelligence to see that by his long rides through the forests round Paris, acting only upon himself and in no way upon the heart or mind of Mathilde, he was leaving the arrangement of his destiny to chance.

It seemed to him that one thing would supply boundless comfort to his grief: namely to speak to Mathilde. And yet what could he venture to say to her?

This was the question upon which one morning at seven o'clock he was pondering deeply, when suddenly he saw her enter the library.

'I know, Sir, that you desire to speak to me.'

'Great God! Who told you that?'

'I know it, what more do you want? If you are lacking in

honour, you may ruin me, or at least attempt to do so; but this danger, which I do not regard as real, will certainly not prevent me from being sincere. I no longer love you, Sir; my wild imagination misled me. . . .'

On receiving this terrible blow, desperate with love and misery, Julien tried to excuse himself. Nothing could be more absurd. Does one excuse oneself for failing to please? But reason no longer held any sway over his actions. A blind instinct urged him to postpone the decision of his fate. It seemed to him that so long as he was still speaking, nothing was definitely settled. Mathilde did not listen to his words, the sound of them irritated her, she could not conceive how he had the audacity to interrupt her.

The twofold remorse of her virtue and her pride made her, that morning, equally unhappy. She was more or less crushed by the frightful idea of having given certain rights over herself to a little cleric, the son of a peasant. 'It is almost,' she told herself in moments when she exaggerated her distress, 'as though I had to reproach myself with a weakness for one of the footmen.'

In bold and proud natures, it is only a step from anger with oneself to fury with other people; one's transports of rage are in such circumstances a source of keen pleasure.

In a moment, Mademoiselle de La Mole reached the stage of heaping on Julien the marks of the most intense scorn. She had infinite cleverness, and this cleverness triumphed in the art of torturing the self-esteem of others and inflicting cruel wounds upon them.

For the first time in his life, Julien found himself subjected to the action of a superior intelligence animated by the most violent hatred of himself. So far from entertaining the slightest idea of defending himself at that moment, his vivid imagination began to make him despise himself. Hearing her heap upon him such cruel marks of scorn, so cleverly calculated to destroy any good opinion that he might have of himself, he felt that Mathilde was right, and that she was not saying enough.

As for her, her pride found an exquisite pleasure in thus

punishing herself and him for the adoration which she had felt a few days earlier.

She had no need to invent or to think for the first time of the cruel words which she now uttered with such complacence. She was only repeating what for the last week had been said in her heart by the counsel of the opposite party to love.

Every word increased Julien's fearful misery an hundred-fold. He tried to escape, Mademoiselle de La Mole held him by the arm with a gesture of authority.

'Please to observe,' he said to her, 'that you are speaking extremely loud; they will hear you in the next room.'

'What of that!' Mademoiselle de La Mole retorted proudly, 'who will dare to say to me that he has heard me? I wish to rid your petty self-esteem for ever of the ideas which it may have formed of me.'

When Julien was able to leave the library, he was so astounded that he already felt his misery less keenly. 'Well! She no longer loves me,' he repeated to himself, speaking aloud as though to inform himself of his position. 'It appears that she loved me for a week or ten days, and I shall love her all my life.

'Is it really possible, she meant nothing, nothing at all to my heart, only a few days ago?'

The delights of satisfied pride flooded Mathilde's bosom; so she had managed to break with him for ever! The thought of so complete a triumph over so strong an inclination made her perfectly happy. 'And so this little gentleman will under-stand, and once for all, that he has not and never will have any power over me.' She was so happy that really she had ceased to feel any love at that moment.

After so atrocious, so humiliating a scene, in anyone less passionate than Julien, love would have become impossible. Without departing for a single instant from what she owed to herself, Mademoiselle de La Mole had addressed to him certain of those disagreeable statements, so well calculated that they can appear to be true, even when one remembers them in cold blood.

The conclusion that Julien drew at the first moment from so astonishing a scene was that Mathilde had an unbounded pride. He believed firmly that everything was at an end for ever between them, and yet, the following day, at luncheon, he was awkward and timid in her presence. This was a fault that could not have been found with him until then. In small matters as in great, he knew clearly what he ought and wished to do, and carried it out.

That day, after luncheon, when Madame de La Mole asked him for a seditious and at the same time quite rare pamphlet, which her parish priest had brought to her secretly that morning, Julien, in taking it from a side table, knocked over an old vase of blue porcelain, the ugliest thing imaginable.

Madame de La Mole rose to her feet with a cry of distress and came across the room to examine the fragments of her beloved vase. 'It was old Japan,' she said, 'it came to me from my great-aunt the Abbess of Chelles; it was a present from the Dutch to the Regent Duke of Orleans who gave it to his daughter....'

Mathilde had followed her mother, delighted to see the destruction of this blue vase which seemed to her horribly ugly. Julien stood silent and not unduly distressed; he saw Mademoiselle de La Mole standing close beside him.

'This vase,' he said to her, 'is destroyed for ever; so is it with a sentiment which was once the master of my heart; I beg you to accept my apologies for all the foolish things it has made me do'; and he left the room.

'Really, one would think,' said Madame de La Mole as he went, 'that this M. Sorel is proud and delighted with what he has done.'

This speech fell like a weight upon Mathilde's heart. 'It is true,' she told herself, 'my mother has guessed aright, such is the sentiment that is animating him.' Then and then only ended her joy in the scene that she had made with him the day before. 'Ah, well, all is at an end,' she said to herself with apparent calm; 'I am left with a great example; my mistake has been fearful, degrading! It will make me wise for all the rest of my life.'

'Was I not speaking the truth?' thought Julien; 'why does the love that I felt for that madwoman torment me still?'

This love, so far from dying, as he hoped, was making rapid strides. 'She is mad, it is true,' he said to himself, 'but is she any less adorable? Is it possible for a girl to be more lovely? Everything that the most elegant civilisation can offer in the way of keen pleasures, was it not all combined to one's heart's content in Mademoiselle de La Mole?' These memories of past happiness took possession of Julien, and rapidly undid all the work of reason.

Reason struggles in vain against memories of this sort; its stern endeavours serve only to enhance their charm.

Twenty-four hours after the breaking of the old Japanese vase, Julien was decidedly one of the unhappiest of men.

CHAPTER FIFTY-ONE

THE SECRET NOTE

Car tout ce que je raconte, je l'ai vu; et si j'ai pu
me tromper en la voyant, bien certainement je ne vous
trompe point en vous le disant.

From a Letter to the Author.

THE Marquis sent for him; M. de La Mole seemed
rejuvenated, there was a gleam in his eye.

'Let us hear a little about your memory,' he said
to Julien. 'I am told it is prodigious! Could you learn four
pages by heart and go and repeat them in London? But without
altering a word!'

The Marquis was feverishly turning the pages of that
morning's *Quotidienne*, and seeking in vain to dissimulate a
highly serious air, which Julien had never seen him display,
not even when they were discussing the Frilair case.

Julien had by this time sufficient experience to feel that he
ought to appear thoroughly deceived by the light manner
that was being assumed for his benefit.

'This number of the *Quotidienne* is perhaps not very amusing;
but, if M. le Marquis will allow me, to-morrow morning I shall
have the honour to recite it to him from beginning to end.'

'What! Even the advertisements?'

'Literally, and without missing a word.'

'Do you give me your word for that?' went on the Marquis
with a sudden gravity.

'Yes, Sir, only the fear of not keeping it might upset my
memory.'

'What I mean is that I forgot to ask you this question yesterday; I do not ask you on your oath never to repeat what you are about to hear; I know you too well to insult you in that way. I have answered for you, I am going to take you to a room where there will be twelve persons assembled; you will take note of what each of them says.

'Do not be uneasy, it is not going to be a confused conversation, each one will speak in his turn, I do not mean a set speech,' the Marquis went on, resuming the tone of careless superiority which came so naturally to him. 'While we are talking, you will write down twenty pages or so; you will return here with me, we shall cut down those twenty pages to four. It is those four pages that you shall recite to me tomorrow morning instead of the whole number of the *Quotidienne*. You will then set off at once; you will have to take post like a young man who is travelling for his pleasure. Your object will be to pass unobserved by anyone. You will arrive in the presence of a great personage. There, you will require more skill. It will be a question of taking in everyone round him; for among his secretaries, among his servants, there are men in the pay of our enemies, who lie in wait for our agents to intercept them. You shall have a formal letter of introduction. When His Excellency looks at you, you will take out my watch here, which I am going to lend you for the journey. Take it now, while you are about it, and give me yours.

'The Duke himself will condescend to copy out at your dictation the four pages which you will have learned by heart.

'When this has been done, but not before, remember, you may, if His Excellency questions you, give him an account of the meeting which you are now about to attend.

'One thing that will prevent you from feeling bored on your journey is that between Paris and the residence of the Minister there are people who would ask for nothing better than to fire a shot at M. l'Abbé Sorel. Then his mission is at an end and I foresee a long delay; for, my dear fellow, how shall we hear of your death? Your zeal cannot go so far as to inform us of it.

423

'Run off at once and buy yourself a complete outfit,' the Marquis went on with a serious air. 'Dress in the style of the year before last. This evening you will have to look a little shabby. On the journey, however, you will dress as usual. Does that surprise you, does your suspicious mind guess the reason? Yes, my friend, one of the venerable personages whom you are about to hear discuss is fully capable of transmitting information by means of which someone may quite possibly administer opium to you, if nothing worse, in the evening, in some respectable inn at which you will have called for supper.'

'It would be better,' said Julien, 'to travel thirty leagues farther and avoid the direct route. My destination is Rome, I suppose. . . .'

The Marquis assumed an air of haughty displeasure which Julien had not seen to so marked a degree since Bray-le-Haut.

'That is what you shall learn, Sir, when I think fit to tell you. I do not like questions.'

'It was not a question,' replied Julien effusively: 'I swear to you, Sir, I was thinking aloud, I was seeking in my own mind the safest route.'

'Yes, it seems that your thoughts were far away. Never forget that an ambassador, one of your youth especially, ought not to appear to be forcing confidences.'

Julien was greatly mortified, he was in the wrong. His self-esteem sought for an excuse and could find none.

'Understand then,' M. de La Mole went on, 'that people always appeal to their hearts when they have done something foolish.'

An hour later, Julien was in the Marquis's waiting-room in the garb of an inferior, with old-fashioned clothes, a doubtfully clean neckcloth and something distinctly smug about his whole appearance.

At the sight of him, the Marquis burst out laughing, and then only was Julien's apology accepted.

'If this young man betrays me,' M. de La Mole asked himself, 'whom can I trust? And yet when it comes to action,

424

one has to trust somebody. My son and his brilliant friends of the same kidney have honest hearts, and loyalty enough for a hundred thousand; if it were a question of fighting, they would perish on the steps of the throne, they know everything ... except just what is required at the moment. Devil take me if I can think of one of them who could learn four pages by heart and travel a hundred leagues without being tracked. Norbert would know how to let himself be killed like his ancestors, but any conscript can do that. ...'

The Marquis fell into a profound meditation: 'And even being killed,' he said with a sigh, 'perhaps this Sorel would manage that as well as he. ...

'The carriage is waiting,' said the Marquis, as though to banish a vexatious thought.

'Sir,' said Julien, 'while they were altering this coat for me, I committed to memory the first page of to-day's *Quotidienne*.'

The Marquis took the paper, Julien repeated the page without a single mistake. 'Good,' said the Marquis, every inch the diplomat that evening; 'meanwhile this young man is not observing the streets through which we are passing.'

They arrived in a large room of a distinctly gloomy aspect, partly panelled and partly hung in green velvet. In the middle of the room, a scowling footman had just set up a large dinner-table, which he proceeded to convert into a writing-table, by means of an immense green cloth covered with ink stains, a relic of some Ministry.

The master of the house was a corpulent man whose name was never uttered; Julien decided that his expression and speech were those of a man engaged in digestion.

At a sign from the Marquis, Julien had remained at the lower end of the table. To keep himself in countenance he began to point the quills. He counted out of the corner of his eye seven speakers, but he could see nothing more of them than their backs. Two of them appeared to him to be addressing M. de La Mole on terms of equality, the others seemed more or less deferential.

Another person entered the room unannounced. 'This is strange,' thought Julien, 'no one is announced in this room.

Can this precaution have been taken in my honour?' Everyone rose to receive the newcomer. He was wearing the same
extremely distinguished decoration as three of the men who
were already in the room. They spoke in low tones. In
judging the newcomer, Julien was restricted to what he could
learn from his features and dress. He was short and stout,
with a high complexion and a gleaming eye devoid of any
expression beyond the savage glare of a wild boar.

Julien's attention was sharply distracted by the almost
immediate arrival of a wholly different person. This was a
tall man, extremely thin and wearing three or four waistcoats. His eye was caressing, his gestures polished.

'That is just the expression of the old Bishop of Besançon,'
thought Julien. This man evidently belonged to the Church,
he did not appear to be more than fifty or fifty-five, no one
could have looked more fatherly.

The young Bishop of Agde appeared, and seemed greatly
surprised when, in making a survey of those present, his eye
rested on Julien. He had not spoken to him since the ceremony at Bray-le-Haut. His look of surprise embarrassed and
irritated Julien. 'What,' the latter said to himself, 'is knowing
a man to be always to my disadvantage? All these great
gentlemen whom I have never seen before do not frighten
me in the least, and the look in this young Bishop's eyes
freezes me! It must be admitted that I am a very strange and
very unfortunate creature.'

A small and extremely dark man presently made a noisy
entrance, and began speaking from the door; he had a sallow
complexion and a slightly eccentric air. On the arrival of this
pitiless talker, groups began to form, apparently to escape
the boredom of listening to him.

As they withdrew from the fireplace they drew near to
the lower end of the table, where Julien was installed. His
countenance became more and more embarrassed, for now
at last, in spite of all his efforts, he could not avoid hearing
them, and however slight his experience might be, he realised
the full importance of the matters that were being discussed
without any attempt at concealment; and yet how careful the

426

evidently exalted personages whom he saw before him ought to be to keep them secret.

Already, working as slowly as possible, Julien had pointed a score of quills; this resource must soon fail him. He looked in vain for an order in the eyes of M. de La Mole; the Marquis had forgotten him.

'What I am doing is absurd,' thought Julien as he pointed his pens; 'but people who are so commonplace in appearance, and are entrusted by others or by themselves with such high interests, must be highly susceptible. My unfortunate expression has a questioning and scarcely respectful effect which would doubtless annoy them. If I lower my eyes too far I shall appear to be making a record of their talk.'

His embarrassment was extreme, he was hearing some strange things said.

CHAPTER FIFTY-TWO

THE DISCUSSION

La république—pour un, aujourd'hui, qui sacrifierait
tout au bien public, il en est des milliers et des millions
qui ne connaissent que leurs jouissances, leur vanité.
On est considéré, à Paris, à cause de sa voiture et non
à cause de sa vertu.

NAPOLÉON *Mémorial.*

THE footman burst in, announcing: 'Monsieur le Duc
de ——.'

'Hold your tongue, you fool,' said the Duke as he
entered the room. He said this so well, and with such majesty
that Julien could not help thinking that knowing how to lose
his temper with a footman was the whole extent of this great
personage's knowledge. Julien raised his eyes and at once
lowered them again. He had so clearly divined the importance of this new arrival that he trembled lest his glance
should be thought an indiscretion.

This Duke was a man of fifty, dressed like a dandy, and
treading as though on springs. He had a narrow head with
a large nose, and a curved face which he kept thrusting forward. It would have been hard for anyone to appear at once
so noble and so insignificant. His coming was a signal for the
opening of the discussion.

Julien was sharply interrupted in his physiognomical studies by the voice of M. de La Mole. 'Let me present to you
M. l'Abbé Sorel,' said the Marquis. 'He is endowed with an
astonishing memory; it was only an hour ago that I spoke

to him of the mission with which he might perhaps be honoured, and, in order to furnish us with a proof of his memory, he has learned by heart the first page of the *Quotidienne.*'

'Ah! The foreign news, from poor N——,' said the master of the house. He picked up the paper eagerly and, looking at Julien with a whimsical air, in the effort to appear important: 'Begin, Sir,' he said to him.

The silence was profound, every eye was fixed on Julien; he repeated his lesson so well that after twenty lines: 'That will do,' said the Duke. The little man with the boar's eyes sat down. He was the chairman for, as soon as he had taken his place, he indicated a card table to Julien, and made a sign to him to bring it up to his side. Julien established himself there with writing materials. He counted twelve people seated round the green cloth.

'M. Sorel,' said the Duke, 'retire to the next room. We shall send for you.'

The master of the house assumed an uneasy expression. 'The shutters are not closed,' he murmured to his neighbour. 'It is no use your looking out of window,' he foolishly exclaimed to Julien. 'Here I am thrust into a conspiracy at the very least,' was the latter's thought. 'Fortunately, it is not one of the kind that end on the Place de Grève. Even if there were danger, I owe that and more to the Marquis. I should be fortunate, were it granted me to atone for all the misery which my follies may one day cause him!'

Without ceasing to think of his follies and of his misery, he studied his surroundings in such a way that he could never forget them. Only then did he remember that he had not heard the Marquis tell his footman the name of the street, and the Marquis had sent for a cab, a thing he never did.

Julien was left for a long time to his reflexions. He was in a parlour hung in green velvet with broad stripes of gold. There was on the side-table a large ivory crucifix, and on the mantelpiece the book *Du Pape*, by M. de Maistre, with gilt edges, and magnificently bound. Julien opened it so as not to appear to be eavesdropping. Every now and then there

429

was a sound of raised voices from the next room. At length the door opened, his name was called.

'Remember, Gentlemen,' said the chairman, 'that from this moment we are addressing the Duc de ——. This gentleman,' he said, pointing to Julien, 'is a young Levite, devoted to our sacred cause, who will have no difficulty in repeating, thanks to his astonishing memory, our most trivial words.

'Monsieur has the floor,' he said, indicating the personage with the fatherly air, who was wearing three or four waistcoats. Julien felt that it would have been more natural to call him the gentleman with the waistcoats. He supplied himself with paper and wrote copiously.

(Here the author would have liked to insert a page of dots. 'That will not look pretty,' says the publisher, 'and for so frivolous a work not to look pretty means death.'

'Politics,' the author resumes, 'are a stone attached to the neck of literature, which, in less than six months, drowns it. Politics in the middle of imaginative interests are like a pistol-shot in the middle of a concert. The noise is deafening without being emphatic. It is not in harmony with the sound of any of the instruments. This mention of politics is going to give deadly offence to half my readers, and to bore the other half, who have already found far more interesting and emphatic politics in their morning paper.'

'If your characters do not talk politics,' the publisher retorts, 'they are no longer Frenchmen of 1830, and your book ceases to hold a mirror, as you claim. . . .')

Julien's report amounted to twenty-six pages; the following is a quite colourless extract; for I have been obliged, as usual, to suppress the absurdities, the frequency of which would have appeared tedious or highly improbable. (Compare the *Gazette des Tribunaux*.)

The man with the waistcoats and the fatherly air (he was a Bishop, perhaps), smiled often, and then his eyes, between their tremulous lids, assumed a strange brilliance and an expression less undecided than was his wont. This personage, who was invited to speak first, before the Duke ('but what Duke?' Julien asked himself), apparently to express opinions and to perform the functions of Attorney General, appeared to Julien to fall into the uncertainty and absence of definite conclusions with which those officers are often reproached. In the course of the discussion the Duke went so far as to rebuke him for this.

After several phrases of morality and indulgent philosophy, the man with the waistcoats said:

'Noble England, guided by a great man, the immortal Pitt, spent forty thousand million francs in destroying the Revolution. If this assembly will permit me to express somewhat boldly a melancholy reflexion, England does not sufficiently understand that with a man like Bonaparte, especially when one had had to oppose to him only a collection of good intentions, there was nothing decisive save personal measures. . . .'

'Ah! Praise of assassination again!' said the master of the house with an uneasy air.

'Spare us your sentimental homilies,' exclaimed the chairman angrily; his boar's eye gleamed with a savage light. 'Continue,' he said to the man with the waistcoats. The chairman's cheeks and brow turned purple.

'Noble England,' the speaker went on, 'is crushed today, for every Englishman, before paying for his daily bread, is obliged to pay the interest on the forty thousand million francs which were employed against the Jacobins. She has no longer a Pitt. . . .'

'She has the Duke of Wellington,' said a military personage who assumed an air of great importance.

'Silence, please, Gentlemen,' cried the chairman; 'if we continue to disagree, there will have been no use in our sending for M. Sorel.'

'We know that Monsieur is full of ideas,' said the Duke with an air of vexation and a glance at the interrupter, one of Napoleon's Generals. Julien saw that this was an allusion to something personal and highly offensive. Everyone smiled; the turncoat General seemed beside himself with rage.

'There is no longer a Pitt,' the speaker went on, with the discouraged air of a man who despairs of making his hearers listen to reason. 'Were there a fresh Pitt in England, one does not hoodwink a nation twice by the same means. . . .'

431

'That is why a conquering General, a Bonaparte is impossible now in France,' cried the military interrupter.

On this occasion, neither the chairman nor the Duke dared shew annoyance, though Julien thought he could read in their eyes that they were tempted to do so. They lowered their eyes, and the Duke contented himself with a sigh loud enough to be audible to them all.

But the speaker had lost his temper.

'You are in a hurry for me to conclude,' he said with heat, entirely discarding that smiling politeness and measured speech which Julien had assumed to be the natural expression of his character: 'you are in a hurry for me to conclude; you give me no credit for the efforts that I am making not to offend the ears of anyone present, however long they may be. Very well, Gentlemen, I shall be brief.

'And I shall say to you in the plainest of words: England has not a halfpenny left for the service of the good cause. Were Pitt to return in person, with all his genius he would not succeed in hoodwinking the small landowners of England, for they know that the brief campaign of Waterloo cost them, by itself, one thousand million francs. Since you wish for plain speaking,' the speaker added, growing more and more animated, 'I shall say to you: *Help yourselves*, for England has not a guinea for your assistance, and if England does not pay, Austria, Russia, Prussia, which have only courage and no money, cannot support more than one campaign or two against France.

'You may hope that the young soldiers collected by Jacobinism will be defeated in the first campaign, in the second perhaps; but in the third (though I pass for a revolutionary in your prejudiced eyes), in the third you will have the soldiers of 1794, who were no longer the recruited peasants of 1792.'

Here the interruption broke out in three or four places at once.

'Sir,' said the chairman to Julien, 'go and make a fair copy in the next room of the first part of the report which you have taken down.' Julien left the room with considerable regret. The speaker had referred to probabilities which formed the subject of his habitual meditations.

432

'They are afraid of my laughing at them,' he thought. When he was recalled, M. de La Mole was saying, with an earnestness, which, to Julien, who knew him, seemed highly amusing:

'Yes, Gentlemen, it is above all of this unhappy race that one can say: "Shall it be a god, a table or a bowl?"

' "*It shall be a god!*" cries the poet. It is to you, Gentlemen, that this saying, so noble and so profound, seems to apply. Act for yourselves, and our noble France will reappear more or less as our ancestors made her and as our own eyes beheld her before the death of Louis XVI.

'England, her noble Lords at least, curses as heartily as we ignoble Jacobinism: without English gold, Austria, Russia, Prussia cannot fight more than two or three battles. Will that suffice to bring about a glorious occupation, like that which M. de Richelieu squandered so stupidly in 1817? I do not think so.'

At this point an interruption occurred, but it was silenced by a general murmur. It arose once more from the former Imperial General, who desired the Blue Riband, and was anxious to appear among the compilers of the secret note.

'I do not think so,' M. de La Mole resumed after the disturbance. He dwelt upon the word 'I' with an insolence which charmed Julien. 'That is well played,' he said to himself as he made his pen fly almost as fast as the Marquis's utterance. With a well-placed word, M. de La Mole annihilated the twenty campaigns of the turncoat.

'It is not to foreigners alone,' the Marquis continued in the most measured tone, 'that we can remain indebted for a fresh military occupation. That youthful band who contribute incendiary articles to the *Globe* will provide you with three or four thousand young captains, among whom may be found a Kléber, a Hoche, a Jourdan, a Pichegru, but less well-intentioned.'

'We did wrong in not crowning him with glory,' said the chairman, 'we ought to have made him immortal.'

'There must, in short, be in France two parties,' went on M. de La Mole, 'but two parties, not in name only, two parties clearly defined, sharply divided. Let us be certain whom

433

we have to crush. On one side the journalists, the electors, public opinion; in a word, youth and all those who admire it. While it is dazed by the sound of its own idle words, we, we have the certain advantage of handling the budget.'

Here came a fresh interruption.

'You, Sir,' M. de La Mole said to the interrupter with a supercilious ease that was quite admirable, 'you do not handle, since the word appears to shock you, you devour forty thousand francs borne on the state budget and eighty thousand which you receive from the Civil List.

'Very well, Sir, since you force me to it, I take you boldly as an example. Like your noble ancestors who followed Saint Louis to the Crusade, you ought, for those hundred and twenty thousand francs, to let us see at least a regiment, a company, shall I say a half-company, were it composed only of fifty men ready to fight, and devoted to the good cause, alive or dead. You have only footmen who, in the event of a revolt, would frighten nobody but yourself.

'The Throne, the Altar, the Nobility may perish any day, Gentlemen, so long as you have not created in each Department a force of five hundred *devoted* men; devoted, I mean, not only with all the gallantry of France but with the constancy of Spain.

'One half of this troop will have to be composed of our sons, our nephews, in short of true gentlemen. Each of them will have by his side, not a glib little cockney ready to hoist the striped cockade if another 1815 should arrive, but an honest peasant, simple and open like Cathelineau; our gentleman will have trained him, it should be his foster-brother, if possible. Let each of us sacrifice the fifth part of his income to form this little devoted troop of five hundred men to a Department. Then you may count upon a foreign occupation. Never will the foreign soldier cross our borders as far as Dijon even, unless he is certain of finding five hundred friendly soldiers in each Department.

'The foreign Kings will listen to you only when you can inform them that there are twenty thousand gentlemen ready to take up arms to open to them the gates of France. This service is arduous, you will say. Gentlemen, it is the price of our heads. Between the liberty of the press and our existence as gentlemen, there is war to the knife. Become manufacturers, peasants, or take up your guns. Be timid if you like, but do not be stupid. Open your eyes.

'*Form your battalions*, I say to you, in the words of the Jacobin song; then there will appear some noble Gustavus-Adolphus, who, moved by the imminent peril to the monarchical principle will come flying three hundred leagues beyond his borders, and do for you what Gustavus did for the Protestant princes. Do you propose to go on talking without acting? In fifty years there will be nothing in Europe but Presidents of Republics, not one King left. And with those four letters K—I—N—G, go the priests and the gentlemen. I can see nothing but *candidates* paying court to draggletailed *majorities*.

'It is no use your saying that France has not at this moment a trustworthy General, known and loved by all, that the army is organised only in the interests of Throne and Altar, that all the old soldiers have been discharged from it, whereas each of the Prussian and Austrian regiments includes fifty non-commissioned officers who have been under fire.

'Two hundred thousand young men of the middle class are in love with the idea of war. . . .'

'Enough unpleasant truths,' came in a tone of importance from a grave personage, apparently high on the ladder of ecclesiastical preferment, for M. de La Mole smiled pleasantly instead of shewing annoyance, which was highly significant to Julien.

'Enough unpleasant truths; Gentlemen, to sum up: the man with whom it was a question of amputating his gangrened leg would be ill-advised to say to his surgeon: this diseased leg is quite sound. Pardon me the simile, Gentlemen, the noble Duke of ——[1] is our surgeon.'

'There is the great secret out at last,' thought Julien; 'it is to the —— that I shall be posting to-night.'

1 The Duke of Wellington. C. K. S. M.

CHAPTER FIFTY-THREE
THE CLERGY, THEIR FORESTS, LIBERTY

The first law for every creature is that of self-preservation, of life. You sow hemlock, and expect to see the corn ripen!

MACHIAVELLI.

T HE grave personage continued; one could see that he knew; he set forth with a gentle and moderate eloquence, which vastly delighted Julien, the following great truths:

(1) England has not a guinea at our service; economy and Hume are the fashion there. Even the *Saints* will not give us any money, and Mr. Brougham will laugh at us.

(2) Impossible to obtain more than two campaigns from the Monarchs of Europe, without English gold; and two campaigns will not be enough against the middle classes.

(3) Necessity of forming an armed party in France, otherwise the monarchical principle in the rest of Europe will not risk even those two campaigns.

'The fourth point which I venture to suggest to you as self-evident is this:

'*The impossibility of forming an armed party in France without the Clergy.* I say it to you boldly, because I am going to prove it to you, Gentlemen. We must give the Clergy everything:

'(1) Because, occupying themselves with their own business night and day, and guided by men of high capacity established out of harm's way three hundred leagues from your frontiers....'

436

'Ah! Rome! Rome!' exclaimed the master of the house. . . .

'Yes, Sir, *Rome*!' the Cardinal answered proudly. 'Whatever be the more or less ingenious pleasantries which were in fashion when you were young, I will proclaim boldly, in 1830, that the Clergy, guided by Rome, speak and speak alone to the lower orders.

'Fifty thousand priests repeat the same words on the day indicated by their leaders, and the people, who, after all, furnish the soldiers, will be more stirred by the voice of their priests than by all the little earthworms in the world. . . .' (This personal allusion gave rise to murmurs.)

'The Clergy have an intellect superior to yours,' the Cardinal went on, raising his voice; 'all the steps that you have taken towards this essential point, *having an armed party here in France*, have been taken by us.' Here facts were cited. Who had sent eighty thousand muskets to the Vendée? and so forth.

'So long as the Clergy are deprived of their forests, they have no tenure. At the first threat of war, the Minister of Finance writes to his agents that there is no more money except for the parish priests. At heart, France is not religious, and loves war. Whoever it be that gives her war, he will be doubly popular, for to make war is to starve the Jesuits, in vulgar parlance; to make war is to deliver those monsters of pride, the French people, from the menace of foreign intervention.'

The Cardinal had a favourable hearing. . . . 'It was essential,' he said, 'that M. de Nerval should leave the Ministry, his name caused needless irritation.'

Upon this, they all rose to their feet and began speaking at once. 'They will be sending me out of the room again,' thought Julien; but the prudent chairman himself had forgotten Julien's presence and indeed his existence.

Every eye turned to a man whom Julien recognised. It was M. de Nerval, the First Minister, whom he had seen at the Duc de Retz's ball.

The disorder was at its height, as the newspapers say, when reporting the sittings of the Chamber. After fully a quarter of an hour, silence began to be restored.

Then M. de Nerval rose and, adopting the tone of an Apostle:

'I shall not for one moment pretend,' he said, in an unnatural voice, 'that I am not attached to office.

'It has been proved to me, Gentlemen, that my name doubles the strength of the Jacobins by turning against us a number of moderate men. I should willingly resign, therefore; but the ways of the Lord are visible to but a small number; but,' he went on, looking fixedly at the Cardinal, 'I have a mission; heaven has said to me: "You shall lay down your head on the scaffold, or you shall re-establish the Monarchy in France, and reduce the Chambers to what Parliament was under Louis XV," and that, Gentlemen, *I will do.*'

He ceased, sat down, and a great silence fell.

'There is a good actor,' thought Julien. He made the mistake, then as always, of crediting people with too much cleverness. Animated by the debates of so lively an evening, and above all by the sincerity of the discussion, at that moment M. de Nerval believed in his mission. With his great courage the man did not combine any sense.

Midnight struck during the silence that followed the fine peroration '*that I will do.*' Julien felt that there was something imposing and funereal in the sound of the clock. He was deeply moved.

The discussion soon began again with increasing energy and above all with an incredible simplicity. 'These men will have me poisoned,' thought Julien, at certain points. 'How can they say such things before a plebeian?'

Two o'clock struck while they were still talking. The master of the house had long been asleep; M. de La Mole was obliged to ring to have fresh candles brought in. M. de Nerval, the Minister, had left at a quarter to two, not without having frequently studied Julien's face in a mirror which hung beside him. His departure had seemed to create an atmosphere of relief.

While the candles were being changed: 'Heaven knows what that fellow is going to say to the King!' the man with the waistcoats murmured to his neighbour. 'He can make us look very foolish and spoil our future.

'You must admit that he shews a very rare presumption, indeed effrontery, in appearing here. He used to come here before he took office; but a portfolio alters everything, swallows up all a man's private interests, he ought to have felt that.'

As soon as the Minister was gone, Bonaparte's General had shut his eyes. He now spoke of his health, his wounds, looked at his watch, and left.

'I would bet,' said the man with the waistcoats, 'that the General is running after the Minister; he is going to make his excuses for being found here, and pretend that he is our leader.'

When the servants, who were half asleep, had finished changing the candles:

'Let us now begin to deliberate, Gentlemen,' said the chairman, 'and no longer attempt to persuade one another. Let us consider the tenor of the note that in forty-eight hours will be before the eyes of our friends abroad. There has been reference to Ministers. We can say, now that M. de Nerval has left us, what do we care for Ministers? We shall control them.'

The Cardinal shewed his approval by a delicate smile.

'Nothing easier, it seems to me, than to sum up our position,' said the young Bishop of Agde with the concentrated and restrained fire of the most exalted fanaticism. Hitherto he had remained silent; his eye, which Julien had watched, at first mild and calm, had grown fiery after the first hour's discussion. Now his heart overflowed like lava from Vesuvius.

'From 1806 to 1814, England made only one mistake,' he said, 'which was her not dealing directly and personally with Napoleon. As soon as that man had created Dukes and Chamberlains, as soon as he had restored the Throne, the mission that God had entrusted to him was at an end; he was ripe only for destruction. The Holy Scriptures teach us in more than one passage the way to make an end of tyrants.' (Here followed several Latin quotations.)

439

'To-day, Gentlemen, it is not a man that we must destroy; it is Paris. The whole of France copies Paris. What is the use of arming your five hundred men in each Department? A hazardous enterprise and one that will never end. What is the use of involving France in a matter which is peculiar to Paris? Paris alone, with her newspapers and her drawing-rooms, has done the harm; let the modern Babylon perish.

'Between the Altar and Paris, there must be a fight to the finish. This catastrophe is indeed to the mundane advantage of the Throne. Why did not Paris dare to breathe under Bonaparte? Ask the artillery of Saint-Roch.'

*   *   *

It was not until three o'clock in the morning that Julien left the house with M. de La Mole.

The Marquis was depressed and tired. For the first time, in speaking to Julien, he used a tone of supplication. He asked him to promise never to disclose the excesses of zeal, such was his expression, which he had chanced to witness. 'Do not mention it to our friend abroad, unless he deliberately insists on knowing the nature of our young hotheads. What does it matter to them if the State be overthrown? They will be Cardinals, and will take refuge in Rome. We, in our country seats, shall be massacred by the peasants.'

The secret note which the Marquis drafted from the long report of six and twenty pages, written by Julien, was not ready until a quarter to five.

'I am dead tired,' said the Marquis, 'and so much can be seen from this note, which is lacking in precision towards the end; I am more dissatisfied with it than with anything I ever did in my life. Now, my friend,' he went on, 'go and lie down for a few hours, and for fear of your being abducted, I am going to lock you into your room.'

Next day, the Marquis took Julien to a lonely mansion, at some distance from Paris. They found there a curious company who, Julien decided, were priests. He was given a pass-port which bore a false name, but did at last indicate the

440

true goal of his journey, of which he had always feigned ignorance. He started off by himself in a calash.

The Marquis had no misgivings as to his memory, Julien had repeated the text of the secret note to him several times; but he was greatly afraid of his being intercepted.

'Remember, whatever you do, to look like a fop who is travelling to kill time,' was his friendly warning, as Julien was leaving the room. 'There may perhaps have been several false brethren in our assembly last night.'

The journey was rapid and very tedious. Julien was barely out of the Marquis's sight before he had forgotten both the secret note and his mission, and was thinking of nothing but Mathilde's scorn.

In a village, some leagues beyond Metz, the postmaster came to inform him that there were no fresh horses. It was ten o'clock at night; Julien, greatly annoyed, ordered supper. He strolled up and down outside the door and passed unperceived into the stable-yard. He saw no horses there.

'The man had a singular expression all the same,' he said to himself; 'his coarse eye was scrutinising me.'

We can see that he was beginning not to believe literally everything that he was told. He thought of making his escape after supper, and in the meanwhile, in order to learn something of the lie of the land, left his room to go and warm himself by the kitchen fire. What was his joy upon finding there Signor Geronimo, the famous singer!

Comfortably ensconced in an armchair which he had made them push up close to the fire, the Neapolitan was groaning aloud and talking more, by himself, than the score of German peasants who were gathered round him openmouthed.

'These people are ruining me,' he cried to Julien, 'I have promised to sing to-morrow at Mayence. Seven Sovereign Princes have assembled there to hear me. But let us take the air,' he added, in a significant tone.

When he had gone a hundred yards along the road, and was well out of earshot:

'Do you know what is happening?' he said to Julien; 'this

postmaster is a rogue. As I was strolling about, I gave a franc to a little ragamuffin who told me everything. There are more than a dozen horses in a stable at the other end of the village. They mean to delay some courier.'

'Indeed?' said Julien, with an innocent air.

It was not enough to have discovered the fraud, they must get on: this was what Geronimo and his friend could not manage to do. 'We must wait for the daylight,' the singer said finally, 'they are suspicious of us. To-morrow morning we shall order a good breakfast; while they are preparing it we go out for a stroll, we escape, hire fresh horses, and reach the next post.'

'And your luggage?' said Julien, who thought that perhaps Geronimo himself might have been sent to intercept him. It was time to sup and retire to bed. Julien was still in his first sleep, when he was awakened with a start by the sound of two people talking in his room, apparently quite unconcerned.

He recognised the postmaster, armed with a dark lantern. Its light was concentrated upon the carriage-trunk, which Julien had had carried up to his room. With the postmaster was another man who was calmly going through the open trunk. Julien could make out only the sleeves of his coat, which were black and close-fitting.

'It is a cassock,' he said to himself, and quietly seized the pocket pistols which he had placed under his pillow.

'You need not be afraid of his waking, Monsieur le Curé,' said the postmaster. 'The wine we gave them was some of what you prepared yourself.'

'I can find no trace of papers,' replied the curé. 'Plenty of linen, oils, pomades and fripperies; he is a young man of the world, occupied with his own pleasures. The envoy will surely be the other, who pretends to speak with an Italian accent.'

The men came up to Julien to search the pockets of his travelling coat. He was strongly tempted to kill them as robbers. This could involve no dangerous consequences. He longed to do it.... 'I should be a mere fool,' he said to himself, 'I should be endangering my mission.' After searching his coat, 'this is no diplomat,' said the priest: he moved away, and wisely.

'If he touches me in my bed, it will be the worse for him!' Julien was saying to himself; 'he may quite well come and stab me, and that I will not allow.'

The curé turned his head, Julien half-opened his eyes; what was his astonishment! It was the Abbé Castanède! And indeed, although the two men had tried to lower their voices, he had felt, from the first, that he recognised the sound of one of them. He was seized with a passionate desire to rid the world of one of its vilest scoundrels....

'But my mission!' he reminded himself.

The priest and his acolyte left the room. A quarter of an hour later, Julien pretended to awake. He called for help and roused the whole house.

'I have been poisoned,' he cried, 'I am in horrible agony!' He wanted a pretext for going to Geronimo's rescue. He found him half asphyxiated by the laudanum that had been in his wine.

Julien, fearing some pleasantry of this kind, had supped upon chocolate which he had brought with him from Paris. He could not succeed in arousing Geronimo sufficiently to make him agree to leave the place.

'Though you offered me the whole Kingdom of Naples,' said the singer, 'I would not forego the pleasure of sleep at this moment.'

'But the seven Sovereign Princes!'

'They can wait.'

Julien set off alone and arrived without further incident at the abode of the eminent personage. He spent a whole morning in vainly soliciting an audience. Fortunately, about four o'clock, the Duke decided to take the air. Julien saw him leave the house on foot, and had no hesitation in going up to him and begging for alms. When within a few feet of the eminent personage, he drew out the Marquis de La Mole's watch, and flourished it ostentatiously. 'Follow me at distance,' said the other, without looking at him.

After walking for a quarter of a league, the Duke turned

abruptly in to a little *Kaffeehaus*. It was in a bedroom of this humblest form of inn that Julien had the honour of reciting his four pages to the Duke. When he had finished: 'Begin again, and go more slowly,' he was told.

The Prince took down notes. 'Go on foot to the next post. Leave your luggage and your calash here. Make your way to Strasbourg as best you can, and on the twenty-second of the month'—it was now the tenth—'be in this coffee-house here at half past twelve. Do not leave here for half an hour. Silence!'

Such were the only words that Julien heard said. They sufficed to fill him with the deepest admiration. 'It is thus,' he thought, 'that one handles affairs; what would this great statesman say if he had heard those hotheaded chatterboxes three days ago?'

Julien took two days to reach Strasbourg, he felt that there was nothing for him to do there. He made a wide circuit. 'If that devil, the Abbé Castanède has recognised me, he is not the man to be easily shaken off.... And what a joy to him to make a fool of me, and to spoil my mission!'

The Abbé Castanède, Chief of Police to the *Congregation* along the whole of the Northern frontier, had mercifully not recognised him. And the Jesuits of Strasbourg, albeit most zealous, never thought of keeping an eye on Julien, who, with his Cross and his blue greatcoat, had the air of a young soldier greatly concerned with his personal appearance.

CHAPTER FIFTY-FOUR

STRASBOURG

Fascination! Thou sharest with love all its energy, all
its capacity for suffering. Its enchanting pleasures, its
sweet delights are alone beyond thy sphere. I could not
say, as I saw her asleep: She is all mine with her angelic
beauty and her sweet frailties! Behold her delivered
into my power, as heaven made her in its compassion
to enchant a man's heart.   SCHILLER.

O BLIGED to spend a week in Strasbourg, Julien sought
to distract himself with thoughts of martial glory
and of devotion to his country. Was he in love, then?
He could not say, only he found in his bruised heart
Mathilde the absolute mistress of his happiness as of his
imagination. He required all his natural energy to keep himself from sinking into despair. To think of anything that bore
no relation to Mademoiselle de La Mole was beyond his
power. Ambition, the mere triumphs of vanity, had distracted
him in the past from the sentiments that Madame de Rênal
inspired in him. Mathilde had absorbed all; he found her
everywhere in his future.

On every hand, in this future, Julien foresaw failure. This
creature whom we saw at Verrières so filled with presumption, so arrogant, had fallen into an absurd extreme of
modesty.

Three days earlier he would have killed the Abbé Castanède with pleasure, and at Strasbourg, had a boy picked a
quarrel with him, he would have offered the boy an apology.

In thinking over the adversaries, the enemies whom he had encountered in the course of his life, he found that invariably he, Julien, had been in the wrong.

The fact was that he had now an implacable enemy in that powerful imagination, which before had been constantly employed in painting such brilliant successes for him in the future.

The absolute solitude of a traveller's existence strengthened the power of this dark imagination. What a treasure would a friend have been! 'But,' Julien asked himself, 'is there a heart in the world that beats for me? And if I had a friend, does not honour impose on me an eternal silence?'

He took a horse and rode sadly about the neighbourhood of Kehl; it is a village on the bank of the Rhine, immortalised by Desaix and Gouvion Saint-Cyr. A German peasant pointed out to him the little streams, the roads, the islands in the Rhine which the valour of those great Generals has made famous. Julien, holding the reins in his left hand, was carrying spread out in his right the superb map which illustrates the *Memoirs* of Marshal Saint-Cyr. A joyful exclamation made him raise his head.

It was Prince Korasoff, his London friend, who had expounded to him some months earlier the first principles of the higher fatuity. Faithful to this great art, Korasoff, who had arrived in Strasbourg the day before, had been an hour at Kehl, and had never in his life read a line about the siege of 1796, began to explain it all to Julien. The German peasant gazed at him in astonishment; for he knew enough French to make out the enormous blunders into which the Prince fell. Julien's thoughts were a thousand leagues away from the peasant's, he was looking with amazement at this handsome young man, and admiring his grace in the saddle.

'A happy nature!' he said to himself. 'How well his breeches fit him, how elegantly his hair is cut! Alas, if I had been like that, perhaps after loving me for three days she would not have taken a dislike to me.'

When the Prince had come to an end of his version of the

siege of Kehl: 'You look like a Trappist,' he said to Julien, 'you are infringing the principle of gravity I taught you in London. A melancholy air can never be the right thing; what you want is a bored air. If you are melancholy, it must be because you want something, there is something in which you have not succeeded.

'*It is shewing your inferiority.* If you are bored, on the other hand, it is the person who has tried in vain to please you who is inferior. Realise, my dear fellow, what a grave mistake you are making.'

Julien flung a crown to the peasant who stood listening to them, open-mouthed.

'Good,' said the Prince, 'that is graceful, a noble disdain! Very good!' And he put his horse into a gallop. Julien followed him, filled with a stupefied admiration.

'Ah! If I had been like that, she would not have preferred Croisenois to me!' The more his reason was shocked by the absurdities of the Prince, the more he despised himself for not admiring them, and deemed himself unfortunate in not sharing them. Self-contempt can be carried no farther.

The Prince found him decidedly melancholy: 'Ah, my dear fellow,' he said to him, as they rode into Strasbourg, 'have you lost all your money, or can you be in love with some little actress?'

The Russians imitate French ways, but always at a distance of fifty years. They have now reached the days of Louis XV.

These jests, at the expense of love, filled Julien's eyes with tears: 'Why should not I consult so friendly a man?' he asked himself suddenly.

'Well, yes, my friend,' he said to the Prince, 'you find me in Strasbourg, madly in love, indeed crossed in love. A charming woman, who lives in a neighbouring town, has abandoned me after three days of passion, and the change is killing me.'

He described to the Prince, under an assumed name, the actions and character of Mathilde.

'Do not go on,' said Korasoff: 'to give you confidence in your physician, I am going to cut short your confidences.

This young woman's husband possesses an enormous fortune, or, what is more likely, she herself belongs to the highest nobility of the place. She must be proud of something.'

Julien nodded his head, he had no longer the heart to speak.

'Very good,' said the Prince, 'here are three medicines, all rather bitter, which you are going to take without delay:

'First: You must every day see Madame ——— what do you call her?'

'Madame de Dubois.'

'What a name!' said the Prince, with a shout of laughter; 'but forgive me, to you it is sublime. It is essential that you see Madame de Dubois every day; above all do not appear to her cold and cross; remember the great principle of your age: be the opposite to what people expect of you. Shew yourself precisely as you were a week before you were honoured with her favours.'

'Ah! I was calm then,' cried Julien, in desperation, 'I thought that I pitied her....'

'The moth singes its wings in the flame of the candle,' the Prince continued, 'a metaphor as old as the world.

'First of all: you will see her every day.

'Secondly: you will pay court to a woman of her acquaintance, but without any appearance of passion, you understand? I do not conceal from you, yours is a difficult part to play: you have to act, and if she discovers that you are acting, you are doomed.'

'She is so clever, and I am not! I am doomed,' said Julien sadly.

'No, you are only more in love than I thought. Madame de Dubois is profoundly taken up with herself, like all women who have received from heaven either too high a rank or too much money. She looks at herself instead of looking at you, and so does not know you. During the two or three amorous impulses to which she has yielded in your favour, by a great effort of imagination, she beheld in you the hero of her dreams and not yourself as you really are....

'But what the devil, these are the elements, my dear Sorel, are you still a schoolboy? . . .

'Egad! Come into this shop; look at that charming black cravat; you would say it was made by John Anderson, of Burlington Street; do me the pleasure of buying it, and of throwing right away that dreadful black rope which you have round your neck.

'And now,' the Prince went on as they left the shop of the first hosier in Strasbourg, 'who are the friends of Madame de Dubois? Good God, what a name! Do not be angry, my dear Sorel, I cannot help it. . . . To whom will you pay court?'

'To a prude of prudes, the daughter of an enormously rich stocking-merchant. She has the loveliest eyes in the world, which please me vastly; she certainly occupies the first place in the district; but amid all her grandeur she blushes and loses her head entirely if anyone refers to trade and a shop. And unfortunately for her, her father was one of the best known tradesmen in Strasbourg.'

'So that if one mentions *industry*,' said the Prince, with a laugh, 'you may be sure that your fair one is thinking of herself and not of you. The weakness is divine and most useful, it will prevent you from ever doing anything foolish in her fair eyes. Your success is assured.'

Julien was thinking of Madame la Maréchale de Fervaques, who often came to the Hôtel de La Mole. She was a beautiful foreigner who had married the Marshal a year before his death. Her whole life seemed to have no other object than to make people forget that she was the daughter of an *industrial*, and in order to count for something in Paris she had set herself at the head of the forces of virtue.

Julien admired the Prince sincerely; what would he not have given to have his absurd affectations! The conversation between the friends was endless; Korasoff was in raptures: never had a Frenchman given him so long a hearing. 'And so I have succeeded at last,' the Prince said to himself with delight, 'in making my voice heard when I give lessons to my masters!

'It is quite understood,' he repeated to Julien for the tenth

449

time, 'not a vestige of passion when you are talking to the young beauty, the Strasbourg stocking-merchant's daughter, in the presence of Madame de Dubois. On the contrary, burning passion when you write. Reading a well written love letter is a prude's supreme pleasure; it is a momentary relaxation. She is not acting a part, she dares to listen to her heart; and so, two letters daily.'

'Never, never!' said Julien, losing courage; 'I would let myself he brayed in a mortar sooner than compose three sentences; I am a corpse, my dear fellow, expect nothing more of me. Leave me to die by the roadside.'

'And who said anything about composing phrases? I have in my hold-all six volumes of love letters in manuscript. There are specimens for every kind of woman, I have a set for the most rigid virtue. Didn't Kalisky make love on Richmond Terrace, you know, a few miles out of London, to the prettiest Quakeress in the whole of England?'

Julien was less wretched when he parted from his friend at two o'clock in the morning.

Next day the Prince sent for a copyist, and two days later Julien had fifty-three love letters carefully numbered, intended to cope with the most sublime and melancholy virtue.

'There would be fifty-four,' said the Prince, 'only Kalisky was shewn the door; but what does it matter to you, being ill-treated by the stocking-merchant's daughter, since you are seeking to influence only the heart of Madame de Dubois?'

Every day they went out riding: the Prince was madly taken with Julien. Not knowing what token to give him of his sudden affection, he ended by offering him the hand of one of his cousins, a wealthy heiress in Moscow; 'and once you are married,' he explained, 'my influence and the Cross you are wearing will make you a Colonel in two years.'

'But this Cross was not given me by Napoleon, quite the reverse.'

'What does that matter,' said the Prince, 'didn't he invent it? It is still the first decoration by far in Europe.'

Julien was on the point of accepting; but duty recalled him to the eminent personage; on parting from Korasoff, he

450

promised to write. He received the reply to the secret note that he had brought, and hastened to Paris; but he had barely been by himself for two days on end, before the thought of leaving France and Mathilde seemed to him a punishment worse than death itself. 'I shall not wed the millions that Korasoff offers me,' he told himself, 'but I shall follow his advice.

'After all, the art of seduction is his business; he has thought of nothing else for more than fifteen years, for he is now thirty. One cannot say that he is lacking in intelligence; he is shrewd and cautious; enthusiasm, poetry are impossible in such a nature: he is calculating; all the more reason why he should not be mistaken.

'There is no help for it, I am going to pay court to Madame de Fervaques.

'She will bore me a little, perhaps. but I shall gaze into those lovely eyes which are so like the eyes that loved me best in the world.

'She is foreign; that is a fresh character to be studied.

'I am mad, I am going under, I must follow the advice of a friend, and pay no heed to myself.'

CHAPTER FIFTY-FIVE

THE OFFICE OF VIRTUE

But if I take this pleasure with so much prudence
and circumspection, it ceases to be a pleasure for me.

LOPE DE VEGA.

IMMEDIATELY on his return to Paris, and on leaving the
study of the Marquis de La Mole, who appeared greatly
disconcerted by the messages that were conveyed to him,
our hero hastened to find Conte Altamira. With the distinction of being under sentence of death, this handsome foreigner combined abundant gravity and had the good fortune
to be devout; these two merits and, more than all, the exalted
birth of the Count were entirely to the taste of Madame de
Fervaques, who saw much of him.

Julien confessed to him gravely that he was deeply in love
with her.

'She represents the purest and loftiest virtue,' replied Altamira, 'only it is a trifle Jesuitical and emphatic. There are
days on which I understand every word that she uses, but I
do not understand the sentence as a whole. She often makes
me think that I do not know French as well as people say.
This acquaintance will make you talked about; it will give
you a position in society. But let us go and see Bustos,' said
Conte Altamira, who had an orderly mind; 'he has made
love to Madame la Maréchale.'

Don Diego Bustos made them explain the matter to him
in detail, without saying a word, like a barrister in chambers. He had a plump, monkish face, with black moustaches,

452

and an unparalleled gravity; in other respects, a good carbonaro.

'I understand,' he said at length to Julien. 'Has the Maréchale de Fervaques had lovers, or has she not? Have you, therefore, any hope of success? That is the question. It is as much as to say that, for my own part, I have failed. Now that I am no longer aggrieved, I put it to myself in this way: often she is out of temper, and, as I shall shortly prove to you, she is nothing if not vindictive.

'I do not find in her that choleric temperament which is a mark of genius and covers every action with a sort of glaze of passion. It is, on the contrary, to her calm and phlegmatic Dutch manner that she owes her rare beauty and the freshness of her complexion.'

Julien was growing impatient with the deliberateness and imperturbable phlegm of the Spaniard; now and again, in spite of himself, he gave vent to a monosyllabic comment.

'Will you listen to me?' Don Diego Bustos inquired gravely.

'Pardon the *furia francese*; I am all ears,' said Julien.

'Well, then, the Maréchale de Fervaques is much given to hatred; she is pitiless in her pursuit of people she has never seen, lawyers, poor devils of literary men who have written songs like Collé, you know?

> 'J'ai la marotte
> D'aimer Marote,' etc.

And Julien was obliged to listen to the quotation to the end. The Spaniard greatly enjoyed singing in French.

That divine song was never listened to with greater impatience. When he had finished: 'The Maréchale,' said Don Diego Bustos, 'has ruined the author of the song:

> 'Un jour l'amant au cabaret....'

Julien was in an agony lest he should wish to sing it. He contented himself with analysing it. It was, as a matter of fact, impious and hardly decent.

'When the Maréchale flew into a passion with that song,'

said Don Diego, 'I pointed out to her that a woman of her rank ought not to read all the stupid things that are published. Whatever progress piety and gravity may make, there will always be in France a literature of the tavern. When Madame de Fervaques had the author, a poor devil on half pay, deprived of a post worth eighteen hundred francs: "Take care," said I to her, "you have attacked this rhymester with your weapons, he may reply to you with his rhymes: he will make a song about virtue. The gilded saloons will be on your side; the people who like to laugh will repeat his epigrams." Do you know, Sir, what answer the Maréchale made me? "In the Lord's service all Paris would see me tread the path of martyrdom; it would be a novel spectacle in France. The people would learn to respect the quality. It would be the happiest day of my life." Never were her eyes more brilliant.'

'And she has superb eyes,' exclaimed Julien.

'I see that you are in love.... Very well, then,' Don Diego Bustos went on gravely, 'she has not the choleric constitution that impels one to vengeance. If she enjoys injuring people, nevertheless, it is because she is unhappy, I suspect *inward suffering*. May she not be a prude who has grown weary of her calling?'

The Spaniard gazed at him in silence for fully a minute.

'That is the whole question,' he went on gravely, 'and it is from this that you may derive some hope. I gave it much thought during the two years in which I professed myself her most humble servant. Your whole future, you, Sir, who are in love, hangs on this great problem. Is she a prude, weary of her calling, and malicious because she is miserable?'

'Or rather,' said Altamira, emerging at last from his profound silence, 'can it be what I have said to you twenty times? Simply and solely French vanity; it is the memory of her father, the famous cloth merchant, that causes the unhappiness of a character naturally morose and dry. There could be only one happiness for her, that of living in Toledo, and being tormented by a confessor, who every day would shew her hell gaping for her.'

As Julien rose to leave: 'Altamira tells me that you are one of us,' Don Diego said to him, graver than ever. 'One day you will help us to reconquer our freedom, and so I wish to help you in this little diversion. It is as well that you should be acquainted with the Maréchale's style; here are four letters in her hand.'

'I shall have them copied,' cried Julien, 'and return them to you.'

'And no one shall ever learn from you a single word of what we have been saying?'

'Never, upon my honour!' cried Julien.

'Then may heaven help you!' the Spaniard concluded; and he accompanied Julien and Altamira in silence to the head of the stair.

This scene cheered our hero somewhat; he almost smiled. 'And here is the devout Altamira,' he said to himself, 'helping me in an adulterous enterprise.'

Throughout the whole of the grave conversation of Don Diego Bustos, Julien had been attentive to the stroke of the hours on the clock of the Hôtel d'Aligre.

The dinner hour was approaching, he was to see Mathilde again! He went home, and dressed himself with great care.

'My first blunder,' he said to himself, as he was going downstairs; 'I must carry out the Prince's orders to the letter.'

He returned to his room, and put on a travelling costume of the utmost simplicity.

'Now,' he thought, 'I must consider how I am to look at her.' It was only half-past five, and dinner was at six. He decided to go down to the drawing-room, which he found deserted. At the sight of the blue sofa, he fell upon his knees and kissed the spot on which Mathilde rested her arm, his tears flowed, his cheeks began to burn. 'I must get rid of this absurd sensibility,' he said to himself angrily; 'it will betray me.' He took up a newspaper to keep himself in countenance, and strolled three or four times from the drawing-room to the garden.

It was only in fear and trembling and safely concealed behind a big oak tree that he ventured to raise his eyes to the window of Mademoiselle de La Mole's room. It was fast shut; he nearly fell to the ground, and stood for a long time leaning against the oak; then, with a tottering step, he went to look at the gardener's ladder.

The link of the chain, forced open by him in circumstances, alas, so different, had not been mended. Carried away by a mad impulse, Julien pressed it to his lips.

After a long course of wandering between drawing-room and garden, he found himself horribly tired; this was an initial success which pleased him greatly. 'My eyes will be dull and will not betray me!' Gradually, the guests arrived in the drawing-room; the door never opened without plunging Julien in mortal dread.

They sat down to table. At length Mademoiselle de La Mole appeared, still faithful to her principle of keeping the others waiting. She blushed a deep red on seeing Julien; she had not been told of his arrival. Following Prince Korasoff's advice, Julien looked at her hands; they were trembling. Disquieted himself, beyond all expression, by this discovery, he was thankful to appear to be merely tired.

M. de La Mole sang his praises. The Marquise addressed him shortly afterwards, and expressed concern at his appearance of fatigue. Julien kept on saying to himself: 'I must not look at Mademoiselle de La Mole too much, but I ought not either to avoid her eye. I must appear to be what I really was a week before my disaster. . . .' He had occasion to be satisfied with his success, and remained in the drawing-room. Attentive for the first time to the lady of the house, he spared no effort to make the men of her circle talk, and to keep the conversation alive.

His politeness was rewarded: about eight o'clock, Madame la Maréchale de Fervaques was announced. Julien left the room and presently reappeared, dressed with the most scrupulous care. Madame de La Mole was vastly flattered by this mark of respect, and sought to give him a proof of her satisfaction by speaking of his travels to Madame de Fervaques. Julien took his seat beside the Maréchale, in such a way that his eyes should not be visible to Mathilde. Thus placed, and following all the rules of the art, he made Madame de Fervaques the object of the most awed admiration. It was with an outburst on this sentiment that the first of the fifty-three letters of which Prince Korasoff had made him a present began.

The Maréchale announced that she was going on to the Opéra-Bouffe. Julien hastened there; he found the Chevalier de Beauvoisis, who took him to the box of the Gentlemen of the Household, immediately beside that of Madame de Fervaques. Julien gazed at her incessantly. 'I must,' he said to himself, as he returned home, 'keep a diary of the siege; otherwise I should lose count of my attacks.' He forced himself to write down two or three pages on this boring subject, and thus succeeded (marvel of marvels!) in hardly giving a thought to Mademoiselle de La Mole.

Mathilde had almost forgotten him during his absence. 'After all, he is only a common person, she thought, 'his name will always remind me of the greatest mistake of my life. I must return in all sincerity to the recognised standards of prudence and honour; a woman has everything to lose in forgetting them.' She shewed herself ready to permit at length the conclusion of the arrangement with the Marquis de Croisenois, begun so long since. He was wild with joy; he would have been greatly astonished had anyone told him that it was resignation that lay at the root of this attitude on Mathilde's part, which was making him so proud.

All Mademoiselle de La Mole's ideas changed at the sight of Julien. 'In reality, that is my husband,' she said to herself; 'if I return in sincerity to the standards of prudence, it is obviously he that I ought to marry.'

She was prepared for importunities, for an air of misery on Julien's part; she prepared her answers: for doubtless, on rising from table, he would endeavour to say a few words to her. Far from it, he remained fixed in the drawing-room, his eyes never even turned towards the garden, heaven knows with how great an effort. 'It would be better to get our explanation over at once,' Mademoiselle de La Mole told herself; she went out by herself to the garden, Julien did not appear there. Mathilde returned and strolled past the drawing-room windows; she saw him busily engaged in describing to Madame de Fervaques the old ruined castles that crown the steep banks of the Rhine and give them so distinctive a character. He was beginning to acquit himself none too badly in the use of the sentimental and picturesque language which is called *wit* in certain drawing-rooms.

Prince Korasoff would indeed have been proud, had he been in Paris: the evening was passing exactly as he had foretold.

He would have approved of the mode of behaviour to which Julien adhered throughout the days that followed.

An intrigue among those constituting the Power behind the Throne was about to dispose of several Blue Ribands; Madame la Maréchale de Fervaques insisted that her great-uncle should be made a Knight of the Order. The Marquis de La Mole was making a similar claim for his father-in-law; they combined their efforts, and the Maréchale came almost every day to the Hôtel de La Mole. It was from her that Julien learned that the Marquis was to become a Minister: he offered the *Camarilla* a highly ingenious plan for destroying the Charter, without any fuss, in three years' time.

Julien might expect a Bishopric, if M. de La Mole entered the Ministry; but to his eyes all these important interests were as though hidden by a veil. His imagination perceived them now only vaguely, and so to speak in the distance. The fearful misery which was driving him mad made him see every interest in life in the state of his relations with Mademoiselle de La Mole. He calculated that after five or six years of patient effort, he might succeed in making her love him once again.

This coolest of heads had, as we see, sunk to a state of absolute unreason. Of all the qualities that had distinguished him in the past, there remained to him only a trace of firmness. Faithful to the letter to the plan of conduct dictated to him by Prince Korasoff, every evening he took his place as near as possible to the armchair occupied by Madame de Fervaques, but found it impossible to think of a word to say to her.

The effort that he was imposing on himself to appear

cured in the eyes of Mathilde absorbed all his spiritual strength, he remained rooted beside the Maréchale like a barely animate being; his eyes even, as in the extremity of physical suffering, had lost all their fire.

Since Madame de La Mole's attitude towards the world was never anything more than a feeble copy of the opinions of that husband who might make her a Duchess, for some days she had been lauding Julien's merits to the skies.

CHAPTER FIFTY-SIX

MORAL LOVE

There also was of course in Adeline
   That calm patrician polish in the address,
Which ne'er can pass the equinoctial line
   Of anything which nature would express;
Just as a mandarin finds nothing fine,
   At least his manner suffers not to guess
That anything he views can greatly please.
                              Don Juan, XIII, 34.

'THERE is a trace of madness in the way the whole of this family have of looking at things,' thought the Maréchale; 'they are infatuated with their little abbé, who can do nothing but sit and stare at one; it is true, his eyes are not bad looking.'

Julien, for his part, found in the Maréchale's manner an almost perfect example of that patrician calm which betokens a scrupulous politeness and still more the impossibility of any keen emotion. Any sudden outburst, a want of self-control, would have shocked Madame de Fervaques almost as much as a want of dignity towards one's inferiors. The least sign of sensibility would have been in her eyes like a sort of moral intoxication for which one ought to blush, and which was highly damaging to what a person of exalted rank owed to herself. Her great happiness was to speak of the King's latest hunt, her favourite book the *Mémoires du duc de Saint-Simon*, especially the genealogical part.

Julien knew the place in the drawing-room which, as the lights were arranged, suited the style of beauty of Madame de Fervaques. He would be there waiting for her, but took great care to turn his chair so that he should not be able to see Mathilde. Astonished by this persistence in hiding from her, one evening she left the blue sofa and came to work at a little table that stood by the Marquise's armchair. Julien could see her at quite a close range from beneath the brim of Madame de Fervaques's hat. Those eyes, which governed his destiny, frightened him at first, seen at such close range, then jerked him violently out of his habitual apathy; he talked, and talked very well.

He addressed himself to the Maréchale, but his sole object was to influence the heart of Mathilde. He grew so animated that finally Madame de Fervaques could not understand what he said.

This was so much to the good. Had it occurred to Julien to follow it up with a few expressions of German mysticism, religious fervour and Jesuitry, the Maréchale would have numbered him straightway among the superior persons called to regenerate the age.

'Since he shews such bad taste,' Mademoiselle de La Mole said to herself, 'as to talk for so long and with such fervour to Madame de Fervaques, I shall not listen to him any more.' For the rest of the evening she kept her word, albeit with difficulty.

At midnight, when she took up her mother's candlestick, to escort her to her room, Madame de La Mole stopped on the stairs to utter a perfect panegyric of Julien. This completed Mathilde's ill humour; she could not send herself to sleep. A thought came to her which soothed her: 'The things that I despise may even be great distinctions in the Maréchale's eyes.'

As for Julien, he had now taken action, he was less wretched; his eyes happened to fall on the Russia-leather portfolio in which Prince Korasoff had placed the fifty-three love letters of which he had made him a present. Julien saw a note at the foot of the first letter: 'Send No. 1 a week after the first meeting.'

'I am late!' exclaimed Julien, 'for it is ever so long now

since I first met Madame de Fervaques. He set to work at once to copy out this first love letter; it was a homily stuffed with phrases about virtue, and of a deadly dulness; Julien was fortunate in falling asleep over the second page.

Some hours later the risen sun surprised him crouching with his head on the table. One of the most painful moments of his life was that in which, every morning, as he awoke, he became conscious of his distress. This morning, he finished copying his letter almost with a laugh. 'Is it possible,' he asked himself, 'that there can ever have been a young man who could write such stuff?' He counted several sentences of nine lines. At the foot of the original he caught sight of a pencilled note.

'One delivers these letters oneself: on horseback, a black cravat, a blue greatcoat. One hands the letter to the porter with a contrite air; profound melancholy in the gaze. If one should see a lady's maid, wipe the eyes furtively. Address a few words to the maid.'

All these instructions were faithfully carried out.

'What I am doing is very bold,' thought Julien, as be rode away from the Hôtel de Fervaques, 'but so much the worse for Korasoff. To dare write to so notorious a prude! I am going to be treated with the utmost contempt, and nothing will amuse me more. This is, really, the only form of comedy to which I can respond. Yes, to cover with ridicule that odious being whom I call *myself* will amuse me. If I obeyed my instincts I should commit some crime for the sake of distraction.'

For a month past, the happiest moment in Julien's day had been that in which he brought his horse back to the stables. Korasoff had expressly forbidden him to look, upon any pretext whatsoever, at the mistress who had abandoned him. But the paces of that horse which she knew so well, the way in which Julien rapped with his whip at the stable door to summon a groom, sometimes drew Mathilde to stand behind her window curtain. The muslin was so fine that Julien could see through it. By looking up in a certain way from under the brim of his hat, he caught a glimpse of Mathilde's form without seeing her eyes. 'Consequently,' he told himself, 'she cannot see mine, and this is not the same as looking at her.'

That evening, Madame de Fervaques behaved to him exactly as though she had not received the philosophical, mystical and religious dissertation which, in the morning, he had handed to her porter with such an air of melancholy. The evening before, chance had revealed to Julien the secret springs of eloquence; he arranged himself so as to be able to see Mathilde's eyes. She, meanwhile, immediately after the arrival of the Maréchale, rose from the blue sofa: this was a desertion of her regular company. M. de Croisenois shewed consternation at this new caprice; his evident distress relieved Julien of the keenest pangs of his own sufferings.

This unexpected turn in his affairs made him talk like an angel; and as self-esteem finds its way even into hearts that serve as temples to the most august virtue: 'Madame de La Mole is right,' the Maréchale said to herself, as she stepped into her carriage, 'that young priest has distinction. My presence must, at first, have frightened him. Indeed, everything that one finds in that house is very frivolous; all the virtue I see there is the result of age, and stood in great need of the congealing hand of time. That young man must have seen the difference; he writes well; but I am much afraid that the request that I should enlighten him with my advice, which he makes in his letter, is in reality only a sentiment unaware of itself.

'And yet, how many conversions have begun in this way! What leads me to augur well of this one is the difference in his style from that of the young men whose letters I have had occasion to see. It is impossible not to recognise unction, a profound earnestness and great conviction in the prose of this young Levite; he must have the soothing virtue of Massillon.'

CHAPTER FIFTY-SEVEN

THE BEST POSITIONS IN THE CHURCH

Des services! des talents! du mérite! bah! soyez d'une coterie.

TÉLÉMAQUE.

THUS the idea of a Bishopric was for the first time blended with that of Julien in the head of a woman who sooner or later would be distributing the best positions in the Church of France. This prospect would have made little difference to him; for the moment his thoughts rose to nothing that was alien to his present misery: everything intensified it; for instance the sight of his bedroom had become intolerable to him. At night, when he came upstairs with his candle, each piece of furniture, every little ornament seemed to acquire the power of speech to inform him harshly of some fresh detail of his misery.

This evening, 'I am a galley slave,' he said to himself, as he entered it, with a vivacity long unfamiliar to him: 'let us hope that the second letter will be as boring as the first.'

It was even more so. What he was copying seemed to him so absurd that he began to transcribe it line for line, without a thought of the meaning.

'It is even more emphatic,' he said to himself, 'than the official documents of the Treaty of Münster, which my tutor in diplomacy made me copy out in London.'

It was only then that he remembered the letters from Madame de Fervaques, the originals of which he had forgotten to restore to the grave Spaniard, Don Diego Bustos. He searched for them; they were really almost as fantastic a rig-marole as those of the young Russian gentleman. They were completely vague. They expressed everything and nothing. 'It is the Æolian harp of style,' thought Julien. 'Amid the most lofty thoughts about annihilation, death, the infinite, etc., I can see no reality save a shocking fear of ridicule.'

The monologue which we have here abridged was repeated nightly for a fortnight. Falling asleep while transcribing a sort of commentary on the Apocalypse, going next day to deliver a letter with a melancholy air, leaving his horse in the stable-yard with the hope of catching a glimpse of Mathilde's gown, working, putting in an appearance in the evening at the Opera when Madame de Fervaques did not come to the Hôtel de La Mole; such were the monotonous events of Julien's existence. They became more interesting when Madame de Fervaques paid a visit to the Marquise; then he could steal a glance at Mathilde's eyes beneath the side of the Maréchale's hat, and would wax eloquent. His picturesque and sentimental phrases began to assume a turn at once more striking and more elegant.

He was fully aware that what he was saying seemed absurd to Mathilde, but he sought to impress her by the elegance of his diction. 'The falser the things I say, the more I ought to appeal to her,' thought Julien; and then, with a shocking boldness, he began to exaggerate certain aspects of nature. He very soon perceived that, if he were not to appear vulgar in the eyes of the Maréchale, he must above all avoid any simple or reasonable idea. He continued on these lines, or abridged his amplifications according as he read success or indifference in the eyes of the two great ladies to whom he must appeal.

On the whole, his life was less horrible than at the time when his days passed in inaction.

'But,' he said to himself one evening, 'here I am transcribing the fifteenth of these abominable dissertations; the first fourteen have been faithfully delivered to the Maréchale's Swiss. I shall soon have the honour of filling all the pigeonholes in her desk. And yet she treats me exactly as though I were not writing! What can be the end of all this? Can my constancy bore her as much as it bores me? I am bound to say that this Russian, Korasoff's friend, who was in love with the fair Quakeress of Richmond, must have been a terrible fellow in his day; no one could be more deadly.'

Like everyone of inferior intelligence whom chance brings into touch with the operations of a great general, Julien understood nothing of the attack launched by the young Russian upon the heart of the fair English maid. The first forty letters were intended only to make her pardon his boldness in writing. It was necessary to make this gentle person, who perhaps was vastly bored, form the habit of receiving letters that were perhaps a trifle less insipid than her everyday life.

One morning, a letter was handed to Julien; he recognized the armorial bearings of Madame de Fervaques, and broke the seal with an eagerness which would have seemed quite impossible to him a few days earlier: it was only an invitation to dine.

He hastened to consult Prince Korasoff's instructions. Unfortunately, the young Russian had chosen to be as frivolous as Dorat, just where he ought to have been simple and intelligible; Julien could not discover the moral attitude which he was supposed to adopt at the Maréchale's table.

Her drawing-room was the last word in magnificence, gilded like the Galerie de Diane in the Tuileries, with oil paintings in the panels. There were blank spaces in these paintings, Julien learned later on that the subjects had seemed hardly decent to the lady of the house, who had had the pictures corrected. 'A moral age!' he thought.

In this drawing-room he remarked three of the gentlemen who had been present at the drafting of the secret note. One of them, the Right Reverend Bishop of ——, the Maréchale's uncle, had the patronage of benefices, and, it was said, could refuse nothing to his niece. 'What a vast stride I have made,' thought Julien, with a melancholy smile, 'and how cold it leaves me! Here I am dining with the famous Bishop of ——.'

The dinner was indifferent and the conversation irritating.

'It is like the table of contents of a dull book,' thought Julien. 'All the greatest subjects of human thought are proudly displayed in it. Listen to it for three minutes, and you ask yourself which is more striking, the emphasis of the speaker or his shocking ignorance.'

The reader has doubtless forgotten that little man of letters, named Tanbeau, the nephew of the Academician and an embryo professor, who, with his vile calumnies, seemed to be employed in poisoning the drawing-room of the Hôtel de La Mole.

It was from this little man that Julien first gleaned the idea that it might well be that Madame de Fervaques, while refraining from answering his letters, looked with indulgence upon the sentiment that dictated them. The black heart of M. Tanbeau was torn asunder by the thought of Julien's successes; but in as much as, looking at it from another angle, a deserving man cannot, any more than a fool, be in two places at once, 'if Sorel becomes the lover of the sublime Maréchale,' the future professor told himself, 'she will place him in the Church in some advantageous manner, and I shall be rid of him at the Hôtel de La Mole.'

M. l'Abbé Pirard also addressed long sermons to Julien on his successes at the Hôtel de Fervaques. There was a *sectarian jealousy* between the austere Jansenist and the Jesuitical, regenerative and monarchical drawing-room of the virtuous Maréchale.

CHAPTER FIFTY-EIGHT

MANON LESCAUT

> Or, une fois qu'il fut bien convaincu de la sottise et
> ânerie du prieur, il réussissait assez ordinairement en
> appelant noir ce qui était blanc, et blanc ce qui était
> noir.
>
> LICHTEMBERG.

THE Russian instructions laid down categorically that one must never contradict in speech the person with whom one corresponded. One must never depart, upon any account, from an attitude of the most ecstatic admiration; the letters were all based upon this supposition.

One evening, at the Opera, in Madame de Fervaques's box, Julien praised to the skies the ballet in *Manon Lescaut*.[1] His sole reason for doing so was that he found it insipid.

The Maréchale said that this ballet was greatly inferior to Abbé Prévost's novel.

'What!' thought Julien, with surprise and amusement, 'a person of such extreme virtue praise a novel!' Madame de Fervaques used to profess, two or three times weekly, the most utter scorn for the writers, who, by means of those vulgar works, sought to corrupt a younger generation only too prone to the errors of the senses.

'In that immoral and pernicious class, *Manon Lescaut*,' the Maréchale went on, 'occupies, they say, one of the first

1 Composed by Halévy upon a libretto by Scribe, and performed in 1830.
C.K.S.M.

places. The frailties and well merited sufferings of a thoroughly criminal heart are, they say, described in it with a truth that is almost profound; which did not prevent your Bonaparte from declaring on Saint Helena that it was a novel written for servants.'

This speech restored all its activity to Julien's spirit. 'People have been trying to damage me with the Maréchale; they have told her of my enthusiasm for Napoleon. This intelligence has stung her sufficiently for her to yield to the temptation to let me feel her resentment.' This discovery kept him amused for the rest of the evening and made him amusing. As he was bidding the Maréchale good night in the vestibule of the Opera: 'Bear in mind, Sir,' she said to him, 'that people must not love Napoleon when they love me; they may, at the most, accept him as a necessity imposed by Providence. Anyhow, the man had not a soul pliant enough to feel great works of art.'

'*When they love me!*' Julien repeated to himself; 'either that means nothing at all, or it means everything. There is one of the secrets of language that are hidden from us poor provincials.' And he thought incessantly of Madame de Rênal as he copied an immensely long letter intended for the Maréchale.

'How is it,' she asked him the following evening, with an air of indifference which seemed to him unconvincing, 'that you speak to me of *London* and *Richmond* in a letter which you wrote last night, it appears, after leaving the Opera?'

Julien was greatly embarrassed; he had copied the letter line for line, without thinking of what he was writing, and apparently had forgotten to substitute for the words *London* and *Richmond*, which occurred in the original, *Paris* and *Saint-Cloud*. He began two or three excuses, but found it impossible to finish any of them; he felt himself on the point of giving way to an outburst of helpless laughter. At length, in his search for the right words, he arrived at the following idea: 'Exalted by the discussion of the most sublime, the highest interests of the human soul, my own, in writing to you, must have become distracted.

'I am creating an impression,' he said to himself, 'therefore

469

I can spare myself the tedium of the rest of the evening.' He left the Hôtel de Fervaques in hot haste. That evening, as he looked over the original text of the letter which he had copied the night before, he very soon came to the fatal passage where the young Russian spoke of *London* and *Richmond*. Julien was quite surprised to find this letter almost tender.

It was the contrast between the apparent frivolity of his talk and the sublime and almost apocalyptic profundity of his letters that had marked him out. The length of his sentences was especially pleasing to the Maréchale; this was not the cursory style brought into fashion by Voltaire, that most immoral of men! Although our hero did everything in the world to banish any suggestion of common sense from his conversation, it had still an anti-monarchical and impious colour which did not escape the notice of Madame de Fervaques. Surrounded by persons who were eminently moral, but who often had not one idea in an evening, this lady was profoundly impressed by everything that bore a semblance of novelty; but, at the same time, she felt that she owed it to herself to be shocked by it. She called this defect, 'retaining the imprint of the frivolity of the age.'

But such drawing-rooms are worth visiting only when one has a favour to ask. All the boredom of this life without interests which Julien was leading is doubtless shared by the reader. These are the barren moorlands on our journey.

Throughout the time usurped in Julien's life by the Fervaques episode, Mademoiselle de La Mole had to make a constant effort not to think of him. Her heart was exposed to violent combats: sometimes she flattered herself that she was despising this gloomy young man; but, in spite of her efforts, his conversation captivated her. What astonished her most of all was his complete insincerity; he never uttered a word to the Maréchale which was not a lie, or at least a shocking travesty of his point of view, which Mathilde knew so perfectly upon almost every subject. This Machiavellism impressed her. 'What profundity!' she said to herself; 'how different from the emphatic blockheads or the common rascals, like M. Tanbeau, who speak the same language!'

Nevertheless, Julien passed some fearful days. It was to perform the most arduous of his duties that he appeared each evening in the Maréchale's drawing-room. His efforts to play a part ended by sapping all his spiritual strength. Often, at night, as he crossed the vast courtyard of the Hôtel de Fervaques, it was only by force of character and reason that he succeeded in keeping himself from sinking into despair.

'I conquered despair at the Seminary,' he said to himself: 'and yet what an appalling prospect I had before me then! I stood to make my fortune or to fail; in either case, I saw myself obliged to spend my whole life in the intimate society of all that is most contemptible and disgusting under heaven. The following spring, when only eleven short months had passed, I was perhaps the happiest of all the young men of my age.'

But often enough all these fine arguments proved futile when faced with the frightful reality. Every day he saw Mathilde at luncheon and at dinner. From the frequent letters which M. de La Mole dictated to him, he knew her to be on the eve of marrying M. de Croisenois. Already that amiable young man was calling twice daily at the Hôtel de La Mole: the jealous eye of an abandoned lover did not miss a single one of his actions.

When he thought he had noticed that Mademoiselle de La Mole was treating her suitor kindly, on returning to his room, Julien could not help casting a loving glance at his pistols.

'Ah, how much wiser I should be,' he said to himself, 'to remove the marks from my linen, and retire to some lonely forest, twenty leagues from Paris, there to end this accursed existence! A stranger to the country-side, my death would remain unknown for a fortnight, and who would think of me after a fortnight had passed?'

This reasoning was extremely sound. But next day, a glimpse of Mathilde's arm, seen between her sleeve and her glove, was enough to plunge our young philosopher in cruel memories, which, at the same time, made him cling to life. 'Very well!' he would then say to himself, 'I shall follow out this Russian policy to the end. How is it going to end?

'As for the Maréchale, certainly, after I have copied these fifty-three letters, I shall write no more.

'As for Mathilde, these six weeks of such painful play-acting, will either fail altogether to appease her anger, or will win me a moment of reconciliation. Great God! I should die of joy!' And he was unable to pursue the idea farther.

When, after a long spell of meditation, he succeeded in recovering the use of his reason: 'Then,' he said to himself, 'I should obtain a day's happiness, after which would begin again her severities, founded, alas, upon the scant power that I have to please her, and I should be left without any further resource, I should be ruined, lost for ever. . . .

'What guarantee can she give me, with her character? Alas, my scant merit is responsible for everything. I must be wanting in elegance in my manners, my way of speaking must be heavy and monotonous. Great God! Why am I myself?'

CHAPTER FIFTY-NINE

BOREDOM

Se sacrifier à ses passions, passe; mais à des passions
qu'on n'a pas! O triste dix-neuvième siècle!

GIRODET.

FTER having read without pleasure at first Julien's long
letters, Madame de Fervaques began to take an
interest in them; but one thing distressed her: 'What
a pity that M. Sorel is not really a priest! One could admit
him to a sort of intimacy: with that Cross and what is almost
a layman's coat, one is exposed to cruel questions, and how
is one to answer them?' She did not complete her thought:
'some malicious friend may suppose and indeed spread the
report that he is some humble little cousin, one of my father's
family, some tradesman decorated by the National Guard.'

Until the moment of her first meeting Julien, Madame
de Fervaques's greatest pleasure had been to write the word
Maréchale before her own name. Thenceforward the vanity
of an upstart, morbid and easily offended, had to fight a
nascent interest.

'It would be so easy for me,' the Maréchale said to herself,
'to make a Grand Vicar of him in some diocese not far from
Paris! But M. Sorel by itself, and to add to that a mere secretary of M. de La Mole! It is deplorable.'

For the first time, this spirit which *dreaded everything* was
stirred by an interest apart from its own pretensions to rank
and to social superiority. Her old porter noticed that, when
he brought her a letter from that handsome young man, who

473

wore such a melancholy air, he was certain to see vanish
the distracted and irritated expression which the Maréchale
always took care to assume when any of her servants entered
the room.

The boredom of a mode of life whose sole ambition was
to create an effect on the public, without there being at the
bottom of her heart any real enjoyment of this kind of success, had become so intolerable since she had begun to think
of Julien, that, if her maids were not to be ill-treated throughout the whole of a day, it was enough that during the previous evening she should have spent an hour with this strange
young man. His growing credit survived anonymous letters,
very well composed. In vain did little Tanbeau supply MM.
de Luz, de Croisenois, de Caylus, with two or three most
adroit calumnies which those gentlemen took pleasure in
spreading abroad, without stopping to consider the truth of
the accusations. The Maréchale, whose mind was not framed
to withstand these vulgar methods, reported her doubts to
Mathilde, and was always comforted.

One day, after having inquired three times whether there
were any letters, Madame de Fervaques suddenly decided to
write to Julien. This was a victory gained by boredom. At
the second letter, the Maréchale was almost brought to a
standstill by the unpleasantness of writing with her own hand
so vulgar an address as: '*à* M. Sorel. *chez* M. le Marquis de
La Mole.'

'You must,' she said to Julien that evening in the driest of
tones, 'bring me some envelopes with your address written
on them.'

'So now I am to combine the lover and the flunkey,'
thought Julien, and bowed, amusing himself by screwing up
his face like Arsène, the Marquis's old footman.

That same evening he brought a supply of envelopes, and
next day, early in the morning, he received a third letter: he
read five or six lines at the beginning, and two or three
towards the end. It covered four pages in a small and very
close script.

Gradually she formed the pleasant habit of writing almost

every day. Julien replied with faithful copies of the Russian letters, and, such is the advantage of the emphatic style, Madame de Fervaques was not at all surprised by the want of connexion between the replies and her own letters.

What would have been the irritation to her pride if little Tanbeau, who had appointed himself a voluntary spy upon Julien's actions, had been able to tell her that all these letters, with their seals unbroken, were flung pell-mell into Julien's drawer!

One morning, the porter brought to him in the library a letter from the Maréchale; Mathilde met the man, saw the letter, and read the address in Julien's hand. She entered the library as the porter left it; the letter was still lying on the edge of the table; Julien, busily engaged in writing, had not placed it in his drawer.

'This is what I cannot endure,' cried Mathilde, seizing the letter; 'you are forgetting me entirely, me who am your wife. Your conduct is appalling, Sir.'

With these words, her pride, astonished by the fearful impropriety of her action, stifled her; she burst into tears, and a moment later appeared to Julien to be unable to breathe.

Surprised, confounded, Julien did not clearly distinguish all the admirable and happy consequences which this scene foreboded for himself. He helped Mathilde to a seat; she almost abandoned herself in his arms.

The first instant in which he perceived this relaxation was one of extreme joy. His second thought was of Korasoff: 'I may ruin everything by a single word.'

His arms ached, so painful was the effort imposed on him by policy. 'I ought not even to allow myself to press to my heart this supple and charming form, or she will despise and abuse me. What a frightful nature!'

And as he cursed Mathilde's nature, he loved her for it a hundred times more; he felt as though he were holding in his arms a queen.

Julien's unfeeling coldness intensified the misery of wounded pride which was tearing the heart of Mademoiselle de La Mole. She was far from possessing the necessary coolness to seek to read in his eyes what he was feeling for her at that moment. She could not bring herself to look at him; she trembled lest she should meet an expression of scorn.

Seated on the divan in the library, motionless and with her head turned away from Julien, she was a prey to the keenest suffering that pride and love can make a human heart feel. Into what a frightful course of action had she fallen!

'It was reserved for me, wretch that I am, to see the most indelicate advances repulsed! And repulsed by whom?' added a pride mad with suffering, 'by one of my father's servants.

'That is what I will not endure,' she said aloud.

And, rising with fury, she opened the drawer of Julien's table, which stood a few feet away from her. She remained frozen with horror on seeing there nine or ten letters unopened, similar in every respect to the letter which the porter had just brought in. On all the envelopes, she recognised Julien's hand, more or less disguised.

'And so,' she cried, beside herself with rage, 'not only have you found favour with her, but you despise her. You, a man of nought, to despise Madame la Maréchale de Fervaques!

'Ah, forgive me, my dear,' she went on, flinging herself at his feet, 'despise me if you wish, but love me, I can no longer live deprived of your love.' And she fell to the ground in a dead faint.

'So there she is, that proud creature, at my feet!' thought Julien.

CHAPTER SIXTY

A BOX AT THE BOUFFES

As the blackest sky
Foretells the heaviest tempest.
Don Juan, I, 73.

IN the thick of all this great commotion, Julien was more bewildered than happy. Mathilde's abuse of him shewed him how wise the Russian policy had been. '*Say little, do little*, that is my one way of salvation.'

He lifted up Mathilde and without a word laid her down again on the divan. Gradually she gave way to tears.

To keep herself in countenance, she took Madame de Fervaques's letters in her hands; she broke the seals slowly. She gave a nervous start on recognising the Maréchale's handwriting. She turned over the sheets of these letters without reading them; the majority of them covered six pages.

'Answer me this, at least,' said Mathilde at length in the most supplicating tone, but without venturing to look at Julien. 'You know very well that I am proud; it is the misfortune of my position, and indeed of my nature, I must admit; so Madame de Fervaques has stolen your heart from me … Has she offered you all the sacrifices to which that fatal passion led me?'

A grim silence was Julien's only answer. 'By what right,' he thought, 'does she ask of me an indiscretion unworthy of an honourable man?'

Mathilde endeavoured to read the letters; the tears that filled her eyes made it impossible for her to do so.

For a month past she had been miserable, but that proud spirit was far from confessing its feelings to itself. Chance alone had brought about this explosion. For an instant jealousy and love had overcome pride. She was seated upon the divan and in close proximity to him. He saw her hair and her throat of alabaster; for a moment he forgot all that he owed to himself; he slipped his arm round her waist, and almost hugged her to his bosom.

She turned her head towards him slowly: he was astonished at the intense grief that was visible in her eyes, and made them quite unrecognisable as hers.

Julien felt his strength begin to fail him, so colossal was the effort involved in the act of courage which he was imposing on himself.

'Those eyes will soon express nothing but the coldest disdain,' he said to himself, 'if I allow myself to be carried away by the joy of loving her.' Meanwhile, in a faint voice and in words which she had barely the strength to utter, she was repeating to him at that moment her assurance of all her regret for the action which an excessive pride might have counselled her to take.

'I too, have my pride,' Julien said to her in a voice that was barely articulate, and his features indicated the extreme limit of physical exhaustion.

Mathilde turned sharply towards him. The sound of his voice was a pleasure the hope of which she had almost abandoned. At that moment she recalled her pride only to curse it, she would fain have discovered some unusual, incredible act to prove to him how greatly she adored him and detested herself.

'It is probably because of that pride,' Julien went on, 'that you have singled me out for an instant; it is certainly because of that courageous firmness, becoming in a man, that you respect me at this moment. I may be in love with the Maréchale. . . .'

Mathilde shuddered; her eyes assumed a strange expression. She was about to hear her sentence uttered. This movement did not pass unobserved by Julien; he felt his courage weaken.

478

'Ah!' he said to himself, listening to the sound of the vain words that came from his lips, as he might have listened to a noise from without; 'if I could only cover those pale cheeks with kisses, and thou not feel them!

'I may be in love with the Maréchale,' he continued ... and his voice grew fainter and fainter; 'but certainly, of her interest in myself I have no decisive proof....'

Mathilde gazed at him; he met her gaze, at least he hoped that his features had not betrayed him. He felt himself penetrated by love to the innermost recesses of his heart. Never had he adored her so intensely; he was scarcely less mad than Mathilde. Could she have found sufficient self-control and courage to manœuvre, he would have fallen at her feet, forswearing all idle play-acting. He had strength enough to be able to continue to speak. 'Ah! Korasoff,' he exclaimed inwardly, 'why are not you here? How I need a word of advice to direct my conduct!' Meanwhile his voice was saying:

'Failing any other sentiment, gratitude would suffice to attach me to the Maréchale; she has shewn me indulgence, she has comforted me when others scorned me.... I may perhaps not repose an unbounded faith in certain signs which are extremely flattering, no doubt, but also, perhaps, are of very brief duration.'

'Ah! Great God!' cried Mathilde.

'Very well! What guarantee will you give me?' Julien went on in sharp, firm accents, seeming to abandon for an instant the prudent forms of diplomacy. 'What guarantee, what god will assure me that the position which you seem disposed to restore to me at this moment will last for more than two days?'

'The intensity of my love and of my misery if you no longer love me,' she said, clasping his hands and turning her face towards him.

The violent movement which she thus made had slightly displaced her pelerine: Julien caught a glimpse of her charming shoulders. Her hair, slightly disordered, recalled to him an exquisite memory....

479

He was about to yield. 'An imprudent word,' he told himself, 'and I begin once more that long succession of days passed in despair. Madame de Rênal used to find reasons for obeying the dictates of her heart: this young girl of high society allows her heart to be moved only when she has proved to herself with good reasons that it ought to be moved.'

He perceived this truth in a flash, and in a flash also regained his courage.

He freed his hands which Mathilde was clasping in her own, and with marked respect withdrew a little way from her. Human courage can go no farther. He then busied himself in gathering together all Madame de Fervaques's letters which were scattered over the divan, and it was with a shew of extreme politeness, so cruel at that moment, that he added:

'Mademoiselle de La Mole will deign to permit me to think over all this.' He withdrew rapidly and left the library; she heard him shut all the doors in turn.

'The monster is not in the least perturbed,' she said to herself. . . .

'But what am I saying, a monster! He is wise, prudent, good; it is I who have done more wrong than could be imagined.'

This point of view persisted. Mathilde was almost happy that day, for she was altogether in love; you would have said that never had that heart been stirred by pride—and such pride!

She shuddered with horror when, that evening in the drawing-room, a footman announced Madame de Fervaques; the man's voice seemed to her to have a sinister sound. She could not endure the sight of the Maréchale, and quickly left the room. Julien, with little pride in his hard-won victory, had been afraid lest his own eyes should betray him, and had not dined at the Hôtel de La Mole.

His love and his happiness increased rapidly as the hour of battle receded; he had already begun to find fault with himself. 'How could I resist her?' he asked himself; 'if she was going to cease to love me! A single moment may alter that proud spirit, and I must confess that I have treated her scandalously.'

In the evening, he felt that he absolutely must appear at the *Bouffes* in Madame de Fervaques's box. She had given him an express invitation: Mathilde would not fail to hear of his presence there or of his discourteous absence. Despite the self-evidence of this argument, he had not the strength, early in the evening, to plunge into society. If he talked, he would forfeit half his happiness.

Ten o'clock struck: he must absolutely shew his face.

Fortunately he found the Maréchale's box filled with women, and was relegated to a place by the door, and entirely concealed by their hats. This position saved him from making a fool of himself; the divine accents of despair of Carolina in *Il matrimonio segreto* made him burst into tears. Madame de Fervaques saw these tears; they were in so marked a contrast to the manly firmness of his usual appearance, that this spirit of a great lady long saturated in all the most corrosive elements of the pride of an upstart was touched by them. What little she had left of a woman's heart led her to speak. She wished to enjoy the sound of her own voice at that moment.

'Have you seen the ladies de La Mole,' she said to him, 'they are in the third tier.' Instantly Julien bent forward into the house, leaning somewhat rudely upon the ledge of the box: he saw Mathilde; her eyes were bright with tears.

'And yet it is not their day for the Opera,' thought Julien; 'what eagerness!'

Mathilde had made her mother come to the *Bouffes*, despite the inferior position of the box which a sycophant of their circle had made haste to offer them. She wished to see whether Julien would spend that evening with the Maréchale.

CHAPTER SIXTY-ONE

MAKING HER AFRAID

Voilà donc le beau miracle de votre civilisation! De
l'amour vous avez fait une affaire ordinaire.

BARNAVE.

JULIEN hurried to Madame de La Mole's box. His eyes
met first the tearful eyes of Mathilde; she was weeping
without restraint, there was no one present but people of
minor importance, the friend who had lent them the box
and some men of her acquaintance. Mathilde laid her hand
upon Julien's; she seemed to have forgotten all fear of her
mother. Almost stifled by her sobs, she said nothing to him
but the single word: *'Guarantees!'*

'Whatever I do, I must not speak to her,' thought Julien,
greatly moved himself, and covering his eyes as best he could
with his hand, ostensibly to avoid the lustre that was blazing
into the boxes on the third tier. 'If I speak, she can no longer
doubt the intensity of my emotion, the sound of my voice
will betray me, all may be lost once more.'

His struggles were far more painful than in the morning,
his spirit had had time to grow disturbed. He was afraid
of seeing Mathilde's vanity wounded. Frantic with love and
passion, he pledged himself not to speak to her.

This is, to my mind, one of the finest traits of his character;
a person capable of such an effort to control himself may go
far, *si fata sinant.*

Mademoiselle de La Mole insisted upon taking Julien home.
Fortunately it was raining in torrents. But the Marquise made

482

him sit facing herself, talked to him continuously, and prevented his saying a word to her daughter. One would have thought that the Marquise was concerned for Julien's happiness; no longer afraid of destroying everything by the intensity of his emotion, he abandoned himself to it with frenzy.

Dare I say that on entering his own room Julien threw himself on his knees and covered with kisses the love letters given him by Prince Korasoff?

'Oh, thou great man! What do I not owe to thee?' he cried in his frenzy.

Gradually a little coolness returned to him. He compared himself to a general who had just won the first half of a great battle. 'The advantage is certain, immense,' he said to himself; 'but what is going to happen to-morrow? An instant may ruin everything.'

He opened with a passionate impulse the *Memoirs dictated at Saint Helena* by Napoleon, and for two solid hours forced himself to read them; his eyes alone read the words, no matter, he forced himself to the task. During this strange occupation, his head and heart, rising to the level of everything that is most great, were at work without his knowledge. 'This is a very different heart from Madame de Rênal's,' he said to himself, but he went no farther.

'*Make her afraid*,' he cried of a sudden, flinging the book from him. 'The enemy will obey me only so long as I make him fear me, then he will not dare to despise me.'

He paced up and down his little room, wild with joy. To be frank, this happiness was due to pride rather than love.

'Make her afraid!' he repeated proudly to himself, and he had reason to be proud. 'Even in her happiest moments, Madame de Rênal always doubted whether my love were equal to hers. Here, it is a demon that I am conquering, I must therefore *conquer*.'

He knew well that next morning, by eight o'clock, Mathilde would be in the library; he did not appear there until nine, burning with love, but his head controlled his heart. Not a single minute passed, perhaps, without his repeating to himself: 'Always keep her mind occupied with the

great uncertainty: "Does he love me?" Her privileged position, the flattery she receives from all who speak to her make
her *a little too much* inclined to self-assurance.'

He found her pale, calm, seated upon the divan, but incapable, apparently, of making any movement. She offered him
her hand.

'Dear, I have offended you, it is true; you are perhaps
vexed with me?'

Julien was not expecting so simple a tone. He was on the
point of betraying himself.

'You wish for guarantees, dear,' she went on after a silence
which she had hoped to see broken; 'that is only fair. Carry
me off, let us start for London. I shall be ruined for ever,
disgraced. . . .' She found the courage to withdraw her hand
from Julien so as to hide her eyes with it. All the sentiments
of modesty and feminine virtue had returned to her heart. . . .
'Very well! Disgrace me,' she said at length with a sigh, 'it
is a guarantee.'

'Yesterday I was happy, because I had the courage to be
severe with myself,' thought Julien. After a brief interval of
silence, he gained sufficient mastery over his heart to say in
an icy tone:

'Once we are on the road to London, once you are disgraced, to use your own words, who can promise me that
you will love me? That my company in the post-chaise will
not seem to you an annoyance? I am not a monster, to have
ruined your reputation will be to me only an additional grief.
It is not your position in society that is the obstacle, it is
unfortunately your own nature. Can you promise yourself
that you will love me for a week?

'(Ah! Let her love me for a week, for a week only,' Julien
murmured to himself, 'and I shall die of joy. What do I care
for the future, what do I care for life itself? And this divine
happiness may begin at this moment if I choose, it depends
entirely upon myself!)'

Mathilde saw him turn pensive.

'So I am altogether unworthy of you,' she said, clasping
his hand.

Julien embraced her, but at once the iron hand of duty gripped his heart. 'If she sees how I adore her, then I lose her.' And, before withdrawing himself from her arms, he had resumed all the dignity that befits a man.

On that day and the days that followed, he managed to conceal the intensity of his bliss; there were moments in which he denied himself even the pleasure of clasping her in his arms.

At other moments, the frenzy of happiness swept aside all the counsels of prudence.

It was beside a bower of honeysuckle arranged so as to hide the ladder, that he was accustomed to take his stand in order to gaze at the distant shutters of Mathilde's window and lament her inconstancy. An oak of great size stood close by, and the trunk of this tree prevented him from being seen by indiscreet persons.

As he passed with Mathilde by this spot which recalled to him so vividly the intensity of his grief, the contrast between past despair and present bliss was too strong for him; tears flooded his eyes, and, carrying to his lips the hand of his mistress: 'Here I lived while I thought of you; from here I gazed at that shutter, I awaited for hours on end the fortunate moment when I should see this hand open it....'

He gave way completely. He portrayed to her, in those true colours which one does not invent, the intensity of his despair at that time. In spasmodic utterances he spoke of his present happiness which had put an end to that cruel suffering....

'What am I doing, Great God!' said Julien, coming suddenly to his senses. 'I am destroying everything.'

In the height of his alarm he thought he already saw less love in the eyes of Mademoiselle de La Mole. This was an illusion; but Julien's face changed rapidly and was flooded with a deathly pallor. His eyes grew dull for a moment, and an expression of arrogance not devoid of malice succeeded that of the most sincere, the most wholehearted love.

'Why, what is the matter with you, dear?' Mathilde tenderly, anxiously inquired.

485

'I am lying,' said Julien savagely, 'and I am lying to you. I reproach myself for it, and yet God knows that I respect you sufficiently not to lie. You love me, you are devoted to me, and I have no need to make fine speeches in order to please you.'

'Great God! They were only fine speeches, all the exquisite things you have been saying to me for the last ten minutes?'

'And I reproach myself for them strongly, dear friend. I made them up long ago for a woman who loved me and used to bore me.... That is the weak spot in my character, I denounce myself to you, forgive me.'

Bitter tears streamed down Mathilde's cheeks.

'Whenever some trifle that has shocked me sets me dreaming for a moment,' Julien went on, 'my execrable memory, which I could curse at this moment, offers me a way of escape, and I abuse it.'

'So I have unconsciously done something that has displeased you?' said Mathilde with a charming simplicity.

'One day, I remember, as you passed by these honeysuckles, you plucked a flower, M. de Luz took it from you, and you let him keep it. I was close beside you.'

'M. de Luz? It is impossible,' replied Mathilde with the dignity that came so naturally to her: 'I never behave like that.'

'I am certain of it,' Julien at once rejoined.

'Ah, well! Then it must be true, dear,' said Mathilde, lowering her eyes sadly. She was positive that for many months past she had never allowed M. de Luz to take any such liberty.

Julien gazed at her with an inexpressible tenderness:

'No,' he said to himself, 'she does not love me any the less.'

She rebuked him that evening, with a laugh, for his fondness for Madame de Fervaques: a *bourgeois* in love with a *parvenue*. 'Hearts of that class are perhaps the only ones that my Julien cannot inflame. She has turned you into a regular dandy,' she said, playing with his hair.

During the period in which he supposed himself to be scorned by Mathilde, Julien had become one of the best-dressed men in Paris. But he had an additional advantage over the other men of this sort; once his toilet was performed, he never gave it another thought.

One thing still vexed Mathilde. Julien continued to copy out the Russian letters, and to send them to the Maréchale.

CHAPTER SIXTY-TWO

THE TIGER

Hélas! pourquoi ces choses et non pas d'autres!
                                    BEAUMARCHAIS.

A<small>N</small> English traveller relates how he lived upon intimate
terms with a tiger; he had reared it and used to play
with it, but always kept a loaded pistol on the table.

Julien abandoned himself to the full force of his happiness
only at those moments when Mathilde could not read the
expression of it in his eyes. He was punctilious in his performance of the duty of addressing a few harsh words to her
from time to time.

When Mathilde's meekness, which he observed with astonishment, and the intensity of her devotion came near to destroying all his self-control, he had the courage to leave her
abruptly.

For the first time Mathilde was in love.

Life, which had always crawled for her at a snail's pace,
now flew.

As it was essential, nevertheless, that her pride should find
some outlet, she sought to expose herself with temerity to all
the risks that her love could make her run. It was Julien who
shewed prudence; and it was only when there was any question of danger that she did not comply with his wishes; but,
submissive, and almost humble towards him, she shewed all
the more arrogance towards anyone else who came near her
in the house, relatives and servants alike.

In the evenings in the drawing-room, she would summon

488

Julien, and would hold long conversations with him in private.

Little Tanbeau took his place one evening beside them; she asked him to go to the library and fetch her the volume of Smollett which dealt with the Revolution of 1688; and as he seemed to hesitate: 'There is no need to hurry,' she went on with an expression of insulting arrogance, which was balm to Julien's spirit.

'Did you notice the look in that little monster's eyes?' he asked her.

'His uncle has done ten or twelve years of service in this drawing-room, otherwise I should have him shewn the door this instant.'

Her behaviour towards MM. de Croisenois, de Luz, and the rest, perfectly polite in form, was scarcely less provoking in substance. Mathilde blamed herself severely for all the confidences she had made to Julien in the past, especially as she did not dare confess to him that she had exaggerated the almost wholly innocent marks of interest of which those gentlemen had been the object.

In spite of the most admirable resolutions, her womanly pride prevented her every day from saying to Julien: 'It was because I was speaking to you that I found pleasure in the thought of my weakness in not withdrawing my hand when M. de Croisenois laid his hand on a marble table beside mine, and managed to touch it.'

Nowadays, whenever one of these gentlemen had spoken to her for a few moments, she found that she had a question to ask Julien, and this was a pretext for keeping him by her side.

She found that she was pregnant, and told the news joyfully to Julien.

'Now will you doubt me? Is not this a guarantee? I am your wife for ever.'

This announcement filled Julien with profound astonishment. He was on the point of forgetting his principle of conduct. 'How can I be deliberately cold and offensive to this poor girl who is ruining herself for me?' Did she appear at all unwell, even on the days on which wisdom made her dread accents heard, he no longer found the courage to address to her one of those cruel speeches, so indispensable, in his experience, to the continuance of their love.

'I mean to write to my father,' Mathilde said to him one day; 'he is more than a father to me; he is a friend; and so I should feel it unworthy of you and of myself to seek to deceive him, were it only for a moment.'

'Great God! What are you going to do?' said Julien in alarm.

'My duty,' she replied, her eyes sparkling with joy.

She felt herself to be more magnanimous than her lover.

'But he will turn me from the house in disgrace!'

'He is within his rights, we must respect them. I shall give you my arm, and we shall go out by the front door, in the full light of day.'

Julien in astonishment begged her to wait for a week.

'I cannot,' she replied, 'the voice of honour speaks. I have seen what is my duty, I must obey, and at once.'

'Very well! I order you to wait,' said Julien at length. 'Your honour is covered, I am your husband. This drastic step is going to alter both our positions. I also am within my rights. To-day is Tuesday; next Tuesday is the day of the Duc de Retz's party; that evening, when M. de La Mole comes home, the porter shall hand him the fatal letter.... He thinks only of making you a Duchess, of that I am certain; think of his grief!'

'Do you mean by that: think of his revenge?'

'I may feel pity for my benefactor, distress at the thought of injuring him; but I do not and never shall fear any man.'

Mathilde submitted. Since she had told Julien of her condition, this was the first time that he had spoken to her with authority; never had he loved her so dearly. It was with gladness that the softer side of his heart seized the pretext of Mathilde's condition to forego the duty of saying a few cruel words. The idea of a confession to M. de La Mole disturbed him greatly. Was he going to be parted from Mathilde? And, however keen the distress with which she saw him go, a month after his departure would she give him a thought?

He felt almost as great a horror of the reproaches which the Marquis might justly heap upon him.

That evening, he admitted to Mathilde this second cause of his distress, and then, carried away by love, admitted the other also.

She changed colour.

'Indeed,' she said, 'six months spent out of my company would be a grief to you!'

'Immense, the only one in the world on which I look with terror.'

Mathilde was delighted. Julien had played his part with such thoroughness that he had succeeded in making her think that of the two she was the more in love.

The fatal Tuesday came all too soon. At midnight, on returning home, the Marquis found a letter with the form of address which indicated that he was to open it himself, and only when he was unobserved.

'MY FATHER,

'Every social tie that binds us is broken, there remain only the ties of nature. After my husband, you are and will ever be the dearest person in the world to me. My eyes fill with tears, I think of the distress that I am causing you, but, that my shame may not be made public, to give you time to deliberate and act, I have been unable to postpone any further the confession that I owe you. If your affection for me, which I know to be extreme, chooses to allow me a small pension, I shall go and settle myself where you please, in Switzerland, for instance, with my husband. His name is so obscure that no one will recognise your daughter in Madame Sorel, daughter-in-law of a carpenter of Verrières. There you have the name I have found it so hard to write. I dread, for Julien, your anger, apparently so righteous. I shall not be a Duchess, Father; but I knew it when I fell in love with him; for it was I that fell in love first, it was I who seduced him. I inherit from you and from our ancestors a spirit too exalted to let my attention be arrested by what is or seems to me vulgar. It is in vain that with the idea of pleasing you I have thought

of M. de Croisenois. Why did you place real merit before
my eyes? You told me yourself on my return from Hyères:
"This young Sorel is the only person who amuses me"; the
poor boy is as greatly distressed as myself, if it be possible,
by the pain which this letter must cause you. I cannot prevent
your being angry with me as a father; but care for me still
as a friend.

'Julien respected me. If he spoke to me now and again, it
was solely because of his profound gratitude to you: for the
natural pride of his character leads him never to reply save
officially to anyone who is placed so far above him. He has
a strong and inborn sense of the differences of social position.
It was I, I admit, with a blush, to my best friend, and never
shall such an admission be made to any other, it was I who
one day in the garden pressed his arm.

'In twenty-four hours from now, why should you be angry
with him? My fault is irreparable. If you require it, I shall
be the channel to convey to you the assurances of his profound respect and of his distress at displeasing you. You need
never set eyes on him; but I shall go and join him wherever
he may choose. It is his right, it is my duty, he is the father
of my child. If in your generosity you are pleased to allow
us six thousand francs upon which to live, I shall accept them
with gratitude: otherwise, Julien intends to settle at Besançon
where he will take up the profession of teacher of Latin and
Literature. However low the degree from which he springs,
I am certain that he will rise. With him, I have no fear of
obscurity. If there be a Revolution, I am sure of a leading
part for him. Could you say as much for any of those who
have sought my hand? They have fine estates? I cannot find
in that single circumstance a reason for admiration. My
Julien would attain to a high position even under the present
form of government, if he had a million and were protected
by my father. . . .'

Mathilde, who knew that the Marquis was a man entirely
governed by first impressions, had written eight pages.

'What is to be done?' Julien said to himself as he paced
the garden at midnight, while M. de La Mole was reading

this letter; 'where do, first of all, my duty, secondly, my interest lie? The debt that I owe him is immense: I should have been, but for him, a rascally understrapper, and not rascal enough to be hated and persecuted by the rest. He has made me a man of the world. My *necessary* rascalities will be, first of all, rarer, and secondly, less ignoble. That is more than if he had given me a million. I owe to him this Cross and the record of so-called diplomatic services which have raised me above my rank.

'If he were to take his pen to prescribe my conduct, what would he write?'

Julien was sharply interrupted by M. de La Mole's old valet.

'The Marquis wishes to see you this moment, dressed or undressed.'

The valet added in an undertone as they were side by side: 'M. le Marquis is furious, beware.'

CHAPTER SIXTY-THREE
THE TORMENT OF THE WEAK

En taillant ce diamant, un lapidaire malhabile lui a ôté quelques-unes de ses plus vives étincelles. Au moyen âge, que dis-je? encore sous Richelieu, le Français avait la *force de vouloir*.

MIRABEAU.

JULIEN found the Marquis furious: for the first time in his life, perhaps, this gentleman was guilty of bad taste; he heaped on Julien all the insults that came to his lips. Our hero was astonished, irritated, but his sense of gratitude was not shaken. 'How many fine projects long cherished in his secret thoughts, the poor man sees crumble in an instant. But I owe it to him to answer him, my silence would increase his rage.' His answer was furnished for him from the part of Tartufe.

'*I am no angel....* I have served you well, you have rewarded me generously.... I was grateful, but I am twenty-two years old.... In this household, my thoughts were intelligible only to yourself, and to that obliging person....'

'Monster!' cried the Marquis. 'Obliging! Obliging! On the day when you found her obliging, you ought to have fled.'

'I made an attempt; I asked you if I might go to Languedoc.'

Tired of pacing the room in fury, the Marquis, broken by grief, threw himself into an armchair; Julien heard him murmur to himself: 'This is no scoundrel.'

'No, I am not one to you,' cried Julien, falling at his feet.

But he felt extremely ashamed of this impulse and rose quickly.

The Marquis was really out of his mind. On seeing this movement he began again to shower upon Julien atrocious insults worthy of a cab-driver. The novelty of these oaths was perhaps a distraction.

'What? My daughter is to be called Madame Sorel! What! My daughter is not to be a Duchess!' Whenever these two ideas presented themselves in such clear terms, the Marquis was in torment, and his impulses were uncontrolled. Julien began to fear a thrashing.

In his lucid intervals, and when the Marquis began to grow accustomed to his disgrace, his reproaches became quite reasonable.

'You ought to have gone, Sir,' he said. 'It was your duty to go. . . . You are the meanest of mankind. . . .'

Julien went to the table and wrote:

'For a long time my life has been insupportable, I am putting an end to it. I beg Monsieur le Marquis to accept, with my expression of a gratitude that knows no bounds, my apologies for the trouble which my death in his house may cause.'

'Will Monsieur le Marquis deign to peruse this paper. . . . Kill me,' said Julien, 'or have me killed by your valet. It is one o'clock in the morning, I am going to stroll in the garden towards the wall at the far end.'

'Go to the devil,' the Marquis shouted after him as he left the room.

'I understand,' thought Julien; 'he would not be sorry to see me spare his valet the responsibility for my death. . . . Let him kill me, well and good, it is a satisfaction that I am offering him. . . . But, by Jove, I am in love with life. . . . I owe myself to my child.'

This idea, which for the first time appeared thus clearly before his imagination, completely absorbed him after the first few minutes of his stroll had been devoted to the sense of danger.

This entirely novel interest made a prudent creature of him. 'I need advice to guide me in dealing with that fiery man.... He has no judgment, he is capable of anything. Fouqué is too far off, besides he would not understand the sentiments of a heart like the Marquis's.

'Conte Altamira.... Can I be sure of eternal silence? My request for advice must not be a definite action, nor complicate my position. Alas! There is no one left but the sombre Abbé Pirard.... His mind is narrowed by Jansenism.... A rascally Jesuit would know the world better, and would be more to my purpose.... M. Pirard is capable of beating me, at the mere mention of my crime.'

The genius of Tartufe came to Julien's aid: 'Very well, I shall go and confess to him.' This was the resolution to which he finally came in the garden, after pacing it for fully two hours. He no longer thought that he might be surprised by a gunshot; sleep was overpowering him.

Next morning, before daybreak, Julien was several leagues from Paris, knocking at the door of the stern Jansenist. He found, greatly to his astonishment, that the other was not unduly surprised at his confession.

'I ought perhaps to blame myself,' the abbé said to himself, more anxious than angry. 'I had thought that I detected this love affair. My affection for yourself, you little wretch, restrained me from warning her father....'

'What will he do?' Julien asked him boldly.

(At that moment, he loved the abbé and a scene would have been most painful to him.)

'I can see three courses,' Julien continued: 'First of all, M. de La Mole may have me put to death'; and he told the abbé of the letter announcing his suicide which he had left with the Marquis; 'secondly, he may have me shot down by Comte Norbert, who will challenge me to a duel.'

'You would accept?' said the abbé in a fury, rising to his feet.

'You do not allow me to finish. Certainly I should never fire at the son of my benefactor.

'Thirdly, he may send me away. If he says to me: "Go to Edinburgh, to New York," I shall obey. Then they can conceal Mademoiselle de La Mole's condition; but I shall never allow them to destroy my child.'

'That, you may be sure, will be the first idea to occur to that corrupt man....'

In Paris, Mathilde was in despair. She had seen her father about seven o'clock. He had shewn her Julien's letter, she trembled lest he should have deemed it noble to put an end to his life: 'And without my permission?' she said to herself with an agony which partook of anger.

'If he is dead, I shall die,' she said to her father. 'It is you that will be the cause of my death.... You will rejoice at it, perhaps.... But I swear to his ghost that I shall at once put on mourning, and shall be publicly *Madame veuve Sorel*, I shall send out the usual announcements, you may count on that.... You will not find me pusillanimous nor a coward.'

Her love rose to the pitch of madness. It was now M. de La Mole's turn to be left speechless.

He began to look upon what had happened more reasonably. At luncheon Mathilde did not put in an appearance. The Marquis was relieved of an immense burden, and flattered as well, when he discovered that she had said nothing to her mother.

About mid-day, Julien returned. The clatter of his horse's hooves could be heard in the courtyard. He dismounted. Mathilde sent for him, and flung herself into his arms almost in the sight of her maid. Julien was not unduly grateful for this transport, he had come away most diplomatic and most calculating from his long conference with the Abbé Pirard. His imagination was extinguished by the calculation of possibilities. Mathilde, with tears in her eyes, informed him that she had seen the letter announcing his suicide.

'My father may change his mind; oblige me by setting off instantly for Villequier. Mount your horse, leave the premises before they rise from table.'

As Julien did not in any way alter his air of cold astonishment, she burst into a flood of tears.

'Allow me to manage our affairs,' she cried to him with a transport, clasping him in her arms. 'You know very well that it is not of my own free will that I part from you. Write

497

under cover to my maid, let the address be in a strange hand; as for me, I shall write you volumes. Farewell! Fly.'

This last word wounded Julien, he obeyed nevertheless. 'It is fated,' he thought, 'that even in their best moments, these people must find a way of hurting me.'

Mathilde put up a firm resistance to all her father's *prudent* plans. She steadfastly refused to set the negotiation upon any other basis than this: She was to be Madame Sorel, and would live in poverty with her husband in Switzerland, or with her father in Paris. She thrust from her the suggestion of a clandestine confinement. 'That would pave the way to the possibility of calumny and dishonour. Two months after our marriage, I shall travel abroad with my husband, and it will be easy for us to pretend that my child was born at a suitable date.'

Received at first with transports of rage, this firmness ended by inspiring the Marquis with doubts.

In a weak moment: 'Here,' he said to his daughter, 'is a transfer of ten thousand livres a year in the Funds, send it to your Julien, and let him speedily make it impossible for me to reclaim it.'

To *obey* Mathilde, whose love of giving orders he knew, Julien had made an unnecessary journey of forty leagues: he was at Villequier, examining the accounts of the agents; this generosity on the part of the Marquis was the occasion of his return. He went to seek asylum with the Abbé Pirard, who, during his absence, had become Mathilde's most effective ally. As often as he was interrogated by the Marquis, he proved to him that any other course than a public marriage would be a crime in the sight of God.

'And happily,' the abbé added, 'the wisdom of the world is here in accordance with religion. Could you reckon for an instant, knowing the fiery character of Mademoiselle de La Mole, upon a secrecy which she had not imposed on herself? If you do not allow the frank course of a public marriage, society will occupy itself for far longer with this strange mis-alliance. Everything must be stated at one time, without the least mystery, apparent or real.'

'It is true,' said the Marquis, growing pensive. 'By this method, to talk of the marriage after three days becomes the chatter of a man who lacks ideas. We ought to profit by some great anti-Jacobin measure by the Government to slip in unobserved in its wake.'

Two or three of M. de La Mole's friends shared the Abbé Pirard's view. The great obstacle, in their eyes, was Mathilde's decided nature. But in spite of all these specious arguments, the Marquis could not grow reconciled to abandoning the hope of a *tabouret* for his daughter.

His memory and his imagination fed upon all sorts of trickeries and pretences which had still been possible in his younger days. To yield to necessity, to go in fear of the law seemed to him an absurd thing and dishonouring to a man of his rank. He was paying dearly for those enchanting dreams in which he had indulged for the last ten years as to the future of his beloved daughter.

'Who could have foreseen it?' he said to himself. 'A girl of so haughty a character, so elevated a mind, prouder than myself of the name she bears! One whose hand had been asked of me in advance by all the most illustrious blood in France!

'We must abandon all prudence. This age is destined to bring everything to confusion! We are marching towards chaos.'

CHAPTER SIXTY-FOUR

A MAN OF SPIRIT

La préfet cheminant sur son cheval se disait: Pourquoi ne serais-je pas ministre, président du conseil,
duc? Voici comment je ferais la guerre.... Par ce
moyen je jetterais les novateurs dans les fers.

Le Globe.

No argument is sufficient to destroy the mastery acquired by ten years of pleasant fancies. The Marquis thought it unreasonable to be angry, but could not bring himself to forgive. 'If this Julien could die by accident,' he said to himself at times.... Thus it was that his sorrowful imagination found some relief in pursuing the most absurd chimeras. They paralysed the influence of the wise counsels of the Abbé Pirard. A month passed in this way without the slightest advance in the negotiations.

In this family affair, as in affairs of politics, the Marquis had brilliant flashes of insight which would leave him enthusiastic for three days on end. At such times a plan of conduct would not please him because it was backed by sound reasons; the reasons found favour in his sight only in so far as they supported his favourite plan. For three days, he would labour with all the ardour and enthusiasm of a poet, to bring matters to a certain position; on the fourth, he no longer gave it a thought.

At first Julien was disconcerted by the dilatoriness of the Marquis; but, after some weeks, he began to discern that M. de La Mole had, in dealing with this affair, no definite plan.

Madame de La Mole and the rest of the household thought that Julien had gone into the country to look after the estates; he was in hiding in the Abbé Pirard's presbytery, and saw Mathilde almost every day; she, each morning, went to spend an hour with her father, but sometimes they remained for weeks on end without mentioning the matter that was occupying all their thoughts.

'I do not wish to know where that man is,' the Marquis said to her one day; 'send him this letter.' Mathilde read:

'The estates in Languedoc bring in 20,600 francs. I give 10,600 francs to my daughter, and 10,000 francs to M. Julien Sorel. I make over the estates themselves, that is to say. Tell the lawyer to draft two separate deeds of gift, and to bring me them to-morrow; after which, no further relations between us. Ah! Sir, how was I to expect such a thing as this?

LE MARQUIS DE LA MOLE.'

'I thank you very much,' said Mathilde gaily. 'We are going to settle in the Château d'Aiguillon, between Agen and Marmande. They say that the country there is as beautiful as Italy.'

This donation came as a great surprise to Julien. He was no longer the severe, cold man that we have known. The destiny of his child absorbed all his thoughts in anticipation. This unexpected fortune, quite considerable for so poor a man, made him ambitious. He now saw, settled on his wife or himself, an income of 30,600 francs. As for Mathilde, all her sentiments were absorbed in one of adoration of her husband, for thus it was that her pride always named Julien. Her great, her sole ambition was to have her marriage recognised. She spent her time in exaggerating the high degree of prudence that she had shown in uniting her destiny with that of a superior man. Personal merit was in fashion in her brain.

Their almost continuous separation, the multiplicity of business, the little time that they had to talk of love, now completed the good effect of the wise policy adopted by Julien in the past.

Finally Mathilde grew impatient at seeing so little of the man whom she had now come to love sincerely.

In a moment of ill humour she wrote to her father, and began her letter like Othello:

'That I have preferred Julien to the attractions which society offered to the daughter of M. le Marquis de La Mole, my choice of him sufficiently proves. These pleasures of reputation and petty vanity are nothing to me. It will soon be six weeks that I have lived apart from my husband. That is enough to prove my respect for you. Before next Thursday, I shall leave the paternal roof. Your generosity has made us rich. No one knows my secret save the estimable Abbé Pirard. I shall go to him; he will marry us, and an hour after the ceremony we shall be on our way to Languedoc, and shall never appear again in Paris save by your order. But what pierces me to the heart is that all this will furnish a savoury anecdote at my expense, and at yours. May not the epigrams of a foolish public oblige our excellent Norbert to seek a quarrel with Julien? In that event, I know him, I should have no control over him. We should find in his heart the plebeian in revolt. I implore you on my knees, O my father, come and attend our wedding, in M. Pirard's church, next Thursday. The point of the malicious ancedote will be blunted, and the life of your only son, my husband's life will be made safe,' etc., etc.

This letter plunged the Marquis in a strange embarrassment. He must now at length *make up his mind.* All his little habits, all his commonplace friends had lost their influence.

In these strange circumstances, the salient features of his character, stamped upon it by the events of his younger days, resumed their full sway. The troubles of the Emigration had made him a man of imagination. After he had enjoyed for two years an immense fortune and all the distinctions of the Court, 1790 had cast him into the fearful hardships of the Emigration. This hard school had changed the heart of a man of two and twenty. Actually he was encamped amid his present wealth rather than dominated by it. But this same

imagination which had preserved his soul from the gangrene
of gold, had left him a prey to an insane passion for seeing
his daughter adorned with a fine-sounding title.

During the six weeks that had just elapsed, urged at one
moment by a caprice, the Marquis had decided to enrich
Julien; poverty seemed to him ignoble, dishonouring to himself, M. de La Mole, impossible in the husband of his daughter; he showered money upon him. Next day, his imagination
taking another direction, it seemed to him that Julien would
hear the silent voice of this generosity in the matter of
money, change his name, retire to America, write to
Mathilde that he was dead to her. M. de La Mole imagined
this letter as written, and traced its effect on his daughter's
character. . . .

On the day on which he was awakened from these youthful
dreams by Mathilde's *real* letter, after having long thought of
killing Julien or of making him disappear, he was dreaming
of building up for him a brilliant future. He was making him
take the name of one of his properties; and why should he
not secure the transmission of his peerage to him? M. le Duc
de Chaulnes, his father-in-law, had spoken to him several
times, since his only son had been killed in Spain, of wishing
to hand on his title to Norbert. . . .

'One cannot deny that Julien shews a singular aptitude for
business, audacity, perhaps even *brilliance*,' the Marquis said
to himself. . . . 'But at the back of that character, I find something alarming. It is the impression that he produces on
everyone, therefore there must be something real in it' (the
more difficult this reality was to grasp, the more it alarmed
the imaginative spirit of the old Marquis).

'My daughter expressed it to me very cleverly the other
day' (in a letter which we have suppressed): ' "Julien belongs
to no drawing-room, to no set." He has not contrived to find
any support against me, not the slightest resource if I abandon him. . . . But is that due to ignorance of the actual state
of society? Two or three times I have said to him: "There is
no real and profitable candidature save that of the drawing-
rooms. . . ."

503

'No, he has not the adroit and cautious spirit of a petti-fogger who never loses a minute or an opportunity.... It is not at all the character of a Louis XI. On the other hand, I see in him the most ungenerous maxims.... I lose track of him.... Does he repeat those maxims to himself, to serve as a *dam* to his passions?

'Anyhow, one thing is clear: he cannot endure contempt, in that way I hold him.

'He has not the religious feeling for high birth, it is true, he does not respect us by instinct.... That is bad; but, after all, the heart of a seminarist should be impatient only of the want of pleasure and money. He is very different; he cannot endure contempt at any price.'

Forced by his daughter's letter, M. de La Mole saw the necessity of making up his mind 'Well, here is the great question: has Julien's audacity gone the length of setting him to make love to my daughter, because he knows that I love her more than anything in the world, and that I have an income of a hundred thousand crowns?

'Mathilde protests the opposite.... No, master Julien, that is a point upon which I wish to be under no illusion.

'Has there been genuine, unpremeditated love? Or rather a vulgar desire to raise himself to a good position? Mathilde is perspicacious, she felt from the first that this suspicion might ruin him with me; hence that admission: it was she who thought first of loving him....

'That a girl of so lofty a character should so far have for-gotten herself as to make tangible advances!... Press his arm in the garden, one evening, how horrible! As though she had not had a hundred less indelicate ways of letting him know that she favoured him.

'*To excuse is to accuse*; I distrust Mathilde....' That day, the Marquis's arguments were more conclusive than usual. Habit, however, prevailed; he resolved to gain time and to write to his daughter; for they communicated by letter between differ-ent parts of the house. M. de La Mole dared not discuss matters with Mathilde and hold out against her. He was afraid of bringing everything to an end by a sudden concession.

LETTER

'Take care not to commit any fresh act of folly; here is a commission as Lieutenant of Hussars for M. le Chevalier Julien Sorel de La Vernaye. You see what I am doing for him. Do not cross me, do not question me. He shall start within twenty-four hours, and report himself at Strasbourg, where his regiment is quartered. Here is a draft upon my banker; I expect obedience.'

Mathilde's love and joy knew no bounds; she sought to profit by her victory and replied at once:

'M. de La Vernaye would be at your feet, speechless with gratitude, if he knew all that you are deigning to do for him. But, in the midst of this generosity, my father has forgotten me; your daughter's honour is in danger. A single indiscretion may leave an everlasting blot, which an income of twenty thousand crowns would not efface. I shall send this commission to M. de La Vernaye only if you give me your word that, in the course of the next month, my marriage shall be celebrated in public, at Villequier. Soon after that period, which I beg you not to prolong, your daughter will be unable to appear in public save with the name of Madame de La Vernaye. How I thank you, dear Papa, for having saved me from the name of Sorel,' etc., etc.

The reply was unexpected.

'Obey or I retract all. Tremble, rash girl, I do not yet know what your Julien is, and you yourself know even less than I. Let him start for Strasbourg, and put his best foot foremost. I shall make my wishes known in a fortnight's time.'

The firmness of this reply astonished Mathilde. 'I do not know Julien'; these words plunged her in a day-dream which presently ended in the most enchanting suppositions; but she believed them to be the truth. 'My Julien's mind has not donned the tawdry little *uniform* of the drawing-rooms, and my father disbelieves in his superiority because of the very fact which proves it. . . .

'Anyhow, if I do not obey this sudden impulse, I foresee the possibility of a public scene; a scandal lowers my position in society, and may make me less attractive in Julien's eyes. After the scandal ... ten years of poverty; and the folly of choosing a husband on account of his merit can only be saved from ridicule by the most brilliant opulence. If I live apart from my father, at his age, be may forget me ... Norbert will marry some attractive, clever woman: the old Louis XIV was beguiled by the Duchesse de Bourgogne....'

She decided to obey, but refrained from communicating her father's letter to Julien; his unaccountable nature might lead him to commit some act of folly.

That evening, when she informed Julien that he was a Lieutenant of Hussars, his joy knew no bounds. We may form an idea of it from the ambition that marked his whole life, and from the passionate love that he now felt for his child. The change of name filled him with astonishment.

'At last,' he thought, 'the tale of my adventures is finished, and the credit is all mine. I have contrived to make myself loved by this monster of pride,' he added, looking at Mathilde; 'her father cannot live without her, nor she without me.'

CHAPTER SIXTY-FIVE

A STORM

Mon Dieu, donnez-moi la médiocrité!
MIRABEAU.

HE was completely absorbed; he made only a half-hearted response to the keen affection that she shewed for him. He remained taciturn and sombre. Never had he appeared so great, so adorable in the eyes of Mathilde. She feared some subtle refinement of his pride which would presently upset the whole position.

Almost every morning, she saw the Abbé Pirard come to the Hôtel. Through his agency might not Julien have penetrated to some extent into her father's intentions? Might not the Marquis himself, in a moment of caprice, have written to him? After so great a happiness, how was she to account for Julien's air of severity? She dared not question him.

Dared not! She, Mathilde! There was, from that moment, in her feeling for Julien, something vague, unaccountable, almost akin to terror. That sere heart felt all the passion that is possible in one brought up amid all that excess of civilisation which Paris admires.

Early next morning, Julien was in the Abbé Pirard's presbytery. A pair of post-horses arrived in the courtyard drawing a dilapidated chaise, hired at the nearest post.

'Such an equipage is no longer in keeping,' the stern abbé told him, with a cantankerous air. 'Here are twenty thousand francs, of which M. de La Mole makes you a present; he expects you to spend them within the year, but to try and make yourself as little ridiculous as possible.' (In so large a sum, bestowed on a young man, the priest saw only an occasion of sin.)

'The Marquis adds: "M. Julien de La Vernaye will have received this money from his father, whom there is no use in my identifying more precisely. M. de La Vernaye will doubtless think it proper to make a present to M. Sorel, carpenter at Verrières, who looked after him in his childhood...." I will undertake this part of the commission,' the abbé went on; 'I have at last made M. de La Mole decide to compromise with that Abbé de Frilair, who is such a Jesuit. His position is unquestionably too strong for us. The implicit recognition of your noble birth by that man who governs Besançon will be one of the implied conditions of the arrangement.'

Julien was no longer able to control his enthusiasm, he embraced the abbé, he saw himself recognised.

'Fie!' said M. Pirard, and thrust him away; 'what is the meaning of this worldly vanity? As for Sorel and his sons, I shall offer them, in my name, an annual pension of five hundred francs, which will be paid to each of them separately, so long as I am satisfied with them.'

Julien was by this time cold and stiff. He thanked the abbé, but in the vaguest terms and without binding himself to anything. 'Can it indeed be possible,' he asked himself, 'that I am the natural son of some great nobleman, banished among our mountains by the terrible Napoleon?' Every moment this idea seemed to him less improbable.... 'My hatred for my father would be a proof.... I should no longer be a monster!'

A few days after this monologue, the Fifteenth Regiment of Hussars, one of the smartest in the Army, was drawn up in order of battle on the parade ground of Strasbourg. M. le Chevalier de La Vernaye was mounted upon the finest horse in Alsace, which had cost him six thousand francs. He had joined as Lieutenant, without having ever been a Second Lieutenant, save on the muster-roll of a Regiment of which he had never even heard.

His impassive air, his severe and almost cruel eyes, his

pallor, his unalterable coolness won him a reputation from the first day. In a short time, his perfect and entirely measured courtesy, his skill with the pistol and sabre, which he made known without undue affectation, removed all temptation to joke audibly at his expense. After five or six days of hesitation, the general opinion of the Regiment declared itself in his favour. 'This young man has everything,' said the older officers who were inclined to banter, 'except youth.'

From Strasbourg, Julien wrote to M. Chélan, the former curé of Verrières, who was now reaching the extreme limits of old age:

'You will have learned with a joy, of which I have no doubt, of the events that have led my family to make me rich. Here are five hundred francs which I beg you to distribute without display, and with no mention of my name, among the needy, who are poor now as I was once, and whom you are doubtless assisting as in the past you assisted me.'

Julien was intoxicated with ambition and not with vanity; he still applied a great deal of his attention to his outward appearance. His horses, his uniforms, the liveries of his servants were kept up with a nicety which would have done credit to the punctiliousness of a great English nobleman. Though only just a Lieutenant, promoted by favour and after two days' service, he was already calculating that, in order to be Commander in Chief at thirty, at latest, like all the great Generals, he would need at three and twenty to be something more than Lieutenant. He could think of nothing but glory and his son.

It was in the midst of the transports of the most frenzied ambition that he was interrupted by a young footman from the Hôtel de La Mole, who arrived with a letter.

'All is lost,' Mathilde wrote to him; 'hasten here as quickly as possible, sacrifice everything, desert if need be. As soon as you arrive, wait for me in a cab, outside the little gate of the garden, No. —— Rue ——. I shall come out to speak to you; perhaps I may be able to let you into the garden. All is lost, and, I fear, beyond hope of repair; count upon me, you will find me devoted and steadfast in adversity. I love you.'

In a few minutes, Julien obtained leave from his Colonel, and left Strasbourg at a gallop; but the fearful anxiety which was devouring him did not allow him to continue this method of travel farther than Metz. He flung himself into a post-chaise; and it was with an almost incredible rapidity that he arrived at the appointed place, outside the little gate of the garden of the Hôtel de La Mole. The gate was flung open, and in a moment, Mathilde, forgetting all self-respect, threw herself into his arms. Fortunately, it was but five o'clock in the morning and the street was still deserted.

'All is lost; my father, dreading my tears, went away on Thursday night. Where? No one knows. Here is his letter; read it.' And she got into the cab with Julien.

'I could forgive everything, except the plan of seducing you because you are rich. That, unhappy girl, is the appalling truth. I give you my word of honour that I will never consent to a marriage with that man. I promise him an income of ten thousand livres if he consents to live abroad, beyond the frontiers of France, or better still in America. Read the letter which I have received in reply to a request for information. The shameless scoundrel had himself invited me to write to Madame de Rênal. Never will I read a line from you about the man. I have a horror of Paris and of you. I request you to cloak with the greatest secrecy what must shortly happen. Renounce *honestly* a vile fellow, and you will regain a father.'

'Where is Madame de Rênal's letter?' said Julien coldly.
'Here it is. I did not wish to shew it to you until you were prepared.'

LETTER

'What I owe to the sacred cause of religion and morals obliges me, Sir, to the painful step which I take in addressing you; a rule, which admits of no relaxation, orders me at this moment to do harm to my neighbour, but in order to avoid a greater scandal. The grief which I feel must be overborne by a sense of duty. It is only too true, Sir, the conduct of the person with regard to whom you ask me to tell the whole truth may have seemed inexplicable or indeed honourable. It may have been thought expedient to conceal or to disguise a part of the truth, prudence required this as well as religion. But that conduct, which you desire to know, has been in fact extremely reprehensible, and more so than I can say. Poor and avaricious, it is by the aid of the most consummate hypocrisy, and by the seduction of a weak and unhappy woman, that this man has sought to make a position for himself and to become somebody. It is a part of my painful duty to add that I am obliged to believe that M. J—— has no religious principles. I am bound in conscience to think that one of his avenues to success in a household is to seek to seduce the woman who has most influence there. Cloaked by a shew of disinterestedness and by phrases from novels, his great and sole object is to contrive to secure control over the master of the house and over his fortune. He leaves in his wake misery and undying regret,' etc., etc., etc.

This letter, extremely long and half obliterated by tears, was certainly in the hand of Madame de Rênal; it was even written with greater care than usual.

'I cannot blame M. de La Mole,' said Julien when he had finished reading it; 'he is just and prudent. What father would give his beloved daughter to such a man! Farewell!'

Julien sprang out of the cab, and ran to his post-chaise which had drawn up at the end of the street. Mathilde, whom he seemed to have forgotten, followed him for a little way; but the sight of the tradesmen who were coming to the doors of their shops, and to whom she was known, forced her to retire in haste into the garden.

Julien had set off for Verrières. On this rapid journey, he was unable to write to Mathilde as he had intended, his hand traced nothing more than an illegible scrawl on the paper.

He arrived at Verrières on a Sunday morning. He entered

the shop of the local gunsmith, who congratulated him effusively on his recent access to fortune. It was the talk of the
town.

Julien had some difficulty in making him understand that
he required a brace of pistols. The gunsmith, at his request,
loaded the pistols.

The *three bells* sounded; this is a signal well known in
French villages, which, after the various peals of the morning, announces that mass is just about to begin.

Julien entered the new church of Verrières. All the tall
windows of the building were screened by crimson curtains.
He found himself standing a few yards behind Madame de
Rênal's bench. He had the impression that she was praying
with fervour. The sight of this woman who had loved him
so dearly made Julien's arm tremble so violently that he
could not at first carry out his design. 'I cannot,' he said to
himself; 'I am physically incapable of it.'

At that moment, the young clerk who was serving mass
rang the bell for the Elevation. Madame de Rênal bowed
her head which for a moment was almost entirely concealed
by the folds of her shawl. Her aspect was less familiar to
Julien; he fired a shot at her with one pistol and missed her,
he fired a second shot; she fell.

CHAPTER SIXTY-SIX

PAINFUL DETAILS

> Do not look for any weakness on my part. I have
> avenged myself. I have deserved death, and here I am.
> Pray for my soul.
>
> SCHILLER.

JULIEN remained motionless, seeing nothing. When he
came to himself a little, he noticed the whole congregation rushing from the church; the priest had left the altar.
Julien set off at a leisurely pace in the wake of some
women who were screaming as they went. One woman, who
was trying to escape faster than the rest, gave him a violent
push; he fell. His feet were caught in a chair overturned by
the crowd; as he rose, he felt himself gripped by the collar;
it was a gendarme in full uniform who was arresting him.
Mechanically Julien's hand went to his pocket pistols; but a
second gendarme seized him by the arms.

He was led away to prison. They took him into a room,
put irons on his wrists, and left him by himself; the door was
shut on him and double-locked; all this was carried out
quickly, and he remained unconscious of it.

'Faith, all is over,' he said aloud on coming to himself....
'Yes, in a fortnight the guillotine ... or suicide between now
and then.'

His reasoning went no farther; he felt a pain in his head
as though it had been gripped with violence. He looked
round to see if anyone was holding it. A few moments later,
he fell into a deep slumber.

513

Madame de Rênal was not mortally wounded. The first bullet had passed through her hat; as she turned round, the second shot had been fired. This bullet had struck her in the shoulder, and, what was surprising, had glanced back from the shoulder-blade, which nevertheless it shattered, against a gothic pillar, from which it broke off a huge splinter of stone.

When, after a long and painful examination, the surgeon, a grave man, said to Madame de Rênal: 'I answer for your life as for my own,' she was deeply affected.

For a long time she had sincerely longed for death. The letter which she had been ordered to write by her confessor of the moment, and had written to M. de La Mole, had dealt the final blow to this creature weakened by an ever-present sorrow. This sorrow was Julien's absence; she herself called it *remorse*. Her director, a young cleric, virtuous and fervent, recently arrived from Dijon, was under no illusion.

'To die thus, but not by my own hand, is not a sin,' thought Madame de Rênal. 'God will pardon me perhaps for rejoicing in my death.' She dared not add: 'And to die by the hand of Julien is the acme of bliss.'

As soon as she was rid of the presence of the surgeon, and of all her friends who had come crowding round her, she sent for Elisa, her maid.

'The gaoler,' she said to her, blushing deeply, 'is a cruel man. Doubtless he intends to maltreat him, thinking that by so doing he will he pleasing me. . . . The thought of such a thing is unendurable. Could you not go, as though on your own behalf, and give the gaoler this packet which contains a few louis? You will tell him that religion does not permit his maltreating him. . . . But on no account must he mention this gift of money.'

It was to this circumstance that Julien was indebted for the humanity of the gaoler of Verrières; he was still that N. Noiroud, the loyal supporter of the government, whom we have seen thrown into such a panic by the arrival of M. Appert.

A magistrate appeared in the prison. 'I have taken life with premeditation,' Julien said to him; 'I bought the pistols and had them loaded by So-and-so, the gunsmith. Article 1342 of the Penal Code is quite clear, I deserve death and await it.' The magistrate, whose mean spirit was incapable of understanding this frank sincerity, sought to multiply his questions so that the accused might contradict himself in his answers.

'But don't you see,' Julien said to him with a smile, 'that I am making myself out as guilty as you can wish? Go, Sir, you shall not lack the quarry that you are pursuing. You shall have the pleasure of passing sentence. Spare me your presence.

'I have still a tiresome duty to perform,' thought Julien, 'I must write to Mademoiselle de La Mole.

'I have avenged myself,' he told her. 'Unfortunately, my name will appear in the newspapers, and I cannot escape from this world *incognito*. I ask your forgiveness. I shall die within two months. My revenge has been terrible, like the grief of being parted from you. From this moment, I forbid myself to write and to utter your name. Never speak of me, even to my son: silence is the only way of honouring me. To the average man I shall be a common murderer. . . . Allow me to tell the truth in this supreme moment: you will forget me. This great catastrophe, as to which I recommend you never to open your lips to a living soul, will suppress for some years all the romantic and unduly adventurous element that I saw in your character. You were made to live among the heroes of the Middle Ages; shew in this crisis their firmness of character. Let what is bound to happen be accomplished in secret and without compromising you. You will take a false name and dispense with a confidant. If you must absolutely have the assistance of a friend, I bequeath to you the Abbé Pirard.

'Do not speak to anyone else, especially to men of your own class; de Luz or Caylus.

'A year after my death, marry M. de Croisenois; I order you as your husband. Do not write to me at all, I should not answer you. Though far less of a villain than Iago, or so it seems to me, I shall say like him: *From this time forth I never will speak word.*

515

'No one shall see me either speak or write; you will have had my last words, with my last adoration.

'J. S.'

It was after he had sent off this letter that for the first time, Julien, having slightly recovered himself, became extremely unhappy. One by one, each of the hopes of his ambition must be wrenched from his heart by those solemn words: 'I am to die.' Death, in itself, was not *horrible* in his eyes. His whole life had been merely a long preparation for misfortune, and he had certainly never forgotten what is reckoned the greatest misfortune of all.

'Why!' he said to himself, 'if in sixty days I had to fight a duel with a man who was a champion fencer, should I be so weak as to think of it incessantly and with terror in my soul?'

He spent more than an hour in seeking to discover his exact sentiments in this connexion.

When he had seen clearly into his soul, and the truth appeared before his eyes as sharply defined as one of the pillars of his prison, he thought of remorse.

'Why should I feel any? I have been outraged in a terrible manner; I have taken life, I deserve death, but that is all. I die after having paid my reckoning with humanity. I leave behind me no unfulfilled obligation, I owe nothing to anyone; there is nothing shameful in my death but the instrument of it: that by itself, it is true, will amply suffice to shame me in the eyes of the townsfolk of Verrières; but, from an intellectual point of view, what could be more contemptible? There remains one way of acquiring distinction in their eyes: namely, by scattering gold coins among the crowd on my way to the scaffold. My memory, linked with the thought of *gold*, will then be resplendent to them.'

After this consideration, which at the end of a minute seemed to him conclusive: 'I have nothing more to do on earth,' Julien said to himself and fell into a deep slumber.

About nine o'clock in the evening, the gaoler awakened him by bringing in his supper.

'What are they saying in Verrières?'

'Monsieur Julien, the oath that I took before the Crucifix, in the King's court, the day I was installed in my post, compels me to keep silence.'

He was silent, but remained in the room. The spectacle of this vulgar hypocrisy amused Julien. 'I must,' he thought, 'keep him waiting a long time for the five francs which he wants as the price of his conscience.'

When the gaoler saw the meal come to an end without any attempt at corruption:

'The friendship that I feel for you, Monsieur Julien,' he began, with a false, winning air, 'obliges me to speak; although they may say that it is against the interests of justice, because it may help you to arrange your defence.... Monsieur Julien, who has a good heart, will be glad if I tell him that Madame de Rênal is going on well.'

'What! She is not dead?' cried Julien, rising from the table, beside himself with amazement.

'What! Didn't you know?' said the gaoler with an air of stupidity which presently turned to one of joyful greed. 'It would only be right for Monsieur to give something to the surgeon who, according to law and justice, ought not to speak. But, to oblige Monsieur, I went to his house, and he told me everything....'

'In short, the injury is not mortal,' said Julien, losing patience and advancing upon him, 'you answer for that with your life?'

The gaoler, a giant six feet in stature, took fright and retreated towards the door. Julien saw that he was going the wrong way to reach the truth, he sat down again and tossed a napoleon to M. Noiroud.

As the man's story began to convince Julien that Madame de Rênal's injury was not mortal, he felt himself overcome by tears. 'Leave me!' he said suddenly.

The gaoler obeyed. As soon as the door was shut: 'Great God! She is not dead!' exclaimed Julien; and he fell on his knees, weeping hot tears.

In this supreme moment he was a believer. What matter

517

the hypocrisies of the priests? Can they destroy anything of
the truth and sublimity of the idea of God?

Only then did Julien begin to repent of the crime that
he had committed. By a coincidence which saved him from
despair, at that moment only had passed away the state of
irritation and semi-insanity in which he had been plunged
since leaving Paris for Verrières.

His tears sprang from a generous source, he had no doubt
as to the sentence that was in store for him.

'And so she will live!' he said to himself.... 'She will live
to pardon me and to love me.'

Late next morning, when the gaoler awakened him:

'You must have a wonderful heart, Monsieur Julien,' the
man said to him. 'Twice I have come in and could not bring
myself to wake you. Here are two bottles of excellent wine
which M. Maslon, our curé, sends you.'

'What? Is that rascal here still?' said Julien.

'Yes, Sir,' replied the gaoler, lowering his voice, 'but do
not speak so loud, it may damage you.'

Julien laughed heartily.

'At the stage I have reached, my friend, you alone could
damage me, if you ceased to be gentle and human.... You
shall be well paid,' Julien broke off, resuming his imperious
air. This air was immediately justified by the gift of a small
coin.

M. Noiroud told him once more, going into the fullest
detail, all that he had heard about Madame de Rênal, but
he did not mention Miss Elisa's visit.

This man was as menial and submissive as possible. An
idea came into Julien's head: 'This sort of ungainly giant may
earn three or four hundred francs, for his prison is never
crowded; I can guarantee him ten thousand francs, if he
cares to escape to Switzerland with me.... The difficulty will
be to persuade him of my sincerity.' The thought of the long
colloquy that he would have to hold with so vile a creature
filled Julien with disgust, he turned his mind to other things.

That evening, there was no longer time. A post-chaise
came to fetch him at midnight. He was charmed with the

gendarmes, his travelling companions. In the morning, when
he arrived at the prison of Besançon, they were so kind as
to lodge him on the upper floor of a gothic dungeon. He
guessed the architecture to date from the beginning of the
fourteenth century; he admired its grace and pointed airi-
ness. Through a narrow gap between two walls on the farther
side of a deep courtyard, there was a glimpse of a superb
view.

Next day he was examined, after which, for several days,
he was left to himself. His spirit was calm. He could find
nothing that was not quite simple in his case: 'I sought to
kill, I must be killed.'

His thoughts did not linger to consider this argument. The
trial, the annoyance of appearing in public, the defence, he
regarded as so many trifling embarrassments, tiresome ceremonies of which it would be time to think when the day
came. The prospect of death detained him almost as little:
'I shall think of that after the sentence.' Life was by no means
tedious to him, he looked at everything in a fresh light. He
had no ambition left. He thought rarely of Mademoiselle de
La Mole. His remorse occupied him a great deal and often
called up before him the image of Madame de Rênal, especially in the silence of the night, disturbed only, in this lofty
dungeon, by the cry of the osprey!

He thanked heaven for not having let him wound her mortally. 'An astonishing thing!' he said to himself, 'I thought
that by her letter to M. de La Mole she had destroyed my
future happiness for all time, and, in less than a fortnight
after the date of that letter, I no longer think of all that was
occupying my mind. . . . Two or three thousand livres a year
to live quietly in a mountain village like Vergy. . . . I was
happy then. . . . I did not recognise my own happiness!'

At other moments, he would rise with a bound from his
chair. 'If I had wounded Madame de Rênal mortally, I
should have killed myself. . . . I require that certainty to make
me feel a horror of myself.

'Kill myself! That is the great question,' he said to himself.
'Those judges so steeped in formalities, so thirsty for the

blood of the wretched prisoner, who would have the best of citizens hanged in order to hang a Cross from their own buttonholes.... I should remove myself from their power, from their insults in bad French, which the local newspaper will proceed to call eloquence.

'I may live for five or six weeks still, more or less.... Kill myself! Faith, no,' he said to himself after a few days, 'Napoleon lived....

'Besides, life is pleasant to me; this is a quiet spot to stay in; I have no worries,' he added, laughing, and set to work to make a list of the books which he wished to have sent to him from Paris.

CHAPTER SIXTY-SEVEN

A DUNGEON

The tomb of a friend.

STERNE.

H E heard a great din in the corridor; it was not the hour for visiting his cell; the osprey flew away screaming, the door opened, and the venerable Curé Chélan, trembling all over and leaning upon his cane, flung himself into Julien's arms.

'Ah, great God! Is it possible, my child.... Monster, I ought to say.'

And the good old man could not add another word. Julien was afraid of his falling. He was obliged to lead him to a chair. The hand of time had fallen heavily upon this man, so vigorous in days gone by. He appeared to Julien to be only the ghost of his former self.

When he had recovered his breath: 'Only the day before yesterday, I received your letter from Strasbourg, with your five hundred francs for the poor of Verrières; it was brought to me up in the mountains at Liveru, where I have gone to live with my nephew Jean. Yesterday, I learned of the catastrophe.... Oh, heavens! Is it possible?' The old man's tears ceased to flow, he seemed incapable of thought and added mechanically: 'You will need your five hundred francs, I have brought them back to you.'

'I need to see you, Father!' Julien exclaimed with emotion. 'I have plenty of money.'

But he could not extract any coherent answer. From time

to time, M. Chélan shed a few tears which rolled in silence down his cheeks; then he gazed at Julien, and was almost stupefied at seeing him take his hands and raise them to his lips. That countenance, once so lively, and so vigorous in its expression of the noblest sentiments, was no longer to be aroused from a state of apathy. A sort of peasant came presently to fetch the old man. 'It does not do to tire him and make him talk too much,' he said to Julien, who realised that this was the nephew. This visit left Julien plunged in bitter grief which stopped his tears. Everything seemed to him sad and comfortless; he felt his heart freeze in his bosom.

This was the most cruel moment that he had experienced since the crime. He had seen death face to face, and in all its ugliness. All the illusions of greatness of soul and generosity had been scattered like a cloud before the storm.

This fearful situation lasted for some hours. After moral poisoning, one requires physical remedies and a bottle of champagne. Julien would have deemed himself a coward had he had recourse to them. Towards the end of a horrible day, the whole of which he had spent in pacing the floor of his narrow dungeon: 'What a fool I am!' he exclaimed. 'It would be if I expected to die in my bed that the sight of that poor old man ought to make me so utterly wretched; but a swift death in the springtide of life is the very thing to save me from that miserable decrepitude.'

Whatever arguments he might thus advance, Julien found that he was moved like any pusillanimous creature and made wretched in consequence by this visit.

There was no longer any trace of rugged grandeur in him, any Roman virtue; death appeared to him on a higher plane, and as a thing less easily to be won.

'This shall be my thermometer,' he said to himself. 'This evening I am ten degrees below the level of courage that must lead me to the guillotine. This morning, I had that courage. What does it matter, after all? Provided that it returns to me at the right moment.' This idea of a thermometer amused him and succeeded finally in distracting him.

Next morning, on waking, he was ashamed of his behaviour

the day before. 'My happiness, my tranquillity are at stake.' He almost made up his mind to write to the Attorney General to ask that nobody should be admitted to his cell. 'And Fouqué?' he thought. 'If he can manage to come to Besançon, how distressed he will he.'

It was perhaps two months since he had given Fouqué a thought. 'I was an utter fool at Strasbourg, my thoughts never went beyond my coat collar.' Memories of Fouqué kept recurring to his mind and left him in a more tender mood. He paced the floor with agitation. 'Now I am certainly twenty degrees below the level of death.... If this weakness increases, it will pay me better to kill myself. What a joy for the Abbé Maslons and the Valenods if I die here like a rat!'

Fouqué arrived; the simple, honest fellow was shattered by grief. His sole idea, if he had one at all, was to sell all that he possessed in order to corrupt the gaoler and so save Julien's life. He spoke to him for hours of the escape of M. de Lavalette.

'You distress me,' Julien said to him; 'M. de Lavalette was innocent, I am guilty. Without meaning to do so, you make me realise the difference....

'But is it true? What! You would sell all that you have?' said Julien, suddenly becoming observant and suspicious once more.

Fouqué, delighted to see his friend at last responsive to his dominant idea, explained to him in full detail, and to within a hundred francs or so, what he expected to receive for each of his properties.

'What a sublime effort in a small landowner!' thought Julien. 'How many savings, how many little cheese-parings, which made me blush so when I saw him make them, he is willing to sacrifice for me! None of those fine young fellows whom I used to see at the Hôtel de La Mole, who read *René*, would have any of his absurdities; but apart from those of them who are very young and have inherited fortunes, as well, and know nothing of the value of money, which of those fine Parisians would be capable of such a sacrifice?'

All Fouqué's mistakes in grammar, all his vulgar mannerisms vanished, he flung himself into his arms. Never have the provinces, when contrasted with Paris, received a nobler homage. Fouqué, delighted by the enthusiasm which he read in his friend's eyes, mistook it for consent to an escape.

This glimpse of the *sublime* restored to Julien all the strength of which M. Chélan's visit had robbed him. He was still very young; but, to my mind, he was a fine plant. Instead of his advancing from tenderness to cunning, like the majority of men, age would have given him an easy access to emotion, he would have been cured of an insane distrust. . . . But what good is there in these vain predictions?

The examinations became more frequent, in spite of the efforts of Julien, whose answers were all aimed at cutting the whole business short. 'I have taken life, or at least I have sought to take life, and with premeditation,' he repeated day after day. But the magistrate was a formalist first and foremost. Julien's statements in no way cut short the examinations; the magistrate's feelings were hurt. Julien did not know that they had proposed to remove him to a horrible cellar, and that it was thanks to Fouqué's intervention that he was allowed to remain in his charming room one hundred and eighty steps from the ground.

M. l'Abbé de Frilair was one of the important persons who contracted with Fouqué for the supply of their firewood. The honest merchant had access even to the all-powerful Grand Vicar. To his inexpressible delight, M. de Frilair informed him that, touched by the good qualities of Julien and by the services which he had rendered in the past to the Seminary, he intended to intervene on his behalf with the judges. Fouqué saw a hope of saving his friend, and on leaving his presence, bowing to the ground, begged the Grand Vicar to expend upon masses, to pray for the acquittal of the prisoner, a sum of ten louis.

Fouqué was strangely in error. M. de Frilair was by no means a Valenod. He refused, and even tried to make the worthy peasant understand that he would do better to keep his money in his pocket. Seeing that it was impossible to make his meaning clear without indiscretion, he advised him to distribute the sum in alms, for the poor prisoners, who, as a matter of fact, were in need of everything.

'This Julien is a strange creature, his action is inexplicable,' thought M. de Frilair, 'and nothing ought to be inexplicable to me.... Perhaps it will be possible to make a martyr of him.... In any case, I shall find out the true *inwardness* of this business and may perhaps find an opportunity of inspiring fear in that Madame de Rênal, who has no respect for us, and detests me in her heart.... Perhaps I may even discover in all this some sensational means of reconciliation with M. de La Mole, who has a weakness for this little Seminarist.'

The settlement of the lawsuit had been signed some weeks earlier, and the Abbé Pirard had left Besançon, not without having spoken of the mystery of Julien's birth, on the very day on which the wretched fellow tried to kill Madame de Rênal in the church of Verrières.

Julien saw only one disagreeable incident in store for him before his death, namely a visit from his father. He consulted Fouqué as to his idea of writing to the Attorney General, asking to be excused any further visitors. This horror at the sight of a father, at such a moment, shocked the honest and respectable heart of the timber-merchant profoundly.

He thought he understood why so many people felt a passionate hatred of his friend. Out of respect for another's grief, he concealed his feelings.

'In any case,' he replied coldly, 'an order for solitary confinement would not apply to your father.'

CHAPTER SIXTY-EIGHT

A MAN OF POWER

> But there is such mystery in her movements, such
> elegance in her form. Who can she be?
>
> SCHILLER.

T HE doors of the dungeon were thrown open at a very
early hour the next morning. Julien awoke with a
start.

'Oh, good God,' he thought, 'here comes my father. What
a disagreeable scene!'

At that moment, a woman dressed as a peasant flung herself into his arms, seizing him in a passionate embrace; he
had difficulty in recognising her. It was Mademoiselle de La
Mole.

'Miscreant, it was only from your letter that I learned
where you were. What you call your crime, though it is nothing but a noble revenge which shews me all the loftiness of
the heart that beats in your bosom, I learned only at
Verrières. ...'

Notwithstanding his prejudices against Mademoiselle de
La Mole, prejudices of which, moreover, he had not himself
formed any definite idea, Julien found her extremely good-
looking. How could he fail to see in all this manner of speech
and action a noble, disinterested sentiment, far above anything that a petty, vulgar spirit would have dared? He imagined once again that he was in love with a queen, and after
a few moments it was with a rare nobility of speech and
thought that he said to her:

'The future was tracing itself quite clearly before my eyes. After my death, I married you to Croisenois, who would be marrying a widow. The noble but slightly romantic spirit of this charming widow, startled and converted to the service of common prudence by an event at once singular, tragic and for her momentous, would have deigned to appreciate the quite genuine merit of the young Marquis. You would have resigned yourself to enjoying the happiness of the rest of the world: esteem, riches, high rank.... But, dear Mathilde, your coming to Besançon, if it is suspected, is going to be a mortal blow to M. de La Mole, and that is what I will never forgive myself. I have already caused him so much sorrow! The Academician will say that he has been warming a serpent in his bosom.'

'I must confess that I hardly expected so much cold reasoning, so much thought for the future,' said Mademoiselle de La Mole, half annoyed. 'My maid, who is almost as prudent as yourself, procured a passport for herself, and it is in the name of Madame Michelet that I have travelled post.'

'And Madame Michelet found it so easy to make her way in to me?'

'Ah! You are still the superior man, the man of my choice! First of all, I offered a hundred francs to a magistrate's secretary, who assured me that it was impossible for me to enter this dungeon. But after taking the money, this honest man made me wait, raised objections, I thought that he meant to rob me....' She broke off.

'Well?' asked Julien.

'Do not be angry with me, my little Julien,' she said, embracing him, 'I was obliged to give my name to this secretary, who took me for a young milliner from Paris, enamoured of the handsome Julien.... Indeed, those are his very words. I swore to him that I was your wife, and I am to have permission to see you every day.'

'That finishes everything,' thought Julien; 'I could not prevent it. After all, M. de La Mole is so great a nobleman that public opinion will easily find an excuse for the young Colonel who will wed this charming widow. My approaching death will cover everything'; and he abandoned himself with ecstasy to Mathilde's love; there followed madness, magnanimity, everything that was most strange. She seriously proposed to him that she should die with him.

After these first transports, and when she had grown used to the happiness of seeing Julien, a keen curiosity suddenly took possession of her soul. She examined her lover, and found him far superior to what she had imagined. Boniface de La Mole seemed to her reincarnate in him, but in a more heroic mould.

Mathilde saw the leading counsel of the place, whom she insulted by offering them gold too crudely; but they ended by accepting.

She speedily came to the conclusion that in doubtful matters of high import, everything in Besançon depended upon M. l'Abbé de Frilair.

Under the obscure name of Madame Michelet, she at first found insuperable obstacles in the way to the presence of the all-powerful leader of the *Congregation*. But the rumour of the beauty of a young milliner, madly in love, who had come from Paris to Besançon to comfort the young Abbé Julien Sorel, began to spread through the town.

Mathilde went alone and on foot through the streets of Besançon; she hoped that she might not be recognised. In any event, she thought that it must help her cause to create a strong impression upon the populace. In her folly she thought of making them revolt, to save Julien on his way to the scaffold. Mademoiselle de La Mole imagined herself to be dressed simply and in a manner becoming a woman stricken with grief; she was dressed in such a fashion as to attract every eye.

She was the sole object of attention in Besançon, when, after a week of solicitation, she obtained an audience of M. Frilair.

Great as her courage might be, the idea of an influential head of the *Congregation* and that of a profound and cautious rascality were so closely associated in her mind that she trembled as she rang the bell at the door of the Bishop's palace. She could barely stand when she had to climb the stair that led to the First Grand Vicar's apartment. The loneliness of the episcopal palace chilled her with fear. 'I may sit down in an armchair, and the armchair grip me by the arms, I shall have vanished. Of whom can my maid ask for news of me? The Captain of Police will decline to interfere.... I am all alone in this great town!'

Her first sight of the apartment set Mademoiselle de La Mole's heart at rest. First of all, it was a footman in the most elegant livery that had opened the door to her. The parlour in which she was asked to wait displayed that refined and delicate luxury, so different from vulgar magnificence, which one finds in Paris only in the best houses. As soon as she caught sight of M. de Frilair, who came towards her with a fatherly air, all thoughts of a dastardly crime vanished. She did not even find on his handsome countenance the imprint of that energetic, that almost wild virtue, so antipathetic to Parisian society. The half-smile that animated the features of the priest who was in supreme control of everything at Besançon, betokened the man used to good society, the cultured prelate, the able administrator. Mathilde imagined herself in Paris.

It needed only a few minutes for M. de Frilair to lead Mathilde on to admit to him that she was the daughter of his powerful adversary, the Marquis de La Mole.

'I am not, as a matter of fact, Madame Michelet,' she said, resuming all the loftiness of her bearing, 'and this admission costs me little, for I have come to consult you, Sir, as to the possibility of procuring the escape of M. de La Vernaye. In the first place he is guilty of nothing worse than a piece of stupidity; the woman at whom he fired is doing well. In the second place, to corrupt the subordinates, I can put down here and now fifty thousand francs, and bind myself to pay double that sum. Lastly, my gratitude and the gratitude of my family will consider no request impossible from the person who has saved M. de La Vernaye.'

M. de Frilair appeared to be surprised at this name. Mathilde shewed him a number of letters from the Ministry of War, addressed to M. Julien Sorel de La Vernaye.

'You see, Sir, that my father undertook to provide for his future. I married him secretly, my father wished him to be a senior officer before making public this marriage, which is a little odd for a La Mole.'

Mathilde remarked that the expression of benevolence and of a mild gaiety speedily vanished as M. de Frilair began to arrive at important discoveries. A subtlety blended with profound insincerity was portrayed on his features.

The abbé had his doubts, he perused the official documents once more slowly.

'What advantage can I gain from these strange confidences?' he asked himself. 'Here I am suddenly brought into close personal contact with a friend of the famous Maréchale de Fervaques, the all-powerful niece of the Lord Bishop of ——, through whom one becomes a Bishop in France.

'What I have always regarded as hidden in the future suddenly presents itself. This may lead me to the goal of all my ambition.'

At first Mathilde was alarmed by the rapid change in the physiognomy of this powerful man, with whom she found herself shut up alone in a remote part of the building. 'But why!' she said to herself presently, 'would it not have been worse to have made no impression upon the cold egoism of a priest sated with the enjoyment of power?'

Dazzled by this rapid and unexpected avenue to the episcopate that was opening before his eyes, astonished at Mathilde's intelligence, for a moment M. de Frilair was off his guard. Mademoiselle de La Mole saw him almost at her feet, trembling nervously with the intensity of his ambition.

'Everything becomes clear,' she thought, 'nothing will be impossible here for a friend of Madame de Fervaques.' Despite a sense of jealousy that was still most painful, she found courage to explain that Julien was an intimate friend of the Maréchale, and almost every evening used to meet, in her house, the Lord Bishop of ——.

'If you were to draw by lot four or five times in succession a list of thirty-six jurymen from among the principal inhabitants of this Department,' said the Grand Vicar with the harsh glare of ambition, dwelling upon each of his words, 'I should consider myself most unfortunate if in each list I did not find eight or nine friends, and those the most intelligent of the lot. Almost invariably I should have a majority, more than is needed to acquit; you see, Mademoiselle, with what ease I can secure an acquittal. . . .'

The abbé broke off suddenly, as though startled by the sound of his words; he was admitting things which are never uttered to the profane.

But Mathilde in turn was stupefied when he informed her that what was most astonishing and interesting to Besançon society in Julien's strange adventure, was that in the past he had inspired a grand passion in Madame de Rênal, which he had long reciprocated. M. de Frilair had no difficulty in perceiving the extreme distress which his story produced.

'I have my revenge!' he thought. 'Here, at last, is a way of controlling this decided young person; I was trembling lest I should not succeed in finding one.' Her distinguished air, as of one not easily led, intensified in his eyes the charm of the rare beauty which he saw almost suppliant before him. He recovered all his self-possession and had no hesitation in turning the knife in the wound.

'I should not be surprised after all,' he said to her lightly, 'were we to learn that it was from jealousy that M. Sorel fired two shots at this woman whom once he loved so dearly. She must have had some relaxation, and for some time past she had been seeing a great deal of a certain Abbé Marquinot of Dijon, a sort of Jansenist, utterly without morals, like all of them.'

M. de Frilair went on torturing with voluptuous relish and at his leisure the heart of this beautiful girl, whose secret he had discovered.

'Why,' he said, fixing a pair of burning eyes on Mathilde, 'should M. Sorel have chosen the church, if not because at that very moment his rival was celebrating mass there? Everyone agrees in ascribing boundless intelligence and even more prudence to the man who is so fortunate as to enjoy your protection. What more simple than to conceal himself in M. de Rênal's gardens, which he knows so well? There, with almost a certainty of not being seen, nor caught, nor suspected, he could have inflicted death on the woman of whom he was jealous.'

These arguments, apparently so well founded, reduced Mathilde to utter despair. Her spirit, haughty enough but saturated with all that dry prudence which passes in society as a faithful portrayal of the human heart, was not made to understand in a moment the joy of defying all prudence which can be so keen a joy to an ardent soul. In the upper classes of Parisian society, in which Mathilde had lived, passion can only very rarely divest itself of prudence, and it is in the attics that girls throw themselves out of windows.

At last the Abbé de Frilair was sure of his control. He gave Mathilde to understand (he was probably lying) that he could influence as he chose the Crown Counsel, who would have to support the charge against Julien.

After the names of the thirty-six jurors for the assize had been drawn by lot, he would make a direct and personal appeal to at least thirty of them.

If M. de Frilair had not thought Mathilde so good-looking, he would not have spoken to her in such plain terms until their fifth or sixth interview.

CHAPTER SIXTY-NINE

INTRIGUE

> March 31, 1676. —He that endeavoured to kill his
> sister in our house, had before killed a man, and it
> had cost his father five hundred écus to get him off;
> by their secret distribution, gaining the favour of the
> counsellors.
>
> LOCKE.[1]

O N leaving the Bishop's palace, Mathilde did not hesitate to send a messenger to Madame de Fervaques;
the fear of compromising herself did not restrain her
for a second. She implored her rival to obtain a letter for M.
de Frilair, written throughout in the hand of the Lord Bishop
of ——. She even went the length of beseeching the other
to hasten, herself, to Besançon. This was a heroic measure
on the part of a proud and jealous spirit.

On the advice of Fouqué, she had taken the precaution of
saying nothing about what she was doing to Julien. Her presence was disturbing enough in itself. A more honourable
man at the approach of death than he had been during his
life, he now felt compunction at the thought not only of M.
de La Mole, but also of Mathilde.

'What is this?' he asked himself, 'I experience in her company moments of abstraction and even of boredom. She is

---

1 I am indebted to the patience and ingenuity of Mr Vyvyan Holland, who has
traced the original text of this motto in *The Life of John Locke, with extracts from
his Correspondence, Journals and Commonplace Books by Lord King* (new edition, 1830).
C.K.S.M.

533

ruining herself for me, and it is thus that I reward her. Can I indeed be wicked?' This question would have troubled him little when he was ambitious; then, not to succeed in life was the only disgrace in his eyes.

His moral uneasiness, in Mathilde's presence, was all the more marked, in that he inspired in her at that moment the most extraordinary and insensate passion. She could speak of nothing but the strange sacrifices which she was anxious to make to save him.

Carried away by a sentiment of which she was proud and which completely overbore her pride, she would have liked not to allow a moment of her life to pass that was not filled with some extraordinary action. The strangest plans, the most perilous to herself, formed the theme of her long conversations with Julien. His gaolers, well rewarded, allowed her to have her way in the prison. Mathilde's ideas were not confined to the sacrifice of her reputation; it mattered nothing to her though she made her condition known to the whole of society. To fling herself on her knees to crave pardon for Julien, in front of the King's carriage as it came by at a gallop, to attract the royal attention, at the risk of a thousand deaths, was one of the tamest fancies of this exalted and courageous imagination. Through her friends who held posts at court, she could count upon being admitted to the reserved parts of the park of Saint-Cloud.

Julien felt himself to be hardly worthy of such devotion, to tell the truth he was tired of heroism. It would have required a simple, artless, almost timid affection to appeal to him, whereas on the contrary, Mathilde's proud spirit must always entertain the idea of a public, of *what people would say*.

In the midst of all her anguish, of all her fears for the life of this lover, whom she was determined not to outlive, Julien felt that she had a secret longing to astonish the public by the intensity of her love and the sublimity of her actions.

He resented the discovery that he was unable to feel at all touched by all this heroism. What would his resentment have been, had he known of all the follies with which Mathilde overpowered the devoted, but eminently reasonable and limited mind of the good Fouqué?

The latter could scarcely find fault with Mathilde's devotion; for he, too, would have sacrificed his whole fortune and exposed his life to the greatest risks to save Julien. He was stupefied by the quantity of gold which Mathilde scattered abroad. At first, the sums thus spent impressed Fouqué, who had for money all the veneration of a provincial.

Later, he discovered that Mademoiselle de La Mole's plans often varied, and, to his great relief, found a word with which to reproach this character which was so exhausting to him: she was *changeable*. To this epithet, that of *wrong-headed*, the direst anathema in the provinces, is the immediate sequel.

'It is strange,' Julien said to himself one day as Mathilde was leaving his prison, 'that so warm a passion, and one of which I am the object, leaves me so unmoved! And I worshipped her two months ago! I have indeed read that at the approach of death we lose interest in everything; but it is frightful to feel oneself ungrateful and to be unable to change. Can I be an egoist?' He heaped on himself, in this connexion, the most humiliating reproaches.

Ambition was dead in his heart, another passion had risen from its ashes; he called it remorse for having murdered Madame de Rênal.

As a matter of fact, he was hopelessly in love with her. He found a strange happiness when, left absolutely alone and without any fear of being disturbed, he could abandon himself entirely to the memory of the happy days which he had spent in the past at Verrières or at Vergy. The most trifling incidents of that time, too swiftly flown, had for him a freshness and a charm that were irresistible. He never gave a thought to his Parisian successes; they bored him.

This tendency, which grew rapidly stronger, was not entirely hidden from the jealous Mathilde. She saw quite plainly that she had to contend with the love of solitude. Now and again, she uttered with terror in her heart the name of Madame de Rênal. She saw Julien shudder. From that moment, her passion knew no bounds nor measure.

'If he dies, I die after him,' she said to herself with absolute sincerity. 'What would the drawing-rooms of Paris say, to see a girl of my rank carry to such a point her adoration of a lover condemned to death? To find such sentiments, we must go back to the days of the heroes; it was love of this nature that set hearts throbbing in the age of Charles IX and Henri III.'

Amid the most impassioned transports, when she pressed Julien's head to her heart: 'What!' she said to herself with horror, 'can this precious head be doomed to fall? Very well!' she added, inflamed by a heroism that was not devoid of happiness, 'my lips, which are now pressed against these dear locks, will be frozen within twenty-four hours after.'

Memories of these moments of heroism and fearful ecstasy seized her in an ineluctable grip. The thought of suicide, so absorbing in itself, and hitherto so remote from that proud spirit, penetrated its defences and soon reigned there with an absolute sway. 'No, the blood of my ancestors has not grown lukewarm in its descent to me,' Mathilde told herself proudly.

'I have a favour to ask you,' her lover said to her one day: 'Put your child out to nurse at Verrières, Madame de Rênal will look after the nurse.'

'That is a very harsh saying. . . .' Mathilde turned pale.

'True, and I ask a thousand pardons,' cried Julien, awakening from his dream and pressing her to his bosom.

Having dried her tears, he returned to the subject of his thoughts, but with more subtlety. He had given the conversation a turn of melancholy philosophy. He spoke of that future which was soon to close for him. 'You must agree, my dear friend, that the passions are an accident in life, but this accident is to be found only in superior beings. . . . The death of my son would be in reality a relief to the pride of your family, so much the subordinate agents will perceive. Neglect will be the lot of that child of misery and shame. . . . I hope that at a date which I do not wish to specify, which however I have the courage to anticipate, you will obey my final behest: You will marry the Marquis de Croisenois.'

'What, dishonoured!'

'Dishonour can have no hold over such a name as yours. You will be a widow, and the widow of a madman, that is all. I shall go farther: my crime, being free from any pecuniary motive, will be in no way dishonouring. Perhaps by that time some philosophical legislator will have secured, from the prejudices of his contemporaries, the suppression of capital punishment. Then, some friendly voice will cite as an instance: "Why, Mademoiselle de La Mole's first husband was mad, but not a wicked man, he was no criminal. It was absurd to cut his head off...." Then my memory will cease to be infamous; at least, after a certain time.... Your position in society, your fortune, and, let me say, your genius will enable M. de Croisenois to play a part, once he is your husband, to which by himself he could not hope to attain. He has only his birth and his gallantry, and those qualities by themselves, which made a man accomplished in 1729, are an anachronism a hundred years later, and only give rise to pretensions. A man must have other things besides if he is to place himself at the head of the youth of France.

'You will bring the support of a firm and adventurous character to the political party in which you will place your husband. You may succeed the Chevreuses and Longuevilles of the Fronde.... But by then, my dear friend, the heavenly fire which animates you at this moment will have cooled a little.

'Allow me to tell you,' he went on, after many other preliminary phrases, 'in fifteen years from now you will regard as an act of folly, pardonable but still an act of folly, the love that you have felt for me....'

He broke off abruptly and returned to his dreams. He found himself once again confronted by that idea, so shocking to Mathilde: 'In fifteen years Madame de Rênal will adore my son, and you will have forgotten him.'

CHAPTER SEVENTY
TRANQUILLITY

It is because I was foolish then that I am now wise.
O philosopher who see nothing save in a flash, how
short is your vision! Your eye is not made to follow the
underground working of the passions.

FRAU VON GOETHE.

THIS conversation was interrupted by a judicial examination, followed by a conference with the lawyer retained for the defence. These were the only absolutely disagreeable moments in a heedless existence full of tender fantasies.

'It was murder, and premeditated murder,' said Julien to magistrate and counsel alike. 'I am sorry, gentlemen, he added, smiling; 'but this reduces your task to a very small matter.

'After all,' thought Julien, when he had succeeded in ridding himself of these two persons, 'I must be brave, and braver, evidently, than these two men. They regard as the worst of evils, as the *king of terrors*, this duel to a fatal issue, of which I shall begin to think seriously only upon the day itself.

'That is because I have known a greater evil,' Julien continued, philosophising to himself. 'I suffered far more keenly on my first journey to Strasbourg, when I thought that I had been abandoned by Mathilde.... And to think that I longed with such passion for this perfect intimacy which to-day leaves me so unmoved! Indeed, I am happier by myself than when that lovely girl shares my solitude....'

The lawyer, a man of rules and formalities, thought him mad, and supposed, with the rest of the public, that it was jealousy that had put the pistol in his hand. One day, he ventured to suggest to Julien that this allegation, whether true or false, would be an excellent line of defence. But the prisoner became in a flash passionate and incisive.

'On your life, Sir,' cried Julien, beside himself with rage, 'bear in mind never again to utter that abominable falsehood.' The prudent advocate was afraid for a moment of being murdered himself.

He prepared his defence, because the decisive moment was rapidly approaching. Besançon and the whole Department could talk of nothing but this *cause célèbre*. Julien was in ignorance of this, he had begged that no one should ever speak to him of such matters.

That very day, Fouqué and Mathilde having sought to inform him of certain public rumours, which seemed to them to furnish grounds for hope, Julien had cut them short at the first word.

'Leave me to enjoy my ideal life. Your petty bickerings, your details of real life, all more or less irritating to me, would bring me down from heaven. One dies as best one can; as for me, I wish to think of death only in my own way. What do I care for *other people*? My relations with *other people* are soon to be cut short. For pity's sake, do not speak to me of them again: it is quite enough to have to degrade myself in the sight of the magistrate and my counsel.

'Indeed,' he said to himself, 'it appears to be my destiny to die in a dream. An obscure creature, like myself, sure of being forgotten within a fortnight, would indeed be foolish, one must admit, were he to play a part....

'It is strange, all the same, that I have learned the art of enjoying life only now that I see its term draw so near.'

He spent these last days in pacing the narrow terrace on the roof of his dungeon, smoking some excellent cigars for which Mathilde had sent a courier to Holland, and with no suspicion that his appearance was daily awaited by all the telescopes in the town. His thoughts were at Vergy. Never did he speak of Madame de Rênal to Fouqué, but on two or three occasions this friend told him that she was recovering rapidly, and these words echoed in his heart.

While Julien's spirit was almost always completely lost in the world of ideas, Mathilde, occupied with realities, as becomes an aristocratic heart, had contrived to increase the intimacy of the direct correspondence between Madame de Fervaques and M. de Frilair to such a point that already the mighty word *Bishopric* had been uttered.

The venerable prelate, in whose hands was the list of bene-fices, added as a postscript to one of his niece's letters: 'That poor Sorel is nothing worse than a fool, I hope that he will be restored to us.'

At the sight of these lines, M. de Frilair was almost out of his mind. He had no doubt of his ability to save Julien.

'But for that Jacobinical law which prescribes the registra-tion of an endless list of jurors, and has no other real object than to take away all influence from well-born people,' he said to Mathilde, on the eve of the drawing by lot of the thirty-six jurors for the assize, 'I could have answered for the verdict. Did I not secure the acquital of the Curé N——?'

It was with pleasure that, on the following day, among the names drawn from the urn, M. de Frilair found those of five members of the *Congregation* of Besançon, and, among those who were strangers to the town, the names of MM. Valenod, de Moirod and de Cholin. 'I can answer at once for these eight jurors,' he told Mathilde. 'The first five are *machines*. Valenod is my agent, Moirod owes all he has to me, Cholin is an imbecile, who is afraid of everything.'

The newspaper published throughout the Department the names of the jurors, and Madame de Rênal, to the inexpres-sible terror of her husband, decided to come to Besançon. All that M. de Rênal could obtain from her was that she would not leave her bed, so that she might not be exposed to the nuisance of being summoned to give evidence. 'You do not understand my position,' said the former Mayor of Verrières. 'I am now a Liberal of the *defection*, as they call it; no doubt but that rascal Valenod and M. de Frilair will easily persuade the Attorney General and the Judges to anything that can be unpleasant for me.'

Madame de Rênal yielded without protest to her husband's orders. 'If I were to appear at the Assize Court,' she told herself, 'I should seem to be demanding vengeance.'

Notwithstanding all the promises of prudence made to her spiritual director and to her husband, no sooner had she arrived in Besançon than she wrote with her own hand to each of the thirty-six jurors:

'I shall not appear in Court upon the day of the trial, Sir, because my presence might prejudice M. Sorel's case. I desire but one thing in the world, and that passionately, namely his acquittal. Be assured of this, the terrible thought that on my account an innocent man has been sent to his death would poison the remainder of my life, and would doubtless shorten it. How could you sentence him to death, while I still live? No, beyond question, society has not the right to take life, especially from such a man as Julien Sorel. Everyone at Verrières has seen him in moments of distraction. This poor young man has powerful enemies; but, even among his enemies (and how many they are!) who is there that has any doubt of his admirable talents and his profound learning? It is not an ordinary person that you are about to judge, Sir. For nearly eighteen months we have all known him to be pious, wise, studious; but, two or three times in the year, he was seized by fits of melancholy which bordered on insanity. The whole town of Verrières, all our neighbours at Vergy where we go in the fine weather, all my family, the Sub-Prefect himself, will bear testimony to his exemplary piety; he knows by heart the whole of the Holy Bible. Would an unbeliever have applied himself for years on end to learning the Holy Scriptures? My sons will have the honour to present this letter to you: they are children. Deign to question them, Sir, they will furnish you with all the details relative to this poor young man that may still be necessary to convince you of the barbarity of condemning him. Far from avenging me, you would be sentencing me to death.

'What is there that his enemies can advance in rebuttal of the following fact? The injury that ensued from one of those moments of insanity which my children themselves used to remark in their tutor was so far from dangerous that within less than two months it has allowed me to post from Verrières to Besançon. If I learn, Sir, that you have even the slightest hesitation in saving from the barbarity of our laws a person who is so little guilty, I shall leave my bed, to which I am confined solely by my husband's orders, and shall come to throw myself at your feet.

'Declare, Sir, that the premeditation is not proven, and you will not have to reproach yourself with the blood of an innocent man,' etc., etc.

CHAPTER SEVENTY-ONE
THE TRIAL

Le pays se souviendra longtemps de ce procès célèbre. L'intéret pour l'accusé était porté jusqu'à l'agitation; c'est que son crime était étonnant et pourtant
pas atroce. L'eût-il été ce jeune homme était si beau!
Sa haute fortune sitôt finie augmentait l'attendrisse-
ment. Le condamneront-ils? demandaient les femmes
aux hommes de leur connaissance, et on les voyait
pâlissantes attendre la réponse.

SAINTE-BEUVE.

At length the day dawned so dreaded by Madame de
Rênal and Mathilde.

The strange appearance of the town increased their
terror, and did not leave even Fouqué's stout heart unmoved.
The whole Province had swarmed into Besançon to witness
the trial of this romantic case.

For some days past there had not been a bed to be had in
the inns. The President of the Assize Court was assailed with
requests for cards of admission; all the ladies of the town
wished to be present at the trial; Julien's portrait was hawked
through the streets, etc., etc.

Mathilde was keeping in reserve for this supreme moment
a letter written throughout in the hand of the Lord Bishop
of ——. This Prelate, who controlled the Church in France
and appointed Bishops, deigned to ask for the acquittal of
Julien. On the eve of the trial, Mathilde took this letter to
the all-powerful Grand Vicar.

At the close of the interview, as she was leaving the room

in a flood of tears: 'I answer for the verdict of the jury,' M. de Frilair told her, emerging at length from his diplomatic reserve, and almost shewing signs of emotion himself. 'Among the twelve persons charged with the duty of finding whether your protégé's crime is proven, and especially whether there was premeditation, I number six friends devoted to my welfare, and I have given them to understand that it rested with them to raise me to the episcopate. Baron de Valenod, whom I have made Mayor of Verrières, has entire control over two of his subordinates, MM. de Moirod and de Cholin. To tell the truth, chance has given us, for dealing with this affair, two jurors who are extremely disaffected; but, although Ultra-Liberals, they loyally obey my orders on great occasions, and I have sent word asking them to vote with M. Valenod. I learn that a sixth juror of the industrial class, an immensely rich and garrulous Liberal, is secretly hoping for a contract from the Ministry of War, and no doubt he would not wish to vex me. I have let him know that M. Valenod has my last word.'

'And who is this M. Valenod?' said Mathilde, anxiously.

'If you knew him, you would have no doubt of our success. He is a bold speaker, impudent, coarse, a man made to be the leader of fools. 1814 raised him from penury, and I am going to make him a Prefect. He is capable of thrashing the other jurors if they refuse to vote as he wishes.'

Mathilde was somewhat reassured.

There was another discussion in store for her that evening. In order not to prolong a painful scene, the outcome of which appeared to him certain, Julien was determined not to open his mouth.

'My counsel will speak, that is quite sufficient,' he said to Mathilde. 'As it is, I shall be all too long exposed as a spectacle to my enemies. These provincials are shocked by the rapid advancement which I owe to you, and, believe me, there is not one of them that does not wish for my conviction, except that he will cry like a fool when I am led to the scaffold.'

'They wish to see you humiliated, it is only too true,'

replied Mathilde, 'but I do not believe that they are cruel. My presence in Besançon and the spectacle of my grief have interested all the women; your handsome face will do the rest. If you say but one word before your judges, the whole court will be on your side,' etc., etc.

The following morning at nine o'clock, when Julien came down from his prison to enter the great hall of the Law Courts, it was with the utmost difficulty that the gendarmes succeeded in clearing a passage through the immense crowd that packed the courtyard. Julien had slept well, he was quite calm, and felt no other sentiment than one of philosophical piety towards this crowd of envious persons who, without cruelty, were ready to applaud his sentence of death. He was quite surprised when, having been detained for more than a quarter of an hour among the crowd, he was obliged to admit that his presence was inspiring a tender pity in the assembly. He did not hear a single unpleasant remark. 'These provincials are less evil-minded than I supposed,' he said to himself.

On entering the court, he was struck by the elegance of the architecture. It was pure gothic, with a number of charming little pillars carved in stone with the most perfect finish. He imagined himself in England.

But presently his whole attention was absorbed in twelve or fifteen pretty women who, seated opposite the dock, filled the three galleries above the bench and the jury-box. On turning round towards the public seats, he saw that the circular gallery which overhung the well of the court was filled with women; most of them were young and seemed to him extremely pretty; their eyes were bright and full of interest. In the rest of the court, the crowd was enormous; people were struggling at the doors, and the sentries were unable to preserve silence.

When all the eyes that were looking for Julien became aware of his presence, on seeing him take his place on the slightly raised bench reserved for the prisoner, he was greeted with a murmur of astonishment and tender interest.

One would have said that morning that he was not yet

twenty; he was dressed quite simply, but with a perfect grace; his hair and brow were charming; Mathilde had insisted on presiding in person over his toilet. His pallor was intense. As soon as he had taken his seat on the bench, he heard people say on all sides: 'Lord, how young he is!....' 'But he is a boy.' 'He is far better looking than his portrait.'

'Prisoner,' said the gendarme seated on his right, 'do you see those six ladies who are on that balcony?' The gendarme pointed to a little gallery which jutted out above the amphitheatre in which the jury was placed. 'That is the Prefect's lady,' the gendarme continued; 'next to her, Madame la Marquise de M——; that one loves you dearly. I heard her speak to the examining magistrate. Next to her is Madame Derville.'

'Madame Derville,' exclaimed Julien, and a vivid blush suffused his brow. 'When she leaves the court,' he thought, 'she will write to Madame de Rênal.' He knew nothing of Madame de Rênal's arrival at Besançon.

The evidence was taken; this occupied some hours. At the first words of the speech for the prosecution made by the Advocate-General, two of the ladies seated on the little balcony burst into tears. 'Madame Derville is not so easily moved,' thought Julien. He noticed, however, that she was extremely flushed.

The Advocate-General indulged in a rhodomontade in bad French on the barbarity of the crime that had been committed; Julien noticed that Madame Derville's neighbours shewed signs of strong disapproval. Several of the jury, evidently friends of these ladies, spoke to them and seemed to reassure them. 'That can only be a good sign,' thought Julien.

Until then he had felt himself penetrated by an unmixed contempt for all the men who were taking part in this trial. The insipid eloquence of the Advocate-General increased this sense of disgust. But gradually the sereneness of Julien's heart melted before the marks of interest of which he was plainly the object.

He was pleased with the firm expression of his counsel.

'No fine language,' he murmured to him as he stood up to speak.

'All the emphasis stolen from Bossuet, which has been displayed against you, has helped your case,' said the counsel. And indeed, he had not been speaking for five minutes before almost all the ladies had their handkerchiefs in their hands. The counsel, encouraged by this, addressed the jury in extremely strong language. Julien shuddered, he felt that he was on the point of bursting into tears. 'Great God! What will my enemies say?'

He was about to yield to the emotion that was overpowering him, when, fortunately for himself, he caught an insolent glance from M. Valenod.

'That wretch's eyes are ablaze,' he said to himself; 'what a triumph for that vile nature! Had my crime led to this alone, I should be bound to abhor it. Heaven knows what he will say of me in the winter evenings to Madame de Rênal!'

This thought obliterated all the rest. Shortly afterwards, Julien was recalled to himself by sounds of approval from the public. His counsel had just concluded his speech. Julien remembered that it was the correct thing to shake hands with him. The time had passed quickly.

Refreshments were brought to counsel and prisoner. It was only then that Julien was struck by a curious circumstance: none of the women had left the court for dinner.

'Faith, I am dying of hunger,' said his counsel, 'and you?'

'I am also,' replied Julien.

'Look, there is the Prefect's lady getting her dinner, too,' his counsel said to him, pointing to the little balcony. 'Cheer up, everything is going well.' The trial was resumed.

As the President was summing up, midnight struck. He was obliged to pause; amid the silence of the universal anxiety, the echoing notes of the clock filled the court.

'Here begins the last day of my life,' thought Julien. Presently he felt himself inflamed by the idea of duty. He had kept his emotion in check until then, and maintained his determination not to speak; but when the President of the Assizes asked him if he had anything to say, he rose. He saw

547

in front of him the eyes of Madame Derville, which, in the lamplight, seemed to shine with a strange brilliance. 'Can she be crying, by any chance,' he wondered.

'Gentlemen of the Jury,

'My horror of the contempt which I believed that I could endure at the moment of my death, impels me to speak. Gentlemen, I have not the honour to belong to your class, you see in me a peasant who has risen in revolt against the lowliness of his station.

'I ask you for no mercy,' Julien went on, his voice growing stronger. 'I am under no illusion; death is in store for me; it will be a just punishment. I have been guilty of attempting the life of the woman most worthy of all respect, of all devotion. Madame de Rênal had been like a mother to me. My crime is atrocious, and it was *premeditated*. I have, therefore, deserved death, Gentlemen of the Jury. But, even were I less guilty, I see before me men who, without pausing to consider what pity may be due to my youth, will seek to punish in me and to discourage forever that class of young men who, born in an inferior station and in a sense burdened with poverty, have the good fortune to secure a sound education, and the audacity to mingle with what the pride of rich people calls society.

'That is my crime, Gentlemen, and it will be punished with all the more severity in as much as actually I am not being tried by my peers. I do not see, anywhere among the jury, a peasant who has grown rich, but only indignant *bourgeois....*'

For twenty minutes Julien continued to speak in this strain; he said everything that was in his heart; the Advocate-General, who aspired to the favour of the aristocracy, kept springing from his seat; but in spite of the somewhat abstract turn which Julien had given the debate, all the women were dissolved in tears. Madame Derville herself had her handkerchief pressed to her eyes. Before concluding, Julien returned to the question of premeditation, to his repentance, to the respect, the filial and unbounded adoration which, in happier times, he had felt for Madame de Rênal.... Madame Derville uttered a cry and fainted.

One o'clock struck as the jury retired to their waiting-room. None of the women had left their seats; several of the men had tears in their eyes. The general conversation was at first most lively; but gradually, as the jury delayed their verdict, the feeling of weariness spread a calm over the assembly. It was a solemn moment; the lamps burned more dimly. Julien, who was dead tired, heard them discussing round him whether this delay augured well or ill. He noticed with pleasure that everyone was on his side; the jury did not return, and still not a woman left the court.

Just as two o'clock had struck, a general stir was audible. The little door of the jury-room opened. M. le Baron de Valenod advanced with a grave, theatrical step, followed by the rest of the jury. He coughed, then declared that on his soul and conscience the unanimous opinion of the jury was that Julien Sorel was guilty of murder, and of murder with premeditation: this verdict inferred a sentence of death; it was pronounced a moment later. Julien looked at his watch, and remembered M. de Lavalette; it was a quarter past two. 'To-day is Friday,' he thought.

'Yes, but this is a lucky day for Valenod, who is sentencing me.... I am too closely guarded for Mathilde to be able to effect my escape, like Madame de Lavalette.... And so, in three days, at this same hour, I shall know what to think of the *great hereafter.*'

At that moment, he heard a cry and was recalled to the things of this world. The women round him were sobbing; he saw that every face was turned towards a little gallery concealed by the capital of a gothic pilaster. He learned afterwards that Mathilde had been hidden there. As the cry was not repeated, everyone turned back to look at Julien, for whom the gendarmes were trying to clear a passage through the crowd.

'Let us try not to give that rascal Valenod any food for laughter,' thought Julien. 'With what a contrite and coaxing air he uttered the verdict that involved the death penalty!

Whereas that poor president, even though he has been a judge for all these years, had tears in his eyes when he sentenced me. What a joy for Valenod to have his revenge for our old rivalry for Madame de Rênal! And so I shall never see her any more! It is all finished.... A last farewell is impossible between us, I feel it.... How happy I should have been to express to her all the horror I feel for my crime!

'These words only: I feel that I am justly condemned.'

CHAPTER SEVENTY-TWO
IN THE PRISON

WHEN Julien was led back to prison he had been put in a cell reserved for those under sentence of death. He, who, as a rule, observed the most trifling details, had never noticed that he was not being taken up to his old dungeon. He was thinking of what he would say to Madame de Rênal, if, before the fatal moment, he should have the good fortune to see her. He felt that she would not allow him to speak, and was seeking a way of expressing his repentance in the first words he would utter. 'After such an action, how am I to convince her that I love her and her only? For after all I sought to kill her either out of ambition or for love of Mathilde.'

On getting into bed he found himself between sheets of a coarse cloth. The scales fell from his eyes. 'Ah! I am in the condemned cell,' he said to himself, 'awaiting my sentence. It is right....

'Conte Altamira told me once that, on the eve of his death, Danton said in his loud voice: "It is strange, the verb to guillotine cannot be conjugated in all its tenses; one can say: I shall be guillotined, thou shalt be guillotined, but one does not say: I have been guillotined."

'Why not,' Julien went on, 'if there is another life? Faith, if I meet the Christian Deity, I am lost: He is a tyrant, and, as such, is full of ideas of vengeance; His Bible speaks of nothing but fearful punishments. I never loved Him! I could never even believe that anyone did love Him sincerely. He is devoid of pity.' (Here Julien recalled several passages from the Bible.) 'He will punish me in some abominable manner....

'But if I meet the God of Fénelon! He will say to me perhaps: "Much shall be pardoned thee, because thou hast loved much...."

'Have I loved much? Ah! I did love Madame de Rênal, but my conduct has been atrocious. There, as elsewhere, I abandoned a simple and modest merit for what was brilliant....

'But then, what a prospect! Colonel of Hussars, should we go to war; Secretary of Legation in time of peace; after that, Ambassador ... for I should soon have learned the business ... and had I been a mere fool, need the son-in-law of the Marquis de La Mole fear any rival? All my foolish actions would have been forgiven me, or rather counted to me as merits. A man of distinction, enjoying the most splendid existence in Vienna or London....

'Not precisely that, Sir, to be guillotined in three days' time.'

Julien laughed heartily at this sally of his own wit. 'Indeed, man has two different beings inside him,' he reflected. 'What devil thought of that malicious touch?

'Very well, yes, my friend, guillotined in three days' time,' he replied to the interrupter. 'M. de Cholin will hire a window, sharing the expense with the Abbé Maslon. Well, for the cost of hiring that window, which of those two worthies will rob the other?'

A passage from Rotrou's *Venceslas* entered his head suddenly.

Ladislas: My soul is well prepared.
The King (his father): So is the scaffold; lay your head thereon.

'A good answer,' he thought, and fell asleep. Someone awakened him in the morning by shaking him violently.

'What, already!' said Julien, opening a haggard eye. He imagined himself to be in the headsman's hands.

It was Mathilde. 'Fortunately, she did not understand.' This reflexion restored all his presence of mind. He found

552

Mathilde changed as though after six months of illness: she was positively unrecognisable.

'That wretch Frilair has betrayed me,' she said to him, wringing her hands; rage prevented her from speaking.

'Was I not fine yesterday when I rose to speak?' replied Julien. 'I was improvising, and for the first time in my life! It is true that there is reason to fear it may also be the last.'

At this moment Julien was playing upon Mathilde's nature with all the calm of a skilled pianist touching the keys of a piano.... 'The advantage of noble birth I lack, it is true,' he went on, 'but the great heart of Mathilde has raised her lover to her own level. Do you suppose that Boniface de La Mole cut a better figure before his judges?'

Mathilde, that morning, was tender without affectation, like any poor girl dwelling in an attic; but she could not win from him any simpler speech. He paid her back, unconsciously, the torment that she had often inflicted on him.

'We do not know the source of the Nile,' Julien said to himself; 'it has not been granted to the eye of man to behold the King of Rivers in the form of a simple rivulet: similarly no human eye shall ever see Julien weak, if only because he is not weak. But I have a heart that is easily moved; the most commonplace words, if they are uttered with an accent of truth, may soften my voice and even make my tears begin to flow. How often have not the sere hearts despised me for this defect! They believed that I was begging for mercy: that is what I cannot endure.

'They say that the thought of his wife overcame Danton at the foot of the scaffold; but Danton had given strength to a nation of coxcombs, and prevented the enemy from reaching Paris.... I alone know what I might have managed to do.... To others, I am at best only a *might-have-been*.

'If Madame de Rênal had been here, in my cell, instead of Mathilde, should I have been able to control myself? The intensity of my despair and of my repentance would have appeared in the eyes of the Valenods, and of all the patricians of the neighbourhood, a craven fear of death; they are so proud, those feeble hearts, whom their financial position places out of reach of temptation! "You see what it is," M. de Moirod and M. de Cholin, who have just sentenced me to death, would have said, "to be born the son of a carpenter! One may become learned, clever, but courage!... Courage is not taught at school." Even this poor Mathilde, who is now weeping, or rather who can no longer weep,' he said, looking at her red eyes ... and he took her in his arms: the sight of genuine grief made him forget his syllogism. 'She has been weeping all night, perhaps,' he said to himself: 'but one day how ashamed she will be when she remembers! She will regard herself as having been led astray, in early youth, by the low opinions of a plebeian.... Croisenois is weak enough to marry her, and, i' faith, he will do well for himself. She will make him play a part,

> 'By that right
> Which a firm spirit planning vast designs
> Has o'er the loutish minds of common men.

'Ah, now; here is a pleasant thing: now that I am to die, all the poetry I ever learned in my life comes back to me. It must be a sign of decadence....'

Mathilde kept on saying to him in a faint voice: 'He is there, in the next room.' At length he began to pay attention to her words. 'Her voice is feeble,' he thought, 'but all her imperious nature is still in its accents. She lowers her voice in order not to lose her temper.

'Who is there?' he asked her gently.

'The lawyer, to make you sign your appeal.'

'I shall not appeal.'

'What! You will not appeal,' she said, rising to her feet, her eyes ablaze with anger, 'and why not, if you please?'

'Because at this moment I feel that I have the courage to die without exciting undue derision. And who can say that in two months' time, after a long confinement in this damp cell, I shall be so well prepared? I foresee interviews with priests, with my father.... I can imagine nothing so unpleasant. Let us die.'

This unexpected obstinacy awoke all the latent pride in

Mathilde's nature. She had not been able to see the Abbé de Frilair before the hour at which the cells in the prison of Besançon were opened; her anger fell upon Julien. She adored him, and for the next quarter of an hour he was reminded by her imprecations against his character, her regrets that she had ever loved him, of that proud spirit which in the past had heaped such poignant insults upon him, in the library of the Hôtel de La Mole.

'Heaven owed it to the glory of your race to bring you into the world a man,' he told her.

'But as for myself,' he thought, 'I should be a rare fool to live two months longer in this disgusting abode, the butt of all the infamous and humiliating lies that the patrician faction is capable of inventing,[1] my sole comfort the imprecations of this madwoman.... Well, the day after to-morrow, I shall be fighting a duel in the morning with a man well known for his coolness and for his remarkable skill.... Very remarkable,' whispered Mephistopheles, 'he never misses his stroke.

'Very well, so be it, all's well that ends well.' (Mathilde's eloquence continued to flow.) 'Begad, no,' he said to himself, 'I shall not appeal.'

Having made this decision, he relapsed into his dreams.... 'The postman on his rounds will bring the newspaper at six o'clock, as usual; at eight, after M. de Rênal has read it, Elisa, entering the room on tiptoe, will lay it down on her bed. Later, she will awake: suddenly, as she reads, she will grow troubled; her lovely hand will tremble; she will come to the words: *At five minutes past ten he had ceased to live.*

'She will shed hot tears, I know her; in vain did I seek to murder her, all will be forgotten, and the person whose life I sought to take will be the only one who will weep sincerely for my death.

'Ah, this is a paradox!' he thought, and, for the next quarter of an hour, while Mathilde continued to make a scene, he thought only of Madame de Rênal. In spite of himself,

---

1 A Jacobin is speaking.

and albeit frequently replying to what Mathilde said to him, he could not free his mind from the memory of that bedroom at Verrières. He saw the *Gazette de Besançon* lying on the counterpane of orange taffeta. He saw that snowy hand clutching it with a convulsive movement; he saw Madame de Rênal weep.... He followed the course of each tear over that charming face.

Mademoiselle de La Mole, having failed to get anything out of Julien, made the lawyer come in. He was fortunately an old Captain of the Army of Italy, of 1796, when he had served with Manuel.

For the sake of form, he opposed the condemned man's decision. Julien, wishing to treat him with respect, explained all his reasons to him.

'Faith, one may think as you do,' M. Félix Vaneau (this was the lawyer's name), said to him at length. 'But you have three clear days in which to appeal, and it is my duty to come back each day. If a volcano opened beneath the prison, in the next two months, you would be saved. You may die a natural death,' he said, looking at Julien.

Julien shook his hand. 'I thank you, you are an honest man. I shall think it over.'

And when Mathilde left him, finally, with the lawyer, he felt far more affection for the lawyer than for her.

CHAPTER SEVENTY-THREE
LAST ADIEUX

An hour later, when he was fast asleep, he was awakened by the tears which he felt trickling over his hand. 'Ah! Mathilde again,' he thought to himself, half awake. 'She has come, faithful to her theory, to attack my resolve by force of tender sentiments.' Irritated by the prospect of this fresh scene in the pathetic manner, he did not open his eyes. The lines of Belphegor flying from his wife came into his mind.

He heard a strange sigh; he opened his eyes; it was Madame de Rênal.

'Ah! Do I see you again before my death? Is it a phantom?' he cried, as he flung himself at her feet.

'But forgive me, Madame, I am nothing but a murderer in your eyes,' he at once added, regaining his composure.

'Sir, . . . I have come to implore you to appeal, I know that you do not wish to. . . .' She was choked by her sobs; she was unable to speak.

'Deign to forgive me.'

'If you wish me to forgive you,' she said to him, rising and throwing herself into his arms, 'appeal at once from the sentence of death.'

Julien covered her with kisses.

'Will you come and see me every day during the next two months?'

'I swear it to you. Every day, unless my husband forbids me.'

557

'Then I sign!' cried Julien. 'What! You forgive me! Is it possible?'

He clasped her in his arms; he was mad. She uttered a faint cry.

'It is nothing,' she told him, 'you hurt me.'

'In your shoulder,' cried Julien, bursting into tears. He stepped back from her, and covered her hand with burning kisses. 'Who would ever have said, last time I saw you, in your bedroom, at Verrières ...?'

'Who would ever have said then that I should write M. de La Mole that infamous letter...?'

'Know that I have always loved you, that I have never loved anyone but you.'

'Is it really possible?' cried Madame de Rênal, equally enraptured. She bowed herself over Julien, who was kneeling at her feet, and for a long time they wept in silence.

At no time in his life had Julien experienced such a moment.

After a long interval, when they were able to speak:

'And that young Madame Michelet,' said Madame de Rênal, 'or rather that Mademoiselle de La Mole; for I am beginning really to believe this strange tale!'

'It is true only in appearance,' replied Julien. 'She is my wife, but she is not my mistress....'

And, each interrupting the other a hundred times, they managed with difficulty, each of them, to tell what the other did not know. The letter sent to M. de La Mole had been written by the young priest who directed Madame de Rênal's conscience, and then copied out by her. 'What a terrible crime religion has made me commit!' she said to him; 'though I did modify the worst passages in the letter....'

Julien's transports of joy proved to her how completely he forgave her. Never had he been so madly in love.

'And yet I regard myself as pious,' Madame de Rênal told him in the course of their conversation. 'I believe sincerely in God; I believe equally, indeed it has been proved to me, that the crime I am committing is fearful, and yet, as soon as I set eyes on you, even after you have fired at me twice with a pistol. . . . ' Here, in spite of her resistance, Julien covered her with kisses.

'Let me alone,' she went on, 'I wish to argue with you, before I forget. . . . As soon as I set eyes on you, all sense of duty vanishes, there is nothing left of me but love for you, or rather love is too feeble a word. I feel for you what I ought to feel only for God: a blend of respect, love, obedience. . . . In truth, I do not know what feeling you inspire in me. Were you to bid me thrust a knife into your gaoler, the crime would be committed before I had had time to think. Explain this to me in simple terms before I leave you, I wish to see clearly into my own heart; for in two months we must part. . . . For that matter, need we part?' she said, with a smile.

'I take back my word,' cried Julien, springing to his feet; 'I shall not appeal from the sentence of death, if by poison, knife, pistol, charcoal or any other means whatsoever, you seek to put an end to, or to endanger your life.'

Madame de Rênal's expression altered suddenly; the warmest affection gave place to a profound abstraction.

'If we were to die at once?' she said to him at length.

'Who knows what we shall find in our next life?' replied Julien; 'torments perhaps, perhaps nothing at all. Can we not spend two months together in a delicious manner? Two months, that is ever so many days. Never shall I have been so happy.'

'You will never have been so happy?'

'Never,' replied Julien with rapture, 'and I am speaking to you as I speak to myself. Heaven preserve me from exaggeration.'

'To speak so is to command me,' she said with a timid and melancholy smile.

'Very well! You swear, by the love that you bear me, not to attempt your life by any direct means, or indirect means. . . . Remember,' he added, 'that you are compelled to live for my son, whom Mathilde will abandon to the care of servants as soon as she is Marquise de Croisenois.'

'I swear,' she replied coldly, 'but I mean to take away with me your appeal written and signed by your hand. I shall go myself to the Attorney-General.'

'Take care, you will compromise yourself.'

'After coming publicly to see you in prison, I am for ever, for Besançon and the whole of the Franche-Comté, a heroine of anecdotes,' she said with an air of profound distress. 'I am a woman who has forfeited her honour; it is true that it was for your sake....'

Her tone was so melancholy that Julien embraced her with a happiness that was quite new to him. It was no longer the intoxication of love, it was extreme gratitude. He had just realised, for the first time, the full extent of the sacrifice that she had made for him.

Some charitable soul doubtless informed M. de Rênal of the long visits which his wife was paying to Julien's prison; for, after three days, he sent his carriage for her, with express orders that she was to return immediately to Verrières.

This cruel parting had begun the day ill for Julien. He was informed, two or three hours later, that a certain intriguing priest, who for all that had not succeeded in making any headway among the Jesuits of Besançon, had taken his stand that morning outside the gate of the prison, in the street. It was raining hard, and outside there the man was trying to pose as a martyr. Julien was out of temper, this piece of foolishness moved him profoundly.

That morning he had already refused a visit from the priest, but the man had made up his mind to hear Julien's confession, and to make a name for himself among the young women of Besançon, on the strength of all the confidences which he would pretend to have received.

He declared in a loud voice that he was going to remain day and night at the gate of the prison: 'God has sent me to touch the heart of that apostate.' And the lower orders, always curious spectators of a scene, began to assemble in crowds.

'Yes, my brethren,' he said to them, 'I shall spend the day here, and the night, and every day and night from now onwards. The Holy Spirit has spoken to me. I have a mission from on high; it is I that am to save the soul of young Sorel. Join with me in my prayers,' etc., etc.

Julien had a horror of scandal, and of anything that might attract attention to himself. He thought of seizing the opportunity to escape from the world unknown; but he had still some hope of seeing Madame de Rênal again, and was desperately in love.

The gate of the prison was situated in one of the most frequented streets. The thought of that mud-bespattered priest, drawing a crowd and creating a scandal, was torture to his soul. 'And, without a doubt, at every instant he is repeating my name!' This moment was more painful than death itself.

He called two or three times, at intervals of an hour, for a turnkey who was devoted to him, to send him out to see whether the priest were still at the gate of the prison.

'Sir, he is on both his knees in the mud,' was the turnkey's invariable answer; 'he is praying aloud, and repeating Litanies for your soul.' 'The impertinent fellow!' thought Julien. At that moment, indeed, he heard a dull roar, it was the crowd responding to the Litany. To increase his impatience, he saw the turnkey move his lips as he repeated the Latin words. 'They are beginning to say,' the turnkey added, 'that your heart must indeed be hardened if you refuse the succour of this holy man.'

'O my country! How barbarous thou still art!' cried Julien in a frenzy of rage. And he continued his reasoning aloud, without a thought of the turnkey's presence.

'The man wants an article in the paper, and now he is certain of obtaining it.

'Oh, cursed provincials! In Paris, I should not have been subjected to all these vexations. They are more adept there in charlatanism.

'Let this holy priest come in,' he said at length to the turnkey, and the sweat trickled in great drops from his brow. The turnkey made the sign of the Cross, and left the cell radiant.

The holy priest proved to be hideously ugly, and was even more foul with mud. The cold rain outside intensified the darkness and dampness of the cell. The priest tried to embrace Julien, and began to shew emotion as he spoke to him. The vilest hypocrisy was all too evident; never in his life had Julien been in such a rage.

A quarter of an hour after the priest had entered, Julien found himself a complete coward. For the first time death appeared to him horrible. He thought of the state of putrefaction in which his body would be two days after his execution, etc., etc.

He was on the point of betraying himself by some sign of weakness, or of flinging himself upon the priest and strangling him with his chain, when it occurred to him to beg the holy man to go and say a good forty-franc mass for him, that very day.

As it was almost mid-day, the priest decamped.

CHAPTER SEVENTY-FOUR

THE SHADOW OF THE GUILLOTINE

As soon as he had gone, Julien began to weep copiously, at the thought of dying. After a while he said to himself that, if Madame de Rênal had been at Besançon, he would have confessed his weakness to her....

At the moment when he most regretted the absence of that beloved woman, he heard Mathilde's step.

'The worst drawback of a prison,' he thought, 'is that one can never close one's door.' All that Mathilde had to say served only to irritate him.

She informed him that, on the day of the trial, M. de Valenod, having in his pocket his appointment as Prefect, had ventured to defy M. de Frilair and indulge himself in the pleasure of condemning Julien to death.

' "Whatever induced your friend," M. de Frilair said to me just now, "to go and arouse and attack the petty vanity of that middle-class aristocracy? Why speak of caste? He shewed them what they ought to do in their own political interest: the fools had never thought of it, and were ready to cry. This caste interest blinded their eyes to the horror of condemning a man to death. You must admit that M. Sorel shews great inexperience. If we do not succeed in saving him by an appeal to clemency, his death will be a sort of suicide...." '

Mathilde did not, of course, mention to Julien a thing which she herself did not yet suspect; namely, that the Abbé de Frilair, seeing Julien irremediably lost, thought that it would serve his own ambition to aspire to become his successor.

Almost out of his mind with helpless rage and vexation: 'Go and hear a mass for me,' he said to Mathilde, 'and leave me a moment's peace.' Mathilde, who was extremely jealous already at Madame de Rênal's visits and had just heard of her departure, realised the cause of Julien's ill humour and burst into tears.

Her grief was genuine, Julien saw this and was all the more irritated. He felt a compelling need of solitude, and how was he to secure it?

Finally Mathilde, having tried every argument to soften him, left him to himself, but almost at that moment Fouqué appeared.

'I want to be alone,' he said to this faithful friend. And, as he saw him hesitate: 'I am composing a memorial for my appeal to clemency ... but anyhow ... do me a favour, never to speak to me of death. If I want any special services on the day, let me be the first to mention them.'

When Julien had at length secured solitude, he found himself more crushed and more of a coward than before. What little strength remained to his enfeebled spirit had been used up in the effort to conceal his condition from Mademoiselle de La Mole and Fouqué.

Towards evening, a comforting thought came to him:

'If this morning, at the moment when death seemed so ugly, I had been warned to prepare for execution, *the eye of the public would have been the incentive to glory*; my gait might perhaps have been a little heavy, like that of a timid fop on entering a drawing-room. A few perspicacious people, if there be any such among these provincials, might have guessed my weakness ... but *no one would have seen it.*'

And he felt himself relieved of part of his load of misery. 'I am a coward at this moment,' he chanted to himself, 'but no one will know of it.'

An almost more disagreeable incident was in store for him on the morrow. For a long time past, his father had been threatening a visit; that morning, before Julien was awake, the white-haired old carpenter appeared in his cell.

Julien felt utterly weak, he expected the most unpleasant

reproaches. To complete his painful sensation, that morning he felt a keen remorse at not loving his father.

'Chance has placed us together on this earth,' he said to himself while the turnkey was making the cell a little tidy, 'and we have done one another almost all the harm imaginable. He comes in the hour of my death to deal me his final blow.'

The old man's severe reproaches began as soon as they were left without a witness.

Julien could not restrain his tears. 'What unworthy weakness!' he said to himself angrily. 'He will go about everywhere exaggerating my want of courage; what a triumph for Valenod and for all the dull hypocrites who reign at Verrières! They are very great people in France, they combine all the social advantages. Until now I could at least say to myself: They receive money, it is true, all the honours are heaped upon them, but I have nobility at heart.

'And here is a witness whom they will all believe, and who will assure the whole of Verrières, exaggerating the facts, that I have been weak in the face of death! I shall be said to have turned coward in this trial which they can all understand!'

Julien was almost in despair. He did not know how to get rid of his father. And to make-believe in such a way as to deceive this sharp-witted old man was, for the moment, utterly beyond his power.

His mind ran swiftly over all the possible ways of escape. 'I have saved money!' he exclaimed suddenly.

This inspired utterance altered the old man's expression and Julien's own position.

'How ought I to dispose of it?' he continued, with more calm: the effect produced by his words had rid him of all sense of inferiority.

The old carpenter was burning with a desire not to allow any of this money to escape, a part of which Julien seemed to wish to leave to his brothers. He spoke at great length and with heat. Julien managed to tease him.

'Well, the Lord has given me inspiration for making my testament. I shall give a thousand francs to each of my brothers, and the remainder to you.'

'Very good,' said the old man, 'that remainder is my due; but since God has been graciously pleased to touch your heart, if you wish to die like a good Christian, you ought first to pay your debts. There is still the cost of your maintenance and education, which I advanced, and which you have forgotten. . . .'

'So that is a father's love!' Julien repeated to himself with despair in his heart, when at length he was alone. Soon the gaoler appeared.

'Sir, after a visit from the family, I always bring my lodgers a bottle of good champagne. It is a trifle dear, six francs the bottle, but it rejoices the heart.'

'Bring three glasses,' Julien told him with boyish glee, 'and send in two of the prisoners whom I hear walking in the corridor.'

The gaoler brought him in two gaolbirds who had repeated their offence and were waiting to be sent back to penal servitude. They were a merry pair of scoundrels and really quite remarkable for cunning, courage and coolness.

'If you give me twenty francs,' one of them said to Julien, 'I will tell you the whole story of my life. It is as good as a play.'

'But you will tell me lies?' said Julien.

'Not at all,' was the answer; 'my friend here, who wants my twenty francs, will give me away if I don't tell the truth.'

His history was abominable. It revealed a courageous heart, in which there survived but a single passion, the lust for money.

After they had left him, Julien was no longer the same man. All his anger with himself had vanished. The piercing grief, envenomed by cowardice, to which he had been a prey since the departure of Madame de Rênal, had turned to melancholy.

'If I had only been less taken in by appearance,' he told himself, 'I should have seen that the drawing-rooms of Paris are inhabited by honest people like my father, or by able rascals like these gaolbirds. They are right, the men in the drawing-rooms never rise in the morning with that poignant thought: "How am I to dine to-day?" And they boast of their probity! And, when summoned to a jury, they proudly condemn the man who has stolen a silver fork because he felt faint with hunger!

'But when there is a Court, when it is a question of securing or losing a Portfolio, my honest men of the drawing-rooms fall into crimes precisely similar to those which the want of food has inspired in this pair of gaolbirds....

'There is no such thing as *natural law*: the expression is merely a hoary piece of stupidity well worthy of the Advocate-General who hunted me down the other day, and whose ancestor was made rich by one of Louis XIV's confiscations. There is no *law*, save when there is a statute to prevent one from doing something, on pain of punishment. Before the statute, there is nothing *natural* save the strength of the lion, or the wants of the creature who suffers from hunger, or cold; in a word, *necessity*.... No, the men whom we honour are merely rascals who have had the good fortune not to be caught red-handed. The accuser whom society sets at my heels has been made rich by a scandalous injustice.... I have committed a murderous assault, and I am rightly condemned, but, short of murder only, the Valenod who condemned me is a hundred times more injurious to society.

'Ah, well,' Julien added sorrowfully, but without anger, 'for all his avarice, my father is worth more than any of those men. He has never loved me. I am now going to fill his cup to overflowing, in dishonouring him by a shameful death. That fear of being in want of money, that exaggerated view of the wickedness of mankind which we call *avarice*, makes him see a prodigious source of consolation and security in a sum of three or four hundred louis which I may leave to him. On Sunday afternoons he will display his gold to all his envious neighbours in Verrières. "To this tune," his glance will say to them, "which of you would not be charmed to have a son guillotined?"'

This philosophy might he true, but it was of a nature to make a man long for death. In this way passed five endless days. He was polite and gentle to Mathilde, whom he saw to be exasperated by the most violent jealousy. One evening Julien thought seriously of taking his life. His spirit was exhausted by the profound dejection into which the departure of Madame de Rênal had cast him. Nothing pleased him any more, either in real life or in imagination. Want of exercise was beginning to affect his health and to give him the weak and excitable character of a young German student. He was losing that manly pride which repels with a forcible oath certain degrading ideas by which the miserable are assailed.

'I have loved the Truth.... Where is it to be found?... Everywhere hypocrisy, or at least charlatanism, even among the most virtuous, even among the greatest'; and his lips curled in disgust.... 'No, man cannot place any trust in man.

'Madame de —, when she was making a collection for her poor orphans, told me that some Prince had just given her ten louis; a lie. But what am I saying? Napoleon at Saint-Helena!... Pure charlatanism, a proclamation in favour of the King of Rome.

'Great God! If such a man as he, at a time, too, when misfortune ought to recall him sternly to a sense of duty, stoops to charlatanism, what is one to expect of the rest of the species?

'Where is Truth? In religion.... Yes,' he added with a bitter smile of the most intense scorn, 'in the mouths of the Maslons, the Frilairs, the Castanèdes.... Perhaps in true Christianity, whose priests would be no more paid than were the Apostles? But Saint Paul was paid with the pleasure of commanding, of speaking, of hearing himself spoken of....

'Ah! If there were a true religion.... Idiot that I am! I see a gothic cathedral, storied windows; my feeble heart imagines the priest from those windows.... My soul would understand him, my soul has need of him. I find only a fop with greasy hair ... little different, in fact, from the Chevalier de Beauvoisis.

'But a true priest, a Massillon, a Fénelon.... Massillon consecrated Dubois. The *Mémoires de Saint-Simon* have spoiled Fénelon for me; but still, a true priest.... Then the tender hearts would have a meeting-place in this world ... We should not remain isolated.... This good priest would speak to us of God. But what God? Not the God of the Bible, a petty despot, cruel and filled with a thirst for vengeance ... but the God of Voltaire, just, good, infinite....'

He was disturbed by all his memories of that Bible which he knew by heart.... But how, whenever *three are gathered together*, how is one to believe in that great name of GOD, after the frightful abuse that our priests make of it?

'To live in isolation! ... What torture!...

'I am becoming foolish and unjust,' said Julien, beating his brow. 'I am isolated here in this cell; but I have not *lived in isolation* on this earth; I had always the compelling idea of *duty*. The duty that I had laid down for myself, rightly or wrongly, was like the trunk of a strong tree against which I leaned during the storm; I tottered, I was shaken. After all, I was only a man ... but I was not carried away.

'It is the damp air of this cell that makes me think of isolation....

'And why be a hypocrite still when I am cursing hypocrisy? It is not death, nor the cell, nor the damp air, it is the absence of Madame de Rênal that is crushing me. If I were at Verrières, and, in order to see her, were obliged to live for weeks on end hidden in the cellars of her house, should I complain?

'The influence of my contemporaries is too strong for me,' he said aloud and with a bitter laugh. 'Talking alone to myself, within an inch of death, I am still a hypocrite.... Oh, nineteenth century!

'A hunter fires his gun in a forest, his quarry falls, he runs forward to seize it. His boot strikes an anthill two feet high, destroys the habitation of the ants, scatters the ants and their eggs to the four winds.... The most philosophical among the ants will never understand that black, enormous, fearful body—the hunter's boot which all of a sudden has burst into their dwelling with incredible speed, preceded by a terrifying noise, accompanied by a flash of reddish flame....

'So it is with death, life, eternity, things that would be

quite simple to anyone who had organs vast enough to conceive them....

'An ephemeral fly is born at nine o'clock in the morning, on one of the long days of summer, to die at five o'clock in the afternoon; how should it understand the word *night*?

'Grant it five hours more of existence, it sees and understands what night is.

'And so with myself, I am to die at three and twenty. Grant me five years more of life, to live with Madame de Rênal.'

Here he gave a satanic laugh. What folly to discuss these great problems!

'*Imprimis:* I am a hypocrite just as much as if there was someone in the cell to hear me.

'*Item:* I am forgetting to live and love, when I have so few days left of life.... Alas! Madame de Rênal is absent; perhaps her husband will not allow her to come to Besançon again, and disgrace herself further.

'That is what is isolating me, that and not the absence of a just, good, all-powerful God, who is not wicked, not hungry for vengeance....

'Ah! If He existed.... Alas! I should fall at His feet. I have deserved death, I should say to him; but, great God, good God, indulgent God, restore to me her whom I love!'

The night was by now far advanced. After an hour or two of peaceful slumber, Fouqué arrived.

Julien felt himself to be strong and resolute like a man who sees clearly into his own heart.

CHAPTER SEVENTY-FIVE

EXIT JULIEN

'I WILL not play that poor Abbé Chas-Bernard the unkind trick of sending for him,' he said to Fouqué; 'he would not be able to eat his dinner for three days afterwards. But try to find me a Jansenist, a friend of M. Pirard and beyond the reach of intrigue.'

Fouqué had been awaiting this development with impatience. Julien acquitted himself in a decent fashion of everything that is due to public opinion in the provinces. Thanks to M. l'Abbé de Frilair, and in spite of his unfortunate choice of a confessor, Julien, in his cell, was under the protection of the *Congregation*; with a little more of the spirit of action, he might have made his escape. But, as the bad air of the cell produced its effect, his mental powers dwindled. This made him all the happier on the return of Madame de Rênal.

'My first duty is towards you,' she said to him as she embraced him; 'I have fled from Verrières....'

Julien had no petty vanity in his relations with her, he told her of all his weak moments. She was kind and charming to him.

That evening, immediately upon leaving the prison, she summoned to her aunt's house the priest who had attached himself to Julien as to a prey; as he wished only to acquire a reputation among the young women belonging to the best society of Besançon, Madame de Rênal easily persuaded him to go and offer a novena at the abbey of Bray-le-Haut.

571

No words could express the intensity and recklessness of Julien's love.

By spending money freely, and by using and abusing the reputation of her aunt, well known for her piety and riches, Madame de Rênal obtained permission to see him twice daily.

On hearing this, Mathilde's jealousy rose to the pitch of insanity. M. de Frilair had assured her that in spite of his position he dared not flout all the conventions so far as to permit her to see her friend more than once daily. Mathilde had Madame de Rênal followed, so as to be kept informed of her most trivial actions. M. de Frilair exhausted every resource of a most cunning mind, in trying to prove to her that Julien was unworthy of her.

In the midst of all these torments, she loved him all the more, and, almost every day, created a horrible scene in his cell.

Julien wished at all costs to behave like an honourable man until the end towards this poor girl whom he had so seriously compromised; but, at every moment, the unbridled passion that he felt for Madame de Rênal overcame him. When, through some flaw in his argument, he failed to convince Mathilde of the innocence of her rival's visits: 'At this stage, the end of the play must be very near,' he said to himself; 'that is some excuse for me if I cannot act better.'

Mademoiselle de La Mole learned of the death of M. de Croisenois. M. de Thaler, that man of boundless wealth, had taken the liberty of saying unpleasant things about Mathilde's disappearance; M. de Croisenois called on him with a request that he would withdraw them: M. de Thaler shewed him certain anonymous letters addressed to himself, and full of details so skilfully put together that it was impossible for the poor Marquis not to discern the true facts.

M. de Thaler indulged in pleasantries that were distinctly broad. Mad with rage and misery, M. de Croisenois insisted upon reparations so drastic that the millionaire preferred a duel. Folly proved triumphant; and one of the men in Paris most worthy of a woman's love met his death in his twenty-fourth year.

This death made a strange and morbid impression on Julien's weakened spirits.

'Poor Croisenois,' he said to Mathilde, 'did really behave quite reasonably and honourably towards us; he had every right to hate me after your imprudent behaviour in your mother's drawing-room, and to seek a quarrel with me; for the hatred that follows on contempt is generally furious.'

The death of M. de Croisenois altered all Julien's ideas with regard to Mathilde's future; he devoted several days to proving to her that she ought to accept the hand of M. de Luz. 'He is a shy man, not too much of a Jesuit,' he told her, 'and a man who no doubt intends to climb. With a more sober and persistent ambition than poor Croisenois, and with no dukedom in his family, he will make no difficulty about marrying Julien Sorel's widow.'

'And a widow who scorns grand passions,' replied Mathilde coldly; 'for she has lived long enough to see, after six months, her lover prefer another woman, and a woman who was the origin of all their troubles.'

'You are unjust; Madame de Rênal's visits will furnish the barrister from Paris, who has been engaged to conduct my appeal, with some striking phrases; he will describe the murderer honoured by the attentions of his victim. That may create an effect, and perhaps one day you will see me the hero of some melodrama,' etc., etc.

A furious jealousy and one that was incapable of wreaking vengeance, the prolongation of a hopeless misery (for, even supposing Julien to be saved, how was she to recapture his heart?), the shame and grief of loving more than ever this faithless lover, had plunged Mademoiselle de La Mole in a grim silence from which the zealous attentions of M. de Frilair were no more capable than the rude frankness of Fouqué, of making her emerge.

As for Julien, except during the moments usurped by the presence of Mathilde, he was living upon love and with hardly a thought of the future. A curious effect of this passion, in its extreme form and free from all pretence, was that Madame de Rênal almost shared his indifference and mild gaiety.

'In the past,' Julien said to her, 'when I might have been so happy during our walks in the woods of Vergy, a burning ambition led my soul into imaginary tracts. Instcad of my pressing to my heart this lovely arm which was so near to my lips, the thought of my future tore me away from you; I was occupied with the countless battles which I should have to fight in order to build up a colossal fortune.... No, I should have died without knowing what happiness meant, had you not come to visit me in this prison.'

Two incidents occurred to disturb this tranquil existence. Julien's confessor, for all that he was a Jansenist, was not immune from an intrigue by the Jesuits, and quite unawares became their instrument.

He came one day to inform him that if he were not to fall into the mortal sin of suicide, he must take every possible step to obtain a reprieve. Now, the clergy having considerable influence at the Ministry of Justice in Paris, an easy method offered itself: he must undergo a sensational conversion....

'Sensational!' Julien repeated. 'Ah! I have caught you at the same game, Father, play-acting like any missionary....'

'Your tender age,' the Jansenist went on gravely, 'the interesting appearance with which Providence has blessed you, the motive itself of your crime, which remains inexplicable, the heroic measures of which Mademoiselle de La Mole is unsparing on your behalf, everything, in short, including the astonishing affection that your victim shews for you, all these have combined to make you the hero of the young women of Besançon. They have forgotten everything for you, even politics....

'Your conversion would strike an echo in their hearts, and would leave a profound impression there. You can be of the greatest service to religion, and am I to hesitate for the frivolous reason that the Jesuits would adopt the same course in similar circumstances! And so, even in this particular case which has escaped their rapacity, they would still be doing harm! Let such a thing never be said.... The tears which will flow at your conversion will annul the corrosive effect of ten editions of the impious works of Voltaire.'

'And what shall I have left,' replied Julien coldly, 'if I

despise myself? I have been ambitious, I have no wish to reproach myself; I acted then according to the expediency of the moment. Now, I am living from day to day. But, generally speaking, I should be making myself extremely unhappy, if I gave way to any cowardly temptation. . . .'

The other incident, which affected Julien far more keenly, arose from Madame de Rênal. Some intriguing friend or other had managed to persuade this simple, timid soul that it was her duty to go to Saint-Cloud, and to throw herself at the feet of King Charles X.

She had made the sacrifice of parting from Julien, and after such an effort, the unpleasantness of making a public spectacle of herself, which at any other time would have seemed to her worse than death, was no longer anything in her eyes.

'I shall go to the King, I shall confess proudly that you are my lover: the life of a man, and of such a man as Julien, must outweigh all other considerations. I shall say that it was out of jealousy that you attempted my life. There are endless examples of poor young men who have been saved in such cases by the humanity of a jury, or by that of the King. . . .'

'I shall cease to see you, I shall bar the door of my prison against you,' cried Julien, 'and most certainly I shall kill myself in despair, the day after, unless you swear to me that you will take no step that will make us both a public spectacle. This idea of going to Paris is not yours. Tell me the name of the intriguing woman who suggested it to you. . . .

'Let us be happy throughout the few remaining days of this brief life. Let us conceal our existence; my crime is only too plain. Mademoiselle de La Mole has unbounded influence in Paris, you may be sure that she is doing all that is humanly possible. Here in the provinces, I have all the wealthy and respectable people against me. Your action would embitter still further these wealthy and above all moderate men, for whom life is such an easy matter. . . . Let us not give food for laughter to the Maslons, the Valenods, and a thousand people better worth than they.'

The bad air of the cell became insupportable to Julien. Fortunately on the day on which he was told that he must die, a bright sun was gladdening the earth, and he himself was in a courageous mood. To walk in the open air was a delicious sensation to him, as is treading solid earth to a mariner who has long been at sea. 'There, all is well,' he said to himself, 'I am not lacking in courage.'

Never had that head been so poetic as at the moment when it was about to fall. The most precious moments that he had known in the past in the woods of Vergy came crowding into his mind with an extreme vividness.

Everything passed simply, decorously, and without affectation on his part.

Two days earlier, he had said to Fouqué: 'For my emotions I cannot answer; this damp and hideous cell gives me moments of fever in which I am not myself; but fear, no; no one shall see me blench.'

He had made arrangements in advance that on the morning of the last day, Fouqué should carry off Mathilde and Madame de Rênal.

'Take them in the same carriage,' he had told him. 'Arrange that the post-horses shall gallop all the time. They will fall into one another's arms, or else will shew a deadly hatred for one another. In either case, the poor women will have some slight distraction from their terrible grief.'

Julien had made Madame de Rênal swear that she would live to look after Mathilde's child.

'Who knows? Perhaps we continue to have sensation after our death,' he said one day to Fouqué. 'I should dearly like to repose, since repose is the word, in that little cave in the high mountain that overlooks Verrières. Many a time, as I have told you, retiring by night to that cave, and casting my gaze afar over the richest provinces of France, I have felt my heart ablaze with ambition: it was my passion then. . . . Anyhow, that cave is precious to me, and no one can deny that it is situated in a spot that a philosopher's heart might envy. . . . Very well! These worthy members of the *Congregation* of Besançon make money out of everything; if you know how to set about it, they will sell you my mortal remains. . . .'

Fouqué was successful in this grim transaction. He was

spending the night alone in his room, by the body of his friend, when to his great surprise, he saw Mathilde appear. A few hours earlier, he had left her ten leagues from Besançon. There was a wild look in her eyes.

'I wish to see him,' she said to him.

Fouqué had not the courage to speak or to rise. He pointed with his finger to a great blue cloak on the floor; in it was wrapped all that remained of Julien.

She fell upon her knees. The memory of Boniface de La Mole and of Marguerite de Navarre gave her, no doubt, a superhuman courage. Her trembling hands unfolded the cloak. Fouqué turned away his eyes.

He heard Mathilde walking rapidly about the room. She lighted a number of candles. When Fouqué had summoned up the strength to look at her, she had placed Julien's head upon a little marble table, in front of her, and was kissing his brow....

Mathilde followed her lover to the tomb which he had chosen for himself. A great number of priests escorted the coffin and, unknown to all, alone in her draped carriage, she carried upon her knees the head of the man whom she had so dearly loved.

Coming thus near to the summit of one of the high mountains of the Jura, in the middle of the night, in that little cave magnificently illuminated with countless candles, a score of priests celebrated the Office of the Dead. All the inhabitants of the little mountain villages, through which the procession passed, had followed it, drawn by the singularity of this strange ceremony.

Mathilde appeared in their midst in a flowing garb of mourning, and, at the end of the service, had several thousands of five franc pieces scattered among them.

Left alone with Fouqué, she insisted upon burying her lover's head with her own hands. Fouqué almost went mad with grief.

By Mathilde's orders, this savage grot was adorned with marbles sculptured at great cost, in Italy.

Madame de Rênal was faithful to her promise. She did not seek in any way to take her own life; but, three days after Julien, died while embracing her children.

ABOUT THE INTRODUCER

JONATHAN KEATES teaches at the City of London School. He has written biographies of Stendhal, Handel and Purcell and a travel book, *Italian Journeys*. His works of fiction include *Strangers' Gallery*, *Allegro Postillions* and *Soon to be a Major Motion Picture*.

ABOUT THE TRANSLATOR

CHARLES KENNETH SCOTT MONCRIEFF was born in Scotland in 1889 and studied Law and English at Edinburgh University. He trained as a professional soldier and spent the First World War in France until wounded in 1917. While convalescing he turned to translating, and his English version of the *Chansons de Roland* was published in 1919. He thereafter translated Proust's *Remembrance of Things Past* and the *Letters of Abelard and Heloïse* before devoting himself to Stendhal, translating *The Charterhouse of Parma* and some of the *Chroniques italiennes* in 1926, *Scarlet and Black* in 1927 and *Armance* in 1928. By this time he had moved to Italy, where he also produced English versions of a number of plays by Pirandello. He died in Rome in 1930.

This book is set in BASKERVILLE. John
Baskerville of Birmingham formed his
ideas of letter-design during his
early career as a writing-master
and engraver of inscriptions.
He retired in middle age,
set up a press of his
own and produced
his first book
in 1757.